R. D. Blackmore

LORNA DOONE

A Romance of Exmoor

Romance CLASSICS

Romance CLASSICS

Published by Trident Press International
801 12th Avenue South
Suite 302
Naples Florida 34102 USA
www.trident-international.com
email: tridentpress@worldnet.att.net

Printed in Australia
ISBN: 1582791775

Preface

This work is called a 'romance,' because the incidents, characters, time, and scenery, are alike romantic. And in shaping this old tale, the Writer neither dares, nor desires, to claim for it the dignity or cumber it with the difficulty of an historic novel.

And yet he thinks that the outlines are filled in more carefully, and the situations (however simple) more warmly coloured and quickened, than a reader would expect to find in what is called a 'legend.'

And he knows that any son of Exmoor, chancing on this volume, cannot fail to bring to mind the nurse-tales of his childhood—the savage deeds of the outlaw Doones in the depth of Bagworthy Forest, the beauty of the hapless maid brought up in the midst of them, the plain John Ridd's Herculean power, and (memory's too congenial food) the exploits of Tom Faggus.

March, 1869.

Chapter I Elements of Education

If anybody cares to read a simple tale told simply, I, John Ridd, of the parish of Oare, in the county of Somerset, yeoman and churchwarden, have seen and had a share in some doings of this neighborhood, which I will try to set down in order, God sparing my life and memory. And they who light upon this book should bear in mind not only that I write for the clearing of our parish from ill fame and calumny, but also a thing which will, I trow, appear too often in it, to wit—that I am nothing more than a plain unlettered man, not read in foreign languages, as a gentleman might be, nor gifted with long words (even in mine own tongue), save what I may have won from the Bible or Master William Shakespeare, whom, in the face of common opinion, I do value highly. In short, I am an ignoramus, but pretty well for a yeoman.

My father being of good substance, at least as we reckon in Exmoor, and seized in his own right, from many generations, of one, and that the best and largest, of the three farms into which our parish is divided (or rather the cultured part thereof), he John Ridd, the elder, churchwarden, and overseer, being a great admirer of learning, and well able to write his name, sent me his only son to be schooled at Tiverton, in the county of Devon. For the chief boast of that ancient town (next to its woollen staple) is a worthy grammar-school, the largest in the west of England, founded and handsomely endowed in the year 1604 by Master Peter Blundell, of that same place, clothier.

Here, by the time I was twelve years old, I had risen into the upper school, and could make bold with Eutropius and Caesar—by aid of an English version—and as much as six lines of Ovid. Some even said that I might, before manhood, rise almost to the third form, being of a perservering nature; albeit, by full consent of all (except my mother), thick-headed. But that would have been, as I now perceive, an ambition beyond a farmer's son; for there is but one form above it, and that made of masterful scholars, entitled rightly 'monitors'. So it came to pass, by the grace of God, that I was called away from learning, whilst sitting at the desk of the junior first in the upper school, and beginning the Greek verb τύπτω.

My eldest grandson makes bold to say that I never could have learned φιλέω, ten pages further on, being all he himself could manage, with plenty of stripes to help him. I know that he hath more head than I—though never will he have such body; and am thankful to have stopped betimes, with a meek and wholesome head-piece.

But if you doubt of my having been there, because now I know so little, go and see my name, 'John Ridd,' graven on that very form. Forsooth, from the time I was strong enough to open a knife and to spell my name, I began to grave it in the oak, first of the block whereon I sate, and then of the desk in front of it, according as I was promoted from one to other of them: and there my grandson reads it now, at this present time of writing, and hath fought a boy for scoffing at it—'John Ridd his name'—and done again in 'winkeys,' a mischievous but cheerful device, in which we took great pleasure.

This is the manner of a 'winkey,' which I here set down, lest child of mine, or grandchild, dare to make one on my premises; if he does, I shall know the mark at once, and score it well upon him. The scholar obtains, by prayer or price, a handful of saltpetre, and then with the knife wherewith he should rather be trying to mend his pens, what does he do but scoop a hole where the desk is some three inches thick. This hole should be left with the middle exalted, and the circumfere dug more deeply. Then let him fill it with saltpetre, all save a little space in the midst, where the boss of the wood is. Upon that boss (and it will be the better if a splinter of timber rise upward) he sticks the end of his candle of tallow, or 'rat's tail,' as we called it, kindled and burning smoothly. Anon, as he reads by that light his lesson, lifting his eyes now and then it may be, the fire of candle lays hold of the petre with a spluttering noise and a leaping. Then should the pupil seize his pen, and, regardless of the nib, stir bravely, and he will see a glow as of burning mountains, and a rich smoke, and sparks going merrily; nor will it cease, if he stir wisely, and there be a good store of petre, until the wood is devoured through, like the sinking of a well-shaft. Now well may it go with the head of a boy intent upon his primer, who betides to sit thereunder! But, above all things, have good care to exercise this art before the master strides up to his desk, in the early gray of the morning.

Other customs, no less worthy, abide in the school of Blundell, such as the singeing of nightcaps; but though they have a pleasant savour, and refreshing to think of, I may not stop to note them, unless it be that goodly one at the incoming of a flood. The school-house stands beside a stream, not very large, called Lowman, which flows into the broad river of Exe, about a mile below. This Lowman stream, although it be not fond of brawl and violence (in the manner of our Lynn), yet is wont to flood into a mighty head of waters when the storms of rain provoke it; and most of all when its little co-mate, called the Taunton Brook—where I have plucked the very best cresses that ever man put salt on—comes foaming down like a great roan horse, and rears at the leap of the hedgerows. Then are the gray stone walls of Blundell on every side encompassed, the vale is spread over with looping waters, and it is a hard thing for the day-boys to get home to their suppers.

And in that time, old Cop, the porter (so called because he hath copper boots to keep the wet from his stomach, and a nose of copper also, in right of other waters), his place is to stand at the gate, attending to the flood-boards grooved into one another, and so to watch the torrents rise, and not be washed away, if it please God he may help it. But long ere the flood hath attained this height, and while it is only waxing, certain boys of deputy will watch at the stoop of the drain-holes, and be apt to look outside the walls when Cop is taking a cordial. And in the very front of the gate, just without the archway, where the ground is paved most handsomely, you may see in copy-letters done a great P.B. of white pebbles. Now, it is the custom and the law that when the invading waters, either fluxing along the wall from below the road-bridge, or pouring sharply across the meadows from a cut called Owen's Ditch—and I myself have seen it come both ways—upon the very instant when the waxing element lips though it be but a single pebble of the founder's letters, it is in the license of any boy, soever small and undoctrined, to rush into the great school-rooms, where a score of masters sit heavily, and scream at the top of his voice, 'P.B.'

Then, with a yell, the boys leap up, or break away from their standing; they toss their caps to the black-beamed roof, and haply the very books after them; and the great boys vex no more the small ones, and the small boys stick up to the great ones. One with another, hard they go, to see the gain of the waters, and the tribulation of Cop, and are prone to kick the day-boys out, with words of scanty compliment. Then the masters look at one another, having no class to look to, and (boys being no more left to watch) in a manner they put their mouths up. With a spirited bang they close their books, and make invitation the one to the other for pipes and foreign cordials, recommending the chance of the time, and the comfort away from cold water.

But, lo! I am dwelling on little things and the pigeons' eggs of the infancy, forgetting the bitter and heavy life gone over me since then. If I am neither a hard man nor a very close one, God knows I have had no lack of rubbing and pounding to make stone of me. Yet can I not somehow believe that we ought to hate one another, to live far asunder, and block the mouth each of his little den; as do the wild beasts of the wood, and the hairy outrangs now brought over, each with a chain upon him. Let that matter be as it will. It is beyond me to unfold, and mayhap of my grandson's grandson. All I know is that wheat is better than when I began to sow it.

Chapter II An Important Item

Now the cause of my leaving Tiverton school, and the way of it, were as follows. On the 29th day of November, in the year of our Lord 1673, the very day when I was twelve years old, and had spent all my substance in sweetmeats, with which I made treat to the little boys, till the large boys ran in and took them, we came out of school at five o'clock, as the rule is upon Tuesdays. According to custom we drove the day-boys in brave rout down the causeway from the school-porch even to the gate where Cop has his dwelling and duty. Little it recked us and helped them less, that they were our founder's citizens, and haply his own grand-nephews (for he left no direct descendants), neither did we much inquire what their lineage was. For it had long been fixed among us, who were of the house and chambers, that these same day-boys were all 'caddes,' as we had discovered to call it, because they paid no groat for their schooling, and brought their own commons with them. In consumption of these we would help them, for our fare in hall fed appetite; and while we ate their victuals, we allowed them freely to talk to us. Nevertheless, we could not feel, when all the victuals were gone, but that these boys required kicking from the premises of Blundell. And some of them were shopkeepers' sons, young grocers, fellmongers, and poulterers, and these to their credit seemed to know how righteous it was to kick them. But others were of high family, as any need be, in Devon—Carews, and Bouchiers, and Bastards, and some of these would turn sometimes, and strike the boy that kicked them. But to do them justice, even these knew that they must be kicked for not paying.

After these 'charity-boys' were gone, as in contumely we called them—'If you break my bag on my head,' said one, 'how will feed thence to morrow?'—and after old Cop with clang of iron had jammed the double gates in under the scruff-stone archway, whereupon are Latin verses, done in brass of small quality, some of us who were not hungry, and cared not for the supper-bell, having sucked much parliament and dumps at my only charges—not that I ever bore much wealth, but because I had been thrifting it for this time of my birth—we were leaning quite at dusk against the iron bars of the gate some six, or it may be seven of us, small boys all, and not conspicuous in the closing of the daylight and the fog that came at eventide, else Cop would have rated us up the green, for he was churly to little boys when his wife had taken their money. There was plenty of room for all of us, for the gate will hold nine boys close-packed, unless they be fed rankly, whereof is little danger; and now we were looking out on the road and wishing we could get there; hoping, moreover, to see a good string of pack-horses come by, with troopers to protect them. For the day-boys had brought us word that some intending their way to the town had lain that morning at Sampford Peveril, and must be in ere nightfall, because Mr. Faggus was after them. Now Mr. Faggus was my first cousin and an honour to the family, being a Northmolton man of great renown on the highway from Barum town even to London. Therefore of course, I hoped that he would catch the packmen, and the boys were asking my opinion as of an oracle, about it.

A certain boy leaning up against me would not allow my elbow room, and struck me very sadly in the stomach part, though his own was full of my parliament. And this I felt so unkindly, that I smote him straightway in the face without tarrying to consider it, or weighing the question duly. Upon this he put his head down, and presented it so vehemently at the middle of my waistcoat, that for a minute or more my breath seemed dropped, as it were, from my pockets, and my life seemed to stop from great want of ease. Before I came to myself again, it had been settled for us that we should move to the 'Ironing-box,' as the triangle of turf is called where the two causeways coming from the school-porch and the hall-porch meet, and our fights are mainly celebrated; only we must wait until the convoy of horses had passed, and then make a ring by candlelight, and the other boys would like it. But suddenly there came round the post where the letters of our founder are, not from the way of Taunton but from the side of Lowman bridge, a very small string of horses, only two indeed (counting for one the pony), and a red-faced man on the bigger nag.

'Plaise ye, worshipful masters,' he said, being feared of the gateway, 'carn 'e tull whur our Jan Ridd be?'

'Hyur a be, ees fai, Jan Ridd,' answered a sharp little chap, making game of John Fry's language.

'Zhow un up, then,' says John Fry poking his whip through the bars at us; 'Zhow un up, and putt un aowt.'

The other little chaps pointed at me, and some began to hallo; but I knew what I was about.

'Oh, John, John,' I cried, 'what's the use of your coming now, and Peggy over the moors, too, and it so cruel cold for her? The holidays don't begin till Wednesday fortnight, John. To think of your not knowing that!'

John Fry leaned forward in the saddle, and turned his eyes away from me; and then there was a noise in his throat like a snail crawling on a window-pane.

'Oh, us knaws that wull enough, Maister Jan; reckon every Oareman knaw that, without go to skoo-ull, like you doth. Your moother have kept arl the apples up, and old Betty toorned the black puddens, and none dare set trap for a blagbird. Arl for thee, lad; every bit of it now for thee!'

He checked himself suddenly, and frightened me. I knew that John Fry's way so well.

'And father, and father—oh, how is father?' I pushed the boys right and left as I said it. 'John, is father up in town! He always used to come for me, and leave nobody else to do it.'

'Vayther'll be at the crooked post, tother zide o' telling-house.* Her coodn't lave 'ouze by raison of the Chirstmas bakkon comin' on, and zome o' the cider welted.'

He looked at the nag's ears as he said it; and, being up to John Fry's ways, I knew that it was a lie. And my heart fell like a lump of lead, and I leaned back on the stay of the gate, and longed no more to fight anybody. A sort of dull power hung over me, like the cloud of a brooding tempest, and I feared to be told anything. I did not even care to stroke the nose of my pony Peggy, although she pushed it in through the rails, where a

*The 'telling-houses' on the moor are rude cots where the shepherds meet to 'tell' their sheep at the end of the pasturing season.

square of broader lattice is, and sniffed at me, and began to crop gently after my fingers. But whatever lives or dies, business must be attended to; and the principal business of good Christians is, beyond all controversy, to fight with one another.

'Come up, Jack,' said one of the boys, lifting me under the chin; 'he hit you, and you hit him, you know.'

'Pay your debts before you go,' said a monitor, striding up to me, after hearing how the honour lay; 'Ridd, you must go through with it.'

'Fight, for the sake of the junior first,' cried the little fellow in my ear, the clever one, the head of our class, who had mocked John Fry, and knew all about the aorists, and tried to make me know it; but I never went more than three places up, and then it was an accident, and I came down after dinner. The boys were urgent round me to fight, though my stomach was not up for it; and being very slow of wit (which is not chargeable on me), I looked from one to other of them, seeking any cure for it. Not that I was afraid of fighting, for now I had been three years at Blundell's, and foughten, all that time, a fight at least once every week, till the boys began to know me; only that the load on my heart was not sprightly as of the hay-field. It is a very sad thing to dwell on; but even now, in my time of wisdom, I doubt it is a fond thing to imagine, and a motherly to insist upon, that boys can do without fighting. Unless they be very good boys, and afraid of one another.

'Nay,' I said, with my back against the wrought-iron stay of the gate, which was socketed into Cop's house-front: 'I will not fight thee now, Robin Snell, but wait till I come back again.'

'Take coward's blow, Jack Ridd, then,' cried half a dozen little boys, shoving Bob Snell forward to do it; because they all knew well enough, having striven with me ere now, and proved me to be their master—they knew, I say, that without great change, I would never accept that contumely. But I took little heed of them, looking in dull wonderment at John Fry, and Smiler, and the blunderbuss, and Peggy. John Fry was scratching his head, I could see, and getting blue in the face, by the light from Cop's parlour-window, and going to and fro upon Smiler, as if he were hard set with it. And all the time he was looking briskly from my eyes to the fist I was clenching, and methought he tried to wink at me in a covert manner; and then Peggy whisked her tail.

'Shall I fight, John?' I said at last; 'I would an you had not come, John.'

'Chraist's will be done; I zim thee had better faight, Jan,' he answered, in a whisper, through the gridiron of the gate; 'there be a dale of faighting avore thee. Best wai to begin gude taime laike. Wull the geatman latt me in, to zee as thee hast vair plai, lad?'

He looked doubtfully down at the colour of his cowskin boots, and the mire upon the horses, for the sloughs were exceedingly mucky. Peggy, indeed, my sorrel pony, being lighter of weight, was not crusted much over the shoulders; but Smiler (our youngest sledder) had been well in over his withers, and none would have deemed him a piebald, save of red mire and black mire. The great blunderbuss, moreover, was choked with a dollop of slough-cake; and John Fry's sad-coloured Sunday hat was indued with a plume of marish-weed. All this I saw while he was dismounting, heavily and wearily, lifting his leg from the saddle-cloth as if with a sore crick in his back.

By this time the question of fighting was gone quite out of our discretion; for sundry of the elder boys, grave and reverend signors, who had taken no small pleasure in teaching our hands to fight, to ward, to parry, to feign and counter, to lunge in the manner of sword-play, and the weaker child to drop on one knee when no cunning of fence might baffle the onset—these great masters of the art, who would far liefer see us little ones practise it than themselves engage, six or seven of them came running down the rounded causeway, having heard that there had arisen 'a snug little mill' at the gate. Now whether that word hath origin in a Greek term meaning a conflict, as the best-read boys asseverated, or whether it is nothing more than a figure of similitude, from the beating arms of a mill, such as I have seen in counties where are no waterbrooks, but folk make bread with wind—it is not for a man devoid of scholarship to determine. Enough that they who made the ring intituled the scene a 'mill,' while we who must be thumped inside it tried to rejoice in their pleasantry, till it turned upon the stomach.

Moreover, I felt upon me now a certain responsibility, a dutiful need to maintain, in the presence of John Fry, the manliness of the Ridd family, and the honour of Exmoor. Hitherto none had worsted me, although in the three years of my schooling, I had fought more than threescore battles, and bedewed with blood every plant of grass towards the middle of the Ironing-box. And this success I owed at first to no skill of my own; until I came to know better; for up to twenty or thirty fights, I struck as nature guided me, no wiser than a father-long-legs in the heat of a lanthorn; but I had conquered, partly through my native strength, and the Exmoor toughness in me, and still more that I could not see when I had gotten my bellyful. But now I was like to have that and more; for my heart was down, to begin with; and then Robert Snell was a bigger boy than I had ever encountered, and as thick in the skull and hard in the brain as even I could claim to be.

I had never told my mother a word about these frequent strivings, because she was soft-hearted; neither had I told by father, because he had not seen it. Therefore, beholding me still an innocent-looking child, with fair curls on my forehead, and no store of bad language, John Fry thought this was the very first fight that ever had befallen me; and so when they let him at the gate, 'with a message to the headmaster,' as one of the monitors told Cop, and Peggy and Smiler were tied to the railings, till I should be through my business, John comes up to me with the tears in his eyes, and says, 'Doon't thee goo for to do it, Jan; doon't thee do it, for gude now.' But I told him that now it was much too late to cry off; so he said, 'The Lord be with thee, Jan, and turn thy thumb-knuckle inwards.'

It was not a very large piece of ground in the angle of the causeways, but quite big enough to fight upon, especially for Christians, who loved to be cheek by jowl at it. The great boys stood in a circle around, being gifted with strong privilege, and the little boys had leave to lie flat and look through the legs of the great boys. But while we were yet preparing, and the candles hissed in the fog-cloud, old Phoebe, of more than fourscore years, whose room was over the hall-porch, came hobbling out, as she always did, to mar the joy of the conflict. No one ever heeded her, neither did she expect it; but the evil was that two senior boys must always lose the first round of the fight, by having to lead her home again.

I marvel how Robin Snell felt. Very likely he thought nothing of it, always having been a boy of a hectoring and unruly sort. But I felt my heart go up and down as the boys came round to strip me; and greatly fearing to be beaten, I blew hot upon my knuckles. Then pulled I off my little cut jerkin, and laid it down on my head cap, and over that my waistcoat, and a boy was proud to take care of them. Thomas Hooper was his name, and I remember how he looked at me. My mother had made that little cut jerkin, in the quiet winter evenings. And taken pride to loop it up in a fashionable way, and I was loth to soil it with blood, and good filberds were in the pocket. Then up to me came Robin Snell (mayor of Exeter thrice since that), and he stood very square, and looking at me, and I lacked not long to look at him. Round his waist he had a kerchief busking up his small-clothes, and on his feet light pumpkin shoes, and all his upper raiment off. And he danced about in a way that made my head swim on my shoulders, and he stood some inches over me. But I, being muddled with much doubt about John Fry and his errand, was only stripped of my jerkin and waistcoat, and not comfortable to begin.

'Come now, shake hands,' cried a big boy, jumping in joy of the spectacle, a third-former nearly six feet high; 'shake hands, you little devils. Keep your pluck up, and show good sport, and Lord love the better man of you.'

Robin took me by the hand, and gazed at me disdainfully, and then smote me painfully in the face, ere I could get my fence up.

'Whutt be 'bout, lad?' cried John Fry; 'hutt un again, Jan, wull 'e? Well done then, our Jan boy.'

For I had replied to Robin now, with all the weight and cadence of penthemimeral caesura (a thing, the name of which I know, but could never make head nor tail of it), and the strife began in a serious style, and the boys looking on were not cheated. Although I could not collect their shouts when the blows were ringing upon me, it was no great loss; for John Fry told me afterwards that their oaths went up like a furnace fire. But to these we paid no heed or hap, being in the thick of swinging, and devoid of judgment. All I know is, I came to my corner, when the round was over, with very hard pumps in my chest, and a great desire to fall away.

'Time is up,' cried head-monitor, ere ever I got my breath again; and when I fain would have lingered awhile on the knee of the boy that held me. John Fry had come up, and the boys were laughing because he wanted a stable lanthorn, and threatened to tell my mother.

'Time is up,' cried another boy, more headlong than head-monitor. 'If we count three before the come of thee, thwacked thou art, and must go to the women.' I felt it hard upon me. He began to count, one, too, three—but before the 'three' was out of his mouth, I was facing my foe, with both hands up, and my breath going rough and hot, and resolved to wait the turn of it. For I had found seat on the knee of a boy sage and skilled to tutor me, who knew how much the end very often differs from the beginning. A rare ripe scholar he was; and now he hath routed up the Germans in the matter of criticism. Sure the clever boys and men have most love towards the stupid ones.

'Finish him off, Bob,' cried a big boy, and that I noticed especially, because I thought it unkind of him, after eating of my toffee as he had that afternoon; 'finish him off, neck and crop; he deserves it for sticking up to a man like you.'

But I was not so to be finished off, though feeling in my knuckles now as if it were a blueness and a sense of chilblain. Nothing held except my legs, and they were good to help me. So this bout, or round, if you please, was foughten warily by me, with gentle recollection of what my tutor, the clever boy, had told me, and some resolve to earn his praise before I came back to his knee again. And never, I think, in all my life, sounded sweeter words in my ears (except when my love loved me) than when my second and backer, who had made himself part of my doings now, and would have wept to see me beaten, said,—

'Famously done, Jack, famously! Only keep your wind up, Jack, and you'll go right through him!'

Meanwhile John Fry was prowling about, asking the boys what they thought of it, and whether I was like to be killed, because of my mother's trouble. But finding now that I had foughten three-score fights already, he came up to me woefully, in the quickness of my breathing, while I sat on the knee of my second, with a piece of spongious coralline to ease me of my bloodshed, and he says in my ears, as if he was clapping spurs into a horse,—

'Never thee knack under, Jan, or never coom naigh Hexmoor no more.'

With that it was all up with me. A simmering buzzed in my heavy brain, and a light came through my eyeplaces. At once I set both fists again, and my heart stuck to me like cobbler's wax. Either Robin Snell should kill me, or I would conquer Robin Snell. So I went in again with my courage up, and Bob came smiling for victory, and I hated him for smiling. He let at me with his left hand, and I gave him my right between his eyes, and he blinked, and was not pleased with it. I feared him not, and spared him not, neither spared myself. My breath came again, and my heart stood cool, and my eyes struck fire no longer. Only I knew that I would die sooner than shame my birthplace. How the rest of it was I know not; only that I had the end of it, and helped to put Robin in bed.

Chapter III The War-Path of the Doones

From Tiverton town to the town of Oare is a very long and painful road, and in good truth the traveller must make his way, as the saying is; for the way is still unmade, at least, on this side of Dulverton, although there is less danger now than in the time of my schooling; for now a good horse may go there without much cost of leaping, but when I was a boy the spurs would fail, when needed most, by reason of the slough-cake. It is to the credit of this age, and our advance upon fatherly ways, that now we have laid down rods and fagots, and even stump-oaks here and there, so that a man in good daylight need not sink, if he be quite sober. There is nothing I have striven at more than doing my duty, way-warden over Exmoor.

But in those days, when I came from school (and good times they were, too, full of a warmth and fine hearth-comfort, which now are dying out), it was a sad and sorry business to find where lay the highway. We are taking now to mark it off with a fence on either side, at least, when a town is handy; but to me his seems of a high pretence, and a sort of landmark, and channel for robbers, though well enough near London, where they have earned a race-course.

We left the town of the two fords, which they say is the meaning of it, very early in the morning, after lying one day to rest, as was demanded by the nags, sore of foot and foundered. For my part, too, I was glad to rest, having aches all over me, and very heavy bruises; and we lodged at the sign of the White Horse Inn, in the street called Gold Street, opposite where the souls are of John and Joan Greenway, set up in gold letters, because we must take the homeward way at cockcrow of the morning. Though still John Fry was dry with me of the reason of his coming, and only told lies about father, and could not keep them agreeable, I hoped for the best, as all boys will, especially after a victory. And I thought, perhaps father had sent for me because he had a good harvest, and the rats were bad in the corn-chamber.

It was high noon before we were got to Dulverton that day, near to which town the river Exe and its big brother Barle have union. My mother had an uncle living there, but we were not to visit his house this time, at which I was somewhat astonished, since we needs must stop for at least two hours, to bait our horses thorough well, before coming to the black bogway. The bogs are very good in frost, except where the hot-springs rise; but as yet there had been no frost this year, save just enough to make the blackbirds look big in the morning. In a hearty black-frost they look small, until the snow falls over them.

The road from Bampton to Dulverton had not been very delicate, yet nothing to complain of much—no deeper, indeed, than the hocks of a horse, except in the rotten places. The day was inclined to be mild and foggy, and both nags sweated freely; but Peggy carrying little weight (for my wardrobe was upon Smiler, and John Fry grumbling always), we could easily keep in front, as far as you may hear a laugh.

John had been rather bitter with me, which methought was a mark of ill taste at coming home for the holidays; and yet I made allowance for John, because he had never been at school, and never would have chance to eat fry upon condition of spelling it; therefore I rode on, thinking that he was hard-set, like a saw, for his dinner, and would soften after tooth-work. And yet at his most hungry times, when his mind was far gone upon bacon, certes he seemed to check himself and look at me as if he were sorry for little things coming over great.

But now, at Dulverton, we dined upon the rarest and choicest victuals that ever I did taste. Even now, at my time of life, to think of it gives me appetite, as once and awhile to think of my first love makes me love all goodness. Hot mutton pasty was a thing I had often heard of from very wealthy boys and men, who made a dessert of dinner; and to hear them talk of it made my lips smack, and my ribs come inwards.

And now John Fry strode into the hostel, with the air and grace of a short-legged man, and shouted as loud as if he was calling sheep upon Exmoor,—

'Hot mooton pasty for twoo trarv'lers, at number vaive, in vaive minnits! Dish un up in the tin with the grahvy, zame as I hardered last Tuesday.'

Of course it did not come in five minutes, nor yet in ten or twenty; but that made it all the better when it came to the real presence; and the smell of it was enough to make an empty man thank God for the room there was inside him. Fifty years have passed me quicker than the taste of that gravy.

It is the manner of all good boys to be careless of apparel, and take no pride in adornment. Good lack, if I see a boy make to do about the fit of his crumpler, and the creasing of his breeches, and desire to be shod for comeliness rather than for use, I cannot 'scape the mark that God took thought to make a girl of him. Not so when they grow older, and court the regard of the maidens; then may the bravery pass from the inside to the outside of them; and no bigger fools are they, even then, than their fathers were before them. But God forbid any man to be a fool to love, and be loved, as I have been. Else would he have prevented it.

When the mutton pasty was done, and Peggy and Smiler had dined well also, out I went to wash at the pump, being a lover of soap and water, at all risk, except of my dinner. And John Fry, who cared very little to wash, save Sabbath days in his own soap, and who had kept me from the pump by threatening loss of the dish, out he came in a satisfied manner, with a piece of quill in his hand, to lean against a door-post, and listen to the horses feeding, and have his teeth ready for supper.

Then a lady's-maid came out, and the sun was on her face, and she turned round to go back again; but put a better face upon it, and gave a trip and hitched her dress, and looked at the sun full body, lest the hostlers should laugh that she was losing her complexion. With a long Italian glass in her fingers very daintily, she came up to the pump in the middle of the yard, where I was running the water off all my head and shoulders, and arms, and some of my breast even, and though I had glimpsed her through the sprinkle, it gave me quite a turn to see her, child as I was, in my open aspect. But she looked at me, no whit abashed, making a baby of me, no doubt, as a woman of thirty will do, even with a very big boy when they catch him on a hayrick, and she said to me in a brazen manner, as if I had been nobody, while I was shrinking behind the pump, and craving to get my shirt on, 'Good leetle boy, come hither to me. Fine heaven! how blue your eyes are, and your skin like snow; but some naughty man has beaten it black. Oh, leetle boy, let me feel it. Ah, how then it must have hurt you! There now, and you shall love me.'

All this time she was touching my breast, here and there, very lightly, with her delicate brown fingers, and I understood from her voice and manner that she was not of this country, but a foreigner by extraction. And then I was not so shy of her, because I could talk better English than she; and yet I longed for my jerkin, but liked not to be rude to her.

'If you please, madam, I must go. John Fry is waiting by the tapster's door, and Peggy neighing to me. If you please, we must get home to-night; and father will be waiting for me this side of the telling-house.'

'There, there, you shall go, leetle dear, and perhaps I will go after you. I have taken much love of you. But the baroness is hard to me. How far you call it now to the bank of the sea at Wash—Wash—'

'At Watchett, likely you mean, madam. Oh, a very long way, and the roads as soft as the road to Oare.'

'Oh-ah, oh-ah—I shall remember; that is the place where my leetle boy live, and some day I will come seek for him. Now make the pump to flow, my dear, and give me the good water. The baroness will not touch unless a nebule be formed outside the glass.'

I did not know what she meant by that; yet I pumped for her very heartily, and marvelled to see her for fifty times throw the water away in the trough, as if it was not good enough. At last the water suited her, with a likeness of fog outside the glass, and the gleam of a crystal under it, and then she made a curtsey to me, in a sort of mocking manner, holding the long glass by the foot, not to take the cloud off; and then she wanted to kiss me; but I was out of breath, and have always been shy of that work, except when I come to offer it; and so I ducked under the pump-handle, and she knocked her chin on the knob of it; and the hostlers came out, and asked whether they would do as well.

Upon this, she retreated up the yard, with a certain dark dignity, and a foreign way of walking, which stopped them at once from going farther, because it was so different from the fashion of their sweethearts. One with another they hung back, where half a cart-load of hay was, and they looked to be sure that she would not turn round; and then each one laughed at the rest of them.

Now, up to the end of Dulverton town, on the northward side of it, where the two new pig-sties be, the Oare folk and the Watchett folk must trudge on together, until we come to a broken cross, where a murdered man lies buried. Peggy and Smiler went up the hill, as if nothing could be too much for them, after the beans they had eaten, and suddenly turning a corner of trees, we happened upon a great coach and six horses labouring very heavily. John Fry rode on with his hat in his hand, as became him towards the quality; but I was amazed to that degree, that I left my cap on my head, and drew bridle without knowing it.

For in the front seat of the coach, which was half-way open, being of the city-make, and the day in want of air, sate the foreign lady, who had met me at the pump and offered to salute me. By her side was a little girl, dark-haired and very wonderful, with a wealthy softness on her, as if she must have her own way. I could not look at her for two glances, and she did not look at me for one, being such a little child, and busy with the hedges. But in the honourable place sate a handsome lady, very warmly dressed, and sweetly delicate of colour. And close to her was a lively child, two or it may be three years old, bearing a white cockade in his hat, and staring at all and everybody. Now, he saw Peggy, and took such a liking to her, that the lady his mother—if so she were—was forced to look at my pony and me. And, to tell the truth, although I am not of those who adore the high folk, she looked at us very kindly, and with a sweetness rarely found in the women who milk the cows for us.

Then I took off my cap to the beautiful lady, without asking wherefore; and she put up her hand and kissed it to me, thinking, perhaps, that I looked like a gentle and good little boy; for folk always called me innocent, though God knows I never was that. But now the foreign lady, or lady's maid, as it might be, who had been busy with little dark eyes, turned upon all this going-on, and looked me straight in the face. I was about to salute her, at a distance, indeed, and not with the nicety she had offered to me, but, strange to say, she stared at my eyes as if she had never seen me before, neither wished to see me again. At this I was so startled, such things beings out of my knowledge, that I startled Peggy also with the muscle of my legs, and she being fresh from stable, and the mire scraped off with cask-hoop, broke away so suddenly that I could do no more than turn round and lower my cap, now five months old, to the beautiful lady. Soon I overtook John Fry, and asked him all about them, and how it was that we had missed their starting from the hostel. But John would never talk much till after a gallon of cider; and all that I could win out of him was that they were 'murdering Papishers,' and little he cared to do with them, or the devil, as they came from. And a good thing for me, and a providence, that I was gone down Dulverton town to buy sweetstuff for Annie, else my stupid head would have gone astray with their great out-coming.

We saw no more of them after that, but turned into the sideway; and soon had the fill of our hands and eyes to look to our own going. For the road got worse and worse, until there was none at all, and perhaps the purest thing it could do was to be ashamed to show itself. But we pushed on as best we might, with doubt of reaching home any time, except by special grace of God.

The fog came down upon the moors as thick as ever I saw it; and there was no sound of any sort, nor a breath of wind to guide us. The little stubby trees that stand here and there, like bushes with a wooden leg to them, were drizzled with a mess of wet, and hung their points with dropping. Wherever the butt-end of a hedgerow came up from the hollow ground, like the withers of a horse, holes of splash were pocked and pimpled in the yellow sand of coneys, or under the dwarf tree's ovens. But soon it was too dark to see that, or anything else, I may say, except the creases in the dusk, where prisoned light crept up the valleys.

After awhile even that was gone, and no other comfort left us except to see our horses' heads jogging to their footsteps, and the dark ground pass below us, lighter where the wet was; and then the splash, foot after foot, more clever than we can do it, and the orderly jerk of the tail, and the smell of what a horse is.

John Fry was bowing forward with sleep upon his saddle, and now I could no longer see the frizzle of wet upon his beard—for he had a very brave one, of a bright red colour, and trimmed into a whale-oil knot, because he was newly married—although that comb of hair had been a subject of some wonder to me, whether I, in God's good time, should have the like of that, handsomely set with shining beads, small above and large below, from the weeping of the heaven. But still I could see the jog of his hat—a Sunday hat with a top to it—and some of his shoulder bowed out in the mist, so that one could say 'Hold up, John,' when Smiler put his foot in. 'Mercy of God! where be us now?' said John Fry, waking suddenly; 'us ought to have passed hold hash, Jan. Zeen it on the road, have 'ee?'

'No indeed, John; no old ash. Nor nothing else to my knowing; nor heard nothing, save thee snoring.'

'Watt a vule thee must be then, Jan; and me myzell no better. Harken, lad, harken!'

We drew our horses up and listened, through the thickness of the air, and with our hands laid to our ears. At first there was nothing to hear, except the panting of the horses and the trickle of the eaving drops from our head-covers and clothing, and the soft sounds of the lonely night, that make us feel, and try not to think. Then there came a mellow noise, very low and mournsome, not a sound to be afraid of, but to long to know the meaning, with a soft rise of the hair. Three times it came and went again, as the shaking of a thread might pass away into the distance; and then I touched John Fry to know that there was something near me.

'Doon't 'e be a vule, Jan! Vaine moozick as iver I 'eer. God bless the man as made un doo it.'

'Have they hanged one of the Doones then, John?'

'Hush, lad; niver talk laike o' thiccy. Hang a Doone! God knoweth, the King would hang pretty quick if her did.'

'Then who is it in the chains, John?'

I felt my spirit rise as I asked; for now I had crossed Exmoor so often as to hope that the people sometimes deserved it, and think that it might be a lesson to the rogues who unjustly loved the mutton they were never born to. But, of course, they were born to hanging, when they set themselves so high.

'It be nawbody,' said John, 'vor us to make a fush about. Belong to t'other zide o' the moor, and come staling shape to our zide. Red Jem Hannaford his name. Thank God for him to be hanged, lad; and good cess to his soul for craikin' zo.'

So the sound of the quiet swinging led us very modestly, as it came and went on the wind, loud and low pretty regularly, even as far as the foot of the gibbet where the four cross-ways are.

'Vamous job this here,' cried John, looking up to be sure of it, because there were so many; 'here be my own nick on the post. Red Jem, too, and no doubt of him; he do hang so handsome like, and his ribs up laike a horse a'most. God bless them as discoovered the way to make a rogue so useful. Good-naight to thee, Jem, my lad; and not break thy drames with the craikin'.'

John Fry shook his bridle-arm, and smote upon Smiler merrily, as he jogged into the homeward track from the guiding of the body. But I was sorry for Red Jem, and wanted to know more about him, and whether he might not have avoided this miserable end, and what his wife and children thought of it, if, indeed, he had any.

But John would talk no more about it; and perhaps he was moved with a lonesome feeling, as the creaking sound came after us.

'Hould thee tongue, lad,' he said sharply; 'us be naigh the Doone-track now, two maile from Dunkery Beacon hill, the haighest place of Hexmoor. So happen they be abroad to-naight, us must crawl on our belly-places, boy.'

I knew at once what he meant—those bloody Doones of Bagworthy, the awe of all Devon and Somerset, outlaws, traitors, murderers. My little legs began to tremble to and fro upon Peggy's sides, as I heard the dead robber in chains behind us, and thought of the live ones still in front.

'But, John,' I whispered warily, sidling close to his saddle-bow; 'dear John, you don't think they will see us in such a fog as this?'

'Never God made vog as could stop their eyesen,' he whispered in answer, fearfully; 'here us be by the hollow ground. Zober, lad, goo zober now, if thee wish to see thy moother.'

For I was inclined, in the manner of boys, to make a run of the danger, and cross the Doone-track at full speed; to rush for it, and be done with it. But even then I wondered why he talked of my mother so, and said not a word of father.

We were come to a long deep 'goyal,' as they call it on Exmoor, a word whose fountain and origin I have nothing to do with. Only I know that when little boys laughed at me at Tiverton, for talking about a 'goyal,' a big boy clouted them on the head, and said that it was in Homer, and meant the hollow of the hand. And another time a Welshman told me that it must be something like the thing they call a 'pant' in those parts. Still I know what it means well enough—to wit, a long trough among wild hills, falling towards the plain country, rounded at the bottom, perhaps, and stiff, more than steep, at the sides of it. Whether it be straight or crooked, makes no difference to it.

We rode very carefully down our side, and through the soft grass at the bottom, and all the while we listened as if the air was a speaking-trumpet. Then gladly we breasted our nags to the rise, and were coming to the comb of it, when I heard something, and caught John's arm, and he bent his hand to the shape of his ear. It was the sound of horses' feet knocking up through splashy ground, as if the bottom sucked them. Then a grunting of weary men, and the lifting noise of stirrups, and sometimes the clank of iron mixed with the wheezy croning of leather and the blowing of hairy nostrils.

'God's sake, Jack, slip round her belly, and let her go where she wull.'

As John Fry whispered, so I did, for he was off Smiler by this time; but our two pads were too fagged to go far, and began to nose about and crop, sniffing more than they need have done. I crept to John's side very softly, with the bridle on my arm.

'Let goo braidle; let goo, lad. Plaise God they take them for forest-ponies, or they'll zend a bullet through us.'

I saw what he meant, and let go the bridle; for now the mist was rolling off, and we were against the sky line to the dark cavalcade below us. John lay on the ground by a barrow of heather, where a little gullet was, and I crept to him, afraid of the noise I made in dragging my legs along, and the creak of my cord breeches. John bleated like a sheep to cover it—a sheep very cold and trembling.

Then just as the foremost horseman passed, scarce twenty yards below us, a puff of wind came up the glen, and the fog rolled off before it. And suddenly a strong red light, cast by the cloud-weight downwards, spread like fingers over the moorland, opened the alleys of darkness, and hung on the steel of the riders.

'Dunkery Beacon,' whispered John, so close into my ear, that I felt his lips and teeth ashake; 'dursn't fire it now except to show the Doones way home again, since the naight as they went up and throwed the watchmen atop of it. Why, wutt be 'bout, lad? God's sake—'

For I could keep still no longer, but wriggled away from his arm, and along the little gullet, still going flat on my breast and thighs, until I was under a grey patch of stone, with a fringe of dry fern round it; there I lay, scarce twenty feet above the heads of the riders, and I feared to draw my breath, though prone to do it with wonder.

For now the beacon was rushing up, in a fiery storm to heaven, and the form of its flame came and went in the folds, and the heavy sky was hovering. All around it was hung with red, deep in twisted columns, and then a giant beard of fire streamed throughout the darkness. The sullen hills were flanked with light, and the valleys chined with shadow, and all the sombrous moors between awoke in furrowed anger.

But most of all the flinging fire leaped into the rocky mouth of the glen below me, where the horsemen passed in silence, scarcely deigning to look round. Heavy men and large of stature, reckless how they bore their guns, or how they sate their horses, with leathern jerkins, and long boots, and iron plates on breast and head, plunder heaped behind their saddles, and flagons slung in front of them; I counted more than thirty pass, like clouds upon red sunset. Some had carcasses of sheep swinging with their skins on, others had deer, and one had a child flung across his saddle-bow. Whether the child were dead, or alive, was more than I could tell, only it hung head downwards there, and must take the chance of it. They had got the child, a very young one, for the sake of the dress, no doubt, which they could not stop to pull off from it; for the dress shone bright, where the fire struck it, as if with gold and jewels. I longed in my heart to know most sadly what they would do with the little thing, and whether they would eat it.

It touched me so to see that child, a prey among those vultures, that in my foolish rage and burning I stood up and shouted to them leaping on a rock, and raving out of all possession. Two of them turned round, and one set his carbine at me, but the other said it was but a pixie, and bade him keep his powder. Little they knew, and less thought I, that the pixie then before them would dance their castle down one day.

John Fry, who in the spring of fright had brought himself down from Smiler's side, as if he were dipped in oil, now came up to me, all risk being over, cross, and stiff, and aching sorely from his wet couch of heather.

'Small thanks to thee, Jan, as my new waife bain't a widder. And who be you to zupport of her, and her son, if she have one? Zarve thee right if I was to chuck thee down into the Doone-track. Zim thee'll come to un, zooner or later, if this be the zample of thee.'

And that was all he had to say, instead of thanking God! For if ever born man was in a fright, and ready to thank God for anything, the name of that man was John Fry not more than five minutes agone.

However, I answered nothing at all, except to be ashamed of myself; and soon we found Peggy and Smiler in company, well embarked on the homeward road, and victualling where the grass was good. Right glad they were to see us again—not for the pleasure of carrying, but because a horse (like a woman) lacks, and is better without, self-reliance.

My father never came to meet us, at either side of the telling-house, neither at the crooked post, nor even at home-linhay although the dogs kept such a noise that he must have heard us. Home-side of the linhay, and under the ashen hedge-row, where father taught me to catch blackbirds, all at once my heart went down, and all my breast was hollow. There was not even the lanthorn light on the peg against the cow's house, and nobody said 'Hold your noise!' to the dogs, or shouted 'Here our Jack is!'

I looked at the posts of the gate, in the dark, because they were tall, like father, and then at the door of the harness-room, where he used to smoke his pipe and sing. Then I thought he had guests perhaps—people lost upon the moors—whom he could not leave unkindly, even for his son's sake. And yet about that I was jealous, and ready to be vexed with him, when he should begin to make much of me. And I felt in my pocket for the new pipe which I had brought him from Tiverton, and said to myself, 'He shall not have it until to-morrow morning.'

Woe is me! I cannot tell. How I knew I know not now—only that I slunk away, without a tear, or thought of weeping, and hid me in a saw-pit. There the timber, over-head, came like streaks across me; and all I wanted was to lack, and none to tell me anything.

By-and-by, a noise came down, as of woman's weeping; and there my mother and sister were, choking and holding together. Although they were my dearest loves, I could not bear to look at them, until they seemed to want my help, and put their hands before their eyes.

Chapter IV A Very Rash Visit

My dear father had been killed by the Doones of Bagworthy, while riding home from Porlock market, on the Saturday evening. With him were six brother-farmers, all of them very sober; for father would have no company with any man who went beyond half a gallon of beer, or a single gallon of cider. The robbers had no grudge against him; for he had never flouted them, neither made overmuch of outcry, because they robbed other people. For he was a man of such strict honesty, and due parish feeling, that he knew it to be every man's own business to defend himself and his goods; unless he belonged to our parish, and then we must look after him.

These seven good farmers were jogging along, helping one another in the troubles of the road, and singing goodly hymns and songs to keep their courage moving, when suddenly a horseman stopped in the starlight full across them.

By dress and arms they knew him well, and by his size and stature, shown against the glimmer of the evening star; and though he seemed one man to seven, it was in truth one man to one. Of the six who had been singing songs and psalms about the power of God, and their own regeneration—such psalms as went the round, in those days, of the public-houses—there was not one but pulled out his money, and sang small beer to a Doone.

But father had been used to think that any man who was comfortable inside his own coat and waistcoat deserved to have no other set, unless he would strike a blow for them. And so, while his gossips doffed their hats, and shook with what was left of them, he set his staff above his head, and rode at the Doone robber. With a trick of his horse, the wild man escaped the sudden onset, although it must have amazed him sadly that any durst resist him. Then when Smiler was carried away with the dash and the weight of my father (not being brought up to battle, nor used to turn, save in plough harness), the outlaw whistled upon his thumb, and plundered the rest of the yeoman. But father, drawing at Smiler's head, to try to come back and help them, was in the midst of a dozen men, who seemed to come out of a turf-rick, some on horse, and some a-foot. Nevertheless, he smote lustily, so far as he could see; and being of great size and strength, and his blood well up, they had no easy job with him. With the play of his wrist, he cracked three or four crowns, being always famous at single-stick; until the rest drew their horses away, and he thought that he was master, and would tell his wife about it.

But a man beyond the range of staff was crouching by the peat-stack, with a long gun set to his shoulder, and he got poor father against the sky, and I cannot tell the rest of it. Only they knew that Smiler came home, with blood upon his withers, and father was found in the morning dead on the moor, with his ivy-twisted cudgel lying broken under him. Now, whether this were an honest fight, God judge betwixt the Doones and me.

It was more of woe than wonder, being such days of violence, that mother knew herself a widow, and her children fatherless. Of children there were only three, none of us fit to be useful yet, only to comfort mother, by making her to work for us. I, John Ridd, was the eldest, and felt it a heavy thing on me; next came sister Annie, with about two years between us; and then the little Eliza.

Now, before I got home and found my sad loss—and no boy ever loved his father more than I loved mine—mother had done a most wondrous thing, which made all the neighbours say that she must be mad, at least. Upon the Monday morning, while her husband lay unburied, she cast a white hood over her hair, and gathered a black cloak round her, and, taking counsel of no one, set off on foot for the Doone-gate.

In the early afternoon she came to the hollow and barren entrance, where in truth there was no gate, only darkness to go through. If I get on with this story, I shall have to tell of it by-and-by, as I saw it afterwards; and will not dwell there now. Enough that no gun was fired at her, only her eyes were covered over, and somebody led her by the hand, without any wish to hurt her.

A very rough and headstrong road was all that she remembered, for she could not think as she wished to do, with the cold iron pushed against her. At the end of this road they delivered her eyes, and she could scarce believe them.

For she stood at the head of a deep green valley, carved from out the mountains in a perfect oval, with a fence of sheer rock standing round it, eighty feet or a hundred high; from whose brink black wooded hills swept up to the sky-line. By her side a little river glided out from underground with a soft dark babble, unawares of daylight; then growing brighter, lapsed away, and fell into the valley. Then, as it ran down the meadow, alders stood on either marge, and grass was blading out upon it, and yellow tufts of rushes gathered, looking at the hurry. But further down, on either bank, were covered houses built of stone, square and roughly cornered, set as if the brook were meant to be the street between them. Only one room high they were, and not placed opposite each other, but in and out as skittles are; only that the first of all, which proved to be the captain's, was a sort of double house, or rather two houses joined together by a plank-bridge, over the river.

Fourteen cots my mother counted, all very much of a pattern, and nothing to choose between them, unless it were the captain's. Deep in the quiet valley there, away from noise, and violence, and brawl, save that of the rivulet, any man would have deemed them homes of simple mind and innocence. Yet not a single house stood there but was the home of murder.

Two men led my mother down a steep and gliddery stair-way, like the ladder of a hay-mow; and thence from the break of the falling water as far as the house of the captain. And there at the door they left her trembling, strung as she was, to speak her mind.

Now, after all, what right had she, a common farmer's widow, to take it amiss that men of birth thought fit to kill her husband. And the Doones were of very high birth, as all we clods of Exmoor knew; and we had enough of good teaching now—let any man say the contrary—to feel that all we had belonged of right to those above us. Therefore my mother was half-ashamed that she could not help complaining.

But after a little while, as she said, remembrance of her husband came, and the way he used to stand by her side and put his strong arm round her, and how he liked his bacon fried, and praised her kindly for it—and so the tears were in her eyes, and nothing should gainsay them.

A tall old man, Sir Ensor Doone, came out with a bill-hook in his hand, hedger's gloves going up his arms, as if he were no better than a labourer at ditch-work. Only in his mouth and eyes, his gait, and most of all his voice, even a child could know and feel that here was no ditch-labourer. Good cause he has found since then, perhaps, to wish that he had been one.

With his white locks moving upon his coat, he stopped and looked down at my mother, and she could not help herself but curtsey under the fixed black gazing.

'Good woman, you are none of us. Who has brought you hither? Young men must be young—but I have had too much of this work.'

And he scowled at my mother, for her comeliness; and yet looked under his eyelids as if he liked her for it. But as for her, in her depth of love-grief, it struck scorn upon her womanhood; and in the flash she spoke.

'What you mean I know not. Traitors! cut-throats! cowards! I am here to ask for my husband.' She could not say any more, because her heart was now too much for her, coming hard in her throat and mouth; but she opened up her eyes at him.

'Madam,' said Sir Ensor Doone—being born a gentleman, although a very bad one—'I crave pardon of you. My eyes are old, or I might have known. Now, if we have your husband prisoner, he shall go free without ransoms, because I have insulted you.'

'Sir,' said my mother, being suddenly taken away with sorrow, because of his gracious manner, 'please to let me cry a bit.'

He stood away, and seemed to know that women want no help for that. And by the way she cried he knew that they had killed her husband.

Then, having felt of grief himself, he was not angry with her, but left her to begin again.

'Loth would I be,' said mother, sobbing with her new red handkerchief, and looking at the pattern of it, 'loth indeed, Sir Ensor Doone, to accuse any one unfairly. But I have lost the very best husband God ever gave to a woman; and I knew him when he was to your belt, and I not up to your knee, sir; and never an unkind word he spoke, nor stopped me short in speaking. All the herbs he left to me, and all the bacon-curing, and when it was best to kill a pig, and how to treat the maidens. Not that I would ever wish—oh, John, it seems so strange to me, and last week you were everything.'

Here mother burst out crying again, not loudly, but turning quietly, because she knew that no one now would ever care to wipe the tears. And fifty or a hundred things, of weekly and daily happening, came across my mother, so that her spirit fell like slackening lime.

'This matter must be seen to; it shall be seen to at once,' the old man answered, moved a little in spite of all his knowledge. 'Madam, if any wrong has been done, trust the honour of a Doone; I will redress it to my utmost. Come inside and rest yourself, while I ask about it. What was your good husband's name, and when and where fell this mishap?'

'Deary me,' said mother, as he set a chair for her very polite, but she would not sit upon it; 'Saturday morning I was a wife, sir; and Saturday night I was a widow, and my children fatherless. My husband's name was John Ridd, sir, as everybody knows; and there was not a finer or better man in Somerset or Devon. He was coming home from Porlock market, and a new gown for me on the crupper, and a shell to put my hair up—oh, John, how good you were to me!'

Of that she began to think again, and not to believe her sorrow, except as a dream from the evil one, because it was too bad upon her, and perhaps she would awake in a minute, and her husband would have the laugh of her. And so she wiped her eyes and smiled, and looked for something.

'Madam, this is a serious thing,' Sir Ensor Doone said graciously, and showing grave concern: 'my boys are a little wild, I know. And yet I cannot think that they would willingly harm any one. And yet—and yet, you do look wronged. Send Counsellor to me,' he shouted, from the door of his house; and down the valley went the call, 'Send Counsellor to Captain.'

Counsellor Doone came in ere yet my mother was herself again; and if any sight could astonish her when all her sense of right and wrong was gone astray with the force of things, it was the sight of the Counsellor. A square-built man of enormous strength, but a foot below the Doone stature (which I shall describe hereafter), he carried a long grey beard descending to the leather of his belt. Great eyebrows overhung his face, like ivy on a pollard oak, and under them two large brown eyes, as of an owl when muting. And he had a power of hiding his eyes, or showing them bright, like a blazing fire. He stood there with his beaver off, and mother tried to look at him, but he seemed not to descry her.

'Counsellor,' said Sir Ensor Doone, standing back in his height from him, 'here is a lady of good repute—'

'Oh, no, sir; only a woman.'

'Allow me, madam, by your good leave. Here is a lady, Counsellor, of great repute in this part of the country, who charges the Doones with having unjustly slain her husband—'

'Murdered him! murdered him!' cried my mother, 'if ever there was a murder. Oh, sir! oh, sir! you know it.'

'The perfect rights and truth of the case is all I wish to know,' said the old man, very loftily: 'and justice shall be done, madam.'

'Oh, I pray you—pray you, sirs, make no matter of business of it. God from Heaven, look on me!'

'Put the case,' said the Counsellor.

'The case is this,' replied Sir Ensor, holding one hand up to mother: 'This lady's worthy husband was slain, it seems, upon his return from the market at Porlock, no longer ago than last Saturday night. Madam, amend me if I am wrong.'

'No longer, indeed, indeed, sir. Sometimes it seems a twelvemonth, and sometimes it seems an hour.'

'Cite his name,' said the Counsellor, with his eyes still rolling inwards.

'Master John Ridd, as I understand. Counsellor, we have heard of him often; a worthy man and a peaceful one, who meddled not with our duties. Now, if any of our boys have been rough, they shall answer it dearly. And yet I can scarce believe it. For the folk about these parts are apt to misconceive of our sufferings, and to have no feeling for us. Counsellor, you are our record, and very stern against us; tell us how this matter was.'

'Oh, Counsellor!' my mother cried; 'Sir Counsellor, you will be fair: I see it in your countenance. Only tell me who it was, and set me face to face with him, and I will bless you, sir, and God shall bless you, and my children.'

The square man with the long grey beard, quite unmoved by anything, drew back to the door and spoke, and his voice was like a fall of stones in the bottom of a mine.

'Few words will be enow for this. Four or five of our best-behaved and most peaceful gentlemen went to the little market at Porlock with a lump of money. They bought some household stores and comforts at a very high price, and pricked upon the homeward road, away from vulgar revellers. When they drew bridle to rest their horses, in the shelter of a peat-rick, the night being dark and sudden, a robber of great size and strength rode into the midst of them, thinking to kill or terrify. His arrogance and hardihood at the first amazed them, but they would not give up without a blow goods which were on trust with them. He had smitten three of them senseless, for the power of his arm was terrible; whereupon the last man tried to ward his blow with a pistol. Carver, sir, it was, our brave and noble Carver, who saved the lives of his brethren and his own; and glad enow they were to escape. Notwithstanding, we hoped it might be only a flesh-wound, and not to speed him in his sins.'

As this atrocious tale of lies turned up joint by joint before her, like a 'devil's coach-horse,'* mother was too much amazed to do any more than look at him, as if the earth must open. But the only thing that opened was the great brown eyes of the Counsellor, which rested on my mother's face with a dew of sorrow, as he spoke of sins.

She, unable to bear them, turned suddenly on Sir Ensor, and caught (as she fancied) a smile on his lips, and a sense of quiet enjoyment.

'All the Doones are gentlemen,' answered the old man gravely, and looking as if he had never smiled since he was a baby. 'We are always glad to explain, madam, any mistake which the rustic people may fall upon about us; and we wish you clearly to conceive that we do not charge your poor husband with any set purpose of robbery, neither will we bring suit for any attainder of his property. Is it not so, Counsellor?'

'Without doubt his land is attainted; unless is mercy you forbear, sir.'

'Counsellor, we will forbear. Madam, we will forgive him. Like enough he knew not right from wrong, at that time of night. The waters are strong at Porlock, and even an honest man may use his staff unjustly in this unchartered age of violence and rapine.'

The Doones to talk of rapine! Mother's head went round so that she curtseyed to them both, scarcely knowing where she was, but calling to mind her manners. All the time she felt a warmth, as if the right was with her, and yet she could not see the way to spread it out before them. With that, she dried her tears in haste and went into the cold air, for fear of speaking mischief.

But when she was on the homeward road, and the sentinels had charge of her, blinding her eyes, as if she were not blind enough with weeping, some one came in haste behind her, and thrust a heavy leathern bag into the limp weight of her hand.

'Captain sends you this,' he whispered; 'take it to the little ones.'

But mother let it fall in a heap, as if it had been a blind worm; and then for the first time crouched before God, that even the Doones should pity her.

Chapter V An Illegal Settlement

Good folk who dwell in a lawful land, if any such there be, may for want of exploration, judge our neighbourhood harshly, unless the whole truth is set before them. In bar of such prejudice, many of us ask leave to explain how and why it was the robbers came to that head in the midst of us. We would rather not have had it so, God knows as well as anybody; but it grew upon us gently, in the following manner. Only let all who read observe that here I enter many things which came to my knowledge in later years.

In or about the year of our Lord 1640, when all the troubles of England were swelling to an outburst, great estates in the North country were

*The cock-tailed beetle has earned this name in the West of England.

suddenly confiscated, through some feud of families and strong influence at Court, and the owners were turned upon the world, and might think themselves lucky to save their necks. These estates were in co-heirship, joint tenancy I think they called it, although I know not the meaning, only so that if either tenant died, the other living, all would come to the live one in spite of any testament.

One of the joint owners was Sir Ensor Doone, a gentleman of brisk intellect; and the other owner was his cousin, the Earl of Lorne and Dykemont.

Lord Lorne was some years the elder of his cousin, Ensor Doone, and was making suit to gain severance of the cumbersome joint tenancy by any fair apportionment, when suddenly this blow fell on them by wiles and woman's meddling; and instead of dividing the land, they were divided from it.

The nobleman was still well-to-do, though crippled in his expenditure; but as for the cousin, he was left a beggar, with many to beg from him. He thought that the other had wronged him, and that all the trouble of law befell through his unjust petition. Many friends advised him to make interest at Court; for having done no harm whatever, and being a good Catholic, which Lord Lorne was not, he would be sure to find hearing there, and probably some favour. But he, like a very hot-brained man, although he had long been married to the daughter of his cousin (whom he liked none the more for that), would have nothing to say to any attempt at making a patch of it, but drove away with his wife and sons, and the relics of his money, swearing hard at everybody. In this he may have been quite wrong; probably, perhaps, he was so; but I am not convinced at all but what most of us would have done the same.

Some say that, in the bitterness of that wrong and outrage, he slew a gentleman of the Court, whom he supposed to have borne a hand in the plundering of his fortunes. Others say that he bearded King Charles the First himself, in a manner beyond forgiveness. One thing, at any rate, is sure—Sir Ensor was attainted, and made a felon outlaw, through some violent deed ensuing upon his dispossession.

He had searched in many quarters for somebody to help him, and with good warrant for hoping it, inasmuch as he, in lucky days, had been open-handed and cousinly to all who begged advice of him. But now all these provided him with plenty of good advice indeed, and great assurance of feeling, but not a movement of leg, or lip, or purse-string in his favour. All good people of either persuasion, royalty or commonalty, knowing his kitchen-range to be cold, no longer would play turnspit. And this, it may be, seared his heart more than loss of land and fame.

In great despair at last, he resolved to settle in some outlandish part, where none could be found to know him; and so, in an evil day for us, he came to the West of England. Not that our part of the world is at all outlandish, according to my view of it (for I never found a better one), but that it was known to be rugged, and large, and desolate. And here, when he had discovered a place which seemed almost to be made for him, so withdrawn, so self-defended, and uneasy of access, some of the country-folk around brought him little offerings—a side of bacon, a keg of cider, hung mutton, or a brisket of venison; so that for a little while he was very honest. But when the newness of his coming began to wear away, and our good folk were apt to think that even a gentleman ought to work or pay other men for doing it, and many farmers were grown weary of manners without discourse to them, and all cried out to one another how unfair it was that owning such a fertile valley young men would not spade or plough by reason of noble lineage—then the young Doones growing up took things they would not ask for.

And here let me, as a solid man, owner of five hundred acres (whether fenced or otherwise, and that is my own business), churchwarden also of this parish (until I go to the churchyard), and proud to be called the parson's friend—for a better man I never knew with tobacco and strong waters, nor one who could read the lessons so well and he has been at Blundell's too—once for all let me declare, that I am a thorough-going Church-and-State man, and Royalist, without any mistake about it. And this I lay down, because some people judging a sausage by the skin, may take in evil part my little glosses of style and glibness, and the mottled nature of my remarks and cracks now and then on the frying-pan. I assure them I am good inside, and not a bit of rue in me; only queer knots, as of marjoram, and a stupid manner of bursting.

There was not more than a dozen of them, counting a few retainers who still held by Sir Ensor; but soon they grew and multiplied in a manner surprising to think of. Whether it was the venison, which we call a strengthening victual, or whether it was the Exmoor mutton, or the keen soft air of the moorlands, anyhow the Doones increased much faster than their honesty. At first they had brought some ladies with them, of good repute with charity; and then, as time went on, they added to their stock by carrying. They carried off many good farmers' daughters, who were sadly displeased at first; but took to them kindly after awhile, and made a new home in their babies. For women, as it seems to me, like strong men more than weak ones, feeling that they need some staunchness, something to hold fast by.

And of all the men in our country, although we are of a thick-set breed, you scarce could find one in three-score fit to be placed among the Doones, without looking no more than a tailor. Like enough, we could meet them man for man (if we chose all around the crown and the skirts of Exmoor), and show them what a cross-buttock means, because we are so stuggy; but in regard of stature, comeliness, and bearing, no woman would look twice at us. Not but what I myself, John Ridd, and one or two I know of—but it becomes me best not to talk of that, although my hair is gray.

Perhaps their den might well have been stormed, and themselves driven out of the forest, if honest people had only agreed to begin with them at once when first they took to plundering. But having respect for their good birth, and pity for their misfortunes, and perhaps a little admiration at the justice of God, that robbed men now were robbers, the squires, and farmers, and shepherds, at first did nothing more than grumble gently, or even make a laugh of it, each in the case of others. After awhile they found the matter gone too far for laughter, as violence and deadly outrage stained the hand of robbery, until every woman clutched her child, and every man turned pale at the very name of Doone. For the sons and grandsons of Sir Ensor grew up in foul liberty, and haughtiness, and hatred, to utter scorn of God and man, and brutality towards dumb animals. There was only one good thing about them, if indeed it were good, to wit, their faith to one another, and truth to their wild eyry. But this only made them feared the more, so certain was the revenge they wreaked upon any who dared to strike a Doone. One night, some ten years ere I was born, when they were sacking a rich man's house not very far from Minehead, a shot was fired at them in the dark, of which they took little notice, and only one of them knew that any harm was done. But when they were well on the homeward road, not having slain either man or woman, or even burned a house down, one of their number fell from his saddle, and died without so much as a groan. The youth had been struck, but would not complain, and perhaps took little heed of the wound, while he was bleeding inwardly. His brothers and cousins laid him softly on a bank of whortle-berries, and just rode back to the lonely hamlet where he had taken his death-wound. No man nor woman was left in the morning, nor house for any to dwell in, only a child with its reason gone.*

This affair made prudent people find more reason to let them alone than to meddle with them; and now they had so entrenched themselves, and waxed so strong in number, that nothing less than a troop of soldiers could wisely enter their premises; and even so it might turn out ill, as perchance we shall see by-and-by.

For not to mention the strength of the place, which I shall describe in its proper order when I come to visit it, there was not one among them but was a mighty man, straight and tall, and wide, and fit to lift four hundredweight. If son or grandson of old Doone, or one of the northern retainers, failed at the age of twenty, while standing on his naked feet to touch with his forehead the lintel of Sir Ensor's door, and to fill the door frame with his shoulders from sidepost even to sidepost, he was led away to the narrow pass which made their valley so desperate, and thrust from the crown with ignominy, to get his own living honestly. Now, the measure of that doorway is, or rather was, I ought to say, six feet and one inch lengthwise, and two feet all but two inches taken crossways in the clear. Yet I not only have heard but know, being so closely mixed with them, that no descendant of old Sir Ensor, neither relative of his (except, indeed, the Counsellor, who was kept by them for his wisdom), and no more than two of their following ever failed of that test, and relapsed to the difficult ways of honesty.

Not that I think anything great of a standard the like of that: for if they had set me in that door-frame at the age of twenty, it is like enough

*This vile deed was done, beyond all doubt.

that I should have walked away with it on my shoulders, though I was not come to my full strength then: only I am speaking now of the average size of our neighbourhood, and the Doones were far beyond that. Moreover, they were taught to shoot with a heavy carbine so delicately and wisely, that even a boy could pass a ball through a rabbit's head at the distance of fourscore yards. Some people may think nought of this, being in practice with longer shots from the tongue than from the shoulder; nevertheless, to do as above is, to my ignorance, very good work, if you can be sure to do it. Not one word do I believe of Robin Hood splitting peeled wands at seven-score yards, and such like. Whoever wrote such stories knew not how slippery a peeled wand is, even if one could hit it, and how it gives to the onset. Now, let him stick one in the ground, and take his bow and arrow at it, ten yards away, or even five.

Now, after all this which I have written, and all the rest which a reader will see, being quicker of mind than I am (who leave more than half behind me, like a man sowing wheat, with his dinner laid in the ditch too near his dog), it is much but what you will understand the Doones far better than I did, or do even to this moment; and therefore none will doubt when I tell them that our good justiciaries feared to make an ado, or hold any public inquiry about my dear father's death. They would all have had to ride home that night, and who could say what might betide them. Least said soonest mended, because less chance of breaking.

So we buried him quietly—all except my mother, indeed, for she could not keep silence—in the sloping little churchyard of Oare, as meek a place as need be, with the Lynn brook down below it. There is not much of company there for anybody's tombstone, because the parish spreads so far in woods and moors without dwelling-house. If we bury one man in three years, or even a woman or child, we talk about it for three months, and say it must be our turn next, and scarcely grow accustomed to it until another goes.

Annie was not allowed to come, because she cried so terribly; but she ran to the window, and saw it all, mooing there like a little calf, so frightened and so left alone. As for Eliza, she came with me, one on each side of mother, and not a tear was in her eyes, but sudden starts of wonder, and a new thing to be looked at unwillingly, yet curiously. Poor little thing! she was very clever, the only one of our family—thank God for the same—but none the more for that guessed she what it is to lose a father.

Chapter VI Necessary Practice

About the rest of all that winter I remember very little, being only a young boy then, and missing my father most out of doors, as when it came to the bird-catching, or the tracking of hares in the snow, or the training of a sheep-dog. Oftentimes I looked at his gun, an ancient piece found in the sea, a little below Glenthorne, and of which he was mighty proud, although it was only a match-lock; and I thought of the times I had held the fuse, while he got his aim at a rabbit, and once even at a red deer rubbing among the hazels. But nothing came of my looking at it, so far as I remember, save foolish tears of my own perhaps, till John Fry took it down one day from the hooks where father's hand had laid it; and it hurt me to see how John handled it, as if he had no memory.

'Bad job for he as her had not got thiccy the naight as her coom acrass them Doones. Rackon Varmer Jan 'ood a-zhown them the wai to kingdom come, 'stead of gooin' herzel zo aisy. And a maight have been gooin' to market now, 'stead of laying banked up over yanner. Maister Jan, thee can zee the grave if thee look alang this here goon-barryel. Buy now, whutt be blubberin' at? Wish I had never told thee.'

'John Fry, I am not blubbering; you make a great mistake, John. You are thinking of little Annie. I cough sometimes in the winter-weather, and father gives me lickerish—I mean—I mean—he used to. Now let me have the gun, John.'

'Thee have the goon, Jan! Thee isn't fit to putt un to thy zhoulder. What a weight her be, for sure!'

'Me not hold it, John! That shows how much you know about it. Get out of the way, John; you are opposite the mouth of it, and likely it is loaded.'

John Fry jumped in a livelier manner than when he was doing day-work; and I rested the mouth on a cross rack-piece, and felt a warm sort of surety that I could hit the door over opposite, or, at least, the cobwall alongside of it, and do no harm in the orchard. But John would not give me link or fuse, and, on the whole, I was glad of it, though carrying on as boys do, because I had heard my father say that the Spanish gun kicked like a horse, and because the load in it came from his hand, and I did not like to undo it. But I never found it kick very hard, and firmly set to the shoulder, unless it was badly loaded. In truth, the thickness of the metal was enough almost to astonish one; and what our people said about it may have been true enough, although most of them are such liars—at least, I mean, they make mistakes, as all mankind must do. Perchance it was no mistake at all to say that this ancient gun had belonged to a noble Spaniard, the captain of a fine large ship in the 'Invincible Armada,' which we of England managed to conquer, with God and the weather helping us, a hundred years ago or more—I can't say to a month or so.

After a little while, when John had fired away at a rat the charge I held so sacred, it came to me as a natural thing to practise shooting with that great gun, instead of John Fry's blunderbuss, which looked like a bell with a stalk to it. Perhaps for a boy there is nothing better than a good windmill to shoot at, as I have seen them in flat countries; but we have no windmills upon the great moorland, yet here and there a few barn-doors, where shelter is, and a way up the hollows. And up those hollows you can shoot, with the help of the sides to lead your aim, and there is a fair chance of hitting the door, if you lay your cheek to the barrel, and try not to be afraid of it.

Gradually I won such skill, that I sent nearly all the lead gutter from the north porch of our little church through our best barn-door, a thing which has often repented me since, especially as churchwarden, and made me pardon many bad boys; but father was not buried on that side of the church.

But all this time, while I was roving over the hills or about the farm, and even listening to John Fry, my mother, being so much older and feeling trouble longer, went about inside the house, or among the maids and fowls, not caring to talk to the best of them, except when she broke out sometimes about the good master they had lost, all and every one of us. But the fowls would take no notice of it, except to cluck for barley; and the maidens, though they had liked him well, were thinking of their sweethearts as the spring came on. Mother thought it wrong of them, selfish and ungrateful; and yet sometimes she was proud that none had such call as herself to grieve for him. Only Annie seemed to go softly in and out, and cry, with nobody along of her, chiefly in the corner where the bees are and the grindstone. But somehow she would never let anybody behold her; being set, as you may say, to think it over by herself, and season it with weeping. Many times I caught her, and many times she turned upon me, and then I could not look at her, but asked how long to dinner-time.

Now in the depth of the winter month, such as we call December, father being dead and quiet in his grave a fortnight, it happened me to be out of powder for practice against his enemies. I had never fired a shot without thinking, 'This for father's murderer'; and John Fry said that I made such faces it was a wonder the gun went off. But though I could hardly hold the gun, unless with my back against a bar, it did me good to hear it go off, and hope to have hitten his enemies.

'Oh, mother, mother,' I said that day, directly after dinner, while she was sitting looking at me, and almost ready to say (as now she did seven times in a week), 'How like your father you are growing! Jack, come here and kiss me'—'oh, mother, if you only knew how much I want a shilling!'

'Jack, you shall never want a shilling while I am alive to give thee one. But what is it for, dear heart, dear heart?'

'To buy something over at Porlock, mother. Perhaps I will tell you afterwards. If I tell not it will be for your good, and for the sake of the children.'

'Bless the boy, one would think he was threescore years of age at least. Give me a little kiss, you Jack, and you shall have the shilling.'

For I hated to kiss or be kissed in those days: and so all honest boys must do, when God puts any strength in them. But now I wanted the powder so much that I went and kissed mother very shyly, looking round the corner first, for Betty not to see me.

But mother gave me half a dozen, and only one shilling for all of them; and I could not find it in my heart to ask her for another, although I would have taken it. In very quick time I ran away with the shilling in my pocket, and got Peggy out on the Porlock road without my mother knowing it. For mother was frightened of that road now, as if all the trees were murderers, and would never let me go alone so much as a hundred yards on it. And, to tell the truth, I was touched with fear for many years about it; and even now, when I ride at dark there, a man by a peat-rick makes me shiver, until I go and collar him. But this time I was very bold, having John Fry's blunderbuss, and keeping a sharp look-out wherever any lurking place was. However, I saw only sheep and small red cattle, and the common deer of the forest, until I was nigh to Porlock town, and then rode straight to Mr. Pooke's, at the sign of the Spit and Gridiron.

Mr. Pooke was asleep, as it happened, not having much to do that day; and so I fastened Peggy by the handle of a warming-pan, at which she had no better manners than to snort and blow her breath; and in I walked with a manful style, bearing John Fry's blunderbuss. Now Timothy Pooke was a peaceful man, glad to live without any enjoyment of mind at danger, and I was tall and large already as most lads of a riper age. Mr. Pooke, as soon as he opened his eyes, dropped suddenly under the counting-board, and drew a great frying-pan over his head, as if the Doones were come to rob him, as their custom was, mostly after the fair-time. It made me feel rather hot and queer to be taken for a robber; and yet methinks I was proud of it.

'Gadzooks, Master Pooke,' said I, having learned fine words at Tiverton; 'do you suppose that I know not then the way to carry firearms? An it were the old Spanish match-lock in the lieu of this good flint-engine, which may be borne ten miles or more and never once go off, scarcely couldst thou seem more scared. I might point at thee muzzle on—just so as I do now—even for an hour or more, and like enough it would never shoot thee, unless I pulled the trigger hard, with a crock upon my finger; so you see; just so, Master Pooke, only a trifle harder.'

'God sake, John Ridd, God sake, dear boy,' cried Pooke, knowing me by this time; 'don't 'e, for good love now, don't 'e show it to me, boy, as if I was to suck it. Put 'un down, for good, now; and thee shall have the very best of all is in the shop.'

'Ho!' I replied with much contempt, and swinging round the gun so that it fetched his hoop of candles down, all unkindled as they were: 'Ho! as if I had not attained to the handling of a gun yet! My hands are cold coming over the moors, else would I go bail to point the mouth at you for an hour, sir, and no cause for uneasiness.'

But in spite of all assurances, he showed himself desirous only to see the last of my gun and me. I dare say 'villainous saltpetre,' as the great playwright calls it, was never so cheap before nor since. For my shilling Master Pooke afforded me two great packages over-large to go into my pockets, as well as a mighty chunk of lead, which I bound upon Peggy's withers. And as if all this had not been enough, he presented me with a roll of comfits for my sister Annie, whose gentle face and pretty manners won the love of everybody.

There was still some daylight here and there as I rose the hill above Porlock, wondering whether my mother would be in a fright, or would not know it. The two great packages of powder, slung behind my back, knocked so hard against one another that I feared they must either spill or blow up, and hurry me over Peggy's ears from the woollen cloth I rode upon. For father always liked a horse to have some wool upon his loins whenever he went far from home, and had to stand about, where one pleased, hot, and wet, and panting. And father always said that saddles were meant for men full-grown and heavy, and losing their activity; and no boy or young man on our farm durst ever get into a saddle, because they all knew that the master would chuck them out pretty quickly. As for me, I had tried it once, from a kind of curiosity; and I could not walk for two or three days, the leather galled my knees so. But now, as Peggy bore me bravely, snorting every now and then into a cloud of air, for the night was growing frosty, presently the moon arose over the shoulder of a hill, and the pony and I were half glad to see her, and half afraid of the shadows she threw, and the images all around us. I was ready at any moment to shoot at anybody, having great faith in my blunderbuss, but hoping not to prove it. And as I passed the narrow place where the Doones had killed my father, such a fear broke out upon me that I leaned upon the neck of Peggy, and shut my eyes, and was cold all over. However, there was not a soul to be seen, until we came home to the old farmyard, and there was my mother crying sadly, and Betty Muxworthy scolding.

'Come along, now,' I whispered to Annie, the moment supper was over; 'and if you can hold your tongue, Annie, I will show you something.'

She lifted herself on the bench so quickly, and flushed so rich with pleasure, that I was obliged to stare hard away, and make Betty look beyond us. Betty thought I had something hid in the closet beyond the clock-case, and she was the more convinced of it by reason of my denial. Not that Betty Muxworthy, or any one else, for that matter, ever found me in a falsehood, because I never told one, not even to my mother—or, which is still a stronger thing, not even to my sweetheart (when I grew up to have one)—but that Betty being wronged in the matter of marriage, a generation or two agone, by a man who came hedging and ditching, had now no mercy, except to believe that men from cradle to grave are liars, and women fools to look at them.

When Betty could find no crime of mine, she knocked me out of the way in a minute, as if I had been nobody; and then she began to coax 'Mistress Annie,' as she always called her, and draw the soft hair down her hands, and whisper into the little ears. Meanwhile, dear mother was falling asleep, having been troubled so much about me; and Watch, my father's pet dog, was nodding closer and closer up into her lap.

'Now, Annie, will you come?' I said, for I wanted her to hold the ladle for melting of the lead; 'will you come at once, Annie? or must I go for Lizzie, and let her see the whole of it?'

'Indeed, then, you won't do that,' said Annie; 'Lizzie to come before me, John; and she can't stir a pot of brewis, and scarce knows a tongue from a ham, John, and says it makes no difference, because both are good to eat! Oh, Betty, what do you think of that to come of all her book-learning?'

'Thank God he can't say that of me,' Betty answered shortly, for she never cared about argument, except on her own side; 'thank he, I says, every marning a'most, never to lead me astray so. Men is desaving and so is galanies; but the most desaving of all is books, with their heads and tails, and the speckots in 'em, lik a peg as have taken the maisles. Some folk purtends to laugh and cry over them. God forgive them for liars!'

It was part of Betty's obstinacy that she never would believe in reading or the possibility of it, but stoutly maintained to the very last that people first learned things by heart, and then pretended to make them out from patterns done upon paper, for the sake of astonishing honest folk just as do the conjurers. And even to see the parson and clerk was not enough to convince her; all she said was, 'It made no odds, they were all the same as the rest of us.' And now that she had been on the farm nigh upon forty years, and had nursed my father, and made his clothes, and all that he had to eat, and then put him in his coffin, she was come to such authority, that it was not worth the wages of the best man on the place to say a word in answer to Betty, even if he would face the risk to have ten for one, or twenty.

Annie was her love and joy. For Annie she would do anything, even so far as to try to smile, when the little maid laughed and danced to her. And in truth I know not how it was, but every one was taken with Annie at the very first time of seeing her. She had such pretty ways and manners, and such a look of kindness, and a sweet soft light in her long blue eyes full of trustful gladness. Everybody who looked at her seemed to grow the better for it, because she knew no evil. And then the turn she had for cooking, you never would have expected it; and how it was her richest mirth to see that she had pleased you. I have been out on the world a vast deal as you will own hereafter, and yet have I never seen Annie's equal for making a weary man comfortable.

Chapter VII Hard It Is To Climb

So many a winter night went by in a hopeful and pleasant manner, with the hissing of the bright round bullets, cast into the water, and the spluttering of the great red apples which Annie was roasting for me. We always managed our evening's work in the chimney of the back-kitchen, where there was room to set chairs and table, in spite of the fire burning. On the right-hand side was a mighty oven, where Betty threatened to bake us; and on the left, long sides of bacon, made of favoured pigs, and growing very brown and comely. Annie knew the names of all, and ran up through the wood-smoke, every now and then, when a gentle memory moved her, and asked them how they were getting on, and when they would like to be eaten. Then she came back with foolish tears, at thinking of that necessity; and I, being soft in a different way, would make up my mind against bacon.

But, Lord bless you! it was no good. Whenever it came to breakfast-time, after three hours upon the moors, I regularly forgot the pigs, but paid good heed to the rashers. For ours is a hungry county, if such there be in England; a place, I mean, where men must eat, and are quick to discharge the duty. The air of the moors is so shrewd and wholesome, stirring a man's recollection of the good things which have betided him, and whetting his hope of something still better in the future, that by the time he sits down to a cloth, his heart and stomach are tuned too well to say 'nay' to one another.

Almost everybody knows, in our part of the world at least, how pleasant and soft the fall of the land is round about Plover's Barrows farm. All above it is strong dark mountain, spread with heath, and desolate, but near our house the valleys cove, and open warmth and shelter. Here are trees, and bright green grass, and orchards full of contentment, and a man may scarce espy the brook, although he hears it everywhere. And indeed a stout good piece of it comes through our farm-yard, and swells sometimes to a rush of waves, when the clouds are on the hill-tops. But all below, where the valley bends, and the Lynn stream comes along with it, pretty meadows slope their breast, and the sun spreads on the water. And nearly all of this is ours, till you come to Nicholas Snowe's land.

But about two miles below our farm, the Bagworthy water runs into the Lynn, and makes a real river of it. Thence it hurries away, with strength and a force of wilful waters, under the foot of a barefaced hill, and so to rocks and woods again, where the stream is covered over, and dark, heavy pools delay it. There are plenty of fish all down this way, and the farther you go the larger they get, having deeper grounds to feed in; and sometimes in the summer months, when mother could spare me off the farm, I came down here, with Annie to help (because it was so lonely), and caught well-nigh a basketful of little trout and minnows, with a hook and a bit of worm on it, or a fern-web, or a blow-fly, hung from a hazel pulse-stick. For of all the things I learned at Blundell's, only two abode with me, and one of these was the knack of fishing, and the other the art of swimming. And indeed they have a very rude manner of teaching children to swim there; for the big boys take the little boys, and put them through a certain process, which they grimly call 'sheep-washing.' In the third meadow from the gate of the school, going up the river, there is a fine pool in the Lowman, where the Taunton brook comes in, and they call it the Taunton Pool. The water runs down with a strong sharp stickle, and then has a sudden elbow in it, where the small brook trickles in; and on that side the bank is steep, four or it may be five feet high, overhanging loamily; but on the other side it is flat, pebbly, and fit to land upon. Now the large boys take the small boys, crying sadly for mercy, and thinking mayhap, of their mothers, with hands laid well at the back of their necks, they bring them up to the crest of the bank upon the eastern side, and make them strip their clothes off. Then the little boys, falling on their naked knees, blubber upwards piteously; but the large boys know what is good for them, and will not be entreated. So they cast them down, one after other into the splash of the water, and watch them go to the bottom first, and then come up and fight for it, with a blowing and a bubbling. It is a very fair sight to watch when you know there is little danger, because, although the pool is deep, the current is sure to wash a boy up on the stones, where the end of the depth is. As for me, they had no need to throw me more than once, because I jumped of my own accord, thinking small things of the Lowman, after the violent Lynn. Nevertheless, I learnt to swim there, as all the other boys did; for the greatest point in learning that is to find that you must do it. I loved the water naturally, and could not long be out of it; but even the boys who hated it most, came to swim in some fashion or other, after they had been flung for a year or two into the Taunton pool.

But now, although my sister Annie came to keep me company, and was not to be parted from me by the tricks of the Lynn stream, because I put her on my back and carried her across, whenever she could not leap it, or tuck up her things and take the stones; yet so it happened that neither of us had been up the Bagworthy water. We knew that it brought a good stream down, as full of fish as of pebbles; and we thought that it must be very pretty to make a way where no way was, nor even a bullock came down to drink. But whether we were afraid or not, I am sure I cannot tell, because it is so long ago; but I think that had something to do with it. For Bagworthy water ran out of Doone valley, a mile or so from the mouth of it.

But when I was turned fourteen years old, and put into good small-clothes, buckled at the knee, and strong blue worsted hosen, knitted by my mother, it happened to me without choice, I may say, to explore the Bagworthy water. And it came about in this wise.

My mother had long been ailing, and not well able to eat much; and there is nothing that frightens us so much as for people to have no love of their victuals. Now I chanced to remember that once at the time of the holidays I had brought dear mother from Tiverton a jar of pickled loaches, caught by myself in the Lowman river, and baked in the kitchen oven, with vinegar, a few leaves of bay, and about a dozen pepper-corns. And mother had said that in all her life she had never tasted anything fit to be compared with them. Whether she said so good a thing out of compliment to my skill in catching the fish and cooking them, or whether she really meant it, is more than I can tell, though I quite believe the latter, and so would most people who tasted them; at any rate, I now resolved to get some loaches for her, and do them in the self-same manner, just to make her eat a bit.

There are many people, even now, who have not come to the right knowledge what a loach is, and where he lives, and how to catch and pickle him. And I will not tell them all about it, because if I did, very likely there would be no loaches left ten or twenty years after the appearance of this book. A pickled minnow is very good if you catch him in a stickle, with the scarlet fingers upon him; but I count him no more than the ropes in beer compared with a loach done properly.

Being resolved to catch some loaches, whatever trouble it cost me, I set forth without a word to any one, in the forenoon of St. Valentine's day, 1675-6, I think it must have been. Annie should not come with me, because the water was too cold; for the winter had been long, and snow lay here and there in patches in the hollow of the banks, like a lady's gloves forgotten. And yet the spring was breaking forth, as it always does in

Devonshire, when the turn of the days is over; and though there was little to see of it, the air was full of feeling.

It puzzles me now, that I remember all those young impressions so, because I took no heed of them at the time whatever; and yet they come upon me bright, when nothing else is evident in the gray fog of experience. I am like an old man gazing at the outside of his spectacles, and seeing, as he rubs the dust, the image of his grandson playing at bo-peep with him.

But let me be of any age, I never could forget that day, and how bitter cold the water was. For I doffed my shoes and hose, and put them into a bag about my neck; and left my little coat at home, and tied my shirt-sleeves back to my shoulders. Then I took a three-pronged fork firmly bound to a rod with cord, and a piece of canvas kerchief, with a lump of bread inside it; and so went into the pebbly water, trying to think how warm it was. For more than a mile all down the Lynn stream, scarcely a stone I left unturned, being thoroughly skilled in the tricks of the loach, and knowing how he hides himself. For being gray-spotted, and clear to see through, and something like a cuttle-fish, only more substantial, he will stay quite still where a streak of weed is in the rapid water, hoping to be overlooked, not caring even to wag his tail. Then being disturbed he flips away, like whalebone from the finger, and hies to a shelf of stone, and lies with his sharp head poked in under it; or sometimes he bellies him into the mud, and only shows his back-ridge. And that is the time to spear him nicely, holding the fork very gingerly, and allowing for the bent of it, which comes to pass, I know not how, at the tickle of air and water.

Or if your loach should not be abroad when first you come to look for him, but keeping snug in his little home, then you may see him come forth amazed at the quivering of the shingles, and oar himself and look at you, and then dart up-stream, like a little grey streak; and then you must try to mark him in, and follow very daintily. So after that, in a sandy place, you steal up behind his tail to him, so that he cannot set eyes on you, for his head is up-stream always, and there you see him abiding still, clear, and mild, and affable. Then, as he looks so innocent, you make full sure to prog him well, in spite of the wry of the water, and the sun making elbows to everything, and the trembling of your fingers. But when you gird at him lovingly, and have as good as gotten him, lo! in the go-by of the river he is gone as a shadow goes, and only a little cloud of mud curls away from the points of the fork.

A long way down that limpid water, chill and bright as an iceberg, went my little self that day on man's choice errand—destruction. All the young fish seemed to know that I was one who had taken out God's certificate, and meant to have the value of it; every one of them was aware that we desolate more than replenish the earth. For a cow might come and look into the water, and put her yellow lips down; a kingfisher, like a blue arrow, might shoot through the dark alleys over the channel, or sit on a dipping withy-bough with his beak sunk into his breast-feathers; even an otter might float downstream likening himself to a log of wood, with his flat head flush with the water-top, and his oily eyes peering quietly; and yet no panic would seize other life, as it does when a sample of man comes.

Now let not any one suppose that I thought of these things when I was young, for I knew not the way to do it. And proud enough in truth I was at the universal fear I spread in all those lonely places, where I myself must have been afraid, if anything had come up to me. It is all very pretty to see the trees big with their hopes of another year, though dumb as yet on the subject, and the waters murmuring gaiety, and the banks spread out with comfort; but a boy takes none of this to heart; unless he be meant for a poet (which God can never charge upon me), and he would liefer have a good apple, or even a bad one, if he stole it.

When I had travelled two miles or so, conquered now and then with cold, and coming out to rub my legs into a lively friction, and only fishing here and there, because of the tumbling water; suddenly, in an open space, where meadows spread about it, I found a good stream flowing softly into the body of our brook. And it brought, so far as I could guess by the sweep of it under my knee-caps, a larger power of clear water than the Lynn itself had; only it came more quietly down, not being troubled with stairs and steps, as the fortune of the Lynn is, but gliding smoothly and forcibly, as if upon some set purpose.

Hereupon I drew up and thought, and reason was much inside me; because the water was bitter cold, and my little toes were aching. So on the bank I rubbed them well with a sprout of young sting-nettle, and having skipped about awhile, was kindly inclined to eat a bit.

Now all the turn of all my life hung upon that moment. But as I sat there munching a crust of Betty Muxworthy's sweet brown bread, and a bit of cold bacon along with it, and kicking my little red heels against the dry loam to keep them warm, I knew no more than fish under the fork what was going on over me. It seemed a sad business to go back now and tell Annie there were no loaches; and yet it was a frightful thing, knowing what I did of it, to venture, where no grown man durst, up the Bagworthy water. And please to recollect that I was only a boy in those days, fond enough of anything new, but not like a man to meet it.

However, as I ate more and more, my spirit arose within me, and I thought of what my father had been, and how he had told me a hundred times never to be a coward. And then I grew warm, and my little heart was ashamed of its pit-a-patting, and I said to myself, 'now if father looks, he shall see that I obey him.' So I put the bag round my back again, and buckled my breeches far up from the knee, expecting deeper water, and crossing the Lynn, went stoutly up under the branches which hang so dark on the Bagworthy river.

I found it strongly over-woven, turned, and torn with thicket-wood, but not so rocky as the Lynn, and more inclined to go evenly. There were bars of chafed stakes stretched from the sides half-way across the current, and light outriders of pithy weed, and blades of last year's water-grass trembling in the quiet places, like a spider's threads, on the transparent stillness, with a tint of olive moving it. And here and there the sun came in, as if his light was sifted, making dance upon the waves, and shadowing the pebbles.

Here, although affrighted often by the deep, dark places, and feeling that every step I took might never be taken backward, on the whole I had very comely sport of loaches, trout, and minnows, forking some, and tickling some, and driving others to shallow nooks, whence I could bail them ashore. Now, if you have ever been fishing, you will not wonder that I was led on, forgetting all about danger, and taking no heed of the time, but shouting in a childish way whenever I caught a 'whacker' (as we called a big fish at Tiverton); and in sooth there were very fine loaches here, having more lie and harbourage than in the rough Lynn stream, though not quite so large as in the Lowman, where I have even taken them to the weight of half a pound.

But in answer to all my shouts there never was any sound at all, except of a rocky echo, or a scared bird hustling away, or the sudden dive of a water-vole; and the place grew thicker and thicker, and the covert grew darker above me, until I thought that the fishes might have good chance of eating me, instead of my eating the fishes.

For now the day was falling fast behind the brown of the hill-tops, and the trees, being void of leaf and hard, seemed giants ready to beat me. And every moment as the sky was clearing up for a white frost, the cold of the water got worse and worse, until I was fit to cry with it. And so, in a sorry plight, I came to an opening in the bushes, where a great black pool lay in front of me, whitened with snow (as I thought) at the sides, till I saw it was only foam-froth.

Now, though I could swim with great ease and comfort, and feared no depth of water, when I could fairly come to it, yet I had no desire to go over head and ears into this great pool, being so cramped and weary, and cold enough in all conscience, though wet only up to the middle, not counting my arms and shoulders. And the look of this black pit was enough to stop one from diving into it, even on a hot summer's day with sunshine on the water; I mean, if the sun ever shone there. As it was, I shuddered and drew back; not alone at the pool itself and the black air there was about it, but also at the whirling manner, and wisping of white threads upon it in stripy circles round and round; and the centre still as jet.

But soon I saw the reason of the stir and depth of that great pit, as well as of the roaring sound which long had made me wonder. For skirting round one side, with very little comfort, because the rocks were high and steep, and the ledge at the foot so narrow, I came to a sudden sight and marvel, such as I never dreamed of. For, lo! I stood at the foot of a long pale slide of water, coming smoothly to me, without any break or hindrance, for a hundred yards or more, and fenced on either side with cliff, sheer, and straight, and shining. The water neither ran nor fell, nor leaped with any spouting, but made one even slope of it, as if it had been combed or planed, and looking like a plank of deal laid down a deep black staircase. However, there was no side-rail, nor any place to walk upon, only the channel a fathom wide, and the perpendicular walls of crag shutting out the evening.

The look of this place had a sad effect, scaring me very greatly, and making me feel that I would give something only to be at home again, with Annie cooking my supper, and our dog Watch sniffing upward. But nothing would come of wishing; that I had long found out; and it only made one the less inclined to work without white feather. So I laid the case before me in a little council; not for loss of time, but only that I wanted rest, and to see things truly.

Then says I to myself—'John Ridd, these trees, and pools, and lonesome rocks, and setting of the sunlight are making a gruesome coward of thee. Shall I go back to my mother so, and be called her fearless boy?'

Nevertheless, I am free to own that it was not any fine sense of shame which settled my decision; for indeed there was nearly as much of danger in going back as in going on, and perhaps even more of labour, the journey being so roundabout. But that which saved me from turning back was a strange inquisitive desire, very unbecoming in a boy of little years; in a word, I would risk a great deal to know what made the water come down like that, and what there was at the top of it.

Therefore, seeing hard strife before me, I girt up my breeches anew, with each buckle one hole tighter, for the sodden straps were stretching and giving, and mayhap my legs were grown smaller from the coldness of it. Then I bestowed my fish around my neck more tightly, and not stopping to look much, for fear of fear, crawled along over the fork of rocks, where the water had scooped the stone out, and shunning thus the ledge from whence it rose like the mane of a white horse into the broad black pool, softly I let my feet into the dip and rush of the torrent.

And here I had reckoned without my host, although (as I thought) so clever; and it was much but that I went down into the great black pool, and had never been heard of more; and this must have been the end of me, except for my trusty loach-fork. For the green wave came down like great bottles upon me, and my legs were gone off in a moment, and I had not time to cry out with wonder, only to think of my mother and Annie, and knock my head very sadly, which made it go round so that brains were no good, even if I had any. But all in a moment, before I knew aught, except that I must die out of the way, with a roar of water upon me, my fork, praise God stuck fast in the rock, and I was borne up upon it. I felt nothing except that here was another matter to begin upon; and it might be worth while, or again it might not, to have another fight for it. But presently the dash of the water upon my face revived me, and my mind grew used to the roar of it, and meseemed I had been worse off than this, when first flung into the Lowman.

Therefore I gathered my legs back slowly, as if they were fish to be landed, stopping whenever the water flew too strongly off my shin-bones, and coming along without sticking out to let the wave get hold of me. And in this manner I won a footing, leaning well forward like a draught-horse, and balancing on my strength as it were, with the ashen stake set behind me. Then I said to my self, 'John Ridd, the sooner you get yourself out by the way you came, the better it will be for you.' But to my great dismay and affright, I saw that no choice was left me now, except that I must climb somehow up that hill of water, or else be washed down into the pool and whirl around it till it drowned me. For there was no chance of fetching back by the way I had gone down into it, and further up was a hedge of rock on either side of the waterway, rising a hundred yards in height, and for all I could tell five hundred, and no place to set a foot in.

Having said the Lord's Prayer (which was all I knew), and made a very bad job of it, I grasped the good loach-stick under a knot, and steadied me with my left hand, and so with a sigh of despair began my course up the fearful torrent-way. To me it seemed half a mile at least of sliding water above me, but in truth it was little more than a furlong, as I came to know afterwards. It would have been a hard ascent even without the slippery slime and the force of the river over it, and I had scanty hope indeed of ever winning the summit. Nevertheless, my terror left me, now I was face to face with it, and had to meet the worst; and I set myself to do my best with a vigour and sort of hardness which did not then surprise me, but have done so ever since.

The water was only six inches deep, or from that to nine at the utmost, and all the way up I could see my feet looking white in the gloom of the hollow, and here and there I found resting-place, to hold on by the cliff and pant awhile. And gradually as I went on, a warmth of courage breathed in me, to think that perhaps no other had dared to try that pass before me, and to wonder what mother would say to it. And then came thought of my father also, and the pain of my feet abated.

How I went carefully, step by step, keeping my arms in front of me, and never daring to straighten my knees is more than I can tell clearly, or even like now to think of, because it makes me dream of it. Only I must acknowledge that the greatest danger of all was just where I saw no jeopardy, but ran up a patch of black ooze-weed in a very boastful manner, being now not far from the summit.

Here I fell very piteously, and was like to have broken my knee-cap, and the torrent got hold of my other leg while I was indulging the bruised one. And then a vile knotting of cramp disabled me, and for awhile I could only roar, till my mouth was full of water, and all of my body was sliding. But the fright of that brought me to again, and my elbow caught in a rock-hole; and so I managed to start again, with the help of more humility.

Now being in the most dreadful fright, because I was so near the top, and hope was beating within me, I laboured hard with both legs and arms, going like a mill and grunting. At last the rush of forked water, where first it came over the lips of the fall, drove me into the middle, and I stuck awhile with my toe-balls on the slippery links of the pop-weed, and the world was green and gliddery, and I durst not look behind me. Then I made up my mind to die at last; for so my legs would ache no more, and my breath not pain my heart so; only it did seem such a pity after fighting so long to give in, and the light was coming upon me, and again I fought towards it; then suddenly I felt fresh air, and fell into it headlong.

Chapter VIII A Boy and a Girl

When I came to myself again, my hands were full of young grass and mould, and a little girl kneeling at my side was rubbing my forehead tenderly with a dock-leaf and a handkerchief.

'Oh, I am so glad,' she whispered softly, as I opened my eyes and looked at her; 'now you will try to be better, won't you?'

I had never heard so sweet a sound as came from between her bright red lips, while there she knelt and gazed at me; neither had I ever seen anything so beautiful as the large dark eyes intent upon me, full of pity and wonder. And then, my nature being slow, and perhaps, for that matter, heavy, I wandered with my hazy eyes down the black shower of her hair, as to my jaded gaze it seemed; and where it fell on the turf, among it (like an early star) was the first primrose of the season. And since that day I think of her, through all the rough storms of my life, when I see an early primrose. Perhaps she liked my countenance, and indeed I know she did, because she said so afterwards; although at the time she was too young to know what made her take to me. Not that I had any beauty, or ever pretended to have any, only a solid healthy face, which many girls have laughed at.

Thereupon I sate upright, with my little trident still in one hand, and was much afraid to speak to her, being conscious of my country-brogue, lest she should cease to like me. But she clapped her hands, and made a trifling dance around my back, and came to me on the other side, as if I were a great plaything.

'What is your name?' she said, as if she had every right to ask me; 'and how did you come here, and what are these wet things in this great bag?'

'You had better let them alone,' I said; 'they are loaches for my mother. But I will give you some, if you like.'

'Dear me, how much you think of them! Why, they are only fish. But how your feet are bleeding! oh, I must tie them up for you. And no shoes nor stockings! Is your mother very poor, poor boy?'

'No,' I said, being vexed at this; 'we are rich enough to buy all this great meadow, if we chose; and here my shoes and stockings be.'

'Why, they are quite as wet as your feet; and I cannot bear to see your feet. Oh, please to let me manage them; I will do it very softly.'

'Oh, I don't think much of that,' I replied; 'I shall put some goose-grease to them. But how you are looking at me! I never saw any one like you before. My name is John Ridd. What is your name?'

'Lorna Doone,' she answered, in a low voice, as if afraid of it, and hanging her head so that I could see only her forehead and eyelashes; 'if you please, my name is Lorna Doone; and I thought you must have known it.'

Then I stood up and touched her hand, and tried to make her look at me; but she only turned away the more. Young and harmless as she was, her name alone made guilt of her. Nevertheless I could not help looking at her tenderly, and the more when her blushes turned into tears, and her tears to long, low sobs.

'Don't cry,' I said, 'whatever you do. I am sure you have never done any harm. I will give you all my fish Lorna, and catch some more for mother; only don't be angry with me.'

She flung her little soft arms up in the passion of her tears, and looked at me so piteously, that what did I do but kiss her. It seemed to be a very odd thing, when I came to think of it, because I hated kissing so, as all honest boys must do. But she touched my heart with a sudden delight, like a cowslip-blossom (although there were none to be seen yet), and the sweetest flowers of spring.

She gave me no encouragement, as my mother in her place would have done; nay, she even wiped her lips (which methought was rather rude of her), and drew away, and smoothed her dress, as if I had used a freedom. Then I felt my cheeks grow burning red, and I gazed at my legs and was sorry. For although she was not at all a proud child (at any rate in her countenance), yet I knew that she was by birth a thousand years in front of me. They might have taken and framed me, or (which would be more to the purpose) my sisters, until it was time for us to die, and then have trained our children after us, for many generations; yet never could we have gotten that look upon our faces which Lorna Doone had naturally, as if she had been born to it.

Here was I, a yeoman's boy, a yeoman every inch of me, even where I was naked; and there was she, a lady born, and thoroughly aware of it, and dressed by people of rank and taste, who took pride in her beauty and set it to advantage. For though her hair was fallen down by reason of her wildness, and some of her frock was touched with wet where she had tended me so, behold her dress was pretty enough for the queen of all the angels. The colours were bright and rich indeed, and the substance very sumptuous, yet simple and free from tinsel stuff, and matching most harmoniously. All from her waist to her neck was white, plaited in close like a curtain, and the dark soft weeping of her hair, and the shadowy light of her eyes (like a wood rayed through with sunset), made it seem yet whiter, as if it were done on purpose. As for the rest, she knew what it was a great deal better than I did, for I never could look far away from her eyes when they were opened upon me.

Now, seeing how I heeded her, and feeling that I had kissed her, although she was such a little girl, eight years old or thereabouts, she turned to the stream in a bashful manner, and began to watch the water, and rubbed one leg against the other.

I, for my part, being vexed at her behaviour to me, took up all my things to go, and made a fuss about it; to let her know I was going. But she did not call me back at all, as I had made sure she would do; moreover, I knew that to try the descent was almost certain death to me, and it looked as dark as pitch; and so at the mouth I turned round again, and came back to her, and said, 'Lorna.'

'Oh, I thought you were gone,' she answered; 'why did you ever come here? Do you know what they would do to us, if they found you here with me?'

'Beat us, I dare say, very hard; or me, at least. They could never beat you,'

'No. They would kill us both outright, and bury us here by the water; and the water often tells me that I must come to that.'

'But what should they kill me for?'

'Because you have found the way up here, and they never could believe it. Now, please to go; oh, please to go. They will kill us both in a moment. Yes, I like you very much'—for I was teasing her to say it—'very much indeed, and I will call you John Ridd, if you like; only please to go, John. And when your feet are well, you know, you can come and tell me how they are.'

'But I tell you, Lorna, I like you very much indeed—nearly as much as Annie, and a great deal more than Lizzie. And I never saw any one like you, and I must come back again to morrow, and so must you, to see me; and I will bring you such lots of things—there are apples still, and a thrush I caught with only one leg broken, and our dog has just had puppies—'

'Oh, dear, they won't let me have a dog. There is not a dog in the valley. They say they are such noisy things—'

'Only put your hand in mine—what little things they are, Lorna! And I will bring you the loveliest dog; I will show you just how long he is.'

'Hush!' A shout came down the valley, and all my heart was trembling, like water after sunset, and Lorna's face was altered from pleasant play to terror. She shrank to me, and looked up at me, with such a power of weakness, that I at once made up my mind to save her or to die with her. A tingle went through all my bones, and I only longed for my carbine. The little girl took courage from me, and put her cheek quite close to mine.

'Come with me down the waterfall. I can carry you easily; and mother will take care of you.'

'No, no,' she cried, as I took her up: 'I will tell you what to do. They are only looking for me. You see that hole, that hole there?'

She pointed to a little niche in the rock which verged the meadow, about fifty yards away from us. In the fading of the twilight I could just descry it.

'Yes, I see it; but they will see me crossing the grass to get there.'

'Look! look!' She could hardly speak. 'There is a way out from the top of it; they would kill me if I told it. Oh, here they come, I can see them.'

The little maid turned as white as the snow which hung on the rocks above her, and she looked at the water and then at me, and she cried, 'Oh dear! oh dear!' And then she began to sob aloud, being so young and unready. But I drew her behind the withy-bushes, and close down to the water, where it was quiet and shelving deep, ere it came to the lip of the chasm. Here they could not see either of us from the upper valley, and might have sought a long time for us, even when they came quite near, if the trees had been clad with their summer clothes. Luckily I had picked up my fish and taken my three-pronged fork away.

Crouching in that hollow nest, as children get together in ever so little compass, I saw a dozen fierce men come down, on the other side of the water, not bearing any fire-arms, but looking lax and jovial, as if they were come from riding and a dinner taken hungrily. 'Queen, queen!' they were shouting, here and there, and now and then: 'where the pest is our little queen gone?'

'They always call me "queen," and I am to be queen by-and-by,' Lorna whispered to me, with her soft cheek on my rough one, and her little heart beating against me: 'oh, they are crossing by the timber there, and then they are sure to see us.'

'Stop,' said I; 'now I see what to do. I must get into the water, and you must go to sleep.'

'To be sure, yes, away in the meadow there. But how bitter cold it will be for you!'

She saw in a moment the way to do it, sooner than I could tell her; and there was no time to lose.

'Now mind you never come again,' she whispered over her shoulder, as she crept away with a childish twist hiding her white front from me; 'only I shall come sometimes—oh, here they are, Madonna!'

Daring scarce to peep, I crept into the water, and lay down bodily in it, with my head between two blocks of stone, and some flood-drift combing over me. The dusk was deepening between the hills, and a white mist lay on the river; but I, being in the channel of it, could see every ripple, and twig, and rush, and glazing of twilight above it, as bright as in a picture; so that to my ignorance there seemed no chance at all but what the men must find me. For all this time they were shouting and swearing, and keeping such a hullabaloo, that the rocks all round the valley rang, and my heart quaked, so (what with this and the cold) that the water began to gurgle round me, and to lap upon the pebbles.

Neither in truth did I try to stop it, being now so desperate, between the fear and the wretchedness; till I caught a glimpse of the little maid, whose beauty and whose kindliness had made me yearn to be with her. And then I knew that for her sake I was bound to be brave and hide myself. She was lying beneath a rock, thirty or forty yards from me, feigning to be fast asleep, with her dress spread beautifully, and her hair drawn over her.

Presently one of the great rough men came round a corner upon her; and there he stopped and gazed awhile at her fairness and her innocence. Then he caught her up in his arms, and kissed her so that I heard him; and if I had only brought my gun, I would have tried to shoot him.

'Here our queen is! Here's the queen, here's the captain's daughter!' he shouted to his comrades; 'fast asleep, by God, and hearty! Now I have first claim to her; and no one else shall touch the child. Back to the bottle, all of you!'

He set her dainty little form upon his great square shoulder, and her narrow feet in one broad hand; and so in triumph marched away, with the purple velvet of her skirt ruffling in his long black beard, and the silken length of her hair fetched out, like a cloud by the wind behind her. This way of her going vexed me so, that I leaped upright in the water, and must have been spied by some of them, but for their haste to the wine-bottle. Of their little queen they took small notice, being in this urgency; although they had thought to find her drowned; but trooped away after one another with kindly challenge to gambling, so far as I could make them out; and I kept sharp watch, I assure you.

Going up that darkened glen, little Lorna, riding still the largest and most fierce of them, turned and put up a hand to me, and I put up a hand to her, in the thick of the mist and the willows.

She was gone, my little dear (though tall of her age and healthy); and when I got over my thriftless fright, I longed to have more to say to her. Her voice to me was so different from all I had ever heard before, as might be a sweet silver bell intoned to the small chords of a harp. But I had no time to think about this, if I hoped to have any supper.

I crept into a bush for warmth, and rubbed my shivering legs on bark, and longed for mother's fagot. Then as daylight sank below the forget-me-not of stars, with a sorrow to be quit, I knew that now must be my time to get away, if there were any.

Therefore, wringing my sodden breaches, I managed to crawl from the bank to the niche in the cliff which Lorna had shown me.

Through the dusk I had trouble to see the mouth, at even the five land-yards of distance; nevertheless, I entered well, and held on by some dead fern-stems, and did hope that no one would shoot me.

But while I was hugging myself like this, with a boyish manner of reasoning, my joy was like to have ended in sad grief both to myself and my mother, and haply to all honest folk who shall love to read this history. For hearing a noise in front of me, and like a coward not knowing where, but afraid to turn round or think of it, I felt myself going down some deep passage into a pit of darkness. It was no good to catch the sides, the whole thing seemed to go with me. Then, without knowing how, I was leaning over a night of water.

This water was of black radiance, as are certain diamonds, spanned across with vaults of rock, and carrying no image, neither showing marge nor end, but centred (at it might be) with a bottomless indrawal.

With that chill and dread upon me, and the sheer rock all around, and the faint light heaving wavily on the silence of this gulf, I must have lost my wits and gone to the bottom, if there were any.

But suddenly a robin sang (as they will do after dark, towards spring) in the brown fern and ivy behind me. I took it for our little Annie's voice (for she could call any robin), and gathering quick warm comfort, sprang up the steep way towards the starlight. Climbing back, as the stones glid down, I heard the cold greedy wave go japping, like a blind black dog, into the distance of arches and hollow depths of darkness.

Chapter IX There Is No Place Like Home

I can assure you, and tell no lie (as John Fry always used to say, when telling his very largest), that I scrambled back to the mouth of that pit as if the evil one had been after me. And sorely I repented now of all my boyish folly, or madness it might well be termed, in venturing, with none to help, and nothing to compel me, into that accursed valley. Once let me get out, thinks I, and if ever I get in again, without being cast in by neck and by crop, I will give our new-born donkey leave to set up for my schoolmaster.

How I kept that resolution we shall see hereafter. It is enough for me now to tell how I escaped from the den that night. First I sat down in the little opening which Lorna had pointed out to me, and wondered whether she had meant, as bitterly occurred to me, that I should run down into the pit, and be drowned, and give no more trouble. But in less than half a minute I was ashamed of that idea, and remembered how she was vexed to think that even a loach should lose his life. And then I said to myself, 'Now surely she would value me more than a thousand loaches; and what she said must be quite true about the way out of this horrible place.'

Therefore I began to search with the utmost care and diligence, although my teeth were chattering, and all my bones beginning to ache with the chilliness and the wetness. Before very long the moon appeared, over the edge of the mountain, and among the trees at the top of it; and then I espied rough steps, and rocky, made as if with a sledge-hammer, narrow, steep, and far asunder, scooped here and there in the side of the entrance, and then round a bulge of the cliff, like the marks upon a great brown loaf, where a hungry child has picked at it. And higher up, where the light of the moon shone broader upon the precipice, there seemed to be a rude broken track, like the shadow of a crooked stick thrown upon a house-wall.

Herein was small encouragement; and at first I was minded to lie down and die; but it seemed to come amiss to me. God has His time for all of us; but He seems to advertise us when He does not mean to do it. Moreover, I saw a movement of lights at the head of the valley, as if lanthorns were coming after me, and the nimbleness given thereon to my heels was in front of all meditation.

Straightway I set foot in the lowest stirrup (as I might almost call it), and clung to the rock with my nails, and worked to make a jump into the second stirrup. And I compassed that too, with the aid of my stick; although, to tell you the truth, I was not at that time of life so agile as boys of smaller frame are, for my size was growing beyond my years, and the muscles not keeping time with it, and the joints of my bones not closely hinged, with staring at one another. But the third step-hole was the hardest of all, and the rock swelled out on me over my breast, and there seemed to be no attempting it, until I espied a good stout rope hanging in a groove of shadow, and just managed to reach the end of it.

How I clomb up, and across the clearing, and found my way home through the Bagworthy forest, is more than I can remember now, for I took all the rest of it then as a dream, by reason of perfect weariness. And indeed it was quite beyond my hopes to tell so much as I have told, for at first beginning to set it down, it was all like a mist before me. Nevertheless, some parts grew clearer, as one by one I remembered them, having taken a little soft cordial, because the memory frightens me.

For the toil of the water, and danger of labouring up the long cascade or rapids, and then the surprise of the fair young maid, and terror of the murderers, and desperation of getting away—all these are much to me even now, when I am a stout churchwarden, and sit by the side of my fire, after going through many far worse adventures, which I will tell, God willing. Only the labour of writing is such (especially so as to construe, and challenge a reader on parts of speech, and hope to be even with him); that by this pipe which I hold in my hand I ever expect to be beaten, as in the days when old Doctor Twiggs, if I made a bad stroke in my exercise, shouted aloud with a sour joy, 'John Ridd, sirrah, down with your smallclothes!'

Let that be as it may, I deserved a good beating that night, after making such a fool of myself, and grinding good fustian to pieces. But when I got home, all the supper was in, and the men sitting at the white table, and mother and Annie and Lizzie near by, all eager, and offering to begin (except, indeed, my mother, who was looking out at the doorway), and by the fire was Betty Muxworthy, scolding, and cooking, and tasting her work, all in a breath, as a man would say. I looked through the door from the dark by the wood-stack, and was half of a mind to stay out like a dog, for fear of the rating and reckoning; but the way my dear mother was looking about and the browning of the sausages got the better of me.

But nobody could get out of me where I had been all the day and evening; although they worried me never so much, and longed to shake me to pieces, especially Betty Muxworthy, who never could learn to let well alone. Not that they made me tell any lies, although it would have served them right almost for intruding on other people's business; but that I just held my tongue, and ate my supper rarely, and let them try their taunts and jibes, and drove them almost wild after supper, by smiling exceeding knowingly. And indeed I could have told them things, as I hinted once or twice; and then poor Betty and our little Lizzie were so mad with eagerness, that between them I went into the fire, being thoroughly overcome with laughter and my own importance.

Now what the working of my mind was (if, indeed it worked at all, and did not rather follow suit of body) it is not in my power to say; only that the result of my adventure in the Doone Glen was to make me dream a good deal of nights, which I had never done much before, and to drive me, with tenfold zeal and purpose, to the practice of bullet-shooting. Not that I ever expected to shoot the Doone family, one by one, or even desired to do so, for my nature is not revengeful; but that it seemed to be somehow my business to understand the gun, as a thing I must be at home with.

I could hit the barn-door now capitally well with the Spanish matchlock, and even with John Fry's blunderbuss, at ten good land-yards distance, without any rest for my fusil. And what was very wrong of me, though I did not see it then, I kept John Fry there, to praise my shots, from dinner-time often until the grey dusk, while he all the time should have been at work spring-ploughing upon the farm. And for that matter so should I have been, or at any rate driving the horses; but John was by no means loath to be there, instead of holding the plough-tail. And indeed, one of our old sayings is,—

For pleasure's sake I would liefer wet,
Than ha' ten lumps of gold for each one of my sweat.

And again, which is not a bad proverb, though unthrifty and unlike a Scotsman's,—

God makes the wheat grow greener,
While farmer be at his dinner.

And no Devonshire man, or Somerset either (and I belong to both of them), ever thinks of working harder than God likes to see him.

Nevertheless, I worked hard at the gun, and by the time that I had sent all the church-roof gutters, so far as I honestly could cut them, through the red pine-door, I began to long for a better tool that would make less noise and throw straighter. But the sheep-shearing came and the hay-season next, and then the harvest of small corn, and the digging of the root called 'batata' (a new but good thing in our neighbourhood, which our folk have made into 'taties'), and then the sweating of the apples, and the turning of the cider-press, and the stacking of the firewood, and netting of the woodcocks, and the springles to be minded in the garden and by the hedgerows, where blackbirds hop to the molehills in the white October mornings, and grey birds come to look for snails at the time when the sun is rising.

It is wonderful how time runs away, when all these things and a great many others come in to load him down the hill and prevent him from stopping to look about. And I for my part can never conceive how people who live in towns and cities, where neither lambs nor birds are (except in some shop windows), nor growing corn, nor meadow-grass, nor even so much as a stick to cut or a stile to climb and sit down upon—how these poor folk get through their lives without being utterly weary of them, and dying from pure indolence, is a thing God only knows, if His mercy allows Him to think of it.

How the year went by I know not, only that I was abroad all day, shooting, or fishing, or minding the farm, or riding after some stray beast, or away by the seaside below Glenthorne, wondering at the great waters, and resolving to go for a sailor. For in those days I had a firm belief, as many other strong boys have, of being born for a seaman. And indeed I had been in a boat nearly twice; but the second time mother found it out, and came and drew me back again; and after that she cried so badly, that I was forced to give my word to her to go no more without telling her.

But Betty Muxworthy spoke her mind quite in a different way about it, the while she was wringing my hosen, and clattering to the drying-horse.

'Zailor, ees fai! ay and zarve un raight. Her can't kape out o' the watter here, whur a' must goo vor to vaind un, zame as a gurt to-ad squalloping, and mux up till I be wore out, I be, wi' the very saight of 's braiches. How wil un ever baide aboard zhip, wi' the watter zinging out under un, and comin' up splash when the wind blow. Latt un goo, missus, latt un goo, zay I for wan, and old Davy wash his clouts for un.'

And this discourse of Betty's tended more than my mother's prayers, I fear, to keep me from going. For I hated Betty in those days, as children always hate a cross servant, and often get fond of a false one. But Betty, like many active women, was false by her crossness only; thinking it just for the moment perhaps, and rushing away with a bucket; ready to stick to it, like a clenched nail, if beaten the wrong way with argument; but melting over it, if you left her, as stinging soap, left along in a basin, spreads all abroad without bubbling.

But all this is beyond the children, and beyond me too for that matter, even now in ripe experience; for I never did know what women mean, and never shall except when they tell me, if that be in their power. Now let that question pass. For although I am now in a place of some authority, I have observed that no one ever listens to me, when I attempt to lay down the law; but all are waiting with open ears until I do enforce it. And so methinks he who reads a history cares not much for the wisdom or folly of the writer (knowing well that the former is far less than his own, and the latter vastly greater), but hurries to know what the people did, and how they got on about it. And this I can tell, if any one can, having been myself in the thick of it.

The fright I had taken that night in Glen Doone satisfied me for a long time thereafter; and I took good care not to venture even in the fields and woods of the outer farm, without John Fry for company. John was greatly surprised and pleased at the value I now set upon him; until, what betwixt the desire to vaunt and the longing to talk things over, I gradually laid bare to him nearly all that had befallen me; except, indeed, about Lorna, whom a sort of shame kept me from mentioning. Not that I did not think of her, and wish very often to see her again; but of course I was only a boy as yet, and therefore inclined to despise young girls, as being unable to do anything, and only meant to listen to orders. And when I got along with the other boys, that was how we always spoke of them, if we deigned to speak at all, as beings of a lower order, only good enough to run errands for us, and to nurse boy-babies.

And yet my sister Annie was in truth a great deal more to me than all the boys of the parish, and of Brendon, and Countisbury, put together; although at the time I never dreamed it, and would have laughed if told so. Annie was of a pleasing face, and very gentle manner, almost like a lady some people said; but without any airs whatever, only trying to give satisfaction. And if she failed, she would go and weep, without letting any one know it, believing the fault to be all her own, when mostly it was of others. But if she succeeded in pleasing you, it was beautiful to see her smile, and stroke her soft chin in a way of her own, which she always used when taking note how to do the right thing again for you. And then her cheeks had a bright clear pink, and her eyes were as blue as the sky in spring, and she stood as upright as a young apple-tree, and no one could help but smile at her, and pat her brown curls approvingly; whereupon she always curtseyed. For she never tried to look away when honest people gazed at her; and even in the court-yard she would come and help to take your saddle, and tell (without your asking her) what there was for dinner.

And afterwards she grew up to be a very comely maiden, tall, and with a well-built neck, and very fair white shoulders, under a bright cloud of curling hair. Alas! poor Annie, like most of the gentle maidens—but tush, I am not come to that yet; and for the present she seemed to me little to look at, after the beauty of Lorna Doone.

Chapter X A Brave Rescue and a Rough Ride

It happened upon a November evening (when I was about fifteen years old, and out-growing my strength very rapidly, my sister Annie being turned thirteen, and a deal of rain having fallen, and all the troughs in the yard being flooded, and the bark from the wood-ricks washed down the gutters, and even our water-shoot going brown) that the ducks in the court made a terrible quacking, instead of marching off to their pen, one behind another. Thereupon Annie and I ran out to see what might be the sense of it. There were thirteen ducks, and ten lily-white (as the fashion then of ducks was), not I mean twenty-three in all, but ten white and three brown-striped ones; and without being nice about their colour, they all quacked very movingly. They pushed their gold-coloured bills here and there (yet dirty, as gold is apt to be), and they jumped on the triangles of their feet, and sounded out of their nostrils; and some of the over-excited ones ran along low on the ground, quacking grievously with their bills snapping and bending, and the roof of their mouths exhibited.

Annie began to cry 'Dilly, dilly, einy, einy, ducksey,' according to the burden of a tune they seem to have accepted as the national duck's anthem; but instead of being soothed by it, they only quacked three times as hard, and ran round till we were giddy. And then they shook their tails together, and looked grave, and went round and round again. Now I am uncommonly fond of ducks, both roasted and roasting and roystering; and it is a fine sight to behold them walk, poddling one after other, with their toes out, like soldiers drilling, and their little eyes cocked all ways at once, and the way that they dib with their bills, and dabble, and throw up their heads and enjoy something, and then tell the others about it. Therefore I knew at once, by the way they were carrying on, that there must be something or other gone wholly amiss in the duck-world. Sister Annie perceived it too, but with a greater quickness; for she counted them like a good duck-wife, and could only tell thirteen of them, when she knew there ought to be fourteen.

And so we began to search about, and the ducks ran to lead us aright, having come that far to fetch us; and when we got down to the foot of the court-yard where the two great ash-trees stand by the side of the little water, we found good reason for the urgence and melancholy of the duck-birds. Lo! the old white drake, the father of all, a bird of high manners and chivalry, always the last to help himself from the pan of barley-meal, and the first to show fight to a dog or cock intruding upon his family, this fine fellow, and pillar of the state, was now in a sad predicament, yet quacking very stoutly. For the brook, wherewith he had been familiar from his callow childhood, and wherein he was wont to quest for water-newts, and tadpoles, and caddis-worms, and other game, this brook, which afforded him very often scanty space to dabble in, and sometimes starved the cresses, was now coming down in a great brown flood, as if the banks never belonged to it. The foaming of it, and the noise, and the cresting of the corners, and the up and down, like a wave of the sea, were enough to frighten any duck, though bred upon stormy waters, which our ducks never had been.

There is always a hurdle six feet long and four and a half in depth, swung by a chain at either end from an oak laid across the channel. And the use of this hurdle is to keep our kine at milking time from straying away there drinking (for in truth they are very dainty) and to fence strange cattle, or Farmer Snowe's horses, from coming along the bed of the brook unknown, to steal our substance. But now this hurdle, which hung in the summer a foot above the trickle, would have been dipped more than two feet deep but for the power against it. For the torrent came down so vehemently that the chains at full stretch were creaking, and the hurdle buffeted almost flat, and thatched (so to say) with the drift-stuff, was going see-saw, with a sulky splash on the dirty red comb of the waters. But saddest to see was between two bars, where a fog was of rushes, and flood-wood, and wild-celery haulm, and dead crowsfoot, who but our venerable mallard jammed in by the joint of his shoulder, speaking aloud as he rose and fell, with his top-knot full of water, unable to comprehend it, with his tail washed far away from him, but often compelled to be silent, being ducked very harshly against his will by the choking fall-to of the hurdle.

For a moment I could not help laughing, because, being borne up high and dry by a tumult of the torrent, he gave me a look from his one little eye (having lost one in fight with the turkey-cock), a gaze of appealing sorrow, and then a loud quack to second it. But the quack came out of time, I suppose, for his throat got filled with water, as the hurdle carried him back again. And then there was scarcely the screw of his tail to be seen until he swung up again, and left small doubt by the way he sputtered, and failed to quack, and hung down his poor crest, but what he must drown in another minute, and frogs triumph over his body.

Annie was crying, and wringing her hands, and I was about to rush into the water, although I liked not the look of it, but hoped to hold on by the hurdle, when a man on horseback came suddenly round the corner of the great ash-hedge on the other side of the stream, and his horse's feet were in the water.

'Ho, there,' he cried; 'get thee back, boy. The flood will carry thee down like a straw. I will do it for thee, and no trouble.'

With that he leaned forward, and spoke to his mare—she was just of the tint of a strawberry, a young thing, very beautiful—and she arched up her neck, as misliking the job; yet, trusting him, would attempt it. She entered the flood, with her dainty fore-legs sloped further and further in front of her, and her delicate ears pricked forward, and the size of her great eyes increasing, but he kept her straight in the turbid rush, by the pressure of his knee on her. Then she looked back, and wondered at him, as the force of the torrent grew stronger, but he bade her go on; and on she went, and it foamed up over her shoulders; and she tossed up her lip and scorned it, for now her courage was waking. Then as the rush of it swept her away, and she struck with her forefeet down the stream, he leaned from his saddle in a manner which I never could have thought possible, and caught up old Tom with his left hand, and set him between his holsters, and smiled at his faint quack of gratitude. In a moment all these were carried downstream, and the rider lay flat on his horse, and tossed the hurdle clear from him, and made for the bend of smooth water.

They landed some thirty or forty yards lower, in the midst of our kitchen-garden, where the winter-cabbage was; but though Annie and I crept in through the hedge, and were full of our thanks and admiring him, he would answer us never a word, until he had spoken in full to the mare, as if explaining the whole to her.

'Sweetheart, I know thou couldst have leaped it,' he said, as he patted her cheek, being on the ground by this time, and she was nudging up to him, with the water pattering off her; 'but I had good reason, Winnie dear, for making thee go through it.'

She answered him kindly with her soft eyes, and smiled at him very lovingly, and they understood one another. Then he took from his waistcoat two peppercorns, and made the old drake swallow them, and tried him softly upon his legs, where the leading gap in the hedge was. Old Tom stood up quite bravely, and clapped his wings, and shook off the wet from his tail-feathers; and then away into the court-yard, and his family gathered around him, and they all made a noise in their throats, and stood up, and put their bills together, to thank God for this great deliverance.

Having taken all this trouble, and watched the end of that adventure, the gentleman turned round to us with a pleasant smile on his face, as if he were lightly amused with himself; and we came up and looked at him. He was rather short, about John Fry's height, or may be a little taller, but very strongly built and springy, as his gait at every step showed plainly, although his legs were bowed with much riding, and he looked as if he lived on horseback. To a boy like me he seemed very old, being over twenty, and well-found in beard; but he was not more than four-and-twenty, fresh and ruddy looking, with a short nose and keen blue eyes, and a merry waggish jerk about him, as if the world were not in earnest. Yet he had a sharp, stern way, like the crack of a pistol, if anything misliked him; and we knew (for children see such things) that it was safer to tickle than buffet him.

'Well, young uns, what be gaping at?' He gave pretty Annie a chuck on the chin, and took me all in without winking.

'Your mare,' said I, standing stoutly up, being a tall boy now; 'I never saw such a beauty, sir. Will you let me have a ride of her?'

'Think thou couldst ride her, lad? She will have no burden but mine. Thou couldst never ride her. Tut! I would be loath to kill thee.'

'Ride her!' I cried with the bravest scorn, for she looked so kind and gentle; 'there never was horse upon Exmoor foaled, but I could tackle in half an hour. Only I never ride upon saddle. Take them leathers off of her.'

He looked at me with a dry little whistle, and thrust his hands into his breeches-pockets, and so grinned that I could not stand it. And Annie laid hold of me in such a way that I was almost mad with her. And he laughed, and approved her for doing so. And the worst of all was—he said nothing.

'Get away, Annie, will you? Do you think I'm a fool, good sir! Only trust me with her, and I will not override her.'

'For that I will go bail, my son. She is liker to override thee. But the ground is soft to fall upon, after all this rain. Now come out into the yard, young man, for the sake of your mother's cabbages. And the mellow straw-bed will be softer for thee, since pride must have its fall. I am thy mother's cousin, boy, and am going up to house. Tom Faggus is my name, as everybody knows; and this is my young mare, Winnie.'

What a fool I must have been not to know it at once! Tom Faggus, the great highwayman, and his young blood-mare, the strawberry! Already her fame was noised abroad, nearly as much as her master's; and my longing to ride her grew tenfold, but fear came at the back of it. Not that I had the smallest fear of what the mare could do to me, by fair play and horse-trickery, but that the glory of sitting upon her seemed to be too great for me; especially as there were rumours abroad that she was not a mare after all, but a witch. However, she looked like a filly all over, and wonderfully beautiful, with her supple stride, and soft slope of shoulder, and glossy coat beaded with water, and prominent eyes full of docile fire. Whether this came from her Eastern blood of the Arabs newly imported, and whether the cream-colour, mixed with our bay, led to that bright strawberry tint, is certainly more than I can decide, being chiefly acquaint with farm-horses. And these come of any colour and form; you never can count what they will be, and are lucky to get four legs to them.

Mr. Faggus gave his mare a wink, and she walked demurely after him, a bright young thing, flowing over with life, yet dropping her soul to a higher one, and led by love to anything; as the manner is of females, when they know what is the best for them. Then Winnie trod lightly upon the straw, because it had soft muck under it, and her delicate feet came back again.

'Up for it still, boy, be ye?' Tom Faggus stopped, and the mare stopped there; and they looked at me provokingly.

'Is she able to leap, sir? There is good take-off on this side of the brook.'

Mr. Faggus laughed very quietly, turning round to Winnie so that she might enter into it. And she, for her part, seemed to know exactly where the fun lay.

'Good tumble-off, you mean, my boy. Well, there can be small harm to thee. I am akin to thy family, and know the substance of their skulls.'

'Let me get up,' said I, waxing wroth, for reasons I cannot tell you, because they are too manifold; 'take off your saddle-bag things. I will try not to squeeze her ribs in, unless she plays nonsense with me.'

Then Mr. Faggus was up on his mettle, at this proud speech of mine; and John Fry was running up all the while, and Bill Dadds, and half a dozen. Tom Faggus gave one glance around, and then dropped all regard for me. The high repute of his mare was at stake, and what was my life compared to it? Through my defiance, and stupid ways, here was I in a duello, and my legs not come to their strength yet, and my arms as limp as a herring.

Something of this occurred to him even in his wrath with me, for he spoke very softly to the filly, who now could scarce subdue herself; but she drew in her nostrils, and breathed to his breath and did all she could to answer him.

'Not too hard, my dear,' he said: 'led him gently down on the mixen. That will be quite enough.' Then he turned the saddle off, and I was up in a moment. She began at first so easily, and pricked her ears so lovingly, and minced about as if pleased to find so light a weight upon her, that I thought she knew I could ride a little, and feared to show any capers. 'Gee wug, Polly!' cried I, for all the men were now looking on, being then at the leaving-off time: 'Gee wug, Polly, and show what thou be'est made of.' With that I plugged my heels into her, and Billy Dadds flung his hat up.

Nevertheless, she outraged not, though her eyes were frightening Annie, and John Fry took a pick to keep him safe; but she curbed to and fro with her strong forearms rising like springs ingathered, waiting and quivering grievously, and beginning to sweat about it. Then her master gave a shrill clear whistle, when her ears were bent towards him, and I felt her form beneath me gathering up like whalebone, and her hind-legs coming under her, and I knew that I was in for it.

First she reared upright in the air, and struck me full on the nose with her comb, till I bled worse than Robin Snell made me; and then down with her fore-feet deep in the straw, and her hind-feet going to heaven. Finding me stick to her still like wax, for my mettle was up as hers was, away she flew with me swifter than ever I went before, or since, I trow. She drove full-head at the cobwall—'Oh, Jack, slip off,' screamed Annie—then she turned like light, when I thought to crush her, and ground my left knee against it. 'Mux me,' I cried, for my breeches were broken, and short words went the furthest—'if you kill me, you shall die with me.' Then she took the court-yard gate at a leap, knocking my words between my teeth, and then right over a quick set hedge, as if the sky were a breath to her; and away for the water-meadows, while I lay on her neck like a child at the breast and wished I had never been born. Straight away, all in the front of the wind, and scattering clouds around her, all I knew of the speed we made was the frightful flash of her shoulders, and her mane like trees in a tempest. I felt the earth under us rushing away, and the air left far behind us, and my breath came and went, and I prayed to God, and was sorry to be so late of it.

All the long swift while, without power of thought, I clung to her crest and shoulders, and dug my nails into her creases, and my toes into her flank-part, and was proud of holding on so long, though sure of being beaten. Then in her fury at feeling me still, she rushed at another device for it, and leaped the wide water-trough sideways across, to and fro, till no breath was left in me. The hazel-boughs took me too hard in the face, and the tall dog-briers got hold of me, and the ache of my back was like crimping a fish; till I longed to give up, thoroughly beaten, and lie there and die in the cresses. But there came a shrill whistle from up the home-hill, where the people had hurried to watch us; and the mare stopped as if with a bullet, then set off for home with the speed of a swallow, and going as smoothly and silently. I never had dreamed of such delicate motion, fluent, and graceful, and ambient, soft as the breeze flitting over the flowers, but swift as the summer lightning. I sat up again, but my strength was all spent, and no time left to recover it, and though she rose at our gate like a bird, I tumbled off into the mixen.

Chapter XI Tom Deserves His Supper

'Well done, lad,' Mr. Faggus said good naturedly; for all were now gathered round me, as I rose from the ground, somewhat tottering, and miry, and crest-fallen, but otherwise none the worse (having fallen upon my head, which is of uncommon substance); nevertheless John Fry was laughing, so that I longed to clout his ears for him; 'Not at all bad work, my boy; we may teach you to ride by-and-by, I see; I thought not to see you stick on so long—'

'I should have stuck on much longer, sir, if her sides had not been wet. She was so slippery—'

'Boy, thou art right. She hath given many the slip. Ha, ha! Vex not, Jack, that I laugh at thee. She is like a sweetheart to me, and better, than any of them be. It would have gone to my heart if thou hadst conquered. None but I can ride my Winnie mare.'

'Foul shame to thee then, Tom Faggus,' cried mother, coming up suddenly, and speaking so that all were amazed, having never seen her wrathful; 'to put my boy, my boy, across her, as if his life were no more than thine! The only son of his father, an honest man, and a quiet man, not a roystering drunken robber! A man would have taken thy mad horse and thee, and flung them both into horse-pond—ay, and what's more, I'll have it done now, if a hair of his head is injured. Oh, my boy, my boy! What could I do without thee? Put up the other arm, Johnny.' All the time mother was scolding so, she was feeling me, and wiping me; while Faggus tried to look greatly ashamed, having sense of the ways of women.

'Only look at his jacket, mother!' cried Annie; 'and a shillingsworth gone from his small-clothes!'

'What care I for his clothes, thou goose? Take that, and heed thine own a bit.' And mother gave Annie a slap which sent her swinging up against Mr. Faggus, and he caught her, and kissed and protected her, and she looked at him very nicely, with great tears in her soft blue eyes. 'Oh, fie upon thee, fie upon thee!' cried mother (being yet more vexed with him, because she had beaten Annie); 'after all we have done for thee, and saved thy worthless neck—and to try to kill my son for me! Never more shall horse of thine enter stable here, since these be thy returns to me. Small thanks to you, John Fry, I say, and you Bill Dadds, and you Jem Slocomb, and all the rest of your coward lot; much you care for your master's son! Afraid of that ugly beast yourselves, and you put a boy just breeched upon him!'

'Wull, missus, what could us do?' began John; 'Jan wudd goo, now wudd't her, Jem? And how was us—'

'Jan indeed! Master John, if you please, to a lad of his years and stature. And now, Tom Faggus, be off, if you please, and think yourself lucky to go so; and if ever that horse comes into our yard, I'll hamstring him myself if none of my cowards dare do it.'

Everybody looked at mother, to hear her talk like that, knowing how quiet she was day by day and how pleasant to be cheated. And the men began to shoulder their shovels, both so as to be away from her, and to go and tell their wives of it. Winnie too was looking at her, being pointed at so much, and wondering if she had done amiss. And then she came to me, and trembled, and stooped her head, and asked my pardon, if she had been too proud with me.

'Winnie shall stop here to-night,' said I, for Tom Faggus still said never a word all the while; but began to buckle his things on, for he knew that women are to be met with wool, as the cannon-balls were at the siege of Tiverton Castle; 'mother, I tell you, Winnie shall stop; else I will go away with her, I never knew what it was, till now, to ride a horse worth riding.'

'Young man,' said Tom Faggus, still preparing sternly to depart, 'you know more about a horse than any man on Exmoor. Your mother may well be proud of you, but she need have had no fear. As if I, Tom Faggus, your father's cousin—and the only thing I am proud of—would ever have let you mount my mare, which dukes and princes have vainly sought, except for the courage in your eyes, and the look of your father about you. I knew you could ride when I saw you, and rarely you have conquered. But women don't understand us. Good-bye, John; I am proud of you, and I hoped to have done you pleasure. And indeed I came full of some courtly tales, that would have made your hair stand up. But though not a crust have I tasted since this time yesterday, having given my meat to a widow, I will go and starve on the moor far sooner than eat the best supper that ever was cooked, in a place that has forgotten me.' With that he fetched a heavy sigh, as if it had been for my father; and feebly got upon Winnie's back, and she came to say farewell to me. He lifted his hat to my mother, with a glance of sorrow, but never a word; and to me he said, 'Open the gate, Cousin John, if you please. You have beaten her so, that she cannot leap it, poor thing.'

But before he was truly gone out of our yard, my mother came softly after him, with her afternoon apron across her eyes, and one hand ready to offer him. Nevertheless, he made as if he had not seen her, though he let his horse go slowly.

'Stop, Cousin Tom,' my mother said, 'a word with you, before you go.'

'Why, bless my heart!' Tom Faggus cried, with the form of his countenance so changed, that I verily thought another man must have leaped into his clothes—'do I see my Cousin Sarah? I thought every one was ashamed of me, and afraid to offer me shelter, since I lost my best cousin, John Ridd. 'Come here,' he used to say, 'Tom, come here, when you are worried, and my wife shall take good care of you.' 'Yes, dear John,' I used to answer, 'I know she promised my mother so; but people have taken to think against me, and so might Cousin Sarah.' Ah, he was a man, a man! If you only heard how he answered me. But let that go, I am nothing now, since the day I lost Cousin Ridd.' And with that he began to push on again; but mother would not have it so.

'Oh, Tom, that was a loss indeed. And I am nothing either. And you should try to allow for me; though I never found any one that did.' And mother began to cry, though father had been dead so long; and I looked on with a stupid surprise, having stopped from crying long ago.

'I can tell you one that will,' cried Tom, jumping off Winnie, in a trice, and looking kindly at mother; 'I can allow for you, Cousin Sarah, in everything but one. I am in some ways a bad man myself; but I know the value of a good one; and if you gave me orders, by God—' And he shook his fists towards Bagworthy Wood, just heaving up black in the sundown.

'Hush, Tom, hush, for God's sake!' And mother meant me, without pointing at me; at least I thought she did. For she ever had weaned me from thoughts of revenge, and even from longings for judgment. 'God knows best, boy,' she used to say, 'let us wait His time, without wishing it.' And so, to tell the truth, I did; partly through her teaching, and partly through my own mild temper, and my knowledge that father, after all, was killed because he had thrashed them.

'Good-night, Cousin Sarah, good-night, Cousin Jack,' cried Tom, taking to the mare again; 'many a mile I have to ride, and not a bit inside of me. No food or shelter this side of Exeford, and the night will be black as pitch, I trow. But it serves me right for indulging the lad, being taken with his looks so.'

'Cousin Tom,' said mother, and trying to get so that Annie and I could not hear her; 'it would be a sad and unkinlike thing for you to despise our dwelling-house. We cannot entertain you, as the lordly inns on the road do; and we have small change of victuals. But the men will go home, being Saturday; and so you will have the fireside all to yourself and the children. There are some few collops of red deer's flesh, and a ham just down from the chimney, and some dried salmon from Lynmouth weir, and cold roast-pig, and some oysters. And if none of those be to your liking, we could roast two woodcocks in half an hour, and Annie would make the toast for them. And the good folk made some mistake last week, going up the country, and left a keg of old Holland cordial in the coving of the wood-rick, having borrowed our Smiler, without asking leave. I fear there is something unrighteous about it. But what can a poor widow do? John Fry would have taken it, but for our Jack. Our Jack was a little too sharp for him.'

Ay, that I was; John Fry had got it, like a billet under his apron, going away in the gray of the morning, as if to kindle his fireplace. 'Why, John,' I said, 'what a heavy log! Let me have one end of it.' 'Thank'e, Jan, no need of thiccy,' he answered, turning his back to me; 'waife wanteth a log as will last all day, to kape the crock a zimmerin.' And he banged his gate upon my heels to make me stop and rub them. 'Why, John,' said I, 'you'm got a log with round holes in the end of it. Who has been cutting gun-wads? Just lift your apron, or I will.'

But, to return to Tom Faggus—he stopped to sup that night with us, and took a little of everything; a few oysters first, and then dried salmon, and then ham and eggs, done in small curled rashers, and then a few collops of venison toasted, and next to that a little cold roast-pig, and a woodcock on toast to finish with, before the Scheidam and hot water. And having changed his wet things first, he seemed to be in fair appetite, and praised Annie's cooking mightily, with a kind of noise like a smack of his lips, and a rubbing of his hands together, whenever he could spare them.

He had gotten John Fry's best small-clothes on, for he said he was not good enough to go into my father's (which mother kept to look at), nor man enough to fill them. And in truth my mother was very glad that he refused, when I offered them. But John was over-proud to have it in his power to say that such a famous man had ever dwelt in any clothes of his; and afterwards he made show of them. For Mr. Faggus's glory, then, though not so great as now it is, was spreading very fast indeed all about our neighbourhood, and even as far as Bridgewater.

Tom Faggus was a jovial soul, if ever there has been one, not making bones of little things, nor caring to seek evil. There was about him such a love of genuine human nature, that if a traveller said a good thing, he would give him back his purse again. It is true that he took people's money more by force than fraud; and the law (being used to the inverse method) was bitterly moved against him, although he could quote precedent. These things I do not understand; having seen so much of robbery (some legal, some illegal), that I scarcely know, as here we say, one crow's foot from the other. It is beyond me and above me, to discuss these subjects; and in truth I love the law right well, when it doth support me, and when I can lay it down to my liking, with prejudice to nobody. Loyal, too, to the King am I, as behoves churchwarden; and ready to make the best of him, as he generally requires. But after all, I could not see (until I grew much older, and came to have some property) why Tom Faggus, working hard, was called a robber and felon of great; while the King, doing nothing at all (as became his dignity), was liege-lord, and paramount owner; with everybody to thank him kindly for accepting tribute.

For the present, however, I learned nothing more as to what our cousin's profession was, only that mother seemed frightened, and whispered to him now and then not to talk of something, because of the children being there; whereupon he always nodded with a sage expression, and applied himself to hollands.

'Now let us go and see Winnie, Jack,' he said to me after supper; 'for the most part I feed her before myself; but she was so hot from the way you drove her. Now she must be grieving for me, and I never let her grieve long.'

I was too glad to go with him, and Annie came slyly after us. The filly was walking to and fro on the naked floor of the stable (for he would not let her have any straw, until he should make a bed for her), and without so much as a headstall on, for he would not have her fastened. 'Do you take my mare for a dog?' he had said when John Fry brought him a halter. And now she ran to him like a child, and her great eyes shone at the lanthorn.

'Hit me, Jack, and see what she will do. I will not let her hurt thee.' He was rubbing her ears all the time he spoke, and she was leaning against him. Then I made believe to strike him, and in a moment she caught me by the waistband, and lifted me clean from the ground, and was casting me down to trample upon me, when he stopped her suddenly.

'What think you of that, boy? Have you horse or dog that would do that for you? Ay, and more than that she will do. If I were to whistle, by-and-by, in the tone that tells my danger, she would break this stable-door down, and rush into the room to me. Nothing will keep her from me then, stone-wall or church-tower. Ah, Winnie, Winnie, you little witch, we shall die together.'

Then he turned away with a joke, and began to feed her nicely, for she was very dainty. Not a husk of oat would she touch that had been under the breath of another horse, however hungry she might be. And with her oats he mixed some powder, fetching it from his saddle-bags. What this was I could not guess, neither would he tell me, but laughed and called it 'star-shavings.' He watched her eat every morsel of it, with two or three drinks of pure water, ministered between whiles; and then he made her bed in a form I had never seen before, and so we said 'Good-night' to her.

Afterwards by the fireside he kept us very merry, sitting in the great chimney-corner, and making us play games with him. And all the while he was smoking tobacco in a manner I never had seen before, not using any pipe for it, but having it rolled in little sticks about as long as my finger, blunt at one end and sharp at the other. The sharp end he would put in his mouth, and lay a brand of wood to the other, and then draw a white cloud of curling smoke, and we never tired of watching him. I wanted him to let me do it, but he said, 'No, my son; it is not meant for boys.' Then Annie put up her lips and asked, with both hands on his knees (for she had taken to him wonderfully), 'Is it meant for girls then cousin Tom?' But she had better not have asked, for he gave it her to try, and she shut both eyes, and sucked at it. One breath, however, was quite enough, for it made her cough so violently that Lizzie and I must thump her back until she was almost crying. To atone for that, cousin Tom set to, and told us whole pages of stories, not about his own doings at all, but strangely enough they seemed to concern almost every one else we had ever heard of. Without halting once for a word or a deed, his tales flowed onward as freely and brightly as the flames of the wood up the chimney, and with no smaller variety. For he spoke with the voices of twenty people, giving each person the proper manner, and the proper place to speak from; so that Annie and Lizzie ran all about, and searched the clock and the linen-press. And he changed his face every moment so, and with such power of mimicry that without so much as a smile of his own, he made even mother laugh so that she broke her new tenpenny waistband; and as for us children, we rolled on the floor, and Betty Muxworthy roared in the wash-up.

Chapter XII A Man Justly Popular

Now although Mr. Faggus was so clever, and generous, and celebrated, I know not whether, upon the whole, we were rather proud of him as a member of our family, or inclined to be ashamed of him. And indeed I think that the sway of the balance hung upon the company we were in. For instance, with the boys at Brendon—for there is no village at Oare—I was exceeding proud to talk of him, and would freely brag of my Cousin Tom. But with the rich parsons of the neighbourhood, or the justices (who came round now and then, and were glad to ride up to a warm farm-house), or even the well-to-do tradesmen of Porlock—in a word, any settled power, which was afraid of losing things—with all of them we were very shy of claiming our kinship to that great outlaw.

And sure, I should pity, as well as condemn him though our ways in the world were so different, knowing as I do his story; which knowledge, methinks, would often lead us to let alone God's prerogative—judgment, and hold by man's privilege—pity. Not that I would find excuse for Tom's downright dishonesty, which was beyond doubt a disgrace to him, and no credit to his kinsfolk; only that it came about without his meaning any harm or seeing how he took to wrong; yet gradually knowing it. And now, to save any further trouble, and to meet those who disparage him (without allowance for the time or the crosses laid upon him), I will tell the history of him, just as if he were not my cousin, and hoping to be heeded. And I defy any man to say that a word of this is either false, or in any way coloured by family. Much cause he had to be harsh with the world; and yet all acknowledged him very pleasant, when a man gave up his money. And often and often he paid the toll for the carriage coming after him, because he had emptied their pockets, and would not add inconvenience. By trade he had been a blacksmith, in the town of Northmolton, in Devonshire, a rough rude place at the end of Exmoor, so that many people marvelled if such a man was bred there. Not only could he read and write, but he had solid substance; a piece of land worth a hundred pounds, and right of common for two hundred sheep, and a score and a half of beasts, lifting up or lying down. And being left an orphan (with all these cares upon him) he began to work right early, and made such a fame at the shoeing of horses, that the farriers of Barum were like to lose their custom. And indeed he won a golden Jacobus for the best-shod nag in the north of Devon, and some say that he never was forgiven.

As to that, I know no more, except that men are jealous. But whether it were that, or not, he fell into bitter trouble within a month of his victory; when his trade was growing upon him, and his sweetheart ready to marry him. For he loved a maid of Southmolton (a currier's daughter I think she was, and her name was Betsy Paramore), and her father had given consent; and Tom Faggus, wishing to look his best, and be clean of course, had a tailor at work upstairs for him, who had come all the way from Exeter. And Betsy's things were ready too—for which they accused him afterwards, as if he could help that—when suddenly, like a thunderbolt, a lawyer's writ fell upon him.

This was the beginning of a law-suit with Sir Robert Bampfylde, a gentleman of the neighbourhood, who tried to oust him from his common, and drove his cattle and harassed them. And by that suit of law poor Tom was ruined altogether, for Sir Robert could pay for much swearing; and then all his goods and his farm were sold up, and even his smithery taken. But he saddled his horse, before they could catch him, and rode away to Southmolton, looking more like a madman than a good farrier, as the people said who saw him. But when he arrived there, instead of comfort, they showed him the face of the door alone; for the news of his loss was before him, and Master Paramore was a sound, prudent man, and a high member of the town council. It is said that they even gave him notice to pay for Betsy's wedding-clothes, now that he was too poor to marry her. This may be false, and indeed I doubt it; in the first place, because Southmolton is a busy place for talking; and in the next, that I do not think the action would have lain at law, especially as the maid lost nothing, but used it all for her wedding next month with Dick Vellacott, of Mockham.

All this was very sore upon Tom; and he took it to heart so grievously, that he said, as a better man might have said, being loose of mind and property, 'The world hath preyed on me like a wolf. God help me now to prey on the world.'

And in sooth it did seem, for a while, as if Providence were with him; for he took rare toll on the highway, and his name was soon as good as gold anywhere this side of Bristowe. He studied his business by night and by day, with three horses all in hard work, until he had made a fine reputation; and then it was competent to him to rest, and he had plenty left for charity. And I ought to say for society too, for he truly loved high society, treating squires and noblemen (who much affected his company) to the very best fare of the hostel. And they say that once the King's Justitiaries, being upon circuit, accepted his invitation, declaring merrily that if never true bill had been found against him, mine host should now be qualified to draw one. And so the landlords did; and he always paid them handsomely, so that all of them were kind to him, and contended for his visits. Let it be known in any township that Mr. Faggus was taking his leisure at the inn, and straightway all the men flocked thither to drink his health without outlay, and all the women to admire him; while the children were set at the cross-roads to give warning of any officers. One of his earliest meetings was with Sir Robert Bampfylde himself, who was riding along the Barum road with only one serving-man after him. Tom Faggus put a pistol to his head, being then obliged to be violent, through want of reputation; while the serving-man pretended to be along way round the corner. Then the baronet pulled out his purse, quite trembling in the hurry of his politeness. Tom took the purse, and his ring, and time-piece, and then handed them back with a very low bow, saying that it was against all usage for him to rob a robber. Then he turned to the unfaithful knave, and trounced him right well for his cowardice, and stripped him of all his property.

But now Mr. Faggus kept only one horse, lest the Government should steal them; and that one was the young mare Winnie. How he came by her he never would tell, but I think that she was presented to him by a certain Colonel, a lover of sport, and very clever in horseflesh, whose life Tom had saved from some gamblers. When I have added that Faggus as yet had never been guilty of bloodshed (for his eyes, and the click of his pistol at first, and now his high reputation made all his wishes respected), and that he never robbed a poor man, neither insulted a woman, but was very good to the Church, and of hot patriotic opinions, and full of jest and jollity, I have said as much as is fair for him, and shown why he was so popular. Everybody cursed the Doones, who lived apart disdainfully. But all good people liked Mr. Faggus—when he had not robbed them—and many a poor sick man or woman blessed him for other people's money; and all the hostlers, stable-boys, and tapsters entirely worshipped him.

I have been rather long, and perhaps tedious, in my account of him, lest at any time hereafter his character should be misunderstood, and his good name disparaged; whereas he was my second cousin, and the lover of my—But let that bide. 'Tis a melancholy story.

He came again about three months afterwards, in the beginning of the spring-time, and brought me a beautiful new carbine, having learned my love of such things, and my great desire to shoot straight. But mother would not let me have the gun, until he averred upon his honour that he had bought it honestly. And so he had, no doubt, so far as it is honest to buy with money acquired rampantly. Scarce could I stop to make my bullets in the mould which came along with it, but must be off to the Quarry Hill, and new target I had made there. And he taught me then how to ride bright Winnie, who was grown since I had seen her, but remembered me most kindly. After making much of Annie, who had a wondrous liking for him—and he said he was her godfather, but God knows how he could have been, unless they confirmed him precociously—away he went, and young Winnie's sides shone like a cherry by candlelight.

Now I feel that of those boyish days I have little more to tell, because everything went quietly, as the world for the most part does with us. I began to work at the farm in earnest, and tried to help my mother, and when I remembered Lorna Doone, it seemed no more than the thought of a dream, which I could hardly call to mind. Now who cares to know how many bushels of wheat we grew to the acre, or how the cattle milched till we ate them, or what the turn of the seasons was? But my stupid self seemed like to be the biggest of all the cattle; for having much to look after the sheep, and being always in kind appetite, I grew four inches longer in every year of my farming, and a matter of two inches wider; until there was no man of my size to be seen elsewhere upon Exmoor. Let that pass: what odds to any how tall or wide I be? There is no Doone's door at Plover's Barrows and if there were I could never go through it. They vexed me so much about my size, long before I had completed it, girding at me with paltry jokes whose wit was good only to stay at home, that I grew shame-faced about the matter, and feared to encounter a looking-glass. But mother was very proud, and said she never could have too much of me.

The worst of all to make me ashamed of bearing my head so high—a thing I saw no way to help, for I never could hang my chin down, and my back was like a gatepost whenever I tried to bend it—the worst of all was our little Eliza, who never could come to a size herself, though she had the wine from the Sacrament at Easter and Allhallowmas, only to be small and skinny, sharp, and clever crookedly. Not that her body was out of the straight (being too small for that perhaps), but that her wit was full of corners, jagged, and strange, and uncomfortable. You never could tell what she might say next; and I like not that kind of women. Now God forgive me for talking so of my own father's daughter, and so much the more by reason that my father could not help it. The right way is to face the matter, and then be sorry for every one. My mother fell grievously on a slide, which John Fry had made nigh the apple-room door, and hidden with straw from the stable, to cover his own great idleness. My father laid John's nose on the ice, and kept him warm in spite of it; but it was too late for Eliza. She was born next day with more mind than body—the worst thing that can befall a man.

But Annie, my other sister, was now a fine fair girl, beautiful to behold. I could look at her by the fireside, for an hour together, when I was not too sleepy, and think of my dear father. And she would do the same thing by me, only wait the between of the blazes. Her hair was done up in a knot behind, but some would fall over her shoulders; and the dancing of the light was sweet to see through a man's eyelashes. There never was a face that showed the light or the shadow of feeling, as if the heart were sun to it, more than our dear Annie's did. To look at her carefully, you might think that she was not dwelling on anything; and then she would know you were looking at her, and those eyes would tell all about it. God knows that I try to be simple enough, to keep to His meaning in me, and not make the worst of His children. Yet often have I been put to shame, and ready to bite my tongue off, after speaking amiss of anybody, and letting out my littleness, when suddenly mine eyes have met the pure soft gaze of Annie.

As for the Doones, they were thriving still, and no one to come against them; except indeed by word of mouth, to which they lent no heed whatever. Complaints were made from time to time, both in high and low quarters (as the rank might be of the people robbed), and once or twice in the highest of all, to wit, the King himself. But His Majesty made a good joke about it (not meaning any harm, I doubt), and was so much pleased with himself thereupon, that he quite forgave the mischief. Moreover, the main authorities were a long way off; and the Chancellor had no cattle on Exmoor; and as for my lord the Chief Justice, some rogue had taken his silver spoons; whereupon his lordship swore that never another man would he hang until he had that one by the neck. Therefore the Doones went on as they listed, and none saw fit to meddle with them. For the only man who would have dared to come to close quarters with them, that is to say Tom Faggus, himself was a quarry for the law, if ever it should be unhooded. Moreover, he had transferred his business to the neighbourhood of Wantage, in the county of Berks, where he found the climate drier, also good downs and commons excellent for galloping, and richer yeomen than ours be, and better roads to rob them on.

Some folk, who had wiser attended to their own affairs, said that I (being sizeable now, and able to shoot not badly) ought to do something against those Doones, and show what I was made of. But for a time I was very bashful, shaking when called upon suddenly, and blushing as deep as a maiden; for my strength was not come upon me, and mayhap I had grown in front of it. And again, though I loved my father still, and would fire at a word about him, I saw not how it would do him good for me to harm his injurers. Some races are of revengeful kind, and will for years pursue their wrong, and sacrifice this world and the next for a moment's foul satisfaction, but methinks this comes of some black blood, perverted and never purified. And I doubt but men of true English birth are stouter than so to be twisted, though some of the women may take that turn, if their own life runs unkindly.

Let that pass—I am never good at talking of things beyond me. All I know is, that if I had met the Doone who had killed my father, I would gladly have thrashed him black and blue, supposing I were able; but would never have fired a gun at him, unless he began that game with me, or fell upon more of my family, or were violent among women. And to do them justice, my mother and Annie were equally kind and gentle, but Eliza would flame and grow white with contempt, and not trust herself to speak to us.

Now a strange thing came to pass that winter, when I was twenty-one years old, a very strange thing, which affrighted the rest, and made me feel uncomfortable. Not that there was anything in it, to do harm to any one, only that none could explain it, except by attributing it to the devil. The weather was very mild and open, and scarcely any snow fell; at any rate, none lay on the ground, even for an hour, in the highest part of Exmoor; a thing which I knew not before nor since, as long as I can remember. But the nights were wonderfully dark, as though with no stars in the heaven; and all day long the mists were rolling upon the hills and down them, as if the whole land were a wash-house. The moorland was full of snipes and teal, and curlews flying and crying, and lapwings flapping heavily, and ravens hovering round dead sheep; yet no redshanks nor dottrell, and scarce any golden plovers (of which we have great store generally) but vast lonely birds, that cried at night, and moved the whole air with their pinions; yet no man ever saw them. It was dismal as well as dangerous now for any man to go fowling (which of late I loved much in the winter) because the fog would come down so thick that the pan of the gun was reeking, and the fowl out of sight ere the powder kindled, and then the sound of the piece was so dead, that the shooter feared harm, and glanced over his shoulder. But the danger of course was far less in this than in losing of the track, and falling into the mires, or over the brim of a precipice.

Nevertheless, I must needs go out, being young and very stupid, and feared of being afraid; a fear which a wise man has long cast by, having learned of the manifold dangers which ever and ever encompass us. And beside this folly and wildness of youth, perchance there was something, I know not what, of the joy we have in uncertainty. Mother, in fear of my missing home—though for that matter, I could smell supper, when hungry, through a hundred land-yards of fog—my dear mother, who thought of me ten times for one thought about herself, gave orders to ring the great sheep-bell, which hung above the pigeon-cote, every ten minutes of the day, and the sound came through the plaits of fog, and I was vexed about it, like the letters of a copy-book. It reminded me, too, of Blundell's bell, and the grief to go into school again.

But during those two months of fog (for we had it all the winter), the saddest and the heaviest thing was to stand beside the sea. To be upon the beach yourself, and see the long waves coming in; to know that they are long waves, but only see a piece of them; and to hear them lifting roundly, swelling over smooth green rocks, plashing down in the hollow corners, but bearing on all the same as ever, soft and sleek and sorrowful, till their little noise is over.

One old man who lived at Lynmouth, seeking to be buried there, having been more than half over the world, though shy to speak about it, and fain to come home to his birthplace, this old Will Watcombe (who dwelt by the water) said that our strange winter arose from a thing he called the 'Gulf-stream', rushing up Channel suddenly. He said it was hot water, almost fit for a man to shave with, and it threw all our cold water out, and ruined the fish and the spawning-time, and a cold spring would come after it. I was fond of going to Lynmouth on Sunday to hear this old man talk, for sometimes he would discourse with me, when nobody else could move him. He told me that this powerful flood set in upon our west so hard sometimes once in ten years, and sometimes not for fifty, and the Lord only knew the sense of it; but that when it came, therewith came warmth and clouds, and fog, and moisture, and nuts, and fruit, and even shells; and all the tides were thrown abroad. As for nuts he winked awhile, and chewed a piece of tobacco; yet did I not comprehend him. Only afterwards I heard that nuts with liquid kernels came, travelling on the Gulf stream; for never before was known so much foreign cordial landed upon our coast, floating ashore by mistake in the fog, and (what with the tossing and the mist) too much astray to learn its duty.

Folk, who are ever too prone to talk, said that Will Watcombe himself knew better than anybody else about this drift of the Gulf-stream, and the places where it would come ashore, and the caves that took the indraught. But De Whichehalse, our great magistrate, certified that there was no proof of unlawful importation; neither good cause to suspect it, at a time of Christian charity. And we knew that it was a foul thing for some quarrymen to say that night after night they had been digging a new cellar at Ley Manor to hold the little marks of respect found in the caverns at high-water weed. Let that be, it is none of my business to speak evil of dignities; duly we common people joked of the 'Gulp-stream,' as we called it.

But the thing which astonished and frightened us so, was not, I do assure you, the landing of foreign spirits, nor the loom of a lugger at twilight in the gloom of the winter moonrise. That which made as crouch in by the fire, or draw the bed-clothes over us, and try to think of something else, was a strange mysterious sound.

At grey of night, when the sun was gone, and no red in the west remained, neither were stars forthcoming, suddenly a wailing voice rose along the valleys, and a sound in the air, as of people running. It mattered not whether you stood on the moor, or crouched behind rocks away from it, or down among reedy places; all as one the sound would come, now from the heart of the earth beneath, now overhead bearing down on you.

And then there was rushing of something by, and melancholy laughter, and the hair of a man would stand on end before he could reason properly.

God, in His mercy, knows that I am stupid enough for any man, and very slow of impression, nor ever could bring myself to believe that our Father would let the evil one get the upper hand of us. But when I had heard that sound three times, in the lonely gloom of the evening fog, and the cold that followed the lines of air, I was loath to go abroad by night, even so far as the stables, and loved the light of a candle more, and the glow of a fire with company.

There were many stories about it, of course, all over the breadth of the moorland. But those who had heard it most often declared that it must be the wail of a woman's voice, and the rustle of robes fleeing horribly, and fiends in the fog going after her. To that, however, I paid no heed, when anybody was with me; only we drew more close together, and barred the doors at sunset.

Chapter XIII Master Huckaback Comes In

Mr. Reuben Huckaback, whom many good folk in Dulverton will remember long after my time, was my mother's uncle, being indeed her mother's brother. He owned the very best shop in the town, and did a fine trade in soft ware, especially when the pack-horses came safely in at Christmas-time. And we being now his only kindred (except indeed his granddaughter, little Ruth Huckaback, of whom no one took any heed), mother beheld it a Christian duty to keep as well as could be with him, both for love of a nice old man, and for the sake of her children. And truly, the Dulverton people said that he was the richest man in their town, and could buy up half the county armigers; 'ay, and if it came to that, they would like to see any man, at Bampton, or at Wivelscombe, and you might say almost Taunton, who could put down golden Jacobus and Carolus against him.

Now this old gentleman—so they called him, according to his money; and I have seen many worse ones, more violent and less wealthy—he must needs come away that time to spend the New Year-tide with us; not that he wanted to do it (for he hated country-life), but because my mother pressing, as mothers will do to a good bag of gold, had wrung a promise from him; and the only boast of his life was that never yet had he broken his word, at least since he opened business.

Now it pleased God that Christmas-time (in spite of all the fogs) to send safe home to Dulverton, and what was more, with their loads quite safe, a goodly string of packhorses. Nearly half of their charge was for Uncle Reuben, and he knew how to make the most of it. Then having balanced his debits and credits, and set the writs running against defaulters, as behoves a good Christian at Christmas-tide, he saddled his horse, and rode off towards Oare, with a good stout coat upon him, and leaving Ruth and his head man plenty to do, and little to eat, until they should see him again.

It had been settled between us that we should expect him soon after noon on the last day of December. For the Doones being lazy and fond of bed, as the manner is of dishonest folk, the surest way to escape them was to travel before they were up and about, to-wit, in the forenoon of the day. But herein we reckoned without our host: for being in high festivity, as became good Papists, the robbers were too lazy, it seems, to take the trouble of going to bed; and forth they rode on the Old Year-morning, not with any view of business, but purely in search of mischief.

We had put off our dinner till one o'clock (which to me was a sad foregoing), and there was to be a brave supper at six of the clock, upon New Year's-eve; and the singers to come with their lanthorns, and do it outside the parlour-window, and then have hot cup till their heads should go round, after making away with the victuals. For although there was nobody now in our family to be churchwarden of Oare, it was well admitted that we were the people entitled alone to that dignity; and though Nicholas Snowe was in office by name, he managed it only by mother's advice; and a pretty mess he made of it, so that every one longed for a Ridd again, soon as ever I should be old enough. This Nicholas Snowe was to come in the evening, with his three tall comely daughters, strapping girls, and well skilled in the dairy; and the story was all over the parish, on a stupid conceit of John Fry's, that I should have been in love with all three, if there had been but one of them. These Snowes were to come, and come they did, partly because Mr. Huckaback liked to see fine young maidens, and partly because none but Nicholas Snowe could smoke a pipe now all around our parts, except of the very high people, whom we durst never invite. And Uncle Ben, as we all knew well, was a great hand at his pipe, and would sit for hours over it, in our warm chimney-corner, and never want to say a word, unless it were inside him; only he liked to have somebody there over against him smoking.

Now when I came in, before one o'clock, after seeing to the cattle—for the day was thicker than ever, and we must keep the cattle close at home, if we wished to see any more of them—I fully expected to find Uncle Ben sitting in the fireplace, lifting one cover and then another, as his favourite manner was, and making sweet mouths over them; for he loved our bacon rarely, and they had no good leeks at Dulverton; and he was a man who always would see his business done himself. But there instead of my finding him with his quaint dry face pulled out at me, and then shut up sharp not to be cheated—who should run out but Betty Muxworthy, and poke me with a saucepan lid.

'Get out of that now, Betty,' I said in my politest manner, for really Betty was now become a great domestic evil. She would have her own way so, and of all things the most distressful was for a man to try to reason.

'Zider-press,' cried Betty again, for she thought it a fine joke to call me that, because of my size, and my hatred of it; 'here be a rare get up, anyhow.'

'A rare good dinner, you mean, Betty. Well, and I have a rare good appetite.' With that I wanted to go and smell it, and not to stop for Betty.

'Troost thee for thiccy, Jan Ridd. But thee must keep it bit langer, I reckon. Her baint coom, Maister Ziderpress. Whatt'e mak of that now?'

'Do you mean to say that Uncle Ben has not arrived yet, Betty?'

'Raived! I knaws nout about that, whuther a hath of noo. Only I tell 'e, her baint coom. Rackon them Dooneses hath gat 'un.'

And Betty, who hated Uncle Ben, because he never gave her a groat, and she was not allowed to dine with him, I am sorry to say that Betty Muxworthy grinned all across, and poked me again with the greasy saucepan cover. But I misliking so to be treated, strode through the kitchen indignantly, for Betty behaved to me even now, as if I were only Eliza.

'Oh, Johnny, Johnny,' my mother cried, running out of the grand show-parlour, where the case of stuffed birds was, and peacock-feathers, and the white hare killed by grandfather; 'I am so glad you are come at last. There is something sadly amiss, Johnny.'

Mother had upon her wrists something very wonderful, of the nature of fal-lal as we say, and for which she had an inborn turn, being of good draper family, and polished above the yeomanry. Nevertheless I could never bear it, partly because I felt it to be out of place in our good farm-house, partly because I hate frippery, partly because it seemed to me to have nothing to do with father, and partly because I never could tell the reason of my hating it. And yet the poor soul had put them on, not to show her hands off (which were above her station) but simply for her children's sake, because Uncle Ben had given them. But another thing, I never could bear for man or woman to call me, 'Johnny,' 'Jack,' or 'John,' I cared not which; and that was honest enough, and no smallness of me there, I say.

'Well, mother, what is the matter, then?'

'I am sure you need not be angry, Johnny. I only hope it is nothing to grieve about, instead of being angry. You are very sweet-tempered, I know, John Ridd, and perhaps a little too sweet at times'—here she meant the Snowe girls, and I hanged my head—'but what would you say if the people there'—she never would call them 'Doones'—'had gotten your poor Uncle Reuben, horse, and Sunday coat, and all?'

'Why, mother, I should be sorry for them. He would set up a shop by the river-side, and come away with all their money.'

'That all you have to say, John! And my dinner done to a very turn, and the supper all fit to go down, and no worry, only to eat and be done with it! And all the new plates come from Watchett, with the Watchett blue upon them, at the risk of the lives of everybody, and the capias from good Aunt Jane for stuffing a curlew with onion before he begins to get cold, and make a woodcock of him, and the way to turn the flap over in the inside of a roasting pig—'

'Well, mother dear, I am very sorry. But let us have our dinner. You know we promised not to wait for him after one o'clock; and you only make us hungry. Everything will be spoiled, mother, and what a pity to think of! After that I will go to seek for him in the thick of the fog, like a needle in a hay-band. That is to say, unless you think'—for she looked very grave about it—'unless you really think, mother, that I ought to go without dinner.'

'Oh no, John, I never thought that, thank God! Bless Him for my children's appetites; and what is Uncle Ben to them?'

So we made a very good dinner indeed, though wishing that he could have some of it, and wondering how much to leave for him; and then, as no sound of his horse had been heard, I set out with my gun to look for him.

I followed the track on the side of the hill, from the farm-yard, where the sledd-marks are—for we have no wheels upon Exmoor yet, nor ever shall, I suppose; though a dunder-headed man tried it last winter, and broke his axle piteously, and was nigh to break his neck—and after that I went all along on the ridge of the rabbit-cleve, with the brook running thin in the bottom; and then down to the Lynn stream and leaped it, and so up the hill and the moor beyond. The fog hung close all around me then, when I turned the crest of the highland, and the gorse both before and behind me looked like a man crouching down in ambush. But still there was a good cloud of daylight, being scarce three of the clock yet, and when a lead of red deer came across, I could tell them from sheep even now. I was half inclined to shoot at them, for the children did love venison; but they drooped their heads so, and looked so faithful, that it seemed hard measure to do it. If one of them had bolted away, no doubt I had let go at him.

After that I kept on the track, trudging very stoutly, for nigh upon three miles, and my beard (now beginning to grow at some length) was full of great drops and prickly, whereat I was very proud. I had not so much as a dog with me, and the place was unkind and lonesome, and the rolling clouds very desolate; and now if a wild sheep ran across he was scared at me as an enemy; and I for my part could not tell the meaning of the marks on him. We called all this part Gibbet-moor, not being in our parish; but though there were gibbets enough upon it, most part of the bodies was gone for the value of the chains, they said, and the teaching of young chirurgeons. But of all this I had little fear, being no more a schoolboy now, but a youth well-acquaint with Exmoor, and the wise art of the sign-posts, whereby a man, who barred the road, now opens it up both ways with his finger-bones, so far as rogues allow him. My carbine was loaded and freshly primed, and I knew myself to be even now a match in strength for any two men of the size around our neighbourhood, except in the Glen Doone. 'Girt Jan Ridd,' I was called already, and folk grew feared to wrestle with me; though I was tired of hearing about it, and often longed to be smaller. And most of all upon Sundays, when I had to make way up our little church, and the maidens tittered at me.

The soft white mist came thicker around me, as the evening fell; and the peat ricks here and there, and the furze-hucks of the summer-time, were all out of shape in the twist of it. By-and-by, I began to doubt where I was, or how come there, not having seen a gibbet lately; and then I heard the draught of the wind up a hollow place with rocks to it; and for the first time fear broke out (like cold sweat) upon me. And yet I knew what a fool I was, to fear nothing but a sound! But when I stopped to listen, there was no sound, more than a beating noise, and that was all inside me. Therefore I went on again, making company of myself, and keeping my gun quite ready.

Now when I came to an unknown place, where a stone was set up endwise, with a faint red cross upon it, and a polish from some conflict, I gathered my courage to stop and think, having sped on the way too hotly. Against that stone I set my gun, trying my spirit to leave it so, but keeping with half a hand for it; and then what to do next was the wonder. As for finding Uncle Ben that was his own business, or at any rate his executor's; first I had to find myself, and plentifully would thank God to find myself at home again, for the sake of all our family.

The volumes of the mist came rolling at me (like great logs of wood, pillowed out with sleepiness), and between them there was nothing more than waiting for the next one. Then everything went out of sight, and glad was I of the stone behind me, and view of mine own shoes. Then a distant noise went by me, as of many horses galloping, and in my fright I set my gun and said, 'God send something to shoot at.' Yet nothing came, and my gun fell back, without my will to lower it.

But presently, while I was thinking 'What a fool I am!' arose as if from below my feet, so that the great stone trembled, that long, lamenting lonesome sound, as of an evil spirit not knowing what to do with it. For the moment I stood like a root, without either hand or foot to help me, and the hair of my head began to crawl, lifting my hat, as a snail lifts his house; and my heart like a shuttle went to and fro. But finding no harm to come of it, neither visible form approaching, I wiped my forehead, and hoped for the best, and resolved to run every step of the way, till I drew our own latch behind me.

Yet here again I was disappointed, for no sooner was I come to the cross-ways by the black pool in the hole, but I heard through the patter of my own feet a rough low sound very close in the fog, as of a hobbled sheep a-coughing. I listened, and feared, and yet listened again, though I wanted not to hear it. For being in haste of the homeward road, and all my heart having heels to it, loath I was to stop in the dusk for the sake of an aged wether. Yet partly my love of all animals, and partly my fear of the farmer's disgrace, compelled me to go to the succour, and the noise was coming nearer. A dry short wheezing sound it was, barred with coughs and want of breath; but thus I made the meaning of it.

'Lord have mercy upon me! O Lord, upon my soul have mercy! An if I cheated Sam Hicks last week, Lord knowest how well he deserved it, and lied in every stocking's mouth—oh Lord, where be I a-going?'

These words, with many jogs between them, came to me through the darkness, and then a long groan and a choking. I made towards the sound, as nigh as ever I could guess, and presently was met, point-blank, by the head of a mountain-pony. Upon its back lay a man bound down, with his feet on the neck and his head to the tail, and his arms falling down like stirrups. The wild little nag was scared of its life by the unaccustomed burden, and had been tossing and rolling hard, in desire to get ease of it.

Before the little horse could turn, I caught him, jaded as he was, by his wet and grizzled forelock, and he saw that it was vain to struggle, but strove to bite me none the less, until I smote him upon the nose.

'Good and worthy sir,' I said to the man who was riding so roughly; 'fear nothing; no harm shall come to thee.'

'Help, good friend, whoever thou art,' he gasped, but could not look at me, because his neck was jerked so; 'God hath sent thee, and not to rob me, because it is done already.'

'What, Uncle Ben!' I cried, letting go the horse in amazement, that the richest man in Dulverton—'Uncle Ben here in this plight! What, Mr. Reuben Huckaback!'

'An honest hosier and draper, serge and longcloth warehouseman'—he groaned from rib to rib—'at the sign of the Gartered Kitten in the loyal town of Dulverton. For God's sake, let me down, good fellow, from this accursed marrow-bone; and a groat of good money will I pay thee, safe in my house to Dulverton; but take notice that the horse is mine, no less than the nag they robbed from me.'

'What, Uncle Ben, dost thou not know me, thy dutiful nephew John Ridd?'

Not to make a long story of it, I cut the thongs that bound him, and set him astride on the little horse; but he was too weak to stay so. Therefore I mounted him on my back, turning the horse into horse-steps, and leading the pony by the cords which I fastened around his nose, set out for Plover's Barrows.

Uncle Ben went fast asleep on my back, being jaded and shaken beyond his strength, for a man of three-score and five; and as soon he felt assured of safety he would talk no more. And to tell the truth he snored so loudly, that I could almost believe that fearful noise in the fog every night came all the way from Dulverton.

Now as soon as ever I brought him in, we set him up in the chimney-corner, comfortable and handsome; and it was no little delight to me to get him off my back; for, like his own fortune, Uncle Ben was of a good round figure. He gave his long coat a shake or two, and he stamped about in the kitchen, until he was sure of his whereabouts, and then he fell asleep again until supper should be ready.

'He shall marry Ruth,' he said by-and-by to himself, and not to me; 'he shall marry Ruth for this, and have my little savings, soon as they be worth the having. Very little as yet, very little indeed; and ever so much gone to-day along of them rascal robbers.'

My mother made a dreadful stir, of course, about Uncle Ben being in such a plight as this; so I left him to her care and Annie's, and soon they fed him rarely, while I went out to see to the comfort of the captured pony. And in truth he was worth the catching, and served us very well afterwards, though Uncle Ben was inclined to claim him for his business at Dulverton, where they have carts and that like. 'But,' I said, 'you shall have him, sir, and welcome, if you will only ride him home as first I found you riding him.' And with that he dropped it.

A very strange old man he was, short in his manner, though long of body, glad to do the contrary things to what any one expected of him, and always looking sharp at people, as if he feared to be cheated. This surprised me much at first, because it showed his ignorance of what we farmers are—an upright race, as you may find, scarcely ever cheating indeed, except upon market-day, and even then no more than may be helped by reason of buyers expecting it. Now our simple ways were a puzzle to him, as I told him very often; but he only laughed, and rubbed his mouth with the back of his dry shining hand, and I think he shortly began to languish for want of some one to higgle with. I had a great mind to give him the pony, because he thought himself cheated in that case; only he would conclude that I did it with some view to a legacy.

Of course, the Doones, and nobody else, had robbed good Uncle Reuben; and then they grew sportive, and took his horse, an especially sober nag, and bound the master upon the wild one, for a little change as they told him. For two or three hours they had fine enjoyment chasing him through the fog, and making much sport of his groanings; and then waxing hungry, they went their way, and left him to opportunity. Now Mr. Huckaback growing able to walk in a few days' time, became thereupon impatient, and could not be brought to understand why he should have been robbed at all.

'I have never deserved it,' he said to himself, not knowing much of Providence, except with a small p to it; 'I have never deserved it, and will not stand it in the name of our lord the King, not I!' At other times he would burst forth thus: 'Three-score years and five have I lived an honest and laborious life, yet never was I robbed before. And now to be robbed in my old age, to be robbed for the first time now!'

Thereupon of course we would tell him how truly thankful he ought to be for never having been robbed before, in spite of living so long in this world, and that he was taking a very ungrateful, not to say ungracious, view, in thus repining, and feeling aggrieved; when anyone else would have knelt and thanked God for enjoying so long an immunity. But say what we would, it was all as one. Uncle Ben stuck fast to it, that he had nothing to thank God for.

Chapter XIV A Motion Which Ends in a Mull

Instead of minding his New-Year pudding, Master Huckaback carried on so about his mighty grievance, that at last we began to think there must be something in it, after all; especially as he assured us that choice and costly presents for the young people of our household were among the goods divested. But mother told him her children had plenty, and wanted no gold and silver, and little Eliza spoke up and said, 'You can give us the pretty things, Uncle Ben, when we come in the summer to see you.'

Our mother reproved Eliza for this, although it was the heel of her own foot; and then to satisfy our uncle, she promised to call Farmer Nicholas Snowe, to be of our council that evening, 'And if the young maidens would kindly come, without taking thought to smoothe themselves, why it would be all the merrier, and who knew but what Uncle Huckaback might bless the day of his robbery, etc., etc.—and thorough good honest girls they were, fit helpmates either for shop or farm.' All of which was meant for me; but I stuck to my platter and answered not.

In the evening Farmer Snowe came up, leading his daughters after him, like fillies trimmed for a fair; and Uncle Ben, who had not seen them on the night of his mishap (because word had been sent to stop them), was mightily pleased and very pleasant, according to his town bred ways. The damsels had seen good company, and soon got over their fear of his wealth, and played him a number of merry pranks, which made our mother quite jealous for Annie, who was always shy and diffident. However, when the hot cup was done, and before the mulled wine was ready, we packed all the maidens in the parlour and turned the key upon them; and then we drew near to the kitchen fire to hear Uncle Ben's proposal. Farmer Snowe sat up in the corner, caring little to bear about anything, but smoking slowly, and nodding backward like a sheep-dog dreaming. Mother was in the settle, of course, knitting hard, as usual; and Uncle Ben took to a three-legged stool, as if all but that had been thieved from him. Howsoever, he kept his breath from speech, giving privilege, as was due, to mother.

'Master Snowe, you are well assured,' said mother, colouring like the furze as it took the flame and fell over, 'that our kinsman here hath received rough harm on his peaceful journey from Dulverton. The times are bad, as we all know well, and there is no sign of bettering them, and if I could see our Lord the King I might say things to move him! nevertheless, I have had so much of my own account to vex for—'

'You are flying out of the subject, Sarah,' said Uncle Ben, seeing tears in her eyes, and tired of that matter.

'Zettle the pralimbinaries,' spoke Farmer Snowe, on appeal from us, 'virst zettle the pralimbinaries; and then us knows what be drivin' at.'

'Preliminaries be damned, sir,' cried Uncle Ben, losing his temper. 'What preliminaries were there when I was robbed; I should like to know? Robbed in this parish as I can prove, to the eternal disgrace of Oare and the scandal of all England. And I hold this parish to answer for it, sir; this parish shall make it good, being a nest of foul thieves as it is; ay, farmers, and yeomen, and all of you. I will beggar every man in this parish, if they be not beggars already, ay, and sell your old church up before your eyes, but what I will have back my tarlatan, time-piece, saddle, and dove-tailed nag.'

Mother looked at me, and I looked at Farmer Snowe, and we all were sorry for Master Huckaback, putting our hands up one to another, that nobody should browbeat him; because we all knew what our parish was, and none the worse for strong language, however rich the man might be. But Uncle Ben took it in a different way. He thought that we all were afraid of him, and that Oare parish was but as Moab or Edom, for him to cast his shoe over.

'Nephew Jack,' he cried, looking at me when I was thinking what to say, and finding only emptiness, 'you are a heavy lout, sir; a bumpkin, a clodhopper; and I shall leave you nothing, unless it be my boots to grease.'

'Well, uncle,' I made answer, 'I will grease your boots all the same for that, so long as you be our guest, sir.'

Now, that answer, made without a thought, stood me for two thousand pounds, as you shall see, by-and-by, perhaps.

'As for the parish,' my mother cried, being too hard set to contain herself, 'the parish can defend itself, and we may leave it to do so. But our Jack is not like that, sir; and I will not have him spoken of. Leave him indeed! Who wants you to do more than to leave him alone, sir; as he might have done you the other night; and as no one else would have dared to do. And after that, to think so meanly of me, and of my children!'

'Hoity, toity, Sarah! Your children, I suppose, are the same as other people's.'

'That they are not; and never will be; and you ought to know it, Uncle Reuben, if any one in the world ought. Other people's children!'

'Well, well!' Uncle Reuben answered, 'I know very little of children; except my little Ruth, and she is nothing wonderful.'

'I never said that my children were wonderful Uncle Ben; nor did I ever think it. But as for being good—'

Here mother fetched out her handkerchief, being overcome by our goodness; and I told her, with my hand to my mouth, not to notice him; though he might be worth ten thousand times ten thousand pounds.

But Farmer Snowe came forward now, for he had some sense sometimes; and he thought it was high time for him to say a word for the parish.

'Maister Huckaback,' he began, pointing with his pipe at him, the end that was done in sealing-wax, 'tooching of what you was plaized to zay 'bout this here parish, and no oother, mind me no oother parish but thees, I use the vreedom, zur, for to tell 'e, that thee be a laiar.'

Then Farmer Nicholas Snowe folded his arms across with the bowl of his pipe on the upper one, and gave me a nod, and then one to mother, to testify how he had done his duty, and recked not what might come of it. However, he got little thanks from us; for the parish was nothing at all to my mother, compared with her children's interests; and I thought it hard that an uncle of mine, and an old man too, should be called a liar, by a visitor at our fireplace. For we, in our rude part of the world, counted it one of the worst disgraces that could befall a man, to receive the lie from any one. But Uncle Ben, as it seems was used to it, in the way of trade, just as people of fashion are, by a style of courtesy.

Therefore the old man only looked with pity at Farmer Nicholas; and with a sort of sorrow too, reflecting how much he might have made in a bargain with such a customer, so ignorant and hot-headed.

'Now let us bandy words no more,' said mother, very sweetly; 'nothing is easier than sharp words, except to wish them unspoken; as I do many and many's the time, when I think of my good husband. But now let us hear from Uncle Reuben what he would have us do to remove this disgrace from amongst us, and to satisfy him of his goods.'

'I care not for my goods, woman,' Master Huckaback answered grandly; 'although they were of large value, about them I say nothing. But what I demand is this, the punishment of those scoundrels.'

'Zober, man, zober!' cried Farmer Nicholas; 'we be too naigh Badgery 'ood, to spake like that of they Dooneses.'

'Pack of cowards!' said Uncle Reuben, looking first at the door, however; 'much chance I see of getting redress from the valour of this Exmoor! And you, Master Snowe, the very man whom I looked to to raise the country, and take the lead as churchwarden—why, my youngest shopman would match his ell against you. Pack of cowards,' cried Uncle Ben, rising and shaking his lappets at us; 'don't pretend to answer me. Shake you all off, that I do—nothing more to do with you!'

We knew it useless to answer him, and conveyed our knowledge to one another, without anything to vex him. However, when the mulled wine was come, and a good deal of it gone (the season being Epiphany), Uncle Reuben began to think that he might have been too hard with us. Moreover, he was beginning now to respect Farmer Nicholas bravely, because of the way he had smoked his pipes, and the little noise made over them. And Lizzie and Annie were doing their best—for now we had let the girls out—to wake more lightsome uproar; also young Faith Snowe was toward to keep the old men's cups aflow, and hansel them to their liking.

So at the close of our entertainment, when the girls were gone away to fetch and light their lanthorns (over which they made rare noise, blowing each the other's out for counting of the sparks to come), Master Huckaback stood up, without much aid from the crock—saw, and looked at mother and all of us.

'Let no one leave this place,' said he, 'until I have said what I want to say; for saving of ill-will among us; and growth of cheer and comfort. May be I have carried things too far, even to the bounds of churlishness, and beyond the bounds of good manners. I will not unsay one word I have said, having never yet done so in my life; but I would alter the manner of it, and set it forth in this light. If you folks upon Exmoor here are loath and wary at fighting, yet you are brave at better stuff; the best and kindest I ever knew, in the matter of feeding.'

Here he sat down with tears in his eyes, and called for a little mulled bastard. All the maids, who were now come back, raced to get it for him, but Annie of course was foremost. And herein ended the expedition, a perilous and a great one, against the Doones of Bagworthy; an enterprise over which we had all talked plainly more than was good for us. For my part, I slept well that night, feeling myself at home again, now that the fighting was put aside, and the fear of it turned to the comfort of talking what we would have done.

Chapter XV Master Huckaback Fails of Warrant

On the following day Master Huckaback, with some show of mystery, demanded from my mother an escort into a dangerous part of the world, to which his business compelled him. My mother made answer to this that he was kindly welcome to take our John Fry with him; at which the good clothier laughed, and said that John was nothing like big enough, but another John must serve his turn, not only for his size, but because if he were carried away, no stone would be left unturned upon Exmoor, until he should be brought back again. Hereupon my mother grew very pale, and found fifty reasons against my going, each of them weightier than the true one, as Eliza (who was jealous of me) managed to whisper to Annie. On the other hand, I was quite resolved (directly the thing was mentioned) to see Uncle Reuben through with it; and it added much to my self-esteem to be the guard of so rich a man. Therefore I soon persuaded mother, with her head upon my breast, to let me go and trust in God, and after that I was greatly vexed to find that this dangerous enterprise was nothing more than a visit to the Baron de Whichehalse, to lay an information, and sue a warrant against the Doones, and a posse to execute it.

Stupid as I always have been, and must ever be no doubt, I could well have told Uncle Reuben that his journey was no wiser than that of the men of Gotham; that he never would get from Hugh de Whichehalse a warrant against the Doones; moreover, that if he did get one, his own wig would be singed with it. But for divers reasons I held my peace, partly from youth and modesty, partly from desire to see whatever please God I should see, and partly from other causes.

We rode by way of Brendon town, Illford Bridge, and Babbrook, to avoid the great hill above Lynmouth; and the day being fine and clear again, I laughed in my sleeve at Uncle Reuben for all his fine precautions. When we arrived at Ley Manor, we were shown very civilly into the hall, and refreshed with good ale and collared head, and the back of a Christmas pudding. I had never been under so fine a roof (unless it were of a church) before; and it pleased me greatly to be so kindly entreated by high-born folk. But Uncle Reuben was vexed a little at being set down side by side with a man in a very small way of trade, who was come upon some business there, and who made bold to drink his health after finishing their horns of ale.

'Sir,' said Uncle Ben, looking at him, 'my health would fare much better, if you would pay me three pounds and twelve shillings, which you have owed me these five years back; and now we are met at the Justice's, the opportunity is good, sir.'

After that, we were called to the Justice-room, where the Baron himself was sitting with Colonel Harding, another Justiciary of the King's peace, to help him. I had seen the Baron de Whichehalse before, and was not at all afraid of him, having been at school with his son as he knew, and it made him very kind to me. And indeed he was kind to everybody, and all our people spoke well of him; and so much the more because we knew that the house was in decadence. For the first De Whichehalse had come from Holland, where he had been a great nobleman, some hundred and fifty years agone. Being persecuted for his religion, when the Spanish power was everything, he fled to England with all he could save, and bought large estates in Devonshire. Since then his descendants had intermarried with ancient county families, Cottwells, and Marwoods, and Walronds, and Welses of Pylton, and Chichesters of Hall; and several of the ladies brought them large increase of property. And so about fifty years before the time of which I am writing, there were few names in the West of England thought more of than De Whichehalse. But now they had lost a great deal of land, and therefore of that which goes with land, as surely as fame belongs to earth—I mean big reputation. How they had lost it, none could tell; except that as the first descendants had a manner of amassing, so the later ones were gifted with a power of scattering. Whether this came of good Devonshire blood opening the sluice of Low Country veins, is beyond both my province and my power to inquire. Anyhow, all people loved this last strain of De Whichehalse far more than the name had been liked a hundred years agone.

Hugh de Whichehalse, a white-haired man, of very noble presence, with friendly blue eyes and a sweet smooth forehead, and aquiline nose quite beautiful (as you might expect in a lady of birth), and thin lips curving delicately, this gentleman rose as we entered the room; while Colonel Harding turned on his chair, and struck one spur against the other. I am sure that, without knowing aught of either, we must have reverenced more of the two the one who showed respect to us. And yet nine gentleman out of ten make this dull mistake when dealing with the class below them!

Uncle Reuben made his very best scrape, and then walked up to the table, trying to look as if he did not know himself to be wealthier than both the gentlemen put together. Of course he was no stranger to them, any more than I was; and, as it proved afterwards, Colonel Harding owed him a lump of money, upon very good security. Of him Uncle Reuben took no notice, but addressed himself to De Whichehalse.

The Baron smiled very gently, so soon as he learned the cause of this visit, and then he replied quite reasonably.

'A warrant against the Doones, Master Huckaback. Which of the Doones, so please you; and the Christian names, what be they?'

'My lord, I am not their godfather; and most like they never had any. But we all know old Sir Ensor's name, so that may be no obstacle.'

'Sir Ensor Doone and his sons—so be it. How many sons, Master Huckaback, and what is the name of each one?'

'How can I tell you, my lord, even if I had known them all as well as my own shop-boys? Nevertheless there were seven of them, and that should be no obstacle.'

'A warrant against Sir Ensor Doone, and seven sons of Sir Ensor Doone, Christian names unknown, and doubted if they have any. So far so good Master Huckaback. I have it all down in writing. Sir Ensor himself was there, of course, as you have given in evidence—'

'No, no, my lord, I never said that: I never said—'

'If he can prove that he was not there, you may be indicted for perjury. But as for those seven sons of his, of course you can swear that they were his sons and not his nephews, or grandchildren, or even no Doones at all?'

'My lord, I can swear that they were Doones. Moreover, I can pay for any mistake I make. Therein need be no obstacle.'

'Oh, yes, he can pay; he can pay well enough,' said Colonel Harding shortly.

'I am heartily glad to hear it,' replied the Baron pleasantly; 'for it proves after all that this robbery (if robbery there has been) was not so very ruinous. Sometimes people think they are robbed, and then it is very sweet afterwards to find that they have not been so; for it adds to their joy in their property. Now, are you quite convinced, good sir, that these people (if there were any) stole, or took, or even borrowed anything at all from you?'

'My lord, do you think that I was drunk?'

'Not for a moment, Master Huckaback. Although excuse might be made for you at this time of the year. But how did you know that your visitors were of this particular family?'

'Because it could be nobody else. Because, in spite of the fog—'

'Fog!' cried Colonel Harding sharply.

'Fog!' said the Baron, with emphasis. 'Ah, that explains the whole affair. To be sure, now I remember, the weather has been too thick for a man to see the head of his own horse. The Doones (if still there be any Doones) could never have come abroad; that is as sure as simony. Master Huckaback, for your good sake, I am heartily glad that this charge has miscarried. I thoroughly understand it now. The fog explains the whole of it.'

'Go back, my good fellow,' said Colonel Harding; 'and if the day is clear enough, you will find all your things where you left them. I know, from my own experience, what it is to be caught in an Exmoor fog.'

Uncle Reuben, by this time, was so put out, that he hardly knew what he was saying.

'My lord, Sir Colonel, is this your justice! If I go to London myself for it, the King shall know how his commission—how a man may be robbed, and the justices prove that he ought to be hanged at back of it; that in his good shire of Somerset—'

'Your pardon a moment, good sir,' De Whichehalse interrupted him; 'but I was about (having heard your case) to mention what need be an obstacle, and, I fear, would prove a fatal one, even if satisfactory proof were afforded of a felony. The mal-feasance (if any) was laid in Somerset; but we, two humble servants of His Majesty, are in commission of his peace for the county of Devon only, and therefore could never deal with it.'

'And why, in the name of God,' cried Uncle Reuben now carried at last fairly beyond himself, 'why could you not say as much at first, and save me all this waste of time and worry of my temper? Gentlemen, you are all in league; all of you stick together. You think it fair sport for an honest trader, who makes no shams as you do, to be robbed and wellnigh murdered, so long as they who did it won the high birthright of felony. If a poor sheep stealer, to save his children from dying of starvation, had dared to look at a two-month lamb, he would swing on the Manor gallows, and all of you cry "Good riddance!" But now, because good birth and bad manners—' Here poor Uncle Ben, not being so strong as before the Doones had played with him, began to foam at the mouth a little, and his tongue went into the hollow where his short grey whiskers were.

I forget how we came out of it, only I was greatly shocked at bearding of the gentry so, and mother scarce could see her way, when I told her all about it. 'Depend upon it you were wrong, John,' was all I could get out of her; though what had I done but listen, and touch my forelock, when called upon. 'John, you may take my word for it, you have not done as you should have done. Your father would have been shocked to think of going to Baron de Whichehalse, and in his own house insulting him! And yet it was very brave of you John. Just like you, all over. And (as none of the men are here, dear John) I am proud of you for doing it.'

All throughout the homeward road, Uncle Ben had been very silent, feeling much displeased with himself and still more so with other people. But before he went to bed that night, he just said to me, 'Nephew Jack, you have not behaved so badly as the rest to me. And because you have no gift of talking, I think that I may trust you. Now, mark my words, this villain job shall not have ending here. I have another card to play.'

'You mean, sir, I suppose, that you will go to the justices of this shire, Squire Maunder, or Sir Richard Blewitt, or—'

'Oaf, I mean nothing of the sort; they would only make a laughing-stock, as those Devonshire people did, of me. No, I will go to the King himself, or a man who is bigger than the King, and to whom I have ready access. I will not tell thee his name at present, only if thou art brought before him, never wilt thou forget it.' That was true enough, by the bye, as I discovered afterwards, for the man he meant was Judge Jeffreys.

'And when are you likely to see him, sir?'

'Maybe in the spring, maybe not until summer, for I cannot go to London on purpose, but when my business takes me there. Only remember my words, Jack, and when you see the man I mean, look straight at him, and tell no lie. He will make some of your zany squires shake in their shoes, I reckon. Now, I have been in this lonely hole far longer than I intended, by reason of this outrage; yet I will stay here one day more upon a certain condition.'

'Upon what condition, Uncle Ben? I grieve that you find it so lonely. We will have Farmer Nicholas up again, and the singers, and—'

'The fashionable milkmaids. I thank you, let me be. The wenches are too loud for me. Your Nanny is enough. Nanny is a good child, and she shall come and visit me.' Uncle Reuben would always call her 'Nanny'; he said that 'Annie' was too fine and Frenchified for us. 'But my condition is this, Jack—that you shall guide me to-morrow, without a word to any one, to a place where I may well descry the dwelling of these scoundrel Doones, and learn the best way to get at them, when the time shall come. Can you do this for me? I will pay you well, boy.'

I promised very readily to do my best to serve him, but, of course, would take no money for it, not being so poor as that came to. Accordingly, on the day following, I managed to set the men at work on the other side of the farm, especially that inquisitive and busybody John Fry, who would pry out almost anything for the pleasure of telling his wife; and then, with Uncle Reuben mounted on my ancient Peggy, I made foot for the westward, directly after breakfast. Uncle Ben refused to go unless I would take a loaded gun, and indeed it was always wise to do so in those days of turbulence; and none the less because of late more than usual of our sheep had left their skins behind them. This, as I need hardly say, was not to be charged to the appetite of the Doones, for they always said that they were not butchers (although upon that subject might well be two opinions); and their practice was to make the shepherds kill and skin, and quarter for them, and sometimes carry to the Doone-gate the prime among the fatlings, for fear of any bruising, which spoils the look at table. But the worst of it was that ignorant folk, unaware of their fastidiousness, scored to them the sheep they lost by lower-born marauders, and so were afraid to speak of it: and the issue of this error was that a farmer, with five or six hundred sheep, could never command, on his wedding-day, a prime saddle of mutton for dinner.

To return now to my Uncle Ben—and indeed he would not let me go more than three land-yards from him—there was very little said between us along the lane and across the hill, although the day was pleasant. I could see that he was half amiss with his mind about the business, and not so full of security as an elderly man should keep himself. Therefore, out I spake, and said,—

'Uncle Reuben, have no fear. I know every inch of the ground, sir; and there is no danger nigh us.'

'Fear, boy! Who ever thought of fear? 'Tis the last thing would come across me. Pretty things those primroses.'

At once I thought of Lorna Doone, the little maid of six years back, and how my fancy went with her. Could Lorna ever think of me? Was I not a lout gone by, only fit for loach-sticking? Had I ever seen a face fit to think of near her? The sudden flash, the quickness, the bright desire to know one's heart, and not withhold her own from it, the soft withdrawal of rich eyes, the longing to love somebody, anybody, anything, not imbrued with wickedness—

My uncle interrupted me, misliking so much silence now, with the naked woods falling over us. For we were come to Bagworthy forest, the blackest and the loneliest place of all that keep the sun out. Even now, in winter-time, with most of the wood unriddled, and the rest of it pinched brown, it hung around us like a cloak containing little comfort. I kept quite close to Peggy's head, and Peggy kept quite close to me, and pricked her ears at everything. However, we saw nothing there, except a few old owls and hawks, and a magpie sitting all alone, until we came to the bank of the hill, where the pony could not climb it. Uncle Ben was very loath to get off, because the pony seemed company, and he thought he could gallop away on her, if the worst came to the worst, but I persuaded him that now he must go to the end of it. Therefore he made Peggy fast, in a place where we could find her, and speaking cheerfully as if there was nothing to be afraid of, he took his staff, and I my gun, to climb the thick ascent.

There was now no path of any kind; which added to our courage all it lessened of our comfort, because it proved that the robbers were not in the habit of passing there. And we knew that we could not go astray, so long as we breasted the hill before us; inasmuch as it formed the rampart, or side-fence of Glen Doone. But in truth I used the right word there for the manner of our ascent, for the ground came forth so steep against us, and withal so woody, that to make any way we must throw ourselves forward, and labour as at a breast-plough. Rough and loamy rungs of oak-root bulged here and there above our heads; briers needs must speak with us, using more of tooth than tongue; and sometimes bulks of rugged stone, like great sheep, stood across us. At last, though very loath to do it, I was forced to leave my gun behind, because I required one hand to drag myself up the difficulty, and one to help Uncle Reuben. And so at last we gained the top, and looked forth the edge of the forest, where the ground was very stony and like the crest of a quarry; and no more trees between us and the brink of cliff below, three hundred yards below it might be, all strong slope and gliddery. And now far the first time I was amazed at the appearance of the Doones's stronghold, and understood its nature. For when I had been even in the valley, and climbed the cliffs to escape from it, about seven years agone, I was no more than a stripling boy, noting little, as boys do, except for their present purpose, and even that soon done with. But now, what with the fame of the Doones, and my own recollections, and Uncle Ben's insistence, all my attention was called forth, and the end was simple astonishment.

The chine of highland, whereon we stood, curved to the right and left of us, keeping about the same elevation, and crowned with trees and brushwood. At about half a mile in front of us, but looking as if we could throw a stone to strike any man upon it, another crest just like our own bowed around to meet it; but failed by reason of two narrow clefts of which we could only see the brink. One of these clefts was the Doone-gate, with a portcullis of rock above it, and the other was the chasm by which I had once made entrance. Betwixt them, where the hills fell back, as in a perfect oval, traversed by the winding water, lay a bright green valley, rimmed with sheer black rock, and seeming to have sunken bodily from the bleak rough heights above. It looked as if no frost could enter neither wind go ruffling; only spring, and hope, and comfort, breathe to one another. Even now the rays of sunshine dwelt and fell back on one another, whenever the clouds lifted; and the pale blue glimpse of the growing day seemed to find young encouragement.

But for all that, Uncle Reuben was none the worse nor better. He looked down into Glen Doone first, and sniffed as if he were smelling it, like a sample of goods from a wholesale house; and then he looked at the hills over yonder, and then he stared at me.

'See what a pack of fools they be?'

'Of course I do, Uncle Ben. "All rogues are fools," was my first copy, beginning of the alphabet.'

'Pack of stuff lad. Though true enough, and very good for young people. But see you not how this great Doone valley may be taken in half an hour?'

'Yes, to be sure I do, uncle; if they like to give it up, I mean.'

'Three culverins on yonder hill, and three on the top of this one, and we have them under a pestle. Ah, I have seen the wars, my lad, from Keinton up to Naseby; and I might have been a general now, if they had taken my advice—'

But I was not attending to him, being drawn away on a sudden by a sight which never struck the sharp eyes of our General. For I had long ago descried that little opening in the cliff through which I made my exit, as before related, on the other side of the valley. No bigger than a rabbit-hole it seemed from where we stood; and yet of all the scene before me, that (from my remembrance perhaps) had the most attraction. Now gazing at it with full thought of all that it had cost me, I saw a little figure come, and pause, and pass into it. Something very light and white, nimble, smooth, and elegant, gone almost before I knew that any one had been there. And yet my heart came to my ribs, and all my blood was in my face, and pride within me fought with shame, and vanity with self-contempt; for though seven years were gone, and I from my boyhood come to manhood, and all must have forgotten me, and I had half-forgotten; at that moment, once for all, I felt that I was face to face with fate (however poor it might be), weal or woe, in Lorna Doone.

Chapter XVI Lorna Growing Formidable

Having reconnoitred thus the position of the enemy, Master Huckaback, on the homeward road, cross-examined me in a manner not at all desirable. For he had noted my confusion and eager gaze at something unseen by him in the valley, and thereupon he made up his mind to know everything about it. In this, however, he partly failed; for although I was no hand at fence, and would not tell him a falsehood, I managed so to hold my peace that he put himself upon the wrong track, and continued thereon with many vaunts of his shrewdness and experience, and some chuckles at my simplicity. Thus much however, he learned aright, that I had been in the Doone valley several years before, and might be brought upon strong inducement to venture there again. But as to the mode of my getting in, the things I saw, and my thoughts upon them, he not only failed to learn the truth, but certified himself into an obstinacy of error, from which no after-knowledge was able to deliver him. And this he did, not only because I happened to say very little, but forasmuch as he disbelieved half of the truth I told him, through his own too great sagacity.

Upon one point, however, he succeeded more easily than he expected, viz. in making me promise to visit the place again, as soon as occasion offered, and to hold my own counsel about it. But I could not help smiling at one thing, that according to his point of view my own counsel meant my own and Master Reuben Huckaback's.

Now he being gone, as he went next day, to his favourite town of Dulverton, and leaving behind him shadowy promise of the mountains he would do for me, my spirit began to burn and pant for something to go on with; and nothing showed a braver hope of movement and adventure than a lonely visit to Glen Doone, by way of the perilous passage discovered in my boyhood. Therefore I waited for nothing more than the slow arrival of new small-clothes made by a good tailor at Porlock, for I was wishful to look my best; and when they were come and approved, I started, regardless of the expense, and forgetting (like a fool) how badly they would take the water.

What with urging of the tailor, and my own misgivings, the time was now come round again to the high-day of St. Valentine, when all our maids were full of lovers, and all the lads looked foolish. And none of them more sheepish or innocent than I myself, albeit twenty-one years old, and not afraid of men much, but terrified of women, at least, if they were comely. And what of all things scared me most was the thought of my own size, and knowledge of my strength, which came like knots upon me daily. In honest truth I tell this thing, (which often since hath puzzled me, when I came to mix with men more), I was to that degree ashamed of my thickness and my stature, in the presence of a woman, that I would not put a trunk of wood on the fire in the kitchen, but let Annie scold me well, with a smile to follow, and with her own plump hands lift up a little log, and fuel it. Many a time I longed to be no bigger than John Fry was; whom now (when insolent) I took with my left hand by the waist-stuff, and set him on my hat, and gave him little chance to tread it; until he spoke of his family, and requested to come down again.

Now taking for good omen this, that I was a seven-year Valentine, though much too big for a Cupidon, I chose a seven-foot staff of ash, and fixed a loach-fork in it, to look as I had looked before; and leaving word upon matters of business, out of the back door I went, and so through the little orchard, and down the brawling Lynn-brook. Not being now so much afraid, I struck across the thicket land between the meeting waters, and came upon the Bagworthy stream near the great black whirlpool. Nothing amazed me so much as to find how shallow the stream now looked to me, although the pool was still as black and greedy as it used to be. And still the great rocky slide was dark and difficult to climb; though the water, which once had taken my knees, was satisfied now with my ankles. After some labour, I reached the top; and halted to look about me well, before trusting to broad daylight.

The winter (as I said before) had been a very mild one; and now the spring was toward so that bank and bush were touched with it. The valley into which I gazed was fair with early promise, having shelter from the wind and taking all the sunshine. The willow-bushes over the stream hung as if they were angling with tasseled floats of gold and silver, bursting like a bean-pod. Between them came the water laughing, like a maid at her own dancing, and spread with that young blue which never lives beyond the April. And on either bank, the meadow ruffled as the breeze came by, opening (through new tuft, of green) daisy-bud or celandine, or a shy glimpse now and then of the love-lorn primrose.

Though I am so blank of wit, or perhaps for that same reason, these little things come and dwell with me, and I am happy about them, and long for nothing better. I feel with every blade of grass, as if it had a history; and make a child of every bud as though it knew and loved me. And being so, they seem to tell me of my own delusions, how I am no more than they, except in self—importance.

While I was forgetting much of many things that harm one, and letting of my thoughts go wild to sounds and sights of nature, a sweeter note than thrush or ouzel ever wooed a mate in, floated on the valley breeze at the quiet turn of sundown. The words were of an ancient song, fit to laugh or cry at.

Love, an if there be one,
Come my love to be,
My love is for the one
Loving unto me.

Not for me the show, love,
Of a gilded bliss;
Only thou must know, love,
What my value is.

If in all the earth, love,
Thou hast none but me,
This shall be my worth, love:
To be cheap to thee.

But, if so thou ever
Strivest to be free,
'Twill be my endeavour
To be dear to thee.

So shall I have plea, love,
Is thy heart andbreath
Clinging still to thee, love,
In the doom of death.

All this I took in with great eagerness, not for the sake of the meaning (which is no doubt an allegory), but for the power and richness, and softness of the singing, which seemed to me better than we ever had even in Oare church. But all the time I kept myself in a black niche of the rock, where the fall of the water began, lest the sweet singer (espying me) should be alarmed, and flee away. But presently I ventured to look forth where a bush was; and then I beheld the loveliest sight—one glimpse of which was enough to make me kneel in the coldest water.

By the side of the stream she was coming to me, even among the primroses, as if she loved them all; and every flower looked the brighter, as her eyes were on them, I could not see what her face was, my heart so awoke and trembled; only that her hair was flowing from a wreath of white violets, and the grace of her coming was like the appearance of the first wind-flower. The pale gleam over the western cliffs threw a shadow of light behind her, as if the sun were lingering. Never do I see that light from the closing of the west, even in these my aged days, without thinking of her. Ah me, if it comes to that, what do I see of earth or heaven, without thinking of her?

The tremulous thrill of her song was hanging on her open lips; and she glanced around, as if the birds were accustomed to make answer. To me it was a thing of terror to behold such beauty, and feel myself the while to be so very low and common. But scarcely knowing what I did, as if a rope were drawing me, I came from the dark mouth of the chasm; and stood, afraid to look at her.

She was turning to fly, not knowing me, and frightened, perhaps, at my stature, when I fell on the grass (as I fell before her seven years agone that day), and I just said, 'Lorna Doone!'

She knew me at once, from my manner and ways, and a smile broke through her trembling, as sunshine comes through aspen-leaves; and being so clever, she saw, of course, that she needed not to fear me.

'Oh, indeed,' she cried, with a feint of anger (because she had shown her cowardice, and yet in her heart she was laughing); 'oh, if you please, who are you, sir, and how do you know my name?'

'I am John Ridd,' I answered; 'the boy who gave you those beautiful fish, when you were only a little thing, seven years ago to-day.'

'Yes, the poor boy who was frightened so, and obliged to hide here in the water.'

'And do you remember how kind you were, and saved my life by your quickness, and went away riding upon a great man's shoulder, as if you had never seen me, and yet looked back through the willow-trees?'

'Oh, yes, I remember everything; because it was so rare to see any except—I mean because I happen to remember. But you seem not to remember, sir, how perilous this place is.'

For she had kept her eyes upon me; large eyes of a softness, a brightness, and a dignity which made me feel as if I must for ever love and yet for ever know myself unworthy. Unless themselves should fill with love, which is the spring of all things. And so I could not answer her, but was overcome with thinking and feeling and confusion. Neither could I look again; only waited for the melody which made every word like a poem to me, the melody of her voice. But she had not the least idea of what was going on with me, any more than I myself had.

'I think, Master Ridd, you cannot know,' she said, with her eyes taken from me, 'what the dangers of this place are, and the nature of the people.'

'Yes, I know enough of that; and I am frightened greatly, all the time, when I do not look at you.'

She was too young to answer me in the style some maidens would have used; the manner, I mean, which now we call from a foreign word 'coquettish.' And more than that, she was trembling from real fear of violence, lest strong hands might be laid on me, and a miserable end of it. And to tell the truth, I grew afraid; perhaps from a kind of sympathy, and because I knew that evil comes more readily than good to us.

Therefore, without more ado, or taking any advantage—although I would have been glad at heart, if needs had been, to kiss her (without any thought of rudeness)—it struck me that I had better go, and have no more to say to her until next time of coming. So would she look the more for me and think the more about me, and not grow weary of my words and the want of change there is in me. For, of course, I knew what a churl I was compared to her birth and appearance; but meanwhile I might improve myself and learn a musical instrument. 'The wind hath a draw after flying straw' is a saying we have in Devonshire, made, peradventure, by somebody who had seen the ways of women.

'Mistress Lorna, I will depart'—mark you, I thought that a powerful word—'in fear of causing disquiet. If any rogue shot me it would grieve you; I make bold to say it, and it would be the death of mother. Few mothers have such a son as me. Try to think of me now and then, and I will bring you some new-laid eggs, for our young blue hen is beginning.'

'I thank you heartily,' said Lorna; 'but you need not come to see me. You can put them in my little bower, where I am almost always—I mean whither daily I repair to read and to be away from them.'

'Only show me where it is. Thrice a day I will come and stop—'

'Nay, Master Ridd, I would never show thee—never, because of peril—only that so happens it thou hast found the way already.'

And she smiled with a light that made me care to cry out for no other way, except to her dear heart. But only to myself I cried for anything at all, having enough of man in me to be bashful with young maidens. So I touched her white hand softly when she gave it to me, and (fancying that she had sighed) was touched at heart about it, and resolved to yield her all my goods, although my mother was living; and then grew angry with myself (for a mile or more of walking) to think she would condescend so; and then, for the rest of the homeward road, was mad with every man in the world who would dare to think of having her.

Chapter XVII John Is Clearly Bewitched

To forget one's luck of life, to forget the cark of care and withering of young fingers; not to feel, or not be moved by, all the change of thought and heart, from large young heat to the sinewy lines and dry bones of old age—this is what I have to do ere ever I can make you know (even as a dream is known) how I loved my Lorna. I myself can never know; never can conceive, or treat it as a thing of reason, never can behold myself dwelling in the midst of it, and think that this was I; neither can I wander far from perpetual thought of it. Perhaps I have two farrows of pigs ready for the chapman; perhaps I have ten stones of wool waiting for the factor. It is all the same. I look at both, and what I say to myself is this: 'Which would Lorna choose of them?' Of course, I am a fool for this; any man may call me so, and I will not quarrel with him, unless he guess my secret. Of course, I fetch my wit, if it be worth the fetching, back again to business. But there my heart is and must be; and all who like to try can cheat me, except upon parish matters.

That week I could do little more than dream and dream and rove about, seeking by perpetual change to find the way back to myself. I cared not for the people round me, neither took delight in victuals; but made believe to eat and drink and blushed at any questions. And being called the master now, head-farmer, and chief yeoman, it irked me much that any one should take advantage of me; yet everybody did so as soon as ever it was known that my wits were gone moon-raking. For that was the way they looked at it, not being able to comprehend the greatness and the loftiness. Neither do I blame them much; for the wisest thing is to laugh at people when we cannot understand them. I, for my part, took no notice; but in my heart despised them as beings of a lesser nature, who never had seen Lorna. Yet I was vexed, and rubbed myself, when John Fry spread all over the farm, and even at the shoeing forge, that a mad dog had come and bitten me, from the other side of Mallond.

This seems little to me now; and so it might to any one; but, at the time, it worked me up to a fever of indignity. To make a mad dog of Lorna, to compare all my imaginings (which were strange, I do assure you—the faculty not being apt to work), to count the raising of my soul no more than hydrophobia! All this acted on me so, that I gave John Fry the soundest threshing that ever a sheaf of good corn deserved, or a bundle of tares was blessed with. Afterwards he went home, too tired to tell his wife the meaning of it; but it proved of service to both of them, and an example for their children.

Now the climate of this country is—so far as I can make of it—to throw no man into extremes; and if he throw himself so far, to pluck him back by change of weather and the need of looking after things. Lest we should be like the Southerns, for whom the sky does everything, and men sit under a wall and watch both food and fruit come beckoning. Their sky is a mother to them; but ours a good stepmother to us—fearing to hurt by indulgence, and knowing that severity and change of mood are wholesome.

The spring being now too forward, a check to it was needful; and in the early part of March there came a change of weather. All the young growth was arrested by a dry wind from the east, which made both face and fingers burn when a man was doing ditching. The lilacs and the woodbines, just crowding forth in little tufts, close kernelling their blossom, were ruffled back, like a sleeve turned up, and nicked with brown at the corners. In the hedges any man, unless his eyes were very dull, could see the mischief doing. The russet of the young elm-bloom was fain to be in its scale again; but having pushed forth, there must be, and turn to a tawny colour. The hangers of the hazel, too, having shed their dust to make the nuts, did not spread their little combs and dry them, as they ought to do; but shrivelled at the base and fell, as if a knife had cut them. And more than all to notice was (at least about the hedges) the shuddering of everything and the shivering sound among them toward the feeble sun; such as we make to a poor fireplace when several doors are open. Sometimes I put my face to warm against the soft, rough maple-stem, which feels like the foot of a red deer; but the pitiless east wind came through all, and took and shook the caved hedge aback till its knees were knocking together, and nothing could be shelter. Then would any one having blood, and trying to keep at home with it, run to a sturdy tree and hope to eat his food behind it, and look for a little sun to come and warm his feet in the shelter. And if it did he might strike his breast, and try to think he was warmer.

But when a man came home at night, after long day's labour, knowing that the days increased, and so his care should multiply; still he found enough of light to show him what the day had done against him in his garden. Every ridge of new-turned earth looked like an old man's muscles, honeycombed, and standing out void of spring, and powdery. Every plant that had rejoiced in passing such a winter now was cowering, turned away, unfit to meet the consequence. Flowing sap had stopped its course; fluted lines showed want of food, and if you pinched the topmost spray, there was no rebound or firmness.

We think a good deal, in a quiet way, when people ask us about them—of some fine, upstanding pear-trees, grafted by my grandfather, who had been very greatly respected. And he got those grafts by sheltering a poor Italian soldier, in the time of James the First, a man who never could do enough to show his grateful memories. How he came to our place is a very difficult story, which I never understood rightly, having heard it from my mother. At any rate, there the pear-trees were, and there they are to this very day; and I wish every one could taste their fruit, old as they are, and rugged.

Now these fine trees had taken advantage of the west winds, and the moisture, and the promise of the spring time, so as to fill the tips of the spray-wood and the rowels all up the branches with a crowd of eager blossom. Not that they were yet in bloom, nor even showing whiteness, only that some of the cones were opening at the side of the cap which pinched them; and there you might count perhaps, a dozen nobs, like very little buttons, but grooved, and lined, and huddling close, to make room for one another. And among these buds were gray-green blades, scarce bigger than a hair almost, yet curving so as if their purpose was to shield the blossom.

Other of the spur-points, standing on the older wood where the sap was not so eager, had not burst their tunic yet, but were flayed and flaked with light, casting off the husk of brown in three-cornered patches, as I have seen a Scotchman's plaid, or as his legs shows through it. These buds, at a distance, looked as if the sky had been raining cream upon them.

Now all this fair delight to the eyes, and good promise to the palate, was marred and baffled by the wind and cutting of the night-frosts. The opening cones were struck with brown, in between the button buds, and on the scapes that shielded them; while the foot part of the cover hung like rags, peeled back, and quivering. And there the little stalk of each, which might have been a pear, God willing, had a ring around its base, and sought a chance to drop and die. The others which had not opened comb, but only prepared to do it, were a little better off, but still very brown and unkid, and shrivelling in doubt of health, and neither peart nor lusty.

Now this I have not told because I know the way to do it, for that I do not, neither yet have seen a man who did know. It is wonderful how we look at things, and never think to notice them; and I am as bad as anybody, unless the thing to be observed is a dog, or a horse, or a maiden. And the last of those three I look at, somehow, without knowing that I take notice, and greatly afraid to do it, only I knew afterwards (when the time of life was in me), not indeed, what the maiden was like, but how she differed from others.

Yet I have spoken about the spring, and the failure of fair promise, because I took it to my heart as token of what would come to me in the budding of my years and hope. And even then, being much possessed, and full of a foolish melancholy, I felt a sad delight at being doomed to blight and loneliness; not but that I managed still (when mother was urgent upon me) to eat my share of victuals, and cuff a man for laziness, and see that a ploughshare made no leaps, and sleep of a night without dreaming. And my mother half-believing, in her fondness and affection, that what the parish said was true about a mad dog having bitten me, and yet arguing that it must be false (because God would have prevented him), my mother gave me little rest, when I was in the room with her. Not that she worried me with questions, nor openly regarded me with any unusual meaning, but that I knew she was watching slyly whenever I took a spoon up; and every hour or so she managed to place a pan of water by me, quite as if by accident, and sometimes even to spill a little upon my shoe or coat-sleeve. But Betty Muxworthy was worst; for, having no fear about my health, she made a villainous joke of it, and used to rush into the kitchen, barking like a dog, and panting, exclaiming that I had bitten her, and justice she would have on me, if it cost her a twelvemonth's wages. And she always took care to do this thing just when I had crossed my legs in the corner after supper, and leaned my head against the oven, to begin to think of Lorna.

However, in all things there is comfort, if we do not look too hard for it; and now I had much satisfaction, in my uncouth state, from labouring, by the hour together, at the hedging and the ditching, meeting the bitter wind face to face, feeling my strength increase, and hoping that some one would be proud of it. In the rustling rush of every gust, in the graceful bend of every tree, even in the 'lords and ladies,' clumped in the scoops of the hedgerow, and most of all in the soft primrose, wrung by the wind, but stealing back, and smiling when the wrath was passed—in all of these, and many others there was aching ecstasy, delicious pang of Lorna.

But however cold the weather was, and however hard the wind blew, one thing (more than all the rest) worried and perplexed me. This was, that I could not settle, turn and twist as I might, how soon I ought to go again upon a visit to Glen Doone. For I liked not at all the falseness of it (albeit against murderers), the creeping out of sight, and hiding, and feeling as a spy might. And even more than this. I feared how Lorna might regard it; whether I might seem to her a prone and blunt intruder, a country youth not skilled in manners, as among the quality, even when they rob us. For I was not sure myself, but that it might be very bad manners to go again too early without an invitation; and my hands and face were chapped so badly by the bitter wind, that Lorna might count them unsightly things, and wish to see no more of them.

However, I could not bring myself to consult any one upon this point, at least in our own neighbourhood, nor even to speak of it near home. But the east wind holding through the month, my hands and face growing worse and worse, and it having occurred to me by this time that possibly Lorna might have chaps, if she came abroad at all, and so might like to talk about them and show her little hands to me, I resolved to take another opinion, so far as might be upon this matter, without disclosing the circumstances.

Now the wisest person in all our parts was reckoned to be a certain wise woman, well known all over Exmoor by the name of Mother Melldrum. Her real name was Maple Durham, as I learned long afterwards; and she came of an ancient family, but neither of Devon nor Somerset. Nevertheless she was quite at home with our proper modes of divination; and knowing that we liked them best—as each man does his own religion—she would always practise them for the people of the country. And all the while, she would let us know that she kept a higher and nobler mode for those who looked down upon this one, not having been bred and born to it.

Mother Melldrum had two houses, or rather she had none at all, but two homes wherein to find her, according to the time of year. In summer she lived in a pleasant cave, facing the cool side of the hill, far inland near Hawkridge and close above Tarr-steps, a wonderful crossing of Barle river, made (as everybody knows) by Satan, for a wager. But throughout the winter, she found sea-air agreeable, and a place where things could be had on credit, and more occasion of talking. Not but what she could have credit (for every one was afraid of her) in the neighbourhood of Tarr-steps; only there was no one handy owning things worth taking.

Therefore, at the fall of the leaf, when the woods grew damp and irk-some, the wise woman always set her face to the warmer cliffs of the Channel; where shelter was, and dry fern bedding, and folk to be seen in the distance, from a bank upon which the sun shone. And there, as I knew from our John Fry (who had been to her about rheumatism, and sheep possessed with an evil spirit, and warts on the hand of his son, young John), any one who chose might find her, towards the close of a winter day, gathering sticks and brown fern for fuel, and talking to herself the while, in a hollow stretch behind the cliffs; which foreigners, who come and go without seeing much of Exmoor, have called the Valley of Rocks.

This valley, or goyal, as we term it, being small for a valley, lies to the west of Linton, about a mile from the town perhaps, and away towards Ley Manor. Our homefolk always call it the Danes, or the Denes, which is no more, they tell me, than a hollow place, even as the word 'den' is. However, let that pass, for I know very little about it; but the place itself is a pretty one, though nothing to frighten anybody, unless he hath lived in a gallipot. It is a green rough-sided hollow, bending at the middle, touched with stone at either crest, and dotted here and there with slabs in and out the brambles. On the right hand is an upward crag, called by some the Castle, easy enough to scale, and giving great view of the Channel. Facing this, from the inland side and the elbow of the valley, a queer old pile of rock arises, bold behind one another, and quite enough to affright a man, if it only were ten times larger. This is called the Devil's Cheese-ring, or the Devil's Cheese-knife, which mean the same thing, as our fathers were used to eat their cheese from a scoop; and perhaps in old time the upmost rock (which has fallen away since I knew it) was like to such an imple-ment, if Satan eat cheese untoasted.

But all the middle of this valley was a place to rest in; to sit and think that troubles were not, if we would not make them. To know the sea out-side the hills, but never to behold it; only by the sound of waves to pity sailors labouring. Then to watch the sheltered sun, coming warmly round the turn, like a guest expected, full of gentle glow and gladness, casting shadow far away as a thing to hug itself, and awakening life from dew, and hope from every spreading bud. And then to fall asleep and dream that the fern was all asparagus.

Alas, I was too young in those days much to care for creature com-forts, or to let pure palate have things that would improve it. Anything went down with me, as it does with most of us. Too late we know the good from bad; the knowledge is no pleasure then; being memory's medicine rather than the wine of hope.

Now Mother Melldrum kept her winter in this vale of rocks, shelter-ing from the wind and rain within the Devil's Cheese-ring, which added greatly to her fame because all else, for miles around, were afraid to go near it after dark, or even on a gloomy day. Under eaves of lichened rock she had a winding passage, which none that ever I knew of durst enter but herself. And to this place I went to seek her, in spite of all misgivings, upon a Sunday in Lenten season, when the sheep were folded.

Our parson (as if he had known my intent) had preached a beautiful sermon about the Witch of Endor, and the perils of them that meddle wantonly with the unseen Powers; and therein he referred especially to the strange noise in the neighbourhood, and upbraided us for want of faith, and many other backslidings. We listened to him very earnestly, for we like to hear from our betters about things that are beyond us, and to be roused up now and then, like sheep with a good dog after them, who can pull some wool without biting. Nevertheless we could not see how our want of faith could have made that noise, especially at night time, notwithstanding which we believed it, and hoped to do a little better.

And so we all came home from church; and most of the people dined with us, as they always do on Sundays, because of the distance to go home, with only words inside them. The parson, who always sat next to mother, was afraid that he might have vexed us, and would not have the best piece of meat, according to his custom. But soon we put him at his ease, and showed him we were proud of him; and then he made no more to do, but accepted the best of the sirloin.

Chapter XVIII Witchery Leads To Witchcraft

Although wellnigh the end of March, the wind blew wild and piercing, as I went on foot that afternoon to Mother Melldrum's dwelling. It was safer not to take a horse, lest (if anything vexed her) she should put a spell upon him; as had been done to Farmer Snowe's stable by the wise woman of Simonsbath.

The sun was low on the edge of the hills by the time I entered the valley, for I could not leave home till the cattle were tended, and the distance was seven miles or more. The shadows of rocks fell far and deep, and the brown dead fern was fluttering, and brambles with their sere leaves hanging, swayed their tatters to and fro, with a red look on them. In patches underneath the crags, a few wild goats were browsing; then they tossed their horns, and fled, and leaped on ledges, and stared at me. Moreover, the sound of the sea came up, and went the length of the valley, and there it lapped on a butt of rocks, and murmured like a shell.

Taking things one with another, and feeling all the lonesomeness, and having no stick with me, I was much inclined to go briskly back, and come at a better season. And when I beheld a tall grey shape, of something or another, moving at the lower end of the valley, where the shade was, it gave me such a stroke of fear, after many others, that my thumb which lay in mother's Bible (brought in my big pocket for the sake of safety) shook so much that it came out, and I could not get it in again. 'This serves me right,' I said to myself, 'for tampering with Beelzebub. Oh that I had listened to parson!'

And thereupon I struck aside; not liking to run away quite, as some people might call it; but seeking to look like a wanderer who was come to see the valley, and had seen almost enough of it. Herein I should have succeeded, and gone home, and then been angry at my want of courage, but that on the very turn and bending of my footsteps, the woman in the distance lifted up her staff to me, so that I was bound to stop.

And now, being brought face to face, by the will of God (as one might say) with anything that might come of it, I kept myself quite straight and stiff, and thrust away all white feather, trusting in my Bible still, hoping that it would protect me, though I had disobeyed it. But upon that remembrance, my conscience took me by the leg, so that I could not go forward.

All this while, the fearful woman was coming near and more near to me; and I was glad to sit down on a rock because my knees were shaking so. I tried to think of many things, but none of them would come to me; and I could not take my eyes away, though I prayed God to be near me.

But when she was come so nigh to me that I could descry her features, there was something in her countenance that made me not dislike her. She looked as if she had been visited by many troubles, and had felt them one by one, yet held enough of kindly nature still to grieve for others. Long white hair, on either side, was falling down below her chin; and through her wrinkles clear bright eyes seemed to spread themselves upon me. Though I had plenty of time to think, I was taken by surprise no less, and unable to say anything; yet eager to hear the silence broken, and longing for a noise or two.

'Thou art not come to me,' she said, looking through my simple face, as if it were but glass, 'to be struck for bone-shave, nor to be blessed for barn-gun. Give me forth thy hand, John Ridd; and tell why thou art come to me.'

But I was so much amazed at her knowing my name and all about me, that I feared to place my hand in her power, or even my tongue by speaking.

'Have no fear of me, my son; I have no gift to harm thee; and if I had, it should be idle. Now, if thou hast any wit, tell me why I love thee.'

'I never had any wit, mother,' I answered in our Devonshire way; 'and never set eyes on thee before, to the furthest of my knowledge.'

'And yet I know thee as well, John, as if thou wert my grandson. Remember you the old Oare oak, and the bog at the head of Exe, and the child who would have died there, but for thy strength and courage, and most of all thy kindness? That was my granddaughter, John; and all I have on earth to love.'

Now that she came to speak of it, with the place and that, so clearly, I remembered all about it (a thing that happened last August), and thought how stupid I must have been not to learn more of the little girl who had fallen into the black pit, with a basketful of whortleberries, and who might have been gulfed if her little dog had not spied me in the distance. I carried her on my back to mother; and then we dressed her all anew, and took her where she ordered us; but she did not tell us who she was, nor anything more than her Christian name, and that she was eight years old, and fond of fried batatas. And we did not seek to ask her more; as our manner is with visitors.

But thinking of this little story, and seeing how she looked at me, I lost my fear of Mother Melldrum, and began to like her; partly because I had helped her grandchild, and partly that if she were so wise, no need would have been for me to save the little thing from drowning. Therefore I stood up and said, though scarcely yet established in my power against hers,—

'Good mother, the shoe she lost was in the mire, and not with us. And we could not match it, although we gave her a pair of sister Lizzie's.'

'My son, what care I for her shoe? How simple thou art, and foolish! according to the thoughts of some. Now tell me, for thou canst not lie, what has brought thee to me.'

Being so ashamed and bashful, I was half-inclined to tell her a lie, until she said that I could not do it; and then I knew that I could not.

'I am come to know,' I said, looking at a rock the while, to keep my voice from shaking, 'when I may go to see Lorna Doone.'

No more could I say, though my mind was charged to ask fifty other questions. But although I looked away, it was plain that I had asked enough. I felt that the wise woman gazed at me in wrath as well as sorrow; and then I grew angry that any one should seem to make light of Lorna.

'John Ridd,' said the woman, observing this (for now I faced her bravely), 'of whom art thou speaking? Is it a child of the men who slew your father?'

'I cannot tell, mother. How should I know? And what is that to thee?'

'It is something to thy mother, John, and something to thyself, I trow; and nothing worse could befall thee.'

I waited for her to speak again, because she had spoken so sadly that it took my breath away.

'John Ridd, if thou hast any value for thy body or thy soul, thy mother, or thy father's name, have nought to do with any Doone.'

She gazed at me in earnest so, and raised her voice in saying it, until the whole valley, curving like a great bell echoed 'Doone,' that it seemed to me my heart was gone for every one and everything. If it were God's will for me to have no more of Lorna, let a sign come out of the rocks, and I would try to believe it. But no sign came, and I turned to the woman, and longed that she had been a man.

'You poor thing, with bones and blades, pails of water, and door-keys, what know you about the destiny of a maiden such as Lorna? Chilblains you may treat, and bone-shave, ringworm, and the scaldings; even scabby sheep may limp the better for your strikings. John the Baptist and his cousins, with the wool and hyssop, are for mares, and ailing dogs, and fowls that have the jaundice. Look at me now, Mother Melldrum, am I like a fool?'

'That thou art, my son. Alas that it were any other! Now behold the end of that; John Ridd, mark the end of it.'

She pointed to the castle-rock, where upon a narrow shelf, betwixt us and the coming stars, a bitter fight was raging. A fine fat sheep, with an honest face, had clomb up very carefully to browse on a bit of juicy grass, now the dew of the land was upon it. To him, from an upper crag, a lean black goat came hurrying, with leaps, and skirmish of the horns, and an angry noise in his nostrils. The goat had grazed the place before, to the utmost of his liking, cropping in and out with jerks, as their manner is of feeding. Nevertheless he fell on the sheep with fury and great malice.

The simple wether was much inclined to retire from the contest, but looked around in vain for any way to peace and comfort. His enemy stood between him and the last leap he had taken; there was nothing left him but to fight, or be hurled into the sea, five hundred feet below.

'Lie down, lie down!' I shouted to him, as if he were a dog, for I had seen a battle like this before, and knew that the sheep had no chance of life except from his greater weight, and the difficulty of moving him.

'Lie down, lie down, John Ridd!' cried Mother Melldrum, mocking me, but without a sign of smiling.

The poor sheep turned, upon my voice, and looked at me so piteously that I could look no longer; but ran with all my speed to try and save him from the combat. He saw that I could not be in time, for the goat was bucking to leap at him, and so the good wether stooped his forehead, with the harmless horns curling aside of it; and the goat flung his heels up, and rushed at him, with quick sharp jumps and tricks of movement, and the points of his long horns always foremost, and his little scut cocked like a gun-hammer.

As I ran up the steep of the rock, I could not see what they were doing, but the sheep must have fought very bravely at last, and yielded his ground quite slowly, and I hoped almost to save him. But just as my head topped the platform of rock, I saw him flung from it backward, with a sad low moan and a gurgle. His body made quite a short noise in the air, like a bucket thrown down a well shaft, and I could not tell when it struck the water, except by the echo among the rocks. So wroth was I with the goat at the moment (being somewhat scant of breath and unable to consider), that I caught him by the right hind-leg, before he could turn from his victory, and hurled him after the sheep, to learn how he liked his own compulsion.

Chapter XIX Another Dangerous Interview

Although I left the Denes at once, having little heart for further questions of the wise woman, and being afraid to visit her house under the Devil's Cheese-ring (to which she kindly invited me), and although I ran most part of the way, it was very late for farm-house time upon a Sunday evening before I was back at Plover's Barrows. My mother had great desire to know all about the matter; but I could not reconcile it with my respect so to frighten her. Therefore I tried to sleep it off, keeping my own counsel; and when that proved of no avail, I strove to work it away, it might be, by heavy outdoor labour, and weariness, and good feeding. These indeed had some effect, and helped to pass a week or two, with more pain of hand than heart to me.

But when the weather changed in earnest, and the frost was gone, and the south-west wind blew softly, and the lambs were at play with the daisies, it was more than I could do to keep from thought of Lorna. For now the fields were spread with growth, and the waters clad with sunshine, and light and shadow, step by step, wandered over the furzy cleves. All the sides of the hilly wood were gathered in and out with green, silver-grey, or russet points, according to the several manner of the trees beginning. And if one stood beneath an elm, with any heart to look at it, lo! all the ground was strewn with flakes (too small to know their meaning), and all the sprays above were rasped and trembling with a redness. And so I stopped beneath the tree, and carved L.D. upon it, and wondered at the buds of thought that seemed to swell inside me.

The upshot of it all was this, that as no Lorna came to me, except in dreams or fancy, and as my life was not worth living without constant sign of her, forth I must again to find her, and say more than a man can tell. Therefore, without waiting longer for the moving of the spring, dressed I was in grand attire (so far as I had gotten it), and thinking my appearance good, although with doubts about it (being forced to dress in the hay-tallat), round the corner of the wood-stack went I very knowingly—for Lizzie's eyes were wondrous sharp—and then I was sure of meeting none who would care or dare to speak of me.

It lay upon my conscience often that I had not made dear Annie secret to this history; although in all things I could trust her, and she loved me like a lamb. Many and many a time I tried, and more than once began the thing; but there came a dryness in my throat, and a knocking under the roof of my mouth, and a longing to put it off again, as perhaps might be the wisest. And then I would remember too that I had no right to speak of Lorna as if she were common property.

This time I longed to take my gun, and was half resolved to do so; because it seemed so hard a thing to be shot at and have no chance of shooting; but when I came to remember the steepness and the slippery nature of the waterslide, there seemed but little likelihood of keeping dry the powder. Therefore I was armed with nothing but a good stout holly staff, seasoned well for many a winter in our back-kitchen chimney.

Although my heart was leaping high with the prospect of some adventure, and the fear of meeting Lorna, I could not but be gladdened by the softness of the weather, and the welcome way of everything. There was that power all round, that power and that goodness, which make us come, as it were, outside our bodily selves, to share them. Over and beside us breathes the joy of hope and promise; under foot are troubles past; in the distance bowering newness tempts us ever forward. We quicken with largesse of life, and spring with vivid mystery.

And, in good sooth, I had to spring, and no mystery about it, ere ever I got to the top of the rift leading into Doone-glade. For the stream was rushing down in strength, and raving at every corner; a mort of rain having fallen last night and no wind come to wipe it. However, I reached the head ere dark with more difficulty than danger, and sat in a place which comforted my back and legs desirably.

Hereupon I grew so happy at being on dry land again, and come to look for Lorna, with pretty trees around me, that what did I do but fall asleep with the holly-stick in front of me, and my best coat sunk in a bed of moss, with water and wood-sorrel. Mayhap I had not done so, nor yet enjoyed the spring so much, if so be I had not taken three parts of a gallon of cider at home, at Plover's Barrows, because of the lowness and sinking ever since I met Mother Melldrum.

There was a little runnel going softly down beside me, falling from the upper rock by the means of moss and grass, as if it feared to make a noise, and had a mother sleeping. Now and then it seemed to stop, in fear of its own dropping, and wait for some orders; and the blades of grass that straightened to it turned their points a little way, and offered their allegiance to wind instead of water. Yet before their carkled edges bent more than a driven saw, down the water came again with heavy drops and pats of running, and bright anger at neglect.

This was very pleasant to me, now and then, to gaze at, blinking as the water blinked, and falling back to sleep again. Suddenly my sleep was broken by a shade cast over me; between me and the low sunlight Lorna Doone was standing.

'Master Ridd, are you mad?' she said, and took my hand to move me.

'Not mad, but half asleep,' I answered, feigning not to notice her, that so she might keep hold of me.

'Come away, come away, if you care for life. The patrol will be here directly. Be quick, Master Ridd, let me hide thee.'

'I will not stir a step,' said I, though being in the greatest fright that might be well imagined,' unless you call me "John."'

'Well, John, then—Master John Ridd, be quick, if you have any to care for you.'

'I have many that care for me,' I said, just to let her know; 'and I will follow you, Mistress Lorna, albeit without any hurry, unless there be peril to more than me.'

Without another word she led me, though with many timid glances towards the upper valley, to, and into, her little bower, where the inlet through the rock was. I am almost sure that I spoke before (though I cannot now go seek for it, and my memory is but a worn-out tub) of a certain deep and perilous pit, in which I was like to drown myself through hurry and fright of boyhood. And even then I wondered greatly, and was vexed with Lorna for sending me in that heedless manner into such an entrance. But now it was clear that she had been right and the fault mine own entirely; for the entrance to the pit was only to he found by seeking it. Inside the niche of native stone, the plainest thing of all to see, at any rate by day light, was the stairway hewn from rock, and leading up the mountain, by means of which I had escaped, as before related. To the right side of this was the mouth of the pit, still looking very formidable; though Lorna laughed at my fear of it, for she drew her water thence. But on the left was a narrow crevice, very difficult to espy, and having a sweep of grey ivy laid, like a slouching beaver, over it. A man here coming from the brightness of the outer air, with eyes dazed by the twilight, would never think of seeing this and following it to its meaning.

Lorna raised the screen for me, but I had much ado to pass, on account of bulk and stature. Instead of being proud of my size (as it seemed to me she ought to be) Lorna laughed so quietly that I was ready to knock my head or elbows against anything, and say no more about it. However, I got through at last without a word of compliment, and broke into the pleasant room, the lone retreat of Lorna.

The chamber was of unhewn rock, round, as near as might be, eighteen or twenty feet across, and gay with rich variety of fern and moss and lichen. The fern was in its winter still, or coiling for the spring-tide; but moss was in abundant life, some feathering, and some gobleted, and some with fringe of red to it. Overhead there was no ceiling but the sky itself, flaked with little clouds of April whitely wandering over it. The floor was made of soft low grass, mixed with moss and primroses; and in a niche of shelter moved the delicate wood-sorrel. Here and there, around the sides, were 'chairs of living stone,' as some Latin writer says, whose name has quite escaped me; and in the midst a tiny spring arose, with crystal beads in it, and a soft voice as of a laughing dream, and dimples like a sleeping babe. Then, after going round a little, with surprise of daylight, the water overwelled the edge, and softly went through lines of light to shadows and an untold bourne.

While I was gazing at all these things with wonder and some sadness, Lorna turned upon me lightly (as her manner was) and said,—

'Where are the new-laid eggs, Master Ridd? Or hath blue hen ceased laying?'

I did not altogether like the way in which she said it with a sort of dialect, as if my speech could be laughed at.

'Here be some,' I answered, speaking as if in spite of her. 'I would have brought thee twice as many, but that I feared to crush them in the narrow ways, Mistress Lorna.'

And so I laid her out two dozen upon the moss of the rock-ledge, unwinding the wisp of hay from each as it came safe out of my pocket. Lorna looked with growing wonder, as I added one to one; and when I had placed them side by side, and bidden her now to tell them, to my amazement what did she do but burst into a flood of tears.

'What have I done?' I asked, with shame, scarce daring even to look at her, because her grief was not like Annie's—a thing that could be coaxed away, and left a joy in going—'oh, what have I done to vex you so?'

'It is nothing done by you, Master Ridd,' she answered, very proudly, as if nought I did could matter; 'it is only something that comes upon me with the scent of the pure true clover-hay. Moreover, you have been too kind; and I am not used to kindness.'

Some sort of awkwardness was on me, at her words and weeping, as if I would like to say something, but feared to make things worse perhaps than they were already. Therefore I abstained from speech, as I would in my own pain. And as it happened, this was the way to make her tell me more about it. Not that I was curious, beyond what pity urged me and the strange affairs around her; and now I gazed upon the floor, lest I should seem to watch her; but none the less for that I knew all that she was doing.

Lorna went a little way, as if she would not think of me nor care for one so careless; and all my heart gave a sudden jump, to go like a mad thing after her; until she turned of her own accord, and with a little sigh came back to me. Her eyes were soft with trouble's shadow, and the proud lift of her neck was gone, and beauty's vanity borne down by woman's want of sustenance.

'Master Ridd,' she said in the softest voice that ever flowed between two lips, 'have I done aught to offend you?'

Hereupon it went hard with me, not to catch her up and kiss her, in the manner in which she was looking; only it smote me suddenly that this would be a low advantage of her trust and helplessness. She seemed to know what I would be at, and to doubt very greatly about it, whether as a child of old she might permit the usage. All sorts of things went through my head, as I made myself look away from her, for fear of being tempted beyond what I could bear. And the upshot of it was that I said, within my heart and through it, 'John Ridd, be on thy very best manners with this lonely maiden.'

Lorna liked me all the better for my good forbearance; because she did not love me yet, and had not thought about it; at least so far as I knew. And though her eyes were so beauteous, so very soft and kindly, there was (to my apprehension) some great power in them, as if she would not have a thing, unless her judgment leaped with it.

But now her judgment leaped with me, because I had behaved so well; and being of quick urgent nature—such as I delight in, for the change from mine own slowness—she, without any let or hindrance, sitting over against me, now raising and now dropping fringe over those sweet eyes that were the road-lights of her tongue, Lorna told me all about everything I wished to know, every little thing she knew, except indeed that point of points, how Master Ridd stood with her.

Although it wearied me no whit, it might be wearisome for folk who cannot look at Lorna, to hear the story all in speech, exactly as she told it; therefore let me put it shortly, to the best of my remembrance.

Nay, pardon me, whosoever thou art, for seeming fickle and rude to thee; I have tried to do as first proposed, to tell the tale in my own words, as of another's fortune. But, lo! I was beset at once with many heavy obstacles, which grew as I went onward, until I knew not where I was, and mingled past and present. And two of these difficulties only were enough to stop me; the one that I must coldly speak without the force of pity, the other that I, off and on, confused myself with Lorna, as might be well expected.

Therefore let her tell the story, with her own sweet voice and manner; and if ye find it wearisome, seek in yourselves the weariness.

Chapter XX Lorna Begins Her Story

'I cannot go through all my thoughts so as to make them clear to you, nor have I ever dwelt on things, to shape a story of them. I know not where the beginning was, nor where the middle ought to be, nor even how at the present time I feel, or think, or ought to think. If I look for help to those around me, who should tell me right and wrong (being older and much wiser), I meet sometimes with laughter, and at other times with anger.

'There are but two in the world who ever listen and try to help me; one of them is my grandfather, and the other is a man of wisdom, whom we call the Counsellor. My grandfather, Sir Ensor Doone, is very old and harsh of manner (except indeed to me); he seems to know what is right and wrong, but not to want to think of it. The Counsellor, on the other hand, though full of life and subtleties, treats my questions as of play, and not gravely worth his while to answer, unless he can make wit of them.

'And among the women there are none with whom I can hold converse, since my Aunt Sabina died, who took such pains to teach me. She was a lady of high repute and lofty ways, and learning, but grieved and harassed more and more by the coarseness, and the violence, and the ignorance around her. In vain she strove, from year to year, to make the young men hearken, to teach them what became their birth, and give them sense of honour. It was her favourite word, poor thing! and they called her "Old Aunt Honour." Very often she used to say that I was her only comfort, and I am sure she was my only one; and when she died it was more to me than if I had lost a mother.

'For I have no remembrance now of father or of mother, although they say that my father was the eldest son of Sir Ensor Doone, and the bravest and the best of them. And so they call me heiress to this little realm of violence; and in sorry sport sometimes, I am their Princess or their Queen.

'Many people living here, as I am forced to do, would perhaps be very happy, and perhaps I ought to be so. We have a beauteous valley, sheltered from the cold of winter and power of the summer sun, untroubled also by the storms and mists that veil the mountains; although I must acknowledge that it is apt to rain too often. The grass moreover is so fresh, and the brook so bright and lively, and flowers of so many hues come after one another that no one need be dull, if only left alone with them.

'And so in the early days perhaps, when morning breathes around me, and the sun is going upward, and light is playing everywhere, I am not so far beside them all as to live in shadow. But when the evening gathers down, and the sky is spread with sadness, and the day has spent itself; then a cloud of lonely trouble falls, like night, upon me. I cannot see the things

I quest for of a world beyond me; I cannot join the peace and quiet of the depth above me; neither have I any pleasure in the brightness of the stars.

'What I want to know is something none of them can tell me—what am I, and why set here, and when shall I be with them? I see that you are surprised a little at this my curiosity. Perhaps such questions never spring in any wholesome spirit. But they are in the depths of mine, and I cannot be quit of them.

'Meantime, all around me is violence and robbery, coarse delight and savage pain, reckless joke and hopeless death. Is it any wonder that I cannot sink with these, that I cannot so forget my soul, as to live the life of brutes, and die the death more horrible because it dreams of waking? There is none to lead me forward, there is none to teach me right; young as I am, I live beneath a curse that lasts for ever.'

Here Lorna broke down for awhile, and cried so very piteously, that doubting of my knowledge, and of any power to comfort, I did my best to hold my peace, and tried to look very cheerful. Then thinking that might be bad manners, I went to wipe her eyes for her.

'Master Ridd,' she began again, 'I am both ashamed and vexed at my own childish folly. But you, who have a mother, who thinks (you say) so much of you, and sisters, and a quiet home; you cannot tell (it is not likely) what a lonely nature is. How it leaps in mirth sometimes, with only heaven touching it; and how it falls away desponding, when the dreary weight creeps on.

'It does not happen many times that I give way like this; more shame now to do so, when I ought to entertain you. Sometimes I am so full of anger, that I dare not trust to speech, at things they cannot hide from me; and perhaps you would be much surprised that reckless men would care so much to elude a young girl's knowledge. They used to boast to Aunt Sabina of pillage and of cruelty, on purpose to enrage her; but they never boast to me. It even makes me smile sometimes to see how awkwardly they come and offer for temptation to me shining packets, half concealed, of ornaments and finery, of rings, or chains, or jewels, lately belonging to other people.

'But when I try to search the past, to get a sense of what befell me ere my own perception formed; to feel back for the lines of childhood, as a trace of gossamer, then I only know that nought lives longer than God wills it. So may after sin go by, for we are children always, as the Counsellor has told me; so may we, beyond the clouds, seek this infancy of life, and never find its memory.

'But I am talking now of things which never come across me when any work is toward. It might have been a good thing for me to have had a father to beat these rovings out of me; or a mother to make a home, and teach me how to manage it. For, being left with none—I think; and nothing ever comes of it. Nothing, I mean, which I can grasp and have with any surety; nothing but faint images, and wonderment, and wandering. But often, when I am neither searching back into remembrance, nor asking of my parents, but occupied by trifles, something like a sign, or message, or a token of some meaning, seems to glance upon me. Whether from the rustling wind, or sound of distant music, or the singing of a bird, like the sun on snow it strikes me with a pain of pleasure.

'And often when I wake at night, and listen to the silence, or wander far from people in the grayness of the evening, or stand and look at quiet water having shadows over it, some vague image seems to hover on the skirt of vision, ever changing place and outline, ever flitting as I follow. This so moves and hurries me, in the eagerness and longing, that straightway all my chance is lost; and memory, scared like a wild bird, flies. Or am I as a child perhaps, chasing a flown cageling, who among the branches free plays and peeps at the offered cage (as a home not to be urged on him), and means to take his time of coming, if he comes at all?

'Often too I wonder at the odds of fortune, which made me (helpless as I am, and fond of peace and reading) the heiress of this mad domain, the sanctuary of unholiness. It is not likely that I shall have much power of authority; and yet the Counsellor creeps up to be my Lord of the Treasury; and his son aspires to my hand, as of a Royal alliance. Well, "honour among thieves," they say; and mine is the first honour: although among decent folk perhaps, honesty is better.

'We should not be so quiet here, and safe from interruption but that I have begged one privilege rather than commanded it. This was that the lower end, just this narrowing of the valley, where it is most hard to come at, might be looked upon as mine, except for purposes of guard. Therefore none beside the sentries ever trespass on me here, unless it be my grandfather, or the Counsellor or Carver.

'By your face, Master Ridd, I see that you have heard of Carver Doone. For strength and courage and resource he bears the first repute among us, as might well be expected from the son of the Counsellor. But he differs from his father, in being very hot and savage, and quite free from argument. The Counsellor, who is my uncle, gives his son the best advice; commending all the virtues, with eloquence and wisdom; yet himself abstaining from them accurately and impartially.

'You must be tired of this story, and the time I take to think, and the weakness of my telling; but my life from day to day shows so little variance. Among the riders there is none whose safe return I watch for—I mean none more than other—and indeed there seems no risk, all are now so feared of us. Neither of the old men is there whom I can revere or love (except alone my grandfather, whom I love with trembling): neither of the women any whom I like to deal with, unless it be a little maiden whom I saved from starving.

'A little Cornish girl she is, and shaped in western manner, not so very much less in width than if you take her lengthwise. Her father seems to have been a miner, a Cornishman (as she declares) of more than average excellence, and better than any two men to be found in Devonshire, or any four in Somerset. Very few things can have been beyond his power of performance, and yet he left his daughter to starve upon a peat-rick. She does not know how this was done, and looks upon it as a mystery, the meaning of which will some day be clear, and redound to her father's honour. His name was Simon Carfax, and he came as the captain of a gang from one of the Cornish stannaries. Gwenny Carfax, my young maid, well remembers how her father was brought up from Cornwall. Her mother had been buried, just a week or so before; and he was sad about it, and had been off his work, and was ready for another job. Then people came to him by night, and said that he must want a change, and everybody lost their wives, and work was the way to mend it. So what with grief, and over-thought, and the inside of a square bottle, Gwenny says they brought him off, to become a mighty captain, and choose the country round. The last she saw of him was this, that he went down a ladder somewhere on the wilds of Exmoor, leaving her with bread and cheese, and his travelling-hat to see to. And from that day to this he never came above the ground again; so far as we can hear of.

'But Gwenny, holding to his hat, and having eaten the bread and cheese (when he came no more to help her), dwelt three days near the mouth of the hole; and then it was closed over, the while that she was sleeping. With weakness and with want of food, she lost herself distressfully, and went away for miles or more, and lay upon a peat-rick, to die before the ravens.

'That very day I chanced to return from Aunt Sabina's dying-place; for she would not die in Glen Doone, she said, lest the angels feared to come for her; and so she was taken to a cottage in a lonely valley. I was allowed to visit her, for even we durst not refuse the wishes of the dying; and if a priest had been desired, we should have made bold with him. Returning very sorrowful, and caring now for nothing, I found this little stray thing lying, her arms upon her, and not a sign of life, except the way that she was biting. Black root-stuff was in her mouth, and a piece of dirty sheep's wool, and at her feet an old egg-shell of some bird of the moorland.

'I tried to raise her, but she was too square and heavy for me; and so I put food in her mouth, and left her to do right with it. And this she did in a little time; for the victuals were very choice and rare, being what I had taken over to tempt poor Aunt Sabina. Gwenny ate them without delay, and then was ready to eat the basket and the ware that contained them.

'Gwenny took me for an angel—though I am little like one, as you see, Master Ridd; and she followed me, expecting that I would open wings and fly when we came to any difficulty. I brought her home with me, so far as this can be a home, and she made herself my sole attendant, without so much as asking me. She has beaten two or three other girls, who used to wait upon me, until they are afraid to come near the house of my grandfather. She seems to have no kind of fear even of our roughest men; and yet she looks with reverence and awe upon the Counsellor. As for the wickedness, and theft, and revelry around her, she says it is no concern of hers, and they know their own business best. By this way of regarding men she has won upon our riders, so that she is almost free from all control of place and season, and is allowed to pass where none even of the youths may go. Being so wide, and short, and flat, she has none to pay her compliments; and, were there any, she would scorn them, as not being Cornishmen. Sometimes she wanders far, by moonlight, on the moors and up the rivers, to give her father (as she says) another chance of finding her, and she comes back not a wit defeated, or discouraged, or depressed, but confident that he is only waiting for the proper time.

'Herein she sets me good example of a patience and contentment hard for me to imitate. Oftentimes I am vexed by things I cannot meddle with, yet which cannot be kept from me, that I am at the point of flying from this dreadful valley, and risking all that can betide me in the unknown outer world. If it were not for my grandfather, I would have done so long ago; but I cannot bear that he should die with no gentle hand to comfort him; and I fear to think of the conflict that must ensue for the government, if there be a disputed succession.

'Ah me! We are to be pitied greatly, rather than condemned, by people whose things we have taken from them; for I have read, and seem almost to understand about it, that there are places on the earth where gentle peace, and love of home, and knowledge of one's neighbours prevail, and are, with reason, looked for as the usual state of things. There honest folk may go to work in the glory of the sunrise, with hope of coming home again quite safe in the quiet evening, and finding all their children; and even in the darkness they have no fear of lying down, and dropping off to slumber, and hearken to the wind of night, not as to an enemy trying to find entrance, but a friend who comes to tell the value of their comfort.

'Of all this golden ease I hear, but never saw the like of it; and, haply, I shall never do so, being born to turbulence. Once, indeed, I had the offer of escape, and kinsman's aid, and high place in the gay, bright world; and yet I was not tempted much, or, at least, dared not to trust it. And it ended very sadly, so dreadfully that I even shrink from telling you about it; for that one terror changed my life, in a moment, at a blow, from childhood and from thoughts of play and commune with the flowers and trees, to a sense of death and darkness, and a heavy weight of earth. Be content now, Master Ridd ask me nothing more about it, so your sleep be sounder.'

But I, John Ridd, being young and new, and very fond of hearing things to make my blood to tingle, had no more of manners than to urge poor Lorna onwards, hoping, perhaps, in depth of heart, that she might have to hold by me, when the worst came to the worst of it. Therefore she went on again.

Chapter XXI Lorna Ends Her Story

'It is not a twelvemonth yet, although it seems ten years agone, since I blew the downy globe to learn the time of day, or set beneath my chin the veinings of the varnished buttercup, or fired the fox-glove cannonade, or made a captive of myself with dandelion fetters; for then I had not very much to trouble me in earnest, but went about, romancing gravely, playing at bo-peep with fear, making for myself strong heroes of gray rock or fir-tree, adding to my own importance, as the children love to do.

'As yet I had not truly learned the evil of our living, the scorn of law, the outrage, and the sorrow caused to others. It even was a point with all to hide the roughness from me, to show me but the gallant side, and keep in shade the other. My grandfather, Sir Ensor Doone, had given strictest order, as I discovered afterwards, that in my presence all should be seemly, kind, and vigilant. Nor was it very difficult to keep most part of the mischief from me, for no Doone ever robs at home, neither do they quarrel much, except at times of gambling. And though Sir Ensor Doone is now so old and growing feeble, his own way he will have still, and no one dare deny him. Even our fiercest and most mighty swordsmen, seared from all sense of right or wrong, yet have plentiful sense of fear, when brought before that white-haired man. Not that he is rough with them, or querulous, or rebukeful; but that he has a strange soft smile, and a gaze they cannot answer, and a knowledge deeper far than they have of themselves. Under his protection, I am as safe from all those men (some of whom are but little akin to me) as if I slept beneath the roof of the King's Lord Justiciary.

'But now, at the time I speak of, one evening of last summer, a horrible thing befell, which took all play of childhood from me. The fifteenth day of last July was very hot and sultry, long after the time of sundown; and I was paying heed of it, because of the old saying that if it rain then, rain will fall on forty days thereafter. I had been long by the waterside at this lower end of the valley, plaiting a little crown of woodbine crocketed with sprigs of heath—to please my grandfather, who likes to see me gay at supper-time. Being proud of my tiara, which had cost some trouble, I set it on my head at once, to save the chance of crushing, and carrying my gray hat, ventured by a path not often trod. For I must be home at the supper-time, or grandfather would be exceeding wrath; and the worst of his anger is that he never condescends to show it.

'Therefore, instead of the open mead, or the windings of the river, I made short cut through the ash-trees covert which lies in the middle of our vale, with the water skirting or cleaving it. You have never been up so far as that—at least to the best of my knowledge—but you see it like a long gray spot, from the top of the cliffs above us. Here I was not likely to meet any of our people because the young ones are afraid of some ancient tale about it, and the old ones have no love of trees where gunshots are uncertain.

'It was more almost than dusk, down below the tree-leaves, and I was eager to go through, and be again beyond it. For the gray dark hung around me, scarcely showing shadow; and the little light that glimmered seemed to come up from the ground. For the earth was strown with the winter-spread and coil of last year's foliage, the lichened claws of chalky twigs, and the numberless decay which gives a light in its decaying. I, for my part, hastened shyly, ready to draw back and run from hare, or rabbit, or small field-mouse.

'At a sudden turn of the narrow path, where it stopped again to the river, a man leaped out from behind a tree, and stopped me, and seized hold of me. I tried to shriek, but my voice was still; I could only hear my heart.

'"Now, Cousin Lorna, my good cousin," he said, with ease and calmness; "your voice is very sweet, no doubt, from all that I can see of you. But I pray you keep it still, unless you would give to dusty death your very best cousin and trusty guardian, Alan Brandir of Loch Awe.'

'"You my guardian!" I said, for the idea was too ludicrous; and ludicrous things always strike me first, through some fault of nature.

'"I have in truth that honour, madam," he answered, with a sweeping bow; "unless I err in taking you for Mistress Lorna Doone."

'"You have not mistaken me. My name is Lorna Doone."

'He looked at me, with gravity, and was inclined to make some claim to closer consideration upon the score of kinship; but I shrunk back, and only said, "Yes, my name is Lorna Doone."

'"Then I am your faithful guardian, Alan Brandir of Loch Awe; called Lord Alan Brandir, son of a worthy peer of Scotland. Now will you confide in me?"

'"I confide in you!" I cried, looking at him with amazement; "why, you are not older than I am!"

'"Yes I am, three years at least. You, my ward, are not sixteen. I, your worshipful guardian, am almost nineteen years of age."

'Upon hearing this I looked at him, for that seemed then a venerable age; but the more I looked the more I doubted, although he was dressed quite like a man. He led me in a courtly manner, stepping at his tallest to an open place beside the water; where the light came as in channel, and was made the most of by glancing waves and fair white stones.

'"Now am I to your liking, cousin?" he asked, when I had gazed at him, until I was almost ashamed, except at such a stripling." Does my Cousin Lorna judge kindly of her guardian, and her nearest kinsman? In a word, is our admiration mutual?"

'"Truly I know not," I said; "but you seem good-natured, and to have no harm in you. Do they trust you with a sword?"

'For in my usage among men of stature and strong presence, this pretty youth, so tricked and slender, seemed nothing but a doll to me. Although he scared me in the wood, now that I saw him in good twilight, lo! he was but little greater than my little self; and so tasselled and so ruffled with a mint of bravery, and a green coat barred with red, and a slim sword hanging under him, it was the utmost I could do to look at him half-gravely.

'"I fear that my presence hath scarce enough of ferocity about it" (he gave a jerk to his sword as he spoke, and clanked it on the brook-stones); "yet do I assure you, cousin, that I am not without some prowess; and many a master of defence hath this good sword of mine disarmed. Now if the boldest and biggest robber in all this charming valley durst so much as breathe the scent of that flower coronal, which doth not adorn but is adorned"—here he talked some nonsense—"I would cleave him from head to foot, ere ever he could fly or cry."

'"Hush!" I said; "talk not so loudly, or thou mayst have to do both thyself, and do them both in vain."

'For he was quite forgetting now, in his bravery before me, where he stood, and with whom he spoke, and how the summer lightning shone above the hills and down the hollow. And as I gazed on this slight fair youth, clearly one of high birth and breeding (albeit over-boastful), a chill of fear crept over me; because he had no strength or substance, and would be no more than a pin-cushion before the great swords of the Doones.

'"I pray you be not vexed with me," he answered, in a softer voice; "for I have travelled far and sorely, for the sake of seeing you. I know right well among whom I am, and that their hospitality is more of the knife than the salt-stand. Nevertheless I am safe enough, for my foot is the fleetest in Scotland, and what are these hills to me? Tush! I have seen some border forays among wilder spirits and craftier men than these be. Once I mind some years agone, when I was quite a stripling lad—"

'"Worshipful guardian," I said, "there is no time now for history. If thou art in no haste, I am, and cannot stay here idling. Only tell me how I am akin and under wardship to thee, and what purpose brings thee here."

'"In order, cousin—all things in order, even with fair ladies. First, I am thy uncle's son, my father is thy mother's brother, or at least thy grandmother's—unless I am deceived in that which I have guessed, and no other man. For my father, being a leading lord in the councils of King Charles the Second, appointed me to learn the law, not for my livelihood, thank God, but because he felt the lack of it in affairs of state. But first your leave, young Mistress Lorna; I cannot lay down legal maxims, without aid of smoke."

'He leaned against a willow-tree, and drawing from a gilded box a little dark thing like a stick, placed it between his lips, and then striking a flint on steel made fire and caught it upon touchwood. With this he kindled the tip of the stick, until it glowed with a ring of red, and then he breathed forth curls of smoke, blue and smelling on the air like spice. I had never seen this done before, though acquainted with tobacco-pipes; and it made me laugh, until I thought of the peril that must follow it.

'"Cousin, have no fear," he said; "this makes me all the safer; they will take me for a glow-worm, and thee for the flower it shines upon. But to return—of law I learned as you may suppose, but little; although I have capacities. But the thing was far too dull for me. All I care for is adventure, moving chance, and hot encounter; therefore all of law I learned was how to live without it. Nevertheless, for amusement's sake, as I must needs be at my desk an hour or so in the afternoon, I took to the sporting branch of the law, the pitfalls, and the ambuscades; and of all the traps to be laid therein, pedigrees are the rarest. There is scarce a man worth a cross of butter, but what you may find a hole in his shield within four generations. And so I struck our own escutcheon, and it sounded hollow. There is a point—but heed not that; enough that being curious now, I followed up the quarry, and I am come to this at last—we, even we, the lords of Loch Awe, have an outlaw for our cousin, and I would we had more, if they be like you."

'"Sir," I answered, being amused by his manner, which was new to me (for the Doones are much in earnest), "surely you count it no disgrace to be of kin to Sir Ensor Doone, and all his honest family!"

'"If it be so, it is in truth the very highest honour and would heal ten holes in our escutcheon. What noble family but springs from a captain among robbers? Trade alone can spoil our blood; robbery purifies it. The robbery of one age is the chivalry of the next. We may start anew, and vie with even the nobility of France, if we can once enrol but half the Doones upon our lineage."

'"I like not to hear you speak of the Doones, as if they were no more than that," I exclaimed, being now unreasonable; "but will you tell me, once for all, sir, how you are my guardian?"

'"That I will do. You are my ward because you were my father's ward, under the Scottish law; and now my father being so deaf, I have succeeded to that right—at least in my own opinion—under which claim I am here to neglect my trust no longer, but to lead you away from scenes and deeds which (though of good repute and comely) are not the best for young gentlewomen. There spoke I not like a guardian? After that can you mistrust me?"

'"But," said I, "good Cousin Alan (if I may so call you), it is not meet for young gentlewomen to go away with young gentlemen, though fifty times their guardians. But if you will only come with me, and explain your tale to my grandfather, he will listen to you quietly, and take no advantage of you."

'"I thank you much, kind Mistress Lorna, to lead the goose into the fox's den! But, setting by all thought of danger, I have other reasons against it. Now, come with your faithful guardian, child. I will pledge my honour against all harm, and to bear you safe to London. By the law of the realm, I am now entitled to the custody of your fair person, and of all your chattels."

'"But, sir, all that you have learned of law, is how to live without it."

'"Fairly met, fair cousin mine! Your wit will do me credit, after a little sharpening. And there is none to do that better than your aunt, my mother. Although she knows not of my coming, she is longing to receive you. Come, and in a few months' time you shall set the mode at Court, instead of pining here, and weaving coronals of daisies."

'I turned aside, and thought a little. Although he seemed so light of mind, and gay in dress and manner, I could not doubt his honesty; and saw, beneath his jaunty air, true mettle and ripe bravery. Scarce had I thought of his project twice, until he spoke of my aunt, his mother, but then the form of my dearest friend, my sweet Aunt Sabina, seemed to come and bid me listen, for this was what she prayed for. Moreover I felt (though not as now) that Doone Glen was no place for me or any proud young maiden. But while I thought, the yellow lightning spread behind a bulk of clouds, three times ere the flash was done, far off and void of thunder; and from the pile of cloud before it, cut as from black paper, and lit to depths of blackness by the blaze behind it, a form as of an aged man, sitting in a chair loose-mantled, seemed to lift a hand and warn.

'This minded me of my grandfather, and all the care I owed him. Moreover, now the storm was rising and I began to grow afraid; for of all things awful to me thunder is the dreadfulest. It doth so growl, like a lion coming, and then so roll, and roar, and rumble, out of a thickening darkness, then crack like the last trump overhead through cloven air and terror, that all my heart lies low and quivers, like a weed in water. I listened now for the distant rolling of the great black storm, and heard it, and was hurried by it. But the youth before me waved his rolled tobacco at it, and drawled in his daintiest tone and manner,—

'"The sky is having a smoke, I see, and dropping sparks, and grumbling. I should have thought these Exmoor hills too small to gather thunder."

'"I cannot go, I will not go with you, Lord Alan Brandir," I answered, being vexed a little by those words of his. "You are not grave enough for me, you are not old enough for me. My Aunt Sabina would not have wished it; nor would I leave my grandfather, without his full permission. I thank you much for coming, sir; but be gone at once by the way you came; and pray how did you come, sir?"

'"Fair cousin, you will grieve for this; you will mourn, when you cannot mend it. I would my mother had been here, soon would she have persuaded you. And yet," he added, with the smile of his accustomed gaiety, "it would have been an unco thing, as we say in Scotland, for her ladyship to have waited upon you, as her graceless son has done, and hopes to do again ere long. Down the cliffs I came, and up them I must make way back again. Now adieu, fair Cousin Lorna, I see you are in haste tonight; but I am right proud of my guardianship. Give me just one flower for token"—here he kissed his hand to me, and I threw him a truss of woodbine—"adieu, fair cousin, trust me well, I will soon be here again."

'"That thou never shalt, sir," cried a voice as loud as a culverin; and Carver Doone had Alan Brandir as a spider hath a fly. The boy made a little shriek at first, with the sudden shock and the terror; then he looked, methought, ashamed of himself, and set his face to fight for it. Very bravely he strove and struggled, to free one arm and grasp his sword; but as well might an infant buried alive attempt to lift his gravestone. Carver Doone, with his great arms wrapped around the slim gay body, smiled (as I saw by the flash from heaven) at the poor young face turned up to him; then (as a nurse bears off a child, who is loath to go to bed), he lifted the youth from his feet, and bore him away into the darkness.

'I was young then. I am older now; older by ten years, in thought, although it is not a twelvemonth since. If that black deed were done again, I could follow, and could combat it, could throw weak arms on the murderer, and strive to be murdered also. I am now at home with violence; and no dark death surprises me.

'But, being as I was that night, the horror overcame me. The crash of thunder overhead, the last despairing look, the death-piece framed with blaze of lightning—my young heart was so affrighted that I could not gasp. My breath went from me, and I knew not where I was, or who, or what. Only that I lay, and cowered, under great trees full of thunder; and could neither count, nor moan, nor have my feet to help me.

'Yet hearkening, as a coward does, through the brushing of the wind, and echo of far noises, I heard a sharp sound as of iron, and a fall of heavy wood. No unmanly shriek came with it, neither cry for mercy. Carver Doone knows what it was; and so did Alan Brandir.'

Here Lorna Doone could tell no more, being overcome with weeping. Only through her tears she whispered, as a thing too bad to tell, that she had seen that giant Carver, in a few days afterwards, smoking a little round brown stick, like those of her poor cousin. I could not press her any more with questions, or for clearness; although I longed very much to know whether she had spoken of it to her grandfather or the Counsellor. But she was now in such condition, both of mind and body, from the force of her own fear multiplied by telling it, that I did nothing more than coax her, at a distance humbly; and so that she could see that some one was at least afraid of her. This (although I knew not women in those days, as now I do, and never shall know much of it), this, I say, so brought her round, that all her fear was now for me, and how to get me safely off, without mischance to any one. And sooth to say, in spite of longing just to see if Master Carver could have served me such a trick—as it grew towards the dusk, I was not best pleased to be there; for it seemed a lawless place, and some of Lorna's fright stayed with me as I talked it away from her.

Chapter XXII

After hearing that tale from Lorna, I went home in sorry spirits, having added fear for her, and misery about, to all my other ailments. And was it not quite certain now that she, being owned full cousin to a peer and lord of Scotland (although he was a dead one), must have nought to do with me, a yeoman's son, and bound to be the father of more yeomen? I had been very sorry when first I heard about that poor young popinjay, and would gladly have fought hard for him; but now it struck me that after all he had no right to be there, prowling (as it were) for Lorna, without any invitation: and we farmers love not trespass. Still, if I had seen the thing, I must have tried to save him.

Moreover, I was greatly vexed with my own hesitation, stupidity, or shyness, or whatever else it was, which had held me back from saying, ere she told her story, what was in my heart to say, videlicet, that I must die unless she let me love her. Not that I was fool enough to think that she would answer me according to my liking, or begin to care about me for a long time yet; if indeed she ever should, which I hardly dared to hope. But that I had heard from men more skillful in the matter that it is wise to be in time, that so the maids may begin to think, when they know that they are thought of. And, to tell the truth, I had bitter fears, on account of her wondrous beauty, lest some young fellow of higher birth and finer parts, and finish, might steal in before poor me, and cut me out altogether. Thinking of which, I used to double my great fist, without knowing it, and keep it in my pocket ready.

But the worst of all was this, that in my great dismay and anguish to see Lorna weeping so, I had promised not to cause her any further trouble from anxiety and fear of harm. And this, being brought to practice, meant that I was not to show myself within the precincts of Glen Doone, for at least another month. Unless indeed (as I contrived to edge into the agreement) anything should happen to increase her present trouble and every day's uneasiness. In that case, she was to throw a dark mantle, or covering of some sort, over a large white stone which hung within the entrance to her retreat—I mean the outer entrance—and which, though unseen from the valley itself, was (as I had observed) conspicuous from the height where I stood with Uncle Reuben.

Now coming home so sad and weary, yet trying to console myself with the thought that love o'erleapeth rank, and must still be lord of all, I found a shameful thing going on, which made me very angry. For it needs must happen that young Marwood de Whichehalse, only son of the Baron, riding home that very evening, from chasing of the Exmoor bustards, with his hounds and serving-men, should take the short cut through our farmyard, and being dry from his exercise, should come and ask for drink. And it needs must happen also that there should be none to give it to him but my sister Annie. I more than suspect that he had heard some report of our Annie's comeliness, and had a mind to satisfy himself upon the subject. Now, as he took the large ox-horn of our quarantine-apple cider (which we always keep apart from the rest, being too good except for the quality), he let his fingers dwell on Annie's, by some sort of accident, while he lifted his beaver gallantly, and gazed on her face in the light from the west. Then what did Annie do (as she herself told me afterwards) but make her very best curtsey to him, being pleased that he was pleased with her, while she thought what a fine young man he was and so much breeding about him! And in truth he was a dark, handsome fellow, hasty, reckless, and changeable, with a look of sad destiny in his black eyes that would make any woman pity him. What he was thinking of our Annie is not for me to say, although I may think that you could not have found another such maiden on Exmoor, except (of course) my Lorna.

Though young Squire Marwood was so thirsty, he spent much time over his cider, or at any rate over the ox-horn, and he made many bows to Annie, and drank health to all the family, and spoke of me as if I had been his very best friend at Blundell's; whereas he knew well enough all the time that we had nought to say to one another; he being three years older, and therefore of course disdaining me. But while he was casting about perhaps for some excuse to stop longer, and Annie was beginning to fear lest mother should come after her, or Eliza be at the window, or Betty up in pigs' house, suddenly there came up to them, as if from the very heart of the earth, that long, low, hollow, mysterious sound which I spoke of in winter.

The young man started in his saddle, let the horn fall on the horse-steps, and gazed all around in wonder; while as for Annie, she turned like a ghost, and tried to slam the door, but failed through the violence of her trembling; (for never till now had any one heard it so close at hand as you might say) or in the mere fall of the twilight. And by this time there was no man, at least in our parish, but knew—for the Parson himself had told us so—that it was the devil groaning because the Doones were too many for him.

Marwood de Whichehalse was not so alarmed but what he saw a fine opportunity. He leaped from his horse, and laid hold of dear Annie in a highly comforting manner; and she never would tell us about it (being so shy and modest), whether in breathing his comfort to her he tried to take some from her pure lips. I hope he did not, because that to me would seem not the deed of a gentleman, and he was of good old family.

At this very moment, who should come into the end of the passage upon them but the heavy writer of these doings I, John Ridd myself, and walking the faster, it may be, on account of the noise I mentioned. I entered the house with some wrath upon me at seeing the gazehounds in the yard; for it seems a cruel thing to me to harass the birds in the breeding-time. And to my amazement there I saw Squire Marwood among the milk-pans with his arm around our Annie's waist, and Annie all blushing and coaxing him off, for she was not come to scold yet.

Perhaps I was wrong; God knows, and if I was, no doubt I shall pay for it; but I gave him the flat of my hand on his head, and down he went in the thick of the milk-pans. He would have had my fist, I doubt, but for having been at school with me; and after that it is like enough he would never have spoken another word. As it was, he lay stunned, with the cream running on him; while I took poor Annie up and carried her in to mother, who had heard the noise and was frightened.

Concerning this matter I asked no more, but held myself ready to bear it out in any form convenient, feeling that I had done my duty, and cared not for the consequence; only for several days dear Annie seemed frightened rather than grateful. But the oddest result of it was that Eliza, who had so despised me, and made very rude verses about me, now came trying to sit on my knee, and kiss me, and give me the best of the pan. However, I would not allow it, because I hate sudden changes.

Another thing also astonished me—namely, a beautiful letter from Marwood de Whichehalse himself (sent by a groom soon afterwards), in which he apologised to me, as if I had been his equal, for his rudeness to my sister, which was not intended in the least, but came of their common alarm at the moment, and his desire to comfort her. Also he begged permission to come and see me, as an old schoolfellow, and set everything straight between us, as should be among honest Blundellites.

All this was so different to my idea of fighting out a quarrel, when once it is upon a man, that I knew not what to make of it, but bowed to higher breeding. Only one thing I resolved upon, that come when he would he should not see Annie. And to do my sister justice, she had no desire to see him.

However, I am too easy, there is no doubt of that, being very quick to forgive a man, and very slow to suspect, unless he hath once lied to me. Moreover, as to Annie, it had always seemed to me (much against my wishes) that some shrewd love of a waiting sort was between her and Tom Faggus: and though Tom had made his fortune now, and everybody respected him, of course he was not to be compared, in that point of respectability, with those people who hanged the robbers when fortune turned against them.

So young Squire Marwood came again, as though I had never smitten him, and spoke of it in as light a way as if we were still at school together. It was not in my nature, of course, to keep any anger against him; and I knew what a condescension it was for him to visit us. And it is a very grievous thing, which touches small landowners, to see an ancient family day by day decaying: and when we heard that Ley Barton itself, and all the Manor of Lynton were under a heavy mortgage debt to John Lovering of Weare-Gifford, there was not much, in our little way, that we would not gladly do or suffer for the benefit of De Whichehalse.

Meanwhile the work of the farm was toward, and every day gave us more ado to dispose of what itself was doing. For after the long dry sweltering wind of March and part of April, there had been a fortnight of soft wet; and when the sun came forth again, hill and valley, wood and meadow, could not make enough of him. Many a spring have I seen since then, but never yet two springs alike, and never one so beautiful. Or was it that my love came forth and touched the world with beauty?

The spring was in our valley now; creeping first for shelter shyly in the pause of the blustering wind. There the lambs came bleating to her, and the orchis lifted up, and the thin dead leaves of clover lay for the new ones to spring through. There the stiffest things that sleep, the stubby oak, and the saplin'd beech, dropped their brown defiance to her, and prepared for a soft reply.

While her over-eager children (who had started forth to meet her, through the frost and shower of sleet), catkin'd hazel, gold-gloved withy, youthful elder, and old woodbine, with all the tribe of good hedge-climbers (who must hasten while haste they may)—was there one of them that did not claim the merit of coming first?

There she stayed and held her revel, as soon as the fear of frost was gone; all the air was a fount of freshness, and the earth of gladness, and the laughing waters prattled of the kindness of the sun.

But all this made it much harder for us, plying the hoe and rake, to keep the fields with room upon them for the corn to tiller. The winter wheat was well enough, being sturdy and strong-sided; but the spring wheat and the barley and the oats were overrun by ill weeds growing faster. Therefore, as the old saying is,—

Farmer, that thy wife may thrive,
Let not burr and burdock wive;
And if thou wouldst keep thy son,
See that bine and gith have none.

So we were compelled to go down the field and up it, striking in and out with care where the green blades hung together, so that each had space to move in and to spread its roots abroad. And I do assure you now, though you may not believe me, it was harder work to keep John Fry, Bill Dadds, and Jem Slocomb all in a line and all moving nimbly to the tune of my own tool, than it was to set out in the morning alone, and hoe half an acre by dinner-time. For, instead of keeping the good ash moving, they would for ever be finding something to look at or to speak of, or at any rate, to stop with; blaming the shape of their tools perhaps, or talking about other people's affairs; or, what was most irksome of all to me, taking advantage as married men, and whispering jokes of no excellence about my having, or having not, or being ashamed of a sweetheart. And this went so far at last that I was forced to take two of them and knock their heads together; after which they worked with a better will.

When we met together in the evening round the kitchen chimney-place, after the men had had their supper and their heavy boots were gone, my mother and Eliza would do their very utmost to learn what I was thinking of. Not that we kept any fire now, after the crock was emptied; but that we loved to see the ashes cooling, and to be together. At these times Annie would never ask me any crafty questions (as Eliza did), but would sit with her hair untwined, and one hand underneath her chin, sometimes looking softly at me, as much as to say that she knew it all and I was no worse off than she. But strange to say my mother dreamed not, even for an instant, that it was possible for Annie to be thinking of such a thing. She was so very good and quiet, and careful of the linen, and clever about the cookery and fowls and bacon-curing, that people used to laugh, and say she would never look at a bachelor until her mother ordered her. But I (perhaps from my own condition and the sense of what it was) felt no certainty about this, and even had another opinion, as was said before.

Often I was much inclined to speak to her about it, and put her on her guard against the approaches of Tom Faggus; but I could not find how to begin, and feared to make a breach between us; knowing that if her mind was set, no words of mine would alter it; although they needs must grieve her deeply. Moreover, I felt that, in this case, a certain homely Devonshire proverb would come home to me; that one, I mean, which records that the crock was calling the kettle smutty. Not, of course, that I compared my innocent maid to a highwayman; but that Annie might think her worse, and would be too apt to do so, if indeed she loved Tom Faggus. And our Cousin Tom, by this time, was living a quiet and godly life; having retired almost from the trade (except when he needed excitement, or came across public officers), and having won the esteem of all whose purses were in his power.

Perhaps it is needless for me to say that all this time while my month was running—or rather crawling, for never month went so slow as that with me—neither weed, nor seed, nor cattle, nor my own mother's anxiety, nor any care for my sister, kept me from looking once every day, and even twice on a Sunday, for any sign of Lorna. For my heart was ever weary; in the budding valleys, and by the crystal waters, looking at the lambs in fold, or the heifers on the mill, labouring in trickled furrows, or among the beaded blades; halting fresh to see the sun lift over the golden-vapoured ridge; or doffing hat, from sweat of brow, to watch him sink in the low gray sea; be it as it would of day, of work, or night, or slumber, it was a weary heart I bore, and fear was on the brink of it.

All the beauty of the spring went for happy men to think of; all the increase of the year was for other eyes to mark. Not a sign of any sunrise for me from my fount of life, not a breath to stir the dead leaves fallen on my heart's Spring.

Chapter XXIII A Royal Invitation

Although I had, for the most part, so very stout an appetite, that none but mother saw any need of encouraging me to eat, I could only manage one true good meal in a day, at the time I speak of. Mother was in despair at this, and tempted me with the whole of the rack, and even talked of sending to Porlock for a druggist who came there twice in a week; and Annie spent all her time in cooking, and even Lizzie sang songs to me; for she could sing very sweetly. But my conscience told me that Betty Muxworthy had some reason upon her side.

'Latt the young ozebird aloun, zay I. Makk zuch ado about un, wi' hogs'-puddens, and hock-bits, and lambs'-mate, and whaten bradd indade, and brewers' ale avore dinner-time, and her not to zit wi' no winder aupen—draive me mad 'e doo, the ov'ee, zuch a passel of voouls. Do 'un good to starve a bit; and takk zome on's wackedness out ov un.'

But mother did not see it so; and she even sent for Nicholas Snowe to bring his three daughters with him, and have ale and cake in the parlour, and advise about what the bees were doing, and when a swarm might be looked for. Being vexed about this and having to stop at home nearly half the evening, I lost good manners so much as to ask him (even in our own house!) what he meant by not mending the swing-hurdle where the Lynn stream flows from our land into his, and which he is bound to maintain. But he looked at me in a superior manner, and said, 'Business, young man, in business time.'

I had other reason for being vexed with Farmer Nicholas just now, viz. that I had heard a rumour, after church one Sunday—when most of all we sorrow over the sins of one another—that Master Nicholas Snowe had been seen to gaze tenderly at my mother, during a passage of the sermon, wherein the parson spoke well and warmly about the duty of Christian love. Now, putting one thing with another, about the bees, and about some ducks, and a bullock with a broken knee-cap, I more than suspected that Farmer Nicholas was casting sheep's eyes at my mother; not only to save all further trouble in the matter of the hurdle, but to override me altogether upon the difficult question of damming. And I knew quite well that John Fry's wife never came to help at the washing without declaring that it was a sin for a well-looking woman like mother, with plenty to live on, and only three children, to keep all the farmers for miles around so unsettled in their minds about her. Mother used to answer 'Oh fie, Mistress Fry! be good enough to mind your own business.' But we always saw that she smoothed her apron, and did her hair up afterwards, and that Mistress Fry went home at night with a cold pig's foot or a bowl of dripping.

Therefore, on that very night, as I could not well speak to mother about it, without seeming undutiful, after lighting the three young ladies—for so in sooth they called themselves—all the way home with our stable-lanthorn, I begged good leave of Farmer Nicholas (who had hung some way behind us) to say a word in private to him, before he entered his own house.

'Wi' all the plaisure in laife, my zon,' he answered very graciously, thinking perhaps that I was prepared to speak concerning Sally.

'Now, Farmer Nicholas Snowe,' I said, scarce knowing how to begin it, 'you must promise not to be vexed with me, for what I am going to say to you.'

'Vaxed wi' thee! Noo, noo, my lad. I 'ave a knowed thee too long for that. And thy veyther were my best friend, afore thee. Never wronged his neighbours, never spak an unkind word, never had no maneness in him. Tuk a vancy to a nice young 'ooman, and never kep her in doubt about it, though there wadn't mooch to zettle on her. Spak his maind laike a man, he did, and right happy he were wi' her. Ah, well a day! Ah, God knoweth best. I never shall zee his laike again. And he were the best judge of a dung-heap anywhere in this county.'

'Well, Master Snowe,' I answered him, 'it is very handsome of you to say so. And now I am going to be like my father, I am going to speak my mind.'

'Raight there, lad; raight enough, I reckon. Us has had enough of pralimbinary.'

'Then what I want to say is this—I won't have any one courting my mother.'

'Coortin' of thy mother, lad?' cried Farmer Snowe, with as much amazement as if the thing were impossible; 'why, who ever hath been dooin' of it?'

'Yes, courting of my mother, sir. And you know best who comes doing it.'

'Wull, wull! What will boys be up to next? Zhud a' thought herzelf wor the proper judge. No thank 'ee, lad, no need of thy light. Know the wai to my own door, at laste; and have a raight to goo there.' And he shut me out without so much as offering me a drink of cider.

The next afternoon, when work was over, I had seen to the horses, for now it was foolish to trust John Fry, because he had so many children, and his wife had taken to scolding; and just as I was saying to myself that in five days more my month would be done, and myself free to seek Lorna, a man came riding up from the ford where the road goes through the Lynn stream. As soon as I saw that it was not Tom Faggus, I went no farther to meet him, counting that it must be some traveller bound for Brendon or Cheriton, and likely enough he would come and beg for a draught of milk or cider; and then on again, after asking the way.

But instead of that, he stopped at our gate, and stood up from his saddle, and halloed as if he were somebody; and all the time he was flourishing a white thing in the air, like the bands our parson weareth. So I crossed the court-yard to speak with him.

'Service of the King!' he saith; 'service of our lord the King! Come hither, thou great yokel, at risk of fine and imprisonment.'

Although not pleased with this, I went to him, as became a loyal man; quite at my leisure, however, for there is no man born who can hurry me, though I hasten for any woman.

'Plover Barrows farm!' said he; 'God only knows how tired I be. Is there any where in this cursed county a cursed place called Plover Barrows farm? For last twenty mile at least they told me 'twere only half a mile farther, or only just round corner. Now tell me that, and I fain would thwack thee if thou wert not thrice my size.'

'Sir,' I replied, 'you shall not have the trouble. This is Plover's Barrows farm, and you are kindly welcome. Sheep's kidneys is for supper, and the ale got bright from the tapping. But why do you think ill of us? We like not to be cursed so.'

'Nay, I think no ill,' he said; 'sheep's kidneys is good, uncommon good, if they do them without burning. But I be so galled in the saddle ten days, and never a comely meal of it. And when they hear "King's service" cried, they give me the worst of everything. All the way down from London, I had a rogue of a fellow in front of me, eating the fat of the land before me, and every one bowing down to him. He could go three miles to my one though he never changed his horse. He might have robbed me at any minute, if I had been worth the trouble. A red mare he rideth, strong in the loins, and pointed quite small in the head. I shall live to see him hanged yet.'

All this time he was riding across the straw of our courtyard, getting his weary legs out of the leathers, and almost afraid to stand yet. A coarse-grained, hard-faced man he was, some forty years of age or so, and of middle height and stature. He was dressed in a dark brown riding suit, none the better for Exmoor mud, but fitting him very differently from the fashion of our tailors. Across the holsters lay his cloak, made of some red skin, and shining from the sweating of the horse. As I looked down on his stiff bright head-piece, small quick eyes and black needly beard, he seemed to despise me (too much, as I thought) for a mere ignoramus and country bumpkin.

'Annie, have down the cut ham,' I shouted, for my sister was come to the door by chance, or because of the sound of a horse in the road, 'and cut a few rashers of hung deer's meat. There is a gentleman come to sup, Annie. And fetch the hops out of the tap with a skewer that it may run more sparkling.'

'I wish I may go to a place never meant for me,' said my new friend, now wiping his mouth with the sleeve of his brown riding coat, 'if ever I fell among such good folk. You are the right sort, and no error therein. All this shall go in your favour greatly, when I make deposition. At least, I mean, if it be as good in the eating as in the hearing. 'Tis a supper quite fit for Tom Faggus himself, the man who hath stolen my victuals so. And that hung deer's meat, now is it of the red deer running wild in these parts?'

'To be sure it is, sir,' I answered; 'where should we get any other?'

'Right, right, you are right, my son. I have heard that the flavour is marvellous. Some of them came and scared me so, in the fog of the morning, that I hungered for them ever since. Ha, ha, I saw their haunches. But the young lady will not forget—art sure she will not forget it?'

'You may trust her to forget nothing, sir, that may tempt a guest to his comfort.'

'In faith, then, I will leave my horse in your hands, and be off for it. Half the pleasure of the mouth is in the nose beforehand. But stay, almost I forgot my business, in the hurry which thy tongue hath spread through my lately despairing belly. Hungry I am, and sore of body, from my heels right upward, and sorest in front of my doublet, yet may I not rest nor bite barley-bread, until I have seen and touched John Ridd. God grant that he be not far away; I must eat my saddle, if it be so.'

'Have no fear, good sir,' I answered; 'you have seen and touched John Ridd. I am he, and not one likely to go beneath a bushel.'

'It would take a large bushel to hold thee, John Ridd. In the name of the King, His Majesty, Charles the Second, these presents!'

He touched me with the white thing which I had first seen him waving, and which I now beheld to be sheepskin, such as they call parchment. It was tied across with cord, and fastened down in every corner with unsightly dabs of wax. By order of the messenger (for I was over-frightened now to think of doing anything), I broke enough of seals to keep an Easter ghost from rising; and there I saw my name in large; God grant such another shock may never befall me in my old age.

'Read, my son; read, thou great fool, if indeed thou canst read,' said the officer to encourage me; 'there is nothing to kill thee, boy, and my supper will be spoiling. Stare not at me so, thou fool; thou art big enough to eat me; read, read, read.'

'If you please, sir, what is your name?' I asked; though why I asked him I know not, except from fear of witchcraft.

'Jeremy Stickles is my name, lad, nothing more than a poor apparitor of the worshipful Court of King's Bench. And at this moment a starving one, and no supper for me unless thou wilt read.'

Being compelled in this way, I read pretty nigh as follows; not that I give the whole of it, but only the gist and the emphasis,—

'To our good subject, John Ridd, etc.'—describing me ever so much better than I knew myself—'by these presents, greeting. These are to require thee, in the name of our lord the King, to appear in person before the Right Worshipful, the Justices of His Majesty's Bench at Westminster, laying aside all thine own business, and there to deliver such evidence as is within thy cognisance, touching certain matters whereby the peace of our said lord the King, and the well-being of this realm, is, are, or otherwise may be impeached, impugned, imperilled, or otherwise detrimented. As witness these presents.' And then there were four seals, and then a signature I could not make out, only that it began with a J, and ended with some other writing, done almost in a circle. Underneath was added in a different handwriting 'Charges will be borne. The matter is full urgent.'

The messenger watched me, while I read so much as I could read of it; and he seemed well pleased with my surprise, because he had expected it. Then, not knowing what else to do, I looked again at the cover, and on the top of it I saw, 'Ride, Ride, Ride! On His Gracious Majesty's business; spur and spare not.'

It may be supposed by all who know me, that I was taken hereupon with such a giddiness in my head and noisiness in my ears, that I was forced to hold by the crook driven in below the thatch for holding of the hay-rakes. There was scarcely any sense left in me, only that the thing was come by power of Mother Melldrum, because I despised her warning, and had again sought Lorna. But the officer was grieved for me, and the danger to his supper.

'My son, be not afraid,' he said; 'we are not going to skin thee. Only thou tell all the truth, and it shall be—but never mind, I will tell thee all about it, and how to come out harmless, if I find thy victuals good, and no delay in serving them.'

'We do our best, sir, without bargain,' said I, 'to please our visitors.'

But when my mother saw that parchment (for we could not keep it from her) she fell away into her favourite bed of stock gilly-flowers, which she had been tending; and when we brought her round again, did nothing but exclaim against the wickedness of the age and people. 'It was useless to tell her; she knew what it was, and so should all the parish know. The King had heard what her son was, how sober, and quiet, and diligent, and the strongest young man in England; and being himself such a reprobate—God forgive her for saying so—he could never rest till he got poor Johnny, and made him as dissolute as himself. And if he did that'—here mother went off into a fit of crying; and Annie minded her face, while Lizzie saw that her gown was in comely order.

But the character of the King improved, when Master Jeremy Stickles (being really moved by the look of it, and no bad man after all) laid it clearly before my mother that the King on his throne was unhappy, until he had seen John Ridd. That the fame of John had gone so far, and his size, and all his virtues—that verily by the God who made him, the King was overcome with it.

Then mother lay back in her garden chair, and smiled upon the whole of us, and most of all on Jeremy; looking only shyly on me, and speaking through some break of tears. 'His Majesty shall have my John; His Majesty is very good: but only for a fortnight. I want no titles for him. Johnny is enough for me; and Master John for the working men.'

Now though my mother was so willing that I should go to London, expecting great promotion and high glory for me, I myself was deeply gone into the pit of sorrow. For what would Lorna think of me? Here was the long month just expired, after worlds of waiting; there would be her lovely self, peeping softly down the glen, and fearing to encourage me; yet there would be nobody else, and what an insult to her! Dwelling upon this, and seeing no chance of escape from it, I could not find one wink of sleep; though Jeremy Stickles (who slept close by) snored loud enough to spare me some. For I felt myself to be, as it were, in a place of some importance; in a situation of trust, I may say; and bound not to depart from it. For who could tell what the King might have to say to me about the Doones—and I felt that they were at the bottom of this strange appearance—or what His Majesty might think, if after receiving a message from him (trusty under so many seals) I were to violate his faith in me as a churchwarden's son, and falsely spread his words abroad?

Perhaps I was not wise in building such a wall of scruples. Nevertheless, all that was there, and weighed upon me heavily. And at last I made up my mind to this, that even Lorna must not know the reason of my going, neither anything about it; but that she might know I was gone a long way from home, and perhaps be sorry for it. Now how was I to let her know even that much of the matter, without breaking compact?

Puzzling on this, I fell asleep, after the proper time to get up; nor was I to be seen at breakfast time; and mother (being quite strange to that) was very uneasy about it. But Master Stickles assured her that the King's writ often had that effect, and the symptom was a good one.

'Now, Master Stickles, when must we start?' I asked him, as he lounged in the yard gazing at our turkey poults picking and running in the sun to the tune of their father's gobble. 'Your horse was greatly foundered, sir, and is hardly fit for the road to-day; and Smiler was sledding yesterday all up the higher Cleve; and none of the rest can carry me.'

'In a few more years,' replied the King's officer, contemplating me with much satisfaction; ''twill be a cruelty to any horse to put thee on his back, John.'

Master Stickles, by this time, was quite familiar with us, calling me 'Jack,' and Eliza 'Lizzie,' and what I liked the least of all, our pretty Annie 'Nancy.'

'That will be as God pleases, sir,' I answered him, rather sharply; 'and the horse that suffers will not be thine. But I wish to know when we must start upon our long travel to London town. I perceive that the matter is of great despatch and urgency.'

'To be sure, so it is, my son. But I see a yearling turkey there, him I mean with the hop in his walk, who (if I know aught of fowls) would roast well to-morrow. Thy mother must have preparation: it is no more than reasonable. Now, have that turkey killed to-night (for his fatness makes me long for him), and we will have him for dinner to-morrow, with, perhaps, one of his brethren; and a few more collops of red deer's flesh for supper, and then on the Friday morning, with the grace of God, we will set our faces to the road, upon His Majesty's business.'

'Nay, but good sir,' I asked with some trembling, so eager was I to see Lorna; 'if His Majesty's business will keep till Friday, may it not keep until Monday? We have a litter of sucking-pigs, excellently choice and white, six weeks old, come Friday. There be too many for the sow, and one of them needeth roasting. Think you not it would be a pity to leave the women to carve it?'

'My son Jack,' replied Master Stickles, 'never was I in such quarters yet: and God forbid that I should be so unthankful to Him as to hurry away. And now I think on it, Friday is not a day upon which pious people love to commence an enterprise. I will choose the young pig to-morrow at noon, at which time they are wont to gambol; and we will celebrate his birthday by carving him on Friday. After that we will gird our loins, and set forth early on Saturday.'

Now this was little better to me than if we had set forth at once. Sunday being the very first day upon which it would be honourable for me to enter Glen Doone. But though I tried every possible means with Master Jeremy Stickles, offering him the choice for dinner of every beast that was on the farm, he durst not put off our departure later than the Saturday. And nothing else but love of us and of our hospitality would have so persuaded him to remain with us till then. Therefore now my only chance of seeing Lorna, before I went, lay in watching from the cliff and espying her, or a signal from her.

This, however, I did in vain, until my eyes were weary and often would delude themselves with hope of what they ached for. But though I lay hidden behind the trees upon the crest of the stony fall, and waited so quiet that the rabbits and squirrels played around me, and even the keen-eyed weasel took me for a trunk of wood—it was all as one; no cast of colour changed the white stone, whose whiteness now was hateful to me; nor did wreath or skirt of maiden break the loneliness of the vale.

Chapter XXIV A Safe Pass for King's Messenger

A journey to London seemed to us in those bygone days as hazardous and dark an adventure as could be forced on any man. I mean, of course, a poor man; for to a great nobleman, with ever so many outriders, attendants, and retainers, the risk was not so great, unless the highwaymen knew of their coming beforehand, and so combined against them. To a poor man, however, the risk was not so much from those gentlemen of the road as from the more ignoble footpads, and the landlords of the lesser hostels, and the loose unguarded soldiers, over and above the pitfalls and the quagmires of the way; so that it was hard to settle, at the first outgoing whether a man were wise to pray more for his neck or for his head.

But nowadays it is very different. Not that highway-men are scarce, in this the reign of our good Queen Anne; for in truth they thrive as well as ever, albeit they deserve it not, being less upright and courteous—but that the roads are much improved, and the growing use of stage-waggons (some of which will travel as much as forty miles in a summer day) has turned our ancient ideas of distance almost upside down; and I doubt whether God be pleased with our flying so fast away from Him. However, that is not my business; nor does it lie in my mouth to speak very strongly upon the subject, seeing how much I myself have done towards making of roads upon Exmoor.

To return to my story (and, in truth, I lose that road too often), it would have taken ten King's messengers to get me away from Plover's Barrows without one goodbye to Lorna, but for my sense of the trust and reliance which His Majesty had reposed in me. And now I felt most bitterly how the very arrangements which seemed so wise, and indeed ingenious, may by the force of events become our most fatal obstacles. For lo! I was blocked entirely from going to see Lorna; whereas we should have fixed it so that I as well might have the power of signalling my necessity.

It was too late now to think of that; and so I made up my mind at last to keep my honour on both sides, both to the King and to the maiden, although I might lose everything except a heavy heart for it. And indeed, more hearts than mine were heavy; for when it came to the tug of parting, my mother was like, and so was Annie, to break down altogether. But I bade them be of good cheer, and smiled in the briskest manner upon them, and said that I should be back next week as one of His Majesty's greatest captains, and told them not to fear me then. Upon which they smiled at the idea of ever being afraid of me, whatever dress I might have on; and so I kissed my hand once more, and rode away very bravely. But bless your heart, I could no more have done so than flown all the way to London if Jeremy Stickles had not been there.

And not to take too much credit to myself in this matter, I must confess that when we were come to the turn in the road where the moor begins, and whence you see the last of the yard, and the ricks and the poultry round them and can (by knowing the place) obtain a glance of the kitchen window under the walnut-tree, it went so hard with me just here that I even made pretence of a stone in ancient Smiler's shoe, to dismount, and to bend my head awhile. Then, knowing that those I had left behind would be watching to see the last of me, and might have false hopes of my coming back, I mounted again with all possible courage, and rode after Jeremy Stickles.

Jeremy, seeing how much I was down, did his best to keep me up with jokes, and tales, and light discourse, until, before we had ridden a league, I began to long to see the things he was describing. The air, the weather, and the thoughts of going to a wondrous place, added to the fine company—at least so Jeremy said it was—of a man who knew all London, made me feel that I should be ungracious not to laugh a little. And being very simple then I laughed no more a little, but something quite considerable (though free from consideration) at the strange things Master Stickles told me, and his strange way of telling them. And so we became very excellent friends, for he was much pleased with my laughing.

Not wishing to thrust myself more forward than need be in this narrative, I have scarcely thought it becoming or right to speak of my own adornments. But now, what with the brave clothes I had on, and the better ones still that were packed up in the bag behind the saddle, it is almost beyond me to forbear saying that I must have looked very pleasing. And many a time I wished, going along, that Lorna could only be here and there, watching behind a furze-bush, looking at me, and wondering how much my clothes had cost. For mother would have no stint in the matter, but had assembled at our house, immediately upon knowledge of what was to be about London, every man known to be a good stitcher upon our side of Exmoor. And for three days they had worked their best, without stint of beer or cider, according to the constitution of each. The result, so they all declared, was such as to create admiration, and defy competition in London. And to me it seemed that they were quite right; though Jeremy Stickles turned up his nose, and feigned to be deaf in the business.

Now be that matter as you please—for the point is not worth arguing—certain it is that my appearance was better than it had been before. For being in the best clothes, one tries to look and to act (so far as may be) up to the quality of them. Not only for the fear of soiling them, but that they enlarge a man's perception of his value. And it strikes me that our sins arise, partly from disdain of others, but mainly from contempt of self, both working the despite of God. But men of mind may not be measured by such paltry rule as this.

By dinner-time we arrived at Porlock, and dined with my old friend, Master Pooke, now growing rich and portly. For though we had plenty of victuals with us we were not to begin upon them, until all chance of victualling among our friends was left behind. And during that first day we had no need to meddle with our store at all; for as had been settled before we left home, we lay that night at Dunster in the house of a worthy tanner, first cousin to my mother, who received us very cordially, and undertook to return old Smiler to his stable at Plover's Barrows, after one day's rest.

Thence we hired to Bridgwater; and from Bridgwater on to Bristowe, breaking the journey between the two. But although the whole way was so new to me, and such a perpetual source of conflict, that the remembrance still abides with me, as if it were but yesterday, I must not be so long in telling as it was in travelling, or you will wish me farther; both because Lorna was nothing there, and also because a man in our neighbourhood had done the whole of it since my time, and feigns to think nothing of it. However, one thing, in common justice to a person who has been traduced, I am bound to mention. And this is, that being two of us, and myself of such magnitude, we never could have made our journey without either fight or running, but for the free pass which dear Annie, by some means (I know not what), had procured from Master Faggus. And when I let it be known, by some hap, that I was the own cousin of Tom Faggus, and honoured with his society, there was not a house upon the road but was proud to entertain me, in spite of my fellow-traveller, bearing the red badge of the King.

'I will keep this close, my son Jack,' he said, having stripped it off with a carving-knife; 'your flag is the best to fly. The man who starved me on the way down, the same shall feed me fat going home.'

Therefore we pursued our way, in excellent condition, having thriven upon the credit of that very popular highwayman, and being surrounded with regrets that he had left the profession, and sometimes begged to intercede that he might help the road again. For all the landlords on the road declared that now small ale was drunk, nor much of spirits called for, because the farmers need not prime to meet only common riders, neither were these worth the while to get drunk with afterwards. Master Stickles himself undertook, as an officer of the King's Justices to plead this case with Squire Faggus (as everybody called him now), and to induce him, for the general good, to return to his proper ministry.

It was a long and weary journey, although the roads are wondrous good on the farther side of Bristowe, and scarcely any man need be bogged, if he keeps his eyes well open, save, perhaps, in Berkshire. In consequence of the pass we had, and the vintner's knowledge of it, we only met two public riders, one of whom made off straightway when he saw my companion's pistols and the stout carbine I bore; and the other came to a parley with us, and proved most kind and affable, when he knew himself in the presence of the cousin of Squire Faggus. 'God save you, gentlemen,' he cried, lifting his hat politely; 'many and many a happy day I have worked this road with him. Such times will never be again. But commend me to his love and prayers. King my name is, and King my nature. Say that, and none will harm you.' And so he made off down the hill, being a perfect gentleman, and a very good horse he was riding.

The night was falling very thick by the time we were come to Tyburn, and here the King's officer decided that it would be wise to halt, because the way was unsafe by night across the fields to Charing village. I for my part was nothing loth, and preferred to see London by daylight.

And after all, it was not worth seeing, but a very hideous and dirty place, not at all like Exmoor. Some of the shops were very fine, and the signs above them finer still, so that I was never weary of standing still to look at them. But in doing this there was no ease; for before one could begin almost to make out the meaning of them, either some of the wayfarers would bustle and scowl, and draw their swords, or the owner, or his apprentice boys, would rush out and catch hold of me, crying, 'Buy, buy,

buy! What d'ye lack, what d'ye lack? Buy, buy, buy!' At first I mistook the meaning of this—for so we pronounce the word 'boy' upon Exmoor—and I answered with some indignation, 'Sirrah, I am no boy now, but a man of one-and-twenty years; and as for lacking, I lack naught from thee, except what thou hast not—good manners.'

The only things that pleased me much, were the river Thames, and the hall and church of Westminster, where there are brave things to be seen, and braver still to think about. But whenever I wandered in the streets, what with the noise the people made, the number of the coaches, the running of the footmen, the swaggering of great courtiers, and the thrusting aside of everybody, many and many a time I longed to be back among the sheep again, for fear of losing temper. They were welcome to the wall for me, as I took care to tell them, for I could stand without the wall, which perhaps was more than they could do. Though I said this with the best intention, meaning no discourtesy, some of them were vexed at it; and one young lord, being flushed with drink, drew his sword and made at me. But I struck it up with my holly stick, so that it flew on the roof of a house, then I took him by the belt with one hand, and laid him in the kennel. This caused some little disturbance; but none of the rest saw fit to try how the matter might be with them.

Now this being the year of our Lord 1683, more than nine years and a half since the death of my father, and the beginning of this history, all London was in a great ferment about the dispute between the Court of the King and the City. The King, or rather perhaps his party (for they said that His Majesty cared for little except to have plenty of money and spend it), was quite resolved to be supreme in the appointment of the chief officers of the corporation. But the citizens maintained that (under their charter) this right lay entirely with themselves; upon which a writ was issued against them for forfeiture of their charter; and the question was now being tried in the court of His Majesty's bench.

This seemed to occupy all the attention of the judges, and my case (which had appeared so urgent) was put off from time to time, while the Court and the City contended. And so hot was the conflict and hate between them, that a sheriff had been fined by the King in 100,000 pounds, and a former lord mayor had even been sentenced to the pillory, because he would not swear falsely. Hence the courtiers and the citizens scarce could meet in the streets with patience, or without railing and frequent blows.

Now although I heard so much of this matter, for nothing else was talked of, and it seeming to me more important even than the churchwardenship of Oare, I could not for the life of me tell which side I should take to. For all my sense of position, and of confidence reposed in me, and of my father's opinions, lay heavily in one scale, while all my reason and my heart went down plump against injustice, and seemed to win the other scale. Even so my father had been, at the breaking out of the civil war, when he was less than my age now, and even less skilled in politics; and my mother told me after this, when she saw how I myself was doubting, and vexed with myself for doing so, that my father used to thank God often that he had not been called upon to take one side or other, but might remain obscure and quiet. And yet he always considered himself to be a good, sound Royalist.

But now as I stayed there, only desirous to be heard and to get away, and scarcely even guessing yet what was wanted of me (for even Jeremy Stickles knew not, or pretended not to know), things came to a dreadful pass between the King and all the people who dared to have an opinion. For about the middle of June, the judges gave their sentence, that the City of London had forfeited its charter, and that its franchise should be taken into the hands of the King. Scarcely was this judgment forth, and all men hotly talking of it, when a far worse thing befell. News of some great conspiracy was spread at every corner, and that a man in the malting business had tried to take up the brewer's work, and lop the King and the Duke of York. Everybody was shocked at this, for the King himself was not disliked so much as his advisers; but everybody was more than shocked, grieved indeed to the heart with pain, at hearing that Lord William Russell and Mr. Algernon Sidney had been seized and sent to the Tower of London, upon a charge of high treason.

Having no knowledge of these great men, nor of the matter how far it was true, I had not very much to say about either of them or it; but this silence was not shared (although the ignorance may have been) by the hundreds of people around me. Such a commotion was astir, such universal sense of wrong, and stern resolve to right it, that each man grasped his fellow's hand, and led him into the vintner's. Even I, although at that time given to excess in temperance, and afraid of the name of cordials, was hard set (I do assure you) not to be drunk at intervals without coarse discourtesy.

However, that (as Betty Muxworthy used to say, when argued down, and ready to take the mop for it) is neither here nor there. I have naught to do with great history and am sorry for those who have to write it; because they are sure to have both friends and enemies in it, and cannot act as they would towards them, without damage to their own consciences.

But as great events draw little ones, and the rattle of the churn decides the uncertainty of the flies, so this movement of the town, and eloquence, and passion had more than I guessed at the time, to do with my own little fortunes. For in the first place it was fixed (perhaps from down right contumely, because the citizens loved him so) that Lord Russell should be tried neither at Westminster nor at Lincoln's Inn, but at the Court of Old Bailey, within the precincts of the city. This kept me hanging on much longer; because although the good nobleman was to be tried by the Court of Common Pleas, yet the officers of King's Bench, to whom I daily applied myself, were in counsel with their fellows, and put me off from day to day.

Now I had heard of the law's delays, which the greatest of all great poets (knowing much of the law himself, as indeed of everything) has specially mentioned, when not expected, among the many ills of life. But I never thought at my years to have such bitter experience of the evil; and it seemed to me that if the lawyers failed to do their duty, they ought to pay people for waiting upon them, instead of making them pay for it. But here I was, now in the second month living at my own charges in the house of a worthy fellmonger at the sign of the Seal and Squirrel, abutting upon the Strand road which leads from Temple Bar to Charing. Here I did very well indeed, having a mattress of good skin-dressings, and plenty to eat every day of my life, but the butter was something to cry 'but' thrice at (according to a conceit of our school days), and the milk must have come from cows driven to water. However, these evils were light compared with the heavy bill sent up to me every Saturday afternoon; and knowing how my mother had pinched to send me nobly to London, and had told me to spare for nothing, but live bravely with the best of them, the tears very nearly came into my eyes, as I thought, while I ate, of so robbing her.

At length, being quite at the end of my money, and seeing no other help for it, I determined to listen to clerks no more, but force my way up to the Justices, and insist upon being heard by them, or discharged from my recognisance. For so they had termed the bond or deed which I had been forced to execute, in the presence of a chief clerk or notary, the very day after I came to London. And the purport of it was, that on pain of a heavy fine or escheatment, I would hold myself ready and present, to give evidence when called upon. Having delivered me up to sign this, Jeremy Stickles was quit of me, and went upon other business, not but what he was kind and good to me, when his time and pursuits allowed of it.

Chapter XXV A Great Man Attends to Business

Having seen Lord Russell murdered in the fields of Lincoln's Inn, or rather having gone to see it, but turned away with a sickness and a bitter flood of tears—for a whiter and a nobler neck never fell before low beast—I strode away towards Westminster, cured of half my indignation at the death of Charles the First. Many people hurried past me, chiefly of the more tender sort, revolting at the butchery. In their ghastly faces, as they turned them back, lest the sight should be coming after them, great sorrow was to be seen, and horror, and pity, and some anger.

In Westminster Hall I found nobody; not even the crowd of crawling varlets, who used to be craving evermore for employment or for payment. I knocked at three doors, one after other, of lobbies going out of it, where I had formerly seen some officers and people pressing in and out, but for my trouble I took nothing, except some thumps from echo. And at last an old man told me that all the lawyers were gone to see the result of their own works, in the fields of Lincoln's Inn.

However, in a few days' time, I had better fortune; for the court was sitting and full of business, to clear off the arrears of work, before the lawyers' holiday. As I was waiting in the hall for a good occasion, a man with horsehair on his head, and a long blue bag in his left hand, touched me gently on the arm, and led me into a quiet place. I followed him very gladly, being confident that he came to me with a message from the Justiciaries. But after taking pains to be sure that none could overhear us, he turned on me suddenly, and asked,—

'Now, John, how is your dear mother?'

'Worshipful sir' I answered him, after recovering from my surprise at his knowledge of our affairs, and kindly interest in them, 'it is two months now since I have seen her. Would to God that I only knew how she is faring now, and how the business of the farm goes!'

'Sir, I respect and admire you,' the old gentleman replied, with a bow very low and genteel; 'few young court-gallants of our time are so reverent and dutiful. Oh, how I did love my mother!' Here he turned up his eyes to heaven, in a manner that made me feel for him and yet with a kind of wonder.

'I am very sorry for you, sir,' I answered most respectfully, not meaning to trespass on his grief, yet wondering at his mother's age; for he seemed to be at least threescore; 'but I am no court-gallant, sir; I am only a farmer's son, and learning how to farm a little.'

'Enough, John; quite enough,' he cried, 'I can read it in thy countenance. Honesty is written there, and courage and simplicity. But I fear that, in this town of London, thou art apt to be taken in by people of no principle. Ah me! Ah me! The world is bad, and I am too old to improve it.'

Then finding him so good and kind, and anxious to improve the age, I told him almost everything; how much I paid the fellmonger, and all the things I had been to see; and how I longed to get away, before the corn was ripening; yet how (despite of these desires) I felt myself bound to walk up and down, being under a thing called 'recognisance.' In short, I told him everything; except the nature of my summons (which I had no right to tell), and that I was out of money.

My tale was told in a little archway, apart from other lawyers; and the other lawyers seemed to me to shift themselves, and to look askew, like sheep through a hurdle, when the rest are feeding.

'What! Good God!' my lawyer cried, smiting his breast indignantly with a roll of something learned; 'in what country do we live? Under what laws are we governed? No case before the court whatever; no primary deposition, so far as we are furnished; not even a King's writ issued—and here we have a fine young man dragged from his home and adoring mother, during the height of agriculture, at his own cost and charges! I have heard of many grievances; but this the very worst of all. Nothing short of a Royal Commission could be warranty for it. This is not only illegal, sir, but most gravely unconstitutional.'

'I had not told you, worthy sir,' I answered him, in a lower tone, 'if I could have thought that your sense of right would be moved so painfully. But now I must beg to leave you, sir—for I see that the door again is open. I beg you, worshipful sir, to accept—'

Upon this he put forth his hand and said, 'Nay, nay, my son, not two, not two:' yet looking away, that he might not scare me.

'To accept, kind sir, my very best thanks, and most respectful remembrances.' And with that, I laid my hand in his. 'And if, sir, any circumstances of business or of pleasure should bring you to our part of the world, I trust you will not forget that my mother and myself (if ever I get home again) will do our best to make you comfortable with our poor hospitality.'

With this I was hasting away from him, but he held my hand and looked round at me. And he spoke without cordiality.

'Young man, a general invitation is no entry for my fee book. I have spent a good hour of business-time in mastering thy case, and stating my opinion of it. And being a member of the bar, called six-and-thirty years agone by the honourable society of the Inner Temple, my fee is at my own discretion; albeit an honorarium. For the honour of the profession, and my position in it, I ought to charge thee at least five guineas, although I would have accepted one, offered with good will and delicacy. Now I will enter it two, my son, and half a crown for my clerk's fee.'

Saying this, he drew forth from his deep, blue bag, a red book having clasps to it, and endorsed in gold letters 'Fee-book'; and before I could speak (being frightened so) he had entered on a page of it, 'To consideration of ease as stated by John Ridd, and advising thereupon, two guineas.'

'But sir, good sir,' I stammered forth, not having two guineas left in the world, yet grieving to confess it, 'I knew not that I was to pay, learned sir. I never thought of it in that way.'

'Wounds of God! In what way thought you that a lawyer listened to your rigmarole?'

'I thought that you listened from kindness, sir, and compassion of my grievous case, and a sort of liking for me.'

'A lawyer like thee, young curmudgeon! A lawyer afford to feel compassion gratis! Either thou art a very deep knave, or the greenest of all greenhorns. Well, I suppose, I must let thee off for one guinea, and the clerk's fee. A bad business, a shocking business!'

Now, if this man had continued kind and soft, as when he heard my story, I would have pawned my clothes to pay him, rather than leave a debt behind, although contracted unwittingly. But when he used harsh language so, knowing that I did not deserve it, I began to doubt within myself whether he deserved my money. Therefore I answered him with some readiness, such as comes sometimes to me, although I am so slow.

'Sir, I am no curmudgeon: if a young man had called me so, it would not have been well with him. This money shall be paid, if due, albeit I had no desire to incur the debt. You have advised me that the Court is liable for my expenses, so far as they be reasonable. If this be a reasonable expense, come with me now to Lord Justice Jeffreys, and receive from him the two guineas, or (it may be) five, for the counsel you have given me to deny his jurisdiction.' With these words, I took his arm to lead him, for the door was open still.

'In the name of God, boy, let me go. Worthy sir, pray let me go. My wife is sick, and my daughter dying—in the name of God, sir, let me go.'

'Nay, nay,' I said, having fast hold of him, 'I cannot let thee go unpaid, sir. Right is right; and thou shalt have it.'

'Ruin is what I shall have, boy, if you drag me before that devil. He will strike me from the bar at once, and starve me, and all my family. Here, lad, good lad, take these two guineas. Thou hast despoiled the spoiler. Never again will I trust mine eyes for knowledge of a greenhorn.'

He slipped two guineas into the hand which I had hooked through his elbow, and spoke in an urgent whisper again, for the people came crowding around us—'For God's sake let me go, boy; another moment will be too late.'

'Learned sir,' I answered him, 'twice you spoke, unless I err, of the necessity of a clerk's fee, as a thing to be lamented.'

'To be sure, to be sure, my son. You have a clerk as much as I have. There it is. Now I pray thee, take to the study of the law. Possession is nine points of it, which thou hast of me. Self-possession is the tenth, and that thou hast more than the other nine.'

Being flattered by this, and by the feeling of the two guineas and half-crown, I dropped my hold upon Counsellor Kitch (for he was no less a man than that), and he was out of sight in a second of time, wig, blue bag, and family. And before I had time to make up my mind what I should do with his money (for of course I meant not to keep it) the crier of the Court (as they told me) came out, and wanted to know who I was. I told him, as shortly as I could, that my business lay with His Majesty's bench, and was very confidential; upon which he took me inside with warning, and showed me to an under-clerk, who showed me to a higher one, and the higher clerk to the head one.

When this gentleman understood all about my business (which I told him without complaint) he frowned at me very heavily, as if I had done him an injury.

'John Ridd,' he asked me with a stern glance, 'is it your deliberate desire to be brought into the presence of the Lord Chief Justice?'

'Surely, sir, it has been my desire for the last two months and more.'

'Then, John, thou shalt be. But mind one thing, not a word of thy long detention, or thou mayst get into trouble.'

'How, sir? For being detained against my own wish?' I asked him; but he turned away, as if that matter were not worth his arguing, as, indeed, I suppose it was not, and led me through a little passage to a door with a curtain across it.

'Now, if my Lord cross-question you,' the gentleman whispered to me, 'answer him straight out truth at once, for he will have it out of thee. And mind, he loves not to be contradicted, neither can he bear a hang-dog look. Take little heed of the other two; but note every word of the middle one; and never make him speak twice.'

I thanked him for his good advice, as he moved the curtain and thrust me in, but instead of entering withdrew, and left me to bear the brunt of it.

The chamber was not very large, though lofty to my eyes, and dark, with wooden panels round it. At the further end were some raised seats, such as I have seen in churches, lined with velvet, and having broad elbows, and a canopy over the middle seat. There were only three men sitting here, one in the centre, and one on each side; and all three were done up wonderfully with fur, and robes of state, and curls of thick gray horsehair, crimped and gathered, and plaited down to their shoulders. Each man had an oak desk before him, set at a little distance, and spread with pens and papers. Instead of writing, however, they seemed to be laughing and talking, or rather the one in the middle seemed to be telling some good story, which the others received with approval. By reason of their great perukes it was hard to tell how old they were; but the one who was speaking seemed the youngest, although he was the chief of them. A thick-set, burly, and bulky man, with a blotchy broad face, and great square jaws, and fierce eyes full of blazes; he was one to be dreaded by gentle souls, and to be abhorred by the noble.

Between me and the three lord judges, some few lawyers were gathering up bags and papers and pens and so forth, from a narrow table in the middle of the room, as if a case had been disposed of, and no other were called on. But before I had time to look round twice, the stout fierce man espied me, and shouted out with a flashing stare'—

'How now, countryman, who art thou?'

'May it please your worship,' I answered him loudly, 'I am John Ridd, of Oare parish, in the shire of Somerset, brought to this London, some two months back by a special messenger, whose name is Jeremy Stickles; and then bound over to be at hand and ready, when called upon to give evidence, in a matter unknown to me, but touching the peace of our lord the King, and the well-being of his subjects. Three times I have met our lord the King, but he hath said nothing about his peace, and only held it towards me, and every day, save Sunday, I have walked up and down the great hall of Westminster, all the business part of the day, expecting to be called upon, yet no one hath called upon me. And now I desire to ask your worship, whether I may go home again?'

'Well, done, John,' replied his lordship, while I was panting with all this speech; 'I will go bail for thee, John, thou hast never made such a long speech before; and thou art a spunky Briton, or thou couldst not have made it now. I remember the matter well, and I myself will attend to it, although it arose before my time'—he was but newly Chief Justice—'but I cannot take it now, John. There is no fear of losing thee, John, any more than the Tower of London. I grieve for His Majesty's exchequer, after keeping thee two months or more.'

'Nay, my lord, I crave your pardon. My mother hath been keeping me. Not a groat have I received.'

'Spank, is it so?' his lordship cried, in a voice that shook the cobwebs, and the frown on his brow shook the hearts of men, and mine as much as the rest of them,—'Spank, is His Majesty come to this, that he starves his own approvers?'

'My lord, my lord,' whispered Mr. Spank, the chief-officer of evidence, 'the thing hath been overlooked, my lord, among such grave matters of treason.'

'I will overlook thy head, foul Spank, on a spike from Temple Bar, if ever I hear of the like again. Vile varlet, what art thou paid for? Thou hast swindled the money thyself, foul Spank; I know thee, though thou art new to me. Bitter is the day for thee that ever I came across thee. Answer me not—one word more and I will have thee on a hurdle.' And he swung himself to and fro on his bench, with both hands on his knees; and every man waited to let it pass, knowing better than to speak to him.

'John Ridd,' said the Lord Chief Justice, at last recovering a sort of dignity, yet daring Spank from the corners of his eyes to do so much as look at him, 'thou hast been shamefully used, John Ridd. Answer me not boy; not a word; but go to Master Spank, and let me know how he behaves to thee;' here he made a glance at Spank, which was worth at least ten pounds to me; 'be thou here again to-morrow, and before any other case is taken, I will see justice done to thee. Now be off boy; thy name is Ridd, and we are well rid of thee.'

I was only too glad to go, after all this tempest; as you may well suppose. For if ever I saw a man's eyes become two holes for the devil to glare from, I saw it that day; and the eyes were those of the Lord Chief Justice Jeffreys.

Mr. Spank was in the lobby before me, and before I had recovered myself—for I was vexed with my own terror—he came up sidling and fawning to me, with a heavy bag of yellow leather.

'Good Master Ridd, take it all, take it all, and say a good word for me to his lordship. He hath taken a strange fancy to thee; and thou must make the most of it. We never saw man meet him eye to eye so, and yet not contradict him, and that is just what he loveth. Abide in London, Master Ridd, and he will make thy fortune. His joke upon thy name proves that. And I pray you remember, Master Ridd, that the Spanks are sixteen in family.'

But I would not take the bag from him, regarding it as a sort of bribe to pay me such a lump of money, without so much as asking how great had been my expenses. Therefore I only told him that if he would kindly keep the cash for me until the morrow, I would spend the rest of the day in counting (which always is sore work with me) how much it had stood me in board and lodging, since Master Stickles had rendered me up; for until that time he had borne my expenses. In the morning I would give Mr. Spank a memorandum, duly signed, and attested by my landlord, including the breakfast of that day, and in exchange for this I would take the exact amount from the yellow bag, and be very thankful for it.

'If that is thy way of using opportunity,' said Spank, looking at me with some contempt, 'thou wilt never thrive in these times, my lad. Even the Lord Chief Justice can be little help to thee; unless thou knowest better than that how to help thyself'

It mattered not to me. The word 'approver' stuck in my gorge, as used by the Lord Chief Justice; for we looked upon an approver as a very low thing indeed. I would rather pay for every breakfast, and even every dinner, eaten by me since here I came, than take money as an approver. And indeed I was much disappointed at being taken in that light, having understood that I was sent for as a trusty subject, and humble friend of His Majesty.

In the morning I met Mr. Spank waiting for me at the entrance, and very desirous to see me. I showed him my bill, made out in fair copy, and he laughed at it, and said, 'Take it twice over, Master Ridd; once for thine own sake, and once for His Majesty's; as all his loyal tradesmen do, when they can get any. His Majesty knows and is proud of it, for it shows their love of his countenance; and he says, "bis dat qui cito dat," then how can I grumble at giving twice, when I give so slowly?'

'Nay, I will take it but once,' I said; 'if His Majesty loves to be robbed, he need not lack of his desire, while the Spanks are sixteen in family.'

The clerk smiled cheerfully at this, being proud of his children's ability; and then having paid my account, he whispered,—

'He is all alone this morning, John, and in rare good humour. He hath been promised the handling of poor Master Algernon Sidney, and he says he will soon make republic of him; for his state shall shortly be headless. He is chuckling over his joke, like a pig with a nut; and that always makes him pleasant. John Ridd, my lord!' With that he swung up the curtain bravely, and according to special orders, I stood, face to face, and alone with Judge Jeffreys.

Chapter XXVI John Is Drained and Cast Aside

His lordship was busy with some letters, and did not look up for a minute or two, although he knew that I was there. Meanwhile I stood waiting to make my bow; afraid to begin upon him, and wondering at his great bull-head. Then he closed his letters, well-pleased with their import, and fixed his bold broad stare on me, as if I were an oyster opened, and he would know how fresh I was.

'May it please your worship,' I said, 'here I am according to order, awaiting your good pleasure.'

'Thou art made to weight, John, more than order. How much dost thou tip the scales to?'

'Only twelvescore pounds, my lord, when I be in wrestling trim. And sure I must have lost weight here, fretting so long in London.'

'Ha, ha! Much fret is there in thee! Hath His Majesty seen thee?'

'Yes, my lord, twice or even thrice; and he made some jest concerning me.'

'A very bad one, I doubt not. His humour is not so dainty as mine, but apt to be coarse and unmannerly. Now John, or Jack, by the look of thee, thou art more used to be called.'

'Yes, your worship, when I am with old Molly and Betty Muxworthy.'

'Peace, thou forward varlet! There is a deal too much of thee. We shall have to try short commons with thee, and thou art a very long common. Ha, ha! Where is that rogue Spank? Spank must hear that by-and-by. It is beyond thy great thick head, Jack.'

'Not so, my lord; I have been at school, and had very bad jokes made upon me.'

'Ha, ha! It hath hit thee hard. And faith, it would be hard to miss thee, even with harpoon. And thou lookest like to blubber, now. Capital, in faith! I have thee on every side, Jack, and thy sides are manifold; many-folded at any rate. Thou shalt have double expenses, Jack, for the wit thou hast provoked in me.'

'Heavy goods lack heavy payment, is a proverb down our way, my lord.'

'Ah, I hurt thee, I hurt thee, Jack. The harpoon hath no tickle for thee. Now, Jack Whale, having hauled thee hard, we will proceed to examine thee.' Here all his manner was changed, and he looked with his heavy brows bent upon me, as if he had never laughed in his life, and would allow none else to do so.

'I am ready to answer, my lord,' I replied, 'if he asks me nought beyond my knowledge, or beyond my honour.'

'Hadst better answer me everything, lump. What hast thou to do with honour? Now is there in thy neighbourhood a certain nest of robbers, miscreants, and outlaws, whom all men fear to handle?'

'Yes, my lord. At least, I believe some of them be robbers, and all of them are outlaws.'

'And what is your high sheriff about, that he doth not hang them all? Or send them up for me to hang, without more to do about them?'

'I reckon that he is afraid, my lord; it is not safe to meddle with them. They are of good birth, and reckless; and their place is very strong.'

'Good birth! What was Lord Russell of, Lord Essex, and this Sidney? 'Tis the surest heirship to the block to be the chip of a good one. What is the name of this pestilent race, and how many of them are there?'

'They are the Doones of Bagworthy forest, may it please your worship. And we reckon there be about forty of them, beside the women and children.'

'Forty Doones, all forty thieves! and women and children! Thunder of God! How long have they been there then?'

'They may have been there thirty years, my lord; and indeed they may have been forty. Before the great war broke out they came, longer back than I can remember.'

'Ay, long before thou wast born, John. Good, thou speakest plainly. Woe betide a liar, whenso I get hold of him. Ye want me on the Western Circuit; by God, and ye shall have me, when London traitors are spun and swung. There is a family called De Whichehalse living very nigh thee, John?'

This he said in a sudden manner, as if to take me off my guard, and fixed his great thick eyes on me. And in truth I was much astonished.

'Yes, my lord, there is. At least, not so very far from us. Baron de Whichehalse, of Ley Manor.'

'Baron, ha! of the Exchequer—eh, lad? And taketh dues instead of His Majesty. Somewhat which halts there ought to come a little further, I trow. It shall be seen to, as well as the witch which makes it so to halt. Riotous knaves in West England, drunken outlaws, you shall dance, if ever I play pipe for you. John Ridd, I will come to Oare parish, and rout out the Oare of Babylon.'

'Although your worship is so learned,' I answered seeing that now he was beginning to make things uneasy; 'your worship, though being Chief Justice, does little justice to us. We are downright good and loyal folk; and I have not seen, since here I came to this great town of London, any who may better us, or even come anigh us, in honesty, and goodness, and duty to our neighbours. For we are very quiet folk, not prating our own virtues—'

'Enough, good John, enough! Knowest thou not that modesty is the maidenhood of virtue, lost even by her own approval? Now hast thou ever heard or thought that De Whichehalse is in league with the Doones of Bagworthy?'

Saying these words rather slowly, he skewered his great eyes into mine, so that I could not think at all, neither look at him, nor yet away. The idea was so new to me that it set my wits all wandering; and looking into me, he saw that I was groping for the truth.

'John Ridd, thine eyes are enough for me. I see thou hast never dreamed of it. Now hast thou ever seen a man whose name is Thomas Faggus?'

'Yes, sir, many and many a time. He is my own worthy cousin; and I fear he that hath intentions'—here I stopped, having no right there to speak about our Annie.

'Tom Faggus is a good man,' he said; and his great square face had a smile which showed me he had met my cousin; 'Master Faggus hath made mistakes as to the title to property, as lawyers oftentimes may do; but take him all for all, he is a thoroughly straightforward man; presents his bill, and has it paid, and makes no charge for drawing it. Nevertheless, we must tax his costs, as of any other solicitor.'

'To be sure, to be sure, my lord!' was all that I could say, not understanding what all this meant.

'I fear he will come to the gallows,' said the Lord Chief Justice, sinking his voice below the echoes; 'tell him this from me, Jack. He shall never be condemned before me; but I cannot be everywhere, and some of our Justices may keep short memory of his dinners. Tell him to change his name, turn parson, or do something else, to make it wrong to hang him. Parson is the best thing, he hath such command of features, and he might take his tithes on horseback. Now a few more things, John Ridd; and for the present I have done with thee.'

All my heart leaped up at this, to get away from London so: and yet I could hardly trust to it.

'Is there any sound round your way of disaffection to His Majesty, His most gracious Majesty?'

'No, my lord: no sign whatever. We pray for him in church perhaps, and we talk about him afterwards, hoping it may do him good, as it is intended. But after that we have naught to say, not knowing much about him—at least till I get home again.'

'That is as it should be, John. And the less you say the better. But I have heard of things in Taunton, and even nearer to you in Dulverton, and even nigher still upon Exmoor; things which are of the pillory kind, and even more of the gallows. I see that you know naught of them. Nevertheless, it will not be long before all England hears of them. Now, John, I have taken a liking to thee, for never man told me the truth, without fear or favour, more thoroughly and truly than thou hast done. Keep thou clear of this, my son. It will come to nothing; yet many shall swing high for it. Even I could not save thee, John Ridd, if thou wert mixed in this affair. Keep from the Doones, keep from De Whichehalse, keep from everything which leads beyond the sight of thy knowledge. I meant to use thee as my tool; but I see thou art too honest and simple. I will send a sharper down; but never let me find thee, John, either a tool for the other side, or a tube for my words to pass through.'

Here the Lord Justice gave me such a glare that I wished myself well rid of him, though thankful for his warnings; and seeing how he had made upon me a long abiding mark of fear, he smiled again in a jocular manner, and said,—

'Now, get thee gone, Jack. I shall remember thee; and I trow, thou wilt'st not for many a day forget me.'

'My lord, I was never so glad to go; for the hay must be in, and the ricks unthatched, and none of them can make spars like me, and two men to twist every hay-rope, and mother thinking it all right, and listening right and left to lies, and cheated at every pig she kills, and even the skins of the sheep to go—'

'John Ridd, I thought none could come nigh your folk in honesty, and goodness, and duty to their neighbours!'

'Sure enough, my lord; but by our folk, I mean ourselves, not the men nor women neither—'

'That will do, John. Go thy way. Not men, nor women neither, are better than they need be.'

I wished to set this matter right; but his worship would not hear me, and only drove me out of court, saying that men were thieves and liars, no more in one place than another, but all alike all over the world, and women not far behind them. It was not for me to dispute this point (though I was not yet persuaded of it), both because my lord was a Judge, and must know more about it, and also that being a man myself I might seem to be defending myself in an unbecoming manner. Therefore I made a low bow, and went; in doubt as to which had the right of it.

But though he had so far dismissed me, I was not yet quite free to go, inasmuch as I had not money enough to take me all the way to Oare, unless indeed I should go afoot, and beg my sustenance by the way, which seemed to be below me. Therefore I got my few clothes packed, and my few debts paid, all ready to start in half an hour, if only they would give me enough to set out upon the road with. For I doubted not, being young and strong, that I could walk from London to Oare in ten days or in twelve at most, which was not much longer than horse-work; only I had been a fool, as you will say when you hear it. For after receiving from Master Spank the amount of the bill which I had delivered—less indeed by fifty shillings than the money my mother had given me, for I had spent fifty shillings, and more, in seeing the town and treating people, which I could not charge to His Majesty—I had first paid all my debts thereout, which were not very many, and then supposing myself to be an established creditor of the Treasury for my coming needs, and already scenting the country air, and foreseeing the joy of my mother, what had I done but spent half my balance, ay and more than three-quarters of it, upon presents for mother, and Annie, and Lizzie, John Fry, and his wife, and Betty Muxworthy, Bill Dadds, Jim Slocombe, and, in a word, half of the rest of the people at Oare, including all the Snowe family, who must have things good and handsome? And if I must while I am about it, hide nothing from those who read me, I had actually bought for Lorna a thing the price of which quite frightened me, till the shopkeeper said it was nothing at all, and that no young man, with a lady to love him, could dare to offer her rubbish, such as the Jew sold across the way. Now the mere idea of beautiful Lorna ever loving me, which he talked about as patly (though of course I never mentioned her) as if it were a settled thing, and he knew all about it, that mere idea so drove me abroad, that if he had asked three times as much, I could never have counted the money.

Now in all this I was a fool of course—not for remembering my friends and neighbours, which a man has a right to do, and indeed is bound to do, when he comes from London—but for not being certified first what cash I had to go on with. And to my great amazement, when I went with another bill for the victuals of only three days more, and a week's expense on the homeward road reckoned very narrowly, Master Spank not only refused to grant me any interview, but sent me out a piece of blue paper, looking like a butcher's ticket, and bearing these words and no more, 'John Ridd, go to the devil. He who will not when he may, when he will, he shall have nay.' From this I concluded that I had lost favour in the sight of Chief Justice Jeffreys. Perhaps because my evidence had not proved of any value! perhaps because he meant to let the matter lie, till cast on him.

Anyhow, it was a reason of much grief, and some anger to me, and very great anxiety, disappointment, and suspense. For here was the time of the hay gone past, and the harvest of small corn coming on, and the trout now rising at the yellow Sally, and the blackbirds eating our white-heart cherries (I was sure, though I could not see them), and who was to do any good for mother, or stop her from weeping continually? And more than this, what was become of Lorna? Perhaps she had cast me away altogether, as a flouter and a changeling; perhaps she had drowned herself in the black well; perhaps (and that was worst of all) she was even married, child as she was, to that vile Carver Doone, if the Doones ever cared about marrying! That last thought sent me down at once to watch for Mr. Spank again, resolved that if I could catch him, spank him I would to a pretty good tune, although sixteen in family.

However, there was no such thing as to find him; and the usher vowed (having orders I doubt) that he was gone to the sea for the good of his health, having sadly overworked himself; and that none but a poor devil like himself, who never had handling of money, would stay in London this foul, hot weather; which was likely to bring the plague with it. Here was another new terror for me, who had heard of the plagues of London, and the horrible things that happened; and so going back to my lodgings at once, I opened my clothes and sought for spots, especially as being so long at a hairy fellmonger's; but finding none, I fell down and thanked God for that same, and vowed to start for Oare to-morrow, with my carbine loaded, come weal come woe, come sun come shower; though all the parish should laugh at me, for begging my way home again, after the brave things said of my going, as if I had been the King's cousin.

But I was saved in some degree from this lowering of my pride, and what mattered more, of mother's; for going to buy with my last crown-piece (after all demands were paid) a little shot and powder, more needful on the road almost than even shoes or victuals, at the corner of the street I met my good friend Jeremy Stickles, newly come in search of me. I took him back to my little room—mine at least till to-morrow morning—and told him all my story, and how much I felt aggrieved by it. But he surprised me very much, by showing no surprise at all.

'It is the way of the world, Jack. They have gotten all they can from thee, and why should they feed thee further? We feed not a dead pig, I trow, but baste him well with brine and rue. Nay, we do not victual him upon the day of killing; which they have done to thee. Thou art a lucky man, John; thou hast gotten one day's wages, or at any rate half a day, after thy work was rendered. God have mercy on me, John! The things I see are manifold; and so is my regard of them. What use to insist on this, or make a special point of that, or hold by something said of old, when a different mood was on? I tell thee, Jack, all men are liars; and he is the least one who presses not too hard on them for lying.'

This was all quite dark to me, for I never looked at things like that, and never would own myself a liar, not at least to other people, nor even to myself, although I might to God sometimes, when trouble was upon me. And if it comes to that, no man has any right to be called a 'liar' for smoothing over things unwitting, through duty to his neighbour.

'Five pounds thou shalt have, Jack,' said Jeremy Stickles suddenly, while I was all abroad with myself as to being a liar or not; 'five pounds, and I will take my chance of wringing it from that great rogue Spank. Ten I would have made it, John, but for bad luck lately. Put back your bits of paper, lad; I will have no acknowledgment. John Ridd, no nonsense with me!'

For I was ready to kiss his hand, to think that any man in London (the meanest and most suspicious place, upon all God's earth) should trust me with five pounds, without even a receipt for it! It overcame me so that I sobbed; for, after all, though big in body, I am but a child at heart. It was not the five pounds that moved me, but the way of giving it; and after so much bitter talk, the great trust in my goodness.

Chapter XXVII Home Again at Last

It was the beginning of wheat-harvest, when I came to Dunster town, having walked all the way from London, and being somewhat footsore. For though five pounds was enough to keep me in food and lodging upon the road, and leave me many a shilling to give to far poorer travellers, it would have been nothing for horse-hire, as I knew too well by the prices Jeremy Stickles had paid upon our way to London. Now I never saw a prettier town than Dunster looked that evening; for sooth to say, I had almost lost all hope of reaching it that night, although the castle was long in view. But being once there, my troubles were gone, at least as regarded wayfaring; for mother's cousin, the worthy tanner (with whom we had slept on the way to London), was in such indignation at the plight in which I came back to him, afoot, and weary, and almost shoeless—not to speak of upper things—that he swore then, by the mercy of God, that if the schemes abrewing round him, against those bloody Papists, should come to any head or shape, and show good chance of succeeding, he would risk a thousand pounds, as though it were a penny.

I told him not to do it, because I had heard otherwise, but was not at liberty to tell one-tenth of what I knew, and indeed had seen in London town. But of this he took no heed, because I only nodded at him; and he could not make it out. For it takes an old man, or at least a middle-aged one, to nod and wink, with any power on the brains of other men. However, I think I made him know that the bad state in which I came to his town, and the great shame I had wrought for him among the folk round the card-table at the Luttrell Arms, was not to be, even there, attributed to King Charles the Second, nor even to his counsellors, but to my own speed of travelling, which had beat post-horses. For being much distraught in mind, and desperate in body, I had made all the way from London to Dunster in six days, and no more. It may be one hundred and seventy miles, I cannot tell to a furlong or two, especially as I lost my way more than a dozen times; but at any rate there in six days I was, and most kindly they received me. The tanner had some excellent daughters, I forget how many; very pretty damsels, and well set up, and able to make good pastry. But though they asked me many questions, and made a sort of lord of me, and offered to darn my stockings (which in truth required it), I fell asleep in the midst of them, although I would not acknowledge it; and they said, 'Poor cousin! he is weary', and led me to a blessed bed, and kissed me all round like swan's down.

In the morning all the Exmoor hills, the thought of which had frightened me at the end of each day's travel, seemed no more than bushels to me, as I looked forth the bedroom window, and thanked God for the sight of them. And even so, I had not to climb them, at least by my own labour. For my most worthy uncle (as we oft call a parent's cousin), finding it impossible to keep me for the day, and owning indeed that I was right in hastening to my mother, vowed that walk I should not, even though he lost his Saturday hides from Minehead and from Watchett. Accordingly he sent me forth on the very strongest nag he had, and the maidens came to wish me God-speed, and kissed their hands at the doorway. It made me proud and glad to think that after seeing so much of the world, and having held my own with it, I was come once more among my own people, and found them kinder, and more warm-hearted, ay and better looking too, than almost any I had happened upon in the mighty city of London.

But how shall I tell you the things I felt, and the swelling of my heart within me, as I drew nearer, and more near, to the place of all I loved and owned, to the haunt of every warm remembrance, the nest of all the fledgling hopes—in a word, to home? The first sheep I beheld on the moor with a great red J.R. on his side (for mother would have them marked with my name, instead of her own as they should have been), I do assure you my spirit leaped, and all my sight came to my eyes. I shouted out, 'Jem, boy!'—for that was his name, and a rare hand he was at fighting—and he knew me in spite of the stranger horse; and I leaned over and stroked his head, and swore he should never be mutton. And when I was passed he set off at full gallop, to call the rest of the J.R.'s together, and tell them young master was come home at last.

But bless your heart, and my own as well, it would take me all the afternoon to lay before you one-tenth of the things which came home to me in that one half-hour, as the sun was sinking, in the real way he ought to sink. I touched my horse with no spur nor whip, feeling that my slow wits would go, if the sights came too fast over them. Here was the pool where we washed the sheep, and there was the hollow that oozed away, where I had shot three wild ducks. Here was the peat-rick that hid my dinner, when I could not go home for it, and there was the bush with the thyme growing round it, where Annie had found a great swarm of our bees. And now was the corner of the dry stone wall, where the moor gave over in earnest, and the partridges whisked from it into the corn lands, and called that their supper was ready, and looked at our house and the ricks as they ran, and would wait for that comfort till winter.

And there I saw—but let me go—Annie was too much for me. She nearly pulled me off my horse, and kissed the very mouth of the carbine.

"I knew you would come. Oh John! Oh John! I have waited here every Saturday night; and I saw you for the last mile or more, but I would not come round the corner, for fear that I should cry, John, and then not cry when I got you. Now I may cry as much as I like, and you need not try to stop me, John, because I am so happy. But you mustn't cry yourself, John; what will mother think of you? She will be so jealous of me.'

What mother thought I cannot tell; and indeed I doubt if she thought at all for more than half an hour, but only managed to hold me tight, and cry, and thank God now and then, but with some fear of His taking me, if she should be too grateful. Moreover she thought it was my own doing, and I ought to have the credit of it, and she even came down very sharply upon John's wife, Mrs. Fry, for saying that we must not be too proud, for all of it was the Lord's doing. However, dear mother was ashamed of that afterwards, and asked Mrs. Fry's humble pardon; and perhaps I ought not to have mentioned it.

Old Smiler had told them that I was coming—all the rest, I mean, except Annie—for having escaped from his halter-ring, he was come out to graze in the lane a bit; when what should he see but a strange horse coming with young master and mistress upon him, for Annie must needs get up behind me, there being only sheep to look at her. Then Smiler gave us a stare and a neigh, with his tail quite stiff with amazement, and then (whether in joy or through indignation) he flung up his hind feet and galloped straight home, and set every dog wild with barking.

Now, methinks, quite enough has been said concerning this mighty return of the young John Ridd (which was known up at Cosgate that evening), and feeling that I cannot describe it, how can I hope that any one else will labour to imagine it, even of the few who are able? For very few can have travelled so far, unless indeed they whose trade it is, or very unsettled people. And even of those who have done so, not one in a hundred can have such a home as I had to come home to.

Mother wept again, with grief and some wrath, and so did Annie also, and even little Eliza, and all were unsettled in loyalty, and talked about a republic, when I told them how I had been left without money for travelling homeward, and expected to have to beg my way, which Farmer Snowe would have heard of. And though I could see they were disappointed at my failure of any promotion, they all declared how glad they were, and how much better they liked me to be no more than what they were accustomed to. At least, my mother and Annie said so, without waiting to hear any more; but Lizzie did not answer to it, until I had opened my bag and shown the beautiful present I had for her. And then she kissed me, almost like Annie, and vowed that she thought very little of captains.

For Lizzie's present was the best of all, I mean, of course, except Lorna's (which I carried in my breast all the way, hoping that it might make her love me, from having lain so long, close to my heart). For I had brought Lizzie something dear, and a precious heavy book it was, and much beyond my understanding; whereas I knew well that to both the others my gifts would be dear, for mine own sake. And happier people could not be found than the whole of us were that evening.

Chapter XXVIII John Has Hope of Lorna

Much as I longed to know more about Lorna, and though all my heart was yearning, I could not reconcile it yet with my duty to mother and Annie, to leave them on the following day, which happened to be a Sunday. For lo, before breakfast was out of our mouths, there came all the men of the farm, and their wives, and even the two crow-boys, dressed as if going to Barnstaple fair, to inquire how Master John was, and whether it was true that the King had made him one of his body-guard; and if so, what was to be done with the belt for the championship of the West-Counties wrestling, which I had held now for a year or more, and none were ready to challenge it. Strange to say, this last point seemed the most important of all to them; and none asked who was to manage the farm, or answer for their wages; but all asked who was to wear the belt.

To this I replied, after shaking hands twice over all round with all of them, that I meant to wear the belt myself, for the honour of Oare parish, so long as ever God gave me strength and health to meet all-comers; for I had never been asked to be body-guard, and if asked I would never have done it. Some of them cried that the King must be mazed, not to keep me for his protection, in these violent times of Popery. I could have told them that the King was not in the least afraid of Papists, but on the contrary, very fond of them; however, I held my tongue, remembering what Judge Jeffreys bade me.

In church, the whole congregation, man, woman, and child (except, indeed, the Snowe girls, who only looked when I was not watching), turned on me with one accord, and stared so steadfastly, to get some reflection of the King from me, that they forgot the time to kneel down and the parson was forced to speak to them. If I coughed, or moved my book, or bowed, or even said 'Amen,' glances were exchanged which meant—'That he hath learned in London town, and most likely from His Majesty.'

However, all this went off in time, and people became even angry with me for not being sharper (as they said), or smarter, or a whit more fashionable, for all the great company I had seen, and all the wondrous things wasted upon me.

But though I may have been none the wiser by reason of my stay in London, at any rate I was much the better in virtue of coming home again. For now I had learned the joy of quiet, and the gratitude for good things round us, and the love we owe to others (even those who must be kind), for their indulgence to us. All this, before my journey, had been too much as a matter of course to me; but having missed it now I knew that it was a gift, and might be lost. Moreover, I had pined so much, in the dust and heat of that great town, for trees, and fields, and running waters, and the sounds of country life, and the air of country winds, that never more could I grow weary of those soft enjoyments; or at least I thought so then.

To awake as the summer sun came slanting over the hill-tops, with hope on every beam adance to the laughter of the morning; to see the leaves across the window ruffling on the fresh new air, and the tendrils of the powdery vine turning from their beaded sleep. Then the lustrous meadows far beyond the thatch of the garden-wall, yet seen beneath the hanging scollops of the walnut-tree, all awaking, dressed in pearl, all amazed at their own glistening, like a maid at her own ideas. Down them troop the lowing kine, walking each with a step of character (even as men and women do), yet all alike with toss of horns, and spread of udders ready. From them without a word, we turn to the farm-yard proper, seen on the right, and dryly strawed from the petty rush of the pitch-paved runnel. Round it stand the snug out-buildings, barn, corn-chamber, cider-press, stables, with a blinker'd horse in every doorway munching, while his driver tightens buckles, whistles and looks down the lane, dallying to begin his labour till the milkmaids be gone by. Here the cock comes forth at last;—where has he been lingering?—eggs may tell to-morrow—he claps his wings and shouts 'cock-a-doodle'; and no other cock dare look at him. Two or three go sidling off, waiting till their spurs be grown; and then the crowd of partlets comes, chattering how their lord has dreamed, and crowed at two in the morning, and praying that the old brown rat would only dare to face him. But while the cock is crowing still, and the pullet world admiring him, who comes up but the old turkey-cock, with all his family round him. Then the geese at the lower end begin to thrust their breasts out, and mum their down-bits, and look at the gander and scream shrill joy for the conflict; while the ducks in pond show nothing but tail, in proof of their strict neutrality.

While yet we dread for the coming event, and the fight which would jar on the morning, behold the grandmother of sows, gruffly grunting right and left with muzzle which no ring may tame (not being matrimonial), hulks across between the two, moving all each side at once, and then all of the other side as if she were chined down the middle, and afraid of spilling the salt from her. As this mighty view of lard hides each combatant from the other, gladly each retires and boasts how he would have slain his neighbour, but that old sow drove the other away, and no wonder he was afraid of her, after all the chicks she had eaten.

And so it goes on; and so the sun comes, stronger from his drink of dew; and the cattle in the byres, and the horses from the stable, and the men from cottage-door, each has had his rest and food, all smell alike of hay and straw, and every one must hie to work, be it drag, or draw, or delve.

So thought I on the Monday morning; while my own work lay before me, and I was plotting how to quit it, void of harm to every one, and let my love have work a little—hardest perhaps of all work, and yet as sure as sunrise. I knew that my first day's task on the farm would be strictly watched by every one, even by my gentle mother, to see what I had learned in London. But could I let still another day pass, for Lorna to think me faithless?

I felt much inclined to tell dear mother all about Lorna, and how I loved her, yet had no hope of winning her. Often and often, I had longed to do this, and have done with it. But the thought of my father's terrible death, at the hands of the Doones, prevented me. And it seemed to me foolish and mean to grieve mother, without any chance of my suit ever speeding. If once Lorna loved me, my mother should know it; and it would be the greatest happiness to me to have no concealment from her, though at first she was sure to grieve terribly. But I saw no more chance of Lorna loving me, than of the man in the moon coming down; or rather of the moon coming down to the man, as related in old mythology.

Now the merriment of the small birds, and the clear voice of the waters, and the lowing of cattle in meadows, and the view of no houses (except just our own and a neighbour's), and the knowledge of everybody around, their kindness of heart and simplicity, and love of their neighbour's doings,—all these could not help or please me at all, and many of them were much against me, in my secret depth of longing and dark tumult of the mind. Many people may think me foolish, especially after coming from London, where many nice maids looked at me (on account of my bulk and stature), and I might have been fitted up with a sweetheart, in spite of my west-country twang, and the smallness of my purse; if only I had said the word. But nay; I have contempt for a man whose heart is like a shirt-stud (such as I saw in London cards), fitted into one to-day, sitting bravely on the breast; plucked out on the morrow morn, and the place that knew it, gone.

Now, what did I do but take my chance; reckless whether any one heeded me or not, only craving Lorna's heed, and time for ten words to her. Therefore I left the men of the farm as far away as might be, after making them work with me (which no man round our parts could do, to his own satisfaction), and then knowing them to be well weary, very unlike to follow me—and still more unlike to tell of me, for each had his London present—I strode right away, in good trust of my speed, without any more misgivings; but resolved to face the worst of it, and to try to be home for supper.

And first I went, I know not why, to the crest of the broken highland, whence I had agreed to watch for any mark or signal. And sure enough at last I saw (when it was too late to see) that the white stone had been covered over with a cloth or mantle,—the sign that something had arisen to make Lorna want me. For a moment I stood amazed at my evil fortune; that I should be too late, in the very thing of all things on which my heart was set! Then after eyeing sorrowfully every crick and cranny to be sure that not a single flutter of my love was visible, off I set, with small respect either for my knees or neck, to make the round of the outer cliffs, and come up my old access.

Nothing could stop me; it was not long, although to me it seemed an age, before I stood in the niche of rock at the head of the slippery watercourse, and gazed into the quiet glen, where my foolish heart was dwelling. Notwithstanding doubts of right, notwithstanding sense of duty, and despite all manly striving, and the great love of my home, there my heart was ever dwelling, knowing what a fool it was, and content to know it.

Many birds came twittering round me in the gold of August; many trees showed twinkling beauty, as the sun went lower; and the lines of water fell, from wrinkles into dimples. Little heeding, there I crouched; though with sense of everything that afterwards should move me, like a picture or a dream; and everything went by me softly, while my heart was gazing.

At last, a little figure came, not insignificant (I mean), but looking very light and slender in the moving shadows, gently here and softly there, as if vague of purpose, with a gloss of tender movement, in and out the wealth of trees, and liberty of the meadow. Who was I to crouch, or doubt, or look at her from a distance; what matter if they killed me now, and one tear came to bury me? Therefore I rushed out at once, as if shot-guns were unknown yet; not from any real courage, but from prisoned love burst forth.

I know not whether my own Lorna was afraid of what I looked, or what I might say to her, or of her own thoughts of me; all I know is that she looked frightened, when I hoped for gladness. Perhaps the power of my joy was more than maiden liked to own, or in any way to answer to; and to tell the truth, it seemed as if I might now forget myself; while she would take good care of it. This makes a man grow thoughtful; unless, as some low fellows do, he believe all women hypocrites.

Therefore I went slowly towards her, taken back in my impulse; and said all I could come to say, with some distress in doing it.

'Mistress Lorna, I had hope that you were in need of me.'

'Oh, yes; but that was long ago; two months ago, or more, sir.' And saying this she looked away, as if it all were over. But I was now so dazed and frightened, that it took my breath away, and I could not answer, feeling sure that I was robbed and some one else had won her. And I tried to turn away, without another word, and go.

But I could not help one stupid sob, though mad with myself for allowing it, but it came too sharp for pride to stay it, and it told a world of things. Lorna heard it, and ran to me, with her bright eyes full of wonder, pity, and great kindness, as if amazed that I had more than a simple liking for her. Then she held out both hands to me; and I took and looked at them.

'Master Ridd, I did not mean,' she whispered, very softly, 'I did not mean to vex you.'

'If you would be loath to vex me, none else in this world can do it,' I answered out of my great love, but fearing yet to look at her, mine eyes not being strong enough.

'Come away from this bright place,' she answered, trembling in her turn; 'I am watched and spied of late. Come beneath the shadows, John.'

I would have leaped into the valley of the shadow of death (as described by the late John Bunyan), only to hear her call me 'John'; though Apollyon were lurking there, and Despair should lock me in.

She stole across the silent grass; but I strode hotly after her; fear was all beyond me now, except the fear of losing her. I could not but behold her manner, as she went before me, all her grace, and lovely sweetness, and her sense of what she was.

She led me to her own rich bower, which I told of once before; and if in spring it were a sight, what was it in summer glory? But although my mind had notice of its fairness and its wonder, not a heed my heart took of it, neither dwelt it in my presence more than flowing water. All that in my presence dwelt, all that in my heart was felt, was the maiden moving gently, and afraid to look at me.

For now the power of my love was abiding on her, new to her, unknown to her; not a thing to speak about, nor even to think clearly; only just to feel and wonder, with a pain of sweetness. She could look at me no more, neither could she look away, with a studied manner—only to let fall her eyes, and blush, and be put out with me, and still more with herself.

I left her quite alone; though close, though tingling to have hold of her. Even her right hand was dropped and lay among the mosses. Neither did I try to steal one glimpse below her eyelids. Life and death to me were hanging on the first glance I should win; yet I let it be so.

After long or short—I know not, yet ere I was weary, ere I yet began to think or wish for any answer—Lorna slowly raised her eyelids, with a gleam of dew below them, and looked at me doubtfully. Any look with so much in it never met my gaze before.

'Darling, do you love me?' was all that I could say to her.

'Yes, I like you very much,' she answered, with her eyes gone from me, and her dark hair falling over, so as not to show me things.

'But do you love me, Lorna, Lorna; do you love me more than all the world?'

'No, to be sure not. Now why should I?'

'In truth, I know not why you should. Only I hoped that you did, Lorna. Either love me not at all, or as I love you for ever.'

'John I love you very much; and I would not grieve you. You are the bravest, and the kindest, and the simplest of all men—I mean of all people—I like you very much, Master Ridd, and I think of you almost every day.'

'That will not do for me, Lorna. Not almost every day I think, but every instant of my life, of you. For you I would give up my home, my love of all the world beside, my duty to my dearest ones, for you I would give up my life, and hope of life beyond it. Do you love me so?'

'Not by any means,' said Lorna; 'no, I like you very much, when you do not talk so wildly; and I like to see you come as if you would fill our valley up, and I like to think that even Carver would be nothing in your hands—but as to liking you like that, what should make it likely? especially when I have made the signal, and for some two months or more you have never even answered it! If you like me so ferociously, why do you leave me for other people to do just as they like with me?'

'To do as they liked! Oh, Lorna, not to make you marry Carver?'

'No, Master Ridd, be not frightened so; it makes me fear to look at you.'

'But you have not married Carver yet? Say quick! Why keep me waiting so?'

'Of course I have not, Master Ridd. Should I be here if I had, think you, and allowing you to like me so, and to hold my hand, and make me laugh, as I declare you almost do sometimes? And at other times you frighten me.'

'Did they want you to marry Carver? Tell me all the truth of it.'

'Not yet, not yet. They are not half so impetuous as you are, John. I am only just seventeen, you know, and who is to think of marrying? But they wanted me to give my word, and be formally betrothed to him in the presence of my grandfather. It seems that something frightened them. There is a youth named Charleworth Doone, every one calls him "Charlie"; a headstrong and a gay young man, very gallant in his looks and manner; and my uncle, the Counsellor, chose to fancy that Charlie looked at me too much, coming by my grandfather's cottage.'

Here Lorna blushed so that I was frightened, and began to hate this Charlie more, a great deal more, than even Carver Doone.

'He had better not,' said I; 'I will fling him over it, if he dare. He shall see thee through the roof, Lorna, if at all he see thee.'

'Master Ridd, you are worse than Carver! I thought you were so kind-hearted. Well, they wanted me to promise, and even to swear a solemn oath (a thing I have never done in my life) that I would wed my eldest cousin, this same Carver Doone, who is twice as old as I am, being thirty-five and upwards. That was why I gave the token that I wished to see you, Master Ridd. They pointed out how much it was for the peace of all the family, and for mine own benefit; but I would not listen for a moment, though the Counsellor was most eloquent, and my grandfather begged me to consider, and Carver smiled his pleasantest, which is a truly frightful thing. Then both he and his crafty father were for using force with me; but Sir Ensor would not hear of it; and they have put off that extreme until he shall be past its knowledge, or, at least, beyond preventing it. And now I am watched, and spied, and followed, and half my little liberty seems to be taken from me. I could not be here speaking with you, even in my own nook and refuge, but for the aid, and skill, and courage of dear little Gwenny Carfax. She is now my chief reliance, and through her alone I hope to baffle all my enemies, since others have forsaken me.'

Tears of sorrow and reproach were lurking in her soft dark eyes, until in fewest words I told her that my seeming negligence was nothing but my bitter loss and wretched absence far away; of which I had so vainly striven to give any tidings without danger to her. When she heard all this, and saw what I had brought from London (which was nothing less than a ring of pearls with a sapphire in the midst of them, as pretty as could well be found), she let the gentle tears flow fast, and came and sat so close beside me, that I trembled like a folded sheep at the bleating of her lamb. But recovering comfort quickly, without more ado, I raised her left hand and observed it with a nice regard, wondering at the small blue veins, and curves, and tapering whiteness, and the points it finished with. My wonder seemed to please her much, herself so well accustomed to it, and not fond of watching it. And then, before she could say a word, or guess what I was up to, as quick as ever I turned hand in a bout of wrestling, on her finger was my ring—sapphire for the veins of blue, and pearls to match white fingers.

'Oh, you crafty Master Ridd!' said Lorna, looking up at me, and blushing now a far brighter blush than when she spoke of Charlie; 'I thought that you were much too simple ever to do this sort of thing. No wonder you can catch the fish, as when first I saw you.'

'Have I caught you, little fish? Or must all my life be spent in hopeless angling for you?'

'Neither one nor the other, John! You have not caught me yet altogether, though I like you dearly John; and if you will only keep away, I shall like you more and more. As for hopeless angling, John—that all others shall have until I tell you otherwise.'

With the large tears in her eyes—tears which seemed to me to rise partly from her want to love me with the power of my love—she put her pure bright lips, half smiling, half prone to reply to tears, against my forehead lined with trouble, doubt, and eager longing. And then she drew my ring from off that snowy twig her finger, and held it out to me; and then, seeing how my face was falling, thrice she touched it with her lips, and sweetly gave it back to me. 'John, I dare not take it now; else I should be cheating you. I will try to love you dearly, even as you deserve and wish. Keep it for me just till then. Something tells me I shall earn it in a very little time. Perhaps you will be sorry then, sorry when it is all too late, to be loved by such as I am.'

What could I do at her mournful tone, but kiss a thousand times the hand which she put up to warn me, and vow that I would rather die with one assurance of her love, than without it live for ever with all beside that the world could give? Upon this she looked so lovely, with her dark eyelashes trembling, and her soft eyes full of light, and the colour of clear sunrise mounting on her cheeks and brow, that I was forced to turn away, being overcome with beauty.

'Dearest darling, love of my life,' I whispered through her clouds of hair; 'how long must I wait to know, how long must I linger doubting whether you can ever stoop from your birth and wondrous beauty to a poor, coarse hind like me, an ignorant unlettered yeoman—'

'I will not have you revile yourself,' said Lorna, very tenderly—just as I had meant to make her. 'You are not rude and unlettered, John. You know a great deal more than I do; you have learned both Greek and Latin, as you told me long ago, and you have been at the very best school in the West of England. None of us but my grandfather, and the Counsellor (who is a great scholar), can compare with you in this. And though I have laughed at your manner of speech, I only laughed in fun, John; I never meant to vex you by it, nor knew that it had done so.'

'Naught you say can vex me, dear,' I answered, as she leaned towards me in her generous sorrow; 'unless you say "Begone, John Ridd; I love another more than you."'

'Then I shall never vex you, John. Never, I mean, by saying that. Now, John, if you please, be quiet—'

For I was carried away so much by hearing her calling me 'John' so often, and the music of her voice, and the way she bent toward me, and the shadow of soft weeping in the sunlight of her eyes, that some of my great hand was creeping in a manner not to be imagined, and far less explained, toward the lithesome, wholesome curving underneath her mantle-fold, and out of sight and harm, as I thought; not being her front waist. However, I was dashed with that, and pretended not to mean it; only to pluck some lady-fern, whose elegance did me no good.

'Now, John,' said Lorna, being so quick that not even a lover could cheat her, and observing my confusion more intently than she need have done. 'Master John Ridd, it is high time for you to go home to your mother. I love your mother very much from what you have told me about her, and I will not have her cheated.'

'If you truly love my mother,' said I, very craftily 'the only way to show it is by truly loving me.'

Upon that she laughed at me in the sweetest manner, and with such provoking ways, and such come-and-go of glances, and beginning of quick blushes, which she tried to laugh away, that I knew, as well as if she herself had told me, by some knowledge (void of reasoning, and the surer for it), I knew quite well, while all my heart was burning hot within me, and mine eyes were shy of hers, and her eyes were shy of mine; for certain and for ever this I knew—as in a glory—that Lorna Doone had now begun and would go on to love me.

Chapter XXIX Reaping Leads to Revelling

Although I was under interdict for two months from my darling—'one for your sake, one for mine,' she had whispered, with her head withdrawn, yet not so very far from me—lighter heart was not on Exmoor than I bore for half the time, and even for three quarters. For she was safe; I knew that daily by a mode of signals well-contrived between us now, on the strength of our experience. 'I have nothing now to fear, John,' she had said to me, as we parted; 'it is true that I am spied and watched, but Gwenny is too keen for them. While I have my grandfather to prevent all violence; and little Gwenny to keep watch on those who try to watch me; and you, above all others, John, ready at a moment, if the worst comes to the worst—this neglected Lorna Doone was never in such case before. Therefore do not squeeze my hand, John; I am safe without it, and you do not know your strength.'

Ah, I knew my strength right well. Hill and valley scarcely seemed to be step and landing for me; fiercest cattle I would play with, making them go backward, and afraid of hurting them, like John Fry with his terrier; even rooted trees seemed to me but as sticks I could smite down, except for my love of everything. The love of all things was upon me, and a softness to them all, and a sense of having something even such as they had.

Then the golden harvest came, waving on the broad hill-side, and nestling in the quiet nooks scooped from out the fringe of wood. A wealth of harvest such as never gladdened all our country-side since my father ceased to reap, and his sickle hung to rust. There had not been a man on Exmoor fit to work that reaping-hook since the time its owner fell, in the prime of life and strength, before a sterner reaper. But now I took it from the wall, where mother proudly stored it, while she watched me, hardly knowing whether she should smile or cry.

All the parish was assembled in our upper courtyard; for we were to open the harvest that year, as had been settled with Farmer Nicholas, and with Jasper Kebby, who held the third or little farm. We started in proper order, therefore, as our practice is: first, the parson Josiah Bowden, wearing his gown and cassock, with the parish Bible in his hand, and a sickle strapped behind him. As he strode along well and stoutly, being a man of substance, all our family came next, I leading mother with one hand, in the other bearing my father's hook, and with a loaf of our own bread and a keg of cider upon my back. Behind us Annie and Lizzie walked, wearing wreaths of corn-flowers, set out very prettily, such as mother would have worn if she had been a farmer's wife, instead of a farmer's widow. Being as she was, she had no adornment, except that her widow's hood was off, and her hair allowed to flow, as if she had been a maiden; and very rich bright hair it was, in spite of all her troubles.

After us, the maidens came, milkmaids and the rest of them, with Betty Muxworthy at their head, scolding even now, because they would not walk fitly. But they only laughed at her; and she knew it was no good to scold, with all the men behind them.

Then the Snowes came trooping forward; Farmer Nicholas in the middle, walking as if he would rather walk to a wheatfield of his own, yet content to follow lead, because he knew himself the leader; and signing every now and then to the people here and there, as if I were nobody. But to see his three great daughters, strong and handsome wenches, making upon either side, as if somebody would run off with them—this was the very thing that taught me how to value Lorna, and her pure simplicity.

After the Snowes came Jasper Kebby, with his wife, new-married; and a very honest pair they were, upon only a hundred acres, and a right of common. After these the men came hotly, without decent order, trying to spy the girls in front, and make good jokes about them, at which their wives laughed heartily, being jealous when alone perhaps. And after these men and their wives came all the children toddling, picking flowers by the way, and chattering and asking questions, as the children will. There must have been threescore of us, take one with another, and the lane was full of people. When we were come to the big field-gate, where the first sickle was to be, Parson Bowden heaved up the rail with the sleeves of his gown done green with it; and he said that everybody might hear him, though his breath was short, 'In the name of the Lord, Amen!'

'Amen! So be it!' cried the clerk, who was far behind, being only a shoemaker.

Then Parson Bowden read some verses from the parish Bible, telling us to lift up our eyes, and look upon the fields already white to harvest;

and then he laid the Bible down on the square head of the gate-post, and despite his gown and cassock, three good swipes he cut off corn, and laid them right end onwards. All this time the rest were huddling outside the gate, and along the lane, not daring to interfere with parson, but whispering how well he did it.

When he had stowed the corn like that, mother entered, leaning on me, and we both said, 'Thank the Lord for all His mercies, and these the first-fruits of His hand!' And then the clerk gave out a psalm verse by verse, done very well; although he sneezed in the midst of it, from a beard of wheat thrust up his nose by the rival cobbler at Brendon. And when the psalm was sung, so strongly that the foxgloves on the bank were shaking, like a chime of bells, at it, Parson took a stoop of cider, and we all fell to at reaping.

Of course I mean the men, not women; although I know that up the country, women are allowed to reap; and right well they reap it, keeping row for row with men, comely, and in due order, yet, meseems, the men must ill attend to their own reaping-hooks, in fear lest the other cut themselves, being the weaker vessel. But in our part, women do what seems their proper business, following well behind the men, out of harm of the swinging hook, and stooping with their breasts and arms up they catch the swathes of corn, where the reapers cast them, and tucking them together tightly with a wisp laid under them, this they fetch around and twist, with a knee to keep it close; and lo, there is a goodly sheaf, ready to set up in stooks! After these the children come, gathering each for his little self, if the farmer be right-minded; until each hath a bundle made as big as himself and longer, and tumbles now and again with it, in the deeper part of the stubble.

We, the men, kept marching onwards down the flank of the yellow wall, with knees bent wide, and left arm bowed and right arm flashing steel. Each man in his several place, keeping down the rig or chine, on the right side of the reaper in front, and the left of the man that followed him, each making farther sweep and inroad into the golden breadth and depth, each casting leftwards his rich clearance on his foregoer's double track.

So like half a wedge of wildfowl, to and fro we swept the field; and when to either hedge we came, sickles wanted whetting, and throats required moistening, and backs were in need of easing, and every man had much to say, and women wanted praising. Then all returned to the other end, with reaping-hooks beneath our arms, and dogs left to mind jackets.

But now, will you believe me well, or will you only laugh at me? For even in the world of wheat, when deep among the varnished crispness of the jointed stalks, and below the feathered yielding of the graceful heads, even as I gripped the swathes and swept the sickle round them, even as I flung them by to rest on brother stubble, through the whirling yellow world, and eagerness of reaping, came the vision of my love, as with downcast eyes she wondered at my power of passion. And then the sweet remembrance glowed brighter than the sun through wheat, through my very depth of heart, of how she raised those beaming eyes, and ripened in my breast rich hope. Even now I could descry, like high waves in the distance, the rounded heads and folded shadows of the wood of Bagworthy. Perhaps she was walking in the valley, and softly gazing up at them. Oh, to be a bird just there! I could see a bright mist hanging just above the Doone Glen. Perhaps it was shedding its drizzle upon her. Oh, to be a drop of rain! The very breeze which bowed the harvest to my bosom gently, might have come direct from Lorna, with her sweet voice laden. Ah, the flaws of air that wander where they will around her, fan her bright cheek, play with lashes, even revel in her hair and reveal her beauties—man is but a breath, we know, would I were such breath as that!

But confound it, while I ponder, with delicious dreams suspended, with my right arm hanging frustrate and the giant sickle drooped, with my left arm bowed for clasping something more germane than wheat, and my eyes not minding business, but intent on distant woods—confound it, what are the men about, and why am I left vapouring? They have taken advantage of me, the rogues! They are gone to the hedge for the cider-jars; they have had up the sledd of bread and meat, quite softly over the stubble, and if I can believe my eyes (so dazed with Lorna's image), they are sitting down to an excellent dinner, before the church clock has gone eleven!

'John Fry, you big villain!' I cried, with John hanging up in the air by the scruff of his neck-cloth, but holding still by his knife and fork, and a goose-leg in between his lips, 'John Fry, what mean you by this, sir?'

'Latt me dowun, or I can't tell 'e,' John answered with some difficulty. So I let him come down, and I must confess that he had reason on his side. 'Plaise your worship'—John called me so, ever since I returned from London, firmly believing that the King had made me a magistrate at least; though I was to keep it secret—'us zeed as how your worship were took with thinkin' of King's business, in the middle of the whate-rigg: and so uz zed, "Latt un coom to his zell, us had better zave taime, by takking our dinner"; and here us be, praise your worship, and hopps no offence with thick iron spoon full of vried taties.'

I was glad enough to accept the ladle full of fried batatas, and to make the best of things, which is generally done by letting men have their own way. Therefore I managed to dine with them, although it was so early.

For according to all that I can find, in a long life and a varied one, twelve o'clock is the real time for a man to have his dinner. Then the sun is at his noon, calling halt to look around, and then the plants and leaves are turning, each with a little leisure time, before the work of the afternoon. Then is the balance of east and west, and then the right and left side of a man are in due proportion, and contribute fairly with harmonious fluids. And the health of this mode of life, and its reclaiming virtue are well set forth in our ancient rhyme,—

Sunrise, breakfast; sun high, dinner;
Sundown, sup; makes a saint of a sinner.

Whish, the wheat falls! Whirl again; ye have had good dinners; give your master and mistress plenty to supply another year. And in truth we did reap well and fairly, through the whole of that afternoon, I not only keeping lead, but keeping the men up to it. We got through a matter of ten acres, ere the sun between the shocks broke his light on wheaten plumes, then hung his red cloak on the clouds, and fell into grey slumber.

Seeing this we wiped our sickles, and our breasts and foreheads, and soon were on the homeward road, looking forward to good supper.

Of course all the reapers came at night to the harvest-supper, and Parson Bowden to say the grace as well as to help to carve for us. And some help was needed there, I can well assure you; for the reapers had brave appetites, and most of their wives having babies were forced to eat as a duty. Neither failed they of this duty; cut and come again was the order of the evening, as it had been of the day; and I had no time to ask questions, but help meat and ladle gravy. All the while our darling Annie, with her sleeves tucked up, and her comely figure panting, was running about with a bucket of taties mashed with lard and cabbage. Even Lizzie had left her books, and was serving out beer and cider; while mother helped plum-pudding largely on pewter-plates with the mutton. And all the time, Betty Muxworthy was grunting in and out everywhere, not having space to scold even, but changing the dishes, serving the meat, poking the fire, and cooking more. But John Fry would not stir a peg, except with his knife and fork, having all the airs of a visitor, and his wife to keep him eating, till I thought there would be no end of it.

Then having eaten all they could, they prepared themselves, with one accord, for the business now of drinking. But first they lifted the neck of corn, dressed with ribbons gaily, and set it upon the mantelpiece, each man with his horn a-froth; and then they sang a song about it, every one shouting in the chorus louder than harvest thunderstorm. Some were in the middle of one verse, and some at the end of the next one; yet somehow all managed to get together in the mighty roar of the burden. And if any farmer up the country would like to know Exmoor harvest-song as sung in my time and will be sung long after I am garnered home, lo, here I set it down for him, omitting only the dialect, which perchance might puzzle him.

EXMOOR HARVEST-SONG

1

The corn, oh the corn, 'tis the ripening of the corn!
Go unto the door, my lad, and look beneath the moon,
Thou canst see, beyond the woodrick, how it is yelloon:
'Tis the harvesting of wheat, and the barley must be shorn.

(Chorus)

The corn, oh the corn, and the yellow, mellow corn!
Here's to the corn, with the cups upon the board!

We've been reaping all the day, and we'll reap again the morn
And fetch it home to mow-yard, and then we'll thank the Lord.

2

The wheat, oh the wheat, 'tis the ripening of the wheat!
All the day it has been hanging down its heavy head,
Bowing over on our bosoms with a beard of red:
'Tis the harvest, and the value makes the labour sweet.

(Chorus)

The wheat, oh the wheat, and the golden, golden wheat!
Here's to the wheat, with the loaves upon the board!
We've been reaping all the day, and we never will be beat,
But fetch it all to mow-yard, and then we'll thank the Lord.

3

The barley, oh the barley, and the barley is in prime!
All the day it has been rustling, with its bristles brown,
Waiting with its beard abowing, till it can be mown!
'Tis the harvest and the barley must abide its time.

(Chorus)

The barley, oh the barley, and the barley ruddy brown!
Here's to the barley, with the beer upon the board!
We'll go amowing, soon as ever all the wheat is down;
When all is in the mow-yard, we'll stop, and thank the Lord.

4

The oats, oh the oats, 'tis the ripening of the oats!
All the day they have been dancing with their flakes of white,
Waiting for the girding-hook, to be the nags' delight:
'Tis the harvest, let them dangle in their skirted coats.

(Chorus)

The oats, oh the oats, and the silver, silver oats!
Here's to the oats with the blackstone on the board!
We'll go among them, when the barley has been laid in rotes:
When all is home to mow-yard, we'll kneel and thank the Lord.

5

The corn, oh the corn, and the blessing of the corn!
Come unto the door, my lads, and look beneath the moon,
We can see, on hill and valley, how it is yelloon,
With a breadth of glory, as when our Lord was born.

(Chorus)

The corn, oh the corn, and the yellow, mellow corn!
Thanks for the corn, with our bread upon the board!
So shall we acknowledge it, before we reap the morn,
With our hands to heaven, and our knees unto the Lord.

Now we sang this song very well the first time, having the parish choir to lead us, and the clarionet, and the parson to give us the time with his cup; and we sang it again the second time, not so but what you might praise it (if you had been with us all the evening), although the parson was gone then, and the clerk not fit to compare with him in the matter of keeping time. But when that song was in its third singing, I defy any man (however sober) to have made out one verse from the other, or even the burden from the verses, inasmuch as every man present, ay, and woman too, sang as became convenient to them, in utterance both of words and tune.

And in truth, there was much excuse for them; because it was a noble harvest, fit to thank the Lord for, without His thinking us hypocrites. For we had more land in wheat, that year, than ever we had before, and twice the crop to the acre; and I could not help now and then remembering, in the midst of the merriment, how my father in the churchyard yonder would have gloried to behold it. And my mother, who had left us now, happening to return just then, being called to have her health drunk (for the twentieth time at least), I knew by the sadness in her eyes that she was thinking just as I was. Presently, therefore, I slipped away from the noise, and mirth, and smoking (although of that last there was not much, except from Farmer Nicholas), and crossing the courtyard in the moonlight, I went, just to cool myself, as far as my father's tombstone.

Chapter XXX Annie Gets The Best of It

I had long outgrown unwholesome feeling as to my father's death, and so had Annie; though Lizzie (who must have loved him least) still entertained some evil will, and longing for a punishment. Therefore I was surprised (and indeed, startled would not be too much to say, the moon being somewhat fleecy), to see our Annie sitting there as motionless as the tombstone, and with all her best fallals upon her, after stowing away the dishes.

My nerves, however, are good and strong, except at least in love matters, wherein they always fail me, and when I meet with witches; and therefore I went up to Annie, although she looked so white and pure; for I had seen her before with those things on, and it struck me who she was.

"What are you doing here, Annie?" I inquired rather sternly, being vexed with her for having gone so very near to frighten me.

"Nothing at all," said our Annie shortly. And indeed it was truth enough for a woman. Not that I dare to believe that women are such liars as men say; only that I mean they often see things round the corner, and know not which is which of it. And indeed I never have known a woman (though right enough in their meaning) purely and perfectly true and transparent, except only my Lorna; and even so, I might not have loved her, if she had been ugly.

'Why, how so?' said I; 'Miss Annie, what business have you here, doing nothing at this time of night? And leaving me with all the trouble to entertain our guests!'

'You seem not to me to be doing it, John,' Annie answered softly; 'what business have you here doing nothing, at this time of night?'

I was taken so aback with this, and the extreme impertinence of it, from a mere young girl like Annie, that I turned round to march away and have nothing more to say to her. But she jumped up, and caught me by the hand, and threw herself upon my bosom, with her face all wet with tears.

'Oh, John, I will tell you. I will tell you. Only don't be angry, John.'

'Angry! no indeed,' said I; 'what right have I to be angry with you, because you have your secrets? Every chit of a girl thinks now that she has a right to her secrets.'

'And you have none of your own, John; of course you have none of your own? All your going out at night—'

'We will not quarrel here, poor Annie,' I answered, with some loftiness; 'there are many things upon my mind, which girls can have no notion of.'

'And so there are upon mine, John. Oh, John, I will tell you everything, if you will look at me kindly, and promise to forgive me. Oh, I am so miserable!'

Now this, though she was behaving so badly, moved me much towards her; especially as I longed to know what she had to tell me. Therefore I allowed her to coax me, and to kiss me, and to lead me away a little, as far as the old yew-tree; for she would not tell me where she was.

But even in the shadow there, she was very long before beginning, and seemed to have two minds about it, or rather perhaps a dozen; and she laid her cheek against the tree, and sobbed till it was pitiful; and I knew what mother would say to her for spoiling her best frock so.

'Now will you stop?' I said at last, harder than I meant it, for I knew that she would go on all night, if any one encouraged her: and though not well acquainted with women, I understood my sisters; or else I must be a born fool—except, of course, that I never professed to understand Eliza.

'Yes, I will stop,' said Annie, panting; 'you are very hard on me, John; but I know you mean it for the best. If somebody else—I am sure I don't know who, and have no right to know, no doubt, but she must be a wicked thing—if somebody else had been taken so with a pain all round the heart, John, and no power of telling it, perhaps you would have coaxed, and kissed her, and come a little nearer, and made opportunity to be very loving.'

Now this was so exactly what I had tried to do to Lorna, that my breath was almost taken away at Annie's so describing it. For a while I could not say a word, but wondered if she were a witch, which had never been in our family: and then, all of a sudden, I saw the way to beat her, with the devil at my elbow.

'From your knowledge of these things, Annie, you must have had them done to you. I demand to know this very moment who has taken such liberties.'

'Then, John, you shall never know, if you ask in that manner. Besides, it was no liberty in the least at all, Cousins have a right to do things—and when they are one's godfather—' Here Annie stopped quite suddenly having so betrayed herself; but met me in the full moonlight, being resolved to face it out, with a good face put upon it.

'Alas, I feared it would come to this,' I answered very sadly; 'I know he has been here many a time, without showing himself to me. There is nothing meaner than for a man to sneak, and steal a young maid's heart, without her people knowing it.'

'You are not doing anything of that sort yourself then, dear John, are you?'

'Only a common highwayman!' I answered, without heeding her; 'a man without an acre of his own, and liable to hang upon any common, and no other right of common over it—'

'John,' said my sister, 'are the Doones privileged not to be hanged upon common land?'

At this I was so thunderstruck, that I leaped in the air like a shot rabbit, and rushed as hard as I could through the gate and across the yard, and back into the kitchen; and there I asked Farmer Nicholas Snowe to give me some tobacco, and to lend me a spare pipe.

This he did with a grateful manner, being now some five-fourths gone; and so I smoked the very first pipe that ever had entered my lips till then; and beyond a doubt it did me good, and spread my heart at leisure.

Meanwhile the reapers were mostly gone, to be up betimes in the morning; and some were led by their wives; and some had to lead their wives themselves, according to the capacity of man and wife respectively. But Betty was as lively as ever, bustling about with every one, and looking out for the chance of groats, which the better off might be free with. And over the kneading-pan next day, she dropped three and sixpence out of her pocket; and Lizzie could not tell for her life how much more might have been in it.

Now by this time I had almost finished smoking that pipe of tobacco, and wondering at myself for having so despised it hitherto, and making up my mind to have another trial to-morrow night, it began to occur to me that although dear Annie had behaved so very badly and rudely, and almost taken my breath away with the suddenness of her allusion, yet it was not kind of me to leave her out there at that time of night, all alone, and in such distress. Any of the reapers going home might be gotten so far beyond fear of ghosts as to venture into the churchyard; and although they would know a great deal better than to insult a sister of mine when sober, there was no telling what they might do in their present state of rejoicing. Moreover, it was only right that I should learn, for Lorna's sake, how far Annie, or any one else, had penetrated our secret.

Therefore, I went forth at once, bearing my pipe in a skilful manner, as I had seen Farmer Nicholas do; and marking, with a new kind of pleasure, how the rings and wreaths of smoke hovered and fluttered in the moonlight, like a lark upon his carol. Poor Annie was gone back again to our father's grave, and there she sat upon the turf, sobbing very gently, and not wishing to trouble any one. So I raised her tenderly, and made much of her, and consoled her, for I could not scold her there; and perhaps after all she was not to be blamed so much as Tom Faggus himself was. Annie was very grateful to me, and kissed me many times, and begged my pardon ever so often for her rudeness to me. And then having gone so far with it, and finding me so complaisant, she must needs try to go a little further, and to lead me away from her own affairs, and into mine concerning Lorna. But although it was clever enough of her she was not deep enough for me there; and I soon discovered that she knew nothing, not even the name of my darling; but only suspected from things she had seen, and put together like a woman. Upon this I brought her back again to Tom Faggus and his doings.

'My poor Annie, have you really promised him to be his wife?'

'Then after all you have no reason, John, no particular reason, I mean, for slighting poor Sally Snowe so?'

'Without even asking mother or me! Oh, Annie, it was wrong of you!'

'But, darling, you know that mother wishes you so much to marry Sally; and I am sure you could have her to-morrow. She dotes on the very ground—'

'I dare say he tells you that, Annie, that he dotes on the ground you walk upon—but did you believe him, child?'

'You may believe me, I assure you, John, and half the farm to be settled upon her, after the old man's time; and though she gives herself little airs, it is only done to entice you; she has the very best hand in the dairy John, and the lightest at a turn-over cake—'

'Now, Annie, don't talk nonsense so. I wish just to know the truth about you and Tom Faggus. Do you mean to marry him?'

'I to marry before my brother, and leave him with none to take care of him! Who can do him a red deer collop, except Sally herself, as I can? Come home, dear, at once, and I will do you one; for you never ate a morsel of supper, with all the people you had to attend upon.'

This was true enough; and seeing no chance of anything more than cross questions and crooked purposes, at which a girl was sure to beat me, I even allowed her to lead me home, with the thoughts of the collop uppermost. But I never counted upon being beaten so thoroughly as I was; for knowing me now to be off my guard, the young hussy stopped at the farmyard gate, as if with a brier entangling her, and while I was stooping to take it away, she looked me full in the face by the moonlight, and jerked out quite suddenly,—

'Can your love do a collop, John?'

'No, I should hope not,' I answered rashly; 'she is not a mere cookmaid I should hope.'

'She is not half so pretty as Sally Snowe; I will answer for that,' said Annie.

'She is ten thousand times as pretty as ten thousand Sally Snowes,' I replied with great indignation.

'Oh, but look at Sally's eyes!' cried my sister rapturously.

'Look at Lorna Doone's,' said I; 'and you would never look again at Sally's.'

'Oh Lorna Doone. Lorna Doone!' exclaimed our Annie half-frightened, yet clapping her hands with triumph, at having found me out so: 'Lorna Doone is the lovely maiden, who has stolen poor somebody's heart so. Ah, I shall remember it; because it is so queer a name. But stop, I had better write it down. Lend me your hat, poor boy, to write on.'

'I have a great mind to lend you a box on the ear,' I answered her in my vexation, 'and I would, if you had not been crying so, you sly good-for-nothing baggage. As it is, I shall keep it for Master Faggus, and add interest for keeping.'

'Oh no, John; oh no, John,' she begged me earnestly, being sobered in a moment. 'Your hand is so terribly heavy, John; and he never would forgive you; although he is so good-hearted, he cannot put up with an insult. Promise me, dear John, that you will not strike him; and I will promise you faithfully to keep your secret, even from mother, and even from Cousin Tom himself.'

'And from Lizzie; most of all, from Lizzie,' I answered very eagerly, knowing too well which of my relations would be hardest with me.

'Of course from little Lizzie,' said Annie, with some contempt; 'a young thing like her cannot be kept too long, in my opinion, from the knowledge of such subjects. And besides, I should be very sorry if Lizzie had the right to know your secrets, as I have, dearest John. Not a soul shall be the wiser for your having trusted me, John; although I shall be very wretched when you are late away at night, among those dreadful people.'

'Well,' I replied, 'it is no use crying over spilt milk Annie. You have my secret, and I have yours; and I scarcely know which of the two is likely to have the worst time of it, when it comes to mother's ears. I could put up with perpetual scolding but not with mother's sad silence.'

'That is exactly how I feel, John.' and as Annie said it she brightened up, and her soft eyes shone upon me; 'but now I shall be much happier, dear; because I shall try to help you. No doubt the young lady deserves it, John. She is not after the farm, I hope?'

'She!' I exclaimed; and that was enough, there was so much scorn in my voice and face.

'Then, I am sure, I am very glad,' Annie always made the best of things; 'for I do believe that Sally Snowe has taken a fancy to our dairy-place, and the pattern of our cream-pans; and she asked so much about our meadows, and the colour of the milk—'

'Then, after all, you were right, dear Annie; it is the ground she dotes upon.'

'And the things that walk upon it,' she answered me with another kiss; 'Sally has taken a wonderful fancy to our best cow, "Nipple-pins." But she never shall have her now; what a consolation!'

We entered the house quite gently thus, and found Farmer Nicholas Snowe asleep, little dreaming how his plans had been overset between us. And then Annie said to me very slyly, between a smile and a blush,—

'Don't you wish Lorna Doone was here, John, in the parlour along with mother; instead of those two fashionable milkmaids, as Uncle Ben will call them, and poor stupid Mistress Kebby?'

'That indeed I do, Annie. I must kiss you for only thinking of it. Dear me, it seems as if you had known all about us for a twelvemonth.'

'She loves you, with all her heart, John. No doubt about that of course.' And Annie looked up at me, as much as to say she would like to know who could help it.

'That's the very thing she won't do,' said I, knowing that Annie would love me all the more for it, 'she is only beginning to like me, Annie; and as for loving, she is so young that she only loves her grandfather. But I hope she will come to it by-and-by.'

'Of course she must,' replied my sister, 'it will be impossible for her to help it.'

'Ah well! I don't know,' for I wanted more assurance of it. 'Maidens are such wondrous things!"

'Not a bit of it,' said Annie, casting her bright eyes downwards: 'love is as simple as milking, when people know how to do it. But you must not let her alone too long; that is my advice to you. What a simpleton you must have been not to tell me long ago. I would have made Lorna wild about you, long before this time, Johnny. But now you go into the parlour, dear, while I do your collop. Faith Snowe is not come, but Polly and Sally. Sally has made up her mind to conquer you this very blessed evening, John. Only look what a thing of a scarf she has on; I should be quite ashamed to wear it. But you won't strike poor Tom, will you?'

'Not I, my darling, for your sweet sake.'

And so dear Annie, having grown quite brave, gave me a little push into the parlour, where I was quite abashed to enter after all I had heard about Sally. And I made up my mind to examine her well, and try a little courting with her, if she should lead me on, that I might be in practice for Lorna. But when I perceived how grandly and richly both the young damsels were apparelled; and how, in their curtseys to me, they retreated, as if I were making up to them, in a way they had learned from Exeter; and how they began to talk of the Court, as if they had been there all their lives, and the latest mode of the Duchess of this, and the profile of the Countess of that, and the last good saying of my Lord something; instead of butter, and cream, and eggs, and things which they understood; I knew there must be somebody in the room besides Jasper Kebby to talk at.

And so there was; for behind the curtain drawn across the window-seat no less a man than Uncle Ben was sitting half asleep and weary; and by his side a little girl very quiet and very watchful. My mother led me to Uncle Ben, and he took my hand without rising, muttering something not over-polite, about my being bigger than ever. I asked him heartily how he was, and he said, 'Well enough, for that matter; but none the better for the noise you great clods have been making.'

'I am sorry if we have disturbed you, sir,' I answered very civilly; 'but I knew not that you were here even; and you must allow for harvest time.'

'So it seems,' he replied; 'and allow a great deal, including waste and drunkenness. Now (if you can see so small a thing, after emptying flagons much larger) this is my granddaughter, and my heiress'—here he glanced at mother—'my heiress, little Ruth Huckaback.'

'I am very glad to see you, Ruth,' I answered, offering her my hand, which she seemed afraid to take, 'welcome to Plover's Barrows, my good cousin Ruth.'

However, my good cousin Ruth only arose, and made me a curtsey, and lifted her great brown eyes at me, more in fear, as I thought, than kinship. And if ever any one looked unlike the heiress to great property, it was the little girl before me.

'Come out to the kitchen, dear, and let me chuck you to the ceiling,' I said, just to encourage her; 'I always do it to little girls; and then they can see the hams and bacon.' But Uncle Reuben burst out laughing; and Ruth turned away with a deep rich colour.

'Do you know how old she is, you numskull?' said Uncle Ben, in his dryest drawl; 'she was seventeen last July, sir.'

'On the first of July, grandfather,' Ruth whispered, with her back still to me; 'but many people will not believe it.'

Here mother came up to my rescue, as she always loved to do; and she said, 'If my son may not dance Miss Ruth, at any rate he may dance with her. We have only been waiting for you, dear John, to have a little harvest dance, with the kitchen door thrown open. You take Ruth; Uncle Ben take Sally; Master Debby pair off with Polly; and neighbour Nicholas will be good enough, if I can awake him, to stand up with fair Mistress Kebby. Lizzie will play us the virginal. Won't you, Lizzie dear?'

'But who is to dance with you, madam?' Uncle Ben asked, very politely. 'I think you must rearrange your figure. I have not danced for a score of years; and I will not dance now, while the mistress and the owner of the harvest sits aside neglected.'

'Nay, Master Huckaback,' cried Sally Snowe, with a saucy toss of her hair; 'Mistress Ridd is too kind a great deal, in handing you over to me. You take her; and I will fetch Annie to be my partner this evening. I like dancing very much better with girls, for they never squeeze and rumple one. Oh, it is so much nicer!'

'Have no fear for me, my dears,' our mother answered smiling: 'Parson Bowden promised to come back again; I expect him every minute; and he intends to lead me off, and to bring a partner for Annie too, a very pretty young gentleman. Now begin; and I will join you.'

There was no disobeying her, without rudeness; and indeed the girls' feet were already jigging; and Lizzie giving herself wonderful airs with a roll of learned music; and even while Annie was doing my collop, her pretty round instep was arching itself, as I could see from the parlour-door. So I took little Ruth, and I spun her around, as the sound of the music came lively and ringing; and after us came all the rest with much laughter, begging me not to jump over her; and anon my grave partner began to smile sweetly, and look up at me with the brightest of eyes, and drop me the prettiest curtseys; till I thought what a great stupe I must have been to dream of putting her in the cheese-rack. But one thing I could not at all understand; why mother, who used to do all in her power to throw me across Sally Snowe, should now do the very opposite; for she would not allow me one moment with Sally, not even to cross in the dance, or whisper, or go anywhere near a corner (which as I said, I intended to do, just by way of practice), while she kept me, all the evening, as close as possible with Ruth Huckaback, and came up and praised me so to Ruth, times and again, that I declare I was quite ashamed. Although of course I knew that I deserved it all, but I could not well say that.

Then Annie came sailing down the dance, with her beautiful hair flowing round her; the lightest figure in all the room, and the sweetest, and the loveliest. She was blushing, with her fair cheeks red beneath her dear blue eyes, as she met my glance of surprise and grief at the partner she was leaning on. It was Squire Marwood de Whichehalse. I would sooner have seen her with Tom Faggus, as indeed I had expected, when I heard of Parson Bowden. And to me it seemed that she had no right to be dancing so with any other; and to this effect I contrived to whisper; but she only said, 'See to yourself, John. No, but let us both enjoy ourselves. You are not dancing with Lorna, John. But you seem uncommonly happy.'

'Tush,' I said; 'could I flip about so, if I had my love with me?'

Chapter XXXI John Fry's Errand

We kept up the dance very late that night, mother being in such wonderful spirits, that she would not hear of our going to bed: while she glanced from young Squire Marwood, very deep in his talk with our Annie, to me and Ruth Huckaback who were beginning to be very pleasant company. Alas, poor mother, so proud as she was, how little she dreamed that her good schemes already were hopelessly going awry!

Being forced to be up before daylight next day, in order to begin right early, I would not go to my bedroom that night for fear of disturbing my mother, but determined to sleep in the tallat awhile, that place being cool, and airy, and refreshing with the smell of sweet hay. Moreover, after my dwelling in town, where I had felt like a horse on a lime-kiln, I could not for a length of time have enough of country life. The mooing of a calf was music, and the chuckle of a fowl was wit, and the snore of the horses was news to me.

'Wult have thee own wai, I reckon,' said Betty, being cross with sleepiness, for she had washed up everything; 'slape in hog-pound, if thee laikes, Jan.'

Letting her have the last word of it (as is the due of women) I stood in the court, and wondered awhile at the glory of the harvest moon, and the yellow world it shone upon. Then I saw, as sure as ever I was standing there in the shadow of the stable, I saw a short wide figure glide across the foot of the courtyard, between me and the six-barred gate. Instead of running after it, as I should have done, I began to consider who it could be, and what on earth was doing there, when all our people were in bed, and the reapers gone home, or to the linhay close against the wheatfield.

Having made up my mind at last, that it could be none of our people—though not a dog was barking—and also that it must have been either a girl or a woman, I ran down with all speed to learn what might be the meaning of it. But I came too late to learn, through my own hesitation, for this was the lower end of the courtyard, not the approach from the parish highway, but the end of the sledd-way, across the fields where the brook goes down to the Lynn stream, and where Squire Faggus had saved the old drake. And of course the dry channel of the brook, being scarcely any water now, afforded plenty of place to hide, leading also to a little coppice, beyond our cabbage-garden, and so further on to the parish highway.

I saw at once that it was vain to make any pursuit by moonlight; and resolving to hold my own counsel about it (though puzzled not a little) and to keep watch there another night, back I returned to the tallatt-ladder, and slept without leaving off till morning.

Now many people may wish to know, as indeed I myself did very greatly, what had brought Master Huckaback over from Dulverton, at that time of year, when the clothing business was most active on account of harvest wages, and when the new wheat was beginning to sample from the early parts up the country (for he meddled as well in corn-dealing) and when we could not attend to him properly by reason of our occupation. And yet more surprising it seemed to me that he should have brought his granddaughter also, instead of the troop of dragoons, without which he had vowed he would never come here again. And how he had managed to enter the house together with his granddaughter, and be sitting quite at home in the parlour there, without any knowledge or even suspicion on my part. That last question was easily solved, for mother herself had admitted them by means of the little passage, during a chorus of the harvest-song which might have drowned an earthquake: but as for his meaning and motive, and apparent neglect of his business, none but himself could interpret them; and as he did not see fit to do so, we could not be rude enough to inquire.

He seemed in no hurry to take his departure, though his visit was so inconvenient to us, as himself indeed must have noticed: and presently Lizzie, who was the sharpest among us, said in my hearing that she believed he had purposely timed his visit so that he might have liberty to pursue his own object, whatsoever it were, without interruption from us. Mother gazed hard upon Lizzie at this, having formed a very different opinion; but Annie and myself agreed that it was worth looking into.

Now how could we look into it, without watching Uncle Reuben, whenever he went abroad, and trying to catch him in his speech, when he was taking his ease at night. For, in spite of all the disgust with which he had spoken of harvest wassailing, there was not a man coming into our kitchen who liked it better than he did; only in a quiet way, and without too many witnesses. Now to endeavour to get at the purpose of any guest, even a treacherous one (which we had no right to think Uncle Reuben) by means of observing him in his cups, is a thing which even the lowest of people would regard with abhorrence. And to my mind it was not clear whether it would be fair-play at all to follow a visitor even at a distance from home and clear of our premises; except for the purpose of fetching him back, and giving him more to go on with. Nevertheless we could not but think, the times being wild and disjointed, that Uncle Ben was not using fairly the part of a guest in our house, to make long expeditions we knew not whither, and involve us in trouble we knew not what.

For his mode was directly after breakfast to pray to the Lord a little (which used not to be his practice), and then to go forth upon Dolly, the which was our Annie's pony, very quiet and respectful, with a bag of good victuals hung behind him, and two great cavalry pistols in front. And he always wore his meanest clothes as if expecting to be robbed, or to disarm the temptation thereto; and he never took his golden chronometer neither his bag of money. So much the girls found out and told me (for I was never at home myself by day); and they very craftily spurred me on, having less noble ideas perhaps, to hit upon Uncle Reuben's track, and follow, and see what became of him. For he never returned until dark or more, just in time to be in before us, who were coming home from the harvest. And then Dolly always seemed very weary, and stained with a muck from beyond our parish.

But I refused to follow him, not only for the loss of a day's work to myself, and at least half a day to the other men, but chiefly because I could not think that it would be upright and manly. It was all very well to creep warily into the valley of the Doones, and heed everything around me, both because they were public enemies, and also because I risked my life at every step I took there. But as to tracking a feeble old man (however subtle he might be), a guest moreover of our own, and a relative through my mother.—'Once for all,' I said, 'it is below me, and I won't do it.'

Thereupon, the girls, knowing my way, ceased to torment me about it: but what was my astonishment the very next day to perceive that instead of fourteen reapers, we were only thirteen left, directly our breakfast was done with—or mowers rather I should say, for we were gone into the barley now.

'Who has been and left his scythe?' I asked; 'and here's a tin cup never been handled!'

'Whoy, dudn't ee knaw, Maister Jan,' said Bill Dadds, looking at me queerly, 'as Jan Vry wur gane avore braxvass.'

'Oh, very well,' I answered, 'John knows what he is doing.' For John Fry was a kind of foreman now, and it would not do to say anything that might lessen his authority. However, I made up my mind to rope him, when I should catch him by himself, without peril to his dignity.

But when I came home in the evening, late and almost weary, there was no Annie cooking my supper, nor Lizzie by the fire reading, nor even little Ruth Huckaback watching the shadows and pondering. Upon this, I went to the girls' room, not in the very best of tempers, and there I found all three of them in the little place set apart for Annie, eagerly listening to John Fry, who was telling some great adventure. John had a great jug of ale beside him, and a horn well drained; and he clearly looked upon himself as a hero, and the maids seemed to be of the same opinion.

'Well done, John,' my sister was saying, 'capitally done, John Fry. How very brave you have been, John. Now quick, let us hear the rest of it.'

'What does all this nonsense mean?' I said, in a voice which frightened them, as I could see by the light of our own mutton candles: 'John Fry, you be off to your wife at once, or you shall have what I owe you now, instead of to-morrow morning.'

John made no answer, but scratched his head, and looked at the maidens to take his part.

'It is you that must be off, I think,' said Lizzie, looking straight at me with all the impudence in the world; 'what right have you to come in here to the young ladies' room, without an invitation even?'

'Very well, Miss Lizzie, I suppose mother has some right here.' And with that, I was going away to fetch her, knowing that she always took my side, and never would allow the house to be turned upside down in that manner. But Annie caught hold of me by the arm, and little Ruth stood in the doorway; and Lizzie said, 'Don't be a fool, John. We know things of you, you know; a great deal more than you dream of.'

Upon this I glanced at Annie, to learn whether she had been telling, but her pure true face reassured me at once, and then she said very gently,—

'Lizzie, you talk too fast, my child. No one knows anything of our John which he need be ashamed of; and working as he does from light to dusk, and earning the living of all of us, he is entitled to choose his own good time for going out and for coming in, without consulting a little girl five years younger than himself. Now, John, sit down, and you shall know all that we have done, though I doubt whether you will approve of it.'

Upon this I kissed Annie, and so did Ruth; and John Fry looked a deal more comfortable, but Lizzie only made a face at us. Then Annie began as follows:—

'You must know, dear John, that we have been extremely curious, ever since Uncle Reuben came, to know what he was come for, especially at this time of year, when he is at his busiest. He never vouchsafed any explanation, neither gave any reason, true or false, which shows his entire ignorance of all feminine nature. If Ruth had known, and refused to tell us, we should have been much easier, because we must have got it out of Ruth before two or three days were over. But darling Ruth knew no more than we did, and indeed I must do her the justice to say that she has been quite as inquisitive. Well, we might have put up with it, if it had not been for his taking Dolly, my own pet Dolly, away every morning, quite as if she belonged to him, and keeping her out until close upon dark, and then bringing her home in a frightful condition. And he even had the impudence, when I told him that Dolly was my pony, to say that we owed him a pony, ever since you took from him that little horse upon which you found him strapped so snugly; and he means to take Dolly to Dulverton with him, to run in his little cart. If there is law in the land he shall not. Surely, John, you will not let him?'

'That I won't,' said I, 'except upon the conditions which I offered him once before. If we owe him the pony, we owe him the straps.'

Sweet Annie laughed, like a bell, at this, and then she went on with her story.

'Well, John, we were perfectly miserable. You cannot understand it, of course; but I used to go every evening, and hug poor Dolly, and kiss her, and beg her to tell me where she had been, and what she had seen, that day. But never having belonged to Balaam, darling Dolly was quite unsuccessful, though often she strove to tell me, with her ears down, and both eyes rolling. Then I made John Fry tie her tail in a knot, with a piece of white ribbon, as if for adornment, that I might trace her among the hills, at any rate for a mile or two. But Uncle Ben was too deep for that; he cut off the ribbon before he started, saying he would have no Doones after him. And then, in despair, I applied to you, knowing how quick of foot you are, and I got Ruth and Lizzie to help me, but you answered us very shortly; and a very poor supper you had that night, according to your deserts.

'But though we were dashed to the ground for a time, we were not wholly discomfited. Our determination to know all about it seemed to increase with the difficulty. And Uncle Ben's manner last night was so dry, when we tried to romp and to lead him out, that it was much worse than Jamaica ginger grated into a poor sprayed finger. So we sent him to bed at the earliest moment, and held a small council upon him. If you remember you, John, having now taken to smoke (which is a hateful practice), had gone forth grumbling about your bad supper and not taking it as a good lesson.'

'Why, Annie,' I cried, in amazement at this, 'I will never trust you again for a supper. I thought you were so sorry.'

'And so I was, dear; very sorry. But still we must do our duty. And when we came to consider it, Ruth was the cleverest of us all; for she said that surely we must have some man we could trust about the farm to go on a little errand; and then I remembered that old John Fry would do anything for money.'

'Not for money, plaize, miss,' said John Fry, taking a pull at the beer; 'but for the love of your swate face.'

'To be sure, John; with the King's behind it. And so Lizzie ran for John Fry at once, and we gave him full directions, how he was to slip out of the barley in the confusion of the breakfast, so that none might miss him; and to run back to the black combe bottom, and there he would find the very same pony which Uncle Ben had been tied upon, and there is no faster upon the farm. And then, without waiting for any breakfast unless he could eat it either running or trotting, he was to travel all up the black combe, by the track Uncle Reuben had taken, and up at the top to look forward carefully, and so to trace him without being seen.'

'Ay; and raight wull a doo'd un,' John cried, with his mouth in the bullock's horn.

'Well, and what did you see, John?' I asked, with great anxiety; though I meant to have shown no interest.

'John was just at the very point of it,' Lizzie answered me sharply, 'when you chose to come in and stop him.'

'Then let him begin again,' said I; 'things being gone so far, it is now my duty to know everything, for the sake of you girls and mother.'

'Hem!' cried Lizzie, in a nasty way; but I took no notice of her, for she was always bad to deal with. Therefore John Fry began again, being heartily glad to do so, that his story might get out of the tumble which all our talk had made in it. But as he could not tell a tale in the manner of my Lorna (although he told it very well for those who understood him) I will take it from his mouth altogether, and state in brief what happened.

When John, upon his forest pony, which he had much ado to hold (its mouth being like a bucket), was come to the top of the long black combe, two miles or more from Plover's Barrows, and winding to the southward, he stopped his little nag short of the crest, and got off and looked ahead of him, from behind a tump of whortles. It was a long flat sweep of moorland over which he was gazing, with a few bogs here and there, and brushy places round them. Of course, John Fry, from his shepherd life and reclaiming of strayed cattle, knew as well as need be where he was, and the spread of the hills before him, although it was beyond our beat, or, rather, I should say, beside it. Not but what we might have grazed there had it been our pleasure, but that it was not worth our while, and scarcely worth Jasper Kebby's even; all the land being cropped (as one might say) with desolation. And nearly all our knowledge of it sprang from the unaccountable tricks of cows who have young calves with them; at which time they have wild desire to get away from the sight of man, and keep calf and milk for one another, although it be in a barren land. At least, our cows have gotten this trick, and I have heard other people complain of it.

John Fry, as I said, knew the place well enough, but he liked it none the more for that, neither did any of our people; and, indeed, all the neighbourhood of Thomshill and Larksborough, and most of all Black Barrow Down lay under grave imputation of having been enchanted with a very evil spell. Moreover, it was known, though folk were loath to speak of it, even on a summer morning, that Squire Thom, who had been murdered there, a century ago or more, had been seen by several shepherds, even in the middle day, walking with his severed head carried in his left hand, and his right arm lifted towards the sun.

Therefore it was very bold in John (as I acknowledged) to venture across that moor alone, even with a fast pony under him, and some whisky by his side. And he would never have done so (of that I am quite certain), either for the sake of Annie's sweet face, or of the golden guinea, which the three maidens had subscribed to reward his skill and valour. But the truth was that he could not resist his own great curiosity. For, carefully spying across the moor, from behind the tuft of whortles, at first he could discover nothing having life and motion, except three or four wild cattle roving in vain search for nourishment, and a diseased sheep banished hither, and some carrion crows keeping watch on her. But when John was taking his very last look, being only too glad to go home again, and acknowledge himself baffled, he thought he saw a figure moving in the farthest distance upon Black Barrow Down, scarcely a thing to be sure of yet, on account of the want of colour. But as he watched, the figure passed between him and a naked cliff, and appeared to be a man on horseback, making his way very carefully, in fear of bogs and serpents. For all about there it is adders' ground, and large black serpents dwell in the marshes, and can swim as well as crawl.

John knew that the man who was riding there could be none but Uncle Reuben, for none of the Doones ever passed that way, and the shepherds were afraid of it. And now it seemed an unkind place for an unarmed man to venture through, especially after an armed one who might not like to be spied upon, and must have some dark object in visiting such drear solitudes. Nevertheless John Fry so ached with unbearable curiosity to know what an old man, and a stranger, and a rich man, and a peaceable could possibly be after in that mysterious manner. Moreover, John so throbbed with hope to find some wealthy secret, that come what would of it he resolved to go to the end of the matter.

Therefore he only waited awhile for fear of being discovered, till Master Huckaback turned to the left and entered a little gully, whence he could not survey the moor. Then John remounted and crossed the rough land and the stony places, and picked his way among the morasses as fast as ever he dared to go; until, in about half an hour, he drew nigh the entrance of the gully. And now it behoved him to be most wary; for Uncle Ben might have stopped in there, either to rest his horse or having reached the end of his journey. And in either case, John had little doubt that he himself would be pistolled, and nothing more ever heard of him. Therefore he made his pony come to the mouth of it sideways, and leaned over and peered in around the rocky corner, while the little horse cropped at the briars.

But he soon perceived that the gully was empty, so far at least as its course was straight; and with that he hastened into it, though his heart was not working easily. When he had traced the winding hollow for half a mile or more, he saw that it forked, and one part led to the left up a steep red bank, and the other to the right, being narrow and slightly tending downwards. Some yellow sand lay here and there between the starving grasses, and this he examined narrowly for a trace of Master Huckaback.

At last he saw that, beyond all doubt, the man he was pursuing had taken the course which led down hill; and down the hill he must follow him. And this John did with deep misgivings, and a hearty wish that he had never started upon so perilous an errand. For now he knew not where he was, and scarcely dared to ask himself, having heard of a horrible hole, somewhere in this neighbourhood, called the Wizard's Slough. Therefore

John rode down the slope, with sorrow, and great caution. And these grew more as he went onward, and his pony reared against him, being scared, although a native of the roughest moorland. And John had just made up his mind that God meant this for a warning, as the passage seemed darker and deeper, when suddenly he turned a corner, and saw a scene which stopped him.

For there was the Wizard's Slough itself, as black as death, and bubbling, with a few scant yellow reeds in a ring around it. Outside these, bright water-grass of the liveliest green was creeping, tempting any unwary foot to step, and plunge, and founder. And on the marge were blue campanula, sundew, and forget-me-not, such as no child could resist. On either side, the hill fell back, and the ground was broken with tufts of rush, and flag, and mares-tail, and a few rough alder-trees overclogged with water. And not a bird was seen or heard, neither rail nor water-hen, wag-tail nor reed-warbler.

Of this horrible quagmire, the worst upon all Exmoor, John had heard from his grandfather, and even from his mother, when they wanted to keep him quiet; but his father had feared to speak of it to him, being a man of piety, and up to the tricks of the evil one. This made John the more desirous to have a good look at it now, only with his girths well up, to turn away and flee at speed, if anything should happen. And now he proved how well it is to be wary and wide-awake, even in lonesome places. For at the other side of the Slough, and a few land-yards beyond it, where the ground was less noisome, he had observed a felled tree lying over a great hole in the earth, with staves of wood, and slabs of stone, and some yellow gravel around it. But the flags of reeds around the morass partly screened it from his eyes, and he could not make out the meaning of it, except that it meant no good, and probably was witchcraft. Yet Dolly seemed not to be harmed by it, for there she was as large as life, tied to a stump not far beyond, and flipping the flies away with her tail.

While John was trembling within himself, lest Dolly should get scent of his pony, and neigh and reveal their presence, although she could not see them, suddenly to his great amazement something white arose out of the hole, under the brown trunk of the tree. Seeing this his blood went back within him, yet he was not able to turn and flee, but rooted his face in among the loose stones, and kept his quivering shoulders back, and prayed to God to protect him. However, the white thing itself was not so very awful, being nothing more than a long-coned night-cap with a tassel on the top, such as criminals wear at hanging-time. But when John saw a man's face under it, and a man's neck and shoulders slowly rising out of the pit, he could not doubt that this was the place where the murderers come to life again, according to the Exmoor story. He knew that a man had been hanged last week, and that this was the ninth day after it.

Therefore he could bear no more, thoroughly brave as he had been, neither did he wait to see what became of the gallows-man; but climbed on his horse with what speed he might, and rode away at full gallop. Neither did he dare go back by the way he came, fearing to face Black Barrow

Down! therefore he struck up the other track leading away towards Cloven Rocks, and after riding hard for an hour and drinking all his whisky, he luckily fell in with a shepherd, who led him on to a public-house somewhere near Exeford. And here he was so unmanned, the excitement being over, that nothing less than a gallon of ale and half a gammon of bacon, brought him to his right mind again. And he took good care to be home before dark, having followed a well-known sheep track.

When John Fry finished his story at last, after many exclamations from Annie, and from Lizzie, and much praise of his gallantry, yet some little disappointment that he had not stayed there a little longer, while he was about it, so as to be able to tell us more, I said to him very sternly,—

'Now, John, you have dreamed half this, my man. I firmly believe that you fell asleep at the top of the black combe, after drinking all your whisky, and never went on the moor at all. You know what a liar you are, John.'

The girls were exceedingly angry at this, and laid their hands before my mouth; but I waited for John to answer, with my eyes fixed upon him steadfastly.

'Bain't for me to denai,' said John, looking at me very honestly, 'but what a maight tull a lai, now and awhiles, zame as other men doth, and most of arl them as spaks again it; but this here be no lai, Maister Jan. I wush to God it wor, boy: a maight slape this naight the better.'

'I believe you speak the truth, John; and I ask your pardon. Now not a word to any one, about this strange affair. There is mischief brewing, I can see; and it is my place to attend to it. Several things come across me now—onlyI will not tell you.'

They were not at all contented with this; but I would give them no better; except to say, when they plagued me greatly, and vowed to sleep at my door all night,—

'Now, my dears, this is foolish of you. Too much of this matter is known already. It is for your own dear sakes that I am bound to be cautious. I have an opinion of my own; but it may be a very wrong one; I will not ask you to share it with me; neither will I make you inquisitive.'

Annie pouted, and Lizzie frowned, and Ruth looked at me with her eyes wide open, but no other mark of regarding me. And I saw that if any one of the three (for John Fry was gone home with the trembles) could be trusted to keep a secret, that one was Ruth Huckaback.

Chapter XXXII Feeding of the Pigs

The story told by John Fry that night, and my conviction of its truth, made me very uneasy, especially as following upon the warning of Judge Jeffreys, and the hints received from Jeremy Stickles, and the outburst of the tanner at Dunster, as well as sundry tales and rumours, and signs of secret understanding, seen and heard on market-days, and at places of entertainment. We knew for certain that at Taunton, Bridgwater, and even Dulverton, there was much disaffection towards the King, and regret for the days of the Puritans. Albeit I had told the truth, and the pure and simple truth, when, upon my examination, I had assured his lordship, that to the best of my knowledge there was nothing of the sort with us.

But now I was beginning to doubt whether I might not have been mistaken; especially when we heard, as we did, of arms being landed at Lynmouth, in the dead of the night, and of the tramp of men having reached some one's ears, from a hill where a famous echo was. For it must be plain to any conspirator (without the example of the Doones) that for the secret muster of men and the stowing of unlawful arms, and communication by beacon lights, scarcely a fitter place could be found than the wilds of Exmoor, with deep ravines running far inland from an unwatched and mostly a sheltered sea. For the Channel from Countisbury Foreland up to Minehead, or even farther, though rocky, and gusty, and full of currents, is safe from great rollers and the sweeping power of the south-west storms, which prevail with us more than all the others, and make sad work on the opposite coast.

But even supposing it probable that something against King Charles the Second (or rather against his Roman advisers, and especially his brother) were now in preparation amongst us, was it likely that Master Huckaback, a wealthy man, and a careful one, known moreover to the Lord Chief Justice, would have anything to do with it? To this I could make no answer; Uncle Ben was so close a man, so avaricious, and so revengeful, that it was quite impossible to say what course he might pursue, without knowing all the chances of gain, or rise, or satisfaction to him. That he hated the Papists I knew full well, though he never spoke much about them; also that he had followed the march of Oliver Cromwell's army, but more as a suttler (people said) than as a real soldier; and that he would go a long way, and risk a great deal of money, to have his revenge on the Doones; although their name never passed his lips during the present visit.

But how was it likely to be as to the Doones themselves? Which side would they probably take in the coming movement, if movement indeed it would be? So far as they had any religion at all, by birth they were Roman Catholics—so much I knew from Lorna; and indeed it was well known all around, that a priest had been fetched more than once to the valley, to soothe some poor outlaw's departure. On the other hand, they were not likely to entertain much affection for the son of the man who had banished them and confiscated their property. And it was not at all impossible that desperate men, such as they were, having nothing to lose, but estates to recover, and not being held by religion much, should cast away all regard for the birth from which they had been cast out, and make common cause with a Protestant rising, for the chance of revenge and replacement.

However I do not mean to say that all these things occurred to me as clearly as I have set them down; only that I was in general doubt, and very sad perplexity. For mother was so warm, and innocent, and kind so to every one, that knowing some little by this time of the English constitution, I feared very greatly lest she should be punished for harbouring malcontents. As well as possible I knew, that if any poor man came to our door, and cried, 'Officers are after me; for God's sake take and hide me,' mother would take him in at once, and conceal, and feed him, even though he had been very violent; and, to tell the truth, so would both my sisters, and so indeed would I do. Whence it will be clear that we were not the sort of people to be safe among disturbances.

Before I could quite make up my mind how to act in this difficulty, and how to get at the rights of it (for I would not spy after Uncle Reuben, though I felt no great fear of the Wizard's Slough, and none of the man with the white night-cap), a difference came again upon it, and a change of chances. For Uncle Ben went away as suddenly as he first had come to us, giving no reason for his departure, neither claiming the pony, and indeed leaving something behind him of great value to my mother. For he begged her to see to his young grand-daughter, until he could find opportunity of fetching her safely to Dulverton. Mother was overjoyed at this, as she could not help displaying; and Ruth was quite as much delighted, although she durst not show it. For at Dulverton she had to watch and keep such ward on the victuals, and the in and out of the shopmen, that it went entirely against her heart, and she never could enjoy herself. Truly she was an altered girl from the day she came to us; catching our unsuspicious manners, and our free goodwill, and hearty noise of laughing.

By this time, the harvest being done, and the thatching of the ricks made sure against south-western tempests, and all the reapers being gone, with good money and thankfulness, I began to burn in spirit for the sight of Lorna. I had begged my sister Annie to let Sally Snowe know, once for all, that it was not in my power to have any thing more to do with her. Of course our Annie was not to grieve Sally, neither to let it appear for a moment that I suspected her kind views upon me, and her strong regard for our dairy: only I thought it right upon our part not to waste Sally's time any longer, being a handsome wench as she was, and many young fellows glad to marry her.

And Annie did this uncommonly well, as she herself told me afterwards, having taken Sally in the sweetest manner into her pure confidence, and opened half her bosom to her, about my very sad love affair. Not that she let Sally know, of course, who it was, or what it was; only that she made her understand, without hinting at any desire of it, that there was no chance now of having me. Sally changed colour a little at this, and then went on about a red cow which had passed seven needles at milking time.

Inasmuch as there are two sorts of month well recognised by the calendar, to wit the lunar and the solar, I made bold to regard both my months, in the absence of any provision, as intended to be strictly lunar. Therefore upon the very day when the eight weeks were expiring forth I went in search of Lorna, taking the pearl ring hopefully, and all the new-laid eggs I could find, and a dozen and a half of small trout from our brook. And the pleasure it gave me to catch those trout, thinking as every one came forth and danced upon the grass, how much she would enjoy him, is more than I can now describe, although I well remember it. And it struck me that after accepting my ring, and saying how much she loved me, it was possible that my Queen might invite me even to stay and sup with her: and so I arranged with dear Annie beforehand, who was now the greatest comfort to me, to account for my absence if I should be late.

But alas, I was utterly disappointed; for although I waited and waited for hours, with an equal amount both of patience and peril, no Lorna ever appeared at all, nor even the faintest sign of her. And another thing occurred as well, which vexed me more than it need have done, for so small a matter. And this was that my little offering of the trout and the new-laid eggs was carried off in the coolest manner by that vile Carver Doone. For thinking to keep them the fresher and nicer, away from so much handling, I laid them in a little bed of reeds by the side of the water, and placed some dog-leaves over them. And when I had quite forgotten about them, and was watching from my hiding-place beneath the willow-tree (for I liked not to enter Lorna's bower, without her permission; except just to peep that she was not there), and while I was turning the ring in my pocket, having just seen the new moon, I became aware of a great man coming eisurely down the valley. He had a broad-brimmed hat, and a leather jerkin, and heavy jack-boots to his middle thigh, and what was worst of all for me, on his shoulder he bore a long carbine. Having nothing to meet him withal but my staff, and desiring to avoid disturbance, I retired promptly into the chasm, keeping the tree betwixt us that he might not descry me, and watching from behind the jut of a rock, where now I had scraped myself a neat little hole for the purpose.

Presently the great man reappeared, being now within fifty yards of me, and the light still good enough, as he drew nearer for me to descry his features: and though I am not a judge of men's faces, there was something in his which turned me cold, as though with a kind of horror. Not that it was an ugly face; nay, rather it seemed a handsome one, so far as mere form and line might go, full of strength, and vigour, and will, and steadfast resolution. From the short black hair above the broad forehead, to the long black beard descending below the curt, bold chin, there was not any curve or glimpse of weakness or of afterthought. Nothing playful, nothing pleasant, nothing with a track of smiles; nothing which a friend could like, and laugh at him for having. And yet he might have been a good man (for I have known very good men so fortified by their own strange ideas of God): I say that he might have seemed a good man, but for the cold and cruel hankering of his steel-blue eyes.

Now let no one suppose for a minute that I saw all this in a moment; for I am very slow, and take a long time to digest things; only I like to set down, and have done with it, all the results of my knowledge, though they not manifold. But what I said to myself, just then, was no more than 'What a fellow to have Lorna!' Having my sense of right so outraged ugh, of course, I would never allow her to go so far as that), I almost longed that he might thrust his head in to look after me. For there I was, with my ash staff clubbed, ready to have at him, and not ill inclined to do so; if only he would come where strength, not firearms, must decide it. However, he suspected nothing of my dangerous neighbourhood, but walked his round like a sentinel, and turned at the brink of the water.

Then as he marched back again, along the margin of the stream, he espied my little hoard, covered up with dog-leaves. He saw that the leaves were upside down, and this of course drew his attention. I saw him stoop, and lay bare the fish, and the eggs set a little way from them and in my simple heart, I thought that now he knew all about me. But to my surprise, he seemed well-pleased; and his harsh short laughter came to me without echo,—

'Ha, ha! Charlie boy! Fisherman Charlie, have I caught thee setting bait for Lorna? Now, I understand thy fishings, and the robbing of Counsellor's hen roost. May I never have good roasting, if I have it not to-night and roast thee, Charlie, afterwards!'

With this he calmly packed up my fish, and all the best of dear Annie's eggs; and went away chuckling steadfastly, to his home, if one may call it so. But I was so thoroughly grieved and mortified by this most impudent robbery, that I started forth from my rocky screen with the intention of pursuing him, until my better sense arrested me, barely in time to escape his eyes. For I said to myself, that even supposing I could contend unarmed with him, it would be the greatest folly in the world to have my secret access known, and perhaps a fatal barrier placed between Lorna and myself, and I knew not what trouble brought upon her, all for the sake of a few eggs and fishes. It was better to bear this trifling loss, however ignominious and goading to the spirit, than to risk my love and Lorna's welfare, and perhaps be shot into the bargain. And I think that all will agree with me, that I acted for the wisest, in withdrawing to my shelter, though deprived of eggs and fishes.

Having waited (as I said) until there was no chance whatever of my love appearing, I hastened homeward very sadly; and the wind of early autumn moaned across the moorland. All the beauty of the harvest, all the gaiety was gone, and the early fall of dusk was like a weight upon me. Nevertheless, I went every evening thenceforward for a fortnight; hoping, every time in vain to find my hope and comfort. And meanwhile, what perplexed me most was that the signals were replaced, in order as agreed upon, so that Lorna could scarcely be restrained by any rigour.

One time I had a narrow chance of being shot and settled with; and it befell me thus. I was waiting very carelessly, being now a little desperate, at the entrance to the glen, instead of watching through my sight-hole, as the proper practice was. Suddenly a ball went by me, with a whizz and whistle, passing through my hat and sweeping it away all folded up. My soft hat fluttered far down the stream, before I had time to go after it, and with the help of both wind and water, was fifty yards gone in a moment. At this I had just enough mind left to shrink back very suddenly, and lurk very still and closely; for I knew what a narrow escape it had been, as I heard the bullet, hard set by the powder, sing mournfully down the chasm, like a drone banished out of the hive. And as I peered through my little cranny, I saw a wreath of smoke still floating where the thickness was of the withy-bed; and presently Carver Doone came forth, having stopped to reload his piece perhaps, and ran very swiftly to the entrance to see what he had shot.

Sore trouble had I to keep close quarters, from the slipperiness of the stone beneath me with the water sliding over it. My foe came quite to the verge of the fall, where the river began to comb over; and there he stopped for a minute or two, on the utmost edge of dry land, upon the very spot indeed where I had fallen senseless when I clomb it in my boyhood. I could hear him breathing hard and grunting, as in doubt and discontent, for he stood within a yard of me, and I kept my right fist ready for him, if he should discover me. Then at the foot of the waterslide, my black hat suddenly appeared, tossing in white foam, and fluttering like a raven wounded. Now I had doubted which hat to take, when I left home that day; till I thought that the black became me best, and might seem kinder to Lorna.

'Have I killed thee, old bird, at last?' my enemy cried in triumph; ''tis the third time I have shot at thee, and thou wast beginning to mock me. No more of thy cursed croaking now, to wake me in the morning. Ha, ha! there are not many who get three chances from Carver Doone; and none ever go beyond it.'

I laughed within myself at this, as he strode away in his triumph; for was not this his third chance of me, and he no whit the wiser? And then I thought that perhaps the chance might some day be on the other side.

For to tell the truth, I was heartily tired of lurking and playing bo-peep so long; to which nothing could have reconciled me, except my fear for Lorna. And here I saw was a man of strength fit for me to encounter, such as I had never met, but would be glad to meet with; having found no man of late who needed not my mercy at wrestling, or at single-stick. And growing more and more uneasy, as I found no Lorna, I would have tried to force the Doone Glen from the upper end, and take my chance of getting back, but for Annie and her prayers.

Now that same night I think it was, or at any rate the next one, that I noticed Betty Muxworthy going on most strangely. She made the queerest signs to me, when nobody was looking, and laid her fingers on her lips, and pointed over her shoulder. But I took little heed of her, being in a kind of dudgeon, and oppressed with evil luck; believing too that all she wanted was to have some little grumble about some petty grievance.

But presently she poked me with the heel of a fire-bundle, and passing close to my ear whispered, so that none else could hear her, 'Larna Doo-un.'

By these words I was so startled, that I turned round and stared at her; but she pretended not to know it, and began with all her might to scour an empty crock with a besom.

'Oh, Betty, let me help you! That work is much too hard for you,' I cried with a sudden chivalry, which only won rude answer.

'Zeed me adooing of thic, every naight last ten year, Jan, wiout vindin' out how hard it wor. But if zo bee thee wants to help, carr peg's bucket for me. Massy, if I ain't forgotten to fade the pegs till now.'

Favouring me with another wink, to which I now paid the keenest heed, Betty went and fetched the lanthorn from the hook inside the door. Then when she had kindled it, not allowing me any time to ask what she was after, she went outside, and pointed to the great bock of wash, and riddlings, and brown hulkage (for we ground our own corn always), and though she knew that Bill Dadds and Jem Slocombe had full work to carry it on a pole (with another to help to sling it), she said to me as quietly as a maiden might ask one to carry a glove, 'Jan Ridd, carr thic thing for me.'

So I carried it for her, without any words; wondering what she was up to next, and whether she had ever heard of being too hard on the willing horse. And when we came to hog-pound, she turned upon me suddenly, with the lanthorn she was bearing, and saw that I had the bock by one hand very easily.

'Jan Ridd,' she said, 'there be no other man in England cud a' dood it. Now thee shalt have Larna.'

While I was wondering how my chance of having Lorna could depend upon my power to carry pig's wash, and how Betty could have any voice in the matter (which seemed to depend upon her decision), and in short, while I was all abroad as to her knowledge and everything, the pigs, who had been fast asleep and dreaming in their emptiness, awoke with one accord at the goodness of the smell around them. They had resigned themselves, as even pigs do, to a kind of fast, hoping to break their fast more sweetly on the morrow morning. But now they tumbled out all headlong, pigs below and pigs above, pigs point-blank and pigs across, pigs courant and pigs rampant, but all alike prepared to eat, and all in good cadence squeaking.

'Tak smarl boocket, and bale un out; wad 'e waste sich stoof as thic here be?' So Betty set me to feed the pigs, while she held the lanthorn; and knowing what she was, I saw that she would not tell me another word until all the pigs were served. And in truth no man could well look at them, and delay to serve them, they were all expressing appetite in so forcible a manner; some running to and fro, and rubbing, and squealing as if from starvation, some rushing down to the oaken troughs, and poking each other away from them; and the kindest of all putting up their fore-feet on the top-rail on the hog-pound, and blinking their little eyes, and grunting prettily to coax us; as who would say, 'I trust you now; you will be kind, I know, and give me the first and the very best of it.'

'Oppen ge-at now, wull 'e, Jan? Maind, young sow wi' the baible back arlway hath first toorn of it, 'cos I brought her up on my lap, I did. Zuck, zuck, zuck! How her stickth her tail up; do me good to zee un! Now thiccy trough, thee zany, and tak thee girt legs out o' the wai. Wish they wud gie thee a good baite, mak thee hop a bit vaster, I reckon. Hit that there girt ozebird over's back wi' the broomstick, he be robbing of my young zow. Choog, choog, choog! and a drap more left in the dripping-pail.'

'Come now, Betty,' I said, when all the pigs were at it sucking, swilling, munching, guzzling, thrusting, and ousting, and spilling the food upon the backs of their brethren (as great men do with their charity), 'come now, Betty, how much longer am I to wait for your message? Surely I am as good as a pig.'

'Dunno as thee be, Jan. No straikiness in thy bakkon. And now I come to think of it, Jan, thee zed, a wake agone last Vriday, as how I had got a girt be-ard. Wull 'e stick to that now, Maister Jan?'

'No, no, Betty, certainly not; I made a mistake about it. I should have said a becoming mustachio, such as you may well be proud of.'

'Then thee be a laiar, Jan Ridd. Zay so, laike a man, lad.'

'Not exactly that, Betty; but I made a great mistake; and I humbly ask your pardon; and if such a thing as a crown-piece, Betty'—

'No fai, no fai!' said Betty, however she put it into her pocket; 'now tak my advice, Jan; thee marry Zally Snowe.'

'Not with all England for her dowry. Oh, Betty, you know better.'

'Ah's me! I know much worse, Jan. Break thy poor mother's heart it will. And to think of arl the danger! Dost love Larna now so much?'

'With all the strength of my heart and soul. I will have her, or I will die, Betty.'

'Wull. Thee will die in either case. But it baint for me to argify. And do her love thee too, Jan?'

'I hope she does, Betty I hope she does. What do you think about it?'

'Ah, then I may hold my tongue to it. Knaw what boys and maidens be, as well as I knew young pegs. I myzell been o' that zort one taime every bit so well as you be.' And Betty held the lanthorn up, and defied me to deny it; and the light through the horn showed a gleam in her eyes, such as I had never seer there before. 'No odds, no odds about that,' she continued; 'mak a fool of myzell to spake of it. Arl gone into churchyard. But it be a lucky foolery for thee, my boy, I can tull 'ee. For I love to see the love in thee. Coom'th over me as the spring do, though I be naigh three score. Now, Jan, I will tell thee one thing, can't abear to zee thee vretting so. Hould thee head down, same as they pegs do.'

So I bent my head quite close to her; and she whispered in my ear, 'Goo of a marning, thee girt soft. Her can't get out of an avening now, her hath zent word to me, to tull 'ee.'

In the glory of my delight at this, I bestowed upon Betty a chaste salute, with all the pigs for witnesses; and she took it not amiss, considering how long she had been out of practice. But then she fell back, like a broom on its handle, and stared at me, feigning anger.

'Oh fai, oh fai! Lunnon impudence, I doubt. I vear thee hast gone on zadly, Jan.'

Chapter XXXIII An Early Morning Call

Of course I was up the very next morning before the October sunrise, and away through the wild and the woodland towards the Bagworthy water, at the foot of the long cascade. The rising of the sun was noble in the cold and warmth of it; peeping down the spread of light, he raised his shoulder heavily over the edge of grey mountain, and wavering length of upland. Beneath his gaze the dew-fogs dipped, and crept to the hollow places; then stole away in line and column, holding skirts, and clinging subtly at the sheltering corners, where rock hung over grass-land; while the brave lines of the hills came forth, one beyond other gliding.

Then the woods arose in folds, like drapery of awakened mountains, stately with a depth of awe, and memory of the tempests. Autumn's mellow hand was on them, as they owned already, touched with gold, and red, and olive; and their joy towards the sun was less to a bridegroom than a father.

Yet before the floating impress of the woods could clear itself, suddenly the gladsome light leaped over hill and valley, casting amber, blue, and purple, and a tint of rich red rose; according to the scene they lit on, and the curtain flung around; yet all alike dispelling fear and the cloven hoof of darkness, all on the wings of hope advancing, and proclaiming, 'God is here.' Then life and joy sprang reassured from every crouching hollow; every flower, and bud, and bird, had a fluttering sense of them; and all the flashing of God's gaze merged into soft beneficence.

So perhaps shall break upon us that eternal morning, when crag and chasm shall be no more, neither hill and valley, nor great unvintaged ocean; when glory shall not scare happiness, neither happiness envy glory; but all things shall arise and shine in the light of the Father's countenance, because itself is risen.

Who maketh His sun to rise upon both the just and the unjust. And surely but for the saving clause, Doone Glen had been in darkness. Now, as I stood with scanty breath—for few men could have won that climb—at the top of the long defile, and the bottom of the mountain gorge all of myself, and the pain of it, and the cark of my discontent fell away into wonder and rapture. For I cannot help seeing things now and then, slow-witted as I have a right to be; and perhaps because it comes so rarely, the sight dwells with me like a picture.

The bar of rock, with the water-cleft breaking steeply through it, stood bold and bare, and dark in shadow, grey with red gullies down it. But the sun was beginning to glisten over the comb of the eastern highland, and through an archway of the wood hung with old nests and ivy. The lines of many a leaning tree were thrown, from the cliffs of the foreland, down upon the sparkling grass at the foot of the western crags. And through the dewy meadow's breast, fringed with shade, but touched on one side with the sun-smile, ran the crystal water, curving in its brightness like diverted hope.

On either bank, the blades of grass, making their last autumn growth, pricked their spears and crisped their tuftings with the pearly purity. The tenderness of their green appeared under the glaucous mantle; while that grey suffusion, which is the blush of green life, spread its damask chastity. Even then my soul was lifted, worried though my mind was: who can see such large kind doings, and not be ashamed of human grief?

Not only unashamed of grief, but much abashed with joy, was I, when I saw my Lorna coming, purer than the morning dew, than the sun more bright and clear. That which made me love her so, that which lifted my heart to her, as the Spring wind lifts the clouds, was the gayness of her nature, and its inborn playfulness. And yet all this with maiden shame, a conscious dream of things unknown, and a sense of fate about them.

Down the valley still she came, not witting that I looked at her, having ceased (through my own misprison) to expect me yet awhile; or at least she told herself so. In the joy of awakened life and brightness of the morning, she had cast all care away, and seemed to float upon the sunrise, like a buoyant silver wave. Suddenly at sight of me, for I leaped forth at once, in fear of seeming to watch her unawares, the bloom upon her cheeks was deepened, and the radiance of her eyes; and she came to meet me gladly.

'At last then, you are come, John. I thought you had forgotten me. I could not make you understand—they have kept me prisoner every evening: but come into my house; you are in danger here.'

Meanwhile I could not answer, being overcome with joy, but followed to her little grotto, where I had been twice before. I knew that the crowning moment of my life was coming—that Lorna would own her love for me.

She made for awhile as if she dreamed not of the meaning of my gaze, but tried to speak of other things, faltering now and then, and mantling with a richer damask below her long eyelashes.

'This is not what I came to know,' I whispered very softly, 'you know what I am come to ask.'

'If you are come on purpose to ask anything, why do you delay so?' She turned away very bravely, but I saw that her lips were trembling.

'I delay so long, because I fear; because my whole life hangs in balance on a single word; because what I have near me now may never more be near me after, though more than all the world, or than a thousand worlds, to me.' As I spoke these words of passion in a low soft voice, Lorna trembled more and more; but she made no answer, neither yet looked up at me.

'I have loved you long and long,' I pursued, being reckless now, 'when you were a little child, as a boy I worshipped you: then when I saw you a comely girl, as a stripling I adored you: now that you are a full-grown maiden all the rest I do, and more—I love you more than tongue can tell, or heart can hold in silence. I have waited long and long; and though I am so far below you I can wait no longer; but must have my answer.'

'You have been very faithful, John,' she murmured to the fern and moss; 'I suppose I must reward you.'

'That will not do for me,' I said; 'I will not have reluctant liking, nor assent for pity's sake; which only means endurance. I must have all love, or none, I must have your heart of hearts; even as you have mine, Lorna.'

While I spoke, she glanced up shyly through her fluttering lashes, to prolong my doubt one moment, for her own delicious pride. Then she opened wide upon me all the glorious depth and softness of her loving eyes, and flung both arms around my neck, and answered with her heart on mine,—

'Darling, you have won it all. I shall never be my own again. I am yours, my own one, for ever and for ever.'

I am sure I know not what I did, or what I said thereafter, being overcome with transport by her words and at her gaze. Only one thing I remember, when she raised her bright lips to me, like a child, for me to kiss, such a smile of sweet temptation met me through her flowing hair, that I almost forgot my manners, giving her no time to breathe.

'That will do,' said Lorna gently, but violently blushing; 'for the present that will do, John. And now remember one thing, dear. All the kindness is to be on my side; and you are to be very distant, as behoves to a young maiden; except when I invite you. But you may kiss my hand, John; oh, yes, you may kiss my hand, you know. Ah to be sure! I had forgotten; how very stupid of me!'

For by this time I had taken one sweet hand and gazed on it, with the pride of all the world to think that such a lovely thing was mine; and then I slipped my little ring upon the wedding finger; and this time Lorna kept it, and looked with fondness on its beauty, and clung to me with a flood of tears.

'Every time you cry,' said I, drawing her closer to me 'I shall consider it an invitation not to be too distant. There now, none shall make you weep. Darling, you shall sigh no more, but live in peace and happiness, with me to guard and cherish you: and who shall dare to vex you?' But she drew a long sad sigh, and looked at the ground with the great tears rolling, and pressed one hand upon the trouble of her pure young breast.

'It can never, never be,' she murmured to herself alone: 'Who am I, to dream of it? Something in my heart tells me it can be so never, never.'

Chapter XXXIV Two Negatives Make An Affirmative

There was, however, no possibility of depressing me at such a time. To be loved by Lorna, the sweet, the pure, the playful one, the fairest creature on God's earth and the most enchanting, the lady of high birth and mind; that I, a mere clumsy, blundering yeoman, without wit, or wealth, or lineage, should have won that loving heart to be my own for ever, was a thought no fears could lessen, and no chance could steal from me.

Therefore at her own entreaty taking a very quick adieu, and by her own invitation an exceeding kind one, I hurried home with deep exulting, yet some sad misgivings, for Lorna had made me promise now to tell my mother everything; as indeed I always meant to do, when my suit should be gone too far to stop. I knew, of course, that my dear mother would be greatly moved and vexed, the heirship of Glen Doone not being a very desirable dower, but in spite of that, and all disappointment as to little Ruth Huckaback, feeling my mother's tenderness and deep affection to me, and forgiving nature, I doubted not that before very long she would view the matter as I did. Moreover, I felt that if once I could get her only to look at Lorna, she would so love and glory in her, that I should obtain all praise and thanks, perchance without deserving them.

Unluckily for my designs, who should be sitting down at breakfast with my mother and the rest but Squire Faggus, as everybody now began to entitle him. I noticed something odd about him, something uncomfortable in his manner, and a lack of that ease and humour which had been wont to distinguish him. He took his breakfast as it came, without a single joke about it, or preference of this to that; but with sly soft looks at Annie, who seemed unable to sit quiet, or to look at any one steadfastly. I feared in my heart what was coming on, and felt truly sorry for poor mother. After breakfast it became my duty to see to the ploughing of a barley-stubble ready for the sowing of a French grass, and I asked Tom Faggus to come with me, but he refused, and I knew the reason. Being resolved to allow him fair field to himself, though with great displeasure that a man of such illegal repute should marry into our family, which had always been counted so honest, I carried my dinner upon my back, and spent the whole day with the furrows.

When I returned, Squire Faggus was gone; which appeared to me but a sorry sign, inasmuch as if mother had taken kindly to him and his intentions, she would surely have made him remain awhile to celebrate the occasion. And presently no doubt was left: for Lizzie came running to meet me, at the bottom of the woodrick, and cried,—

'Oh, John, there is such a business. Mother is in such a state of mind, and Annie crying her eyes out. What do you think? You would never guess, though I have suspected it, ever so long.'

'No need for me to guess,' I replied, as though with some indifference, because of her self-important air; 'I knew all about it long ago. You have not been crying much, I see. I should like you better if you had.'

'Why should I cry? I like Tom Faggus. He is the only one I ever see with the spirit of a man.'

This was a cut, of course, at me. Mr. Faggus had won the goodwill of Lizzie by his hatred of the Doones, and vows that if he could get a dozen men of any courage to join him, he would pull their stronghold about their ears without any more ado. This malice of his seemed strange to me, as he had never suffered at their hands, so far at least as I knew; was it to be attributed to his jealousy of outlaws who excelled him in his business? Not being good at repartee, I made no answer to Lizzie, having found this course more irksome to her than the very best invective: and so we entered the house together; and mother sent at once for me, while I was trying to console my darling sister Annie.

'Oh, John! speak one good word for me,' she cried with both hands laid in mine, and her tearful eyes looking up at me.

'Not one, my pet, but a hundred,' I answered, kindly embracing her: 'have no fear, little sister: I am going to make your case so bright, by comparison, I mean, that mother will send for you in five minutes, and call you her best, her most dutiful child, and praise Cousin Tom to the skies, and send a man on horseback after him; and then you will have a harder task to intercede for me, my dear.'

'Oh, John, dear John, you won't tell her about Lorna—oh, not to-day, dear.'

'Yes, to-day, and at once, Annie. I want to have it over, and be done with it.'

'Oh, but think of her, dear. I am sure she could not bear it, after this great shock already.'

'She will bear it all the better,' said I; 'the one will drive the other out. I know exactly what mother is. She will be desperately savage first with you, and then with me, and then for a very little while with both of us together; and then she will put one against the other (in her mind I mean) and consider which was most to blame; and in doing that she will be compelled to find the best in either's case, that it may beat the other; and so as the pleas come before her mind, they will gain upon the charges, both of us being her children, you know: and before very long (particularly if we both keep out of the way) she will begin to think that after all she has been a little too hasty, and then she will remember how good we have always been to her; and how like our father. Upon that, she will think of her own love-time, and sigh a good bit, and cry a little, and then smile, and send for both of us, and beg our pardon, and call us her two darlings.'

'Now, John, how on earth can you know all that?' exclaimed my sister, wiping her eyes, and gazing at me with a soft bright smile. 'Who on earth can have told you, John? People to call you stupid indeed! Why, I feel that all you say is quite true, because you describe so exactly what I should do myself; I mean—I mean if I had two children, who had behaved as we have done. But tell me, darling John, how you learned all this.'

'Never you mind,' I replied, with a nod of some conceit, I fear: 'I must be a fool if I did not know what mother is by this time.'

Now inasmuch as the thing befell according to my prediction, what need for me to dwell upon it, after saying how it would be? Moreover, I would regret to write down what mother said about Lorna, in her first surprise and tribulation; not only because I was grieved by the gross injustice of it, and frightened mother with her own words (repeated deeply after her); but rather because it is not well, when people repent of hasty speech, to enter it against them.

That is said to be the angels' business; and I doubt if they can attend to it much, without doing injury to themselves.

However, by the afternoon, when the sun began to go down upon us, our mother sat on the garden bench, with her head on my great otter-skin waistcoat (which was waterproof), and her right arm round our Annie's waist, and scarcely knowing which of us she ought to make the most of, or which deserved most pity. Not that she had forgiven yet the rivals to her love—Tom Faggus, I mean, and Lorna—but that she was beginning to think a tattle better of them now, and a vast deal better of her own children.

And it helped her much in this regard, that she was not thinking half so well as usual of herself, or rather of her own judgment; for in good truth she had no self, only as it came home to her, by no very distant road, but by way of her children. A better mother never lived; and can I, after searching all things, add another word to that?

And indeed poor Lizzie was not so very bad; but behaved (on the whole) very well for her. She was much to be pitied, poor thing, and great allowances made for her, as belonging to a well-grown family, and a very comely one; and feeling her own shortcomings. This made her leap to the other extreme, and reassert herself too much, endeavouring to exalt the mind at the expense of the body; because she had the invisible one (so far as can be decided) in better share than the visible. Not but what she had her points, and very comely points of body; lovely eyes to wit, and very beautiful hands and feet (almost as good as Lorna's), and a neck as white as snow; but Lizzie was not gifted with our gait and port, and bounding health.

Now, while we sat on the garden bench, under the great ash-tree, we left dear mother to take her own way, and talk at her own pleasure. Children almost always are more wide-awake than their parents. The fathers and the mothers laugh; but the young ones have the best of them. And now both Annie knew, and I, that we had gotten the best of mother; and therefore we let her lay down the law, as if we had been two dollies.

'Darling John,' my mother said, 'your case is a very hard one. A young and very romantic girl—God send that I be right in my charitable view of her—has met an equally simple boy, among great dangers and difficulties, from which my son has saved her, at the risk of his life at every step. Of course, she became attached to him, and looked up to him in every way, as a superior being'—

'Come now, mother,' I said; 'if you only saw Lorna, you would look upon me as the lowest dirt'—

'No doubt I should,' my mother answered; 'and the king and queen, and all the royal family. Well, this poor angel, having made up her mind to take compassion upon my son, when he had saved her life so many times, persuades him to marry her out of pure pity, and throw his poor mother overboard. And the saddest part of it all is this—'

'That my mother will never, never, never understand the truth,' said I.

'That is all I wish,' she answered; 'just to get at the simple truth from my own perception of it. John, you are very wise in kissing me; but perhaps you would not be so wise in bringing Lorna for an afternoon, just to see what she thinks of me. There is a good saddle of mutton now; and there are some very good sausages left, on the blue dish with the anchor, Annie, from the last little sow we killed.'

'As if Lorna would eat sausages!' said I, with appearance of high contempt, though rejoicing all the while that mother seemed to have her name so pat; and she pronounced it in a manner which made my heart leap to my ears: 'Lorna to eat sausages!'

'I don't see why she shouldn't,' my mother answered smiling, 'if she means to be a farmer's wife, she must take to farmer's ways, I think. What do you say, Annie?'

'She will eat whatever John desires, I should hope,' said Annie gravely; 'particularly as I made them.'

'Oh that I could only get the chance of trying her!' I answered, 'if you could once behold her, mother, you would never let her go again. And she would love you with all her heart, she is so good and gentle.'

'That is a lucky thing for me'; saying this my mother wept, as she had been doing off and on, when no one seemed to look at her; 'otherwise I suppose, John, she would very soon turn me out of the farm, having you so completely under her thumb, as she seems to have. I see now that my time is over. Lizzie and I will seek our fortunes. It is wiser so.'

'Now, mother,' I cried; 'will you have the kindness not to talk any nonsense? Everything belongs to you; and so, I hope, your children do. And you, in turn, belong to us; as you have proved ever since—oh, ever since we can remember. Why do you make Annie cry so? You ought to know better than that.'

Mother upon this went over all the things she had done before; how many times I know not; neither does it matter. Only she seemed to enjoy it more, every time of doing it. And then she said she was an old fool; and Annie (like a thorough girl) pulled her one grey hair out.

Chapter XXXV Ruth Is Not Like Lorna

Although by our mother's reluctant consent a large part of the obstacles between Annie and her lover appeared to be removed, on the other hand Lorna and myself gained little, except as regarded comfort of mind, and some ease to the conscience. Moreover, our chance of frequent meetings and delightful converse was much impaired, at least for the present; because though mother was not aware of my narrow escape from Carver Doone, she made me promise never to risk my life by needless visits. And upon this point, that is to say, the necessity of the visit, she was well content, as she said, to leave me to my own good sense and honour; only begging me always to tell her of my intention beforehand. This pledge, however, for her own sake, I declined to give; knowing how wretched she would be during all the time of my absence; and, on that account, I promised instead, that I would always give her a full account of my adventure upon returning.

Now my mother, as might be expected, began at once to cast about for some means of relieving me from all further peril, and herself from great anxiety. She was full of plans for fetching Lorna, in some wonderful manner, out of the power of the Doones entirely, and into her own hands, where she was to remain for at least a twelve-month, learning all mother and Annie could teach her of dairy business, and farm-house life, and the best mode of packing butter. And all this arose from my happening to say, without meaning anything, how the poor dear had longed for quiet, and a life of simplicity, and a rest away from violence! Bless thee, mother—now long in heaven, there is no need to bless thee; but it often makes a dimness now in my well-worn eyes, when I think of thy loving-kindness, warmth, and romantic innocence.

As to stealing my beloved from that vile Glen Doone, the deed itself was not impossible, nor beyond my daring; but in the first place would she come, leaving her old grandfather to die without her tendence? And even if, through fear of Carver and that wicked Counsellor, she should consent to fly, would it be possible to keep her without a regiment of soldiers? Would not the Doones at once ride forth to scour the country for their queen, and finding her (as they must do), burn our house, and murder us, and carry her back triumphantly?

All this I laid before my mother, and to such effect that she acknowledged, with a sigh that nothing else remained for me (in the present state of matters) except to keep a careful watch upon Lorna from safe distance, observe the policy of the Doones, and wait for a tide in their affairs. Meanwhile I might even fall in love (as mother unwisely hinted) with a certain more peaceful heiress, although of inferior blood, who would be daily at my elbow. I am not sure but what dear mother herself would have been disappointed, had I proved myself so fickle; and my disdain and indignation at the mere suggestion did not so much displease her; for she only smiled and answered,—

'Well, it is not for me to say; God knows what is good for us. Likings will not come to order; otherwise I should not be where I am this day. And of one thing I am rather glad; Uncle Reuben well deserves that his pet scheme should miscarry. He who called my boy a coward, an ignoble coward, because he would not join some crack-brained plan against the valley which sheltered his beloved one! And all the time this dreadful "coward" risking his life daily there, without a word to any one! How glad I am that you will not have, for all her miserable money, that little dwarfish granddaughter of the insolent old miser!'

She turned, and by her side was standing poor Ruth Huckaback herself, white, and sad, and looking steadily at my mother's face, which became as red as a plum while her breath deserted her.

'If you please, madam,' said the little maiden, with her large calm eyes unwavering, 'it is not my fault, but God Almighty's, that I am a little dwarfish creature. I knew not that you regarded me with so much contempt on that account; neither have you told my grandfather, at least within my hearing, that he was an insolent old miser. When I return to

Dulverton, which I trust to do to-morrow (for it is too late to-day), I shall be careful not to tell him your opinion of him, lest I should thwart any schemes you may have upon his property. I thank you all for your kindness to me, which has been very great, far more than a little dwarfish creature could, for her own sake, expect. I will only add for your further guidance one more little truth. It is by no means certain that my grandfather will settle any of his miserable money upon me. If I offend him, as I would in a moment, for the sake of a brave and straightforward man'—here she gave me a glance which I scarcely knew what to do with—'my grandfather, upright as he is, would leave me without a shilling. And I often wish it were so. So many miseries come upon me from the miserable money—' Here she broke down, and burst out crying, and ran away with a faint good-bye; while we three looked at one another, and felt that we had the worst of it.

'Impudent little dwarf!' said my mother, recovering her breath after ever so long. 'Oh, John, how thankful you ought to be! What a life she would have led you!'

'Well, I am sure!' said Annie, throwing her arms around poor mother: 'who could have thought that little atomy had such an outrageous spirit! For my part I cannot think how she can have been sly enough to hide it in that crafty manner, that John might think her an angel!'

'Well, for my part,' I answered, laughing, 'I never admired Ruth Huckaback half, or a quarter so much before. She is rare stuff. I would have been glad to have married her to-morrow, if I had never seen my Lorna.'

'And a nice nobody I should have been, in my own house!' cried mother: 'I never can be thankful enough to darling Lorna for saving me. Did you see how her eyes flashed?'

'That I did; and very fine they were. Now nine maidens out of ten would have feigned not to have heard one word that was said, and have borne black malice in their hearts. Come, Annie, now, would not you have done so?'

'I think,' said Annie, 'although of course I cannot tell, you know, John, that I should have been ashamed at hearing what was never meant for me, and should have been almost as angry with myself as anybody.'

'So you would,' replied my mother; 'so any daughter of mine would have done, instead of railing and reviling. However, I am very sorry that any words of mine which the poor little thing chose to overhear should have made her so forget herself. I shall beg her pardon before she goes, and I shall expect her to beg mine.'

'That she will never do,' said I; 'a more resolute little maiden never yet had right upon her side; although it was a mere accident. I might have said the same thing myself, and she was hard upon you, mother dear.'

After this, we said no more, at least about that matter; and little Ruth, the next morning, left us, in spite of all that we could do. She vowed an everlasting friendship to my younger sister Eliza; but she looked at Annie with some resentment, when they said good-bye, for being so much taller.

At any rate so Annie fancied, but she may have been quite wrong. I rode beside the little maid till far beyond Exeford, when all danger of the moor was past, and then I left her with John Fry, not wishing to be too particular, after all the talk about her money. She had tears in her eyes when she bade me farewell, and she sent a kind message home to mother, and promised to come again at Christmas, if she could win permission.

Upon the whole, my opinion was that she had behaved uncommonly well for a maid whose self-love was outraged, with spirit, I mean, and proper pride; and yet with a great endeavour to forgive, which is, meseems, the hardest of all things to a woman, outside of her own family.

After this, for another month, nothing worthy of notice happened, except of course that I found it needful, according to the strictest good sense and honour, to visit Lorna immediately after my discourse with mother, and to tell her all about it. My beauty gave me one sweet kiss with all her heart (as she always did, when she kissed at all), and I begged for one more to take to our mother, and before leaving, I obtained it. It is not for me to tell all she said, even supposing (what is not likely) that any one cared to know it, being more and more peculiar to ourselves and no one else. But one thing that she said was this, and I took good care to carry it, word for word, to my mother and Annie:—

'I never can believe, dear John, that after all the crime and outrage wrought by my reckless family, it ever can be meant for me to settle down to peace and comfort in a simple household. With all my heart I long for home; any home, however dull and wearisome to those used to it, would seem a paradise to me, if only free from brawl and tumult, and such as I could call my own. But even if God would allow me this, in lieu of my wild inheritance, it is quite certain that the Doones never can and never will.'

Again, when I told her how my mother and Annie, as well as myself, longed to have her at Plover's Barrows, and teach her all the quiet duties in which she was sure to take such delight, she only answered with a bright blush, that while her grandfather was living she would never leave him; and that even if she were free, certain ruin was all she should bring to any house that received her, at least within the utmost reach of her amiable family. This was too plain to be denied, and seeing my dejection at it, she told me bravely that we must hope for better times, if possible, and asked how long I would wait for her.

'Not a day if I had my will,' I answered very warmly; at which she turned away confused, and would not look at me for awhile; 'but all my life,' I went on to say, 'if my fortune is so ill. And how long would you wait for me, Lorna?'

'Till I could get you,' she answered slyly, with a smile which was brighter to me than the brightest wit could be. 'And now,' she continued, 'you bound me, John, with a very beautiful ring to you, and when I dare not wear it, I carry it always on my heart. But I will bind you to me, you dearest, with the very poorest and plainest thing that ever you set eyes on. I could give you fifty fairer ones, but they would not be honest; and I love you for your honesty, and nothing else of course, John; so don't you be conceited. Look at it, what a queer old thing! There are some ancient marks upon it, very grotesque and wonderful; it looks like a cat in a tree almost, but never mind what it looks like. This old ring must have been a giant's; therefore it will fit you perhaps, you enormous John. It has been on the front of my old glass necklace (which my grandfather found them taking away, and very soon made them give back again) ever since I can remember; and long before that, as some woman told me. Now you seem very greatly amazed; pray what thinks my lord of it?'

'That is worth fifty of the pearl thing which I gave you, you darling; and that I will not take it from you.'

'Then you will never take me, that is all. I will have nothing to do with a gentleman'—

'No gentleman, dear—a yeoman.'

'Very well, a yeoman—nothing to do with a yeoman who will not accept my love-gage. So, if you please, give it back again, and take your lovely ring back.'

She looked at me in such a manner, half in earnest, half in jest, and three times three in love, that in spite of all good resolutions, and her own faint protest, I was forced to abandon all firm ideas, and kiss her till she was quite ashamed, and her head hung on my bosom, with the night of her hair shed over me. Then I placed the pearl ring back on the soft elastic bend of the finger she held up to scold me; and on my own smallest finger drew the heavy hoop she had given me. I considered this with satisfaction, until my darling recovered herself; and then I began very gravely about it, to keep her (if I could) from chiding me:—

'Mistress Lorna, this is not the ring of any giant. It is nothing more nor less than a very ancient thumb-ring, such as once in my father's time was ploughed up out of the ground in our farm, and sent to learned doctors, who told us all about it, but kept the ring for their trouble. I will accept it, my own one love; and it shall go to my grave with me.' And so it shall, unless there be villains who would dare to rob the dead.

Now I have spoken about this ring (though I scarcely meant to do so, and would rather keep to myself things so very holy) because it holds an important part in the history of my Lorna. I asked her where the glass necklace was from which the ring was fastened, and which she had worn in her childhood, and she answered that she hardly knew, but remembered that her grandfather had begged her to give it up to him, when she was ten years old or so, and had promised to keep it for her until she could take care of it; at the same time giving her back the ring, and fastening it from her pretty neck, and telling her to be proud of it. And so she always had been, and now from her sweet breast she took it, and it became John Ridd's delight.

All this, or at least great part of it, I told my mother truly, according to my promise; and she was greatly pleased with Lorna for having been so good to me, and for speaking so very sensibly; and then she looked at the great gold ring, but could by no means interpret it. Only she was quite certain, as indeed I myself was, that it must have belonged to an ancient race of great consideration, and high rank, in their time. Upon which I was for taking it off, lest it should be degraded by a common farmer's finger. But mother said 'No,' with tears in her eyes; 'if the common farmer had won the great lady of the ancient race, what were rings and old-world trinkets, when compared to the living jewel?' Being quite of her opinion in this, and loving the ring (which had no gem in it) as the token of my priceless gem, I resolved to wear it at any cost, except when I should be ploughing, or doing things likely to break it; although I must own that it felt very queer (for I never had throttled a finger before), and it looked very queer, for a length of time, upon my great hard-working hand.

And before I got used to my ring, or people could think that it belonged to me (plain and ungarnished though it was), and before I went to see Lorna again, having failed to find any necessity, and remembering my duty to mother, we all had something else to think of, not so pleasant, and more puzzling.

Chapter XXXVI John Returns to Business

Now November was upon us, and we had kept Allhallowmass, with roasting of skewered apples (like so many shuttlecocks), and after that the day of Fawkes, as became good Protestants, with merry bonfires and burned batatas, and plenty of good feeding in honour of our religion; and then while we were at wheat-sowing, another visitor arrived.

This was Master Jeremy Stickles, who had been a good friend to me (as described before) in London, and had earned my mother's gratitude, so far as ever he chose to have it. And he seemed inclined to have it all; for he made our farm-house his headquarters, and kept us quite at his beck and call, going out at any time of the evening, and coming back at any time of the morning, and always expecting us to be ready, whether with horse, or man, or maiden, or fire, or provisions. We knew that he was employed somehow upon the service of the King, and had at different stations certain troopers and orderlies quite at his disposal; also we knew that he never went out, nor even slept in his bedroom, without heavy firearms well loaded, and a sharp sword nigh his hand; and that he held a great commission, under royal signet, requiring all good subjects, all officers of whatever degree, and especially justices of the peace, to aid him to the utmost, with person, beast, and chattel, or to answer it at their peril.

Now Master Jeremy Stickles, of course, knowing well what women are, durst not open to any of them the nature of his instructions. But, after awhile, perceiving that I could be relied upon, and that it was a great discomfort not to have me with him, he took me aside in a lonely place, and told me nearly everything; having bound me first by oath, not to impart to any one, without his own permission, until all was over.

But at this present time of writing, all is over long ago; ay and forgotten too, I ween, except by those who suffered. Therefore may I tell the whole without any breach of confidence. Master Stickles was going forth upon his usual night journey, when he met me coming home, and I said something half in jest, about his zeal and secrecy; upon which he looked all round the yard, and led me to an open space in the clover field adjoining.

'John,' he said, 'you have some right to know the meaning of all this, being trusted as you were by the Lord Chief Justice. But he found you scarcely supple enough, neither gifted with due brains.'

'Thank God for that same,' I answered, while he tapped his head, to signify his own much larger allowance. Then he made me bind myself, which in an evil hour I did, to retain his secret; and after that he went on solemnly, and with much importance,—

'There be some people fit to plot, and others to be plotted against, and others to unravel plots, which is the highest gift of all. This last hath fallen to my share, and a very thankless gift it is, although a rare and choice one. Much of peril too attends it; daring courage and great coolness are as needful for the work as ready wit and spotless honour. Therefore His Majesty's advisers have chosen me for this high task, and they could not have chosen a better man. Although you have been in London, Jack, much longer than you wished it, you are wholly ignorant, of course, in matters of state, and the public weal.'

'Well,' said I, 'no doubt but I am, and all the better for me. Although I heard a deal of them; for everybody was talking, and ready to come to blows; if only it could be done without danger. But one said this, and one said that; and they talked so much about Birminghams, and Tantivies, and Whigs and Tories, and Protestant flails and such like, that I was only too glad to have my glass and clink my spoon for answer.'

'Right, John, thou art right as usual. Let the King go his own gait. He hath too many mistresses to be ever England's master. Nobody need fear him, for he is not like his father: he will have his own way, 'tis true, but without stopping other folk of theirs: and well he knows what women are, for he never asks them questions. Now heard you much in London town about the Duke of Monmouth?'

'Not so very much,' I answered; 'not half so much as in Devonshire: only that he was a hearty man, and a very handsome one, and now was banished by the Tories; and most people wished he was coming back, instead of the Duke of York, who was trying boots in Scotland.'

'Things are changed since you were in town. The Whigs are getting up again, through the folly of the Tories killing poor Lord Russell; and now this Master Sidney (if my Lord condemns him) will make it worse again. There is much disaffection everywhere, and it must grow to an outbreak. The King hath many troops in London, and meaneth to bring more from Tangier; but he cannot command these country places; and the trained bands cannot help him much, even if they would. Now, do you understand me, John?'

'In truth, not I. I see not what Tangier hath to do with Exmoor; nor the Duke of Monmouth with Jeremy Stickles.'

'Thou great clod, put it the other way. Jeremy Stickles may have much to do about the Duke of Monmouth. The Whigs having failed of Exclusion, and having been punished bitterly for the blood they shed, are ripe for any violence. And the turn of the balance is now to them. See-saw is the fashion of England always; and the Whigs will soon be the top-sawyers.'

'But,' said I, still more confused, '"The King is the top-sawyer," according to our proverb. How then can the Whigs be?'

'Thou art a hopeless ass, John. Better to sew with a chestnut than to teach thee the constitution. Let it be so, let it be. I have seen a boy of five years old more apt at politics than thou. Nay, look not offended, lad. It is my fault for being over-deep to thee. I should have considered thy intellect.'

'Nay, Master Jeremy, make no apologies. It is I that should excuse myself; but, God knows, I have no politics.'

'Stick to that, my lad,' he answered; 'so shalt thou die easier. Now, in ten words (without parties, or trying thy poor brain too much), I am here to watch the gathering of a secret plot, not so much against the King as against the due succession.'

'Now I understand at last. But, Master Stickles, you might have said all that an hour ago almost.'

'It would have been better, if I had, to thee,' he replied with much compassion; 'thy hat is nearly off thy head with the swelling of brain I have given thee. Blows, blows, are thy business, Jack. There thou art in thine element. And, haply, this business will bring thee plenty even for thy great head to take. Now hearken to one who wishes thee well, and plainly sees the end of it—stick thou to the winning side, and have naught to do with the other one.'

'That,' said I, in great haste and hurry, 'is the very thing I want to do, if I only knew which was the winning side, for the sake of Lorna—that is to say, for the sake of my dear mother and sisters, and the farm.'

'Ha!' cried Jeremy Stickles, laughing at the redness of my face—'Lorna, saidst thou; now what Lorna? Is it the name of a maiden, or a light-o'-love?'

'Keep to your own business,' I answered, very proudly; 'spy as much as e'er thou wilt, and use our house for doing it, without asking leave or telling; but if I ever find thee spying into my affairs, all the King's life-guards in London, and the dragoons thou bringest hither, shall not save thee from my hand—or one finger is enough for thee.'

Being carried beyond myself by his insolence about Lorna, I looked at Master Stickles so, and spake in such a voice, that all his daring courage and his spotless honour quailed within him, and he shrank—as if I would strike so small a man.

Then I left him, and went to work at the sacks upon the corn-floor, to take my evil spirit from me before I should see mother. For (to tell the truth) now my strength was full, and troubles were gathering round me, and people took advantage so much of my easy temper, sometimes when I was over-tried, a sudden heat ran over me, and a glowing of all my muscles, and a tingling for a mighty throw, such as my utmost self-command, and fear of hurting any one, could but ill refrain. Afterwards, I was always very sadly ashamed of myself, knowing how poor a thing bodily strength is, as compared with power of mind, and that it is a coward's part to misuse it upon weaker folk. For the present there was a little breach between Master Stickles and me, for which I blamed myself very sorely. But though, in full memory of his kindness and faithfulness in London, I asked his pardon many times for my foolish anger with him, and offered to undergo any penalty he would lay upon me, he only said it was no matter, there was nothing to forgive. When people say that, the truth often is that they can forgive nothing.

So for the present a breach was made between Master Jeremy and myself, which to me seemed no great loss, inasmuch as it relieved me from any privity to his dealings, for which I had small liking. All I feared was lest I might, in any way, be ungrateful to him; but when he would have no more of me, what could I do to help it? However, in a few days' time I was of good service to him, as you shall see in its proper place.

But now my own affairs were thrown into such disorder that I could think of nothing else, and had the greatest difficulty in hiding my uneasiness. For suddenly, without any warning, or a word of message, all my Lorna's signals ceased, which I had been accustomed to watch for daily, and as it were to feed upon them, with a glowing heart. The first time I stood on the wooded crest, and found no change from yesterday, I could hardly believe my eyes, or thought at least that it must be some great mistake on the part of my love. However, even that oppressed me with a heavy heart, which grew heavier, as I found from day to day no token.

Three times I went and waited long at the bottom of the valley, where now the stream was brown and angry with the rains of autumn, and the weeping trees hung leafless. But though I waited at every hour of day, and far into the night, no light footstep came to meet me, no sweet voice was in the air; all was lonely, drear, and drenched with sodden desolation. It seemed as if my love was dead, and the winds were at her funeral.

Once I sought far up the valley, where I had never been before, even beyond the copse where Lorna had found and lost her brave young cousin. Following up the river channel, in shelter of the evening fog, I gained a corner within stone's throw of the last outlying cot. This was a gloomy, low, square house, without any light in the windows, roughly built of wood and stone, as I saw when I drew nearer. For knowing it to be Carver's dwelling (or at least suspecting so, from some words of Lorna's), I was led by curiosity, and perhaps by jealousy, to have a closer look at it. Therefore, I crept up the stream, losing half my sense of fear, by reason of anxiety. And in truth there was not much to fear, the sky being now too dark for even a shooter of wild fowl to make good aim. And nothing else but guns could hurt me, as in the pride of my strength I thought, and in my skill of single-stick.

Nevertheless, I went warily, being now almost among this nest of cockatrices. The back of Carver's house abutted on the waves of the rushing stream; and seeing a loop-hole, vacant for muskets, I looked in, but all was quiet. So far as I could judge by listening, there was no one now inside, and my heart for a moment leaped with joy, for I had feared to find

Lorna there. Then I took a careful survey of the dwelling, and its windows, and its door, and aspect, as if I had been a robber meaning to make privy entrance. It was well for me that I did this, as you will find hereafter.

Having impressed upon my mind (a slow but, perhaps retentive mind), all the bearings of the place, and all its opportunities, and even the curve of the stream along it, and the bushes near the door, I was much inclined to go farther up, and understand all the village. But a bar of red light across the river, some forty yards on above me, and crossing from the opposite side like a chain, prevented me. In that second house there was a gathering of loud and merry outlaws, making as much noise as if they had the law upon their side. Some, indeed, as I approached, were laying down both right and wrong, as purely, and with as high a sense, as if they knew the difference. Cold and troubled as I was, I could hardly keep from laughing.

Before I betook myself home that night, and eased dear mother's heart so much, and made her pale face spread with smiles, I had resolved to penetrate Glen Doone from the upper end, and learn all about my Lorna. Not but what I might have entered from my unsuspected channel, as so often I had done; but that I saw fearful need for knowing something more than that. Here was every sort of trouble gathering upon me, here was Jeremy Stickles stealing upon every one in the dark; here was Uncle Reuben plotting Satan only could tell what; here was a white night-capped man coming bodily from the grave; here was my own sister Annie committed to a highwayman, and mother in distraction; most of all—here, there, and where—was my Lorna stolen, dungeoned, perhaps out-raged. It was no time for shilly shally, for the balance of this and that, or for a man with blood and muscle to pat his nose and ponder. If I left my Lorna so; if I let those black-soul'd villains work their pleasure on my love; if the heart that clave to mine could find no vigour in it—then let maidens cease from men, and rest their faith in tabby-cats.

Rudely rolling these ideas in my heavy head and brain I resolved to let the morrow put them into form and order, but not contradict them. And then, as my constitution willed (being like that of England), I slept, and there was no stopping me.

Chapter XXXVII A Very Desperate Venture

That the enterprise now resolved upon was far more dangerous than any hitherto attempted by me, needs no further proof than this:—I went and made my will at Porlock, with a middling honest lawyer there; not that I had much to leave, but that none could say how far the farm, and all the farming stock, might depend on my disposition. It makes me smile when I remember how particular I was, and how for the life of me I was puzzled to bequeath most part of my clothes, and hats, and things altogether my own, to Lorna, without the shrewd old lawyer knowing who she was and where she lived. At last, indeed, I flattered myself that I had baffled old

Tape's curiosity; but his wrinkled smile and his speech at parting made me again uneasy.

'A very excellent will, young sir. An admirably just and virtuous will; all your effects to your nearest of kin; filial and fraternal duty thoroughly exemplified; nothing diverted to alien channels, except a small token of esteem and reverence to an elderly lady, I presume: and which may or may not be valid, or invalid, on the ground of uncertainty, or the absence of any legal status on the part of the legatee. Ha, ha! Yes, yes! Few young men are so free from exceptionable entanglements. Two guineas is my charge, sir: and a rare good will for the money. Very prudent of you, sir. Does you credit in every way. Well, well; we all must die; and often the young before the old.'

Not only did I think two guineas a great deal too much money for a quarter of an hour's employment, but also I disliked particularly the words with which he concluded; they sounded, from his grating voice, like the evil omen of a croaking raven. Nevertheless I still abode in my fixed resolve to go, and find out, if I died for it, what was become of Lorna. And herein I lay no claim to courage; the matter being simply a choice between two evils, of which by far the greater one was, of course, to lose my darling.

The journey was a great deal longer to fetch around the Southern hills, and enter by the Doone-gate, than to cross the lower land and steal in by the water-slide. However, I durst not take a horse (for fear of the Doones who might be abroad upon their usual business), but started betimes in the evening, so as not to hurry, or waste any strength upon the way. And thus I came to the robbers' highway, walking circumspectly, scanning the sky-line of every hill, and searching the folds of every valley, for any moving figure.

Although it was now well on towards dark, and the sun was down an hour or so, I could see the robbers' road before me, in a trough of the winding hills, where the brook ploughed down from the higher barrows, and the coving banks were roofed with furze. At present, there was no one passing, neither post nor sentinel, so far as I could descry; but I thought it safer to wait a little, as twilight melted into night; and then I crept down a seam of the highland, and stood upon the Doone-track.

As the road approached the entrance, it became more straight and strong, like a channel cut from rock, with the water brawling darkly along the naked side of it. Not a tree or bush was left, to shelter a man from bullets: all was stern, and stiff, and rugged, as I could not help perceiving, even through the darkness, and a smell as of churchyard mould, a sense of being boxed in and cooped, made me long to be out again.

And here I was, or seemed to be, particularly unlucky; for as I drew near the very entrance, lightly of foot and warily, the moon (which had often been my friend) like an enemy broke upon me, topping the eastward ridge of rock, and filling all the open spaces with the play of wavering light. I shrank back into the shadowy quarter on the right side of the road; and gloomily employed myself to watch the triple entrance, on which the moonlight fell askew.

All across and before the three rude and beetling archways hung a felled oak overhead, black, and thick, and threatening. This, as I heard before, could be let fall in a moment, so as to crush a score of men, and bar the approach of horses. Behind this tree, the rocky mouth was spanned, as by a gallery with brushwood and piled timber, all upon a ledge of stone, where thirty men might lurk unseen, and fire at any invader. From that rampart it would be impossible to dislodge them, because the rock fell sheer below them twenty feet, or it may be more; while overhead it towered three hundred, and so jutted over that nothing could be cast upon them; even if a man could climb the height. And the access to this portcullis place—if I may so call it, being no portcullis there—was through certain rocky chambers known to the tenants only.

But the cleverest of their devices, and the most puzzling to an enemy, was that, instead of one mouth only, there were three to choose from, with nothing to betoken which was the proper access; all being pretty much alike, and all unfenced and yawning. And the common rumour was that in times of any danger, when any force was known to be on muster in their neighbourhood, they changed their entrance every day, and diverted the other two, by means of sliding doors to the chasms and dark abysses.

Now I could see those three rough arches, jagged, black, and terrible; and I knew that only one of them could lead me to the valley; neither gave the river now any further guidance; but dived underground with a sullen roar, where it met the cross-bar of the mountain. Having no means at all of judging which was the right way of the three, and knowing that the other two would lead to almost certain death, in the ruggedness and darkness,—for how could a man, among precipices and bottomless depths of water, without a ray of light, have any chance to save his life?—I do declare that I was half inclined to go away, and have done with it.

However, I knew one thing for certain, to wit, that the longer I stayed debating the more would the enterprise pall upon me, and the less my relish be. And it struck me that, in times of peace, the middle way was the likeliest; and the others diverging right and left in their farther parts might be made to slide into it (not far from the entrance), at the pleasure of the warders. Also I took it for good omen that I remembered (as rarely happened) a very fine line in the Latin grammar, whose emphasis and meaning is 'middle road is safest.'

Therefore, without more hesitation, I plunged into the middle way, holding a long ash staff before me, shodden at the end with iron. Presently I was in black darkness groping along the wall, and feeling a deal more fear than I wished to feel; especially when upon looking back I could no longer see the light, which I had forsaken. Then I stumbled over something hard, and sharp, and very cold, moreover so grievous to my legs that it needed my very best doctrine and humour to forbear from swearing, in the manner they use in London. But when I arose and felt it, and knew it to be a culverin, I was somewhat reassured thereby, inasmuch as it was not likely that they would plant this engine except in the real and true entrance.

Therefore I went on again, more painfully and wearily, and presently found it to be good that I had received that knock, and borne it with such patience; for otherwise I might have blundered full upon the sentries, and been shot without more ado. As it was, I had barely time to draw back, as I turned a corner upon them; and if their lanthorn had been in its place, they could scarce have failed to descry me, unless indeed I had seen the gleam before I turned the corner.

There seemed to be only two of them, of size indeed and stature as all the Doones must be, but I need not have feared to encounter them both, had they been unarmed, as I was. It was plain, however, that each had a long and heavy carbine, not in his hands (as it should have been), but standing close beside him. Therefore it behoved me now to be exceedingly careful, and even that might scarce avail, without luck in proportion. So I kept well back at the corner, and laid one cheek to the rock face, and kept my outer eye round the jut, in the wariest mode I could compass, watching my opportunity: and this is what I saw.

The two villains looked very happy—which villains have no right to be, but often are, meseemeth—they were sitting in a niche of rock, with the lanthorn in the corner, quaffing something from glass measures, and playing at push-pin, or shepherd's chess, or basset; or some trivial game of that sort. Each was smoking a long clay pipe, quite of new London shape, I could see, for the shadow was thrown out clearly; and each would laugh from time to time, as he fancied he got the better of it. One was sitting with his knees up, and left hand on his thigh; and this one had his back to me, and seemed to be the stouter. The other leaned more against the rock, half sitting and half astraddle, and wearing leathern overalls, as if newly come from riding. I could see his face quite clearly by the light of the open lanthorn, and a handsomer or a bolder face I had seldom, if ever, set eyes upon; insomuch that it made me very unhappy to think of his being so near my Lorna.

'How long am I to stand crouching here?' I asked of myself, at last, being tired of hearing them cry, 'score one,' 'score two,' 'No, by—, Charlie,' 'By—, I say it is, Phelps.' And yet my only chance of slipping by them unperceived was to wait till they quarrelled more, and came to blows about it. Presently, as I made up my mind to steal along towards them (for the cavern was pretty wide, just there), Charlie, or Charleworth Doone, the younger and taller man, reached forth his hand to seize the money, which he swore he had won that time. Upon this, the other jerked his arm, vowing that he had no right to it; whereupon Charlie flung at his face the contents of the glass he was sipping, but missed him and hit the candle, which sputtered with a flare of blue flame (from the strength perhaps of the spirit) and then went out completely. At this, one swore, and the other laughed; and before they had settled what to do, I was past them and round the corner.

And then, like a giddy fool as I was, I needs must give them a startler—the whoop of an owl, done so exactly, as John Fry had taught me, and echoed by the roof so fearfully, that one of them dropped the tinder box; and the other caught up his gun and cocked it, at least as I judged by the sounds they made. And then, too late, I knew my madness, for if either of them had fired, no doubt but what all the village would have risen and rushed upon me. However, as the luck of the matter went, it proved for my advantage; for I heard one say to the other,—

'Curse it, Charlie, what was that? It scared me so, I have dropped my box; my flint is gone, and everything. Will the brimstone catch from your pipe, my lad?'

'My pipe is out, Phelps, ever so long. Damn it, I am not afraid of an owl, man. Give me the lanthorn, and stay here. I'm not half done with you yet, my friend.'

'Well said, my boy, well said! Go straight to Carver's, mind you. The other sleepy heads be snoring, as there is nothing up to-night. No dallying now under Captain's window. Queen will have nought to say to you; and Carver will punch your head into a new wick for your lanthorn.'

'Will he though? Two can play at that.' And so after some rude jests, and laughter, and a few more oaths, I heard Charlie (or at any rate somebody) coming toward me, with a loose and not too sober footfall. As he reeled a little in his gait, and I would not move from his way one inch, after his talk of Lorna, but only longed to grasp him (if common sense permitted it), his braided coat came against my thumb, and his leathern gaiters brushed my knee. If he had turned or noticed it, he would have been a dead man in a moment; but his drunkenness saved him.

So I let him reel on unharmed; and thereupon it occurred to me that I could have no better guide, passing as he would exactly where I wished to be; that is to say under Lorna's window. Therefore I followed him without any especial caution; and soon I had the pleasure of seeing his form against the moonlit sky. Down a steep and winding path, with a handrail at the corners (such as they have at Ilfracombe), Master Charlie tripped along—and indeed there was much tripping, and he must have been an active fellow to recover as he did—and after him walked I, much hoping (for his own poor sake) that be might not turn and espy me.

But Bacchus (of whom I read at school, with great wonder about his meaning—and the same I may say of Venus) that great deity preserved Charlie, his pious worshipper, from regarding consequences. So he led me very kindly to the top of the meadow land, where the stream from underground broke forth, seething quietly with a little hiss of bubbles. Hence I had fair view and outline of the robbers' township, spread with bushes here and there, but not heavily overshadowed. The moon, approaching now the full, brought the forms in manner forth, clothing each with character, as the moon (more than the sun) does, to an eye accustomed.

I knew that the Captain's house was first, both from what Lorna had said of it, and from my mother's description, and now again from seeing Charlie halt there for a certain time, and whistle on his fingers, and hurry on, fearing consequence. The tune that he whistled was strange to me, and lingered in my ears, as having something very new and striking, and fantastic in it. And I repeated it softly to myself, while I marked the position of the houses and the beauty of the village. For the stream, in lieu of any street, passing between the houses, and affording perpetual change, and twinkling, and reflections moreover by its sleepy murmur soothing all the dwellers there, this and the snugness of the position, walled with rock and spread with herbage, made it look, in the quiet moonlight, like a little paradise. And to think of all the inmates there, sleeping with good consciences, having plied their useful trade of making others work for them, enjoying life without much labour, yet with great renown.

Master Charlie went down the village, and I followed him carefully, keeping as much as possible in the shadowy places, and watching the windows of every house, lest any light should be burning. As I passed Sir Ensor's house, my heart leaped up, for I spied a window, higher than the rest above the ground, and with a faint light moving. This could hardly fail to be the room wherein my darling lay; for here that impudent young fellow had gazed while he was whistling. And here my courage grew tenfold, and my spirit feared no evil—for lo, if Lorna had been surrendered to that scoundrel, Carver, she would not have been at her grandfather's house, but in Carver's accursed dwelling.

Warm with this idea, I hurried after Charleworth Doone, being resolved not to harm him now, unless my own life required it. And while I watched from behind a tree, the door of the farthest house was opened; and sure enough it was Carver's self, who stood bareheaded, and half undressed in the doorway. I could see his great black chest, and arms, by the light of the lamp he bore.

'Who wants me this time of night?' he grumbled, in a deep gruff voice; 'any young scamp prowling after the maids shall have sore bones for his trouble.'

'All the fair maids are for thee, are they, Master Carver?' Charlie answered, laughing; 'we young scamps must be well-content with coarser stuff than thou wouldst have.'

'Would have? Ay, and will have,' the great beast muttered angrily. 'I bide my time; but not very long. Only one word for thy good, Charlie. I will fling thee senseless into the river, if ever I catch thy girl-face there again.'

'Mayhap, Master Carver, it is more than thou couldst do. But I will not keep thee; thou art not pleasant company to-night. All I want is a light for my lanthorn, and a glass of schnapps, if thou hast it.'

'What is become of thy light, then? Good for thee I am not on duty.'

'A great owl flew between me and Phelps, as we watched beside the culvern, and so scared was he at our fierce bright eyes that he fell and knocked the light out.'

'Likely tale, or likely lie, Charles! We will have the truth to-morrow. Here take thy light, and be gone with thee. All virtuous men are in bed now.'

'Then so will I be, and why art thou not? Ha, have I earned my schnapps now?'

'If thou hast, thou hast paid a bad debt; there is too much in thee already. Be off! my patience is done with.'

Then he slammed the door in the young man's face, having kindled his lanthorn by this time: and Charlie went up to the watchplace again, muttering as he passed me, 'Bad look-out for all of us, when that surly old beast is Captain. No gentle blood in him, no hospitality, not even pleasant language, nor a good new oath in his frowsy pate! I've a mind to cut the whole of it; and but for the girls I would so.'

My heart was in my mouth, as they say, when I stood in the shade by Lorna's window, and whispered her name gently. The house was of one story only, as the others were, with pine-ends standing forth the stone, and only two rough windows upon that western side of it, and perhaps both of them were Lorna's. The Doones had been their own builders, for no one should know their ins and outs; and of course their work was clumsy. As for their windows, they stole them mostly from the houses round about. But though the window was not very close, I might have whispered long enough, before she would have answered me; frightened as she was, no doubt by many a rude overture. And I durst not speak aloud because I saw another watchman posted on the western cliff, and commanding all the valley. And now this man (having no companion for drinking or for gambling) espied me against the wall of the house, and advanced to the brink, and challenged me.

'Who are you there? Answer! One, two, three; and I fire at thee.'

The nozzle of his gun was pointed full upon me, as I could see, with the moonlight striking on the barrel; he was not more than fifty yards off, and now he began to reckon. Being almost desperate about it, I began to whistle, wondering how far I should get before I lost my windpipe: and as luck would have it, my lips fell into that strange tune I had practised last; the one I had heard from Charlie. My mouth would scarcely frame the notes, being parched with terror; but to my surprise, the man fell back, dropped his gun, and saluted. Oh, sweetest of all sweet melodies!

That tune was Carver Doone's passport (as I heard long afterwards), which Charleworth Doone had imitated, for decoy of Lorna. The sentinel took me for that vile Carver; who was like enough to be prowling there, for private talk with Lorna; but not very likely to shout forth his name, if it might be avoided. The watchman, perceiving the danger perhaps of intruding on Carver's privacy, not only retired along the cliff, but withdrew himself to good distance.

Meanwhile he had done me the kindest service; for Lorna came to the window at once, to see what the cause of the shout was, and drew back the curtain timidly. Then she opened the rough lattice; and then she watched the cliff and trees; and then she sighed very sadly.

'Oh, Lorna, don't you know me?' I whispered from the side, being afraid of startling her by appearing over suddenly.

Quick though she always was of thought, she knew me not from my whisper, and was shutting the window hastily when I caught it back, and showed myself.

'John!' she cried, yet with sense enough not to speak aloud: 'oh, you must be mad, John.'

'As mad as a March hare,' said I, 'without any news of my darling. You knew I would come: of course you did.'

'Well, I thought, perhaps—you know: now, John, you need not eat my hand. Do you see they have put iron bars across?'

'To be sure. Do you think I should be contented, even with this lovely hand, but for these vile iron bars. I will have them out before I go. Now, darling, for one moment—just the other hand, for a change, you know.'

So I got the other, but was not honest; for I kept them both, and felt their delicate beauty trembling, as I laid them to my heart.

'Oh, John, you will make me cry directly'—she had been crying long ago—'if you go on in that way. You know we can never have one another; every one is against it. Why should I make you miserable? Try not to think of me any more.'

'And will you try the same of me, Lorna?'

'Oh yes, John; if you agree to it. At least I will try to try it.'

'Then you won't try anything of the sort,' I cried with great enthusiasm, for her tone was so nice and melancholy: 'the only thing we will try to try, is to belong to one another. And if we do our best, Lorna, God alone can prevent us.'

She crossed herself, with one hand drawn free as I spoke so boldly; and something swelled in her little throat, and prevented her from answering.

'Now tell me,' I said; 'what means all this? Why are you so pent up here? Why have you given me no token? Has your grandfather turned against you? Are you in any danger?'

'My poor grandfather is very ill: I fear that he will not live long. The Counsellor and his son are now the masters of the valley; and I dare not venture forth, for fear of anything they might do to me. When I went forth, to signal for you, Carver tried to seize me; but I was too quick for him. Little Gwenny is not allowed to leave the valley now; so that I could send no message. I have been so wretched, dear, lest you should think me false to you. The tyrants now make sure of me. You must watch this house, both night and day, if you wish to save me. There is nothing they would shrink from; if my poor grandfather—oh, I cannot bear to think of myself, when I ought to think of him only; dying without a son to tend him, or a daughter to shed a tear.'

'But surely he has sons enough; and a deal too many,' I was going to say, but stopped myself in time: 'why do none of them come to him?'

'I know not. I cannot tell. He is a very strange old man; and few have ever loved him. He was black with wrath at the Counsellor, this very afternoon—but I must not keep you here—you are much too brave, John; and I am much too selfish: there, what was that shadow?'

'Nothing more than a bat, darling, come to look for his sweetheart. I will not stay long; you tremble so: and yet for that very reason, how can I leave you, Lorna?'

'You must—you must,' she answered; 'I shall die if they hurt you. I hear the old nurse moving. Grandfather is sure to send for me. Keep back from the window.'

However, it was only Gwenny Carfax, Lorna's little handmaid: my darling brought her to the window and presented her to me, almost laughing through her grief.

'Oh, I am so glad, John; Gwenny, I am so glad you came. I have wanted long to introduce you to my "young man," as you call him. It is rather dark, but you can see him. I wish you to know him again, Gwenny.'

'Whoy!' cried Gwenny, with great amazement, standing on tiptoe to look out, and staring as if she were weighing me: 'her be bigger nor any Doone! Heared as her have bate our Cornish champion awrastling. 'Twadn't fair play nohow: no, no; don't tell me, 'twadn't fair play nohow.'

'True enough, Gwenny,' I answered her; for the play had been very unfair indeed on the side of the Bodmin champion; 'it was not a fair bout, little maid; I am free to acknowledge that.' By that answer, or rather by the construction she put upon it, the heart of the Cornish girl was won, more than by gold and silver.

'I shall knoo thee again, young man; no fear of that,' she answered, nodding with an air of patronage. 'Now, missis, gae on coortin', and I wall gae outside and watch for 'ee.' Though expressed not over delicately, this proposal arose, no doubt, from Gwenny's sense of delicacy; and I was very thankful to her for taking her departure.

'She is the best little thing in the world,' said Lorna, softly laughing; 'and the queerest, and the truest. Nothing will bribe her against me. If she seems to be on the other side, never, never doubt her. Now no more of your "coortin'," John! I love you far too well for that. Yes, yes, ever so much! If you will take a mean advantage of me. And as much as ever you like to imagine; and then you may double it, after that. Only go, do go, good John; kind, dear, darling John; if you love me, go.'

'How can I go without settling anything?' I asked very sensibly. 'How shall I know of your danger now? Hit upon something; you are so quick. Anything you can think of; and then I will go, and not frighten you.'

'I have been thinking long of something,' Lorna answered rapidly, with that peculiar clearness of voice which made every syllable ring like music of a several note, 'you see that tree with the seven rooks' nests bright against the cliffs there? Can you count them, from above, do you think? From a place where you will be safe, dear'—

'No doubt, I can; or if I cannot, it will not take me long to find a spot, whence I can do it.'

'Gwenny can climb like any cat. She has been up there in the summer, watching the young birds, day by day, and daring the boys to touch them. There are neither birds, nor eggs there now, of course, and nothing doing. If you see but six rooks' nests; I am in peril and want you. If you see but five, I am carried off by Carver.'

'Good God!' said I, at the mere idea; in a tone which frightened Lorna.

'Fear not, John,' she whispered sadly, and my blood grew cold at it: 'I have means to stop him; or at least to save myself. If you can come within one day of that man's getting hold of me, you will find me quite unharmed. After that you will find me dead, or alive, according to circumstances, but in no case such that you need blush to look at me.'

Her dear sweet face was full of pride, as even in the gloom I saw: and I would not trespass on her feelings by such a thing, at such a moment, as an attempt at any caress. I only said, 'God bless you, darling!' and she said the same to me, in a very low sad voice. And then I stole below Carver's house, in the shadow from the eastern cliff; and knowing enough of the village now to satisfy all necessity, betook myself to my well-known track in returning from the valley; which was neither down the waterslide (a course I feared in the darkness) nor up the cliffs at Lorna's bower; but a way of my own inventing, which there is no need to dwell upon.

A weight of care was off my mind; though much of trouble hung there still. One thing was quite certain—if Lorna could not have John Ridd, no one else should have her. And my mother, who sat up for me, and with me long time afterwards, agreed that this was comfort.

Chapter XXXVIII A Good Turn for Jeremy

John Fry had now six shillings a week of regular and permanent wage, besides all harvest and shearing money, as well as a cottage rent-free, and enough of garden-ground to rear pot-herbs for his wife and all his family. Now the wages appointed by our justices, at the time of sessions, were four-and-sixpence a week for summer, and a shilling less for the winter-time; and we could be fined, and perhaps imprisoned, for giving more than the sums so fixed. Therefore John Fry was looked upon as the richest man upon Exmoor, I mean of course among labourers, and there were many jokes about robbing him, as if he were the mint of the King; and Tom Faggus promised to try his hand, if he came across John on the highway, although he had ceased from business, and was seeking a Royal pardon.

Now is it according to human nature, or is it a thing contradictory (as I would fain believe)? But anyhow, there was, upon Exmoor, no more discontented man, no man more sure that he had not his worth, neither half so sore about it, than, or as, John Fry was. And one thing he did which I could not wholly (or indeed I may say, in any measure) reconcile with my sense of right, much as I laboured to do John justice, especially because of his roguery; and this was, that if we said too much, or accused him at all of laziness (which he must have known to be in him), he regularly turned round upon us, and quite compelled us to hold our tongues, by threatening to lay information against us for paying him too much wages!

Now I have not mentioned all this of John Fry, from any disrespect for his memory (which is green and honest amongst us), far less from any desire to hurt the feelings of his grandchildren; and I will do them the justice, once for all, to avow, thus publicly, that I have known a great many bigger rogues, and most of themselves in the number. But I have referred, with moderation, to this little flaw in a worthy character (or foible, as we call it, when a man is dead) for this reason only—that without it there was no explaining John's dealings with Jeremy Stickles.

Master Jeremy, being full of London and Norwich experience, fell into the error of supposing that we clods and yokels were the simplest of the simple, and could be cheated at his good pleasure. Now this is not so: when once we suspect that people have that idea of us, we indulge them in it to the top of their bent, and grieve that they should come out of it, as they do at last in amazement, with less money than before, and the laugh now set against them.

Ever since I had offended Jeremy, by threatening him (as before related) in case of his meddling with my affairs, he had more and more allied himself with simple-minded John, as he was pleased to call him. John Fry was everything: it was 'run and fetch my horse, John'—'John, are my pistols primed well?'—'I want you in the stable, John, about something very particular', until except for the rudeness of it, I was longing to tell Master Stickles that he ought to pay John's wages. John for his part was not backward, but gave himself the most wonderful airs of secrecy and importance, till half the parish began to think that the affairs of the nation were in his hand, and he scorned the sight of a dungfork.

It was not likely that this should last; and being the only man in the parish with any knowledge of politics, I gave John Fry to understand that he must not presume to talk so freely, as if he were at least a constable, about the constitution; which could be no affair of his, and might bring us all into trouble. At this he only tossed his nose, as if he had been in London at least three times for my one; which vexed me so that I promised him the thick end of the plough-whip if even the name of a knight of the shire should pass his lips for a fortnight.

Now I did not suspect in my stupid noddle that John Fry would ever tell Jeremy Stickles about the sight at the Wizard's Slough and the man in the white nightcap; because John had sworn on the blade of his knife not to breathe a word to any soul, without my full permission. However, it appears that John related, for a certain consideration, all that he had seen, and doubtless more which had accrued to it. Upon this Master Stickles was much astonished at Uncle Reuben's proceedings, having always accounted him a most loyal, keen, and wary subject.

All this I learned upon recovering Jeremy's good graces, which came to pass in no other way than by the saving of his life. Being bound to keep the strictest watch upon the seven rooks' nests, and yet not bearing to be idle and to waste my mother's stores, I contrived to keep my work entirely at the western corner of our farm, which was nearest to Glen Doone, and whence I could easily run to a height commanding the view I coveted.

One day Squire Faggus had dropped in upon us, just in time for dinner; and very soon he and King's messenger were as thick as need be. Tom had brought his beloved mare to show her off to Annie, and he mounted his pretty sweetheart upon her, after giving Winnie notice to be on her very best behaviour. The squire was in great spirits, having just accomplished a purchase of land which was worth ten times what he gave for it; and this he did by a merry trick upon old Sir Roger Bassett, who never supposed him to be in earnest, as not possessing the money. The whole thing was done on a bumper of claret in a tavern where they met; and the old knight having once pledged his word, no lawyers could hold him back from it. They could only say that Master Faggus, being attainted of felony, was not a capable grantee. 'I will soon cure that,' quoth Tom, 'my pardon has been ready for months and months, so soon as I care to sue it.'

And now he was telling our Annie, who listened very rosily, and believed every word he said, that, having been ruined in early innocence by the means of lawyers, it was only just, and fair turn for turn, that having become a match for them by long practice upon the highway, he should reinstate himself, at their expense, in society. And now he would go to London at once, and sue out his pardon, and then would his lovely darling Annie, etc., etc.—things which I had no right to hear, and in which I was not wanted.

Therefore I strode away up the lane to my afternoon's employment, sadly comparing my love with theirs (which now appeared so prosperous), yet heartily glad for Annie's sake; only remembering now and then the old proverb 'Wrong never comes right.'

I worked very hard in the copse of young ash, with my billhook and a shearing-knife; cutting out the saplings where they stooled too close together, making spars to keep for thatching, wall-crooks to drive into the cob, stiles for close sheep hurdles, and handles for rakes, and hoes, and two-bills, of the larger and straighter stuff. And all the lesser I bound in faggots, to come home on the sledd to the woodrick. It is not to be supposed that I did all this work, without many peeps at the seven rooks' nests, which proved my Lorna's safety. Indeed, whenever I wanted a change, either from cleaving, or hewing too hard, or stooping too much at binding, I was up and away to the ridge of the hill, instead of standing and doing nothing.

Soon I forgot about Tom and Annie; and fell to thinking of Lorna only; and how much I would make of her; and what I should call our children; and how I would educate them, to do honour to her rank; yet all the time I worked none the worse, by reason of meditation. Fresh-cut spars are not so good as those of a little seasoning; especially if the sap was not gone down at the time of cutting. Therefore we always find it needful to have plenty still in stock.

It was very pleasant there in the copse, sloping to the west as it was, and the sun descending brightly, with rocks and banks to dwell upon. The stems of mottled and dimpled wood, with twigs coming out like elbows, hung and clung together closely, with a mode of bending in, as children do at some danger; overhead the shrunken leaves quivered and rustled ripely, having many points like stars, and rising and falling delicately, as fingers play sad music. Along the bed of the slanting ground, all between the stools of wood, there were heaps of dead brown leaves, and sheltered mats of lichen, and drifts of spotted stick gone rotten, and tufts of rushes here and there, full of fray and feathering.

All by the hedge ran a little stream, a thing that could barely name itself, flowing scarce more than a pint in a minute, because of the sunny weather. Yet had this rill little crooks and crannies dark and bravely bearded, and a gallant rush through a reeden pipe—the stem of a flag that was grounded; and here and there divided threads, from the points of a branching stick, into mighty pools of rock (as large as a grown man's hat almost) napped with moss all around the sides and hung with corded grasses. Along and down the tiny banks, and nodding into one another, even across main channel, hung the brown arcade of ferns; some with gold tongues languishing; some with countless ear-drops jerking, some with great quilled ribs uprising and long saws aflapping; others cupped, and fanning over with the grace of yielding, even as a hollow fountain spread by winds that have lost their way.

Deeply each beyond other, pluming, stooping, glancing, glistening, weaving softest pillow lace, coying to the wind and water, when their fleeting image danced, or by which their beauty moved,—God has made no lovelier thing; and only He takes heed of them.

It was time to go home to supper now, and I felt very friendly towards it, having been hard at work for some hours, with only the voice of the little rill, and some hares and a pheasant for company. The sun was gone down behind the black wood on the farther cliffs of Bagworthy, and the russet of the tufts and spear-beds was becoming gray, while the greyness of the sapling ash grew brown against the sky; the hollow curves of the little stream became black beneath the grasses and the fairy fans innumerable, while outside the hedge our clover was crimping its leaves in the dewfall, like the cocked hats of wood-sorrel,—when, thanking God for all this scene, because my love had gifted me with the key to all things lovely, I prepared to follow their example, and to rest from labour.

Therefore I wiped my bill-hook and shearing-knife very carefully, for I hate to leave tools dirty; and was doubting whether I should try for another glance at the seven rooks' nests, or whether it would be too dark for it. It was now a quarter of an hour mayhap, since I had made any chopping noise, because I had been assorting my spars, and tying them in bundles, instead of plying the bill-hook; and the gentle tinkle of the stream was louder than my doings. To this, no doubt, I owe my life, which then (without my dreaming it) was in no little jeopardy.

For, just as I was twisting the bine of my very last faggot, before tucking the cleft tongue under, there came three men outside the hedge, where the western light was yellow; and by it I could see that all three of them carried firearms. These men were not walking carelessly, but following down the hedge-trough, as if to stalk some enemy: and for a moment it struck me cold to think it was I they were looking for. With the swiftness of terror I concluded that my visits to Glen Doone were known, and now my life was the forfeit.

It was a most lucky thing for me, that I heard their clothes catch in the brambles, and saw their hats under the rampart of ash, which is made by what we call 'splashing,' and lucky, for me that I stood in a goyal, and had the dark coppice behind me. To this I had no time to fly, but with a sort of instinct, threw myself flat in among the thick fern, and held my breath, and lay still as a log. For I had seen the light gleam on their gun-barrels, and knowing the faults of the neighbourhood, would fain avoid swelling their number. Then the three men came to the gap in the hedge, where I had been in and out so often; and stood up, and looked in over.

It is all very well for a man to boast that, in all his life, he has never been frightened, and believes that he never could be so. There may be men of that nature—I will not dare to deny it; only I have never known them. The fright I was now in was horrible, and all my bones seemed to creep inside me; when lying there helpless, with only a billet and the comb of fern to hide me, in the dusk of early evening, I saw three faces in the gap; and what was worse, three gun-muzzles.

'Somebody been at work here—' it was the deep voice of Carver Doone; 'jump up, Charlie, and look about; we must have no witnesses.'

'Give me a hand behind,' said Charlie, the same handsome young Doone I had seen that night; 'this bank is too devilish steep for me.'

'Nonsense, man!' cried Marwood de Whichehalse, who to my amazement was the third of the number; 'only a hind cutting faggots; and of course he hath gone home long ago. Blind man's holiday, as we call it. I can see all over the place; and there is not even a rabbit there.'

At that I drew my breath again, and thanked God I had gotten my coat on.

'Squire is right,' said Charlie, who was standing up high (on a root perhaps), 'there is nobody there now, captain; and lucky for the poor devil that he keepeth workman's hours. Even his chopper is gone, I see.'

'No dog, no man, is the rule about here, when it comes to coppice work,' continued young de Whichehalse; there is not a man would dare work there, without a dog to scare the pixies.'

'There is a big young fellow upon this farm,' Carver Doone muttered sulkily, 'with whom I have an account to settle, if ever I come across him. He hath a cursed spite to us, because we shot his father. He was going to bring the lumpers upon us, only he was afeared, last winter. And he hath been in London lately, for some traitorous job, I doubt.'

'Oh, you mean that fool, John Ridd,' answered the young squire; 'a very simple clod-hopper. No treachery in him I warrant; he hath not the head for it. All he cares about is wrestling. As strong as a bull, and with no more brains.'

'A bullet for that bull,' said Carver; and I could see the grin on his scornful face; 'a bullet for ballast to his brain, the first time I come across him.'

'Nonsense, captain! I won't have him shot, for he is my old school-fellow, and hath a very pretty sister. But his cousin is of a different mould, and ten times as dangerous.'

'We shall see, lads, we shall see,' grumbled the great black-bearded man. 'Ill bodes for the fool that would hinder me. But come, let us onward. No lingering, or the viper will be in the bush from us. Body and soul, if he give us the slip, both of you shall answer it.'

'No fear, captain, and no hurry,' Charlie answered gallantly, 'would I were as sure of living a twelvemonth as he is of dying within the hour! Extreme unction for him in my bullet patch. Remember, I claim to be his confessor, because he hath insulted me.'

'Thou art welcome to the job for me,' said Marwood, as they turned away, and kept along the hedge-row; 'I love to meet a man sword to sword; not to pop at him from a foxhole.'

What answer was made I could not hear, for by this time the stout ashen hedge was between us, and no other gap to be found in it, until at the very bottom, where the corner of the copse was. Yet I was not quit of danger now; for they might come through that second gap, and then would be sure to see me, unless I crept into the uncut thicket, before they could enter the clearing. But in spite of all my fear, I was not wise enough to do that. And in truth the words of Carver Doone had filled me with such anger, knowing what I did about him and his pretence to Lorna; and the sight of Squire Marwood, in such outrageous company, had so moved my curiosity, and their threats against some unknown person so aroused my pity, that much of my prudence was forgotten, or at least the better part of courage, which loves danger at long distance.

Therefore, holding fast my bill-hook, I dropped myself very quietly into the bed of the runnel, being resolved to take my chance of their entrance at the corner, where the water dived through the hedge-row. And so I followed them down the fence, as gently as a rabbit goes, only I was inside it, and they on the outside; but yet so near that I heard the branches rustle as they pushed them.

Perhaps I had never loved ferns so much as when I came to the end of that little gully, and stooped betwixt two patches of them, now my chiefest shelter, for cattle had been through the gap just there, in quest of fodder and coolness, and had left but a mound of trodden earth between me and the outlaws. I mean at least on my left hand (upon which side they were), for in front where the brook ran out of the copse was a good stiff hedge of holly. And now I prayed Heaven to lead them straight on; for if they once turned to their right, through the gap, the muzzles of their guns would come almost against my forehead.

I heard them, for I durst not look; and could scarce keep still for trembling—I heard them trampling outside the gap, uncertain which track they should follow. And in that fearful moment, with my soul almost looking out of my body, expecting notice to quit it, what do you think I did? I counted the threads in a spider's web, and the flies he had lately eaten, as their skeletons shook in the twilight.

'We shall see him better in there,' said Carver, in his horrible gruff voice, like the creaking of the gallows chain; 'sit there, behind holly hedge, lads, while he cometh down yonder hill; and then our good-evening to him; one at his body, and two at his head; and good aim, lest we baulk the devil.'

'I tell you, captain, that will not do,' said Charlie, almost whispering: 'you are very proud of your skill, we know, and can hit a lark if you see it: but he may not come until after dark, and we cannot be too nigh to him. This holly hedge is too far away. He crosses down here from Slocomslade, not from Tibbacot, I tell you; but along that track to the left there, and so by the foreland to Glenthorne, where his boat is in the cove. Do you think I have tracked him so many evenings, without knowing his line to a hair? Will you fool away all my trouble?'

'Come then, lad, we will follow thy lead. Thy life for his, if we fail of it.'

'After me then, right into the hollow; thy legs are growing stiff, captain.'

'So shall thy body be, young man, if thou leadest me astray in this.'

I heard them stumbling down the hill, which was steep and rocky in that part; and peering through the hedge, I saw them enter a covert, by the side of the track which Master Stickles followed, almost every evening, when he left our house upon business. And then I knew who it was they were come on purpose to murder—a thing which I might have guessed long before, but for terror and cold stupidity.

'Oh that God,' I thought for a moment, waiting for my blood to flow; 'Oh that God had given me brains, to meet such cruel dastards according to their villainy! The power to lie, and the love of it; the stealth to spy, and the glory in it; above all, the quiet relish for blood, and joy in the death of an enemy—these are what any man must have, to contend with the Doones upon even terms. And yet, I thank God that I have not any of these.'

It was no time to dwell upon that, only to try, if might be, to prevent the crime they were bound upon. To follow the armed men down the hill would have been certain death to me, because there was no covert there, and the last light hung upon it. It seemed to me that my only chance to stop the mischief pending was to compass the round of the hill, as fast as feet could be laid to ground; only keeping out of sight from the valley, and then down the rocks, and across the brook, to the track from Slocombslade: so as to stop the King's messenger from travelling any farther, if only I could catch him there.

And this was exactly what I did; and a terrible run I had for it, fearing at every step to hear the echo of shots in the valley, and dropping down the scrubby rocks with tearing and violent scratching. Then I crossed Bagworthy stream, not far below Doone-valley, and breasted the hill towards Slocombslade, with my heart very heavily panting. Why Jeremy chose to ride this way, instead of the more direct one which would have been over Oare-hill), was more than I could account for: but I had nothing to do with that; all I wanted was to save his life.

And this I did by about a minute; and (which was the hardest thing of all) with a great horse-pistol at my head as I seized upon his bridle.

'Jeremy, Jerry,' was all I could say, being so fearfully short of breath; for I had crossed the ground quicker than any horse could.

'Spoken just in time, John Ridd!' cried Master Stickles, still however pointing the pistol at me: 'I might have known thee by thy size, John. What art doing here?'

'Come to save your life. For God's sake, go no farther. Three men in the covert there, with long guns, waiting for thee.'

'Ha! I have been watched of late. That is why I pointed at thee, John. Back round this corner, and get thy breath, and tell me all about it. I never saw a man so hurried. I could beat thee now, John.'

Jeremy Stickles was a man of courage, and presence of mind, and much resource: otherwise he would not have been appointed for this business; nevertheless he trembled greatly when he heard what I had to tell him. But I took good care to keep back the name of young Marwood de Whichehalse; neither did I show my knowledge of the other men; for reasons of my own not very hard to conjecture.

'We will let them cool their heels, John Ridd,' said Jeremy, after thinking a little. 'I cannot fetch my musketeers either from Glenthorne or Lynmouth, in time to seize the fellows. And three desperate Doones, well-armed, are too many for you and me. One result this attempt will have, it will make us attack them sooner than we had intended. And one more it will have, good John, it will make me thy friend for ever. Shake hands my lad, and forgive me freely for having been so cold to thee. Mayhap, in the troubles coming, it will help thee not a little to have done me this good turn.'

Upon this he shook me by the hand, with a pressure such as we feel not often; and having learned from me how to pass quite beyond view of his enemies, he rode on to his duty, whatever it might be. For my part I was inclined to stay, and watch how long the three fusiliers would have the patience to lie in wait; but seeing less and less use in that, as I grew more and more hungry, I swung my coat about me, and went home to Plover's Barrows.

Chapter XXXIX Troubled State and a Foolish Joke

Stickles took me aside the next day, and opened all his business to me, whether I would or not. But I gave him clearly to understand that he was not to be vexed with me, neither to regard me as in any way dishonest, if I should use for my own purpose, or for the benefit of my friends, any part of the knowledge and privity thus enforced upon me. To this he agreed quite readily; but upon the express provision that I should do nothing to thwart his schemes, neither unfold them to any one; but otherwise be allowed to act according to my own conscience, and as consisted with the honour of a loyal gentleman—for so he was pleased to term me. Now what he said lay in no great compass and may be summed in smaller still; especially as people know the chief part of it already. Disaffection to the King, or rather dislike to his brother James, and fear of Roman ascendancy, had existed now for several years, and of late were spreading rapidly; partly through the downright arrogance of the Tory faction, the cruelty and austerity of the Duke of York, the corruption of justice, and confiscation of ancient rights and charters; partly through jealousy of the French king, and his potent voice in our affairs; and partly (or perhaps one might even say, mainly) through that natural tide in all political channels, which verily moves as if it had the moon itself for its mistress. No sooner is a thing done and fixed, being set far in advance perhaps of all that was done before (like a new mole in the sea), but immediately the waters retire, lest they should undo it; and every one says how fine it is, but leaves other people to walk on it. Then after awhile, the vague endless ocean, having retired and lain still without a breeze or murmur, frets and heaves again with impulse, or with lashes laid on it, and in one great surge advances over every rampart.

And so there was at the time I speak of, a great surge in England, not rolling yet, but seething; and one which a thousand Chief Justices, and a million Jeremy Stickles, should never be able to stop or turn, by stringing up men in front of it; any more than a rope of onions can repulse a volcano. But the worst of it was that this great movement took a wrong channel at first; not only missing legitimate line, but roaring out that the back ditchway was the true and established course of it.

Against this rash and random current nearly all the ancient mariners of the State were set; not to allow the brave ship to drift there, though some little boats might try it. For the present there seemed to be a pause, with no open onset, but people on the shore expecting, each according to his wishes, and the feel of his own finger, whence the rush of wind should come which might direct the water.

Now,—to reduce high figures of speech into our own little numerals,—all the towns of Somersetshire and half the towns of Devonshire were full of pushing eager people, ready to swallow anything, or to make others swallow it. Whether they believed the folly about the black box, and all that stuff, is not for me to say; only one thing I know, they pretended to do so, and persuaded the ignorant rustics. Taunton, Bridgwater, Minehead, and Dulverton took the lead of the other towns in utterance of their discontent, and threats of what they meant to do if ever a Papist dared to climb the Protestant throne of England. On the other hand, the Tory leaders were not as yet under apprehension of an immediate outbreak, and feared to damage their own cause by premature coercion, for the struggle was not very likely to begin in earnest during the life of the present King; unless he should (as some people hoped) be so far emboldened as to make public profession of the faith which he held (if any). So the Tory policy was to watch, not indeed permitting their opponents to gather strength, and muster in armed force or with order, but being well apprised of all their schemes and intended movements, to wait for some bold overt act, and then to strike severely. And as a Tory watchman—or spy, as the Whigs would call him—Jeremy Stickles was now among us; and his duty was threefold.

First, and most ostensibly, to see to the levying of poundage in the little haven of Lynmouth, and farther up the coast, which was now becoming a place of resort for the folk whom we call smugglers, that is to say, who land their goods without regard to King's revenue as by law established. And indeed there had been no officer appointed to take toll, until one had been sent to Minehead, not so very long before. The excise as well (which had been ordered in the time of the Long Parliament) had been little heeded by the people hereabouts.

Second, his duty was (though only the Doones had discovered it) to watch those outlaws narrowly, and report of their manners (which were scanty), doings (which were too manifold), reputation (which was execrable), and politics, whether true to the King and the Pope, or otherwise.

Jeremy Stickles' third business was entirely political; to learn the temper of our people and the gentle families, to watch the movements of the trained bands (which could not always be trusted), to discover any collecting of arms and drilling of men among us, to prevent (if need were, by open force) any importation of gunpowder, of which there had been some rumour; in a word, to observe and forestall the enemy.

Now in providing for this last-mentioned service, the Government had made a great mistake, doubtless through their anxiety to escape any public attention. For all the disposable force at their emissary's command amounted to no more than a score of musketeers, and these so divided along the coast as scarcely to suffice for the duty of sentinels. He held a commission, it is true, for the employment of the train-bands, but upon the understanding that he was not to call upon them (except as a last resource), for any political object; although he might use them against the Doones as private criminals, if found needful; and supposing that he could get them.

'So you see, John,' he said in conclusion, 'I have more work than tools to do it with. I am heartily sorry I ever accepted such a mixed and meagre commission. At the bottom of it lies (I am well convinced) not only the desire to keep things quiet, but the paltry jealousy of the military people. Because I am not a Colonel, forsooth, or a Captain in His Majesty's service, it would never do to trust me with a company of soldiers! And yet they would not send either Colonel or Captain, for fear of a stir in the rustic mind. The only thing that I can do with any chance of success, is to rout out these vile Doone fellows, and burn their houses over their heads. Now what think you of that, John Ridd?'

'Destroy the town of the Doones,' I said, 'and all the Doones inside it! Surely, Jeremy, you would never think of such a cruel act as that!'

'A cruel act, John! It would be a mercy for at least three counties. No doubt you folk, who live so near, are well accustomed to them, and would miss your liveliness in coming home after nightfall, and the joy of finding your sheep and cattle right, when you not expected it. But after awhile you might get used to the dullness of being safe in your beds, and not losing your sisters and sweethearts. Surely, on the whole, it is as pleasant not to be robbed as to be robbed.'

'I think we should miss them very much,' I answered after consideration; for the possibility of having no Doones had never yet occurred to me, and we all were so thoroughly used to them, and allowed for it in our year's reckoning; 'I am sure we should miss them very sadly; and something worse would come of it.'

'Thou art the staunchest of all staunch Tories,' cried Stickles, laughing, as he shook my hand; 'thou believest in the divine right of robbers, who are good enough to steal thy own fat sheep. I am a jolly Tory, John, but thou art ten times jollier: oh! the grief in thy face at the thought of being robbed no longer!'

He laughed in a very unseemly manner; while I descried nothing to laugh about. For we always like to see our way; and a sudden change upsets us. And unless it were in the loss of the farm, or the death of the King, or of Betty Muxworthy, there was nothing that could so unsettle our minds as the loss of the Doones of Bagworthy.

And beside all this, I was thinking, of course, and thinking more than all the rest, about the troubles that might ensue to my own beloved Lorna. If an attack of Glen Doone were made by savage soldiers and rude train-bands, what might happen, or what might not, to my delicate, innocent darling? Therefore, when Jeremy Stickles again placed the matter before me, commending my strength and courage and skill (to flatter me of the highest), and finished by saying that I would be worth at least four common men to him, I cut him short as follows:

'Master Stickles, once for all, I will have naught to do with it. The reason why is no odds of thine, nor in any way disloyal. Only in thy plans remember that I will not strike a blow, neither give any counsel, neither guard any prisoners.'

'Not strike a blow,' cried Jeremy, 'against thy father's murderers, John!'

'Not a single blow, Jeremy; unless I knew the man who did it, and he gloried in his sin. It was a foul and dastard deed, yet not done in cold blood; neither in cold blood will I take God's task of avenging it.'

'Very well, John,' answered Master Stickles, 'I know thine obstinacy. When thy mind is made up, to argue with thee is pelting a rock with peppercorns. But thou hast some other reason, lad, unless I am much mistaken, over and above thy merciful nature and Christian forgiveness. Anyhow, come and see it, John. There will be good sport, I reckon; especially when we thrust our claws into the nest of the ravens. Many a yeoman will find his daughter, and some of the Porlock lads their sweethearts. A nice young maiden, now, for thee, John; if indeed, any—'

'No more of this!' I answered very sternly: 'it is no business of thine, Jeremy; and I will have no joking upon this matter.'

'Good, my lord; so be it. But one thing I tell thee in earnest. We will have thy old double-dealing uncle, Huckaback of Dulverton, and march him first to assault Doone Castle, sure as my name is Stickles. I hear that he hath often vowed to storm the valley himself, if only he could find a dozen musketeers to back him. Now, we will give him chance to do it, and prove his loyalty to the King, which lies under some suspicion of late.'

With regard to this, I had nothing to say; for it seemed to me very reasonable that Uncle Reuben should have first chance of recovering his stolen goods, about which he had made such a sad to-do, and promised himself such vengeance. I made bold, however, to ask Master Stickles at what time he intended to carry out this great and hazardous attempt. He answered that he had several things requiring first to be set in order, and that he must make an inland Journey, even as far as Tiverton, and perhaps Crediton and Exeter, to collect his forces and ammunition for them. For he meant to have some of the yeomanry as well as of the trained bands, so that if the Doones should sally forth, as perhaps they would, on horseback, cavalry might be there to meet them, and cut them off from returning.

All this made me very uncomfortable, for many and many reasons, the chief and foremost being of course my anxiety about Lorna. If the attack succeeded, what was to become of her? Who would rescue her from the brutal soldiers, even supposing that she escaped from the hands of her own people, during the danger and ferocity? And in smaller ways, I was much put out; for instance, who would ensure our corn-ricks, sheep, and cattle, ay, and even our fat pigs, now coming on for bacon, against the spreading all over the country of unlicensed marauders? The Doones had their rights, and understood them, and took them according to prescription, even as the parsons had, and the lords of manors, and the King himself, God save him! But how were these low soldiering fellows (half-starved at home very likely, and only too glad of the fat of the land, and ready, according to our proverb, to burn the paper they fried in), who were they to come hectoring and heroing over us, and Heliogabalising, with our pretty sisters to cook for them, and be chucked under chin perhaps afterwards? There is nothing England hates so much, according to my sense of it, as that fellows taken from plough-tail, cart-tail, pot-houses and parish-stocks, should be hoisted and foisted upon us (after a few months' drilling, and their lying shaped into truckling) as defenders of the public weal, and heroes of the universe.

In another way I was vexed, moreover—for after all we must consider the opinions of our neighbours—namely, that I knew quite well how everybody for ten miles round (for my fame must have been at least that wide, after all my wrestling), would lift up hands and cry out thus—'Black shame on John Ridd, if he lets them go without him!'

Putting all these things together, as well as many others, which our own wits will suggest to you, it is impossible but what you will freely acknowledge that this unfortunate John Ridd was now in a cloven stick. There was Lorna, my love and life, bound by her duty to that old vil—nay, I mean to her good grandfather, who could now do little mischief, and therefore deserved all praise—Lorna bound, at any rate, by her womanly feelings, if not by sense of duty, to remain in the thick danger, with nobody to protect her, but everybody to covet her, for beauty and position. Here was all the country roused with violent excitement, at the chance of snapping at the Doones; and not only getting tit for tat; but every young man promising his sweetheart a gold chain, and his mother at least a shilling. And here was our own mow-yard, better filled than we could remember, and perhaps every sheaf in it destined to be burned or stolen, before we had finished the bread we had baked.

Among all these troubles, there was, however, or seemed to be, one comfort. Tom Faggus returned from London very proudly and very happily, with a royal pardon in black and white, which everybody admired the more, because no one could read a word of it. The Squire himself acknowledged cheerfully that he could sooner take fifty purses than read a single line of it. Some people indeed went so far as to say that the parchment was made from a sheep Tom had stolen, and that was why it prevaricated so in giving him a character. But I, knowing something by this time, of lawyers, was able to contradict them; affirming that the wolf had more than the sheep to do with this matter.

For, according to our old saying, the three learned professions live by roguery on the three parts of a man. The doctor mauls our bodies; the parson starves our souls, but the lawyer must be the adroitest knave, for he has to ensnare our minds. Therefore he takes a careful delight in covering his traps and engines with a spread of dead-leaf words, whereof himself knows little more than half the way to spell them.

But now Tom Faggus, although having wit to gallop away on his strawberry mare, with the speed of terror, from lawyers (having paid them with money too honest to stop), yet fell into a reckless adventure, ere ever he came home, from which any lawyer would have saved him, although he ought to have needed none beyond common thought for dear Annie. Now I am, and ever have been, so vexed about this story that I cannot tell it pleasantly (as I try to write in general) in my own words and manner. Therefore I will let John Fry (whom I have robbed of another story, to which he was more entitled, and whom I have robbed of many speeches (which he thought very excellent), lest I should grieve any one with his lack of education,—the last lack he ever felt, by the bye), now with your good leave, I will allow poor John to tell this tale, in his own words and style; which he has a perfect right to do, having been the first to tell us. For Squire Faggus kept it close; not trusting even Annie with it (or at least she said so); because no man knows much of his sweetheart's tongue, until she has borne him a child or two.

Only before John begins his story, this I would say, in duty to him, and in common honesty,—that I dare not write down some few of his words, because they are not convenient, for dialect or other causes; and that I cannot find any way of spelling many of the words which I do repeat, so that people, not born on Exmoor, may know how he pronounced them; even if they could bring their lips and their legs to the proper attitude. And in this I speak advisedly; having observed some thousand times that the manner a man has of spreading his legs, and bending his knees, or stiffening, and even the way he will set his heel, make all the difference in his tone, and time of casting his voice aright, and power of coming home to you.

We always liked John's stories, not for any wit in them; but because we laughed at the man, rather than the matter. The way he held his head was enough, with his chin fixed hard like a certainty (especially during his biggest lie), not a sign of a smile in his lips or nose, but a power of not laughing; and his eyes not turning to anybody, unless somebody had too much of it (as young girls always do) and went over the brink of laughter. Thereupon it was good to see John Fry; how he looked gravely first at the laughter, as much as to ask, 'What is it now?' then if the fool went laughing more, as he or she was sure to do upon that dry inquiry, John would look again, to be sure of it, and then at somebody else to learn whether the laugh had company; then if he got another grin, all his mirth came out in glory, with a sudden break; and he wiped his lips, and was grave again.

Now John, being too much encouraged by the girls (of which I could never break them), came into the house that December evening, with every inch of him full of a tale. Annie saw it, and Lizzie, of course; and even I, in the gloom of great evils, perceived that John was a loaded gun; but I did not care to explode him. Now nothing primed him so hotly as this: if you wanted to hear all John Fry had heard, the surest of all sure ways to it was, to pretend not to care for a word of it.

'I wor over to Exeford in the morning,' John began from the chimney-corner, looking straight at Annie; 'for to zee a little calve, Jan, as us cuddn't get thee to lave houze about. Meesus have got a quare vancy vor un, from wutt her have heer'd of the brade. Now zit quite, wull 'e Miss Luzzie, or a 'wunt goo on no vurder. Vaine little tayl I'll tull' ee, if so be thee zits quite. Wull, as I coom down the hill, I zeed a saight of volks astapping of the ro-udwai. Arl on 'em wi' girt goons, or two men out of dree wi' 'em. Rackon there wor dree score on 'em, tak smarl and beg togather laike; latt aloun the women and chillers; zum on em wi' matches blowing, tothers wi' flint-lacks. "Wutt be up now?" I says to Bill Blacksmith, as had knowledge of me: "be the King acoomin? If her be, do 'ee want to shutt 'un?"

'"Thee not knaw!" says Bill Blacksmith, just the zame as I be a tullin of it: "whai, man, us expex Tam Faggus, and zum on us manes to shutt 'un."

'"Shutt 'un wi'out a warrant!" says I: "sure 'ee knaws better nor thic, Bill! A man mayn't shutt to another man, wi'out have a warrant, Bill. Warship zed so, last taime I zeed un, and nothing to the contrairy."

'"Haw, haw! Never frout about that," saith Bill, zame as I be tullin you; "us has warrants and warships enow, dree or vour on 'em. And more nor a dizzen warranties; fro'ut I know to contrairy. Shutt 'un, us manes; and shutt 'un, us will—" Whai, Miss Annie, good Lord, whuttiver maks 'ee stear so?'

'Nothing at all, John,' our Annie answered; 'only the horrible ferocity of that miserable blacksmith.'

'That be nayther here nor there,' John continued, with some wrath at his own interruption: 'Blacksmith knawed whutt the Squire had been; and veared to lose his own custom, if Squire tuk to shooin' again. Shutt any man I would myzell as intervared wi' my trade laike. "Lucky for thee," said Bill Blacksmith, "as thee bee'st so shart and fat, Jan. Dree on us wor a gooin' to shutt 'ee, till us zeed how fat thee waz, Jan."

'"Lor now, Bill!" I answered 'un, wi' a girt cold swat upon me: "shutt me, Bill; and my own waife niver drame of it!'

Here John Fry looked round the kitchen; for he had never said anything of the kind, I doubt; but now made it part of his discourse, from thinking that Mistress Fry was come, as she generally did, to fetch him.

'Wull done then, Jan Vry,' said the woman, who had entered quietly, but was only our old Molly. 'Wutt handsome manners thee hast gat, Jan, to spake so well of thy waife laike; after arl the laife she leads thee!'

'Putt thee pot on the fire, old 'ooman, and bile thee own bakkon,' John answered her, very sharply: 'nobody no raight to meddle wi' a man's bad ooman but himzell. Wull, here was all these here men awaitin', zum wi' harses, zum wi'out; the common volk wi' long girt guns, and tha quarlity wi' girt broad-swords. Who wor there? Whay latt me zee. There wor Squire Maunder,' here John assumed his full historical key, 'him wi' the pot to his vittle-place; and Sir Richard Blewitt shaking over the zaddle, and Squaire Sandford of Lee, him wi' the long nose and one eye, and Sir Gronus Batchildor over to Ninehead Court, and ever so many more on 'em, tulling up how they was arl gooin' to be promoted, for kitching of Tom Faggus.

'"Hope to God," says I to myzell, "poor Tom wun't coom here today: arl up with her, if 'a doeth: and who be there to suckzade 'un?" Mark me now, all these charps was good to shutt 'un, as her coom crass the watter; the watter be waide enow there and stony, but no deeper than my knee-place.

'"Thee cas'n goo no vurder," Bill Blacksmith saith to me: "nawbody 'lowed to crass the vord, until such time as Faggus coom; plaise God us may mak sure of 'un."

'"Amen, zo be it," says I; "God knoweth I be never in any hurry, and would zooner stop nor goo on most taimes."

'Wi' that I pulled my vittles out, and zat a horsebarck, atin' of 'em, and oncommon good they was. "Won't us have 'un this taime just," saith Tim Potter, as keepeth the bull there; "and yet I be zorry for 'un. But a man must kape the law, her must; zo be her can only learn it. And now poor Tom will swing as high as the tops of they girt hashes there."

'"Just thee kitch 'un virst," says I; "maisure rope, wi' the body to maisure by."

'"Hurrah! here be another now," saith Bill Blacksmith, grinning; "another coom to help us. What a grave gentleman! A warship of the pace, at laste!"

'For a gentleman, on a cue-ball horse, was coming slowly down the hill on tother zide of watter, looking at us in a friendly way, and with a long papper standing forth the lining of his coat laike. Horse stapped to drink in the watter, and gentleman spak to 'un kindly, and then they coom raight on to ussen, and the gentleman's face wor so long and so grave, us veared 'a wor gooin' to prache to us.

'"Coort o' King's Bench," saith one man; "Checker and Plays," saith another; "Spishal Commission, I doubt," saith Bill Blacksmith; "backed by the Mayor of Taunton."

'"Any Justice of the King's Peace, good people, to be found near here?" said the gentleman, lifting his hat to us, and very gracious in his manner.

'"Your honour," saith Bill, with his hat off his head; "there be sax or zeven warships here: arl on 'em very wise 'uns. Squaire Maunder there be the zinnyer."

'So the gentleman rode up to Squire Maunder, and raised his cocked hat in a manner that took the Squire out of countenance, for he could not do the like of it.

'"Sir," said he, "good and worshipful sir, I am here to claim your good advice and valour; for purposes of justice. I hold His Majesty's commission, to make to cease a notorious rogue, whose name is Thomas Faggus." With that he offered his commission; but Squire Maunder told the truth, that he could not rade even words in print, much less written karakters.* Then the other magistrates rode up, and put their heads together, how to meet the London gentleman without loss of importance. There wor one of 'em as could rade purty vair, and her made out King's mark upon it: and he bowed upon his horse to the gentleman, and he laid his hand on his heart and said, "Worshipful sir, we, as has the honour of His Gracious Majesty's commission, are entirely at your service, and crave instructions from you."

'Then a waving of hats began, and a bowing, and making of legs to wan anather, sich as nayver wor zeed afore; but none of 'em arl, for air and brading, cud coom anaigh the gentleman with the long grave face.

'"Your warships have posted the men right well," saith he with anather bow all round; "surely that big rogue will have no chance left among so many valiant musketeers. Ha! what see I there, my friend? Rust in the pan of your gun! That gun would never go off, sure as I am the King's Commissioner. And I see another just as bad; and lo, there the third! Pardon me, gentlemen, I have been so used to His Majesty's Ordnance-yards. But I fear that bold rogue would ride through all of you, and laugh at your worship's beards, by George."

'"But what shall us do?" Squire Maunder axed; "I vear there be no oil here."

'"Discharge your pieces, gentlemen, and let the men do the same; or at least let us try to discharge them, and load again with fresh powder. It is the fog of the morning hath spoiled the priming. That rogue is not in sight yet: but God knows we must not be asleep with him, or what will His Majesty say to me, if we let him slip once more?"

'"Excellent, wondrous well said, good sir," Squire Maunder answered him; "I never should have thought of that now. Bill Blacksmith, tell all the men to be ready to shoot up into the air, directly I give the word. Now, are you ready there, Bill?"

*Lest I seem to under-rate the erudition of Devonshire magistrates, I venture to offer copy of a letter from a Justice of the Peace to his bookseller, circa 1810 A.D., now in my possession:—

'Sur. 'plez to zen me the aks relatting to A-GUSTUS-PAKS,'—Ed. of L. D.

'"All ready, your worship," saith Bill, saluting like a soldier.

'"Then, one, two, dree, and shutt!" cries Squire Maunder, standing up in the irons of his stirrups.

'Thereupon they all blazed out, and the noise of it went all round the hills; with a girt thick cloud arising, and all the air smelling of powder. Before the cloud was gone so much as ten yards on the wind, the gentleman on the cue-bald horse shuts up his face like a pair of nut-cracks, as wide as it was long before, and out he pulls two girt pistols longside of zaddle, and clap'th one to Squire Maunder's head, and tother to Sir Richard Blewitt's.

'"Hand forth your money and all your warrants," he saith like a clap of thunder; "gentlemen, have you now the wit to apprehend Tom Faggus?"

'Squire Maunder swore so that he ought to he fined; but he pulled out his purse none the slower for that, and so did Sir Richard Blewitt.

'"First man I see go to load a gun, I'll gi'e 'un the bullet to do it with," said Tom; for you see it was him and no other, looking quietly round upon all of them. Then he robbed all the rest of their warships, as pleasant as might be; and he saith, "Now, gentlemen, do your duty: serve your warrants afore you imprison me"; with that he made them give up all the warrants, and he stuck them in the band of his hat, and then he made a bow with it.

'"Good morning to your warships now, and a merry Christmas all of you! And the merrier both for rich and poor, when gentlemen see their almsgiving. Lest you deny yourselves the pleasure, I will aid your warships. And to save you the trouble of following me, when your guns be loaded—this is my strawberry mare, gentlemen, only with a little cream on her. Gentlemen all, in the name of the King, I thank you."

'All this while he was casting their money among the poor folk by the handful; and then he spak kaindly to the red mare, and wor over the back of the hill in two zeconds, and best part of two maile away, I reckon, afore ever a gun wor loaded.'*

Chapter XL Two Fools Together

That story of John Fry's, instead of causing any amusement, gave us great disquietude; not only because it showed that Tom Faggus could not resist sudden temptation and the delight of wildness, but also that we greatly feared lest the King's pardon might be annulled, and all his kindness cancelled, by a reckless deed of that sort. It was true (as Annie insisted continually, even with tears, to wear in her arguments) that Tom had not brought away anything, except the warrants, which were of no use at all, after receipt of the pardon; neither had he used any violence, except just to

*The truth of this story is well established by first-rate tradition.

frighten people; but could it be established, even towards Christmas-time, that Tom had a right to give alms, right and left, out of other people's money?

Dear Annie appeared to believe that it could; saying that if the rich continually chose to forget the poor, a man who forced them to remember, and so to do good to themselves and to others, was a public benefactor, and entitled to every blessing. But I knew, and so Lizzie knew—John Fry being now out of hearing—that this was not sound argument. For, if it came to that, any man might take the King by the throat, and make him cast away among the poor the money which he wanted sadly for Her Grace the Duchess, and the beautiful Countess, of this, and of that. Lizzie, of course, knew nothing about His Majesty's diversions, which were not fit for a young maid's thoughts; but I now put the form of the argument as it occurred to me.

Therefore I said, once for all (and both my sisters always listened when I used the deep voice from my chest):

'Tom Faggus hath done wrong herein; wrong to himself, and to our Annie. All he need have done was to show his pardon, and the magistrates would have rejoiced with him. He might have led a most godly life, and have been respected by everybody; and knowing how brave Tom is, I thought that he would have done as much. Now if I were in love with a maid'—I put it thus for the sake of poor Lizzie—'never would I so imperil my life, and her fortune in life along with me, for the sake of a poor diversion. A man's first duty is to the women, who are forced to hang upon him'—

'Oh, John, not that horrible word,' cried Annie, to my great surprise, and serious interruption; 'oh, John, any word but that!' And she burst forth crying terribly.

'What word, Lizzie? What does the wench mean?' I asked, in the saddest vexation; seeing no good to ask Annie at all, for she carried on most dreadfully.

'Don't you know, you stupid lout?' said Lizzie, completing my wonderment, by the scorn of her quicker intelligence; 'if you don't know, axe about?'

And with that, I was forced to be content; for Lizzie took Annie in such a manner (on purpose to vex me, as I could see) with her head drooping down, and her hair coming over, and tears and sobs rising and falling, to boot, without either order or reason, that seeing no good for a man to do (since neither of them was Lorna), I even went out into the courtyard, and smoked a pipe, and wondered what on earth is the meaning of women.

Now in this I was wrong and unreasonable (as all women will acknowledge); but sometimes a man is so put out, by the way they take on about nothing, that he really cannot help thinking, for at least a minute, that women are a mistake for ever, and hence are for ever mistaken. Nevertheless I could not see that any of these great thoughts and ideas applied at all to my Lorna; but that she was a different being; not woman enough to do anything bad, yet enough of a woman for man to adore.

And now a thing came to pass which tested my adoration pretty sharply, inasmuch as I would far liefer faced Carver Doone and his father, nay, even the roaring lion himself with his hoofs and flaming nostrils, than have met, in cold blood, Sir Ensor Doone, the founder of all the colony, and the fear of the very fiercest.

But that I was forced to do at this time, and in the manner following. When I went up one morning to look for my seven rooks' nests, behold there were but six to be seen; for the topmost of them all was gone, and the most conspicuous. I looked, and looked, and rubbed my eyes, and turned to try them by other sights; and then I looked again; yes, there could be no doubt about it; the signal was made for me to come, because my love was in danger. For me to enter the valley now, during the broad daylight, could have brought no comfort, but only harm to the maiden, and certain death to myself. Yet it was more than I could do to keep altogether at distance; therefore I ran to the nearest place where I could remain unseen, and watched the glen from the wooded height, for hours and hours, impatiently.

However, no impatience of mine made any difference in the scene upon which I was gazing. In the part of the valley which I could see, there was nothing moving, except the water, and a few stolen cows, going sadly along, as if knowing that they had no honest right there. It sank very heavily into my heart, with all the beds of dead leaves around it, and there was nothing I cared to do, except blow on my fingers, and long for more wit.

For a frost was beginning, which made a great difference to Lorna and to myself, I trow; as well as to all the five million people who dwell in this island of England; such a frost as never I saw before,* neither hope ever to see again; a time when it was impossible to milk a cow for icicles, or for a man to shave some of his beard (as I liked to do for Lorna's sake, because she was so smooth) without blunting his razor on hard gray ice. No man could 'keep yatt' (as we say), even though he abandoned his work altogether, and thumped himself, all on the chest and the front, till his frozen hands would have been bleeding except for the cold that kept still all his veins.

However, at present there was no frost, although for a fortnight threatening; and I was too young to know the meaning of the way the dead leaves hung, and the worm-casts prickling like women's combs, and the leaden tone upon everything, and the dead weight of the sky. Will Watcombe, the old man at Lynmouth, who had been half over the world almost, and who talked so much of the Gulf-stream, had (as I afterwards called to mind) foretold a very bitter winter this year. But no one would listen to him because there were not so many hips and haws as usual; whereas we have all learned from our grandfathers that Providence never

*If John Ridd lived until the year 1740 (as so strong a man was bound to do), he must have seen almost a harder frost; and perhaps it put an end to him; for then he would be some fourscore years old. But tradition makes him 'keep yatt,' as he says, up to fivescore years.—ED.

sends very hard winters, without having furnished a large supply of berries for the birds to feed upon.

It was lucky for me, while I waited here, that our very best sheep-dog, old Watch, had chosen to accompany me that day. For otherwise I must have had no dinner, being unpersuaded, even by that, to quit my survey of the valley. However, by aid of poor Watch, I contrived to obtain a supply of food; for I sent him home with a note to Annie fastened upon his chest; and in less than an hour back he came, proud enough to wag his tail off, with his tongue hanging out from the speed of his journey, and a large lump of bread and of bacon fastened in a napkin around his neck. I had not told my sister, of course, what was toward; for why should I make her anxious?

When it grew towards dark, I was just beginning to prepare for my circuit around the hills; but suddenly Watch gave a long low growl; I kept myself close as possible, and ordered the dog to be silent, and presently saw a short figure approaching from a thickly-wooded hollow on the left side of my hiding-place. It was the same figure I had seen once before in the moonlight, at Plover's Barrows; and proved, to my great delight, to be the little maid Gwenny Carfax. She started a moment, at seeing me, but more with surprise than fear; and then she laid both her hands upon mine, as if she had known me for twenty years.

'Young man,' she said, 'you must come with me. I was gwain' all the way to fetch thee. Old man be dying; and her can't die, or at least her won't, without first considering thee.'

'Considering me!' I cried; 'what can Sir Ensor Doone want with considering me? Has Mistress Lorna told him?'

'All concerning thee, and thy doings; when she knowed old man were so near his end. That vexed he was about thy low blood, a' thought her would come to life again, on purpose for to bate 'ee. But after all, there can't be scarcely such bad luck as that. Now, if her strook thee, thou must take it; there be no denaying of un. Fire I have seen afore, hot and red, and raging; but I never seen cold fire afore, and it maketh me burn and shiver.'

And in truth, it made me both burn and shiver, to know that I must either go straight to the presence of Sir Ensor Doone, or give up Lorna, once for all, and rightly be despised by her. For the first time of my life, I thought that she had not acted fairly. Why not leave the old man in peace, without vexing him about my affair? But presently I saw again that in this matter she was right; that she could not receive the old man's blessing (supposing that he had one to give, which even a worse man might suppose), while she deceived him about herself, and the life she had undertaken.

Therefore, with great misgiving of myself, but no ill thought of my darling, I sent Watch home, and followed Gwenny; who led me along very rapidly, with her short broad form gliding down the hollow, from which she had first appeared. Here at the bottom, she entered a thicket of gray ash stubs and black holly, with rocks around it gnarled with roots, and hung with masks of ivy. Here in a dark and lonely corner, with a pixie ring before it, she came to a narrow door, very brown and solid, looking like a trunk of wood at a little distance. This she opened, without a key, by stooping down and pressing it, where the threshold met the jamb; and then she ran in very nimbly, but I was forced to be bent in two, and even so without comfort. The passage was close and difficult, and as dark as any black pitch; but it was not long (be it as it might), and in that there was some comfort. We came out soon at the other end, and were at the top of Doone valley. In the chilly dusk air, it looked most untempting, especially during that state of mind under which I was labouring. As we crossed towards the Captain's house, we met a couple of great Doones lounging by the waterside. Gwenny said something to them, and although they stared very hard at me, they let me pass without hindrance. It is not too much to say that when the little maid opened Sir Ensor's door, my heart thumped, quite as much with terror as with hope of Lorna's presence.

But in a moment the fear was gone, for Lorna was trembling in my arms, and my courage rose to comfort her. The darling feared, beyond all things else, lest I should be offended with her for what she had said to her grandfather, and for dragging me into his presence; but I told her almost a falsehood (the first, and the last, that ever I did tell her), to wit, that I cared not that much—and showed her the tip of my thumb as I said it—for old Sir Ensor, and all his wrath, so long as I had his granddaughter's love.

Now I tried to think this as I said it, so as to save it from being a lie; but somehow or other it did not answer, and I was vexed with myself both ways. But Lorna took me by the hand as bravely as she could, and led me into a little passage where I could hear the river moaning and the branches rustling.

Here I passed as long a minute as fear ever cheated time of, saying to myself continually that there was nothing to be frightened at, yet growing more and more afraid by reason of so reasoning. At last my Lorna came back very pale, as I saw by the candle she carried, and whispered, 'Now be patient, dearest. Never mind what he says to you; neither attempt to answer him. Look at him gently and steadfastly, and, if you can, with some show of reverence; but above all things, no compassion; it drives him almost mad. Now come; walk very quietly.'

She led me into a cold, dark room, rough and very gloomy, although with two candles burning. I took little heed of the things in it, though I marked that the window was open. That which I heeded was an old man, very stern and comely, with death upon his countenance; yet not lying in his bed, but set upright in a chair, with a loose red cloak thrown over him. Upon this his white hair fell, and his pallid fingers lay in a ghastly fashion without a sign of life or movement or of the power that kept him up; all rigid, calm, and relentless. Only in his great black eyes, fixed upon me solemnly, all the power of his body dwelt, all the life of his soul was burning.

I could not look at him very nicely, being afeared of the death in his face, and most afeared to show it. And to tell the truth, my poor blue eyes fell away from the blackness of his, as if it had been my coffin-plate.

Therefore I made a low obeisance, and tried not to shiver. Only I groaned that Lorna thought it good manners to leave us two together.

'Ah,' said the old man, and his voice seemed to come from a cavern of skeletons; 'are you that great John Ridd?'

'John Ridd is my name, your honour,' was all that I could answer; 'and I hope your worship is better.'

'Child, have you sense enough to know what you have been doing?'

'Yes, I knew right well,' I answered, 'that I have set mine eyes far above my rank.'

'Are you ignorant that Lorna Doone is born of the oldest families remaining in North Europe?'

'I was ignorant of that, your worship; yet I knew of her high descent from the Doones of Bagworthy.'

The old man's eyes, like fire, probed me whether I was jesting; then perceiving how grave I was, and thinking that I could not laugh (as many people suppose of me), he took on himself to make good the deficiency with a very bitter smile.

'And know you of your own low descent from the Ridds of Oare?'

'Sir,' I answered, being as yet unaccustomed to this style of speech, 'the Ridds, of Oare, have been honest men twice as long as the Doones have been rogues.'

'I would not answer for that, John,' Sir Ensor replied, very quietly, when I expected fury. 'If it be so, thy family is the very oldest in Europe. Now hearken to me, boy, or clown, or honest fool, or whatever thou art; hearken to an old man's words, who has not many hours to live. There is nothing in this world to fear, nothing to revere or trust, nothing even to hope for; least of all, is there aught to love.'

'I hope your worship is not quite right,' I answered, with great misgivings; 'else it is a sad mistake for anybody to live, sir.'

'Therefore,' he continued, as if I had never spoken, 'though it may seem hard for a week or two, like the loss of any other toy, I deprive you of nothing, but add to your comfort, and (if there be such a thing) to your happiness, when I forbid you ever to see that foolish child again. All marriage is a wretched farce, even when man and wife belong to the same rank of life, have temper well assorted, similar likes and dislikes, and about the same pittance of mind. But when they are not so matched, the farce would become a long, dull tragedy, if anything were worth lamenting. There, I have reasoned enough with you; I am not in the habit of reasoning. Though I have little confidence in man's honour, I have some reliance in woman's pride. You will pledge your word in Lorna's presence never to see or to seek her again; never even to think of her more. Now call her, for I am weary.'

He kept his great eyes fixed upon me with their icy fire (as if he scorned both life and death), and on his haughty lips some slight amusement at my trouble; and then he raised one hand (as if I were a poor dumb creature), and pointed to the door. Although my heart rebelled and kindled at his proud disdain, I could not disobey him freely; but made a low salute, and went straightway in search of Lorna.

I found my love (or not my love; according as now she should behave; for I was very desperate, being put upon so sadly); Lorna Doone was crying softly at a little window, and listening to the river's grief. I laid my heavy arm around her, not with any air of claiming or of forcing her thoughts to me, but only just to comfort her, and ask what she was thinking of. To my arm she made no answer, neither to my seeking eyes; but to my heart, once for all, she spoke with her own upon it. Not a word, nor sound between us; not even a kiss was interchanged; but man, or maid, who has ever loved hath learned our understanding.

Therefore it came to pass, that we saw fit to enter Sir Ensor's room in the following manner. Lorna, with her right hand swallowed entirely by the palm of mine, and her waist retired from view by means of my left arm. All one side of her hair came down, in a way to be remembered, upon the left and fairest part of my favourite otter-skin waistcoat; and her head as well would have lain there doubtless, but for the danger of walking so. I, for my part, was too far gone to lag behind in the matter; but carried my love bravely, fearing neither death nor hell, while she abode beside me.

Old Sir Ensor looked much astonished. For forty years he had been obeyed and feared by all around him; and he knew that I had feared him vastly, before I got hold of Lorna. And indeed I was still afraid of him; only for loving Lorna so, and having to protect her.

Then I made him a bow, to the very best of all I had learned both at Tiverton and in London; after that I waited for him to begin, as became his age and rank in life.

'Ye two fools!' he said at last, with a depth of contempt which no words may express; 'ye two fools!'

'May it please your worship,' I answered softly; 'maybe we are not such fools as we look. But though we be, we are well content, so long as we may be two fools together.'

'Why, John,' said the old man, with a spark, as of smiling in his eyes; 'thou art not altogether the clumsy yokel, and the clod, I took thee for.'

'Oh, no, grandfather; oh, dear grandfather,' cried Lorna, with such zeal and flashing, that her hands went forward; 'nobody knows what John Ridd is, because he is so modest. I mean, nobody except me, dear.' And here she turned to me again, and rose upon tiptoe, and kissed me.

'I have seen a little o' the world,' said the old man, while I was half ashamed, although so proud of Lorna; 'but this is beyond all I have seen, and nearly all I have heard of. It is more fit for southern climates than for the fogs of Exmoor.'

'It is fit for all the world, your worship; with your honour's good leave, and will,' I answered in humility, being still ashamed of it; 'when it happens so to people, there is nothing that can stop it, sir.'

Now Sir Ensor Doone was leaning back upon his brown chair-rail, which was built like a triangle, as in old farmhouses (from one of which it had come, no doubt, free from expense or gratitude); and as I spoke he coughed a little; and he sighed a good deal more; and perhaps his dying heart desired to open time again, with such a lift of warmth and hope as he descried in our eyes, and arms. I could not understand him then; any more than a baby playing with his grandfather's spectacles; nevertheless I wondered whether, at his time of life, or rather on the brink of death, he was thinking of his youth and pride.

'Fools you are; be fools for ever,' said Sir Ensor Doone, at last; while we feared to break his thoughts, but let each other know our own, with little ways of pressure; 'it is the best thing I can wish you; boy and girl, be boy and girl, until you have grandchildren.'

Partly in bitterness he spoke, and partly in pure weariness, and then he turned so as not to see us; and his white hair fell, like a shroud, around him.

Chapter XLI Cold Comfort

All things being full of flaw, all things being full of holes, the strength of all things is in shortness. If Sir Ensor Doone had dwelled for half an hour upon himself, and an hour perhaps upon Lorna and me, we must both have wearied of him, and required change of air. But now I longed to see and know a great deal more about him, and hoped that he might not go to Heaven for at least a week or more. However, he was too good for this world (as we say of all people who leave it); and I verily believe his heart was not a bad one, after all.

Evil he had done, no doubt, as evil had been done to him; yet how many have done evil, while receiving only good! Be that as it may; and not vexing a question (settled for ever without our votes), let us own that he was, at least, a brave and courteous gentleman.

And his loss aroused great lamentation, not among the Doones alone, and the women they had carried off, but also of the general public, and many even of the magistrates, for several miles round Exmoor. And this, not only from fear lest one more wicked might succeed him (as appeared indeed too probable), but from true admiration of his strong will, and sympathy with his misfortunes.

I will not deceive any one, by saying that Sir Ensor Doone gave (in so many words) his consent to my resolve about Lorna. This he never did, except by his speech last written down; from which as he mentioned grandchildren, a lawyer perhaps might have argued it. Not but what he may have meant to bestow on us his blessing; only that he died next day, without taking the trouble to do it.

He called indeed for his box of snuff, which was a very high thing to take; and which he never took without being in very good humour, at least for him. And though it would not go up his nostrils, through the failure of his breath, he was pleased to have it there, and not to think of dying.

'Will your honour have it wiped?' I asked him very softly, for the brown appearance of it spoiled (to my idea) his white mostacchio; but he seemed to shake his head; and I thought it kept his spirits up. I had never before seen any one do, what all of us have to do some day; and it greatly kept my spirits down, although it did not so very much frighten me.

For it takes a man but a little while, his instinct being of death perhaps, at least as much as of life (which accounts for his slaying his fellow men so, and every other creature), it does not take a man very long to enter into another man's death, and bring his own mood to suit it. He knows that his own is sure to come; and nature is fond of the practice. Hence it came to pass that I, after easing my mother's fears, and seeing a little to business, returned (as if drawn by a polar needle) to the death-bed of Sir Ensor.

There was some little confusion, people wanting to get away, and people trying to come in, from downright curiosity (of all things the most hateful), and others making great to-do, and talking of their own time to come, telling their own age, and so on. But every one seemed to think, or feel, that I had a right to be there; because the women took that view of it. As for Carver and Counsellor, they were minding their own affairs, so as to win the succession; and never found it in their business (at least so long as I was there) to come near the dying man.

He, for his part, never asked for any one to come near him, not even a priest, nor a monk or friar; but seemed to be going his own way, peaceful, and well contented. Only the chief of the women said that from his face she believed and knew that he liked to have me at one side of his bed, and Lorna upon the other. An hour or two ere the old man died, when only we two were with him, he looked at us both very dimly and softly, as if he wished to do something for us, but had left it now too late. Lorna hoped that he wanted to bless us; but he only frowned at that, and let his hand drop downward, and crooked one knotted finger.

'He wants something out of the bed, dear,' Lorna whispered to me; 'see what it is, upon your side, there.'

I followed the bent of his poor shrunken hand, and sought among the pilings; and there I felt something hard and sharp, and drew it forth and gave it to him. It flashed, like the spray of a fountain upon us, in the dark winter of the room. He could not take it in his hand, but let it hang, as daisies do; only making Lorna see that he meant her to have it.

'Why, it is my glass necklace!' Lorna cried, in great surprise; 'my necklace he always promised me; and from which you have got the ring, John. But grandfather kept it, because the children wanted to pull it from my neck. May I have it now, dear grandfather? Not unless you wish, dear.'

Darling Lorna wept again, because the old man could not tell her (except by one very feeble nod) that she was doing what he wished. Then she gave to me the trinket, for the sake of safety; and I stowed it in my breast. He seemed to me to follow this, and to be well content with it.

Before Sir Ensor Doone was buried, the greatest frost of the century had set in, with its iron hand, and step of stone, on everything. How it came is not my business, nor can I explain it; because I never have watched the skies; as people now begin to do, when the ground is not to their liking. Though of all this I know nothing, and less than nothing I may say (because I ought to know something); I can hear what people tell me; and I can see before my eyes.

The strong men broke three good pickaxes, ere they got through the hard brown sod, streaked with little maps of gray where old Sir Ensor was to lie, upon his back, awaiting the darkness of the Judgment-day. It was in the little chapel-yard; I will not tell the name of it; because we are now such Protestants, that I might do it an evil turn; only it was the little place where Lorna's Aunt Sabina lay.

Here was I, remaining long, with a little curiosity; because some people told me plainly that I must be damned for ever by a Papist funeral; and here came Lorna, scarcely breathing through the thick of stuff around her, yet with all her little breath steaming on the air, like frost.

I stood apart from the ceremony, in which of course I was not entitled, either by birth or religion, to bear any portion; and indeed it would have been wiser in me to have kept away altogether; for now there was no one to protect me among those wild and lawless men; and both Carver and the Counsellor had vowed a fearful vengeance on me, as I heard from Gwenny. They had not dared to meddle with me while the chief lay dying; nor was it in their policy, for a short time after that, to endanger their succession by an open breach with Lorna, whose tender age and beauty held so many of the youths in thrall.

The ancient outlaw's funeral was a grand and moving sight; more perhaps from the sense of contrast than from that of fitness. To see those dark and mighty men, inured to all of sin and crime, reckless both of man and God, yet now with heads devoutly bent, clasped hands, and downcast eyes, following the long black coffin of their common ancestor, to the place where they must join him when their sum of ill was done; and to see the feeble priest chanting, over the dead form, words the living would have laughed at, sprinkling with his little broom drops that could not purify; while the children, robed in white, swung their smoking censers slowly over the cold and twilight grave; and after seeing all, to ask, with a shudder unexpressed, 'Is this the end that God intended for a man so proud and strong?'

Not a tear was shed upon him, except from the sweetest of all sweet eyes; not a sigh pursued him home. Except in hot anger, his life had been cold, and bitter, and distant; and now a week had exhausted all the sorrow of those around him, a grief flowing less from affection than fear. Aged men will show his tombstone; mothers haste with their infants by it; children shrink from the name upon it, until in time his history shall lapse and be forgotten by all except the great Judge and God.

After all was over, I strode across the moors very sadly; trying to keep the cold away by virtue of quick movement. Not a flake of snow had fallen yet; all the earth was caked and hard, with a dry brown crust upon it; all the sky was banked with darkness, hard, austere, and frowning. The fog of the last three weeks was gone, neither did any rime remain; but all things had a look of sameness, and a kind of furzy colour. It was freezing hard and sharp, with a piercing wind to back it; and I had observed that the holy water froze upon Sir Ensor's coffin.

One thing struck me with some surprise, as I made off for our fire-side (with a strong determination to heave an ash-tree up the chimney-place), and that was how the birds were going, rather than flying as they used to fly. All the birds were set in one direction, steadily journeying westward, not with any heat of speed, neither flying far at once; but all (as if on business bound), partly running, partly flying, partly fluttering along; silently, and without a voice, neither pricking head nor tail. This movement of the birds went on, even for a week or more; every kind of thrushes passed us, every kind of wild fowl, even plovers went away, and crows, and snipes and wood-cocks. And before half the frost was over, all we had in the snowy ditches were hares so tame that we could pat them; partridges that came to hand, with a dry noise in their crops; heath-poults, making cups of snow; and a few poor hopping redwings, flipping in and out the hedge, having lost the power to fly. And all the time their great black eyes, set with gold around them, seemed to look at any man, for mercy and for comfort.

Annie took a many of them, all that she could find herself, and all the boys would bring her; and she made a great hutch near the fire, in the back-kitchen chimney-place. Here, in spite of our old Betty (who sadly wanted to roast them), Annie kept some fifty birds, with bread and milk, and raw chopped meat, and all the seed she could think of, and lumps of rotten apples, placed to tempt them, in the corners. Some got on, and some died off; and Annie cried for all that died, and buried them under the woodrick; but, I do assure you, it was a pretty thing to see, when she went to them in the morning. There was not a bird but knew her well, after one day of comforting; and some would come to her hand, and sit, and shut one eye, and look at her. Then she used to stroke their heads, and feel their breasts, and talk to them; and not a bird of them all was there but liked to have it done to him. And I do believe they would eat from her hand things unnatural to them, lest she should he grieved and hurt by not knowing what to do for them. One of them was a noble bird, such as I never had seen before, of very fine bright plumage, and larger than a missel-thrush. He was the hardest of all to please: and yet he tried to do his best. I have heard since then, from a man who knows all about birds, and beasts, and fishes, that he must have been a Norwegian bird, called in this country a Roller, who never comes to England but in the most tremendous winters.

Another little bird there was, whom I longed to welcome home, and protect from enemies, a little bird no native to us, but than any native dearer. But lo, in the very night which followed old Sir Ensor's funeral, such a storm of snow began as never have I heard nor read of, neither could have dreamed it. At what time of night it first began is more than I can say, at least from my own knowledge, for we all went to bed soon after supper, being cold and not inclined to talk. At that time the wind was moaning sadly, and the sky as dark as a wood, and the straw in the yard swirling round and round, and the cows huddling into the great cow-house, with their chins upon one another. But we, being blinder than they, I suppose, and not having had a great snow for years, made no preparation against the storm, except that the lambing ewes were in shelter.

It struck me, as I lay in bed, that we were acting foolishly; for an ancient shepherd had dropped in and taken supper with us, and foretold a heavy fall and great disaster to live stock. He said that he had known a frost beginning, just as this had done, with a black east wind, after days of raw cold fog, and then on the third night of the frost, at this very time of year (to wit on the 15th of December) such a snow set in as killed half of the sheep and many even of the red deer and the forest ponies. It was three-score years agone,* he said; and cause he had to remember it, inasmuch as two of his toes had been lost by frost-nip, while he dug out his sheep on the other side of the Dunkery. Hereupon mother nodded at him, having heard from her father about it, and how three men had been frozen to death, and how badly their stockings came off from them.

Remembering how the old man looked, and his manner of listening to the wind and shaking his head very ominously (when Annie gave him a glass of schnapps), I grew quite uneasy in my bed, as the room got colder and colder; and I made up my mind, if it only pleased God not to send the snow till the morning, that every sheep, and horse, and cow, ay, and even the poultry, should be brought in snug, and with plenty to eat, and fodder enough to roast them.

Alas what use of man's resolves, when they come a day too late; even if they may avail a little, when they are most punctual!

In the bitter morning I arose, to follow out my purpose, knowing the time from the force of habit, although the room was so dark and gray. An odd white light was on the rafters, such as I never had seen before; while all the length of the room was grisly, like the heart of a mouldy oat-rick. I went to the window at once, of course; and at first I could not understand what was doing outside of it. It faced due east (as I may have said), with the walnut-tree partly sheltering it; and generally I could see the yard, and the woodrick, and even the church beyond.

But now, half the lattice was quite blocked up, as if plastered with gray lime; and little fringes, like ferns, came through, where the joining of the lead was; and in the only undarkened part, countless dots came swarming, clustering, beating with a soft, low sound, then gliding down in a slippery manner, not as drops of rain do, but each distinct from his neighbour. Inside the iron frame (which fitted, not to say too comfortably, and went along the stonework), at least a peck of snow had entered, following its own bend and fancy; light as any cobweb.

With some trouble, and great care, lest the ancient frame should yield, I spread the lattice open; and saw at once that not a moment must

*The frost of 1625.

he lost, to save our stock. All the earth was flat with snow, all the air was thick with snow; more than this no man could see, for all the world was snowing.

I shut the window and dressed in haste; and when I entered the kitchen, not even Betty, the earliest of all early birds, was there. I raked the ashes together a little, just to see a spark of warmth; and then set forth to find John Fry, Jem Slocombe, and Bill Dadds. But this was easier thought than done; for when I opened the courtyard door, I was taken up to my knees at once, and the power of the drifting cloud prevented sight of anything. However, I found my way to the woodrick, and there got hold of a fine ash-stake, cut by myself not long ago. With this I ploughed along pretty well, and thundered so hard at John Fry's door, that he thought it was the Doones at least, and cocked his blunderbuss out of the window.

John was very loth to come down, when he saw the meaning of it; for he valued his life more than anything else; though he tried to make out that his wife was to blame. But I settled his doubts by telling him, that I would have him on my shoulder naked, unless he came in five minutes; not that he could do much good, but because the other men would be sure to skulk, if he set them the example. With spades, and shovels, and pitch-forks, and a round of roping, we four set forth to dig out the sheep; and the poor things knew that it was high time.

Chapter XLII The Great Winter

It must have snowed most wonderfully to have made that depth of covering in about eight hours. For one of Master Stickles' men, who had been out all the night, said that no snow began to fall until nearly midnight. And here it was, blocking up the doors, stopping the ways, and the water courses, and making it very much worse to walk than in a saw-pit newly used. However, we trudged along in a line; I first, and the other men after me; trying to keep my track, but finding legs and strength not up to it. Most of all, John Fry was groaning; certain that his time was come, and sending messages to his wife, and blessings to his children. For all this time it was snowing harder than it ever had snowed before, so far as a man might guess at it; and the leaden depth of the sky came down, like a mine turned upside down on us. Not that the flakes were so very large; for I have seen much larger flakes in a shower of March, while sowing peas; but that there was no room between them, neither any relaxing, nor any change of direction.

Watch, like a good and faithful dog, followed us very cheerfully, leaping out of the depth, which took him over his back and ears already, even in the level places; while in the drifts he might have sunk to any distance out of sight, and never found his way up again. However, we helped him now and then, especially through the gaps and gateways; and so after a deal of floundering, some laughter, and a little swearing, we came all safe to the lower meadow, where most of our flock was hurdled.

But behold, there was no flock at all! None, I mean, to be seen anywhere; only at one corner of the field, by the eastern end, where the snow drove in, a great white billow, as high as a barn, and as broad as a house. This great drift was rolling and curling beneath the violent blast, tufting and combing with rustling swirls, and carved (as in patterns of cornice) where the grooving chisel of the wind swept round. Ever and again the tempest snatched little whiffs from the channelled edges, twirled them round and made them dance over the chime of the monster pile, then let them lie like herring-bones, or the seams of sand where the tide has been. And all the while from the smothering sky, more and more fiercely at every blast, came the pelting, pitiless arrows, winged with murky white, and pointed with the barbs of frost.

But although for people who had no sheep, the sight was a very fine one (so far at least as the weather permitted any sight at all); yet for us, with our flock beneath it, this great mount had but little charm. Watch began to scratch at once, and to howl along the sides of it; he knew that his charge was buried there, and his business taken from him. But we four men set to in earnest, digging with all our might and main, shovelling away at the great white pile, and fetching it into the meadow. Each man made for himself a cave, scooping at the soft, cold flux, which slid upon him at every stroke, and throwing it out behind him, in piles of castled fancy. At last we drove our tunnels in (for we worked indeed for the lives of us), and all converging towards the middle, held our tools and listened.

The other men heard nothing at all; or declared that they heard nothing, being anxious now to abandon the matter, because of the chill in their feet and knees. But I said, 'Go, if you choose all of you. I will work it out by myself, you pie-crusts,' and upon that they gripped their shovels, being more or less of Englishmen; and the least drop of English blood is worth the best of any other when it comes to lasting out.

But before we began again, I laid my head well into the chamber; and there I hears a faint 'ma-a-ah,' coming through some ells of snow, like a plaintive, buried hope, or a last appeal. I shouted aloud to cheer him up, for I knew what sheep it was, to wit, the most valiant of all the wethers, who had met me when I came home from London, and been so glad to see me. And then we all fell to again; and very soon we hauled him out. Watch took charge of him at once, with an air of the noblest patronage, lying on his frozen fleece, and licking all his face and feet, to restore his warmth to him. Then fighting Tom jumped up at once, and made a little butt at Watch, as if nothing had ever ailed him, and then set off to a shallow place, and looked for something to nibble at.

Further in, and close under the bank, where they had huddled themselves for warmth, we found all the rest of the poor sheep packed, as closely as if they were in a great pie. It was strange to observe how their vapour and breath, and the moisture exuding from their wool had scooped, as it were, a coved room for them, lined with a ribbing of deep yellow snow. Also the churned snow beneath their feet was as yellow as gamboge. Two or three of the weaklier hoggets were dead, from want of air, and from pressure; but more than three-score were as lively as ever; though cramped and stiff for a little while.

'However shall us get 'em home?' John Fry asked in great dismay, when we had cleared about a dozen of them; which we were forced to do very carefully, so as not to fetch the roof down. 'No manner of maning to draive 'un, drough all they girt driftnesses.'

'You see to this place, John,' I replied, as we leaned on our shovels a moment, and the sheep came rubbing round us; 'let no more of them out for the present; they are better where they be. Watch, here boy, keep them!'

Watch came, with his little scut of a tail cocked as sharp as duty, and I set him at the narrow mouth of the great snow antre. All the sheep sidled away, and got closer, that the other sheep might be bitten first, as the foolish things imagine; whereas no good sheep-dog even so much as lips a sheep to turn it.

Then of the outer sheep (all now snowed and frizzled like a lawyer's wig) I took the two finest and heaviest, and with one beneath my right arm, and the other beneath my left, I went straight home to the upper sheppey, and set them inside and fastened them. Sixty and six I took home in that way, two at a time on each joumey; and the work grew harder and harder each time, as the drifts of the snow were deepening. No other man should meddle with them; I was resolved to try my strength against the strength of the elements; and try it I did, ay, and proved it. A certain fierce delight burned in me, as the struggle grew harder; but rather would I die than yield; and at last I finished it. People talk of it to this day; but none can tell what the labour was, who have not felt that snow and wind.

Of the sheep upon the mountain, and the sheep upon the western farm, and the cattle on the upper barrows, scarcely one in ten was saved; do what we would for them, and this was not through any neglect (now that our wits were sharpened), but from the pure impossibility of finding them at all. That great snow never ceased a moment for three days and nights; and then when all the earth was filled, and the topmost hedges were unseen, and the trees broke down with weight (wherever the wind had not lightened them), a brilliant sun broke forth and showed the loss of all our customs.

All our house was quite snowed up, except where we had purged a way, by dint of constant shovellings. The kitchen was as dark and darker than the cider-cellar, and long lines of furrowed scollops ran even up to the chimney-stacks. Several windows fell right inwards, through the weight of the snow against them; and the few that stood, bulged in, and bent like an old bruised lanthorn. We were obliged to cook by candle-light; we were forced to read by candle-light; as for baking, we could not do it, because the oven was too chill; and a load of faggots only brought a little wet down the sides of it.

For when the sun burst forth at last upon that world of white, what he brought was neither warmth, nor cheer, nor hope of softening; only a clearer shaft of cold, from the violet depths of sky. Long-drawn alleys of white haze seemed to lead towards him, yet such as he could not come down, with any warmth remaining. Broad white curtains of the frost-fog looped around the lower sky, on the verge of hill and valley, and above the laden trees. Only round the sun himself, and the spot of heaven he claimed, clustered a bright purple-blue, clear, and calm, and deep.

That night such a frost ensued as we had never dreamed of, neither read in ancient books, or histories of Frobisher. The kettle by the fire froze, and the crock upon the hearth-cheeks; many men were killed, and cattle rigid in their head-ropes. Then I heard that fearful sound, which never I had heard before, neither since have heard (except during that same winter), the sharp yet solemn sound of trees burst open by the frost-blow. Our great walnut lost three branches, and has been dying ever since; though growing meanwhile, as the soul does. And the ancient oak at the cross was rent, and many score of ash trees. But why should I tell all this? the people who have not seen it (as I have) will only make faces, and disbelieve; till such another frost comes; which perhaps may never be.

This terrible weather kept Tom Faggus from coming near our house for weeks; at which indeed I was not vexed a quarter so much as Annie was; for I had never half approved of him, as a husband for my sister; in spite of his purchase from Squire Bassett, and the grant of the Royal pardon. It may be, however, that Annie took the same view of my love for Lorna, and could not augur well of it; but if so, she held her peace, though I was not so sparing. For many things contributed to make me less good-humoured now than my real nature was; and the very least of all these things would have been enough to make some people cross, and rude, and fractious. I mean the red and painful chapping of my face and hands, from working in the snow all day, and lying in the frost all night. For being of a fair complexion, and a ruddy nature, and pretty plump withal, and fed on plenty of hot victuals, and always forced by my mother to sit nearer the fire than I wished, it was wonderful to see how the cold ran revel on my cheeks and knuckles. And I feared that Lorna (if it should ever please God to stop the snowing) might take this for a proof of low and rustic blood and breeding.

And this I say was the smallest thing; for it was far more serious that we were losing half our stock, do all we would to shelter them. Even the horses in the stables (mustered all together for the sake of breath and steaming) had long icicles from their muzzles, almost every morning. But of all things the very gravest, to my apprehension, was the impossibility of hearing, or having any token of or from my loved one. Not that those three days alone of snow (tremendous as it was) could have blocked the country so; but that the sky had never ceased, for more than two days at a time, for full three weeks thereafter, to pour fresh piles of fleecy mantle; neither had the wind relaxed a single day from shaking them. As a rule, it snowed all day, cleared up at night, and froze intensely, with the stars as bright as jewels, earth spread out in lustrous twilight, and the sounds in the air as sharp and crackling as artillery; then in the morning, snow again; before the sun could come to help.

It mattered not what way the wind was. Often and often the vanes went round, and we hoped for change of weather; the only change was that it seemed (if possible) to grow colder. Indeed, after a week or so, the wind would regularly box the compass (as the sailors call it) in the course of every day, following where the sun should be, as if to make a mock of him. And this of course immensely added to the peril of the drifts; because they shifted every day; and no skill or care might learn them.

I believe it was on Epiphany morning, or somewhere about that period, when Lizzie ran into the kitchen to me, where I was thawing my goose-grease, with the dogs among the ashes—the live dogs, I mean, not the iron ones, for them we had given up long ago,—and having caught me, by way of wonder (for generally I was out shoveling long before my 'young lady' had her nightcap off), she positively kissed me, for the sake of warming her lips perhaps, or because she had something proud to say.

'You great fool, John,' said my lady, as Annie and I used to call her, on account of her airs and graces; 'what a pity you never read, John!'

'Much use, I should think, in reading!' I answered, though pleased with her condescension; 'read, I suppose, with roof coming in, and only this chimney left sticking out of the snow!'

'The very time to read, John,' said Lizzie, looking grander; 'our worst troubles are the need, whence knowledge can deliver us.'

'Amen,' I cried out; 'are you parson or clerk? Whichever you are, good-morning.'

Thereupon I was bent on my usual round (a very small one nowadays), but Eliza took me with both hands, and I stopped of course; for I could not bear to shake the child, even in play, for a moment, because her back was tender. Then she looked up at me with her beautiful eyes, so large, unhealthy and delicate, and strangely shadowing outward, as if to spread their meaning; and she said,—

'Now, John, this is no time to joke. I was almost frozen in bed last night; and Annie like an icicle. Feel how cold my hands are. Now, will you listen to what I have read about climates ten times worse than this; and where none but clever men can live?'

'Impossible for me to listen now, I have hundreds of things to see to; but I will listen after breakfast to your foreign climates, child. Now attend to mother's hot coffee.'

She looked a little disappointed, but she knew what I had to do; and after all she was not so utterly unreasonable; although she did read books. And when I had done my morning's work, I listened to her patiently; and it was out of my power to think that all she said was foolish.

For I knew common sense pretty well, by this time, whether it happened to be my own, or any other person's, if clearly laid before me. And Lizzie had a particular way of setting forth very clearly whatever she wished to express and enforce. But the queerest part of it all was this, that if she could but have dreamed for a moment what would be the first application made me by of her lesson, she would rather have bitten her tongue off than help me to my purpose.

She told me that in the Arctic Regions, as they call some places, a long way north, where the Great Bear lies all across the heavens, and no sun is up, for whole months at a time, and yet where people will go exploring, out of pure contradiction, and for the sake of novelty, and love of being frozen—that here they always had such winters as we were having now. It never ceased to freeze, she said; and it never ceased to snow; except when it was too cold; and then all the air was choked with glittering spikes; and a man's skin might come off of him, before he could ask the reason. Nevertheless the people there (although the snow was fifty feet deep, and all their breath fell behind them frozen, like a log of wood dropped from their shoulders), yet they managed to get along, and make the time of the year to each other, by a little cleverness. For seeing how the snow was spread, lightly over everything, covering up the hills and valleys, and the foreskin of the sea, they contrived a way to crown it, and to glide like a flake along. Through the sparkle of the whiteness, and the wreaths of windy tossings, and the ups and downs of cold, any man might get along with a boat on either foot, to prevent his sinking.

She told me how these boats were made; very strong and very light, of ribs with skin across them; five feet long, and one foot wide; and turned up at each end, even as a canoe is. But she did not tell me, nor did I give it a moment's thought myself, how hard it was to walk upon them without early practice. Then she told me another thing equally useful to me; although I would not let her see how much I thought about it. And this concerned the use of sledges, and their power of gliding, and the lightness of their following; all of which I could see at once, through knowledge of our own farm-sleds; which we employ in lieu of wheels, used in flatter districts. When I had heard all this from her, a mere chit of a girl as she was, unfit to make a snowball even, or to fry snow pancakes, I looked down on her with amazement, and began to wish a little that I had given more time to books.

But God shapes all our fitness, and gives each man his meaning, even as he guides the wavering lines of snow descending. Our Eliza was meant for books; our dear Annie for loving and cooking; I, John Ridd, for sheep, and wrestling, and the thought of Lorna; and mother to love all three of us, and to make the best of her children. And now, if I must tell the truth, as at every page I try to do (though God knows it is hard enough), I had felt through all this weather, though my life was Lorna's, something of a satisfaction in so doing duty to my kindest and best of mothers, and to none but her. For (if you come to think of it) a man's young love is very pleasant, very sweet, and tickling; and takes him through the core of heart; without his knowing how or why. Then he dwells upon it sideways, without people looking, and builds up all sorts of fancies, growing hot with working so at his own imaginings. So his love is a crystal Goddess, set upon an obelisk; and whoever will not bow the knee (yet without glancing at her), the lover makes it a sacred rite either to kick or to stick him. I am not speaking of me and Lorna, but of common people.

Then (if you come to think again) lo!—or I will not say lo! for no one can behold it—only feel, or but remember, what a real mother is. Ever loving, ever soft, ever turning sin to goodness, vices into virtues; blind to all nine-tenths of wrong; through a telescope beholding (though herself so nigh to them) faintest decimal of promise, even in her vilest child. Ready to thank God again, as when her babe was born to her; leaping (as at kingdom-come) at a wandering syllable of Gospel for her lost one.

All this our mother was to us, and even more than all of this; and hence I felt a pride and joy in doing my sacred duty towards her, now that the weather compelled me. And she was as grateful and delighted as if she had no more claim upon me than a stranger's sheep might have. Yet from time to time I groaned within myself and by myself, at thinking of my sad debarment from the sight of Lorna, and of all that might have happened to her, now she had no protection.

Therefore, I fell to at once, upon that hint from Lizzie, and being used to thatching-work, and the making of traps, and so on, before very long I built myself a pair of strong and light snow-shoes, framed with ash and ribbed of withy, with half-tanned calf-skin stretched across, and an inner sole to support my feet. At first I could not walk at all, but floundered about most piteously, catching one shoe in the other, and both of them in the snow-drifts, to the great amusement of the girls, who were come to look at me. But after a while I grew more expert, discovering what my errors were, and altering the inclination of the shoes themselves, according to a print which Lizzie found in a book of adventures. And this made such a difference, that I crossed the farmyard and came back again (though turning was the worst thing of all) without so much as falling once, or getting my staff entangled.

But oh, the aching of my ankles, when I went to bed that night; I was forced to help myself upstairs with a couple of mopsticks! and I rubbed the joints with neatsfoot oil, which comforted them greatly. And likely enough I would have abandoned any further trial, but for Lizzie's ridicule, and pretended sympathy; asking if the strong John Ridd would have old Betty to lean upon. Therefore I set to again, with a fixed resolve not to notice pain or stiffness, but to warm them out of me. And sure enough, before dark that day, I could get along pretty freely; especially improving every time, after leaving off and resting. The astonishment of poor John Fry, Bill Dadds, and Jem Slocombe, when they saw me coming down the hill upon them, in the twilight, where they were clearing the furze rick and trussing it for cattle, was more than I can tell you; because they did not let me see it, but ran away with one accord, and floundered into a snowdrift. They believed, and so did every one else (especially when I grew able to glide along pretty rapidly), that I had stolen Mother Melldrum's sieves, on which she was said to fly over the foreland at midnight every Saturday.

Upon the following day, I held some council with my mother; not liking to go without her permission, yet scarcely daring to ask for it. But here she disappointed me, on the right side of disappointment; saying that she had seen my pining (which she never could have done; because I had been too hard at work), and rather than watch me grieving so, for somebody or other, who now was all in all to me, I might go upon my course, and God's protection go with me! At this I was amazed, because it was not at all like mother; and knowing how well I had behaved, ever since the time of our snowing up, I was a little moved to tell her that she could not understand me. However my sense of duty kept me, and my knowledge of the catechism, from saying such a thing as that, or even thinking twice of it. And so I took her at her word, which she was not prepared for; and telling her how proud I was of her trust in Providence, and how I could run in my new snow-shoes, I took a short pipe in my mouth, and started forth accordingly.

Chapter XLIII Not Too Soon

When I started on my road across the hills and valleys (which now were pretty much alike), the utmost I could hope to do was to gain the crest of hills, and look into the Doone Glen. Hence I might at least descry whether Lorna still was safe, by the six nests still remaining, and the view of the Captain's house. When I was come to the open country, far beyond the sheltered homestead, and in the full brunt of the wind, the keen blast of the cold broke on me, and the mighty breadth of snow. Moor and highland, field and common, cliff and vale, and watercourse, over all the rolling folds of misty white were flung. There was nothing square or jagged left, there was nothing perpendicular; all the rugged lines were eased, and all the breaches smoothly filled. Curves, and mounds, and rounded heavings, took the place of rock and stump; and all the country looked as if a woman's hand had been on it.

Through the sparkling breadth of white, which seemed to glance my eyes away, and outside the humps of laden trees, bowing their backs like a woodman, I contrived to get along, half-sliding and half-walking, in places where a plain-shodden man must have sunk, and waited freezing till the thaw should come to him. For although there had been such violent frost, every night, upon the snow, the snow itself, having never thawed, even for an hour, had never coated over. Hence it was as soft and light as if all had fallen yesterday. In places where no drift had been, but rather off than on to them, three feet was the least of depth; but where the wind had chased it round, or any draught led like a funnel, or anything opposed it; there you might very safely say that it ran up to twenty feet, or thirty, or even fifty, and I believe some times a hundred.

At last I got to my spy-hill (as I had begun to call it), although I never should have known it but for what it looked on. And even to know this last ...ain required all the eyes of love, soever sharp and vigilant. For all the ...ful Glen Doone (shaped from out the mountains, as if on purpose ...oones, and looking in the summer-time like a sharp cut vase of ...as besnowed half up the sides, and at either end so, that it was more like the white basins wherein we boil plum-puddings. Not a patch of grass was there, not a black branch of a tree; all was white; and the little river flowed beneath an arch of snow; if it managed to flow at all.

Now this was a great surprise to me; not only because I believed Glen Doone to be a place outside all frost, but also because I thought perhaps that it was quite impossible to be cold near Lorna. And now it struck me all at once that perhaps her ewer was frozen (as mine had been for the last three weeks, requiring embers around it), and perhaps her window would not shut, any more than mine would; and perhaps she wanted blankets. This idea worked me up to such a chill of sympathy, that seeing no Doones now about, and doubting if any guns would go off, in this state of the weather, and knowing that no man could catch me up (except with shoes like mine), I even resolved to slide the cliffs, and bravely go to Lorna.

It helped me much in this resolve, that the snow came on again, thick enough to blind a man who had not spent his time among it, as I had done now for days and days. Therefore I took my neatsfoot oil, which now was clogged like honey, and rubbed it hard into my leg-joints, so far as I could reach them. And then I set my back and elbows well against a snow-drift, hanging far adown the cliff, and saying some of the Lord's Prayer, threw myself on Providence. Before there was time to think or dream, I landed very beautifully upon a ridge of run-up snow in a quiet corner. My good shoes, or boots, preserved me from going far beneath it; though one of them was sadly strained, where a grub had gnawed the ash, in the early summer-time. Having set myself aright, and being in good spirits, I made boldly across the valley (where the snow was furrowed hard), being now afraid of nobody.

If Lorna had looked out of the window she would not have known me, with those boots upon my feet, and a well-cleaned sheepskin over me, bearing my own (J.R.) in red, just between my shoulders, but covered now in snow-flakes. The house was partly drifted up, though not so much as ours was; and I crossed the little stream almost without knowing that it was under me. At first, being pretty safe from interference from the other huts, by virtue of the blinding snow and the difficulty of walking, I examined all the windows; but these were coated so with ice, like ferns and flowers and dazzling stars, that no one could so much as guess what might be inside of them. Moreover I was afraid of prying narrowly into them, as it was not a proper thing where a maiden might be; only I wanted to know just this, whether she were there or not.

Taking nothing by this movement, I was forced, much against my will, to venture to the door and knock, in a hesitating manner, not being sure but what my answer might be the mouth of a carbine. However it was not so, for I heard a pattering of feet and a whispering going on, and then a shrill voice through the keyhole, asking, 'Who's there?'

'Only me, John Ridd,' I answered; upon which I heard a little laughter, and a little sobbing, or something that was like it; and then the door was opened about a couple of inches, with a bar behind it still; and then the little voice went on,—

'Put thy finger in, young man, with the old ring on it. But mind thee, if it be the wrong one, thou shalt never draw it back again.'

Laughing at Gwenny's mighty threat, I showed my finger in the opening; upon which she let me in, and barred the door again like lightning.

'What is the meaning of all this, Gwenny?' I asked, as I slipped about on the floor, for I could not stand there firmly with my great snow-shoes on.

'Maning enough, and bad maning too,' the Cornish girl made answer. Us be shut in here, and starving, and durstn't let anybody in upon us. I wish thou wer't good to ate, young man: I could manage most of thee.'

I was so frightened by her eyes, full of wolfish hunger, that I could only say 'Good God!' having never seen the like before. Then drew I forth a large piece of bread, which I had brought in case of accidents, and placed it in her hands. She leaped at it, as a starving dog leaps at sight of his supper, and she set her teeth in it, and then withheld it from her lips, with something very like an oath at her own vile greediness; and then away round the corner with it, no doubt for her young mistress. I meanwhile was occupied, to the best of my ability, in taking my snow-shoes off, yet wondering much within myself why Lorna did not come to me.

But presently I knew the cause, for Gwenny called me, and I ran, and found my darling quite unable to say so much as, 'John, how are you?' Between the hunger and the cold, and the excitement of my coming, she had fainted away, and lay back on a chair, as white as the snow around us. In betwixt her delicate lips, Gwenny was thrusting with all her strength the hard brown crust of the rye-bread, which she had snatched from me so.

'Get water, or get snow,' I said; 'don't you know what fainting is, you very stupid child?'

'Never heerd on it, in Cornwall,' she answered, trusting still to the bread; 'be un the same as bleeding?'

'It will be directly, if you go on squeezing away with that crust so. Eat a piece: I have got some more. Leave my darling now to me.'

Hearing that I had some more, the starving girl could resist no longer, but tore it in two, and had swallowed half before I had coaxed my Lorna back to sense, and hope, and joy, and love.

'I never expected to see you again. I had made up my mind to die, John; and to die without your knowing it.'

As I repelled this fearful thought in a manner highly fortifying, the tender hue flowed back again into her famished cheeks and lips, and a softer brilliance glistened from the depth of her dark eyes. She gave me one little shrunken hand, and I could not help a tear for it.

'After all, Mistress Lorna,' I said, pretending to be gay, for a smile might do her good; 'you do not love me as Gwenny does; for she even wanted to eat me.'

'And shall, afore I have done, young man,' Gwenny answered laughing; 'you come in here with they red chakes, and make us think o' sirloin.'

'Eat up your bit of brown bread, Gwenny. It is not good enough for your mistress. Bless her heart, I have something here such as she never tasted the like of, being in such appetite. Look here, Lorna; smell it first. I have had it ever since Twelfth Day, and kept it all the time for you. Annie made it. That is enough to warrant it good cooking.'

And then I showed my great mince-pie in a bag of tissue paper, and I told them how the mince-meat was made of golden pippins finely shred, with the undercut of the sirloin, and spice and fruit accordingly and far beyond my knowledge. But Lorna would not touch a morsel until she had thanked God for it, and given me the kindest kiss, and put a piece in Gwenny's mouth.

I have eaten many things myself, with very great enjoyment, and keen perception of their merits, and some thanks to God for them. But I never did enjoy a thing, that had found its way between my own lips, half, or even a quarter as much as I now enjoyed beholding Lorna, sitting proudly upwards (to show that she was faint no more) entering into that mince-pie, and moving all her pearls of teeth (inside her little mouth-place) exactly as I told her. For I was afraid lest she should be too fast in going through it, and cause herself more damage so, than she got of nourishment. But I had no need to fear at all, and Lorna could not help laughing at me for thinking that she had no self-control.

Some creatures require a deal of food (I myself among the number), and some can do with a very little; making, no doubt, the best of it. And I have often noticed that the plumpest and most perfect women never eat so hard and fast as the skinny and three-cornered ones. These last be often ashamed of it, and eat most when the men be absent. Hence it came to pass that Lorna, being the loveliest of all maidens, had as much as she could do to finish her own half of pie; whereas Gwenny Carfax (though generous more than greedy), ate up hers without winking, after finishing the brown loaf; and then I begged to know the meaning of this state of things.

'The meaning is sad enough,' said Lorna; 'and I see no way out of it. We are both to be starved until I let them do what they like with me.

'That is to say until you choose to marry Carver Doone, and be slowly killed by him?'

'Slowly! No, John, quickly. I hate him so intensely, that less than a week would kill me.'

'Not a doubt of that,' said Gwenny; 'oh, she hates him nicely then; but not half so much as I do.'

I told them that this state of things could be endured no longer, on which point they agreed with me, but saw no means to help it. For even if Lorna could make up her mind to come away with me and live at Plover's Barrows farm, under my good mother's care, as I had urged so often, behold the snow was all around us, heaped as high as mountains, and how could any delicate maiden ever get across it?

Then I spoke with a strange tingle upon both sides of my heart, knowing that this undertaking was a serious one for all, and might burn our farm down,—

'If I warrant to take you safe, and without much fright or hardship, Lorna, will you come with me?'

'To be sure I will, dear,' said my beauty, with a smile and a glance to follow it; 'I have small alternative, to starve, or go with you, John.'

'Gwenny, have you courage for it? Will you come with your young mistress?'

'Will I stay behind?' cried Gwenny, in a voice that settled it. And so we began to arrange about it; and I was much excited. It was useless now to leave it longer; if it could be done at all, it could not be too quickly done. It was the Counsellor who had ordered, after all other schemes had failed, that his niece should have no food until she would obey him. He had strictly watched the house, taking turns with Carver, to ensure that none came nigh it bearing food or comfort. But this evening, they had thought it needless to remain on guard; and it would have been impossible, because themselves were busy offering high festival to all the valley, in right of their own commandership. And Gwenny said that nothing made her so nearly mad with appetite as the account she received from a woman of all the dishes preparing. Nevertheless she had answered bravely,—

'Go and tell the Counsellor, and go and tell the Carver, who sent you to spy upon us, that we shall have a finer dish than any set before them.' And so in truth they did, although so little dreaming it; for no Doone that was ever born, however much of a Carver, might vie with our Annie for mince-meat.

Now while we sat reflecting much, and talking a good deal more, in spite of all the cold—for I never was in a hurry to go, when I had Lorna with me—she said, in her silvery voice, which always led me so along, as if I were a slave to a beautiful bell,—

'Now, John, we are wasting time, dear. You have praised my hair, till it curls with pride, and my eyes till you cannot see them, even if they are brown diamonds which I have heard for the fiftieth time at least; though I never saw such a jewel. Don't you think it is high time to put on your snow-shoes, John?'

'Certainly not,' I answered, 'till we have settled something more. I was so cold when I came in; and now I am as warm as a cricket. And so are you, you lively soul; though you are not upon my hearth yet.'

'Remember, John,' said Lorna, nestling for a moment to me; 'the severity of the weather makes a great difference between us. And you must never take advantage.'

'I quite understand all that, dear. And the harder it freezes the better, while that understanding continues. Now do try to be serious.'

'I try to be serious! And I have been trying fifty times, and could not bring you to it, John! Although I am sure the situation, as the Counsellor says at the beginning of a speech, the situation, to say the least, is serious enough for anything. Come, Gwenny, imitate him.'

Gwenny was famed for her imitation of the Counsellor making a speech; and she began to shake her hair, and mount upon a footstool; but I really could not have this, though even Lorna ordered it. The truth was that my darling maiden was in such wild spirits, at seeing me so unexpected, and at the prospect of release, and of what she had never known, quiet life and happiness, that like all warm and loving natures, she could scarce control herself.

'Come to this frozen window, John, and see them light the stack-fire. They will little know who looks at them. Now be very good, John. You stay in that corner, dear, and I will stand on this side; and try to breathe yourself a peep-hole through the lovely spears and banners. Oh, you don't know how to do it. I must do it for you. Breathe three times, like that, and that; and then you rub it with your fingers, before it has time to freeze again.'

All this she did so beautifully, with her lips put up like cherries, and her fingers bent half back, as only girls can bend them, and her little waist thrown out against the white of the snowed-up window, that I made her do it three times over; and I stopped her every time and let it freeze again, that so she might be the longer. Now I knew that all her love was mine, every bit as much as mine was hers; yet I must have her to show it, dwelling upon every proof, lengthening out all certainty. Perhaps the jealous heart is loath to own a life worth twice its own. Be that as it may, I know that we thawed the window nicely.

And then I saw, far down the stream (or rather down the bed of it, for there was no stream visible), a little form of fire arising, red, and dark, and flickering. Presently it caught on something, and went upward boldly; and then it struck into many forks, and then it fell, and rose again.

'Do you know what all that is, John?' asked Lorna, smiling cleverly at the manner of my staring.

'How on earth should I know? Papists burn Protestants in the flesh; and Protestants burn Papists in effigy, as we mock them. Lorna, are they going to burn any one to-night?'

'No, you dear. I must rid you of these things. I see that you are bigoted. The Doones are firing Dunkery beacon, to celebrate their new captain.'

'But how could they bring it here through the snow? If they have sledges, I can do nothing.'

'They brought it before the snow began. The moment poor grandfather was gone, even before his funeral, the young men, having none to check them, began at once upon it. They had always borne a grudge against it; not that it ever did them harm; but because it seemed so insolent. "Can't a gentleman go home, without a smoke behind him?" I have often heard them saying. And though they have done it no serious harm, since they threw the firemen on the fire, many, many years ago, they have often promised to bring it here for their candle; and now they have done it. Ah, now look! The tar is kindled.'

Though Lorna took it so in joke, I looked upon it very gravely, knowing that this heavy outrage to the feelings of the neighbourhood would cause more stir than a hundred sheep stolen, or a score of houses sacked. Not of course that the beacon was of the smallest use to any one, neither stopped anybody from stealing, nay, rather it was like the parish knell, which begins when all is over, and depresses all the survivors; yet I knew that we valued it, and were proud, and spoke of it as a mighty institution; and even more than that, our vestry had voted, within the last two years, seven shillings and six-pence to pay for it, in proportion with other parishes. And one of the men who attended to it, or at least who was paid for doing so, was our Jem Slocombe's grandfather.

However, in spite of all my regrets, the fire went up very merrily, blazing red and white and yellow, as it leaped on different things. And the light danced on the snow-drifts with a misty lilac hue. I was astonished at its burning in such mighty depths of snow; but Gwenny said that the wicked men had been three days hard at work, clearing, as it were, a cock-pit, for their fire to have its way. And now they had a mighty pile, which must have covered five land-yards square, heaped up to a goodly height, and eager to take fire.

In this I saw great obstacle to what I wished to manage. For when this pyramid should be kindled thoroughly, and pouring light and blazes round, would not all the valley be like a white room full of candles? Thinking thus, I was half inclined to abide my time for another night: and then my second thoughts convinced me that I would be a fool in this. For lo, what an opportunity! All the Doones would be drunk, of course, in about three hours' time, and getting more and more in drink as the night went on. As for the fire, it must sink in about three hours or more, and only cast uncertain shadows friendly to my purpose. And then the outlaws must cower round it, as the cold increased on them, helping the weight of the liquor; and in their jollity any noise would be cheered as a false alarm. Most of all, and which decided once for all my action,—when these wild and reckless villains should be hot with ardent spirits, what was door, or wall, to stand betwixt them and my Lorna?

This thought quickened me so much that I touched my darling reverently, and told her in a few short words how I hoped to manage it.

'Sweetest, in two hours' time, I shall be again with you. Keep the bar up, and have Gwenny ready to answer any one. You are safe while they are dining, dear, and drinking healths, and all that stuff; and before they have done with that, I shall be again with you. Have everything you care to take in a very little compass, and Gwenny must have no baggage. I shall knock loud, and then wait a little; and then knock twice, very softly.'

With this I folded her in my arms; and she looked frightened at me; not having perceived her danger; and then I told Gwenny over again what I had told her mistress: but she only nodded her head and said, 'Young man, go and teach thy grandmother.'

Chapter XLIV Brought Home At Last

To my great delight I found that the weather, not often friendly to lovers, and lately seeming so hostile, had in the most important matter done me a signal service. For when I had promised to take my love from the power of those wretches, the only way of escape apparent lay through the main

Doone-gate. For though I might climb the cliffs myself, especially with the snow to aid me, I durst not try to fetch Lorna up them, even if she were not half-starved, as well as partly frozen; and as for Gwenny's door, as we called it (that is to say, the little entrance from the wooded hollow), it was snowed up long ago to the level of the hills around. Therefore I was at my wit's end how to get them out; the passage by the Doone-gate being long, and dark, and difficult, and leading to such a weary circuit among the snowy moors and hills.

But now, being homeward-bound by the shortest possible track, I slipped along between the bonfire and the boundary cliffs, where I found a caved way of snow behind a sort of avalanche: so that if the Doones had been keeping watch (which they were not doing, but revelling), they could scarcely have discovered me. And when I came to my old ascent, where I had often scaled the cliff and made across the mountains, it struck me that I would just have a look at my first and painful entrance, to wit, the water-slide. I never for a moment imagined that this could help me now; for I never had dared to descend it, even in the finest weather; still I had a curiosity to know what my old friend was like, with so much snow upon him. But, to my very great surprise, there was scarcely any snow there at all, though plenty curling high overhead from the cliff, like bolsters over it. Probably the sweeping of the north-east wind up the narrow chasm had kept the showers from blocking it, although the water had no power under the bitter grip of frost. All my water-slide was now less a slide than path of ice; furrowed where the waters ran over fluted ridges; seamed where wind had tossed and combed them, even while congealing; and crossed with little steps wherever the freezing torrent lingered. And here and there the ice was fibred with the trail of sludge-weed, slanting from the side, and matted, so as to make resting-place.

Lo it was easy track and channel, as if for the very purpose made, down which I could guide my sledge with Lorna sitting in it. There were only two things to be feared; one lest the rolls of snow above should fall in and bury us; the other lest we should rush too fast, and so be carried headlong into the black whirlpool at the bottom, the middle of which was still unfrozen, and looking more horrible by the contrast. Against this danger I made provision, by fixing a stout bar across; but of the other we must take our chance, and trust ourselves to Providence.

I hastened home at my utmost speed, and told my mother for God's sake to keep the house up till my return, and to have plenty of fire blazing, and plenty of water boiling, and food enough hot for a dozen people, and the best bed aired with the warming-pan. Dear mother smiled softly at my excitement, though her own was not much less, I am sure, and enhanced by sore anxiety. Then I gave very strict directions to Annie, and praised her a little, and kissed her; and I even endeavoured to flatter Eliza, lest she should be disagreeable.

After this I took some brandy, both within and about me; the former, because I had sharp work to do; and the latter in fear of whatever might happen, in such great cold, to my comrades. Also I carried some other provisions, grieving much at their coldness: and then I went to the upper linhay, and took our new light pony-sledd, which had been made almost as much for pleasure as for business; though God only knows how our girls could have found any pleasure in bumping along so. On the snow, however, it ran as sweetly as if it had been made for it; yet I durst not take the pony with it; in the first place, because his hoofs would break through the ever-shifting surface of the light and piling snow; and secondly, because these ponies, coming from the forest, have a dreadful trick of neighing, and most of all in frosty weather.

Therefore I girded my own body with a dozen turns of hay-rope, twisting both the ends in under at the bottom of my breast, and winding the hay on the skew a little, that the hempen thong might not slip between, and so cut me in the drawing. I put a good piece of spare rope in the sledd, and the cross-seat with the back to it, which was stuffed with our own wool, as well as two or three fur coats; and then, just as I was starting, out came Annie, in spite of the cold, panting for fear of missing me, and with nothing on her head, but a lanthorn in one hand.

'Oh, John, here is the most wonderful thing! Mother has never shown it before; and I can't think how she could make up her mind. She had gotten it in a great well of a cupboard, with camphor, and spirits, and lavender. Lizzie says it is a most magnificent sealskin cloak, worth fifty pounds, or a farthing.'

'At any rate it is soft and warm,' said I, very calmly flinging it into the bottom of the sledd. 'Tell mother I will put it over Lorna's feet.'

'Lorna's feet! Oh, you great fool,' cried Annie, for the first time reviling me; 'over her shoulders; and be proud, you very stupid John.'

'It is not good enough for her feet,' I answered, with strong emphasis; 'but don't tell mother I said so, Annie. Only thank her very kindly.'

With that I drew my traces hard, and set my ashen staff into the snow, and struck out with my best foot foremost (the best one at snow-shoes, I mean), and the sledd came after me as lightly as a dog might follow; and Annie, with the lanthorn, seemed to be left behind and waiting like a pretty lamp-post.

The full moon rose as bright behind me as a paten of pure silver, casting on the snow long shadows of the few things left above, burdened rock, and shaggy foreland, and the labouring trees. In the great white desolation, distance was a mocking vision; hills looked nigh, and valleys far; when hills were far and valleys nigh. And the misty breath of frost, piercing through the ribs of rock, striking to the pith of trees, creeping to the heart of man, lay along the hollow places, like a serpent sloughing. Even as my own gaunt shadow (travestied as if I were the moonlight's daddy-longlegs), went before me down the slope; even I, the shadow's master, who had tried in vain to cough, when coughing brought good liquorice, felt a pressure on my bosom, and a husking in my throat.

However, I went on quietly, and at a very tidy speed; being only too thankful that the snow had ceased, and no wind as yet arisen. And from the ring of low white vapour girding all the verge of sky, and from the rosy blue above, and the shafts of starlight set upon a quivering bow, as well as from the moon itself and the light behind it, having learned the signs of frost from its bitter twinges, I knew that we should have a night as keen as ever England felt. Nevertheless, I had work enough to keep me warm if I managed it. The question was, could I contrive to save my darling from it?

Daring not to risk my sledd by any fall from the valley-cliffs, I dragged it very carefully up the steep incline of ice, through the narrow chasm, and so to the very brink and verge where first I had seen my Lorna, in the fishing days of boyhood. As I then had a trident fork, for sticking of the loaches, so I now had a strong ash stake, to lay across from rock to rock, and break the speed of descending. With this I moored the sledd quite safe, at the very lip of the chasm, where all was now substantial ice, green and black in the moonlight; and then I set off up the valley, skirting along one side of it.

The stack-fire still was burning strongly, but with more of heat than blaze; and many of the younger Doones were playing on the verge of it, the children making rings of fire, and their mothers watching them. All the grave and reverend warriors having heard of rheumatism, were inside of log and stone, in the two lowest houses, with enough of candles burning to make our list of sheep come short.

All these I passed, without the smallest risk or difficulty, walking up the channel of drift which I spoke of once before. And then I crossed, with more of care, and to the door of Lorna's house, and made the sign, and listened, after taking my snow-shoes off.

But no one came, as I expected, neither could I espy a light. And I seemed to hear a faint low sound, like the moaning of the snow-wind. Then I knocked again more loudly, with a knocking at my heart: and receiving no answer, set all my power at once against the door. In a moment it flew inwards, and I glided along the passage with my feet still slippery. There in Lorna's room I saw, by the moonlight flowing in, a sight which drove me beyond sense.

Lorna was behind a chair, crouching in the corner, with her hands up, and a crucifix, or something that looked like it. In the middle of the room lay Gwenny Carfax, stupid, yet with one hand clutching the ankle of a struggling man. Another man stood above my Lorna, trying to draw the chair away. In a moment I had him round the waist, and he went out of the window with a mighty crash of glass; luckily for him that window had no bars like some of them. Then I took the other man by the neck; and he could not plead for mercy. I bore him out of the house as lightly as I would bear a baby, yet squeezing his throat a little more than I fain would do to an infant. By the bright moonlight I saw that I carried Marwood de Whichehalse. For his father's sake I spared him, and because he had been my schoolfellow; but with every muscle of my body strung with indignation, I cast him, like a skittle, from me into a snowdrift, which closed over him. Then I looked for the other fellow, tossed through Lorna's window, and found him lying stunned and bleeding, neither able to groan yet. Charleworth Doone, if his gushing blood did not much mislead me.

It was no time to linger now; I fastened my shoes in a moment, and caught up my own darling with her head upon my shoulder, where she whispered faintly; and telling Gwenny to follow me, or else I would come back for her, if she could not walk the snow, I ran the whole distance to my sledd, caring not who might follow me. Then by the time I had set up Lorna, beautiful and smiling, with the seal-skin cloak all over her, sturdy Gwenny came along, having trudged in the track of my snow-shoes, although with two bags on her back. I set her in beside her mistress, to support her, and keep warm; and then with one look back at the glen, which had been so long my home of heart, I hung behind the sledd, and launched it down the steep and dangerous way.

Though the cliffs were black above us, and the road unseen in front, and a great white grave of snow might at a single word come down, Lorna was as calm and happy as an infant in its bed. She knew that I was with her; and when I told her not to speak, she touched my hand in silence. Gwenny was in a much greater fright, having never seen such a thing before, neither knowing what it is to yield to pure love's confidence. I could hardly keep her quiet, without making a noise myself. With my staff from rock to rock, and my weight thrown backward, I broke the sledd's too rapid way, and brought my grown love safely out, by the selfsame road which first had led me to her girlish fancy, and my boyish slavery.

Unpursued, yet looking back as if some one must be after us, we skirted round the black whirling pool, and gained the meadows beyond it. Here there was hard collar work, the track being all uphill and rough; and Gwenny wanted to jump out, to lighten the sledd and to push behind. But I would not hear of it; because it was now so deadly cold, and I feared that Lorna might get frozen, without having Gwenny to keep her warm. And after all, it was the sweetest labour I had ever known in all my life, to be sure that I was pulling Lorna, and pulling her to our own farmhouse.

Gwenny's nose was touched with frost, before we had gone much farther, because she would not keep it quiet and snug beneath the seal-skin. And here I had to stop in the moonlight (which was very dangerous) and rub it with a clove of snow, as Eliza had taught me; and Gwenny scolding all the time, as if myself had frozen it. Lorna was now so far oppressed with all the troubles of the evening, and the joy that followed them, as well as by the piercing cold and difficulty of breathing, that she lay quite motionless, like fairest wax in the moonlight—when we stole a glance at her, beneath the dark folds of the cloak; and I thought that she was falling into the heavy snow-sleep, whence there is no awaking.

Therefore, I drew my traces tight, and set my whole strength to the business; and we slipped along at a merry pace, although with many joltings, which must have sent my darling out into the cold snowdrifts but for the short strong arm of Gwenny. And so in about an hour's time, in spite of many hindrances, we came home to the old courtyard, and all the dogs saluted us. My heart was quivering, and my cheeks as hot as the Doones' bonfire, with wondering both what Lorna would think of our farm-yard, and what my mother would think of her. Upon the former subject my anxiety was wasted, for Lorna neither saw a thing, nor even opened her heavy eyes. And as to what mother would think of her, she was certain not to think at all, until she had cried over her.

And so indeed it came to pass. Even at this length of time, I can hardly tell it, although so bright before my mind, because it moves my heart so. The sledd was at the open door, with only Lorna in it; for Gwenny Carfax had jumped out, and hung back in the clearing, giving any reason rather than the only true one—that she would not be intruding. At the door were all our people; first, of course, Betty Muxworthy, teaching me how to draw the sledd, as if she had been born in it, and flourishing with a great broom, wherever a speck of snow lay. Then dear Annie, and old Molly (who was very quiet, and counted almost for nobody), and behind them, mother, looking as if she wanted to come first, but doubted how the manners lay. In the distance Lizzie stood, fearful of encouraging, but unable to keep out of it.

Betty was going to poke her broom right in under the sealskin cloak, where Lorna lay unconscious, and where her precious breath hung frozen, like a silver cobweb; but I caught up Betty's broom, and flung it clean away over the corn chamber; and then I put the others by, and fetched my mother forward.

'You shall see her first,' I said: 'is she not your daughter? Hold the light there, Annie.'

Dear mother's hands were quick and trembling, as she opened the shining folds; and there she saw my Lorna sleeping, with her black hair all dishevelled, and she bent and kissed her forehead, and only said, 'God bless her, John!' And then she was taken with violent weeping, and I was forced to hold her.

'Us may tich of her now, I rackon,' said Betty in her most jealous way; 'Annie, tak her by the head, and I'll tak her by the toesen. No taime to stand here like girt gawks. Don'ee tak on zo, missus. Ther be vainer vish in the zea—Lor, but, her be a booty!'

With this, they carried her into the house, Betty chattering all the while, and going on now about Lorna's hands, and the others crowding round her, so that I thought I was not wanted among so many women, and should only get the worst of it, and perhaps do harm to my darling. Therefore I went and brought Gwenny in, and gave her a potful of bacon and peas, and an iron spoon to eat it with, which she did right heartily.

Then I asked her how she could have been such a fool as to let those two vile fellows enter the house where Lorna was; and she accounted for it so naturally, that I could only blame myself. For my agreement had been to give one loud knock (if you happen to remember) and after that two little knocks. Well these two drunken rogues had come; and one, being very drunk indeed, had given a great thump; and then nothing more to do with it; and the other, being three-quarters drunk, had followed his leader (as one might say) but feebly, and making two of it. Whereupon up jumped Lorna, and declared that her John was there.

All this Gwenny told me shortly, between the whiles of eating, and even while she licked the spoon; and then there came a message for me that my love was sensible, and was seeking all around for me. Then I told Gwenny to hold her tongue (whatever she did among us), and not to trust to women's words; and she told me they all were liars, as she had found out long ago; and the only thing to believe in was an honest man, when found. Thereupon I could have kissed her as a sort of tribute, liking to be appreciated; yet the peas upon her lips made me think about it; and thought is fatal to action. So I went to see my dear.

That sight I shall not forget; till my dying head falls back, and my breast can lift no more. I know not whether I were then more blessed, or harrowed by it. For in the settle was my Lorna, propped with pillows round her, and her clear hands spread sometimes to the blazing fireplace. In her eyes no knowledge was of anything around her, neither in her neck the sense of leaning towards anything. Only both her lovely hands were entreating something, to spare her, or to love her; and the lines of supplication quivered in her sad white face.

'All go away, except my mother,' I said very quietly, but so that I would be obeyed; and everybody knew it. Then mother came to me alone; and she said, 'The frost is in her brain; I have heard of this before, John.' 'Mother, I will have it out,' was all that I could answer her; 'leave her to me altogether; only you sit there and watch.' For I felt that Lorna knew me, and no other soul but me; and that if not interfered with, she would soon come home to me. Therefore I sat gently by her, leaving nature, as it were, to her own good time and will. And presently the glance that watched me, as at distance and in doubt, began to flutter and to brighten, and to deepen into kindness, then to beam with trust and love, and then with gathering tears to falter, and in shame to turn away. But the small entreating hands found their way, as if by instinct, to my great projecting palms; and trembled there, and rested there.

For a little while we lingered thus, neither wishing to move away, neither caring to look beyond the presence of the other; both alike so full of hope, and comfort, and true happiness; if only the world would let us be. And then a little sob disturbed us, and mother tried to make believe that she was only coughing. But Lorna, guessing who she was, jumped up so very rashly that she almost set her frock on fire from the great ash log; and away she ran to the old oak chair, where mother was by the clock-case pretending to be knitting, and she took the work from mother's hands, and laid them both upon her head, kneeling humbly, and looking up.

'God bless you, my fair mistress!' said mother, bending nearer, and then as Lorna's gaze prevailed, 'God bless you, my sweet child!'

And so she went to mother's heart by the very nearest road, even as she had come to mine; I mean the road of pity, smoothed by grace, and youth, and gentleness.

Chapter XLV A Change Long Needed

Jeremy Stickles was gone south, ere ever the frost set in, for the purpose of mustering forces to attack the Doone Glen. But, of course, this weather had put a stop to every kind of movement; for even if men could have borne the cold, they could scarcely be brought to face the perils of the snow-drifts. And to tell the truth I cared not how long this weather lasted, so long as we had enough to eat, and could keep ourselves from freezing. Not only that I did not want Master Stickles back again, to make more disturbances; but also that the Doones could not come prowling after Lorna while the snow lay piled between us, with the surface soft and dry. Of course they would very soon discover where their lawful queen was, although the track of sledd and snow-shoes had been quite obliterated by another shower, before the revellers could have grown half as drunk as they intended. But Marwood de Whichehalse, who had been snowed up among them (as Gwenny said), after helping to strip the beacon, that young Squire was almost certain to have recognised me, and to have told the vile Carver. And it gave me no little pleasure to think how mad that Carver must be with me, for robbing him of the lovely bride whom he was starving into matrimony. However, I was not pleased at all with the prospect of the consequences; but set all hands on to thresh the corn, ere the Doones could come and burn the ricks. For I knew that they could not come yet, inasmuch as even a forest pony could not traverse the country, much less the heavy horses needed to carry such men as they were. And hundreds of the forest ponies died in this hard weather, some being buried in the snow, and more of them starved for want of grass.

Going through this state of things, and laying down the law about it (subject to correction), I very soon persuaded Lorna that for the present she was safe, and (which made her still more happy) that she was not only welcome, but as gladdening to our eyes as the flowers of May. Of course, so far as regarded myself, this was not a hundredth part of the real truth; and even as regarded others, I might have said it ten times over. For Lorna had so won them all, by her kind and gentle ways, and her mode of hearkening to everybody's trouble, and replying without words, as well as by her beauty, and simple grace of all things, that I could almost wish sometimes the rest would leave her more to me. But mother could not do enough; and Annie almost worshipped her; and even Lizzie could not keep her bitterness towards her; especially when she found that Lorna knew as much of books as need be.

As for John Fry, and Betty, and Molly, they were a perfect plague when Lorna came into the kitchen. For betwixt their curiosity to see a live Doone in the flesh (when certain not to eat them), and their high respect for birth (with or without honesty), and their intense desire to know all about Master John's sweetheart (dropped, as they said, from the snow-clouds), and most of all their admiration of a beauty such as never even their angels could have seen—betwixt and between all this, I say, there was no getting the dinner cooked, with Lorna in the kitchen.

And the worst of it was that Lorna took the strangest of all strange fancies for this very kitchen; and it was hard to keep her out of it. Not that she had any special bent for cooking, as our Annie had; rather indeed the contrary, for she liked to have her food ready cooked; but that she loved the look of the place, and the cheerful fire burning, and the racks of bacon to be seen, and the richness, and the homeliness, and the pleasant smell of everything. And who knows but what she may have liked (as the very best of maidens do) to be admired, now and then, between the times of business?

Therefore if you wanted Lorna (as I was always sure to do, God knows how many times a day), the very surest place to find her was our own old kitchen. Not gossiping, I mean, nor loitering, neither seeking into things, but seeming to be quite at home, as if she had known it from a child, and seeming (to my eyes at least) to light it up, and make life and colour out of all the dullness; as I have seen the breaking sun do among brown shocks of wheat.

But any one who wished to learn whether girls can change or not, as the things around them change (while yet their hearts are steadfast, and for ever anchored), he should just have seen my Lorna, after a fortnight of our life, and freedom from anxiety. It is possible that my company—although I am accounted stupid by folk who do not know my way—may have had something to do with it; but upon this I will not say much, lest I lose my character. And indeed, as regards company, I had all the threshing to see to, and more than half to do myself (though any one would have thought that even John Fry must work hard this weather), else I could not hope at all to get our corn into such compass that a good gun might protect it.

But to come back to Lorna again (which I always longed to do, and must long for ever), all the change between night and day, all the shifts of cloud and sun, all the difference between black death and brightsome liveliness, scarcely may suggest or equal Lorna's transformation. Quick she had always been and 'peart' (as we say on Exmoor) and gifted with a leap of thought too swift for me to follow; and hence you may find fault with much, when I report her sayings. But through the whole had always run, as a black string goes through pearls, something dark and touched with shadow, coloured as with an early end.

But, now, behold! there was none of this! There was no getting her, for a moment, even to be serious. All her bright young wit was flashing, like a newly-awakened flame, and all her high young spirits leaped, as if dancing to its fire. And yet she never spoke a word which gave more pain than pleasure.

And even in her outward look there was much of difference. Whether it was our warmth, and freedom, and our harmless love of God, and trust in one another; or whether it were our air, and water, and the pea-fed bacon; anyhow my Lorna grew richer and more lovely, more perfect and more firm of figure, and more light and buoyant, with every passing day that laid its tribute on her cheeks and lips. I was allowed one kiss a day; only one for manners' sake, because she was our visitor; and I might have it before breakfast, or else when I came to say 'good-night!'

according as I decided. And I decided every night, not to take it in the morning, but put it off till the evening time, and have the pleasure to think about, through all the day of working. But when my darling came up to me in the early daylight, fresher than the daystar, and with no one looking; only her bright eyes smiling, and sweet lips quite ready, was it likely I could wait, and think all day about it? For she wore a frock of Annie's, nicely made to fit her, taken in at the waist and curved—I never could explain it, not being a mantua-maker; but I know how her figure looked in it, and how it came towards me.

But this is neither here nor there; and I must on with my story. Those days are very sacred to me, and if I speak lightly of them, trust me, 'tis with lip alone; while from heart reproach peeps sadly at the flippant tricks of mind.

Although it was the longest winter ever known in our parts (never having ceased to freeze for a single night, and scarcely for a single day, from the middle of December till the second week in March), to me it was the very shortest and the most delicious; and verily I do believe it was the same to Lorna. But when the Ides of March were come (of which I do remember something dim from school, and something clear from my favourite writer) lo, there were increasing signals of a change of weather.

One leading feature of that long cold, and a thing remarked by every one (however unobservant) had been the hollow moaning sound ever present in the air, morning, noon, and night-time, and especially at night, whether any wind were stirring, or whether it were a perfect calm. Our people said that it was a witch cursing all the country from the caverns by the sea, and that frost and snow would last until we could catch and drown her. But the land, being thoroughly blocked with snow, and the inshore parts of the sea with ice (floating in great fields along), Mother Melldrum (if she it were) had the caverns all to herself, for there was no getting at her. And speaking of the sea reminds me of a thing reported to us, and on good authority; though people might be found hereafter who would not believe it, unless I told them that from what I myself beheld of the channel I place perfect faith in it: and this is, that a dozen sailors at the beginning of March crossed the ice, with the aid of poles from Clevedon to Penarth, or where the Holm rocks barred the flotage.

But now, about the tenth of March, that miserable moaning noise, which had both foregone and accompanied the rigour, died away from out the air; and we, being now so used to it, thought at first that we must be deaf. And then the fog, which had hung about (even in full sunshine) vanished, and the shrouded hills shone forth with brightness manifold. And now the sky at length began to come to its true manner, which we had not seen for months, a mixture (if I so may speak) of various expressions. Whereas till now from Allhallows-tide, six weeks ere the great frost set in, the heavens had worn one heavy mask of ashen gray when clouded, or else one amethystine tinge with a hazy rim, when cloudless. So it was pleasant to behold, after that monotony, the fickle sky which suits our England, though abused by foreign folk.

And soon the dappled softening sky gave some earnest of its mood; for a brisk south wind arose, and the blessed rain came driving, cold indeed, yet most refreshing to the skin, all parched with snow, and the eyeballs so long dazzled. Neither was the heart more sluggish in its thankfulness to God. People had begun to think, and somebody had prophesied, that we should have no spring this year, no seed-time, and no harvest; for that the Lord had sent a judgment on this country of England, and the nation dwelling in it, because of the wickedness of the Court, and the encouragement shown to Papists. And this was proved, they said, by what had happened in the town of London; where, for more than a fortnight, such a chill of darkness lay that no man might behold his neighbour, even across the narrowest street; and where the ice upon the Thames was more than four feet thick, and crushing London Bridge in twain. Now to these prophets I paid no heed, believing not that Providence would freeze us for other people's sins; neither seeing how England could for many generations have enjoyed good sunshine, if Popery meant frost and fogs. Besides, why could not Providence settle the business once for all by freezing the Pope himself; even though (according to our view) he were destined to extremes of heat, together with all who followed him?

Not to meddle with that subject, being beyond my judgment, let me tell the things I saw, and then you must believe me. The wind, of course, I could not see, not having the powers of a pig; but I could see the laden branches of the great oaks moving, hoping to shake off the load packed and saddled on them. And hereby I may note a thing which some one may explain perhaps in the after ages, when people come to look at things. This is that in desperate cold all the trees were pulled awry, even though the wind had scattered the snow burden from them. Of some sorts the branches bended downwards, like an archway; of other sorts the boughs curved upwards, like a red deer's frontlet. This I know no reason* for; but am ready to swear that I saw it.

Now when the first of the rain began, and the old familiar softness spread upon the window glass, and ran a little way in channels (though from the coldness of the glass it froze before reaching the bottom), knowing at once the difference from the short sharp thud of snow, we all ran out, and filled our eyes and filled our hearts with gazing. True, the snow was piled up now all in mountains round us; true, the air was still so cold that our breath froze on the doorway, and the rain was turned to ice wherever it struck anything; nevertheless that it was rain there was no denying, as we watched it across black doorways, and could see no sign of white. Mother, who had made up her mind that the farm was not worth having

*The reason is very simple, as all nature's reasons are; though the subject has not yet been investigated thoroughly. In some trees the vascular tissue is more open on the upper side, in others on the under side, of the spreading branches; according to the form of growth, and habit of the sap. Hence in very severe cold, when the vessels (comparatively empty) are constricted, some have more power of contraction on the upper side, and some upon the under.

after all those prophesies, and that all of us must starve, and holes be scratched in the snow for us, and no use to put up a tombstone (for our church had been shut up long ago) mother fell upon my breast, and sobbed that I was the cleverest fellow ever born of woman. And this because I had condemned the prophets for a pack of fools; not seeing how business could go on, if people stopped to hearken to them.

Then Lorna came and glorified me, for I had predicted a change of weather, more to keep their spirits up, than with real hope of it; and then came Annie blushing shyly, as I looked at her, and said that Winnie would soon have four legs now. This referred to some stupid joke made by John Fry or somebody, that in this weather a man had no legs, and a horse had only two.

But as the rain came down upon us from the southwest wind, and we could not have enough of it, even putting our tongues to catch it, as little children might do, and beginning to talk of primroses; the very noblest thing of all was to hear and see the gratitude of the poor beasts yet remaining and the few surviving birds. From the cowhouse lowing came, more than of fifty milking times; moo and moo, and a turn-up noise at the end of every bellow, as if from the very heart of kine. Then the horses in the stables, packed as closely as they could stick, at the risk of kicking, to keep the warmth in one another, and their spirits up by discoursing, these began with one accord to lift up their voices, snorting, snaffling, whinnying, and neighing, and trotting to the door to know when they should have work again. To whom, as if in answer, came the feeble bleating of the sheep, what few, by dint of greatest care, had kept their fleeces on their backs, and their four legs under them.

Neither was it a trifling thing, let whoso will say the contrary, to behold the ducks and geese marching forth in handsome order from their beds of fern and straw. What a goodly noise they kept, what a flapping of their wings, and a jerking of their tails, as they stood right up and tried with a whistling in their throats to imitate a cockscrow! And then how daintily they took the wet upon their dusty plumes, and ducked their shoulders to it, and began to dress themselves, and laid their grooved bills on the snow, and dabbled for more ooziness!

Lorna had never seen, I dare say, anything like this before, and it was all that we could do to keep her from rushing forth with only little lambswool shoes on, and kissing every one of them. 'Oh, the dear things, oh, the dear things!' she kept saying continually, 'how wonderfully clever they are! Only look at that one with his foot up, giving orders to the others, John!'

'And I must give orders to you, my darling,' I answered, gazing on her face, so brilliant with excitement; 'and that is, that you come in at once, with that worrisome cough of yours; and sit by the fire, and warm yourself.'

'Oh, no, John! Not for a minute, if you please, good John. I want to see the snow go away, and the green meadows coming forth. And here comes our favourite robin, who has lived in the oven so long, and sang us a song every morning. I must see what he thinks of it!'

'You will do nothing of the sort,' I answered very shortly, being only too glad of a cause for having her in my arms again. So I caught her up, and carried her in; and she looked and smiled so sweetly at me instead of pouting (as I had feared) that I found myself unable to go very fast along the passage. And I set her there in her favourite place, by the sweet-scented wood-fire; and she paid me porterage without my even asking her; and for all the beauty of the rain, I was fain to stay with her; until our Annie came to say that my advice was wanted.

Now my advice was never much, as everybody knew quite well; but that was the way they always put it, when they wanted me to work for them. And in truth it was time for me to work; not for others, but myself, and (as I always thought) for Lorna. For the rain was now coming down in earnest; and the top of the snow being frozen at last, and glazed as hard as a china cup, by means of the sun and frost afterwards, all the rain ran right away from the steep inclines, and all the outlets being blocked with ice set up like tables, it threatened to flood everything. Already it was ponding up, like a tide advancing at the threshold of the door from which we had watched the duck-birds; both because great piles of snow trended in that direction, in spite of all our scraping, and also that the gulley hole, where the water of the shoot went out (I mean when it was water) now was choked with lumps of ice, as big as a man's body. For the 'shoot,' as we called our little runnel of everlasting water, never known to freeze before, and always ready for any man either to wash his hands, or drink, where it spouted from a trough of bark, set among white flint-stones; this at last had given in, and its music ceased to lull us, as we lay in bed.

It was not long before I managed to drain off this threatening flood, by opening the old sluice-hole; but I had much harder work to keep the stables, and the cow-house, and the other sheds, from flooding. For we have a sapient practice (and I never saw the contrary round about our parts, I mean), of keeping all rooms underground, so that you step down to them. We say that thus we keep them warmer, both for cattle and for men, in the time of winter, and cooler in the summer-time. This I will not contradict, though having my own opinion; but it seems to me to be a relic of the time when people in the western countries lived in caves beneath the ground, and blocked the mouths with neat-skins.

Let that question still abide, for men who study ancient times to inform me, if they will; all I know is, that now we had no blessings for the system. If after all their cold and starving, our weak cattle now should have to stand up to their knees in water, it would be certain death to them; and we had lost enough already to make us poor for a long time; not to speak of our kind love for them. And I do assure you, I loved some horses, and even some cows for that matter, as if they had been my blood-relations; knowing as I did their virtues. And some of these were lost to us; and I could not bear to think of them. Therefore I worked hard all night to try and save the rest of them.

Chapter XLVI Squire Faggus Makes Some Lucky Hits

Through that season of bitter frost the red deer of the forest, having nothing to feed upon, and no shelter to rest in, had grown accustomed to our ricks of corn, and hay, and clover. There we might see a hundred of them almost any morning, come for warmth, and food, and comfort, and scarce willing to move away. And many of them were so tame, that they quietly presented themselves at our back door, and stood there with their coats quite stiff, and their flanks drawn in and panting, and icicles sometimes on their chins, and their great eyes fastened wistfully upon any merciful person; craving for a bit of food, and a drink of water; I suppose that they had not sense enough to chew the snow and melt it; at any rate, all the springs being frozen, and rivers hidden out of sight, these poor things suffered even more from thirst than they did from hunger.

But now there was no fear of thirst, and more chance indeed of drowning; for a heavy gale of wind arose, with violent rain from the south-west, which lasted almost without a pause for three nights and two days. At first the rain made no impression on the bulk of snow, but ran from every sloping surface and froze on every flat one, through the coldness of the earth; and so it became impossible for any man to keep his legs without the help of a shodden staff. After a good while, however, the air growing very much warmer, this state of things began to change, and a worse one to succeed it; for now the snow came thundering down from roof, and rock, and ivied tree, and floods began to roar and foam in every trough and gulley. The drifts that had been so white and fair, looked yellow, and smirched, and muddy, and lost their graceful curves, and moulded lines, and airiness. But the strangest sight of all to me was in the bed of streams, and brooks, and especially of the Lynn river. It was worth going miles to behold such a thing, for a man might never have the chance again.

Vast drifts of snow had filled the valley, and piled above the river-course, fifty feet high in many places, and in some as much as a hundred. These had frozen over the top, and glanced the rain away from them, and being sustained by rock and tree, spanned the water mightily. But meanwhile the waxing flood, swollen from every moorland hollow and from every spouting crag, had dashed away all icy fetters, and was rolling gloriously. Under white fantastic arches, and long tunnels freaked and fretted, and between pellucid pillars jagged with nodding architraves, the red impetuous torrent rushed, and the brown foam whirled and flashed. I was half inclined to jump in and swim through such glorious scenery; for nothing used to please me more than swimming in a flooded river. But I thought of the rocks, and I thought of the cramp, and more than all, of Lorna; and so, between one thing and another, I let it roll on without me.

It was now high time to work very hard; both to make up for the farm-work lost during the months of frost and snow, and also to be ready for a great and vicious attack from the Doones, who would burn us in our beds at the earliest opportunity. Of farm-work there was little yet for even the most zealous man to begin to lay his hand to; because when the ground appeared through the crust of bubbled snow (as at last it did, though not as my Lorna had expected, at the first few drops of rain) it was all so soaked and sodden, and as we call it, 'mucksy,' that to meddle with it in any way was to do more harm than good. Nevertheless, there was yard work, and house work, and tendence of stock, enough to save any man from idleness.

As for Lorna, she would come out. There was no keeping her in the house. She had taken up some peculiar notion that we were doing more for her than she had any right to, and that she must earn her living by the hard work of her hands. It was quite in vain to tell her that she was expected to do nothing, and far worse than vain (for it made her cry sadly) if any one assured her that she could do no good at all. She even began upon mother's garden before the snow was clean gone from it, and sowed a beautiful row of peas, every one of which the mice ate.

But though it was very pretty to watch her working for her very life, as if the maintenance of the household hung upon her labours, yet I was grieved for many reasons, and so was mother also. In the first place, she was too fair and dainty for this rough, rude work; and though it made her cheeks so bright, it surely must be bad for her to get her little feet so wet. Moreover, we could not bear the idea that she should labour for her keep; and again (which was the worst of all things) mother's garden lay exposed to a dark deceitful coppice, where a man might lurk and watch all the fair gardener's doings. It was true that none could get at her thence, while the brook which ran between poured so great a torrent. Still the distance was but little for a gun to carry, if any one could be brutal enough to point a gun at Lorna. I thought that none could be found to do it; but mother, having more experience, was not so certain of mankind.

Now in spite of the floods, and the sloughs being out, and the state of the roads most perilous, Squire Faggus came at last, riding his famous strawberry mare. There was a great ado between him and Annie, as you may well suppose, after some four months of parting. And so we left them alone awhile, to coddle over their raptures. But when they were tired of that, or at least had time enough to do so, mother and I went in to know what news Tom had brought with him. Though he did not seem to want us yet, he made himself agreeable; and so we sent Annie to cook the dinner while her sweetheart should tell us everything.

Tom Faggus had very good news to tell, and he told it with such force of expression as made us laugh very heartily. He had taken up his purchase from old Sir Roger Bassett of a nice bit of land, to the south of the moors, and in the parish of Molland. When the lawyers knew thoroughly who he was, and how he had made his money, they behaved uncommonly well to him, and showed great sympathy with his pursuits. He put them up to a thing or two; and they poked him in the ribs, and laughed, and said that he was quite a boy; but of the right sort, none the less. And so they made old Squire Bassett pay the bill for both sides; and all he got for three hundred acres was a hundred and twenty pounds; though Tom had paid five hundred. But lawyers know that this must be so, in spite of all their endeavours; and the old gentleman, who now expected to find a bill for him to pay, almost thought himself a rogue, for getting anything out of them.

It is true that the land was poor and wild, and the soil exceeding shallow; lying on the slope of rock, and burned up in hot summers. But with us, hot summers are things known by tradition only (as this great winter may be); we generally have more moisture, especially in July, than we well know what to do with. I have known a fog for a fortnight at the summer solstice, and farmers talking in church about it when they ought to be praying. But it always contrives to come right in the end, as other visitations do, if we take them as true visits, and receive them kindly.

Now this farm of Squire Faggus (as he truly now had a right to be called) was of the very finest pasture, when it got good store of rain. And Tom, who had ridden the Devonshire roads with many a reeking jacket, knew right well that he might trust the climate for that matter. The herbage was of the very sweetest, and the shortest, and the closest, having perhaps from ten to eighteen inches of wholesome soil between it and the solid rock. Tom saw at once what it was fit for—the breeding of fine cattle.

Being such a hand as he was at making the most of everything, both his own and other people's (although so free in scattering, when the humour lay upon him) he had actually turned to his own advantage that extraordinary weather which had so impoverished every one around him. For he taught his Winnie (who knew his meaning as well as any child could, and obeyed not only his word of mouth, but every glance be gave her) to go forth in the snowy evenings when horses are seeking everywhere (be they wild or tame) for fodder and for shelter; and to whinny to the forest ponies, miles away from home perhaps, and lead them all with rare appetites and promise of abundance, to her master's homestead. He shod good Winnie in such a manner that she could not sink in the snow; and he clad her over the loins with a sheep-skin dyed to her own colour, which the wild horses were never tired of coming up and sniffing at; taking it for an especial gift, and proof of inspiration. And Winnie never came home at night without at least a score of ponies trotting shyly after her, tossing their heads and their tails in turn, and making believe to be very wild, although hard pinched by famine. Of course Tom would get them all into his pound in about five minutes, for he himself could neigh in a manner which went to the heart of the wildest horse. And then he fed them well, and turned them into his great cattle pen, to abide their time for breaking, when the snow and frost should be over.

He had gotten more than three hundred now, in this sagacious manner; and he said it was the finest sight to see their mode of carrying on, how they would snort, and stamp, and fume, and prick their ears, and rush backwards, and lash themselves with their long rough tails, and shake their jagged manes, and scream, and fall upon one another, if a strange man came anigh them. But as for feeding time, Tom said it was better than fifty plays to watch them, and the tricks they were up to, to cheat their feeders, and one another. I asked him how on earth he had managed to get fodder, in such impassable weather, for such a herd of horses; but he said that they lived upon straw and sawdust; and he knew that I did not believe him, any more than about his star-shavings. And this was just the thing he loved—to mystify honest people, and be a great deal too knowing. However, I may judge him harshly, because I myself tell everything.

I asked him what he meant to do with all that enormous lot of horses, and why he had not exerted his wits to catch the red deer as well. He said that the latter would have been against the laws of venery, and might have brought him into trouble, but as for disposing of his stud, it would give him little difficulty. He would break them, when the spring weather came on, and deal with them as they required, and keep the handsomest for breeding. The rest he would despatch to London, where he knew plenty of horse-dealers; and he doubted not that they would fetch him as much as ten pounds apiece all round, being now in great demand. I told him I wished that he might get it; but as it proved afterwards, he did.

Then he pressed us both on another point, the time for his marriage to Annie; and mother looked at me to say when, and I looked back at mother. However, knowing something of the world, and unable to make any further objection, by reason of his prosperity, I said that we must even do as the fashionable people did, and allow the maid herself to settle, when she would leave home and all. And this I spoke with a very bad grace, being perhaps of an ancient cast, and over fond of honesty—I mean, of course, among lower people.

But Tom paid little heed to this, knowing the world a great deal better than ever I could pretend to do; and being ready to take a thing, upon which he had set his mind, whether it came with a good grace, or whether it came with a bad one. And seeing that it would be awkward to provoke my anger, he left the room, before more words, to submit himself to Annie.

Upon this I went in search of Lorna, to tell her of our cousin's arrival, and to ask whether she would think fit to see him, or to dine by herself that day; for she should do exactly as it pleased her in everything, while remaining still our guest. But I rather wished that she might choose not to sit in Tom's company, though she might be introduced to him. Not but what he could behave quite as well as could, and much better, as regarded elegance and assurance, only that his honesty had not been as one might desire. But Lorna had some curiosity to know what this famous man was like, and declared that she would by all means have the pleasure of dining with him, if he did not object to her company on the ground of the Doones' dishonesty; moreover, she said that it would seem a most foolish air on her part, and one which would cause the greatest pain to Annie, who had been so good to her, if she should refuse to sit at table with a man who held the King's pardon, and was now a pattern of honesty.

Against this I had not a word to say; and could not help acknowledging in my heart that she was right, as well as wise, in her decision. And afterwards I discovered that mother would have been much displeased, if she had decided otherwise.

Accordingly she turned away, with one of her very sweetest smiles (whose beauty none can describe) saying that she must not meet a man of such fashion and renown, in her common gardening frock; but must try to look as nice as she could, if only in honour of dear Annie. And truth to tell, when she came to dinner, everything about her was the neatest and prettiest that can possibly be imagined. She contrived to match the colours so, to suit one another and her own, and yet with a certain delicate harmony of contrast, and the shape of everything was so nice, so that when she came into the room, with a crown of winning modesty upon the consciousness of beauty, I was quite as proud as if the Queen of England entered.

My mother could not help remarking, though she knew that it was not mannerly, how like a princess Lorna looked, now she had her best things on; but two things caught Squire Faggus's eyes, after he had made a most gallant bow, and received a most graceful courtesy; and he kept his bright bold gaze upon them, first on one, and then on the other, until my darling was hot with blushes, and I was ready to knock him down if he had not been our visitor. But here again I should have been wrong, as I was apt to be in those days, for Tom intended no harm whatever, and his gaze was of pure curiosity; though Annie herself was vexed with it. The two objects of his close regard, were first, and most worthily, Lorna's face, and secondly, the ancient necklace restored to her by Sir Ensor Doone.

Now wishing to save my darling's comfort, and to keep things quiet, I shouted out that dinner was ready, so that half the parish could hear me; upon which my mother laughed, and chid me, and despatched her guests before her. And a very good dinner we made, I remember, and a very happy one; attending to the women first, as now is the manner of eating; except among the workmen. With them, of course, it is needful that the man (who has his hours fixed) should be served first, and make the utmost of his time for feeding, while the women may go on, as much as ever they please, afterwards. But with us, who are not bound to time, there is no such reason to be quoted; and the women being the weaker vessels, should be the first to begin to fill. And so we always arranged it.

Now, though our Annie was a graceful maid, and Lizzie a very learned one, you should have seen how differently Lorna managed her dining; she never took more than about a quarter of a mouthful at a time, and she never appeared to be chewing that, although she must have done so. Indeed, she appeared to dine as if it were a matter of no consequence, and as if she could think of other things more than of her business. All this, and her own manner of eating, I described to Eliza once, when I wanted to vex her for something very spiteful that she had said; and I never succeeded so well before, for the girl was quite outrageous, having her own perception of it, which made my observation ten times as bitter to her. And I am not sure but what she ceased to like poor Lorna from that day; and if so, I was quite paid out, as I well deserved, for my bit of satire.

For it strikes me that of all human dealings, satire is the very lowest, and most mean and common. It is the equivalent in words of what bullying is in deeds; and no more bespeaks a clever man, than the other does a brave one. These two wretched tricks exalt a fool in his own low esteem, but never in his neighbour's; for the deep common sense of our nature tells that no man of a genial heart, or of any spread of mind, can take pride in either. And though a good man may commit the one fault or the other, now and then, by way of outlet, he is sure to have compunctions soon, and to scorn himself more than the sufferer.

Now when the young maidens were gone—for we had quite a high dinner of fashion that day, with Betty Muxworthy waiting, and Gwenny Carfax at the gravy—and only mother, and Tom, and I remained at the white deal table, with brandy, and schnapps, and hot water jugs; Squire Faggus said quite suddenly, and perhaps on purpose to take us aback, in case of our hiding anything,—'What do you know of the history of that beautiful maiden, good mother?'

'Not half so much as my son does,' mother answered, with a soft smile at me; 'and when John does not choose to tell a thing, wild horses will not pull it out of him.'

'That is not at all like me, mother,' I replied rather sadly; 'you know almost every word about Lorna, quite as well as I do.'

'Almost every word, I believe, John; for you never tell a falsehood. But the few unknown may be of all the most important to me.'

To this I made no answer, for fear of going beyond the truth, or else of making mischief. Not that I had, or wished to have, any mystery with mother; neither was there in purest truth, any mystery in the matter; to the utmost of my knowledge. And the only things that I had kept back, solely for mother's comfort, were the death of poor Lord Alan Brandir (if indeed he were dead) and the connection of Marwood de Whichehalse with the dealings of the Doones, and the threats of Carver Doone against my own prosperity; and, may be, one or two little things harrowing more than edifying.

'Come, come,' said Master Faggus, smiling very pleasantly, 'you two understand each other, if any two on earth do. Ah, if I had only had a mother, how different I might have been!' And with that he sighed, in the tone which always overcame mother upon that subject, and had something to do with his getting Annie; and then he produced his pretty box, full of rolled tobacco, and offered me one, as I now had joined the goodly company of smokers. So I took it, and watched what he did with his own, lest I might go wrong about mine.

But when our cylinders were both lighted, and I enjoying mine wonderfully, and astonishing mother by my skill, Tom Faggus told us that he was sure he had seen my Lorna's face before, many and many years ago, when she was quite a little child, but he could not remember where it was, or anything more about it at present; though he would try to do so afterwards. He could not be mistaken, he said, for he had noticed her eyes especially; and had never seen such eyes before, neither again, until this day. I asked him if he had ever ventured into the Doone-valley; but he shook his head, and replied that he valued his life a deal too much for that. Then we put it to him, whether anything might assist his memory; but he said that he knew not of aught to do so, unless it were another glass of schnapps.

This being provided, he grew very wise, and told us clearly and candidly that we were both very foolish. For he said that we were keeping Lorna, at the risk not only of our stock, and the house above our heads, but also of our precious lives; and after all was she worth it, although so very beautiful? Upon which I told him, with indignation, that her beauty was the least part of her goodness, and that I would thank him for his opinion when I had requested it.

'Bravo, our John Ridd!' he answered; 'fools will be fools till the end of the chapter; and I might be as big a one, if I were in thy shoes, John. Nevertheless, in the name of God, don't let that helpless child go about with a thing worth half the county on her.'

'She is worth all the county herself,' said I, 'and all England put together; but she has nothing worth half a rick of hay upon her; for the ring I gave her cost only,'—and here I stopped, for mother was looking, and I never would tell her how much it had cost me; though she had tried fifty times to find out.

'Tush, the ring!' Tom Faggus cried, with a contempt that moved me: 'I would never have stopped a man for that. But the necklace, you great oaf, the necklace is worth all your farm put together, and your Uncle Ben's fortune to the back of it; ay, and all the town of Dulverton.'

'What,' said I, 'that common glass thing, which she has had from her childhood!'

'Glass indeed! They are the finest brilliants ever I set eyes on; and I have handled a good many.'

'Surely,' cried mother, now flushing as red as Tom's own cheeks with excitement, 'you must be wrong, or the young mistress would herself have known it.'

I was greatly pleased with my mother, for calling Lorna 'the young mistress'; it was not done for the sake of her diamonds, whether they were glass or not; but because she felt as I had done, that Tom Faggus, a man of no birth whatever, was speaking beyond his mark, in calling a lady like Lorna a helpless child; as well as in his general tone, which displayed no deference. He might have been used to the quality, in the way of stopping their coaches, or roystering at hotels with them; but he never had met a high lady before, in equality, and upon virtue; and we both felt that he ought to have known it, and to have thanked us for the opportunity, in a word, to have behaved a great deal more humbly than he had even tried to do.

'Trust me,' answered Tom, in his loftiest manner, which Annie said was 'so noble,' but which seemed to me rather flashy, 'trust me, good mother, and simple John, for knowing brilliants, when I see them. I would have stopped an eight-horse coach, with four carabined out-riders, for such a booty as that. But alas, those days are over; those were days worth living in. Ah, I never shall know the like again. How fine it was by moonlight!'

'Master Faggus,' began my mother, with a manner of some dignity, such as she could sometimes use, by right of her integrity, and thorough kindness to every one, 'this is not the tone in which you have hitherto spoken to me about your former pursuits and life, I fear that the spirits'—but here she stopped, because the spirits were her own, and Tom was our visitor,—'what I mean, Master Faggus, is this: you have won my daughter's heart somehow; and you won my consent to the matter through your honest sorrow, and manly undertaking to lead a different life, and touch no property but your own. Annie is my eldest daughter, and the child of a most upright man. I love her best of all on earth, next to my boy John here'—here mother gave me a mighty squeeze, to be sure that she would have me at least—'and I will not risk my Annie's life with a man who yearns for the highway.'

Having made this very long speech (for her), mother came home upon my shoulder, and wept so that (but for heeding her) I would have taken Tom by the nose, and thrown him, and Winnie after him, over our farm-yard gate. For I am violent when roused; and freely hereby acknowledge it; though even my enemies will own that it takes a great deal to rouse me. But I do consider the grief and tears (when justly caused) of my dearest friends, to be a great deal to rouse me.

Chapter XLVII Jeremy in Danger

Nothing very long abides, as the greatest of all writers (in whose extent I am for ever lost in raptured wonder, and yet for ever quite at home, as if his heart were mine, although his brains so different), in a word as Mr. William Shakespeare, in every one of his works insists, with a humoured melancholy. And if my journey to London led to nothing else of advancement, it took me a hundred years in front of what I might else have been, by the most simple accident.

Two women were scolding one another across the road, very violently, both from upstair windows; and I in my hurry for quiet life, and not knowing what might come down upon me, quickened my step for the nearest corner. But suddenly something fell on my head; and at first I was afraid to look, especially as it weighed heavily. But hearing no breakage of ware, and only the other scold laughing heartily, I turned me about and espied a book, which one had cast at the other, hoping to break her window. So I took the book, and tendered it at the door of the house from which it had fallen; but the watchman came along just then, and the man at the door declared that it never came from their house, and begged me to say no more. This I promised readily, never wishing to make mischief; and I said, 'Good sir, now take the book; I will go on to my business.' But he answered that he would do no such thing; for the book alone, being hurled so hard, would convict his people of a lewd assault; and he begged me, if I would do a good turn, to put the book under my coat and go. And so I did: in part at least. For I did not put the book under my coat, but went along with it openly, looking for any to challenge it. Now this book, so acquired, has been not only the joy of my younger days, and main delight of my manhood, but also the comfort, and even the hope, of my now declining years. In a word, it is next to my Bible to me, and written in equal English; and if you espy any goodness whatever in my own loose style of writing, you must not thank me, John Ridd, for it, but the writer who holds the champion's belt in wit, as I once did in wrestling.

Now, as nothing very long abides, it cannot be expected that a woman's anger should last very long, if she be at all of the proper sort. And my mother, being one of the very best, could not long retain her wrath against the Squire Faggus especially when she came to reflect, upon Annie's suggestion, how natural, and one might say, how inevitable it was that a young man fond of adventure and change and winning good profits by jeopardy, should not settle down without some regrets to a fixed abode and a life of sameness, however safe and respectable. And even as Annie put the case, Tom deserved the greater credit for vanquishing so nobly these yearnings of his nature; and it seemed very hard to upbraid him, considering how good his motives were; neither could Annie understand how mother could reconcile it with her knowledge of the Bible, and the one sheep that was lost, and the hundredth piece of silver, and the man that went down to Jericho.

Whether Annie's logic was good and sound, I am sure I cannot tell; but it seemed to me that she ought to have let the Jericho traveller alone, inasmuch as he rather fell among Tom Fagusses, than resembled them. However, her reasoning was too much for mother to hold out against; and Tom was replaced, and more than that, being regarded now as an injured man. But how my mother contrived to know, that because she had been too hard upon Tom, he must be right about the necklace, is a point which I never could clearly perceive, though no doubt she could explain it.

To prove herself right in the conclusion, she went herself to fetch Lorna, that the trinket might be examined, before the day grew dark. My darling came in, with a very quick glance and smile at my cigarro (for I was having the third by this time, to keep things in amity); and I waved it towards her, as much as to say, 'you see that I can do it.' And then mother led her up to the light, for Tom to examine her necklace.

On the shapely curve of her neck it hung, like dewdrops upon a white hyacinth; and I was vexed that Tom should have the chance to see it there. But even if she had read my thoughts, or outrun them with her own, Lorna turned away, and softly took the jewels from the place which so much adorned them. And as she turned away, they sparkled through the rich dark waves of hair. Then she laid the glittering circlet in my mother's hands; and Tom Faggus took it eagerly, and bore it to the window.

'Don't you go out of sight,' I said; 'you cannot resist such things as those, if they be what you think them.'

'Jack, I shall have to trounce thee yet. I am now a man of honour, and entitled to the duello. What will you take for it, Mistress Lorna? At a hazard, say now.'

'I am not accustomed to sell things, sir,' replied Lorna, who did not like him much, else she would have answered sportively, 'What is it worth, in your opinion?'

'Do you think it is worth five pounds, now?'

'Oh, no! I never had so much money as that in all my life. It is very bright, and very pretty; but it cannot be worth five pounds, I am sure.'

'What a chance for a bargain! Oh, if it were not for Annie, I could make my fortune.'

'But, sir, I would not sell it to you, not for twenty times five pounds. My grandfather was so kind about it; and I think it belonged to my mother.'

'There are twenty-five rose diamonds in it, and twenty-five large brilliants that cannot be matched in London. How say you, Mistress Lorna, to a hundred thousand pounds?'

My darling's eyes so flashed at this, brighter than any diamonds, that I said to myself, 'Well, all have faults; and now I have found out Lorna's—she is fond of money!' And then I sighed rather heavily; for of all faults this seems to me one of the worst in a woman. But even before my sigh was finished, I had cause to condemn myself. For Lorna took the necklace very quietly from the hands of Squire Faggus, who had not half done with admiring it, and she went up to my mother with the sweetest smile I ever saw.

'Dear kind mother, I am so glad,' she said in a whisper, coaxing mother out of sight of all but me; 'now you will have it, won't you, dear? And I shall be so happy; for a thousandth part of your kindness to me no jewels in the world can match.'

I cannot lay before you the grace with which she did it, all the air of seeking favour, rather than conferring it, and the high-bred fear of giving offence, which is of all fears the noblest. Mother knew not what to say. Of course she would never dream of taking such a gift as that; and yet she saw how sadly Lorna would be disappointed. Therefore, mother did, from habit, what she almost always did, she called me to help her. But knowing that my eyes were full—for anything noble moves me so, quite as rashly as things pitiful—I pretended not to hear my mother, but to see a wild cat in the dairy.

Therefore I cannot tell what mother said in reply to Lorna; for when I came back, quite eager to let my love know how I worshipped her, and how deeply I was ashamed of myself, for meanly wronging her in my heart, behold Tom Faggus had gotten again the necklace which had such charms for him, and was delivering all around (but especially to Annie, who was wondering at his learning) a dissertation on precious stones, and his sentiments about those in his hand. He said that the work was very ancient, but undoubtedly very good; the cutting of every line was true, and every angle was in its place. And this he said, made all the difference in the lustre of the stone, and therefore in its value. For if the facets were ill-matched, and the points of light so ever little out of perfect harmony, all the lustre of the jewel would be loose and wavering, and the central fire dulled; instead of answering, as it should, to all possibilities of gaze, and overpowering any eye intent on its deeper mysteries. We laughed at the Squire's dissertation; for how should he know all these things, being nothing better, and indeed much worse than a mere Northmolton blacksmith? He took our laughter with much good nature; having Annie to squeeze his hand and convey her grief at our ignorance: but he said that of one thing he was quite certain, and therein I believed him. To wit, that a trinket of this kind never could have belonged to any ignoble family, but to one of the very highest and most wealthy in England. And looking at Lorna, I felt that she must have come from a higher source than the very best of diamonds.

Tom Faggus said that the necklace was made, he would answer for it, in Amsterdam, two or three hundred years ago, long before London jewellers had begun to meddle with diamonds; and on the gold clasp he found some letters, done in some inverted way, the meaning of which was beyond him; also a bearing of some kind, which he believed was a mountain-cat. And thereupon he declared that now he had earned another glass of schnapps, and would Mistress Lorna mix it for him?

I was amazed at his impudence; and Annie, who thought this her business, did not look best pleased; and I hoped that Lorna would tell him at once to go and do it for himself. But instead of that she rose to do it with a soft humility, which went direct to the heart of Tom; and he leaped up with a curse at himself, and took the hot water from her, and would not allow her to do anything except to put the sugar in; and then he bowed to her grandly. I knew what Lorna was thinking of; she was thinking all the time that her necklace had been taken by the Doones with violence upon some great robbery; and that Squire Faggus knew it, though he would not show his knowledge; and that this was perhaps the reason why mother had refused it so.

We said no more about the necklace for a long time afterwards; neither did my darling wear it, now that she knew its value, but did not know its history. She came to me the very next day, trying to look cheerful, and begged me if I loved her (never mind how little) to take charge of it again, as I once had done before, and not even to let her know in what place I stored it. I told her that this last request I could not comply with; for having been round her neck so often, it was now a sacred thing, more than a million pounds could be. Therefore it should dwell for the present in the neighbourhood of my heart; and so could not be far from her. At this she smiled her own sweet smile, and touched my forehead with her lips. and wished that she could only learn how to deserve such love as mine.

Tom Faggus took his good departure, which was a kind farewell to me, on the very day I am speaking of, the day after his arrival. Tom was a thoroughly upright man, according to his own standard; and you might rely upon him always, up to a certain point I mean, to be there or thereabouts. But sometimes things were too many for Tom, especially with ardent spirits, and then he judged, perhaps too much, with only himself for the jury. At any rate, I would trust him fully, for candour and for honesty, in almost every case in which he himself could have no interest. And so we got on very well together; and he thought me a fool; and I tried my best not to think anything worse of him.

Scarcely was Tom clean out of sight, and Annie's tears not dry yet (for she always made a point of crying upon his departure), when in came Master Jeremy Stickles, splashed with mud from head to foot, and not in the very best of humours, though happy to get back again.

'Curse those fellows!' he cried, with a stamp which sent the water hissing from his boot upon the embers; 'a pretty plight you may call this, for His Majesty's Commissioner to return to his headquarters in! Annie, my dear,' for he was always very affable with Annie, 'will you help me off with my overalls, and then turn your pretty hand to the gridiron? Not a blessed morsel have I touched for more than twenty-four hours.'

'Surely then you must be quite starving, sir,' my sister replied with the greatest zeal; for she did love a man with an appetite; 'how glad I am that the fire is clear!' But Lizzie, who happened to be there, said with her peculiar smile,—

'Master Stickles must be used to it; for he never comes back without telling us that.'

'Hush!' cried Annie, quite shocked with her; 'how would you like to be used to it? Now, Betty, be quick with the things for me. Pork, or mutton, or deer's meat, sir? We have some cured since the autumn.'

'Oh, deer's meat, by all means,' Jeremy Stickles answered; 'I have tasted none since I left you, though dreaming of it often. Well, this is better than being chased over the moors for one's life, John. All the way from Landacre Bridge, I have ridden a race for my precious life, at the peril of my limbs and neck. Three great Doones galloping after me, and a good job for me that they were so big, or they must have overtaken me. Just go and see to my horse, John, that's an excellent lad. He deserves a good turn this day, from me; and I will render it to him.'

However he left me to do it, while he made himself comfortable: and in truth the horse required care; he was blown so that he could hardly stand, and plastered with mud, and steaming so that the stable was quite full with it. By the time I had put the poor fellow to rights, his master had finished dinner, and was in a more pleasant humour, having even offered to kiss Annie, out of pure gratitude, as he said; but Annie answered with spirit that gratitude must not be shown by increasing the obligation. Jeremy made reply to this that his only way to be grateful then was to tell us his story: and so he did, at greater length than I can here repeat it; for it does not bear particularly upon Lorna's fortunes.

It appears that as he was riding towards us from the town of Southmolton in Devonshire, he found the roads very soft and heavy, and the floods out in all directions; but met with no other difficulty until he came to Landacre Bridge. He had only a single trooper with him, a man not of the militia but of the King's army, whom Jeremy had brought from Exeter. As these two descended towards the bridge they observed that both the

Kensford water and the River Barle were pouring down in mighty floods from the melting of the snow. So great indeed was the torrent, after they united, that only the parapets of the bridge could be seen above the water, the road across either bank being covered and very deep on the hither side. The trooper did not like the look of it, and proposed to ride back again, and round by way of Simonsbath, where the stream is smaller. But Stickles would not have it so, and dashing into the river, swam his horse for the bridge, and gained it with some little trouble; and there he found the water not more than up to his horse's knees perhaps. On the crown of the bridge he turned his horse to watch the trooper's passage, and to help him with directions; when suddenly he saw him fall headlong into the torrent, and heard the report of a gun from behind, and felt a shock to his own body, such as lifted him out of the saddle. Turning round he beheld three men, risen up from behind the hedge on one side of his onward road, two of them ready to load again, and one with his gun unfired, waiting to get good aim at him. Then Jeremy did a gallant thing, for which I doubt whether I should have had the presence of mind in danger. He saw that to swim his horse back again would be almost certain death; as affording such a target, where even a wound must be fatal. Therefore he struck the spurs into the nag, and rode through the water straight at the man who was pointing the long gun at him. If the horse had been carried off his legs, there must have been an end of Jeremy; for the other men were getting ready to have another shot at him. But luckily the horse galloped right on without any need for swimming, being himself excited, no doubt, by all he had seen and heard of it. And Jeremy lay almost flat on his neck, so as to give little space for good aim, with the mane tossing wildly in front of him. Now if that young fellow with the gun had his brains as ready as his flint was, he would have shot the horse at once, and then had Stickles at his mercy; but instead of that he let fly at the man, and missed him altogether, being scared perhaps by the pistol which Jeremy showed him the mouth of. And galloping by at full speed, Master Stickles tried to leave his mark behind him, for he changed the aim of his pistol to the biggest man, who was loading his gun and cursing like ten cannons. But the pistol missed fire, no doubt from the flood which had gurgled in over the holsters; and Jeremy seeing three horses tethered at a gate just up the hill, knew that he had not yet escaped, but had more of danger behind him. He tried his other great pistol at one of the horses tethered there, so as to lessen (if possible) the number of his pursuers. But the powder again failed him; and he durst not stop to cut the bridles, bearing the men coming up the hill. So he even made the most of his start, thanking God that his weight was light, compared at least to what theirs was.

And another thing he had noticed which gave him some hope of escaping, to wit that the horses of the Doones, although very handsome animals, were suffering still from the bitter effects of the late long frost, and the scarcity of fodder. 'If they do not catch me up, or shoot me, in the course of the first two miles, I may see my home again'; this was what he said to himself as he turned to mark what they were about, from the brow of the steep hill. He saw the flooded valley shining with the breadth of water, and the trooper's horse on the other side, shaking his drenched flanks and neighing; and half-way down the hill he saw the three Doones mounting hastily. And then he knew that his only chance lay in the stoutness of his steed.

The horse was in pretty good condition; and the rider knew him thoroughly, and how to make the most of him; and though they had travelled some miles that day through very heavy ground, the bath in the river had washed the mud off, and been some refreshment. Therefore Stickles encouraged his nag, and put him into a good hard gallop, heading away towards Withycombe. At first he had thought of turning to the right, and making off for Withypool, a mile or so down the valley; but his good sense told him that no one there would dare to protect him against the Doones, so he resolved to go on his way; yet faster than he had intended.

The three villains came after him, with all the speed they could muster, making sure from the badness of the road that he must stick fast ere long, and so be at their mercy. And this was Jeremy's chiefest fear, for the ground being soft and thoroughly rotten, after so much frost and snow, the poor horse had terrible work of it, with no time to pick the way; and even more good luck than skill was needed to keep him from foundering. How Jeremy prayed for an Exmoor fog (such as he had often sworn at), that he might turn aside and lurk, while his pursuers went past him! But no fog came, nor even a storm to damp the priming of their guns; neither was wood or coppice nigh, nor any place to hide in; only hills, and moor, and valleys; with flying shadows over them, and great banks of snow in the corners. At one time poor Stickles was quite in despair; for after leaping a little brook which crosses the track at Newland, be stuck fast in a 'dancing bog,' as we call them upon Exmoor. The horse had broken through the crust of moss and sedge and marishweed, and could do nothing but wallow and sink, with the black water spirting over him. And Jeremy, struggling with all his might, saw the three villains now topping the crest, less than a furlong behind him; and heard them shout in their savage delight. With the calmness of despair, he yet resolved to have one more try for it; and scrambling over the horse's head, gained firm land, and tugged at the bridle. The poor nag replied with all his power to the call upon his courage, and reared his forefeet out of the slough, and with straining eyeballs gazed at him. 'Now,' said Jeremy, 'now, my fine fellow!' lifting him with the bridle, and the brave beast gathered the roll of his loins, and sprang from his quagmired haunches. One more spring, and he was on earth again, instead of being under it; and Jeremy leaped on his back, and stooped, for he knew that they would fire. Two bullets whistled over him, as the horse, mad with fright, dashed forward; and in five minutes more he had come to the Exe, and the pursuers had fallen behind him. The Exe, though a much smaller stream than the Barle, now ran in a foaming torrent, unbridged, and too wide for leaping. But Jeremy's horse took the water well; and both he and his rider were lightened, as well as comforted by it. And as they passed towards Lucott hill, and struck upon the founts of Lynn, the horses of the three pursuers began to tire under them. Then Jeremy Stickles knew that if he could only escape the sloughs, he was safe for the present; and so he stood up in his stirrups, and gave them a loud halloo, as if they had been so many foxes.

Their only answer was to fire the remaining charge at him; but the distance was too great for any aim from horseback; and the dropping bullet idly ploughed the sod upon one side of him. He acknowledged it with a wave of his hat, and laid one thumb to his nose, in the manner fashionable in London for expression of contempt. However, they followed him yet farther; hoping to make him pay out dearly, if he should only miss the track, or fall upon morasses. But the neighbourhood of our Lynn stream is not so very boggy; and the King's messenger now knew his way as well as any of his pursuers did; and so he arrived at Plover's Barrows, thankful, and in rare appetite.

'But was the poor soldier drowned?' asked Annie; 'and you never went to look for him! Oh, how very dreadful!'

'Shot, or drowned; I know not which. Thank God it was only a trooper. But they shall pay for it, as dearly as if it had been a captain.'

'And how was it you were struck by a bullet, and only shaken in your saddle? Had you a coat of mail on, or of Milanese chain-armour? Now, Master Stickles, had you?'

'No, Mistress Lizzie; we do not wear things of that kind nowadays. You are apt, I perceive, at romances. But I happened to have a little flat bottle of the best stoneware slung beneath my saddle-cloak, and filled with the very best eau de vie, from the George Hotel, at Southmolton. The brand of it now is upon my back. Oh, the murderous scoundrels, what a brave spirit they have spilled!'

'You had better set to and thank God,' said I, 'that they have not spilled a braver one.'

Chapter XLVIII Every Man Must Defend Himself

It was only right in Jeremy Stickles, and of the simplest common sense, that he would not tell, before our girls, what the result of his journey was. But he led me aside in the course of the evening, and told me all about it; saying that I knew, as well as he did, that it was not woman's business. This I took, as it was meant, for a gentle caution that Lorna (whom he had not seen as yet) must not he informed of any of his doings. Herein I quite agreed with him; not only for his furtherance, but because I always think that women, of whatever mind, are best when least they meddle with the things that appertain to men.

Master Stickles complained that the weather had been against him bitterly, closing all the roads around him; even as it had done with us. It had taken him eight days, he said, to get from Exeter to Plymouth; whither he found that most of the troops had been drafted off from Exeter. When all were told, there was but a battalion of one of the King's horse regiments, and two companies of foot soldiers; and their commanders had orders, later than the date of Jeremy's commission, on no account to quit the southern coast, and march inland. Therefore, although they would gladly have come for a brush with the celebrated Doones, it was more than they durst attempt, in the face of their instructions. However, they spared him a single trooper, as a companion of the road, and to prove to the justices of the county, and the lord lieutenant, that he had their approval.

To these authorities Master Stickles now was forced to address himself, although he would rather have had one trooper than a score from the very best trained bands. For these trained bands had afforded very good soldiers, in the time of the civil wars, and for some years afterwards; but now their discipline was gone; and the younger generation had seen no real fighting. Each would have his own opinion, and would want to argue it; and if he were not allowed, he went about his duty in such a temper as to prove that his own way was the best.

Neither was this the worst of it; for Jeremy made no doubt but what (if he could only get the militia to turn out in force) he might manage, with the help of his own men, to force the stronghold of the enemy; but the truth was that the officers, knowing how hard it would be to collect their men at that time of the year, and in that state of the weather, began with one accord to make every possible excuse. And especially they pressed this point, that Bagworthy was not in their county; the Devonshire people affirming vehemently that it lay in the shire of Somerset, and the Somersetshire folk averring, even with imprecations, that it lay in Devonshire. Now I believe the truth to be that the boundary of the two counties, as well as of Oare and Brendon parishes, is defined by the Bagworthy river; so that the disputants on both sides were both right and wrong.

Upon this, Master Stickles suggested, and as I thought very sensibly, that the two counties should unite, and equally contribute to the extirpation of this pest, which shamed and injured them both alike. But hence arose another difficulty; for the men of Devon said they would march when Somerset had taken the field; and the sons of Somerset replied that indeed they were quite ready, but what were their cousins of Devonshire doing? And so it came to pass that the King's Commissioner returned without any army whatever; but with promise of two hundred men when the roads should be more passable. And meanwhile, what were we to do, abandoned as we were to the mercies of the Doones, with only our own hands to help us? And herein I grieved at my own folly, in having let Tom Faggus go, whose wit and courage would have been worth at least half a dozen men to us. Upon this matter I held long council with my good friend Stickles; telling him all about Lorna's presence, and what I knew of her history. He agreed with me that we could not hope to escape an attack from the outlaws, and the more especially now that they knew himself to be returned to us. Also he praised me for my forethought in having threshed out all our corn, and hidden the produce in such a manner that they were not likely to find it. Furthermore, he recommended that all the entrances to the house should at once be strengthened, and a watch must be maintained at night; and he thought it wiser that I should go (late as it was) to Lynmouth, if a horse could pass the valley, and fetch every one of his mounted troopers, who might now be quartered there. Also if any men of courage, though capable only of handling a pitchfork, could be found in the neighbourhood, I was to try to summon them. But our district is so thinly peopled, that I had little faith in this; however my errand was given me, and I set forth upon it; for John Fry was afraid of the waters.

Knowing how fiercely the floods were out, I resolved to travel the higher road, by Cosgate and through Countisbury; therefore I swam my horse through the Lynn, at the ford below our house (where sometimes you may step across), and thence galloped up and along the hills. I could see all the inland valleys ribbon'd with broad waters; and in every winding crook, the banks of snow that fed them; while on my right the turbid sea was flaked with April showers. But when I descended the hill towards Lynmouth, I feared that my journey was all in vain.

For the East Lynn (which is our river) was ramping and roaring frightfully, lashing whole trunks of trees on the rocks, and rending them, and grinding them. And into it rushed, from the opposite side, a torrent even madder; upsetting what it came to aid; shattering wave with boiling billow, and scattering wrath with fury. It was certain death to attempt the passage: and the little wooden footbridge had been carried away long ago. And the men I was seeking must be, of course, on the other side of this deluge, for on my side there was not a single house.

I followed the bank of the flood to the beach, some two or three hundred yards below; and there had the luck to see Will Watcombe on the opposite side, caulking an old boat. Though I could not make him hear a word, from the deafening roar of the torrent, I got him to understand at last that I wanted to cross over. Upon this he fetched another man, and the two of them launched a boat; and paddling well out to sea, fetched round the mouth of the frantic river. The other man proved to be Stickles's chief mate; and so he went back and fetched his comrades, bringing their weapons, but leaving their horses behind. As it happened there were but four of them; however, to have even these was a help; and I started again at full speed for my home; for the men must follow afoot, and cross our river high up on the moorland.

This took them a long way round, and the track was rather bad to find, and the sky already darkening; so that I arrived at Plover's Barrows more than two hours before them. But they had done a sagacious thing, which was well worth the delay; for by hoisting their flag upon the hill, they fetched the two watchmen from the Foreland, and added them to their number.

It was lucky that I came home so soon; for I found the house in a great commotion, and all the women trembling. When I asked what the matter was, Lorna, who seemed the most self-possessed, answered that it was all her fault, for she alone had frightened them. And this in the following manner. She had stolen out to the garden towards dusk, to watch some favourite hyacinths just pushing up, like a baby's teeth, and just attracting the fatal notice of a great house-snail at night-time. Lorna at last had discovered the glutton, and was bearing him off in triumph to the tribunal of the ducks, when she descried two glittering eyes glaring at her steadfastly, from the elder-bush beyond the stream. The elder was smoothing its wrinkled leaves, being at least two months behind time; and among them this calm cruel face appeared; and she knew it was the face of Carver Doone.

The maiden, although so used to terror (as she told me once before), lost all presence of mind hereat, and could neither shriek nor fly, but only gaze, as if bewitched. Then Carver Doone, with his deadly smile, gloating upon her horror, lifted his long gun, and pointed full at Lorna's heart. In vain she strove to turn away; fright had stricken her stiff as stone. With the inborn love of life, she tried to cover the vital part wherein the winged death must lodge—for she knew Carver's certain aim—but her hands hung numbed, and heavy; in nothing but her eyes was life.

With no sign of pity in his face, no quiver of relenting, but a well-pleased grin at all the charming palsy of his victim, Carver Doone lowered, inch by inch, the muzzle of his gun. When it pointed to the ground, between her delicate arched insteps, he pulled the trigger, and the bullet flung the mould all over her. It was a refinement of bullying, for which I swore to God that night, upon my knees, in secret, that I would smite down Carver Doone or else he should smite me down. Base beast! what largest humanity, or what dreams of divinity, could make a man put up with this?

My darling (the loveliest, and most harmless, in the world of maidens), fell away on a bank of grass, and wept at her own cowardice; and trembled, and wondered where I was; and what I would think of this. Good God! What could I think of it? She over-rated my slow nature, to admit the question.

While she leaned there, quite unable yet to save herself, Carver came to the brink of the flood, which alone was between them; and then he stroked his jet-black beard, and waited for Lorna to begin. Very likely, be thought that she would thank him for his kindness to her. But she was now recovering the power of her nimble limbs; and ready to be off like hope, and wonder at her own cowardice.

'I have spared you this time,' he said, in his deep calm voice, 'only because it suits my plans; and I never yield to temper. But unless you come back to-morrow, pure, and with all you took away, and teach me to destroy that fool, who has destroyed himself for you, your death is here, your death is here, where it has long been waiting.'

Although his gun was empty, he struck the breech of it with his finger; and then he turned away, not deigning even once to look back again; and Lorna saw his giant figure striding across the meadow-land, as if the Ridds were nobodies, and he the proper owner. Both mother and I were greatly hurt at hearing of this insolence: for we had owned that meadow, from the time of the great Alfred; and even when that good king lay in the Isle of Athelney, he had a Ridd along with him.

Now I spoke to Lorna gently, seeing how much she had been tried; and I praised her for her courage, in not having run away, when she was so unable; and my darling was pleased with this, and smiled upon me for saying it; though she knew right well that, in this matter, my judgment was not impartial. But you may take this as a general rule, that a woman likes praise from the man whom she loves, and cannot stop always to balance it.

Now expecting a sharp attack that night—when Jeremy Stickles the more expected, after the words of Carver, which seemed to be meant to mislead us—we prepared a great quantity of knuckles of pork, and a ham in full cut, and a fillet of hung mutton. For we would almost surrender rather than keep our garrison hungry. And all our men were exceedingly brave; and counted their rounds of the house in half-pints.

Before the maidens went to bed, Lorna made a remark which seemed to me a very clever one, and then I wondered how on earth it had never occurred to me before. But first she had done a thing which I could not in the least approve of: for she had gone up to my mother, and thrown herself into her arms, and begged to be allowed to return to Glen Doone.

'My child, are you unhappy here?' mother asked her, very gently, for she had begun to regard her now as a daughter of her own.

'Oh, no! Too happy, by far too happy, Mrs. Ridd. I never knew rest or peace before, or met with real kindness. But I cannot be so ungrateful, I cannot be so wicked, as to bring you all into deadly peril, for my sake alone. Let me go: you must not pay this great price for my happiness.'

'Dear child, we are paying no price at all,' replied my mother, embracing her; 'we are not threatened for your sake only. Ask John, he will tell you. He knows every bit about politics, and this is a political matter.'

Dear mother was rather proud in her heart, as well as terribly frightened, at the importance now accruing to Plover's Barrows farm; and she often declared that it would be as famous in history as the Rye House, or the Meal-tub, or even the great black box, in which she was a firm believer: and even my knowledge of politics could not move her upon that matter. 'Such things had happened before,' she would say, shaking her head with its wisdom, 'and why might they not happen again? Women would be women, and men would be men, to the end of the chapter; and if she had been in Lucy Water's place, she would keep it quiet, as she had done'; and then she would look round, for fear, lest either of her daughters had heard her; 'but now, can you give me any reason, why it may not have been so? You are so fearfully positive, John: just as men always are.' 'No,' I used to say; 'I can give you no reason, why it may not have been so, mother. But the question is, if it was so, or not; rather than what it might have been. And, I think, it is pretty good proof against it, that what nine men of every ten in England would only too gladly believe, if true, is nevertheless kept dark from them.' 'There you are again, John,' mother would reply, 'all about men, and not a single word about women. If you had any argument at all, you would own that marriage is a question upon which women are the best judges.' 'Oh!' I would groan in my spirit, and go; leaving my dearest mother quite sure, that now at last she must have convinced me. But if mother had known that Jeremy Stickles was working against the black box, and its issue, I doubt whether he would have fared so well, even though he was a visitor. However, she knew that something was doing and something of importance; and she trusted in God for the rest of it. Only she used te tell me, very seriously, of an evening, 'The very least they can give you, dear John, is a coat of arms. Be sure you take nothing less, dear; and the farm can well support it.'

But lo! I have left Lorna ever so long, anxious to consult me upon political matters. She came to me, and her eyes alone asked a hundred questions, which I rather had answered upon her lips than troubled her pretty ears with them. Therefore I told her nothing at all, save that the attack (if any should be) would not be made on her account; and that if she should hear, by any chance, a trifle of a noise in the night, she was to wrap the clothes around her, and shut her beautiful eyes again. On no account, whatever she did, was she to go to the window. She liked my expression about her eyes, and promised to do the very best she could and then she crept so very close, that I needs must have her closer; and with her head on my breast she asked,—

'Can't you keep out of this fight, John?'

'My own one,' I answered, gazing through the long black lashes, at the depths of radiant love; 'I believe there will be nothing: but what there is I must see out.'

'Shall I tell you what I think, John? It is only a fancy of mine, and perhaps it is not worth telling.'

'Let us have it, dear, by all means. You know so much about their ways.'

'What I believe is this, John. You know how high the rivers are, higher than ever they were before, and twice as high, you have told me. I believe that Glen Doone is flooded, and all the houses under water.'

'You little witch,' I answered; 'what a fool I must be not to think of it! Of course it is: it must be. The torrent from all the Bagworthy forest, and all the valleys above it, and the great drifts in the glen itself, never could have outlet down my famous waterslide. The valley must be under water twenty feet at least. Well, if ever there was a fool, I am he, for not having thought of it.'

'I remember once before,' said Lorna, reckoning on her fingers, 'when there was heavy rain, all through the autumn and winter, five or it may be six years ago, the river came down with such a rush that the water was two feet deep in our rooms, and we all had to camp by the cliff-edge. But you think that the floods are higher now, I believe I heard you say, John.'

'I don't think about it, my treasure,' I answered; 'you may trust me for understanding floods, after our work at Tiverton. And I know that the deluge in all our valleys is such that no living man can remember, neither will ever behold again. Consider three months of snow, snow, snow, and a fortnight of rain on the top of it, and all to be drained in a few days away! And great barricades of ice still in the rivers blocking them up, and ponding them. You may take my word for it, Mistress Lorna, that your pretty bower is six feet deep.'

'Well, my bower has served its time', said Lorna, blushing as she remembered all that had happened there; 'and my bower now is here, John. But I am so sorry to think of all the poor women flooded out of their houses and sheltering in the snowdrifts. However, there is one good of it: they cannot send many men against us, with all this trouble upon them.'

'You are right,' I replied; 'how clever you are! and that is why there were only three to cut off Master Stickles. And now we shall beat them, I make no doubt, even if they come at all. And I defy them to fire the house: the thatch is too wet for burning.'

We sent all the women to bed quite early, except Gwenny Carfax and our old Betty. These two we allowed to stay up, because they might be useful to us, if they could keep from quarreling. For my part, I had little fear, after what Lorna had told me, as to the result of the combat. It was not likely that the Doones could bring more than eight or ten men against us, while their homes were in such danger: and to meet these we had eight good men, including Jeremy, and myself, all well armed and resolute, besides our three farm-servants, and the parish-clerk, and the shoemaker. These five could not be trusted much for any valiant conduct, although they spoke very confidently over their cans of cider. Neither were their weapons fitted for much execution, unless it were at close quarters, which they would be likely to avoid. Bill Dadds had a sickle, Jem Slocombe a flail, the cobbler had borrowed the constable's staff (for the constable would not attend, because there was no warrant), and the parish clerk had brought his pitch-pipe, which was enough to break any man's head. But John Fry, of course, had his blunderbuss, loaded with tin-tacks and marbles, and more likely to kill the man who discharged it than any other person: but we knew that John had it only for show, and to describe its qualities.

Now it was my great desire, and my chiefest hope, to come across Carver Doone that night, and settle the score between us; not by any shot in the dark, but by a conflict man to man. As yet, since I came to full-grown power, I had never met any one whom I could not play teetotum with: but now at last I had found a man whose strength was not to be laughed at. I could guess it in his face, I could tell it in his arms, I could see it in his stride and gait, which more than all the rest betray the substance of a man. And being so well used to wrestling, and to judge antagonists, I felt that here (if anywhere) I had found my match.

Therefore I was not content to abide within the house, or go the rounds with the troopers; but betook myself to the rick yard, knowing that the Doones were likely to begin their onset there. For they had a pleasant custom, when they visited farm-houses, of lighting themselves towards picking up anything they wanted, or stabbing the inhabitants, by first creating a blaze in the rick yard. And though our ricks were all now of mere straw (except indeed two of prime clover-hay), and although on the top they were so wet that no firebrands might hurt them; I was both unwilling to have them burned, and fearful that they might kindle, if well roused up with fire upon the windward side.

By the bye, these Doones had got the worst of this pleasant trick one time. For happening to fire the ricks of a lonely farm called Yeanworthy, not far above Glenthorne, they approached the house to get people's goods, and to enjoy their terror. The master of the farm was lately dead, and had left, inside the clock-case, loaded, the great long gun, wherewith he had used to sport at the ducks and the geese on the shore. Now Widow Fisher took out this gun, and not caring much what became of her (for she had loved her husband dearly), she laid it upon the window-sill, which looked upon the rick-yard; and she backed up the butt with a chest of oak drawers, and she opened the window a little back, and let the muzzle out on the slope. Presently five or six fine young Doones came dancing a reel (as their manner was) betwixt her and the flaming rick. Upon which she pulled the trigger with all the force of her thumb, and a quarter of a pound of duck-shot went out with a blaze on the dancers. You may suppose what their dancing was, and their reeling how changed to staggering, and their music none of the sweetest. One of them fell into the rick, and was burned, and buried in a ditch next day; but the others were set upon their horses, and carried home on a path of blood. And strange to say, they never avenged this very dreadful injury; but having heard that a woman had fired this desperate shot among them, they said that she ought to be a Doone, and inquired how old she was.

Now I had not been so very long waiting in our mow-yard, with my best gun ready, and a big club by me, before a heaviness of sleep began to creep upon me. The flow of water was in my ears, and in my eyes a hazy spreading, and upon my brain a closure, as a cobbler sews a vamp up. So I leaned back in the clover-rick, and the dust of the seed and the smell came round me, without any trouble; and I dozed about Lorna, just once or twice, and what she had said about new-mown hay; and then back went my head, and my chin went up; and if ever a man was blest with slumber, down it came upon me, and away went I into it.

Now this was very vile of me, and against all good resolutions, even such as I would have sworn to an hour ago or less. But if you had been in the water as I had, ay, and had long fight with it, after a good day's work, and then great anxiety afterwards, and brain-work (which is not fair for me), and upon that a stout supper, mayhap you would not be so hard on my sleep; though you felt it your duty to wake me.

Chapter XLIX Maiden Sentinels Are Best

It was not likely that the outlaws would attack out premises until some time after the moon was risen; because it would be too dangerous to cross the flooded valleys in the darkness of the night. And but for this consideration, I must have striven harder against the stealthy approach of slumber. But even so, it was very foolish to abandon watch, especially in such as I, who sleep like any dormouse. Moreover, I had chosen the very worst place in the world for such employment, with a goodly chance of awakening in a bed of solid fire.

And so it might have been, nay, it must have been, but for Lorna's vigilance. Her light hand upon my arm awoke me, not too readily; and leaping up, I seized my club, and prepared to knock down somebody.

'Who's that?' I cried; 'stand back, I say, and let me have fair chance at you.'

'Are you going to knock me down, dear John?' replied the voice I loved so well; 'I am sure I should never get up again, after one blow from you, John.'

'My darling, is it you?' I cried; 'and breaking all your orders? Come back into the house at once: and nothing on your head, dear!'

'How could I sleep, while at any moment you might he killed beneath my window? And now is the time of real danger; for men can see to travel.'

I saw at once the truth of this. The moon was high and clearly lighting all the watered valleys. To sleep any longer might be death, not only to myself, but all.

'The man on guard at the back of the house is fast asleep,' she continued; 'Gwenny, who let me out, and came with me, has heard him snoring for two hours. I think the women ought to be the watch, because they have had no travelling. Where do you suppose little Gwenny is?'

'Surely not gone to Glen Doone?' I was not sure, however: for I could believe almost anything of the Cornish maiden's hardihood.

'No,' replied Lorna, 'although she wanted even to do that. But of course I would not hear of it, on account of the swollen waters. But she is perched on yonder tree, which commands the Barrow valley. She says that they are almost sure to cross the streamlet there; and now it is so wide and large, that she can trace it in the moonlight, half a mile beyond her. If they cross, she is sure to see them, and in good time to let us know.'

'What a shame,' I cried, 'that the men should sleep, and the maidens be the soldiers! I will sit in that tree myself, and send little Gwenny back to you. Go to bed, my best and dearest; I will take good care not to sleep again.'

'Please not to send me away, dear John,' she answered very mournfully; 'you and I have been together through perils worse than this. I shall only be more timid, and more miserable, indoors.'

'I cannot let you stay here,' I said; 'it is altogether impossible. Do you suppose that I can fight, with you among the bullets, Lorna? If this is the way you mean to take it, we had better go both to the apple-room, and lock ourselves in, and hide under the tiles, and let them burn all the rest of the premises.'

At this idea Lorna laughed, as I could see by the moonlight; and then she said,—

'You are right, John. I should only do more harm than good: and of all things I hate fighting most, and disobedience next to it. Therefore I will go indoors, although I cannot go to bed. But promise me one thing, dearest John. You will keep yourself out of the way, now won't you, as much as you can, for my sake?'

'Of that you may be quite certain, Lorna. I will shoot them all through the hay-ricks.'

'That is right, dear,' she answered, never doubting but what I could do it; 'and then they cannot see you, you know. But don't think of climbing that tree, John; it is a great deal too dangerous. It is all very well for Gwenny; she has no bones to break.'

'None worth breaking, you mean, I suppose. Very well; I will not climb the tree, for I should defeat my own purpose, I fear; being such a conspicuous object. Now go indoors, darling, without more words. The more you linger, the more I shall keep you.'

She laughed her own bright laugh at this, and only said, 'God keep you, love!' and then away she tripped across the yard, with the step I loved to watch so. And thereupon I shouldered arms, and resolved to tramp till morning. For I was vexed at my own neglect, and that Lorna should have to right it.

But before I had been long on duty, making the round of the ricks and stables, and hailing Gwenny now and then from the bottom of her tree, a short wide figure stole towards me, in and out the shadows, and I saw that it was no other than the little maid herself, and that she bore some tidings.

'Ten on 'em crossed the watter down yonner,' said Gwenny, putting her hand to her mouth, and seeming to regard it as good news rather than otherwise: 'be arl craping up by hedgerow now. I could shutt dree on 'em from the bar of the gate, if so be I had your goon, young man.'

'There is no time to lose, Gwenny. Run to the house and fetch Master Stickles, and all the men; while I stay here, and watch the rick-yard.'

Perhaps I was wrong in heeding the ricks at such a time as that; especially as only the clover was of much importance. But it seemed to me like a sort of triumph that they should be even able to boast of having fired our mow-yard. Therefore I stood in a nick of the clover, whence we had cut some trusses, with my club in hand, and gun close by.

The robbers rode into our yard as coolly as if they had been invited, having lifted the gate from the hinges first on account of its being fastened. Then they actually opened our stable-doors, and turned our honest horses out, and put their own rogues in the place of them. At this my breath was quite taken away; for we think so much of our horses. By this time I could see our troopers, waiting in the shadow of the house, round the corner from where the Doones were, and expecting the order to fire. But Jeremy Stickles very wisely kept them in readiness, until the enemy should advance upon them.

'Two of you lazy fellows go,' it was the deep voice of Carver Doone, 'and make us a light, to cut their throats by. Only one thing, once again. If any man touches Lorna, I will stab him where he stands. She belongs to me. There are two other young damsels here, whom you may take away if you please. And the mother, I hear, is still comely. Now for our rights. We have borne too long the insolence of these yokels. Kill every man, and every child, and burn the cursed place down.'

As he spoke thus blasphemously, I set my gun against his breast; and by the light buckled from his belt, I saw the little 'sight' of brass gleaming alike upon either side, and the sleek round barrel glimmering. The aim was sure as death itself. If I only drew the trigger (which went very lighily) Carver Doone would breathe no more. And yet—will you believe me?—I could not pull the trigger. Would to God that I had done so!

For I never had taken human life, neither done bodily harm to man; beyond the little bruises, and the trifling aches and pains, which follow a good and honest bout in the wrestling ring. Therefore I dropped my carbine, and grasped again my club, which seemed a more straight-forward implement.

Presently two young men came towards me, bearing brands of resined hemp, kindled from Carver's lamp. The foremost of them set his torch to the rick within a yard of me, and smoke concealing me from him. I struck him with a back-handed blow on the elbow, as he bent it; and I heard the bone of his arm break, as clearly as ever I heard a twig snap. With a roar of pain he fell on the ground, and his torch dropped there, and singed him. The other man stood amazed at this, not having yet gained sight of me; till I caught his firebrand from his hand, and struck it into his countenance. With that he leaped at me; but I caught him, in a manner learned from early wrestling, and snapped his collar-bone, as I laid him upon the top of his comrade.

This little success so encouraged me, that I was half inclined to advance, and challenge Carver Doone to meet me; but I bore in mind that he would be apt to shoot me without ceremony; and what is the utmost of human strength against the power of powder? Moreover, I remembered my promise to sweet Lorna; and who would be left to defend her, if the rogues got rid of me?

While I was hesitating thus (for I always continue to hesitate, except in actual conflict), a blaze of fire lit up the house, and brown smoke hung around it. Six of our men had let go at the Doones, by Jeremy Stickles' order, as the villains came swaggering down in the moonlight ready for rape or murder. Two of them fell, and the rest hung back, to think at their leisure what this was. They were not used to this sort of thing: it was neither just nor courteous.

Being unable any longer to contain myself, as I thought of Lorna's excitement at all this noise of firing, I came across the yard, expecting whether they would shoot at me. However, no one shot at me; and I went up to Carver Doone, whom I knew by his size in the moonlight, and I took him by the beard, and said, 'Do you call yourself a man?'

For a moment he was so astonished that he could not answer. None had ever dared, I suppose, to look at him in that way; and he saw that he had met his equal, or perhaps his master. And then he tried a pistol at me, but I was too quick for him.

'Now, Carver Doone, take warning,' I said to him, very soberly; 'you have shown yourself a fool by your contempt of me. I may not be your match in craft; but I am in manhood. You are a despicable villain. Lie low in your native muck.'

And with that word, I laid him flat upon his back in our straw-yard, by a trick of the inner heel, which he could not have resisted (though his strength had been twice as great as mine), unless he were a wrestler. Seeing him down the others ran, though one of them made a shot at me, and some of them got their horses, before our men came up; and some went away without them. And among these last was Captain Carver who arose, while I was feeling myself (for I had a little wound), and strode away with a train of curses enough to poison the light of the moon.

We gained six very good horses, by this attempted rapine, as well as two young prisoners, whom I had smitten by the clover-rick. And two dead Doones were left behind, whom (as we buried them in the churchyard, without any service over them), I for my part was most thankful that I had not killed. For to have the life of a fellow-man laid upon one's conscience—deserved he his death, or deserved it not—is to my sense of right and wrong the heaviest of all burdens; and the one that wears most deeply inwards, with the dwelling of the mind on this view and on that of it.

I was inclined to pursue the enemy and try to capture more of them; but Jeremy Stickles would not allow it, for he said that all the advantage would be upon their side, if we went hurrying after them, with only the moon to guide us. And who could tell but what there might be another band of them, ready to fall upon the house, and burn it, and seize the women, if we left them unprotected? When he put the case thus, I was glad enough to abide by his decision. And one thing was quite certain, that the Doones had never before received so rude a shock, and so violent a blow to their supremacy, since first they had built up their power, and become the Lords of Exmoor. I knew that Carver Doone would gnash those mighty teeth of his, and curse the men around him, for the blunder (which was in truth his own) of over-confidence and carelessness. And at the same time, all the rest would feel that such a thing had never happened, while old Sir Ensor was alive; and that it was caused by nothing short of gross mismanagement.

I scarcely know who made the greatest fuss about my little wound, mother, or Annie, or Lorna. I was heartily ashamed to be so treated like a milksop; but most unluckily it had been impossible to hide it. For the ball had cut along my temple, just above the eyebrow; and being fired so near at hand, the powder too had scarred me. Therefore it seemed a great deal worse than it really was; and the sponging, and the plastering, and the sobbing, and the moaning, made me quite ashamed to look Master Stickles in the face.

However, at last I persuaded them that I had no intention of giving up the ghost that night; and then they all fell to, and thanked God with an emphasis quite unknown in church. And hereupon Master Stickles said, in his free and easy manner (for no one courted his observation), that I was the luckiest of all mortals in having a mother, and a sister, and a sweetheart, to make much of me. For his part, he said, he was just as well off in not having any to care for him. For now he might go and get shot, or stabbed, or knocked on the head, at his pleasure, without any one being offended. I made bold, upon this, to ask him what was become of his wife; for I had heard him speak of having one. He said that he neither knew nor cared; and perhaps I should be like him some day. That Lorna should hear such sentiments was very grievous to me. But she looked at me with a smile, which proved her contempt for all such ideas; and lest anything still more unfit might be said, I dismissed the question.

But Master Stickles told me afterwards, when there was no one with us, to have no faith in any woman, whatever she might seem to be. For he assured me that now he possessed very large experience, for so small a matter; being thoroughly acquainted with women of every class, from ladies of the highest blood, to Bonarobas, and peasants' wives: and that they all might be divided into three heads and no more; that is to say as follows. First, the very hot and passionate, who were only contemptible; second, the cold and indifferent, who were simply odious; and third, the mixture of the other two, who had the bad qualities of both. As for reason, none of them had it; it was like a sealed book to them, which if they ever tried to open, they began at the back of the cover.

Now I did not like to hear such things; and to me they appeared to be insolent, as well as narrow-minded. For if you came to that, why might not men, as well as women, be divided into the same three classes, and be pronounced upon by women, as beings even more devoid than their gentle judges of reason? Moreover, I knew, both from my own sense, and from the greatest of all great poets, that there are, and always have been, plenty of women, good, and gentle, warm-hearted, loving, and lovable; very keen, moreover, at seeing the right, be it by reason, or otherwise. And upon the whole, I prefer them much to the people of my own sex, as goodness of heart is more important than to show good reason for having it. And so I said to Jeremy,—

'You have been ill-treated, perhaps, Master Stickles, by some woman or other?'

'Ah, that have I,' he replied with an oath; 'and the last on earth who should serve me so, the woman who was my wife. A woman whom I never struck, never wronged in any way, never even let her know that I like another better. And yet when I was at Berwick last, with the regiment on guard there against those vile moss-troopers, what does that woman do but fly in the face of all authority, and of my especial business, by running away herself with the biggest of all moss-troopers? Not that I cared a groat about her; and I wish the fool well rid of her: but the insolence of the thing was such that everybody laughed at me; and back I went to London, losing a far better and safer job than this; and all through her. Come, let's have another onion.'

Master Stickles's view of the matter was so entirely unromantic, that I scarcely wondered at Mistress Stickles for having run away from him to an adventurous moss-trooper. For nine women out of ten must have some kind of romance or other, to make their lives endurable; and when their love has lost this attractive element, this soft dew-fog (if such it be), the love itself is apt to languish; unless its bloom be well replaced by the budding hopes of children. Now Master Stickles neither had, nor wished to have, any children.

Without waiting for any warrant, only saying something about 'captus in flagrante delicto,'—if that be the way to spell it—Stickles sent our prisoners off, bound and looking miserable, to the jail at Taunton. I was desirous to let them go free, if they would promise amendment; but although I had taken them, and surely therefore had every right to let them go again, Master Stickles said, 'Not so.' He assured me that it was a matter of public polity; and of course, not knowing what he meant, I could not contradict him; but thought that surely my private rights ought to be respected. For if I throw a man in wrestling, I expect to get his stakes; and if I take a man prisoner—why, he ought, in common justice, to belong to me, and I have a good right to let him go, if I think proper to do so. However, Master Stickles said that I was quite benighted, and knew nothing of the Constitution; which was the very thing I knew, beyond any man in our parish!

Nevertheless, it was not for me to contradict a commissioner; and therefore I let my prisoners go, and wished them a happy deliverance. Stickles replied, with a merry grin, that if ever they got it, it would be a jail deliverance, and the bliss of dancing; and he laid his hand to his throat in a manner which seemed to me most uncourteous. However, his foresight proved too correct; for both those poor fellows were executed, soon after the next assizes. Lorna had done her very best to earn another chance for them; even going down on her knees to that common Jeremy, and pleading with great tears for them. However, although much moved by her, he vowed that he durst do nothing else. To set them free was more than his own life was worth; for all the country knew, by this time, that two captive Doones were roped to the cider-press at Plover's Barrows. Annie bound the broken arm of the one whom I had knocked down with the club, and I myself supported it; and then she washed and rubbed with lard the face of the other poor fellow, which the torch had injured; and I fetched back his collar-bone to the best of my ability. For before any surgeon could arrive, they were off with a well-armed escort. That day we were reinforced so strongly from the stations along the coast, even as far as Minehead, that we not only feared no further attack, but even talked of assaulting Glen Doone, without waiting for the train-bands. However, I thought that it would be mean to take advantage of the enemy in the thick of the floods and confusion; and several of the others thought so too, and did not like fighting in water. Therefore it was resolved to wait and keep a watch upon the valley, and let the floods go down again.

Chapter L A Merry Meeting a Sad One

Now the business I had most at heart (as every one knows by this time) was to marry Lorna as soon as might be, if she had no objection, and then to work the farm so well, as to nourish all our family. And herein I saw no difficulty; for Annie would soon be off our hands, and somebody might come and take a fancy to little Lizzie (who was growing up very nicely now, though not so fine as Annie); moreover, we were almost sure to have great store of hay and corn after so much snow, if there be any truth in the old saying,—

"A foot deep of rain
Will kill hay and grain;
But three feet of snow
Will make them come mo'."

And although it was too true that we had lost a many cattle, yet even so we had not lost money; for the few remaining fetched such prices as were never known before. And though we grumbled with all our hearts, and really believed, at one time, that starvation was upon us, I doubt whether, on the whole, we were not the fatter, and the richer, and the wiser for that winter. And I might have said the happier, except for the sorrow which we felt at the failures among our neighbours. The Snowes lost every sheep they had, and nine out of ten horned cattle; and poor Jasper Kebby would have been forced to throw up the lease of his farm, and perhaps to go to prison, but for the help we gave him.

However, my dear mother would have it that Lorna was too young, as yet, to think of being married: and indeed I myself was compelled to admit that her form was becoming more perfect and lovely; though I had not thought it possible. And another difficulty was, that as we had all been Protestants from the time of Queen Elizabeth, the maiden must be converted first, and taught to hate all Papists. Now Lorna had not the smallest idea of ever being converted. She said that she loved me truly, but wanted not to convert me; and if I loved her equally, why should I wish to convert her? With this I was tolerably content, not seeing so very much difference between a creed and a credo, and believing God to be our Father, in Latin as well as English. Moreover, my darling knew but little of the Popish ways—whether excellent or otherwise—inasmuch as the Doones, though they stole their houses, or at least the joiner's work, had never been tempted enough by the devil to steal either church or chapel.

Lorna came to our little church, when Parson Bowden reappeared after the snow was over; and she said that all was very nice, and very like what she had seen in the time of her Aunt Sabina, when they went far away to the little chapel, with a shilling in their gloves. It made the tears come into her eyes, by the force of memory, when Parson Bowden did the things, not so gracefully nor so well, yet with pleasant imitation of her old Priest's sacred rites.

'He is a worthy man,' she said, being used to talk in the service time, and my mother was obliged to cough: 'I like him very much indeed: but I wish he would let me put his things the right way on his shoulders.'

Everybody in our parish, who could walk at all, or hire a boy and a wheelbarrow, ay, and half the folk from Countisbury, Brendon, and even Lynmouth, was and were to be found that Sunday, in our little church of Oare. People who would not come anigh us, when the Doones were threatening with carbine and with fire-brand, flocked in their very best clothes, to see a lady Doone go to church. Now all this came of that vile John Fry; I knew it as well as possible; his tongue was worse than the clacker of a charity-school bell, or the ladle in the frying-pan, when the bees are swarming.

However, Lorna was not troubled; partly because of her natural dignity and gentleness; partly because she never dreamed that the people were come to look at her. But when we came to the Psalms of the day, with some vague sense of being stared at more than ought to be, she dropped the heavy black lace fringing of the velvet hat she wore, and concealed from the congregation all except her bright red lips, and the oval snowdrift of her chin. I touched her hand, and she pressed mine; and we felt that we were close together, and God saw no harm in it.

As for Parson Bowden (as worthy a man as ever lived, and one who could shoot flying), he scarcely knew what he was doing, without the clerk to help him. He had borne it very well indeed, when I returned from London; but to see a live Doone in his church, and a lady Doone, and a lovely Doone, moreover one engaged to me, upon whom he almost looked as the Squire of his parish (although not rightly an Armiger), and to feel that this lovely Doone was a Papist, and therefore of higher religion—as all our parsons think—and that she knew exactly how he ought to do all the service, of which he himself knew little; I wish to express my firm belief that all these things together turned Parson Bowden's head a little, and made him look to me for orders.

My mother, the very best of women, was (as I could well perceive) a little annoyed and vexed with things. For this particular occasion, she had procured from Dulverton, by special message to Ruth Huckaback (whereof more anon), a head-dress with a feather never seen before upon Exmoor, to the best of every one's knowledge. It came from a bird called a flaming something—a flaming oh, or a flaming ah, I will not be positive—but I can assure you that it did flame; and dear mother had no other thought, but that all the congregation would neither see nor think of any other mortal thing, or immortal even, to the very end of the sermon.

Herein she was so disappointed, that no sooner did she get home, but upstairs she went at speed, not even stopping at the mirror in our little parlour, and flung the whole thing into a cupboard, as I knew by the bang of the door, having eased the lock for her lately. Lorna saw there was something wrong; and she looked at Annie and Lizzie (as more likely to understand it) with her former timid glance; which I knew so well, and which had first enslaved me.

'I know not what ails mother,' said Annie, who looked very beautiful, with lilac lute-string ribbons, which I saw the Snowe girls envying; 'but she has not attended to one of the prayers, nor said "Amen," all the morning. Never fear, darling Lorna, it is nothing about you. It is something about our John, I am sure; for she never worries herself very much about anybody but him.' And here Annie made a look at me, such as I had had five hundred of.

'You keep your opinions to yourself,' I replied; because I knew the dear, and her little bits of jealousy; 'it happens that you are quite wrong, this time. Lorna, come with me, my darling.'

'Oh yes, Lorna; go with him,' cried Lizzie, dropping her lip, in a way which you must see to know its meaning; 'John wants nobody now but you; and none can find fault with his taste, dear.'

'You little fool, I should think not,' I answered, very rudely; for, betwixt the lot of them, my Lorna's eyelashes were quivering; 'now, dearest angel, come with me; and snap your hands at the whole of them.'

My angel did come, with a sigh, and then with a smile, when we were alone; but without any unangelic attempt at snapping her sweet white fingers.

These little things are enough to show that while every one so admired Lorna, and so kindly took to her, still there would, just now and then, be petty and paltry flashes of jealousy concerning her; and perhaps it could not be otherwise among so many women. However, we were always doubly kind to her afterwards; and although her mind was so sensitive and quick that she must have suffered, she never allowed us to perceive it, nor lowered herself by resenting it.

Possibly I may have mentioned that little Ruth Huckaback had been asked, and had even promised to spend her Christmas with us; and this was the more desirable, because she had left us through some offence, or sorrow, about things said of her. Now my dear mother, being the kindest and best-hearted of all women, could not bear that poor dear Ruth (who would some day have such a fortune), should be entirely lost to us. 'It is our duty, my dear children,' she said more than once about it, 'to forgive and forget, as freely as we hope to have it done to us. If dear little Ruth has not behaved quite as we might have expected, great allowance should be made for a girl with so much money. Designing people get hold of her, and flatter her, and coax her, to obtain a base influence over her; so that when she falls among simple folk, who speak the honest truth of her, no wonder the poor child is vexed, and gives herself airs, and so on. Ruth can be very useful to us in a number of little ways; and I consider it quite a duty to pardon her freak of petulance.'

Now one of the little ways in which Ruth had been very useful, was the purchase of the scarlet feathers of the flaming bird; and now that the house was quite safe from attack, and the mark on my forehead was healing, I was begged, over and over again, to go and see Ruth, and make all things straight, and pay for the gorgeous plumage. This last I was very desirous to do, that I might know the price of it, having made a small bet on the subject with Annie; and having held counsel with myself, whether or not it were possible to get something of the kind for Lorna, of still more distinguished appearance. Of course she could not wear scarlet as yet, even if I had wished it; but I believed that people of fashion often wore purple for mourning; purple too was the royal colour, and Lorna was by right a queen; therefore I was quite resolved to ransack Uncle Reuben's stores, in search of some bright purple bird, if nature had kindly provided one.

All this, however, I kept to myself, intending to trust Ruth Huckaback, and no one else in the matter. And so, one beautiful spring morning, when all the earth was kissed with scent, and all the air caressed with song, up the lane I stoutly rode, well armed, and well provided.

Now though it is part of my life to heed, it is no part of my tale to tell, how the wheat was coming on. I reckon that you, who read this story, after I am dead and gone (and before that none shall read it), will say, 'Tush! What is his wheat to us? We are not wheat: we are human beings: and all we care for is human doings.' This may be very good argument, and in the main, I believe that it is so. Nevertheless, if a man is to tell only what he thought and did, and not what came around him, he must not mention his own clothes, which his father and mother bought for him. And more than my own clothes to me, ay, and as much as my own skin, are the works of nature round about, whereof a man is the smallest.

And now I will tell you, although most likely only to be laughed at, because I cannot put it in the style of Mr. Dryden—whom to compare to Shakespeare! but if once I begin upon that, you will never hear the last of me—nevertheless, I will tell you this; not wishing to be rude, but only just because I know it; the more a man can fling his arms (so to say) round Nature's neck, the more he can upon her bosom, like an infant, lie and suck,—the more that man shall earn the trust and love of all his fellow men.

In this matter is no jealousy (when the man is dead); because thereafter all others know how much of the milk be had; and he can suck no longer; and they value him accordingly, for the nourishment he is to them. Even as when we keep a roaster of the sucking-pigs, we choose, and praise at table most, the favourite of its mother. Fifty times have I seen this, and smiled, and praised our people's taste, and offered them more of the vitals.

Now here am I upon Shakespeare (who died, of his own fruition, at the age of fifty-two, yet lived more than fifty thousand men, within his little span of life), when all the while I ought to be riding as hard as I can to Dulverton. But, to tell the truth, I could not ride hard, being held at every turn, and often without any turn at all, by the beauty of things around me. These things grow upon a man if once he stops to notice them.

It wanted yet two hours to noon, when I came to Master Huckaback's door, and struck the panels smartly. Knowing nothing of their manners, only that people in a town could not be expected to entertain (as we do in farm-houses), having, moreover, keen expectation of Master

Huckaback's avarice, I had brought some stuff to eat, made by Annie, and packed by Lorna, and requiring no thinking about it.

Ruth herself came and let me in, blushing very heartily; for which colour I praised her health, and my praises heightened it. That little thing had lovely eyes, and could be trusted thoroughly. I do like an obstinate little woman, when she is sure that she is right. And indeed if love had never sped me straight to the heart of Lorna (compared to whom, Ruth was no more than the thief is to the candle), who knows but what I might have yielded to the law of nature, that thorough trimmer of balances, and verified the proverb that the giant loves the dwarf?

'I take the privilege, Mistress Ruth, of saluting you according to kinship, and the ordering of the Canons.' And therewith I bussed her well, and put my arm around her waist, being so terribly restricted in the matter of Lorna, and knowing the use of practice. Not that I had any warmth—all that was darling Lorna's—only out of pure gallantry, and my knowledge of London fashions. Ruth blushed to such a pitch at this, and looked up at me with such a gleam; as if I must have my own way; that all my love of kissing sunk, and I felt that I was wronging her. Only my mother had told me, when the girls were out of the way, to do all I could to please darling Ruth, and I had gone about it accordingly.

Now Ruth as yet had never heard a word about dear Lorna, and when she led me into the kitchen (where everything looked beautiful), and told me not to mind, for a moment, about the scrubbing of my boots, because she would only be too glad to clean it all up after me, and told me how glad she was to see me, blushing more at every word, and recalling some of them, and stooping down for pots and pans, when I looked at her too ruddily—all these things came upon me so, without any legal notice, that I could only look at Ruth, and think how very good she was, and how bright her handles were; and wonder if I had wronged her. Once or twice, I began—this I say upon my honour—to endeavour to explain exactly, how we were at Plover's Barrows; how we all had been bound to fight, and had defeated the enemy, keeping their queen amongst us. But Ruth would make some great mistake between Lorna and Gwenny Carfax, and gave me no chance to set her aright, and cared about nothing much, except some news of Sally Snowe.

What could I do with this little thing? All my sense of modesty, and value for my dinner, were against my over-pressing all the graceful hints I had given about Lorna. Ruth was just a girl of that sort, who will not believe one word, except from her own seeing; not so much from any doubt, as from the practice of using eyes which have been in business.

I asked Cousin Ruth (as we used to call her, though the cousinship was distant) what was become of Uncle Ben, and how it was that we never heard anything of or from him now. She replied that she hardly knew what to make of her grandfather's manner of carrying on, for the last half-year or more. He was apt to leave his home, she said, at any hour of the day or night; going none knew whither, and returning no one might say when. And his dress, in her opinion, was enough to frighten a hodman, of a scavenger of the roads, instead of the decent suit of kersey, or of Sabbath doeskins, such as had won the respect and reverence of his fellow-townsmen. But the worst of all things was, as she confessed with tears in her eyes, that the poor old gentleman had something weighing heavily on his mind.

'It will shorten his days, Cousin Ridd,' she said, for she never would call me Cousin John; 'he has no enjoyment of anything that he eats or drinks, nor even in counting his money, as he used to do all Sunday; indeed no pleasure in anything, unless it be smoking his pipe, and thinking and staring at bits of brown stone, which he pulls, every now and then, out of his pockets. And the business he used to take such pride in is now left almost entirely to the foreman, and to me.'

'And what will become of you, dear Ruth, if anything happens to the old man?'

'I am sure I know not,' she answered simply; 'and I cannot bear to think of it. It must depend, I suppose, upon dear grandfather's pleasure about me.'

'It must rather depend,' said I, though having no business to say it, 'upon your own good pleasure, Ruth; for all the world will pay court to you.'

'That is the very thing which I never could endure. I have begged dear grandfather to leave no chance of that. When he has threatened me with poverty, as he does sometimes, I have always met him truly, with the answer that I feared one thing a great deal worse than poverty; namely, to be an heiress. But I cannot make him believe it. Only think how strange, Cousin Ridd, I cannot make him believe it.'

'It is not strange at all,' I answered; 'considering how he values money. Neither would any one else believe you, except by looking into your true, and very pretty eyes, dear.'

Now I beg that no one will suspect for a single moment, either that I did not mean exactly what I said, or meant a single atom more, or would not have said the same, if Lorna had been standing by. What I had always liked in Ruth, was the calm, straightforward gaze, and beauty of her large brown eyes. Indeed I had spoken of them to Lorna, as the only ones to be compared (though not for more than a moment) to her own, for truth and light, but never for depth and softness. But now the little maiden dropped them, and turned away, without reply.

'I will go and see to my horse,' I said; 'the boy that has taken him seemed surprised at his having no horns on his forehead. Perhaps he will lead him into the shop, and feed him upon broadcloth.'

'Oh, he is such a stupid boy,' Ruth answered with great sympathy: 'how quick of you to observe that now: and you call yourself "Slow John Ridd!" I never did see such a stupid boy: sometimes he spoils my temper. But you must be back in half an hour, at the latest, Cousin Ridd. You see I remember what you are; when once you get among horses, or cows, or things of that sort.'

'Things of that sort! Well done, Ruth! One would think you were quite a Cockney.'

Uncle Reuben did not come home to his dinner; and his granddaughter said she had strictest orders never to expect him. Therefore we had none to dine with us, except the foreman of the shop, a worthy man, named Thomas Cockram, fifty years of age or so. He seemed to me to have strong intentions of his own about little Ruth, and on that account to regard me with a wholly undue malevolence. And perhaps, in order to justify him, I may have been more attentive to her than otherwise need have been; at any rate, Ruth and I were pleasant; and he the very opposite.

'My dear Cousin Ruth,' I said, on purpose to vex Master Cockram, because he eyed us so heavily, and squinted to unluckily, 'we have long been looking for you at our Plover's Barrows farm. You remember how you used to love hunting for eggs in the morning, and hiding up in the tallat with Lizzie, for me to seek you among the hay, when the sun was down. Ah, Master Cockram, those are the things young people find their pleasure in, not in selling a yard of serge, and giving twopence-halfpenny change, and writing "settled" at the bottom, with a pencil that has blacked their teeth. Now, Master Cockram, you ought to come as far as our good farm, at once, and eat two new-laid eggs for breakfast, and be made to look quite young again. Our good Annie would cook for you; and you should have the hot new milk and the pope's eye from the mutton; and every foot of you would become a yard in about a fortnight.' And hereupon, I spread my chest, to show him an example. Ruth could not keep her countenance: but I saw that she thought it wrong of me; and would scold me, if ever I gave her the chance of taking those little liberties. However, he deserved it all, according to my young ideas, for his great impertinence in aiming at my cousin.

But what I said was far less grievous to a man of honest mind than little Ruth's own behaviour. I could hardly have believed that so thoroughly true a girl, and one so proud and upright, could have got rid of any man so cleverly as she got rid of Master Thomas Cockram. She gave him not even a glass of wine, but commended to his notice, with a sweet and thoughtful gravity, some invoice which must be corrected, before her dear grandfather should return; and to amend which three great ledgers must be searched from first to last. Thomas Cockram winked at me, with the worst of his two wrong eyes; as much as to say, 'I understand it; but I cannot help myself. Only you look out, if ever'—and before he had finished winking, the door was shut behind him. Then Ruth said to me in the simplest manner, 'You have ridden far today, Cousin Ridd; and have far to ride to get home again. What will dear Aunt Ridd say, if we send you away without nourishment? All the keys are in my keeping, and dear grandfather has the finest wine, not to be matched in the west of England, as I have heard good judges say; though I know not wine from cider. Do you like the wine of Oporto, or the wine of Xeres?'

'I know not one from the other, fair cousin, except by the colour,' I answered: 'but the sound of Oporto is nobler, and richer. Suppose we try wine of Oporto.'

The good little creature went and fetched a black bottle of an ancient cast, covered with dust and cobwebs. These I was anxious to shake aside; and indeed I thought that the wine would be better for being roused up a little. Ruth, however, would not hear a single word to that purport; and seeing that she knew more about it, I left her to manage it. And the result was very fine indeed, to wit, a sparkling rosy liquor, dancing with little flakes of light, and scented like new violets. With this I was so pleased and gay, and Ruth so glad to see me gay, that we quite forgot how the time went on; and though my fair cousin would not be persuaded to take a second glass herself, she kept on filling mine so fast that it was never empty, though I did my best to keep it so.

'What is a little drop like this to a man of your size and strength, Cousin Ridd?' she said, with her cheeks just brushed with rose, which made her look very beautiful; 'I have heard you say that your head is so thick—or rather so clear, you ought to say—that no liquor ever moves it.'

'That is right enough,' I answered; 'what a witch you must be, dear Ruth, to have remembered that now!'

'Oh, I remember every word I have ever heard you say, Cousin Ridd; because your voice is so deep, you know, and you talk so little. Now it is useless to say "no". These bottles hold almost nothing. Dear grandfather will not come home, I fear, until long after you are gone. What will Aunt Ridd think of me, I am sure? You are all so dreadfully hospitable. Now not another "no," Cousin Ridd. We must have another bottle.'

'Well, must is must,' I answered, with a certain resignation. 'I cannot bear bad manners, dear; and how old are you next birthday?'

'Eighteen, dear John;' said Ruth, coming over with the empty bottle; and I was pleased at her calling me 'John,' and had a great mind to kiss her. However, I thought of my Lorna suddenly, and of the anger I should feel if a man went on with her so; therefore I lay back in my chair, to wait for the other bottle.

'Do you remember how we danced that night?' I asked, while she was opening it; 'and how you were afraid of me first, because I looked so tall, dear?'

'Yes, and so very broad, Cousin Ridd. I thought that you would eat me. But I have come to know, since then, how very kind and good you are.'

'And will you come and dance again, at my wedding, Cousin Ruth?'

She nearly let the bottle fall, the last of which she was sloping carefully into a vessel of bright glass; and then she raised her hand again, and finished it judiciously. And after that, she took the window, to see that all her work was clear; and then she poured me out a glass and said, with very pale cheeks, but else no sign of meaning about her, 'What did you ask me, Cousin Ridd?'

'Nothing of any importance, Ruth; only we are so fond of you. I mean to be married as soon as I can. Will you come and help us?'

'To be sure I will, Cousin Ridd—unless, unless, dear grandfather cannot spare me from the business.' She went away; and her breast was heaving, like a rick of under-carried hay. And she stood at the window long, trying to make yawns of sighs.

For my part, I knew not what to do. And yet I could think about it, as I never could with Lorna; with whom I was always in a whirl, from the power of my love. So I thought some time about it; and perceived that it was the manliest way, just to tell her everything; except that I feared she liked me. But it seemed to me unaccountable that she did not even ask the name of my intended wife. Perhaps she thought that it must be Sally; or perhaps she feared to trust her voice.

'Come and sit by me, dear Ruth; and listen to a long, long story, how things have come about with me.'

'No, thank you, Cousin Ridd,' she answered; 'at least I mean that I shall be happy—that I shall be ready to hear you—to listen to you, I mean of course. But I would rather stay where I am, and have the air—or rather be able to watch for dear grandfather coming home. He is so kind and good to me. What should I do without him?'

Then I told her how, for years and years, I had been attached to Lorna, and all the dangers and difficulties which had so long beset us, and how I hoped that these were passing, and no other might come between us, except on the score of religion; upon which point I trusted soon to overcome my mother's objections. And then I told her how poor, and helpless, and alone in the world, my Lorna was; and how sad all her youth had been, until I brought her away at last. And many other little things I mentioned, which there is no need for me again to dwell upon. Ruth heard it all without a word, and without once looking at me; and only by her attitude could I guess that she was weeping. Then when all my tale was told, she asked in a low and gentle voice, but still without showing her face to me,—

'And does she love you, Cousin Ridd? Does she say that she loves you with—with all her heart?'

'Certainly, she does,' I answered. 'Do you think it impossible for one like her to do so?'

She said no more; but crossed the room before I had time to look at her, and came behind my chair, and kissed me gently on the forehead.

'I hope you may be very happy, with—I mean in your new life,' she whispered very softly; 'as happy as you deserve to be, and as happy as you can make others be. Now how I have been neglecting you! I am quite ashamed of myself for thinking only of grandfather: and it makes me so low-spirited. You have told me a very nice romance, and I have never even helped you to a glass of wine. Here, pour it for yourself, dear cousin; I shall be back again directly.'

With that she was out of the door in a moment; and when she came back, you would not have thought that a tear had dimmed those large bright eyes, or wandered down those pale clear cheeks. Only her hands were cold and trembling: and she made me help myself.

Uncle Reuben did not appear at all; and Ruth, who had promised to come and see us, and stay for a fortnight at our house (if her grandfather could spare her), now discovered, before I left, that she must not think of doing so. Perhaps she was right in deciding thus; at any rate it had now become improper for me to press her. And yet I now desired tenfold that she should consent to come, thinking that Lorna herself would work the speediest cure of her passing whim.

For such, I tried to persuade myself, was the nature of Ruth's regard for me: and upon looking back I could not charge myself with any misconduct towards the little maiden. I had never sought her company, I had never trifled with her (at least until that very day), and being so engrossed with my own love, I had scarcely ever thought of her. And the maiden would never have thought of me, except as a clumsy yokel, but for my mother's and sister's meddling, and their wily suggestions. I believe they had told the little soul that I was deeply in love with her; although they both stoutly denied it. But who can place trust in a woman's word, when it comes to a question of match-making?

Chapter LI A Visit From the Counsellor

Now while I was riding home that evening, with a tender conscience about Ruth, although not a wounded one, I guessed but little that all my thoughts were needed much for my own affairs. So however it proved to be; for as I came in, soon after dark, my sister Eliza met me at the corner of the cheese-room, and she said, 'Don't go in there, John,' pointing to mother's room; 'until I have had a talk with you.'

'In the name of Moses,' I inquired, having picked up that phrase at Dulverton; 'what are you at about me now? There is no peace for a quiet fellow.'

'It is nothing we are at,' she answered; 'neither may you make light of it. It is something very important about Mistress Lorna Doone.'

'Let us have it at once,' I cried; 'I can bear anything about Lorna, except that she does not care for me.'

'It has nothing to do with that, John. And I am quite sure that you never need fear anything of that sort. She perfectly wearies me sometimes, although her voice is so soft and sweet, about your endless perfections.'

'Bless her little heart!' I said; 'the subject is inexhaustible.'

'No doubt ' replied Lizzie, in the driest manner; 'especially to your sisters. However this is no time to joke. I fear you will get the worst of it, John. Do you know a man of about Gwenny's shape, nearly as broad as he is long, but about six times the size of Gwenny, and with a length of snow-white hair, and a thickness also; as the copses were last winter. He never can comb it, that is quite certain, with any comb yet invented.'

'Then you go and offer your services. There are few things you cannot scarify. I know the man from your description, although I have never seen him. Now where is my Lorna? '

'Your Lorna is with Annie, having a good cry, I believe; and Annie too glad to second her. She knows that this great man is here, and knows that he wants to see her. But she begged to defer the interview, until dear John's return.'

'What a nasty way you have of telling the very commonest piece of news!' I said, on purpose to pay her out. 'What man will ever fancy you, you unlucky little snapper? Now, no more nursery talk for me. I will go and settle this business. You had better go and dress your dolls; if you can give them clothes unpoisoned.' Hereupon Lizzie burst into a perfect roar of tears; feeling that she had the worst of it. And I took her up, and begged her pardon; although she scarcely deserved it; for she knew that I was out of luck, and she might have spared her satire.

I was almost sure that the man who was come must be the Counsellor himself; of whom I felt much keener fear than of his son Carver. And knowing that his visit boded ill to me and Lorna, I went and sought my dear; and led her with a heavy heart, from the maiden's room to mother's, to meet our dreadful visitor.

Mother was standing by the door, making curtseys now and then, and listening to a long harangue upon the rights of state and land, which the Counsellor (having found that she was the owner of her property, and knew nothing of her title to it) was encouraged to deliver it. My dear mother stood gazing at him, spell-bound by his eloquence, and only hoping that he would stop. He was shaking his hair upon his shoulders, in the power of his words, and his wrath at some little thing, which he declared to be quite illegal.

Then I ventured to show myself, in the flesh, before him; although he feigned not to see me; but he advanced with zeal to Lorna; holding out both hands at once.

'My darling child, my dearest niece; how wonderfully well you look! Mistress Ridd, I give you credit. This is the country of good things. I never would have believed our Queen could have looked so royal. Surely of all virtues, hospitality is the finest, and the most romantic. Dearest Lorna, kiss your uncle; it is quite a privilege.'

'Perhaps it is to you, sir,' said Lorna, who could never quite check her sense of oddity; 'but I fear that you have smoked tobacco, which spoils reciprocity.'

'You are right, my child. How keen your scent is! It is always so with us. Your grandfather was noted for his olfactory powers. Ah, a great loss, dear Mrs. Ridd, a terrible loss to this neighbourhood! As one of our great writers says—I think it must be Milton—"We ne'er shall look upon his like again."'

'With your good leave sir,' I broke in, 'Master Milton could never have written so sweet and simple a line as that. It is one of the great Shakespeare.'

'Woe is me for my neglect!' said the Counsellor, bowing airily; 'this must be your son, Mistress Ridd, the great John, the wrestler. And one who meddles with the Muses! Ah, since I was young, how everything is changed, madam! Except indeed the beauty of women, which seems to me to increase every year.' Here the old villain bowed to my mother; and she blushed, and made another curtsey, and really did look very nice.

'Now though I have quoted the poets amiss, as your son informs me (for which I tender my best thanks, and must amend my reading), I can hardly be wrong in assuming that this young armiger must be the too attractive cynosure to our poor little maiden. And for my part, she is welcome to him. I have never been one of those who dwell upon distinctions of rank, and birth, and such like; as if they were in the heart of nature, and must be eternal. In early youth, I may have thought so, and been full of that little pride. But now I have long accounted it one of the first axioms of political economy—you are following me, Mistress Ridd?'

'Well, sir, I am doing my best; but I cannot quite keep up with you.'

'Never mind, madam; I will be slower. But your son's intelligence is so quick—'

'I see, sir; you thought that mine must be. But no; it all comes from his father, sir. His father was that quick and clever—'

'Ah, I can well suppose it, madam. And a credit he is to both of you. Now, to return to our muttons—a figure which you will appreciate—I may now be regarded, I think, as this young lady's legal guardian; although I have not had the honour of being formally appointed such. Her father was the eldest son of Sir Ensor Doone; and I happened to be the second son; and as young maidens cannot be baronets, I suppose I am "Sir Counsellor." Is it so, Mistress Ridd, according to your theory of genealogy?'

'I am sure I don't know, sir,' my mother answered carefully; 'I know not anything of that name, sir, except in the Gospel of Matthew: but I see not why it should be otherwise.'

'Good, madam! I may look upon that as your sanction and approval: and the College of Heralds shall hear of it. And in return, as Lorna's guardian, I give my full and ready consent to her marriage with your son, madam.'

'Oh, how good of you, sir, how kind! Well, I always did say, that the learnedest people were, almost always, the best and kindest, and the most simple-hearted.'

'Madam, that is a great sentiment. What a goodly couple they will be! and if we can add him to our strength—'

'Oh no, sir, oh no!' cried mother: 'you really must not think of it. He has always been brought up so honest—'

'Hem! that makes a difference. A decided disqualification for domestic life among the Doones. But, surely, he might get over those prejudices, madam?'

'Oh no, sir! he never can: he never can indeed. When he was only that high, sir, he could not steal even an apple, when some wicked boys tried to mislead him.'

'Ah,' replied the Counsellor, shaking his white head gravely; 'then I greatly fear that his case is quite incurable. I have known such cases; violent prejudice, bred entirely of education, and anti-economical to the last degree. And when it is so, it is desperate: no man, after imbibing ideas of that sort, can in any way be useful.'

'Oh yes, sir, John is very useful. He can do as much work as three other men; and you should see him load a sledd, sir.'

'I was speaking, madam, of higher usefulness,—power of the brain and heart. The main thing for us upon earth is to take a large view of things. But while we talk of the heart, what is my niece Lorna doing, that she does not come and thank me, for my perhaps too prompt concession to her youthful fancies? Ah, if I had wanted thanks, I should have been more stubborn.'

Lorna, being challenged thus, came up and looked at her uncle, with her noble eyes fixed full upon his, which beneath his white eyebrows glistened, like dormer windows piled with snow.

'For what am I to thank you, uncle?'

'My dear niece, I have told you. For removing the heaviest obstacle, which to a mind so well regulated could possibly have existed, between your dutiful self and the object of your affections.'

'Well, uncle, I should be very grateful, if I thought that you did so from love of me; or if I did not know that you have something yet concealed from me.'

'And my consent,' said the Counsellor, 'is the more meritorious, the more liberal, frank, and candid, in the face of an existing fact, and a very clearly established one; which might have appeared to weaker minds in the light of an impediment; but to my loftier view of matrimony seems quite a recommendation.'

'What fact do you mean, sir? Is it one that I ought to know?'

'In my opinion it is, good niece. It forms, to my mind, so fine a basis for the invariable harmony of the matrimonial state. To be brief—as I always endeavour to be, without becoming obscure—you two young people (ah, what a gift is youth! one can never be too thankful for it) you will have the rare advantage of commencing married life, with a subject of common interest to discuss, whenever you weary of—well, say of one another; if you can now, by any means, conceive such a possibility. And perfect justice meted out: mutual goodwill resulting, from the sense of reciprocity.'

'I do not understand you, sir. Why can you not say what you mean, at once?'

'My dear child, I prolong your suspense. Curiosity is the most powerful of all feminine instincts; and therefore the most delightful, when not prematurely satisfied. However, if you must have my strong realities, here they are. Your father slew dear John's father, and dear John's father slew yours.'

Having said thus much, the Counsellor leaned back upon his chair, and shaded his calm white-bearded eyes from the rays of our tallow candles. He was a man who liked to look, rather than to be looked at. But Lorna came to me for aid; and I went up to Lorna and mother looked at both of us.

Then feeling that I must speak first (as no one would begin it), I took my darling round the waist, and led her up to the Counsellor; while she tried to bear it bravely; yet must lean on me, or did.

'Now, Sir Counsellor Doone,' I said, with Lorna squeezing both my hands, I never yet knew how (considering that she was walking all the time, or something like it); 'you know right well, Sir Counsellor, that Sir Ensor Doone gave approval.' I cannot tell what made me think of this: but so it came upon me.

'Approval to what, good rustic John? To the slaughter so reciprocal?'

'No, sir, not to that; even if it ever happened; which I do not believe. But to the love betwixt me and Lorna; which your story shall not break, without more evidence than your word. And even so, shall never break; if Lorna thinks as I do.'

The maiden gave me a little touch, as much as to say, 'You are right, darling: give it to him, again, like that.' However, I held my peace, well knowing that too many words do mischief.

Then mother looked at me with wonder, being herself too amazed to speak; and the Counsellor looked, with great wrath in his eyes, which he tried to keep from burning.

'How say you then, John Ridd,' he cried, stretching out one hand, like Elijah; 'is this a thing of the sort you love? Is this what you are used to?'

'So please your worship,' I answered; 'no kind of violence can surprise us, since first came Doones upon Exmoor. Up to that time none heard of harm; except of taking a purse, maybe, or cutting a strange sheep's throat. And the poor folk who did this were hanged, with some benefit of clergy. But ever since the Doones came first, we are used to anything.'

'Thou varlet,' cried the Counsellor, with the colour of his eyes quite changed with the sparkles of his fury; 'is this the way we are to deal with such a low-bred clod as thou? To question the doings of our people, and to talk of clergy! What, dream you not that we could have clergy, and of the right sort, too, if only we cared to have them? Tush! Am I to spend my time arguing with a plough-tail Bob?'

'If your worship will hearken to me,' I answered very modestly, not wishing to speak harshly, with Lorna looking up at me; 'there are many things that might be said without any kind of argument, which I would never wish to try with one of your worship's learning. And in the first place it seems to me that if our fathers hated one another bitterly, yet neither won the victory, only mutual discomfiture; surely that is but a reason why we should be wiser than they, and make it up in this generation by goodwill and loving'—

'Oh, John, you wiser than your father!' mother broke upon me here; 'not but what you might be as wise, when you come to be old enough.'

'Young people of the present age,' said the Counsellor severely, 'have no right feeling of any sort, upon the simplest matter. Lorna Doone, stand forth from contact with that heir of parricide; and state in your own mellifluous voice, whether you regard this slaughter as a pleasant trifle.'

'You know, without any words of mine,' she answered very softly, yet not withdrawing from my hand, 'that although I have been seasoned well to every kind of outrage, among my gentle relatives, I have not yet so purely lost all sense of right and wrong as to receive what you have said, as lightly as you declared it. You think it a happy basis for our future concord. I do not quite think that, my uncle; neither do I quite believe that a word of it is true. In our happy valley, nine-tenths of what is said is false; and you were always wont to argue that true and false are but a blind turned upon a pivot. Without any failure of respect for your character, good uncle, I decline politely to believe a word of what you have told me. And even if it were proved to me, all I can say is this, if my John will have me, I am his for ever.'

This long speech was too much for her; she had overrated her strength about it, and the sustenance of irony. So at last she fell into my arms, which had long been waiting for her; and there she lay with no other sound, except a gurgling in her throat.

'You old villain,' cried my mother, shaking her fist at the Counsellor, while I could do nothing else but hold, and bend across, my darling, and whisper to deaf ears; 'What is the good of the quality; if this is all that comes of it? Out of the way! You know the words that make the deadly mischief; but not the ways that heal them. Give me that bottle, if hands you have; what is the use of Counsellors?'

I saw that dear mother was carried away; and indeed I myself was something like it; with the pale face upon my bosom, and the heaving of the heart, and the heat and cold all through me, as my darling breathed or lay. Meanwhile the Counsellor stood back, and seemed a little sorry; although of course it was not in his power to be at all ashamed of himself.

'My sweet love, my darling child,' our mother went on to Lorna, in a way that I shall never forget, though I live to be a hundred; 'pretty pet, not a word of it is true, upon that old liar's oath; and if every word were true, poor chick, you should have our John all the more for it. You and John were made by God and meant for one another, whatever falls between you. Little lamb, look up and speak: here is your own John and I; and the devil take the Counsellor.'

I was amazed at mother's words, being so unlike her; while I loved her all the more because she forgot herself so. In another moment in ran Annie, ay and Lizzie also, knowing by some mystic sense (which I have often noticed, but never could explain) that something was astir, belonging to the world of women, yet foreign to the eyes of men. And now the Counsellor, being well-born, although such a heartless miscreant, beckoned to me to come away; which I, being smothered with women, was only too glad to do, as soon as my own love would let go of me.

'That is the worst of them,' said the old man; when I had led him into our kitchen, with an apology at every step, and given him hot schnapps and water, and a cigarro of brave Tom Faggus: 'you never can say much, sir, in the way of reasoning (however gently meant and put) but what these women will fly out. It is wiser to put a wild bird in a cage, and expect him to sit and look at you, and chirp without a feather rumpled, than it is to expect a woman to answer reason reasonably.' Saying this, he looked at his puff of smoke as if it contained more reason.

'I am sure I do not know, sir,' I answered according to a phrase which has always been my favourite, on account of its general truth: moreover, he was now our guest, and had right to be treated accordingly: 'I am, as you see, not acquainted with the ways of women, except my mother and sisters.'

'Except not even them, my son, said the Counsellor, now having finished his glass, without much consultation about it; 'if you once understand your mother and sisters—why you understand the lot of them.'

He made a twist in his cloud of smoke, and dashed his finger through it, so that I could not follow his meaning, and in manners liked not to press him.

'Now of this business, John,' he said, after getting to the bottom of the second glass, and having a trifle or so to eat, and praising our chimney-corner; 'taking you on the whole, you know, you are wonderfully good people; and instead of giving me up to the soldiers, as you might have done, you are doing your best to make me drunk.'

'Not at all, sir,' I answered; 'not at all, your worship. Let me mix you another glass. We rarely have a great gentleman by the side of our embers and oven. I only beg your pardon, sir, that my sister Annie (who knows where to find all the good pans and the lard) could not wait upon you this evening; and I fear they have done it with dripping instead, and in a pan with the bottom burned. But old Betty quite loses her head sometimes, by dint of over-scolding.'

'My son,' replied the Counsellor, standing across the front of the fire, to prove his strict sobriety: 'I meant to come down upon you to-night; but you have turned the tables upon me. Not through any skill on your part, nor through any paltry weakness as to love (and all that stuff, which boys and girls spin tops at, or knock dolls' noses together), but through your simple way of taking me, as a man to be believed; combined with the comfort of this place, and the choice tobacco and cordials. I have not enjoyed an evening so much, God bless me if I know when!'

'Your worship,' said I, 'makes me more proud than I well know what to do with. Of all the things that please and lead us into happy sleep at night, the first and chiefest is to think that we have pleased a visitor.'

'Then, John, thou hast deserved good sleep; for I am not pleased easily. But although our family is not so high now as it hath been, I have enough of the gentleman left to be pleased when good people try me. My father, Sir Ensor, was better than I in this great element of birth, and my son Carver is far worse. Aetas parentum, what is it, my boy? I hear that you have been at a grammar-school.'

'So I have, your worship, and at a very good one; but I only got far enough to make more tail than head of Latin.'

'Let that pass,' said the Counsellor; 'John, thou art all the wiser.' And the old man shook his hoary locks, as if Latin had been his ruin. I looked at him sadly, and wondered whether it might have so ruined me, but for God's mercy in stopping it.

Chapter LII The Way to Make the Cream Rise

That night the reverend Counsellor, not being in such state of mind as ought to go alone, kindly took our best old bedstead, carved in panels, well enough, with the woman of Samaria. I set him up, both straight and heavy, so that he need but close both eyes, and keep his mouth just open; and in the morning he was thankful for all that he could remember.

I, for my part, scarcely knew whether he really had begun to feel goodwill towards us, and to see that nothing else could be of any use to him; or whether he was merely acting, so as to deceive us. And it had struck me, several times, that he had made a great deal more of the spirit he had taken than the quantity would warrant, with a man so wise and solid. Neither did I quite understand a little story which Lorna told me, how that in the night awaking, she had heard, or seemed to hear, a sound of feeling in her room; as if there had been some one groping carefully among the things within her drawers or wardrobe-closet. But the noise had ceased at once, she said, when she sat up in bed and listened; and knowing how many mice we had, she took courage and fell asleep again.

After breakfast, the Counsellor (who looked no whit the worse for schnapps, but even more grave and venerable) followed our Annie into the dairy, to see how we managed the clotted cream, of which he had eaten a basinful. And thereupon they talked a little; and Annie thought him a fine old gentleman, and a very just one; for he had nobly condemned the people who spoke against Tom Faggus.

'Your honour must plainly understand,' said Annie, being now alone with him, and spreading out her light quick hands over the pans, like butterflies, 'that they are brought in here to cool, after being set in the basin-holes, with the wood-ash under them, which I showed you in the back-kitchen. And they must have very little heat, not enough to simmer even; only just to make the bubbles rise, and the scum upon the top set thick; and after that, it clots as firm—oh, as firm as my two hands be.'

'Have you ever heard,' asked the Counsellor, who enjoyed this talk with Annie, 'that if you pass across the top, without breaking the surface, a string of beads, or polished glass, or anything of that kind, the cream will set three times as solid, and in thrice the quantity?'

'No, sir; I have never heard that,' said Annie, staring with all her simple eyes; 'what a thing it is to read books, and grow learned! But it is very easy to try it: I will get my coral necklace; it will not be witchcraft, will it, sir?'

'Certainly not,' the old man replied; 'I will make the experiment myself; and you may trust me not to be hurt, my dear. But coral will not do, my child, neither will anything coloured. The beads must be of plain common glass; but the brighter they are the better.'

'Then I know the very thing,' cried Annie; 'as bright as bright can be, and without any colour in it, except in the sun or candle light. Dearest Lorna has the very thing, a necklace of some old glass-beads, or I think they called them jewels: she will be too glad to lend it to us. I will go for it, in a moment.'

'My dear, it cannot be half so bright as your own pretty eyes. But remember one thing, Annie, you must not say what it is for; or even that I am going to use it, or anything at all about it; else the charm will be broken. Bring it here, without a word; if you know where she keeps it.'

'To be sure I do,' she answered; 'John used to keep it for her. But she took it away from him last week, and she wore it when—I mean when somebody was here; and he said it was very valuable, and spoke with great learning about it, and called it by some particular name, which I forget at this moment. But valuable or not, we cannot hurt it, can we, sir, by passing it over the cream-pan?'

'Hurt it!' cried the Counsellor: 'nay, we shall do it good, my dear. It will help to raise the cream: and you may take my word for it, young maiden, none can do good in this world, without in turn receiving it.' Pronouncing this great sentiment, he looked so grand and benevolent, that Annie (as she said afterwards) could scarce forbear from kissing him, yet feared to take the liberty. Therefore, she only ran away to fetch my Lorna's necklace.

Now as luck would have it—whether good luck or otherwise, you must not judge too hastily,—my darling had taken it into her head, only a day or two before, that I was far too valuable to be trusted with her necklace. Now that she had some idea of its price and quality, she had begun to fear that some one, perhaps even Squire Faggus (in whom her faith was illiberal), might form designs against my health, to win the bauble from me. So, with many pretty coaxings, she had led me to give it up; which, except for her own sake, I was glad enough to do, misliking a charge of such importance.

Therefore Annie found it sparkling in the little secret hole, near the head of Lorna's bed, which she herself had recommended for its safer custody; and without a word to any one she brought it down, and danced it in the air before the Counsellor, for him to admire its lustre.

'Oh, that old thing!' said the gentleman, in a tone of some contempt; 'I remember that old thing well enough. However, for want of a better, no doubt it will answer our purpose. Three times three, I pass it over. Crinkleum, crankum, grass and clover! What are you feared of, you silly child?'

'Good sir, it is perfect witchcraft! I am sure of that, because it rhymes. Oh, what would mother say to me? Shall I ever go to heaven again? Oh, I see the cream already!'

'To be sure you do; but you must not look, or the whole charm will be broken, and the devil will fly away with the pan, and drown every cow you have got in it.'

'Oh, sir, it is too horrible. How could you lead me to such a sin? Away with thee, witch of Endor!'

For the door began to creak, and a broom appeared suddenly in the opening, with our Betty, no doubt, behind it. But Annie, in the greatest terror, slammed the door, and bolted it, and then turned again to the Counsellor; yet looking at his face, had not the courage to reproach him.

For his eyes rolled like two blazing barrels, and his white shagged brows were knit across them, and his forehead scowled in black furrows, so that Annie said that if she ever saw the devil, she saw him then, and no mistake. Whether the old man wished to scare her, or whether he was trying not to laugh, is more than I can tell you.

'Now,' he said, in a deep stern whisper; 'not a word of this to a living soul; neither must you, nor any other enter this place for three hours at least. By that time the charm will have done its work: the pan will be cream to the bottom; and you will bless me for a secret which will make your fortune. Put the bauble under this pannikin; which none must lift for a day and a night. Have no fear, my simple wench; not a breath of harm shall come to you, if you obey my orders'

'Oh, that I will, sir, that I will: if you will only tell me what to do.'

'Go to your room, without so much as a single word to any one. Bolt yourself in, and for three hours now, read the Lord's Prayer backwards.'

Poor Annie was only too glad to escape, upon these conditions; and the Counsellor kissed her upon the forehead and told her not to make her eyes red, because they were much too sweet and pretty. She dropped them at this, with a sob and a curtsey, and ran away to her bedroom; but as for reading the Lord's Prayer backwards, that was much beyond her; and she had not done three words quite right, before the three hours expired.

Meanwhile the Counsellor was gone. He bade our mother adieu, with so much dignity of bearing, and such warmth of gratitude, and the high-bred courtesy of the old school (now fast disappearing), that when he was gone, dear mother fell back on the chair which he had used last night, as if it would teach her the graces. And for more than an hour she made believe not to know what there was for dinner.

'Oh, the wickedness of the world! Oh, the lies that are told of people—or rather I mean the falsehoods—because a man is better born, and has better manners! Why, Lorna, how is it that you never speak about your charming uncle? Did you notice, Lizzie, how his silver hair was waving upon his velvet collar, and how white his hands were, and every nail like an acorn; only pink like shell-fish, or at least like shells? And the way he bowed, and dropped his eyes, from his pure respect for me! And then, that he would not even speak, on account of his emotion; but pressed my hand in silence! Oh, Lizzie, you have read me beautiful things about Sir Gallyhead, and the rest; but nothing to equal Sir Counsellor.'

'You had better marry him, madam,' said I, coming in very sternly; though I knew I ought not to say it: 'he can repay your adoration. He has stolen a hundred thousand pounds.'

'John,' cried my mother, 'you are mad!' And yet she turned as pale as death; for women are so quick at turning; and she inkled what it was.

'Of course I am, mother; mad about the marvels of Sir Galahad. He has gone off with my Lorna's necklace. Fifty farms like ours can never make it good to Lorna.'

Hereupon ensued grim silence. Mother looked at Lizzie's face, for she could not look at me; and Lizzie looked at me, to know: and as for me,

I could have stamped almost on the heart of any one. It was not the value of the necklace—I am not so low a hound as that—nor was it even the damned folly shown by every one of us—it was the thought of Lorna's sorrow for her ancient plaything; and even more, my fury at the breach of hospitality.

But Lorna came up to me softly, as a woman should always come; and she laid one hand upon my shoulder; and she only looked at me. She even seemed to fear to look, and dropped her eyes, and sighed at me. Without a word, I knew by that, how I must have looked like Satan; and the evil spirit left my heart; when she had made me think of it.

'Darling John, did you want me to think that you cared for my money, more than for me?'

I led her away from the rest of them, being desirous of explaining things, when I saw the depth of her nature opened, like an everlasting well, to me. But she would not let me say a word, or do anything by ourselves, as it were: she said, 'Your duty is to your mother: this blow is on her, and not on me.'

I saw that she was right; though how she knew it is beyond me; and I asked her just to go in front, and bring my mother round a little. For I must let my passion pass: it may drop its weapons quickly; but it cannot come and go, before a man has time to think.

Then Lorna went up to my mother, who was still in the chair of elegance; and she took her by both hands, and said,—

'Dearest mother, I shall fret so, if I see you fretting. And to fret will kill me, mother. They have always told me so.'

Poor mother bent on Lorna's shoulder, without thought of attitude, and laid her cheek on Lorna's breast, and sobbed till Lizzie was jealous, and came with two pocket-handkerchiefs. As for me, my heart was lighter (if they would only dry their eyes, and come round by dinnertime) than it had been since the day on which Tom Faggus discovered the value of that blessed and cursed necklace. None could say that I wanted Lorna for her money now. And perhaps the Doones would let me have her; now that her property was gone.

But who shall tell of Annie's grief? The poor little thing would have staked her life upon finding the trinket, in all its beauty, lying under the pannikin. She proudly challenged me to lift it—which I had done, long ere that, of course—if only I would take the risk of the spell for my incredulity. I told her not to talk of spells, until she could spell a word backwards; and then to look into the pan where the charmed cream should be. She would not acknowledge that the cream was the same as all the rest was: and indeed it was not quite the same, for the points of poor Lorna's diamonds had made a few star-rays across the rich firm crust of yellow.

But when we raised the pannikin, and there was nothing under it, poor Annie fell against the wall, which had been whitened lately; and her face put all the white to scorn. My love, who was as fond of her, as if she had known her for fifty years, hereupon ran up and caught her, and abused all diamonds. I will dwell no more upon Annie's grief, because we felt it all so much. But I could not help telling her, if she wanted a witch, to seek good Mother Melldrum, a legitimate performer.

That same night Master Jeremy Stickles (of whose absence the Counsellor must have known) came back, with all equipment ready for the grand attack. Now the Doones knew, quite as well as we did, that this attack was threatening; and that but for the wonderful weather it would have been made long ago. Therefore we, or at least our people (for I was doubtful about going), were sure to meet with a good resistance, and due preparation.

It was very strange to hear and see, and quite impossible to account for, that now some hundreds of country people (who feared to whisper so much as a word against the Doones a year ago, and would sooner have thought of attacking a church, in service time, than Glen Doone) now sharpened their old cutlasses, and laid pitch-forks on the grindstone, and bragged at every village cross, as if each would kill ten Doones himself, neither care to wipe his hands afterwards. And this fierce bravery, and tall contempt, had been growing ever since the news of the attack upon our premises had taken good people by surprise; at least as concerned the issue.

Jeremy Stickles laughed heartily about Annie's new manner of charming the cream; but he looked very grave at the loss of the jewels, so soon as he knew their value.

'My son,' he exclaimed, 'this is very heavy. It will go ill with all of you to make good this loss, as I fear that you will have to do.'

'What!' cried I, with my blood running cold. 'We make good the loss, Master Stickles! Every farthing we have in the world, and the labour of our lives to boot, will never make good the tenth of it.'

'It would cut me to the heart,' he answered, laying his hand on mine, 'to hear of such a deadly blow to you and your good mother. And this farm; how long, John, has it been in your family?'

'For at least six hundred years,' I said, with a foolish pride that was only too like to end in groans; 'and some people say, by a Royal grant, in the time of the great King Alfred. At any rate, a Ridd was with him throughout all his hiding-time. We have always held by the King and crown: surely none will turn us out, unless we are guilty of treason?'

'My son,' replied Jeremy very gently, so that I could love him for it, 'not a word to your good mother of this unlucky matter. Keep it to yourself, my boy, and try to think but little of it. After all, I may be wrong: at any rate, least said best mended.'

'But Jeremy, dear Jeremy, how can I bear to leave it so? Do you suppose that I can sleep, and eat my food, and go about, and look at other people, as if nothing at all had happened? And all the time have it on my mind, that not an acre of all the land, nor even our old sheep-dog, belongs to us, of right at all! It is more than I can do, Jeremy. Let me talk, and know the worst of it.'

'Very well,' replied Master Stickles, seeing that both the doors were closed; 'I thought that nothing could move you, John; or I never would have told you. Likely enough I am quite wrong; and God send that I be so. But what I guessed at some time back seems more than a guess, now that you have told me about these wondrous jewels. Now will you keep, as close as death, every word I tell you?'

'By the honour of a man, I will. Until you yourself release me.'

'That is quite enough, John. From you I want no oath; which, according to my experience, tempts a man to lie the more, by making it more important. I know you now too well to swear you, though I have the power. Now, my lad, what I have to say will scare your mind in one way, and ease it in another. I think that you have been hard pressed—I can read you like a book, John—by something which that old villain said, before he stole the necklace. You have tried not to dwell upon it; you have even tried to make light of it for the sake of the women: but on the whole it has grieved you more than even this dastard robbery.'

'It would have done so, Jeremy Stickles, if I could once have believed it. And even without much belief, it is so against our manners, that it makes me miserable. Only think of loving Lorna, only think of kissing her; and then remembering that her father had destroyed the life of mine!'

'Only think,' said Master Stickles, imitating my very voice, 'of Lorna loving you, John, of Lorna kissing you, John; and all the while saying to herself, "this man's father murdered mine." Now look at it in Lorna's way as well as in your own way. How one-sided all men are!'

'I may look at it in fifty ways, and yet no good will come of it. Jeremy, I confess to you, that I tried to make the best of it; partly to baffle the Counsellor, and partly because my darling needed my help, and bore it so, and behaved to me so nobly. But to you in secret, I am not ashamed to say that a woman may look over this easier than a man may.'

'Because her nature is larger, my son, when she truly loves; although her mind be smaller. Now, if I can ease you from this secret burden, will you bear, with strength and courage, the other which I plant on you?'

'I will do my best,' said I.

'No man can do more,' said he and so began his story.

Chapter LIII Jeremy Finds Out Something

'You know, my son,' said Jeremy Stickles, with a good pull at his pipe, because he was going to talk so much, and putting his legs well along the settle; 'it has been my duty, for a wearier time than I care to think of (and which would have been unbearable, except for your great kindness), to search this neighbourhood narrowly, and learn everything about everybody. Now the neighbourhood itself is queer; and people have different ways of thinking from what we are used to in London. For instance now, among your folk, when any piece of news is told, or any man's conduct spoken of, the very first question that arises in your mind is this—"Was this action kind and good?" Long after that, you say to yourselves, "does the law enjoin or forbid this thing?" Now here is your fundamental error:

for among all truly civilised people the foremost of all questions is, "how stands the law herein?" And if the law approve, no need for any further questioning. That this is so, you may take my word: for I know the law pretty thoroughly.

'Very well; I need not say any more about that, for I have shown that you are all quite wrong. I only speak of this savage tendency, because it explains so many things which have puzzled me among you, and most of all your kindness to men whom you never saw before; which is an utterly illegal thing. It also explains your toleration of these outlaw Doones so long. If your views of law had been correct, and law an element of your lives, these robbers could never have been indulged for so many years amongst you: but you must have abated the nuisance.'

'Now, Stickles,' I cried, 'this is too bad!' he was delivering himself so grandly. 'Why you yourself have been amongst us, as the balance, and sceptre, and sword of law, for nigh upon a twelvemonth; and have you abated the nuisance, or even cared to do it, until they began to shoot at you?'

'My son,' he replied, 'your argument is quite beside the purpose, and only tends to prove more clearly that which I have said of you. However, if you wish to hear my story, no more interruptions. I may not have a chance to tell you, perhaps for weeks, or I know not when, if once those yellows and reds arrive, and be blessed to them, the lubbers! Well, it may be six months ago, or it may be seven, at any rate a good while before that cursed frost began, the mere name of which sends a shiver down every bone of my body, when I was riding one afternoon from Dulverton to Watchett'—

'Dulverton to Watchett!' I cried. 'Now what does that remind me of? I am sure, I remember something—'

'Remember this, John, if anything—that another word from thee, and thou hast no more of mine. Well, I was a little weary perhaps, having been plagued at Dulverton with the grossness of the people. For they would tell me nothing at all about their fellow-townsmen, your worthy Uncle Huckaback, except that he was a God-fearing man, and they only wished I was like him. I blessed myself for a stupid fool, in thinking to have pumped them; for by this time I might have known that, through your Western homeliness, every man in his own country is something more than a prophet. And I felt, of course, that I had done more harm than good by questioning; inasmuch as every soul in the place would run straightway and inform him that the King's man from the other side of the forest had been sifting out his ways and works.'

'Ah,' I cried, for I could not help it; 'you begin to understand at last, that we are not quite such a set of oafs, as you at first believed us.'

'I was riding on from Dulverton,' he resumed, with great severity, yet threatening me no more, which checked me more than fifty threats: 'and it was late in the afternoon, and I was growing weary. The road (if road it could be called) 'turned suddenly down from the higher land to the very brink of the sea; and rounding a little jut of cliff, I met the roar of the breakers. My horse was scared, and leaped aside; for a northerly wind was piping, and driving hunks of foam across, as children scatter snow-balls. But he only sank to his fetlocks in the dry sand, piled with pop-weed: and I tried to make him face the waves; and then I looked about me.

'Watchett town was not to be seen, on account of a little foreland, a mile or more upon my course, and standing to the right of me. There was room enough below the cliffs (which are nothing there to yours, John), for horse and man to get along, although the tide was running high with a northerly gale to back it. But close at hand and in the corner, drawn above the yellow sands and long eye-brows of rackweed, as snug a little house blinked on me as ever I saw, or wished to see.

'You know that I am not luxurious, neither in any way given to the common lusts of the flesh, John. My father never allowed his hair to grow a fourth part of an inch in length, and he was a thoroughly godly man; and I try to follow in his footsteps, whenever I think about it. Nevertheless, I do assure you that my view of that little house and the way the lights were twinkling, so different from the cold and darkness of the rolling sea, moved the ancient Adam in me, if he could he found to move. I love not a house with too many windows: being out of house and doors some three-quarters of my time, when I get inside a house I like to feel the difference. Air and light are good for people who have any lack of them; and if a man once talks about them, 'tis enough to prove his need of them. But, as you well know, John Ridd, the horse who has been at work all day, with the sunshine in his eyes, sleeps better in dark stables, and needs no moon to help him.

'Seeing therefore that this same inn had four windows, and no more, I thought to myself how snug it was, and how beautiful I could sleep there. And so I made the old horse draw hand, which he was only too glad to do, and we clomb above the spring-tide mark, and over a little piece of turf, and struck the door of the hostelry. Some one came and peeped at me through the lattice overhead, which was full of bulls' eyes; and then the bolt was drawn back, and a woman met me very courteously. A dark and foreign-looking woman, very hot of blood, I doubt, but not altogether a bad one. And she waited for me to speak first, which an Englishwoman would not have done.

'"Can I rest here for the night?" I asked, with a lift of my hat to her; for she was no provincial dame, who would stare at me for the courtesy; "my horse is weary from the sloughs, and myself but little better: beside that, we both are famished."

'"Yes, sir, you can rest and welcome. But of food, I fear, there is but little, unless of the common order. Our fishers would have drawn the nets, but the waves were violent. However, we have—what you call it? I never can remember, it is so hard to say—the flesh of the hog salted."

'"Bacon!" said I; "what can be better? And half dozen of eggs with it, and a quart of fresh-drawn ale. You make me rage with hunger, madam. Is it cruelty, or hospitality?"

'"Ah, good!" she replied, with a merry smile, full of southern sunshine: "you are not of the men round here; you can think, and you can laugh!"

'"And most of all, I can eat, good madam. In that way I shall astonish you; even more than by my intellect."

'She laughed aloud, and swung her shoulders, as your natives cannot do; and then she called a little maid to lead my horse to stable. However, I preferred to see that matter done myself, and told her to send the little maid for the frying-pan and the egg-box.

'Whether it were my natural wit and elegance of manner; or whether it were my London freedom and knowledge of the world; or (which is perhaps the most probable, because the least pleasing supposition) my ready and permanent appetite, and appreciation of garlic—I leave you to decide, John: but perhaps all three combined to recommend me to the graces of my charming hostess. When I say "charming," I mean of course by manners and by intelligence, and most of all by cooking; for as regards external charms (most fleeting and fallacious) hers had ceased to cause distress, for I cannot say how many years. She said that it was the climate—for even upon that subject she requested my opinion—and I answered, "if there be a change, let madam blame the seasons."

'However, not to dwell too much upon our little pleasantries (for I always get on with these foreign women better than with your Molls and Pegs), I became, not inquisitive, but reasonably desirous to know, by what strange hap or hazard, a clever and a handsome woman, as she must have been some day, a woman moreover with great contempt for the rustic minds around her, could have settled here in this lonely inn, with only the waves for company, and a boorish husband who slaved all day in turning a potter's wheel at Watchett. And what was the meaning of the emblem set above her doorway, a very unattractive cat sitting in a ruined tree?

'However, I had not very long to strain my curiosity; for when she found out who I was, and how I held the King's commission, and might be called an officer, her desire to tell me all was more than equal to mine of hearing it. Many and many a day, she had longed for some one both skilful and trustworthy, most of all for some one bearing warrant from a court of justice. But the magistrates of the neighbourhood would have nothing to say to her, declaring that she was a crack-brained woman, and a wicked, and even a foreign one.

'With many grimaces she assured me that never by her own free-will would she have lived so many years in that hateful country, where the sky for half the year was fog, and rain for nearly the other half. It was so the very night when first her evil fortune brought her there; and so no doubt it would be, long after it had killed her. But if I wished to know the reason of her being there, she would tell me in few words, which I will repeat as briefly.

'By birth she was an Italian, from the mountains of Apulia, who had gone to Rome to seek her fortunes, after being badly treated in some love-affair. Her Christian name was Benita; as for her surname, that could make no difference to any one. Being a quick and active girl, and resolved to work down her troubles, she found employment in a large hotel; and rising gradually, began to send money to her parents. And here she might have thriven well, and married well under sunny skies, and been a happy woman, but that some black day sent thither a rich and noble English family, eager to behold the Pope. It was not, however, their fervent longing for the Holy Father which had brought them to St. Peter's roof; but rather their own bad luck in making their home too hot to hold them. For although in the main good Catholics, and pleasant receivers of anything, one of their number had given offence, by the folly of trying to think for himself. Some bitter feud had been among them, Benita knew not how it was; and the sister of the nobleman who had died quite lately was married to the rival claimant, whom they all detested. It was something about dividing land; Benita knew not what it was.

'But this Benita did know, that they were all great people, and rich, and very liberal; so that when they offered to take her, to attend to the children, and to speak the language for them, and to comfort the lady, she was only too glad to go, little foreseeing the end of it. Moreover, she loved the children so, from their pretty ways and that, and the things they gave her, and the style of their dresses, that it would have broken her heart almost never to see the dears again.

'And so, in a very evil hour, she accepted the service of the noble Englishman, and sent her father an old shoe filled to the tongue with money, and trusted herself to fortune. But even before she went, she knew that it could not turn out well; for the laurel leaf which she threw on the fire would not crackle even once, and the horn of the goat came wrong in the twist, and the heel of her foot was shining. This made her sigh at the starting-time; and after that what could you hope for?

'However, at first all things went well. My Lord was as gay as gay could be: and never would come inside the carriage, when a decent horse could be got to ride. He would gallop in front, at a reckless pace, without a weapon of any kind, delighted with the pure blue air, and throwing his heart around him. Benita had never seen any man so admirable, and so childish. As innocent as an infant; and not only contented, but noisily happy with anything. Only other people must share his joy; and the shadow of sorrow scattered it, though it were but the shade of poverty.

'Here Benita wept a little; and I liked her none the less, and believed her ten times more; in virtue of a tear or two.

'And so they travelled through Northern Italy, and throughout the south of France, making their way anyhow; sometimes in coaches, sometimes in carts, sometimes upon mule-back, sometimes even a-foot and weary; but always as happy as could be. The children laughed, and grew, and throve (especially the young lady, the elder of the two), and Benita began to think that omens must not be relied upon. But suddenly her faith in omens was confirmed for ever.

'My Lord, who was quite a young man still, and laughed at English arrogance, rode on in front of his wife and friends, to catch the first of a famous view, on the French side of the Pyrenee hills. He kissed his hand to his wife, and said that he would save her the trouble of coming. For those two were so one in one, that they could make each other know whatever he or she had felt. And so my Lord went round the corner, with a fine young horse leaping up at the steps.

'They waited for him, long and long; but he never came again; and within a week, his mangled body lay in a little chapel-yard; and if the priests only said a quarter of the prayers they took the money for, God knows they can have no throats left; only a relaxation.

'My lady dwelled for six months more—it is a melancholy tale (what true tale is not so?)—scarcely able to believe that all her fright was not a dream. She would not wear a piece or shape of any mourning-clothes; she would not have a person cry, or any sorrow among us. She simply disbelieved the thing, and trusted God to right it. The Protestants, who have no faith, cannot understand this feeling. Enough that so it was; and so my Lady went to heaven.

'For when the snow came down in autumn on the roots of the Pyrenees, and the chapel-yard was white with it, many people told the lady that it was time for her to go. And the strongest plea of all was this, that now she bore another hope of repeating her husband's virtues. So at the end of October, when wolves came down to the farm-lands, the little English family went home towards their England.

'They landed somewhere on the Devonshire coast, ten or eleven years agone, and stayed some days at Exeter; and set out thence in a hired coach, without any proper attendance, for Watchett, in the north of Somerset. For the lady owned a quiet mansion in the neighbourhood of that town, and her one desire was to find refuge there, and to meet her lord, who was sure to come (she said) when he heard of his new infant. Therefore with only two serving-men and two maids (including Benita), the party set forth from Exeter, and lay the first night at Bampton.

'On the following morn they started bravely, with earnest hope of arriving at their journey's end by daylight. But the roads were soft and very deep, and the sloughs were out in places; and the heavy coach broke down in the axle, and needed mending at Dulverton; and so they lost three hours or more, and would have been wiser to sleep there. But her ladyship would not hear of it; she must be home that night, she said, and her husband would be waiting. How could she keep him waiting now, after such a long, long time?

'Therefore, although it was afternoon, and the year now come to December, the horses were put to again, and the heavy coach went up the hill, with the lady and her two children, and Benita, sitting inside of it; the other maid, and two serving-men (each man with a great blunderbuss) mounted upon the outside; and upon the horses three Exeter postilions. Much had been said at Dulverton, and even back at Bampton, about some great freebooters, to whom all Exmoor owed suit and service, and paid them very punctually. Both the serving-men were scared, even over their ale, by this. But the lady only said, "Drive on; I know a little of highwaymen: they never rob a lady."

'Through the fog and through the muck the coach went on, as best it might; sometimes foundered in a slough, with half of the horses splashing it, and some-times knuckled up on a bank, and straining across the middle, while all the horses kicked at it. However, they went on till dark as well as might be expected. But when they came, all thanking God, to the pitch and slope of the sea-bank, leading on towards Watchett town, and where my horse had shied so, there the little boy jumped up, and clapped his hands at the water; and there (as Benita said) they met their fate, and could not fly it.

'Although it was past the dusk of day, the silver light from the sea flowed in, and showed the cliffs, and the gray sand-line, and the drifts of wreck, and wrack-weed. It showed them also a troop of horsemen, waiting under a rock hard by, and ready to dash upon them. The postilions lashed towards the sea, and the horses strove in the depth of sand, and the serving-men cocked their blunder-busses, and cowered away behind them; but the lady stood up in the carriage bravely, and neither screamed nor spoke, but hid her son behind her. Meanwhile the drivers drove into the sea, till the leading horses were swimming.

'But before the waves came into the coach, a score of fierce men were round it. They cursed the postilions for mad cowards, and cut the traces, and seized the wheel-horses, all-wild with dismay in the wet and the dark. Then, while the carriage was heeling over, and well-nigh upset in the water, the lady exclaimed, "I know that man! He is our ancient enemy;" and Benita (foreseeing that all their boxes would be turned inside out, or carried away), snatched the most valuable of the jewels, a magnificent necklace of diamonds, and cast it over the little girl's head, and buried it under her travelling-cloak, hoping to save it. Then a great wave, crested with foam, rolled in, and the coach was thrown on its side, and the sea rushed in at the top and the windows, upon shrieking, and clashing, and fainting away.

'What followed Benita knew not, as one might well suppose, herself being stunned by a blow on the head, beside being palsied with terror. "See, I have the mark now," she said, "where the jamb of the door came down on me!" But when she recovered her senses, she found herself lying upon the sand, the robbers were out of sight, and one of the serving-men was bathing her forehead with sea water. For this she rated him well, having taken already too much of that article; and then she arose and ran to her mistress, who was sitting upright on a little rock, with her dead boy's face to her bosom, sometimes gazing upon him, and sometimes questing round for the other one.

'Although there were torches and links around, and she looked at her child by the light of them, no one dared to approach the lady, or speak, or try to help her. Each man whispered his fellow to go, but each hung back himself, and muttered that it was too awful to meddle with. And there she would have sat all night, with the fine little fellow stone dead in her arms, and her tearless eyes dwelling upon him, and her heart but not her mind thinking, only that the Italian women stole up softly to her side, and whispered; "It is the will of God."

'"So it always seems to be," were all the words the mother' answered; and then she fell on Benita's neck; and the men were ashamed to be near her weeping; and a sailor lay down and bellowed. Surely these men are the best.

'Before the light of the morning came along the tide to Watchett my Lady had met her husband. They took her into the town that night, but not to her own castle; and so the power of womanhood (which is itself maternity) came over swiftly upon her. The lady, whom all people loved (though at certain times particular), lies in Watchett little churchyard, with son and heir at her right hand, and a little babe, of sex unknown, sleeping on her bosom.

'This is a miserable tale,' said Jeremy Stickles brightly; 'hand me over the schnapps, my boy. What fools we are to spoil our eyes for other people's troubles! Enough of our own to keep them clean, although we all were chimney-sweeps. There is nothing like good hollands, when a man becomes too sensitive. Restore the action of the glands; that is my rule, after weeping. Let me make you another, John. You are quite low-spirited.'

But although Master Jeremy carried on so (as became his manhood), and laughed at the sailor's bellowing; bless his heart, I knew as well that tears were in his brave keen eyes, as if I had dared to look for them, or to show mine own.

'And what was the lady's name?' I asked; 'and what became of the little girl? And why did the woman stay there?'

'Well!' cried Jeremy Stickles, only too glad to be cheerful again: 'talk of a woman after that! As we used to say at school—"Who dragged whom, how many times, in what manner, round the wall of what?" But to begin, last first, my John (as becomes a woman): Benita stayed in that blessed place, because she could not get away from it. The Doones—if Doones indeed they were, about which you of course know best—took every stiver out of the carriage: wet or dry they took it. And Benita could never get her wages: for the whole affair is in Chancery, and they have appointed a receiver.'

'Whew!' said I, knowing something of London, and sorry for Benita's chance.

'So the poor thing was compelled to drop all thought of Apulia, and settle down on the brink of Exmoor, where you get all its evils, without the good to balance them. She married a man who turned a wheel for making the blue Watchett ware, partly because he could give her a house, and partly because he proved himself a good soul towards my Lady. There they are, and have three children; and there you may go and visit them.'

'I understand all that, Jeremy, though you do tell things too quickly, and I would rather have John Fry's style; for he leaves one time for his words to melt. Now for my second question. What became of the little maid?'

'You great oaf!' cried Jeremy Stickles: 'you are rather more likely to know, I should think, than any one else in all the kingdoms.'

'If I knew, I should not ask you. Jeremy Stickles, do try to be neither conceited nor thick-headed.'

'I will when you are neither,' answered Master Jeremy; 'but you occupy all the room, John. No one else can get in with you there.'

'Very well then, let me out. Take me down in both ways.'

'If ever you were taken down; you must have your double joints ready now. And yet in other ways you will be as proud and set up as Lucifer. As certain sure as I stand here, that little maid is Lorna Doone.'

Chapter LIV Mutual Discomfiture

It must not be supposed that I was altogether so thick-headed as Jeremy would have made me out. But it is part of my character that I like other people to think me slow, and to labour hard to enlighten me, while all the time I can say to myself, 'This man is shallower than I am; it is pleasant to see his shoals come up while he is sounding mine so!' Not that I would so behave, God forbid, with anybody (be it man or woman) who in simple heart approached me, with no gauge of intellect. But when the upper hand is taken, upon the faith of one's patience, by a man of even smaller wits (not that Jeremy was that, neither could he have lived to be thought so), why, it naturally happens, that we knuckle under, with an ounce of indignation.

Jeremy's tale would have moved me greatly both with sorrow and anger, even without my guess at first, and now my firm belief, that the child of those unlucky parents was indeed my Lorna. And as I thought of the lady's troubles, and her faith in Providence, and her cruel, childless death, and then imagined how my darling would be overcome to hear it, you may well believe that my quick replies to Jeremy Stickles's banter were but as the flourish of a drum to cover the sounds of pain.

For when he described the heavy coach and the persons in and upon it, and the breaking down at Dulverton, and the place of their destination, as well as the time and the weather, and the season of the year, my heart began to burn within me, and my mind replaced the pictures, first of the foreign lady's-maid by the pump caressing me, and then of the coach struggling up the hill, and the beautiful dame, and the fine little boy, with the white cockade in his hat; but most of all the little girl, dark-haired and very lovely, and having even in those days the rich soft look of Lorna.

But when he spoke of the necklace thrown over the head of the little maiden, and of her disappearance, before my eyes arose at once the flashing of the beacon-fire, the lonely moors embrowned with the light, the tramp of the outlaw cavalcade, and the helpless child head-downward, lying across the robber's saddle-bow.

Then I remembered my own mad shout of boyish indignation, and marvelled at the strange long way by which the events of life come round. And while I thought of my own return, and childish attempt to hide myself from sorrow in the sawpit, and the agony of my mother's tears, it did not fail to strike me as a thing of omen, that the selfsame day should be, both to my darling and myself, the blackest and most miserable of all youthful days.

The King's Commissioner thought it wise, for some good reason of his own, to conceal from me, for the present, the name of the poor lady supposed to be Lorna's mother; and knowing that I could easily now discover it, without him, I let that question abide awhile. Indeed I was half afraid to hear it, remembering that the nobler and the wealthier she proved to be, the smaller was my chance of winning such a wife for plain John Ridd. Not that she would give me up: that I never dreamed of. But that others would interfere; or indeed I myself might find it only honest to relinquish her. That last thought was a dreadful blow, and took my breath away from me.

Jeremy Stickles was quite decided—and of course the discovery being his, he had a right to be so—that not a word of all these things must be imparted to Lorna herself, or even to my mother, or any one whatever. 'Keep it tight as wax, my lad,' he cried, with a wink of great expression; 'this belongs to me, mind, and the credit, ay, and the premium, and the right of discount, are altogether mine. It would have taken you fifty years to put two and two together so, as I did, like a clap of thunder. Ah, God has given some men brains; and others have good farms and money, and a certain skill in the lower beasts. Each must use his special talent. You work your farm: I work my brains. In the end, my lad, I shall beat you.'

'Then, Jeremy, what a fool you must be, if you cudgel your brains to make money of this, to open the barn-door to me, and show me all your threshing.'

'Not a whit, my son. Quite the opposite. Two men always thresh better than one. And here I have you bound to use your flail, one two, with mine, and yet in strictest honour bound not to bushel up, till I tell you.'

'But,' said I, being much amused by a Londoner's brave, yet uncertain, use of simplest rural metaphors, for he had wholly forgotten the winnowing: 'surely if I bushel up, even when you tell me, I must take half-measure.'

'So you shall, my boy,' he answered, 'if we can only cheat those confounded knaves of Equity. You shall take the beauty, my son, and the elegance, and the love, and all that—and, my boy, I will take the money.'

This he said in a way so dry, and yet so richly unctuous, that being gifted somehow by God, with a kind of sense of queerness, I fell back in my chair, and laughed, though the underside of my laugh was tears.

'Now, Jeremy, how if I refuse to keep this half as tight as wax. You bound me to no such partnership, before you told the story; and I am not sure, by any means, of your right to do so afterwards.'

'Tush!' he replied: 'I know you too well, to look for meanness in you. If from pure goodwill, John Ridd, and anxiety to relieve you, I made no condition precedent, you are not the man to take advantage, as a lawyer might. I do not even want your promise. As sure as I hold this glass, and drink your health and love in another drop (forced on me by pathetic words), so surely will you be bound to me, until I do release you. Tush! I know men well by this time: a mere look of trust from one is worth another's ten thousand oaths.'

'Jeremy, you are right,' I answered; 'at least as regards the issue. Although perhaps you were not right in leading me into a bargain like this, without my own consent or knowledge. But supposing that we should both be shot in this grand attack on the valley (for I mean to go with you now, heart and soul), is Lorna to remain untold of that which changes all her life?'

'Both shot!' cried Jeremy Stickles: 'my goodness, boy, talk not like that! And those Doones are cursed good shots too. Nay, nay, the yellows shall go in front; we attack on the Somerset side, I think. I from a hill will reconnoitre, as behoves a general, you shall stick behind a tree, if we can only find one big enough to hide you. You and I to be shot, John Ridd, with all this inferior food for powder anxious to be devoured?'

I laughed, for I knew his cool hardihood, and never-flinching courage; and sooth to say no coward would have dared to talk like that.

'But when one comes to think of it,' he continued, smiling at himself; 'some provision should be made for even that unpleasant chance. I will leave the whole in writing, with orders to be opened, etc., etc.—Now no more of that, my boy; a cigarro after schnapps, and go to meet my yellow boys.'

His 'yellow boys,' as he called the Somersetshire trained bands, were even now coming down the valley from the London Road, as every one since I went up to town, grandly entitled the lane to the moors. There was one good point about these men, that having no discipline at all, they made pretence to none whatever. Nay, rather they ridiculed the thing, as below men of any spirit. On the other hand, Master Stickles's troopers looked down on these native fellows from a height which I hope they may never tumble, for it would break the necks of all of them.

Now these fine natives came along, singing, for their very lives, a song the like of which set down here would oust my book from modest people, and make everybody say, 'this man never can have loved Lorna.' Therefore, the less of that the better; only I thought, 'what a difference from the goodly psalms of the ale house!'

Having finished their canticle, which contained more mirth than melody, they drew themselves up, in a sort of way supposed by them to be military, each man with heel and elbow struck into those of his neighbour, and saluted the King's Commissioner. 'Why, where are your officers?' asked Master Stickles; 'how is it that you have no officers?' Upon this there arose a general grin, and a knowing look passed along their faces, even up to the man by the gatepost. 'Are you going to tell me, or not,' said Jeremy, 'what is become of your officers?'

'Plaise zur,' said one little fellow at last, being nodded at by the rest to speak, in right of his known eloquence; 'hus tould Harfizers, as a wor no nade of un, now King's man hiszell wor coom, a puppose vor to command us laike.'

'And do you mean to say, you villains,' cried Jeremy, scarce knowing whether to laugh, or to swear, or what to do; 'that your officers took their dismissal thus, and let you come on without them?'

'What could 'em do?' asked the little man, with reason certainly on his side: 'hus zent 'em about their business, and they was glad enough to goo.'

'Well!' said poor Jeremy, turning to me; 'a pretty state of things, John! Threescore cobblers, and farming men, plasterers, tailors, and kettles-to-mend; and not a man to keep order among them, except my blessed self, John! And I trow there is not one among them could hit all in-door flying. The Doones will make riddles of all of us.'

However, he had better hopes when the sons of Devon appeared, as they did in about an hour's time; fine fellows, and eager to prove themselves. These had not discarded their officers, but marched in good obedience to them, and were quite prepared to fight the men of Somerset (if need be) in addition to the Doones. And there was scarcely a man among them but could have trounced three of the yellow men, and would have done it gladly too, in honour of the red facings.

'Do you mean to suppose, Master Jeremy Stickles,' said I, looking on with amazement, beholding also all our maidens at the upstair windows wondering; 'that we, my mother a widow woman, and I a young man of small estate, can keep and support all these precious fellows, both yellow ones, and red ones, until they have taken the Doone Glen?'

'God forbid it, my son!' he replied, laying a finger upon his lip: 'Nay, nay, I am not of the shabby order, when I have the strings of government. Kill your sheep at famine prices, and knead your bread at a figure expressing the rigours of last winter. Let Annie make out the bill every day, and I at night will double it. You may take my word for it, Master John, this spring-harvest shall bring you in three times as much as last autumn's did. If they cheated you in town, my lad, you shall have your change in the country. Take thy bill, and write down quickly.'

However this did not meet my views of what an honest man should do; and I went to consult my mother about it, as all the accounts would be made in her name.

Dear mother thought that if the King paid only half again as much as other people would have to pay, it would be perhaps the proper thing; the half being due for loyalty: and here she quoted an ancient saying,—

The King and his staff.
Be a man and a half:

which, according to her judgment, ruled beyond dispute the law of the present question. To argue with her after that (which she brought up with such triumph) would have been worse than useless. Therefore I just told Annie to make the bills at a third below the current market prices; so that the upshot would be fair. She promised me honestly that she would; but with a twinkle in her bright blue eyes, which she must have caught from Tom Faggus. It always has appeared to me that stern and downright honesty upon money matters is a thing not understood of women; be they as good as good can be.

The yellows and the reds together numbered a hundred and twenty men, most of whom slept in our barns and stacks; and besides these we had fifteen troopers of the regular army. You may suppose that all the country was turned upside down about it; and the folk who came to see them drill—by no means a needless exercise—were a greater plague than the soldiers. The officers too of the Devonshire hand were such a torment to us, that we almost wished their men had dismissed them, as the Somerset troop had done with theirs. For we could not keep them out of our house, being all young men of good family, and therefore not to be met with bars. And having now three lovely maidens (for even Lizzie might he called so, when she cared to please), mother and I were at wit's ends, on account of those blessed officers. I never got a wink of sleep; they came whistling under the window so; and directly I went out to chase them, there was nothing but a cat to see.

Therefore all of us were right glad (except perhaps Farmer Snowe, from whom we had bought some victuals at rare price), when Jeremy Stickles gave orders to march, and we began to try to do it. A good deal of boasting went overhead, as our men defiled along the lane; and the thick broad patins of pennywort jutted out between the stones, ready to heal their bruises. The parish choir came part of the way, and the singing-loft from Countisbury; and they kept our soldiers' spirits up with some of the most pugnacious Psalms. Parson Bowden marched ahead, leading all our van and file, as against the Papists; and promising to go with us, till we came to bullet distance. Therefore we marched bravely on, and children came to look at us. And I wondered where Uncle Reuben was, who ought to have led the culverins (whereof we had no less than three), if Stickles could only have found him; and then I thought of little Ruth; and without any fault on my part, my heart went down within me.

The culverins were laid on bark; and all our horses pulling them, and looking round every now and then, with their ears curved up like a squirrel'd nut, and their noses tossing anxiously, to know what sort of plough it was man had been pleased to put behind them—man, whose endless whims and wildness they could never understand, any more than they could satisfy. However, they pulled their very best—as all our horses always do—and the culverins went up the hill, without smack of whip, or swearing. It had been arranged, very justly, no doubt, and quite in keeping with the spirit of the Constitution, but as it proved not too wisely, that either body of men should act in its own county only. So when we reached the top of the hill, the sons of Devon marched on, and across the track leading into Doone-gate, so as to fetch round the western side, and attack with their culverin from the cliffs, whence the sentry had challenged me on the night of my passing the entrance. Meanwhile the yellow lads were to stay upon the eastern highland, whence Uncle Reuben and myself had reconnoitred so long ago; and whence I had leaped into the valley at the time of the great snow-drifts. And here they were not to show themselves; but keep their culverin in the woods, until their cousins of Devon appeared on the opposite parapet of the glen.

The third culverin was entrusted to the fifteen troopers; who, with ten picked soldiers from either trained hand, making in all five-and-thirty men, were to assault the Doone-gate itself, while the outlaws were placed between two fires from the eastern cliff and the western. And with this force went Jeremy Stickles, and with it went myself, as knowing more about the passage than any other stranger did. Therefore, if I have put it clearly, as I strive to do, you will see that the Doones must repulse at once three simultaneous attacks, from an army numbering in the whole one hundred and thirty-five men, not including the Devonshire officers; fifty men on each side, I mean, and thirty-five at the head of the valley.

The tactics of this grand campaign appeared to me so clever, and beautifully ordered, that I commended Colonel Stickles, as everybody now called him, for his great ability and mastery of the art of war. He admitted that he deserved high praise; but said that he was not by any means equally certain of success, so large a proportion of his forces being only a raw militia, brave enough no doubt for anything, when they saw their way to it; but knowing little of gunnery, and wholly unused to be shot at. Whereas all the Doones were practised marksmen, being compelled when lads (like the Balearic slingers) to strike down their meals before tasting them. And then Colonel Stickles asked me, whether I myself could stand fire; he knew that I was not a coward, but this was a different question. I told him that I had been shot at, once or twice before; but nevertheless disliked it, as much as almost anything. Upon that he said that I would do; for that when a man got over the first blush of diffidence, he soon began to look upon it as a puff of destiny.

I wish I could only tell what happened, in the battle of that day, especially as nearly all the people round these parts, who never saw gun-fire in it, have gotten the tale so much amiss; and some of them will even stand in front of my own hearth, and contradict me to the teeth; although at the time they were not born, nor their fathers put into breeches. But in truth, I cannot tell, exactly, even the part in which I helped, how then can I be expected, time by time, to lay before you, all the little ins and outs of places, where I myself was not? Only I can contradict things, which I know could not have been; and what I plainly saw should not be controverted in my own house.

Now we five-and-thirty men lay back a little way round the corner, in the hollow of the track which leads to the strong Doone-gate. Our culverin was in amongst us, loaded now to the muzzle, and it was not comfortable to know that it might go off at any time. Although the yeomanry were not come (according to arrangement), some of us had horses there; besides the horses who dragged the cannon, and now were sniffing at it. And there were plenty of spectators to mind these horses for us, as soon as we should charge; inasmuch as all our friends and neighbours, who had so keenly prepared for the battle, now resolved to take no part, but look on, and praise the winners.

At last we heard the loud bang-bang, which proved that Devon and Somerset were pouring their indignation hot into the den of malefactors, or at least so we supposed; therefore at double quick march we advanced round the bend of the cliff which had hidden us, hoping to find the gate undefended, and to blow down all barriers with the fire of our cannon. And indeed it seemed likely at first to be so, for the wild and mountainous gorge of rock appeared to be all in pure loneliness, except where the coloured coats of our soldiers, and their metal trappings, shone with the sun behind them. Therefore we shouted a loud hurrah, as for an easy victory.

But while the sound of our cheer rang back among the crags above us, a shrill clear whistle cleft the air for a single moment, and then a dozen carbines bellowed, and all among us flew murderous lead. Several of our men rolled over, but the rest rushed on like Britons, Jeremy and myself in front, while we heard the horses plunging at the loaded gun behind us. 'Now, my lads,' cried Jeremy, 'one dash, and we are beyond them!' For he saw that the foe was overhead in the gallery of brushwood.

Our men with a brave shout answered him, for his courage was fine example; and we leaped in under the feet of the foe, before they could load their guns again. But here, when the foremost among us were past, an awful crash rang behind us, with the shrieks of men, and the din of metal, and the horrible screaming of horses. The trunk of the tree had been launched overhead, and crashed into the very midst of us. Our cannon was under it, so were two men, and a horse with his poor back broken. Another horse vainly struggled to rise, with his thigh-bone smashed and protruding.

Now I lost all presence of mind at this, for I loved both those good horses, and shouting for any to follow me, dashed headlong into the cavern. Some five or six men came after me, the foremost of whom was Jeremy, when a storm of shot whistled and patted around me, with a blaze of light and a thunderous roar. On I leaped, like a madman, and pounced on one gunner, and hurled him across his culverin; but the others had fled, and a heavy oak door fell to with a bang, behind them. So utterly were my senses gone, and naught but strength remaining, that I caught up the cannon with both hands, and dashed it, breech-first, at the doorway. The solid oak burst with the blow, and the gun stuck fast, like a builder's putlog.

But here I looked round in vain for any one to come and follow up my success. The scanty light showed me no figure moving through the length of the tunnel behind me; only a heavy groan or two went to my heart, and chilled it. So I hurried back to seek Jeremy, fearing that he must be smitten down.

And so indeed I found him, as well as three other poor fellows, struck by the charge of the culverin, which had passed so close beside me. Two of the four were as dead as stones, and growing cold already, but Jeremy and the other could manage to groan, just now and then. So I turned my attention to them, and thought no more of fighting.

Having so many wounded men, and so many dead among us, we loitered at the cavern's mouth, and looked at one another, wishing only for somebody to come and take command of us. But no one came; and I was griefed so much about poor Jeremy, besides being wholly unused to any violence of bloodshed, that I could only keep his head up, and try to stop him from bleeding. And he looked up at me pitifully, being perhaps in a haze of thought, as a calf looks at a butcher.

The shot had taken him in the mouth; about that no doubt could be, for two of his teeth were in his beard, and one of his lips was wanting. I laid his shattered face on my breast, and nursed him, as a woman might. But he looked at me with a jerk at this; and I saw that he wanted coolness.

While here we stayed, quite out of danger (for the fellows from the gallery could by no means shoot us, even if they remained there, and the oaken door whence the others fled was blocked up by the culverin), a boy who had no business there (being in fact our clerk's apprentice to the art of shoe-making) came round the corner upon us in the manner which boys, and only boys, can use with grace and freedom; that is to say, with a sudden rush, and a sidelong step, and an impudence,—

'Got the worst of it!' cried the boy; 'better be off all of you. Zoomerzett and Devon a vighting; and the Doones have drashed 'em both. Maister Ridd, even thee be drashed.'

We few, who yet remained of the force which was to have won the Doone-gate, gazed at one another, like so many fools, and nothing more. For we still had some faint hopes of winning the day, and recovering our reputation, by means of what the other men might have done without us. And we could not understand at all how Devonshire and Somerset, being embarked in the same cause, should be fighting with one another.

Finding nothing more to be done in the way of carrying on the war, we laid poor Master Stickles and two more of the wounded upon the carriage of bark and hurdles, whereon our gun had lain; and we rolled the gun into the river, and harnessed the horses yet alive, and put the others out of their pain, and sadly wended homewards, feeling ourselves to be thoroughly beaten, yet ready to maintain that it was no fault of ours whatever. And in this opinion the women joined, being only too glad and thankful to see us home alive again.

Now, this enterprise having failed so, I prefer not to dwell too long upon it; only just to show the mischief which lay at the root of the failure. And this mischief was the vile jealousy betwixt red and yellow uniform. Now I try to speak impartially, belonging no more to Somerset than I do to Devonshire, living upon the borders, and born of either county. The tale was told me by one side first; and then quite to a different tune by the other; and then by both together, with very hot words of reviling. and a desire to fight it out again. And putting this with that, the truth appears to be as follows:—

The men of Devon, who bore red facings, had a long way to go round the hills, before they could get into due position on the western side of the Doone Glen. And knowing that their cousins in yellow would claim the whole of the glory, if allowed to be first with the firing, these worthy fellows waited not to take good aim with their cannons, seeing the others about to shoot; but fettled it anyhow on the slope, pointing in a general direction; and trusting in God for aimworthiness, laid the rope to the breech, and fired. Now as Providence ordained it, the shot, which was a casual mixture of anything considered hard—for instance, jug-bottoms and knobs of doors—the whole of this pernicious dose came scattering and shattering among the unfortunate yellow men upon the opposite cliff; killing one and wounding two.

Now what did the men of Somerset do, but instead of waiting for their friends to send round and beg pardon, train their gun full mouth upon them, and with a vicious meaning shoot. Not only this, but they loudly cheered, when they saw four or five red coats lie low; for which savage feeling not even the remarks of the Devonshire men concerning their coats could entirely excuse them. Now I need not tell the rest of it, for the tale makes a man discontented. Enough that both sides waxed hotter and hotter with the fire of destruction. And but that the gorge of the cliffs lay between, very few would have lived to tell of it; for our western blood becomes stiff and firm, when churned with the sense of wrong in it.

At last the Doones (who must have laughed at the thunder passing overhead) recalling their men from the gallery, issued out of Gwenny's gate (which had been wholly overlooked) and fell on the rear of the Somerset men, and slew four beside their cannon. Then while the survivors ran away, the outlaws took the hot culverin, and rolled it down into their valley. Thus, of the three guns set forth that morning, only one ever came home again, and that was the gun of the Devonshire men, who dragged it home themselves, with the view of making a boast about it.

This was a melancholy end of our brave setting out, and everybody blamed every one else; and several of us wanted to have the whole thing over again, as then we must have righted it. But upon one point all agreed, by some reason not clear to me, that the root of the evil was to be found in the way Parson Bowden went up the hill, with his hat on, and no cassock.

Chapter LV Getting Into Chancery

Two of the Devonshire officers (Captains Pyke and Dallan) now took command of the men who were left, and ordered all to go home again, commending much the bravery which had been displayed on all sides, and the loyalty to the King, and the English constitution. This last word always seems to me to settle everything when said, because nobody understands it, and yet all can puzzle their neighbours. So the Devonshire men, having beans to sow (which they ought to have done on Good Friday) went home; and our Somerset friends only stayed for two days more to backbite them.

To me the whole thing was purely grievous; not from any sense of defeat (though that was bad enough) but from the pain and anguish caused by death, and wounds, and mourning. 'Surely we have woes enough,' I used to think of an evening, when the poor fellows could not sleep or rest, or let others rest around them; 'surely all this smell of wounds is not incense men should pay to the God who made them. Death, when it comes and is done with, may be a bliss to any one; but the doubt of life or death, when a man lies, as it were, like a trunk upon a sawpit and a grisly head looks up at him, and the groans of pain are cleaving him, this would be beyond all bearing—but for Nature's sap—sweet hope.'

Jeremy Stickles lay and tossed, and thrust up his feet in agony, and bit with his lipless mouth the clothes, and was proud to see blood upon them. He looked at us ever so many times, as much as to say, 'Fools, let me die, then I shall have some comfort'; but we nodded at him sagely, especially the women, trying to convey to him, on no account to die yet. And then we talked to one another (on purpose for him to hear us), how brave he was, and not the man to knock under in a hurry, and how he should have the victory yet; and how well he looked, considering.

These things cheered him a little now, and a little more next time; and every time we went on so, he took it with less impatience. Then once when he had been very quiet, and not even tried to frown at us, Annie leaned over, and kissed his forehead, and spread the pillows and sheet, with a curve as delicate as his own white ears; and then he feebly lifted hands, and prayed to God to bless her. And after that he came round gently; though never to the man he had been, and never to speak loud again.

For a time (as I may have implied before) Master Stickles's authority, and manner of levying duties, had not been taken kindly by the people round our neighbourhood. The manors of East Lynn and West Lynn, and even that of Woolhanger—although just then all three were at issue about some rights of wreck, and the hanging of a sheep-stealer (a man of no great eminence, yet claimed by each for the sake of his clothes)—these three, having their rights impugned, or even superseded, as they declared by the quartering of soldiers in their neighbourhood, united very kindly to oppose the King's Commissioner. However, Jeremy had contrived to conciliate the whole of them, not so much by anything engaging in his deportment or delicate address, as by holding out bright hopes that the plunder of the Doone Glen might become divisible among the adjoining manors. Now I have never discovered a thing which the lords of manors (at least in our part of the world) do not believe to belong to themselves, if only they could get their rights. And it did seem natural enough that if the Doones were ousted, and a nice collection of prey remained, this should be parted among the people having ancient rights of plunder. Nevertheless, Master Jeremy knew that the soldiers would have the first of it, and the King what they could not carry.

And perhaps he was punished justly for language so misleading, by the general indignation of the people all around us, not at his failure, but at himself, for that which he could in no wise prevent. And the stewards of the manors rode up to our house on purpose to reproach him, and were greatly vexed with all of us, because he was too ill to see them.

To myself (though by rights the last to be thought of, among so much pain and trouble) Jeremy's wound was a great misfortune, in more ways than one. In the first place, it deferred my chance of imparting either to my mother or to Mistress Lorna my firm belief that the maid I loved was not sprung from the race which had slain my father; neither could he in any way have offended against her family. And this discovery I was yearning more and more to declare to them; being forced to see (even in the midst of all our warlike troubles) that a certain difference was growing betwixt them both, and betwixt them and me. For although the words of the Counsellor had seemed to fail among us, being bravely met and scattered, yet our courage was but as wind flinging wide the tare-seeds, when the sower casts them from his bag. The crop may not come evenly, many places may long lie bare, and the field be all in patches; yet almost every vetch will spring, and tiller out, and stretch across the scatterings where the wind puffed.

And so dear mother and darling Lorna now had been for many a day thinking, worrying, and wearing, about the matter between us. Neither liked to look at the other, as they used to do; with mother admiring Lorna's eyes, and grace, and form of breeding; and Lorna loving mother's goodness, softness, and simplicity. And the saddest and most hurtful thing was that neither could ask the other of the shadow falling between them. And so it went on, and deepened.

In the next place Colonel Stickles's illness was a grievous thing to us, in that we had no one now to command the troopers. Ten of these were still alive, and so well approved to us, that they could never fancy aught, whether for dinner or supper, without its being forth-coming. If they wanted trout they should have it; if colloped venison, or broiled ham, or salmon from Lynmouth and Trentisoe, or truffles from the woodside, all these were at the warriors' service, until they lusted for something else. Even the wounded men ate nobly; all except poor Jeremy, who was forced to have a young elder shoot, with the pith drawn, for to feed him. And once, when they wanted pickled loach (from my description of it), I took up my boyish sport again, and pronged them a good jarful. Therefore, none of them could complain; and yet they were not satisfied; perhaps for want of complaining.

Be that as it might, we knew that if they once resolved to go (as they might do at any time, with only a corporal over them) all our house, and all our goods, ay, and our own precious lives, would and must be at the mercy of embittered enemies. For now the Doones, having driven back, as every one said, five hundred men—though not thirty had ever fought with them—were in such feather all round the country, that nothing was too good for them. Offerings poured in at the Doone gate, faster than Doones could away with them, and the sympathy both of Devon and Somerset became almost oppressive. And perhaps this wealth of congratulation, and mutual good feeling between plundered and victim, saved us from any piece of spite; kindliness having won the day, and every one loving every one.

But yet another cause arose, and this the strongest one of all, to prove the need of Stickles's aid, and calamity of his illness. And this came to our knowledge first, without much time to think of it. For two men appeared at our gate one day, stripped to their shirts, and void of horses, and looking very sorrowful. Now having some fear of attack from the Doones, and scarce knowing what their tricks might be, we received these strangers cautiously, desiring to know who they were before we let them see all our premises.

However, it soon became plain to us that although they might not be honest fellows, at any rate they were not Doones; and so we took them in, and fed, and left them to tell their business. And this they were glad enough to do; as men who have been maltreated almost always are. And it was not for us to contradict them, lest our victuals should go amiss.

These two very worthy fellows—nay, more than that by their own account, being downright martyrs—were come, for the public benefit, from the Court of Chancery, sitting for everybody's good, and boldly redressing evil. This court has a power of scent unknown to the Common-law practitioners, and slowly yet surely tracks its game; even as the great lumbering dogs, now introduced from Spain, and called by some people 'pointers,' differ from the swift gaze-hound, who sees his prey and runs him down in the manner of the common lawyers. If a man's ill fate should drive him to make a choice between these two, let him rather be chased by the hounds of law, than tracked by the dogs of Equity.

Now, as it fell in a very black day (for all except the lawyers) His Majesty's Court of Chancery, if that be what it called itself, gained scent of poor Lorna's life, and of all that might be made of it. Whether through that brave young lord who ran into such peril, or through any of his friends, or whether through that deep old Counsellor, whose game none might penetrate; or through any disclosures of the Italian woman, or even of Jeremy himself; none just now could tell us; only this truth was too clear—Chancery had heard of Lorna, and then had seen how rich she was; and never delaying in one thing, had opened mouth, and swallowed her.

The Doones, with a share of that dry humour which was in them hereditary, had welcomed the two apparitors (if that be the proper name for them) and led them kindly down the valley, and told them then to serve their writ. Misliking the look of things, these poor men began to fumble among their clothes; upon which the Doones cried, 'off with them! Let us see if your message he on your skins.' And with no more manners than that, they stripped, and lashed them out of the valley; only bidding them come to us, if they wanted Lorna Doone; and to us they came accordingly. Neither were they sure at first but that we should treat them so; for they had no knowledge of the west country, and thought it quite a godless place, wherein no writ was holy.

We however comforted and cheered them so considerably, that, in gratitude, they showed their writs, to which they had stuck like leeches. And these were twofold; one addressed to Mistress Lorna Doone, so called, and bidding her keep in readiness to travel whenever called upon, and commit herself to nobody, except the accredited messengers of the right honourable Court; while the other was addressed to all subjects of His Majesty, having custody of Lorna Doone, or any power over her. And this last threatened and exhorted, and held out hopes of recompense, if she were rendered truly. My mother and I held consultation, over both these documents, with a mixture of some wrath and fear, and a fork of great sorrow to stir them. And now having Jeremy Stickles's leave, which he gave with a nod when I told him all, and at last made him understand it, I laid bare to my mother as well what I knew, as what I merely surmised, or guessed, concerning Lorna's parentage. All this she received with great tears, and wonder, and fervent thanks to God, and still more fervent praise of her son, who had nothing whatever to do with it. However, now the question was, how to act about these writs. And herein it was most unlucky that we could not have Master Stickles, with his knowledge of the world, and especially of the law-courts, to advise us what to do, and to help in doing it. And firstly of the first I said, 'We have rogues to deal with; but try we not to rogue them.'

To this, in some measure, dear mother agreed, though she could not see the justice of it, yet thought that it might he wiser, because of our want of practice. And then I said, 'Now we are bound to tell Lorna, and to serve her citation upon her, which these good fellows have given us.'

'Then go, and do it thyself, my son,' mother replied with a mournful smile, misdoubting what the end might be. So I took the slip of brown parchment, and went to seek my darling.

Lorna was in her favourite place, the little garden which she tended with such care and diligence. Seeing how the maiden loved it, and was happy there, I had laboured hard to fence it from the dangers of the wood. And here she had corrected me, with better taste, and sense of pleasure, and the joys of musing. For I meant to shut out the brook, and build my fence inside of it; but Lorna said no; if we must have a fence, which could not but be injury, at any rate leave the stream inside, and a pleasant bank beyond it. And soon I perceived that she was right, though not so much as afterwards; for the fairest of all things in a garden, and in summer-time most useful, is a brook of crystal water; where a man may come and meditate, and the flowers may lean and see themselves, and the rays of the sun are purfied. Now partly with her own white hands, and partly with Gwenny's red ones, Lorna had made of this sunny spot a haven of beauty to dwell in. It was not only that colours lay in the harmony we would seek of them, neither was it the height of plants, sloping to one another; nor even the delicate tone of foliage following suit, and neighbouring. Even the breathing of the wind, soft and gentle in and out, moving things that need not move, and passing longer-stalked ones, even this was not enough among the flush of fragrance, to tell a man the reason of his quiet satisfaction. But so it shall for ever be. As the river we float upon (with wine, and flowers, and music,) is nothing at the well-spring but a bubble without reason.

Feeling many things, but thinking without much to guide me, over the grass-plats laid between, I went up to Lorna. She in a shower of damask roses, raised her eyes and looked at me. And even now, in those sweet eyes, so deep with loving-kindness, and soft maiden dreamings, there seemed to be a slight unwilling, half confessed withdrawal; overcome by love and duty, yet a painful thing to see.

'Darling,' I said, 'are your spirits good? Are you strong enough today, to bear a tale of cruel sorrow; but which perhaps, when your tears are shed, will leave you all the happier?'

'What can you mean?' she answered trembling, not having been vey strong of late, and now surprised at my manner; 'are you come to give me up, John?'

'Not very likely,' I replied; 'neither do I hope such a thing would leave you all the happier. Oh, Lorna, if you can think that so quickly as you seem to have done, now you have every prospect and strong temptation to it. You are far, far above me in the world, and I have no right to claim you. Perhaps, when you have heard these tidings you will say, "John Ridd, begone; your life and mine are parted."'

'Will I?' cried Lorna, with all the brightness of her playful ways returning: 'you very foolish and jealous John, how shall I punish you for this? Am I to forsake every flower I have, and not even know that the world goes round, while I look up at you, the whole day long and say, "John, I love, love, love you?"'

During these words she leaned upon me, half in gay imitation of what I had so often made her do, and half in depth of earnestness, as the thrice-repeated word grew stronger, and grew warmer, with and to her heart. And as she looked up at the finish, saying, 'you,' so musically, I was much inclined to clasp her round; but remembering who she was, forbore; at which she seemed surprised with me.

'Mistress Lorna, I replied, with I know not what temptation, making little of her caresses, though more than all my heart to me: 'Mistress Lorna, you must keep your rank and proper dignity. You must never look at me with anything but pity now.'

'I shall look at you with pity, John,' said Lorna, trying to laugh it off, yet not knowing what to make of me, 'if you talk any more of this nonsense, knowing me as you ought to do. I shall even begin to think that you, and your friends, are weary of me, and of so long supporting me; and are only seeking cause to send me back to my old misery. If it be so, I will go. My life matters little to any one.' Here the great bright tears arose; but the maiden was too proud to sob.

'Sweetest of all sweet loves,' I cried, for the sign of a tear defeated me; 'what possibility could make me ever give up Lorna?'

'Dearest of all dears,' she answered; 'if you dearly love me, what possibility could ever make me give you up, dear?'

Upon that there was no more forbearing, but I kissed and clasped her, whether she were Countess, or whether Queen of England; mine she was, at least in heart; and mine she should be wholly. And she being of the same opinion, nothing was said between us.

'Now, Lorna,' said I, as she hung on my arm, willing to trust me anywhere, 'come to your little plant-house, and hear my moving story.'

'No story can move me much, dear,' she answered rather faintly, for any excitement stayed with her; 'since I know your strength of kindness, scarcely any tale can move me, unless it be of yourself, love; or of my poor mother.'

'It is of your poor mother, darling. Can you bear to hear it?' And yet I wondered why she did not say as much of her father.

'Yes, I can bear anything. But although I cannot see her, and have long forgotten, I could not bear to hear ill of her.'

'There is no ill to hear, sweet child, except of evil done to her. Lorna, you are of an ill-starred race.'

'Better that than a wicked race,' she answered with her usual quickness, leaping at conclusion; 'tell me I am not a Doone, and I will—but I cannot love you more.'

'You are not a Doone, my Lorna, for that, at least, I can answer; though I know not what your name is.'

'And my father—your father—what I mean is—'

'Your father and mine never met one another. Your father was killed by an accident in the Pyrenean mountains, and your mother by the Doones; or at least they caused her death, and carried you away from her.'

All this, coming as in one breath upon the sensitive maiden, was more than she could bear all at once; as any but a fool like me must of course have known. She lay back on the garden bench, with her black hair shed on the oaken bark, while her colour went and came and only by that, and her quivering breath, could any one say that she lived and thought. And yet she pressed my hand with hers, that I might tell her all of it.

Chapter LVI John Becomes Too Popular

No flower that I have ever seen, either in shifting of light and shade, or in the pearly morning, may vie with a fair young woman's face when tender thought and quick emotion vary, enrich, and beautify it. Thus my Lorna hearkened softly, almost without word or gesture, yet with sighs and glances telling, and the pressure of my hand, how each word was moving her.

When at last my tale was done, she turned away, and wept bitterly for the sad fate of her parents. But to my surprise she spoke not even a word of wrath or rancour. She seemed to take it all as fate.

'Lorna, darling,' I said at length, for men are more impatient in trials of time than women are, 'do you not even wish to know what your proper name is?'

'How can it matter to me, John?' she answered, with a depth of grief which made me seem a trifler. 'It can never matter now, when there are none to share it.'

'Poor little soul!' was all I said in a tone of purest pity; and to my surprise she turned upon me, caught me in her arms, and loved me as she had never done before.

'Dearest, I have you,' she cried; 'you, and only you, love. Having you I want no other. All my life is one with yours. Oh, John, how can I treat you so?'

Blushing through the wet of weeping, and the gloom of pondering, yet she would not hide her eyes, but folded me, and dwelled on me.

'I cannot believe,' in the pride of my joy, I whispered into one little ear, 'that you could ever so love me, beauty, as to give up the world for me.'

'Would you give up your farm for me, John?' cried Lorna, leaping back and looking, with her wondrous power of light at me; 'would you give up your mother, your sisters, your home, and all that you have in the world and every hope of your life, John?'

'Of course I would. Without two thoughts. You know it; you know it, Lorna.'

'It is true that I do, 'she answered in a tone of deepest sadness; 'and it is this power of your love which has made me love you so. No good can come of it, no good. God's face is set against selfishness.'

As she spoke in that low tone I gazed at the clear lines of her face (where every curve was perfect) not with love and wonder only, but with a strange new sense of awe.

'Darling,' I said, 'come nearer to me. Give me surety against that. For God's sake never frighten me with the thought that He would part us.'

'Does it then so frighten you?' she whispered, coming close to me; 'I know it, dear; I have known it long; but it never frightens me. It makes me sad, and very lonely, till I can remember.'

'Till you can remember what?' I asked, with a long, deep shudder; for we are so superstitious.

'Until I do remember, love, that you will soon come back to me, and be my own for ever. This is what I always think of, this is what I hope for.'

Although her eyes were so glorious, and beaming with eternity, this distant sort of beatitude was not much to my liking. I wanted to have my love on earth; and my dear wife in my own home; and children in good time, if God should please to send us any. And then I would be to them, exactly what my father was to me. And beside all this, I doubted much about being fit for heaven; where no ploughs are, and no cattle, unless sacrificed bulls went thither.

Therefore I said, 'Now kiss me, Lorna; and don't talk any nonsense.' And the darling came and did it; being kindly obedient, as the other world often makes us.

'You sweet love,' I said at this, being slave to her soft obedience; 'do you suppose I should be content to leave you until Elysium?'

'How on earth can I tell, dear John, what you will be content with?'

'You, and only you,' said I; 'the whole of it lies in a syllable. Now you know my entire want; and want must be my comfort.'

'But surely if I have money, sir, and birth, and rank, and all sorts of grandeur, you would never dare to think of me.'

She drew herself up with an air of pride, as she gravely pronounced these words, and gave me a scornful glance, or tried; and turned away as if to enter some grand coach or palace; while I was so amazed and grieved in my raw simplicity especially after the way in which she had first received my news, so loving and warm-hearted, that I never said a word, but stared and thought, 'How does she mean it?'

She saw the pain upon my forehead, and the wonder in my eyes, and leaving coach and palace too, back she flew to me in a moment, as simple as simplest milkmaid.

'Oh, you fearful stupid, John, you inexpressibly stupid, John,' she cried with both arms round my neck, and her lips upon my forehead; 'you have called yourself thick-headed, John, and I never would believe it. But now I do with all my heart. Will you never know what I am, love?'

'No, Lorna, that I never shall. I can understand my mother well, and one at least of my sisters, and both the Snowe girls very easily, but you I never understand; only love you all the more for it.'

'Then never try to understand me, if the result is that, dear John. And yet I am the very simplest of all foolish simple creatures. Nay, I am wrong; therein I yield the palm to you, my dear. To think that I can act so! No wonder they want me in London, as an ornament for the stage, John.'

Now in after days, when I heard of Lorna as the richest, and noblest, and loveliest lady to be found in London, I often remembered that little scene, and recalled every word and gesture, wondering what lay under it. Even now, while it was quite impossible once to doubt those clear deep eyes, and the bright lips trembling so; nevertheless I felt how much the world would have to do with it; and that the best and truest people cannot shake themselves quite free. However, for the moment, I was very proud and showed it.

And herein differs fact from fancy, things as they befall us from things as we would have them, human ends from human hopes; that the first are moved by a thousand and the last on two wheels only, which (being named) are desire and fear. Hope of course is nothing more than desire with a telescope, magnifying distant matters, overlooking near ones; opening one eye on the objects, closing the other to all objections. And if hope be the future tense of desire, the future of fear is religion—at least with too many of us.

Whether I am right or wrong in these small moralities, one thing is sure enough, to wit, that hope is the fastest traveller, at any rate, in the time of youth. And so I hoped that Lorna might be proved of blameless family, and honourable rank and fortune; and yet none the less for that, love me and belong to me. So I led her into the house, and she fell into my mother's arms; and I left them to have a good cry of it, with Annie ready to help them.

If Master Stickles should not mend enough to gain his speech a little, and declare to us all he knew, I was to set out for Watchett, riding upon horseback, and there to hire a cart with wheels, such as we had not begun, as yet, to use on Exmoor. For all our work went on broad wood, with runners and with earthboards; and many of us still looked upon wheels (though mentioned in the Bible) as the invention of the evil one, and Pharoah's especial property.

Now, instead of getting better, Colonel Stickles grew worse and worse, in spite of all our tendance of him, with simples and with nourishment, and no poisonous medicine, such as doctors would have given him. And the fault of this lay not with us, but purely with himself and his unquiet constitution. For he roused himself up to a perfect fever, when through Lizzie's giddiness he learned the very thing which mother and Annie were hiding from him, with the utmost care; namely, that Sergeant Bloxham had taken upon himself to send direct to London by the Chancery officers, a full report of what had happened, and of the illness of his chief, together with an urgent prayer for a full battalion of King's troops, and a plenary commander.

This Sergeant Bloxham, being senior of the surviving soldiers, and a very worthy man in his way, but a trifle over-zealous, had succeeded to the captaincy upon his master's disablement. Then, with desire to serve his country and show his education, he sat up most part of three nights, and wrote this very wonderful report by the aid of our stable lanthorn. It was a very fine piece of work, as three men to whom he read it (but only one at a time) pronounced, being under seal of secrecy. And all might have gone well with it, if the author could only have held his tongue, when near the ears of women. But this was beyond his sense as it seems, although so good a writer. For having heard that our Lizzie was a famous judge of literature (as indeed she told almost every one), he could not contain himself, but must have her opinion upon his work.

Lizzie sat on a log of wood, and listened with all her ears up, having made proviso that no one else should be there to interrupt her. And she put in a syllable here and there, and many a time she took out one (for the Sergeant overloaded his gun, more often than undercharged it; like a liberal man of letters), and then she declared the result so good, so chaste, and the style to be so elegant, and yet so fervent, that the Sergeant broke his pipe in three, and fell in love with her on the spot. Now this has led me out of my way; as things are always doing, partly through their own perverseness, partly through my kind desire to give fair turn to all of them, and to all the people who do them. If any one expects of me a strict and well-drilled story, standing 'at attention' all the time, with hands at the side like two wens on my trunk, and eyes going neither right nor left; I trow that man has been disappointed many a page ago, and has left me to my evil ways; and if not, I love his charity. Therefore let me seek his grace, and get back, and just begin again.

That great despatch was sent to London by the Chancery officers, whom we fitted up with clothes, and for three days fattened them; which in strict justice they needed much, as well as in point of equity. They were kind enough to be pleased with us, and accepted my new shirts generously; and urgent as their business was, another week (as they both declared) could do no harm to nobody, and might set them upon their legs again. And knowing, although they were London men, that fish do live in water, these two fellows went fishing all day, but never landed anything. However, their holiday was cut short; for the Sergeant, having finished now his narrative of proceedings, was not the man to let it hang fire, and be quenched perhaps by Stickles.

Therefore, having done their business, and served both citations, these two good men had a pannier of victuals put up by dear Annie, and borrowing two of our horses, rode to Dunster, where they left them, and hired on towards London. We had not time to like them much, and so we did not miss them, especially in our great anxiety about poor Master Stickles.

Jeremy lay between life and death, for at least a fortnight. If the link of chain had flown upwards (for half a link of chain it was which took him in the mouth so), even one inch upwards, the poor man could have needed no one except Parson Bowden; for the bottom of his skull, which holds the brain as in the egg-cup, must have clean gone from him. But striking him horizontally, and a little upon the skew, the metal came out at the back of his neck, and (the powder not being strong, I suppose) it lodged in his leather collar.

Now the rust of this iron hung in the wound, or at least we thought so; though since I have talked with a man of medicine, I am not so sure of it. And our chief aim was to purge this rust; when rather we should have stopped the hole, and let the oxide do its worst, with a plug of new flesh on both sides of it.

At last I prevailed upon him by argument, that he must get better, to save himself from being ignobly and unjustly superseded; and hereupon I reviled Sergeant Bloxham more fiercely than Jeremy's self could have done, and indeed to such a pitch that Jeremy almost forgave him, and became much milder. And after that his fever and the inflammation of his wound, diminished very rapidly.

However, not knowing what might happen, or even how soon poor Lorna might be taken from our power, and, falling into lawyers' hands, have cause to wish herself most heartily back among the robbers, I set forth one day for Watchett, taking advantage of the visit of some troopers from an outpost, who would make our house quite safe. I rode alone, being fully primed, and having no misgivings. For it was said that even the Doones had begun to fear me, since I cast their culverin through the door, as above related; and they could not but believe, from my being still untouched (although so large an object) in the thickest of their fire, both of gun and cannon, that I must bear a charmed life, proof against ball and bullet. However, I knew that Carver Doone was not a likely man to hold any superstitious opinions; and of him I had an instinctive dread, although quite ready to face him.

Riding along, I meditated upon Lorna's history; how many things were now beginning to unfold themselves, which had been obscure and dark! For instance, Sir Ensor Doone's consent, or to say the least his indifference, to her marriage with a yeoman; which in a man so proud (though dying) had greatly puzzled both of us. But now, if she not only proved to be no grandchild of the Doone, but even descended from his enemy, it was natural enough that he should feel no great repugnance to her humiliation. And that Lorna's father had been a foe to the house of Doone I gathered from her mother's cry when she beheld their leader. Moreover that fact would supply their motive in carrying off the unfortunate little creature, and rearing her among them, and as one of their own family; yet hiding her true birth from her. She was a 'great card,' as we say, when playing All-fours at Christmas-time; and if one of them could marry her, before she learned of right and wrong, vast property, enough to buy pardons for a thousand Doones, would be at their mercy. And since I was come to know Lorna better, and she to know me thoroughly—many things had been outspoken, which her early bashfulness had kept covered from me. Attempts I mean to pledge her love to this one, or that other; some of which perhaps might have been successful, if there had not been too many.

And then, as her beauty grew richer and brighter, Carver Doone was smitten strongly, and would hear of no one else as a suitor for her; and by the terror of his claim drove off all the others. Here too may the explanation of a thing which seemed to be against the laws of human nature, and upon which I longed, but dared not to cross-question Lorna. How could such a lovely girl, although so young, and brave, and distant, have escaped the vile affections of a lawless company?

But now it was as clear as need be. For any proven violence would have utterly vitiated all claim upon her grand estate; at least as those claims must be urged before a court of equity. And therefore all the elders (with views upon her real estate) kept strict watch on the youngers, who confined their views to her personality.

Now I do not mean to say that all this, or the hundred other things which came, crowding consideration, were half as plain to me at the time, as I have set them down above. Far be it from me to deceive you so. No doubt my thoughts were then dark and hazy, like an oil-lamp full of fungus; and I have trimmed them, as when they burned, with scissors sharpened long afterwards. All I mean to say is this, that jogging along to a certain tune of the horse's feet, which we call 'three-halfpence and twopence,' I saw my way a little into some things which had puzzled me.

When I knocked at the little door, whose sill was gritty and grimed with sand, no one came for a very long time to answer me, or to let me in. Not wishing to be unmannerly, I waited a long time, and watched the sea, from which the wind was blowing; and whose many lips of waves—though the tide was half-way out—spoke to and refreshed me. After a while I knocked again, for my horse was becoming hungry; and a good while after that again, a voice came through the key-hole,—

'Who is that wishes to enter?'

'The boy who was at the pump,' said I, 'when the carriage broke down at Dulverton. The boy that lives at oh—ah; and some day you would come seek for him.'

'Oh, yes, I remember certainly. My leetle boy, with the fair white skin. I have desired to see him, oh many, yes, many times.'

She was opening the door, while saying this, and then she started back in affright that the little boy should have grown so.

'You cannot be that leetle boy. It is quite impossible. Why do you impose on me?'

'Not only am I that little boy, who made the water to flow for you, till the nebule came upon the glass; but also I am come to tell you all about your little girl.'

'Come in, you very great leetle boy,' she answered, with her dark eyes brightened. And I went in, and looked at her. She was altered by time, as much as I was. The slight and graceful shape was gone; not that I remembered anything of her figure, if you please; for boys of twelve are not yet prone to note the shapes of women; but that her lithe straight gait had struck me as being so unlike our people. Now her time for walking so was past, and transmitted to her children. Yet her face was comely still, and full of strong intelligence. I gazed at her, and she at me; and we were sure of one another.

'Now what will ye please to eat?' she asked, with a lively glance at the size of my mouth: 'that is always the first thing you people ask, in these barbarous places.'

'I will tell you by-and-by,' I answered, misliking this satire upon us; 'but I might begin with a quart of ale, to enable me to speak, madam.'

'Very well. One quevart of be-or;' she called out to a little maid, who was her eldest child, no doubt. 'It is to be expected, sir. Be-or, be-or, be-or, all day long, with you Englishmen!'

'Nay,' I replied, 'not all day long, if madam will excuse me. Only a pint at breakfast-time, and a pint and a half at eleven o'clock, and a quart or so at dinner. And then no more till the afternoon; and half a gallon at supper-time. No one can object to that.'

'Well, I suppose it is right,' she said, with an air of resignation; 'God knows. But I do not understand it. It is "good for business," as you say, to preclude everything.'

'And it is good for us, madam,' I answered with indignation, for beer is my favourite beverage; 'and I am a credit to beer, madam; and so are all who trust to it.'

'At any rate, you are, young man. If beer has made you grow so large, I will put my children upon it; it is too late for me to begin. The smell to me is hateful.'

Now I only set down that to show how perverse those foreign people are. They will drink their wretched heartless stuff, such as they call claret, or wine of Medoc, or Bordeaux, or what not, with no more meaning than sour rennet, stirred with the pulp from the cider press, and strained through the cap of our Betty. This is very well for them; and as good as they deserve, no doubt, and meant perhaps by the will of God, for those unhappy natives. But to bring it over to England and set it against our home-brewed ale (not to speak of wines from Portugal) and sell it at ten times the price, as a cure for British bile, and a great enlightenment; this I say is the vilest feature of the age we live in.

Madam Benita Odam—for the name of the man who turned the wheel proved to be John Odam—showed me into a little room containing two chairs and a fir-wood table, and sat down on a three-legged seat and studied me very steadfastly. This she had a right to do; and I, having all my clothes on now, was not disconcerted. It would not become me to repeat her judgment upon my appearance, which she delivered as calmly as if I were a pig at market, and as proudly as if her own pig. And she asked me whether I had ever got rid of the black marks on my breast.

Not wanting to talk about myself (though very fond of doing so, when time and season favour) I led her back to that fearful night of the day when first I had seen her. She was not desirous to speak of it, because of her own little children; however, I drew her gradually to recollection of Lorna, and then of the little boy who died, and the poor mother buried with him. And her strong hot nature kindled, as she dwelled upon these things; and my wrath waxed within me; and we forgot reserve and prudence under the sense of so vile a wrong. She told me (as nearly as might be) the very same story which she had told to Master Jeremy Stickles; only she dwelled upon it more, because of my knowing the outset. And being a woman, with an inkling of my situation, she enlarged upon the little maid, more than to dry Jeremy.

'Would you know her again?' I asked, being stirred by these accounts of Lorna, when she was five years old: 'would you know her as a full-grown maiden?'

'I think I should,' she answered; 'it is not possible to say until one sees the person; but from the eyes of the little girl, I think that I must know her. Oh, the poor young creature! Is it to be believed that the cannibals devoured her! What a people you are in this country! Meat, meat, meat!'

As she raised her hands and eyes in horror at our carnivorous propensities, to which she clearly attributed the disappearance of Lorna, I could scarce help laughing, even after that sad story. For though it is said at the present day, and will doubtless be said hereafter, that the Doones had devoured a baby once, as they came up Porlock hill, after fighting hard in the market-place, I knew that the tale was utterly false; for cruel and brutal as they were, their taste was very correct and choice, and indeed one might say fastidious. Nevertheless I could not stop to argue that matter with her.

'The little maid has not been devoured,' I said to Mistress Odam: 'and now she is a tall young lady, and as beautiful as can be. If I sleep in your good hostel to-night after going to Watchett town, will you come with me to Oare to-morrow, and see your little maiden?'

'I would like—and yet I fear. This country is so barbarous. And I am good to eat—my God, there is much picking on my bones!'

She surveyed herself with a glance so mingled of pity and admiration, and the truth of her words was so apparent (only that it would have taken a week to get at the bones, before picking) that I nearly lost good manners; for she really seemed to suspect even me of cannibal inclinations. However, at last I made her promise to come with me on the morrow, presuming that Master Odam could by any means be persuaded to keep her company in the cart, as propriety demanded. Having little doubt that Master Odam was entirely at his wife's command, I looked upon that matter as settled, and set off for Watchett, to see the grave of Lorna's poor mother, and to hire a cart for the morrow.

And here (as so often happens with men) I succeeded without any trouble or hindrance, where I had looked for both of them, namely, in finding a suitable cart; whereas the other matter, in which I could have expected no difficulty, came very near to defeat me. For when I heard that Lorna's father was the Earl of Dugal—as Benita impressed upon me with a strong enforcement, as much as to say, 'Who are you, young man, to come even asking about her?'—then I never thought but that everybody in Watchett town must know all about the tombstone of the Countess of Dugal.

This, however, proved otherwise. For Lord Dugal had never lived at Watchett Grange, as their place was called; neither had his name become familiar as its owner. Because the Grange had only devolved to him by will, at the end of a long entail, when the last of the Fitz-Pains died out; and though he liked the idea of it, he had gone abroad, without taking seisin. And upon news of his death, John Jones, a rich gentleman from Llandaff, had taken possession, as next of right, and hushed up all the story. And though, even at the worst of times, a lady of high rank and wealth could not be robbed, and as bad as murdered, and then buried in a little place, without moving some excitement, yet it had been given out, on purpose and with diligence, that this was only a foreign lady travelling for her health and pleasure, along the seacoast of England. And as the poor thing never spoke, and several of her servants and her baggage looked so foreign, and she herself died in a collar of lace unlike any made in England, all Watchett, without hesitation, pronounced her to be a foreigner. And the English serving man and maid, who might have cleared up everything, either were bribed by Master Jones, or else decamped of their own accord with the relics of the baggage. So the poor Countess of Dugal, almost in sight of her own grand house, was buried in an unknown grave, with her pair of infants, without a plate, without a tombstone (worse than all) without a tear, except from the hired Italian woman.

Surely my poor Lorna came of an ill-starred family.

Now in spite of all this, if I had only taken Benita with me, or even told her what I wished, and craved her directions, there could have been no trouble. But I do assure you that among the stupid people at Watchett (compared with whom our folk of Oare, exceeding dense though being, are as Hamlet against Dogberry) what with one of them and another, and the firm conviction of all the town that I could be come only to wrestle, I do assure you (as I said before) that my wits almost went out of me. And what vexed me yet more about it was, that I saw my own mistake, in coming myself to seek out the matter, instead of sending some unknown person. For my face and form were known at that time (and still are so) to nine people out of every ten living in forty miles of me. Not through any excellence, or anything of good desert, in either the one or the other, but simply because folks will be fools on the rivalry of wrestling. The art is a fine one in itself, and demands a little wit of brain, as well as strength of body; it binds the man who studies it to temperance, and chastity, to self-respect, and most of all to an even and sweet temper; for I have thrown stronger men than myself (when I was a mere sapling, and before my strength grew hard on me) through their loss of temper. But though the art is an honest one, surely they who excel therein have a right (like all the rest of man-kind) to their own private life.

Be that either way—and I will not speak too strongly, for fear of indulging my own annoyance—anyhow, all Watchett town cared ten times as much to see John Ridd, as to show him what he wanted. I was led to every public-house, instead of to the churchyard; and twenty tables were ready for me, in lieu of a single gravestone. 'Zummerzett thou bee'st, Jan Ridd, and Zummerzett thou shalt be. Thee carl theezell a Davonsheer man! Whoy, thee lives in Zummerzett; and in Zummerzett thee wast barn, lad.' And so it went on, till I was weary; though very much obliged to them.

Dull and solid as I am, and with a wild duck waiting for me at good Mistress Odam's, I saw that there was nothing for it but to yield to these good people, and prove me a man of Somerset, by eating a dinner at their expense. As for the churchyard, none would hear of it; and I grieved for broaching the matter.

But how was I to meet Lorna again, without having done the thing of all things which I had promised to see to? It would never do to tell her that so great was my popularity, and so strong the desire to feed me, that I could not attend to her mother. Least of all could I say that every one in Watchett knew John Ridd; while none had heard of the Countess of Dugal. And yet that was about the truth, as I hinted very delicately to Mistress Odam that evening. But she (being vexed about her wild duck, and not having English ideas on the matter of sport, and so on) made a poor unwitting face at me. Nevertheless Master Odam restored me to my self-respect; for he stared at me till I went to bed; and he broke his hose with excitement. For being in the leg-line myself, I wanted to know what the muscles were of a man who turned a wheel all day. I had never seen a treadmill (though they have one now at Exeter), and it touched me much to learn whether it were good exercise. And herein, from what I saw of Odam, I incline to think that it does great harm; as moving the muscles too much in a line, and without variety.

Chapter LVII Lorna Knows Her Nurse

Having obtained from Benita Odam a very close and full description of the place where her poor mistress lay, and the marks whereby to know it, I hastened to Watchett the following morning, before the sun was up, or any people were about. And so, without interruption, I was in the churchyard at sunrise.

In the farthest and darkest nook, overgrown with grass, and overhung by a weeping-tree a little bank of earth betokened the rounding off of a hapless life. There was nothing to tell of rank, or wealth, of love, or even pity; nameless as a peasant lay the last (as supposed) of a mighty race. Only some unskilful hand, probably Master Odam's under his wife's teaching, had carved a rude L., and a ruder D., upon a large pebble from the beach, and set it up as a headstone.

I gathered a little grass for Lorna and a sprig of the weeping-tree, and then returned to the Forest Cat, as Benita's lonely inn was called. For the way is long from Watchett to Oare; and though you may ride it rapidly, as the Doones had done on that fatal night, to travel on wheels, with one horse only, is a matter of time and of prudence. Therefore, we set out pretty early, three of us and a baby, who could not well be left behind. The wife of the man who owned the cart had undertaken to mind the business, and the other babies, upon condition of having the keys of all the taps left with her.

As the manner of journeying over the moor has been described oft enough already, I will say no more, except that we all arrived before dusk of the summer's day, safe at Plover's Barrows. Mistress Benita was delighted with the change from her dull hard life; and she made many excellent observations, such as seem natural to a foreigner looking at our country.

As luck would have it, the first who came to meet us at the gate was Lorna, with nothing whatever upon her head (the weather being summerly) but her beautiful hair shed round her; and wearing a sweet white frock tucked in, and showing her figure perfectly. In her joy she ran straight up to the cart; and then stopped and gazed at Benita. At one glance her old nurse knew her: 'Oh, the eyes, the eyes!' she cried, and was over the rail of the cart in a moment, in spite of all her substance. Lorna, on the other hand, looked at her with some doubt and wonder, as though having right to know much about her, and yet unable to do so. But when the foreign woman said something in Roman language, and flung new hay from the cart upon her, as if in a romp of childhood, the young maid cried, 'Oh, Nita, Nita!' and fell upon her breast, and wept; and after that looked round at us.

This being so, there could be no doubt as to the power of proving Lady Lorna's birth, and rights, both by evidence and token. For though we had not the necklace now—thanks to Annie's wisdom—we had the ring of heavy gold, a very ancient relic, with which my maid (in her simple way) had pledged herself to me. And Benita knew this ring as well as she knew her own fingers, having heard a long history about it; and the effigy on it of the wild cat was the bearing of the house of Lorne.

For though Lorna's father was a nobleman of high and goodly lineage, her mother was of yet more ancient and renowned descent, being the last in line direct from the great and kingly chiefs of Lorne. A wild and headstrong race they were, and must have everything their own way. Hot blood was ever among them, even of one household; and their sovereignty (which more than once had defied the King of Scotland) waned and fell among themselves, by continual quarrelling. And it was of a piece with this, that the Doones (who were an offset, by the mother's side, holding in co-partnership some large property, which had come by the spindle, as we say) should fall out with the Earl of Lorne, the last but one of that title.

The daughter of this nobleman had married Sir Ensor Doone; but this, instead of healing matters, led to fiercer conflict. I never could quite understand all the ins and outs of it; which none but a lawyer may go through, and keep his head at the end of it. The motives of mankind are plainer than the motions they produce. Especially when charity (such as found among us) sits to judge the former, and is never weary of it; while reason does not care to trace the latter complications, except for fee or title.

Therefore it is enough to say, that knowing Lorna to be direct in heirship to vast property, and bearing especial spite against the house of which she was the last, the Doones had brought her up with full intention of lawful marriage; and had carefully secluded her from the wildest of their young gallants. Of course, if they had been next in succession, the child would have gone down the waterfall, to save any further trouble; but there was an intercepting branch of some honest family; and they being outlaws, would have a poor chance (though the law loves outlaws) against them. Only Lorna was of the stock; and Lorna they must marry. And what a triumph against the old earl, for a cursed Doone to succeed him!

As for their outlawry, great robberies, and grand murders, the veriest child, nowadays, must know that money heals the whole of that. Even if they had murdered people of a good position, it would only cost about twice as much to prove their motives loyal. But they had never slain any man above the rank of yeoman; and folk even said that my father was the highest of their victims; for the death of Lorna's mother and brother was never set to their account.

Pure pleasure it is to any man, to reflect upon all these things. How truly we discern clear justice, and how well we deal it. If any poor man steals a sheep, having ten children starving, and regarding it as mountain game (as a rich man does a hare), to the gallows with him. If a man of rank beats down a door, smites the owner upon the head, and honours the wife with attention, it is a thing to be grateful for, and to slouch smitten head the lower.

While we were full of all these things, and wondering what would happen next, or what we ought ourselves to do, another very important matter called for our attention. This was no less than Annie's marriage to the Squire Faggus. We had tried to put it off again; for in spite of all advantages, neither my mother nor myself had any real heart for it. Not that we dwelled upon Tom's short-comings or rather perhaps his going too far, at the time when he worked the road so. All that was covered by the King's pardon, and universal respect of the neighbourhood. But our scruple was this—and the more we talked the more it grew upon us—that we both had great misgivings as to his future steadiness.

For it would be a thousand pities, we said, for a fine, well-grown, and pretty maiden (such as our Annie was), useful too, in so many ways, and lively, and warm-hearted, and mistress of 500 pounds, to throw herself away on a man with a kind of a turn for drinking. If that last were even hinted, Annie would be most indignant, and ask, with cheeks as red as roses, who had ever seen Master Faggus any the worse for liquor indeed? Her own opinion was, in truth, that be took a great deal too little, after all his hard work, and hard riding, and coming over the hills to be insulted! And if ever it lay in her power, and with no one to grudge him his trumpery glass, she would see that poor Tom had the nourishment which his cough and his lungs required.

His lungs being quite as sound as mine, this matter was out of all argument; so mother and I looked at one another, as much as to say, 'let her go upstairs, she will cry and come down more reasonable.' And while she was gone, we used to say the same thing over and over again; but without perceiving a cure for it. And we almost always finished up with the following reflection, which sometimes came from mother's lips, and sometimes from my own: 'Well, well, there is no telling. None can say how a man may alter; when he takes to matrimony. But if we could only make Annie promise to be a little firm with him!'

I fear that all this talk on our part only hurried matters forward, Annie being more determined every time we pitied her. And at last Tom Faggus came, and spoke as if he were on the King's road, with a pistol at my head, and one at mother's. 'No more fast and loose,' he cried. 'either one thing or the other. I love the maid, and she loves me; and we will have one another, either with your leave, or without it. How many more times am I to dance over these vile hills, and leave my business, and get nothing more than a sigh or a kiss, and "Tom, I must wait for mother"? You are famous for being straightforward, you Ridds. Just treat me as I would treat you now.'

I looked at my mother; for a glance from her would have sent Tom out of the window; but she checked me with her hand, and said, 'You have some ground of complaint, sir; I will not deny it. Now I will be as straightforward with you, as even a Ridd is supposed to be. My son and myself have all along disliked your marriage with Annie. Not for what you have been so much, as for what we fear you will be. Have patience, one moment, if you please. We do not fear your taking to the highway life again; for that you are too clever, no doubt, now that you have property. But we fear that you will take to drinking, and to squandering money. There are many examples of this around us; and we know what the fate of the wife is. It has been hard to tell you this, under our own roof, and with our own—' Here mother hesitated.

'Spirits, and cider, and beer,' I broke in; 'out with it, like a Ridd, mother; as he will have all of it.'

'Spirits, and cider, and beer,' said mother very firmly after me; and then she gave way and said, 'You know, Tom, you are welcome to every drop and more of it.'

Now Tom must have had a far sweeter temper than ever I could claim; for I should have thrust my glass away, and never have taken another drop in the house where such a check had met me. But instead of that, Master Faggus replied, with a pleasant smile,—

'I know that I am welcome, good mother; and to prove it, I will have some more.'

And thereupon be mixed himself another glass of hollands with lemon and hot water, yet pouring it very delicately.

'Oh, I have been so miserable—take a little more, Tom,' said mother, handing the bottle.

'Yes, take a little more,' I said; 'you have mixed it over weak, Tom.'

'If ever there was a sober man,' cried Tom, complying with our request; 'if ever there was in Christendom a man of perfect sobriety, that man is now before you. Shall we say to-morrow week, mother? It will suit your washing day.'

'How very thoughtful you are, Tom! Now John would never have thought of that, in spite of all his steadiness.'

'Certainly not,' I answered proudly; 'when my time comes for Lorna, I shall not study Betty Muxworthy.'

In this way the Squire got over us; and Farmer Nicholas Snowe was sent for, to counsel with mother about the matter and to set his two daughters sewing.

When the time for the wedding came, there was such a stir and commotion as had never been known in the parish of Oare since my father's marriage. For Annie's beauty and kindliness had made her the pride of the neighbourhood; and the presents sent her, from all around, were enough to stock a shop with. Master Stickles, who now could walk, and who certainly owed his recovery, with the blessing of God, to Annie, presented her with a mighty Bible, silver-clasped, and very handsome, beating the parson's out and out, and for which he had sent to Taunton. Even the common troopers, having tasted her cookery many times (to help out their poor rations), clubbed together, and must have given at least a week's pay apiece, to have turned out what they did for her. This was no less than a silver pot, well-designed, but suited surely rather to the bridegroom's taste than bride's. In a word, everybody gave her things.

And now my Lorna came to me, with a spring of tears in appealing eyes—for she was still somewhat childish, or rather, I should say, more childish now than when she lived in misery—and she placed her little hand in mine, and she was half afraid to speak, and dropped her eyes for me to ask.

'What is it, little darling?' I asked, as I saw her breath come fast; for the smallest emotion moved her form.

'You don't think, John, you don't think, dear, that you could lend me any money?'

'All I have got,' I answered; 'how much do you want, dear heart?'

'I have been calculating; and I fear that I cannot do any good with less than ten pounds, John.'

Here she looked up at me, with horror at the grandeur of the sum, and not knowing what I could think of it. But I kept my eyes from her. 'Ten pounds!' I said in my deepest voice, on purpose to have it out in comfort, when she should be frightened; 'what can you want with ten pounds, child?'

'That is my concern, said Lorna, plucking up her spirit at this: 'when a lady asks for a loan, no gentleman pries into the cause of her asking it.'

'That may be as may be,' I answered in a judicial manner; 'ten pounds, or twenty, you shall have. But I must know the purport.'

'Then that you never shall know, John. I am very sorry for asking you. It is not of the smallest consequence. Oh, dear, no.' Herewith she was running away.

'Oh, dear, yes,' I replied; 'it is of very great consequence; and I understand the whole of it. You want to give that stupid Annie, who has lost you a hundred thousand pounds, and who is going to be married before us, dear—God only can tell why, being my younger sister—you want to give her a wedding present. And you shall do it, darling; because it is so good of you. Don't you know your title, love? How humble you are with us humble folk. You are Lady Lorna something, so far as I can make out yet: and you ought not even to speak to us. You will go away and disdain us.'

'If you please, talk not like that, John. I will have nothing to do with it, if it comes between you and me, John.'

'You cannot help yourself,' said I. And then she vowed that she could and would. And rank and birth were banished from between our lips in no time.

'What can I get her good enough? I am sure I do not know,' she asked: 'she has been so kind and good to me, and she is such a darling. How I shall miss her, to be sure! By the bye, you seem to think, John, that I shall be rich some day.'

'Of course you will. As rich as the French King who keeps ours. Would the Lord Chancellor trouble himself about you, if you were poor?'

'Then if I am rich, perhaps you would lend me twenty pounds, dear John. Ten pounds would be very mean for a wealthy person to give her.'

To this I agreed, upon condition that I should make the purchase myself, whatever it might be. For nothing could be easier than to cheat Lorna about the cost, until time should come for her paying me. And this was better than to cheat her for the benefit of our family. For this end, and for many others, I set off to Dulverton, bearing more commissions, more messages, and more questions than a man of thrice my memory might carry so far as the corner where the sawpit is. And to make things worse, one girl or other would keep on running up to me, or even after me (when started) with something or other she had just thought of, which she could not possibly do without, and which I must be sure to remember, as the most important of the whole.

To my dear mother, who had partly outlived the exceeding value of trifles, the most important matter seemed to ensure Uncle Reuben's countenance and presence at the marriage. And if I succeeded in this, I might well forget all the maidens' trumpery. This she would have been wiser to tell me when they were out of hearing; for I left her to fight her own battle with them; and laughing at her predicament, promised to do the best I could for all, so far as my wits would go.

Uncle Reuben was not at home, but Ruth, who received me very kindly, although without any expressions of joy, was sure of his return in the afternoon, and persuaded me to wait for him. And by the time that I had finished all I could recollect of my orders, even with paper to help me, the old gentleman rode into the yard, and was more surprised than pleased to see me. But if he was surprised, I was more than that—I was utterly astonished at the change in his appearance since the last time I had seen him. From a hale, and rather heavy man, gray-haired, but plump, and ruddy, he was altered to a shrunken, wizened, trembling, and almost decrepit figure. Instead of curly and comely locks, grizzled indeed, but plentiful, he had only a few lank white hairs scattered and flattened upon his forehead. But the greatest change of all was in the expression of his eyes, which had been so keen, and restless, and bright, and a little sarcastic. Bright indeed they still were, but with a slow unhealthy lustre; their keenness was turned to perpetual outlook, their restlessness to a haggard want. As for the humour which once gleamed there (which people who fear it call sarcasm) it had been succeeded by stares of terror, and then mistrust, and shrinking. There was none of the interest in mankind, which is needful even for satire.

'Now what can this be?' thought I to myself, 'has the old man lost all his property, or taken too much to strong waters?'

'Come inside, John Ridd,' he said; 'I will have a talk with you. It is cold out here; and it is too light. Come inside, John Ridd, boy.'

I followed him into a little dark room, quite different from Ruth Huckaback's. It was closed from the shop by an old division of boarding, hung with tanned canvas; and the smell was very close and faint. Here there was a ledger desk, and a couple of chairs, and a long-legged stool.

'Take the stool,' said Uncle Reuben, showing me in very quietly, 'it is fitter for your height, John. Wait a moment; there is no hurry.'

Then he slipped out by another door, and closing it quickly after him, told the foreman and waiting-men that the business of the day was done. They had better all go home at once; and he would see to the fastenings. Of course they were only too glad to go; but I wondered at his sending them, with at least two hours of daylight left.

However, that was no business of mine, and I waited, and pondered whether fair Ruth ever came into this dirty room, and if so, how she kept her hands from it. For Annie would have had it upside down in about two minutes, and scrubbed, and brushed, and dusted, until it looked quite another place; and yet all this done without scolding and crossness; which are the curse of clean women, and ten times worse than the dustiest dust.

Uncle Ben came reeling in, not from any power of liquor, but because he was stiff from horseback, and weak from work and worry.

'Let me be, John, let me be,' he said, as I went to help him; 'this is an unkind dreary place; but many a hundred of good gold Carolus has been turned in this place, John.'

'Not a doubt about it, sir,' I answered in my loud and cheerful manner; 'and many another hundred, sir; and may you long enjoy them!'

'My boy, do you wish me to die?' he asked, coming up close to my stool, and regarding me with a shrewd though blear-eyed gaze; 'many do. Do you, John?'

'Come,' said I, 'don't ask such nonsense. You know better than that, Uncle Ben. Or else, I am sorry for you. I want you to live as long as possible, for the sake of—' Here I stopped.

'For the sake of what, John? I knew it is not for my own sake. For the sake of what, my boy?'

'For the sake of Ruth,' I answered; 'if you must have all the truth. Who is to mind her when you are gone?'

'But if you knew that I had gold, or a manner of getting gold, far more than ever the sailors got out of the Spanish galleons, far more than ever was heard of; and the secret was to be yours, John; yours after me and no other soul's—then you would wish me dead, John.' Here he eyed me as if a speck of dust in my eyes should not escape him.

'You are wrong, Uncle Ben; altogether wrong. For all the gold ever heard or dreamed of, not a wish would cross my heart to rob you of one day of life.'

At last he moved his eyes from mine; but without any word, or sign, to show whether he believed, or disbelieved. Then he went to a chair, and sat with his chin upon the ledger-desk; as if the effort of probing me had been too much for his weary brain. 'Dreamed of! All the gold ever dreamed of! As if it were but a dream!' he muttered; and then he closed his eyes to think.

'Good Uncle Reuben,' I said to him, 'you have been a long way today, sir. Let me go and get you a glass of good wine. Cousin Ruth knows where to find it.'

'How do you know how far I have been?' he asked, with a vicious look at me. 'And Cousin Ruth! You are very pat with my granddaughter's name, young man!'

'It would be hard upon me, sir, not to know my own cousin's name.'

'Very well. Let that go by. You have behaved very badly to Ruth. She loves you; and you love her not.'

At this I was so wholly amazed—not at the thing itself, I mean, but at his knowledge of it—that I could not say a single word; but looked, no doubt, very foolish.

'You may well be ashamed, young man,' he cried, with some triumph over me, 'you are the biggest of all fools, as well as a conceited coxcomb. What can you want more than Ruth? She is a little damsel, truly; but finer men than you, John Ridd, with all your boasted strength and wrestling, have wedded smaller maidens. And as for quality, and value—bots! one inch of Ruth is worth all your seven feet put together.'

Now I am not seven feet high; nor ever was six feet eight inches, in my very prime of life; and nothing vexes me so much as to make me out a giant, and above human sympathy, and human scale of weakness. It cost me hard to hold my tongue; which luckily is not in proportion to my stature. And only for Ruth's sake I held it. But Uncle Ben (being old and worn) was vexed by not having any answer, almost as much as a woman is.

'You want me to go on,' he continued, with a look of spite at me, 'about my poor Ruth's love for you, to feed your cursed vanity. Because a set of asses call you the finest man in England; there is no maid (I suppose) who is not in love with you. I believe you are as deep as you are long, John Ridd. Shall I ever get to the bottom of your character?'

This was a little too much for me. Any insult I could take (with goodwill) from a white-haired man, and one who was my relative; unless it touched my love for Lorna, or my conscious modesty. Now both of these were touched to the quick by the sentences of the old gentleman. Therefore, without a word, I went; only making a bow to him.

But women who are (beyond all doubt) the mothers of all mischief, also nurse that babe to sleep, when he is too noisy. And there was Ruth, as I took my horse (with a trunk of frippery on him), poor little Ruth was at the bridle, and rusting all the knops of our town-going harness with tears.

'Good-bye dear,' I said, as she bent her head away from me; 'shall I put you up on the saddle, dear?'

'Cousin Ridd, you may take it lightly,' said Ruth, turning full upon me, 'and very likely you are right, according to your nature'—this was the only cutting thing the little soul ever said to me—'but oh, Cousin Ridd, you have no idea of the pain you will leave behind you.'

'How can that be so, Ruth, when I am as good as ordered to be off the premises?'

'In the first place, Cousin Ridd, grandfather will be angry with himself, for having so ill-used you. And now he is so weak and poorly, that he is always repenting. In the next place I shall scold him first, until he admits his sorrow; and when he has admitted it, I shall scold myself for scolding him. And then he will come round again, and think that I was hard on him; and end perhaps by hating you—for he is like a woman now, John.'

That last little touch of self-knowledge in Ruth, which she delivered with a gleam of some secret pleasantry, made me stop and look closely at her: but she pretended not to know it. 'There is something in this child,' I thought, 'very different from other girls. What it is I cannot tell; for one very seldom gets at it.'

At any rate the upshot was that the good horse went back to stable, and had another feed of corn, while my wrath sank within me. There are two things, according to my experience (which may not hold with another man) fitted beyond any others to take hot tempers out of us. The first is to see our favourite creatures feeding, and licking up their food, and happily snuffling over it, yet sparing time to be grateful, and showing taste and perception; the other is to go gardening boldly, in the spring of the year, without any misgiving about it, and hoping the utmost of everything. If there be a third anodyne, approaching these two in power, it is to smoke good tobacco well, and watch the setting of the moon; and if this should only be over the sea, the result is irresistible.

Master Huckaback showed no especial signs of joy at my return; but received me with a little grunt, which appeared to me to mean, 'Ah, I thought he would hardly be fool enough to go.' I told him how sorry I was for having in some way offended him; and he answered that I did well to grieve for one at least of my offences. To this I made no reply, as behoves a man dealing with cross and fractious people; and presently he became better-tempered, and sent little Ruth for a bottle of wine. She gave me a beautiful smile of thanks for my forbearance as she passed; and I knew by her manner that she would bring the best bottle in all the cellar.

As I had but little time to spare (although the days were long and light) we were forced to take our wine with promptitude and rapidity; and whether this loosened my uncle's tongue, or whether he meant beforehand to speak, is now almost uncertain. But true it is that he brought his chair very near to mine, after three or four glasses, and sent Ruth away upon some errand which seemed of small importance. At this I was vexed, for the room always looked so different without her.

'Come, Jack,' he said, 'here's your health, young fellow, and a good and obedient wife to you. Not that your wife will ever obey you though; you are much too easy-tempered. Even a bitter and stormy woman might live in peace with you, Jack. But never you give her the chance to try. Marry some sweet little thing, if you can. If not, don't marry any. Ah, we have the maid to suit you, my lad, in this old town of Dulverton.'

'Have you so, sir? But perhaps the maid might have no desire to suit me.'

'That you may take my word she has. The colour of this wine will prove it. The little sly hussy has been to the cobwebbed arch of the cellar, where she has no right to go, for any one under a magistrate. However, I am glad to see it, and we will not spare it, John. After my time, somebody, whoever marries little Ruth, will find some rare wines there, I trow, and perhaps not know the difference.'

Thinking of this the old man sighed, and expected me to sigh after him. But a sigh is not (like a yawn) infectious; and we are all more prone to be sent to sleep than to sorrow by one another. Not but what a sigh sometimes may make us think of sighing.

'Well, sir,' cried I, in my sprightliest manner, which rouses up most people, 'here's to your health and dear little Ruth's: and may you live to knock off the cobwebs from every bottle in under the arch. Uncle Reuben, your life and health, sir?'

With that I took my glass thoughtfully, for it was wondrous good; and Uncle Ben was pleased to see me dwelling pleasantly on the subject with parenthesis, and self-commune, and oral judgment unpronounced, though smacking of fine decision. 'Curia vult advisari,' as the lawyers say; which means, 'Let us have another glass, and then we can think about it.'

'Come now, John,' said Uncle Ben, laying his wrinkled hand on my knee, when he saw that none could heed us, 'I know that you have a sneaking fondness for my grandchild Ruth. Don't interrupt me now; you have; and to deny it will only provoke me.'

'I do like Ruth, sir,' I said boldly, for fear of misunderstanding; 'but I do not love her.'

'Very well; that makes no difference. Liking may very soon be loving (as some people call it) when the maid has money to help her.'

'But if there be, as there is in my case—'

'Once for all, John, not a word. I do not attempt to lead you into any engagement with little Ruth; neither will I blame you (though I may be disappointed) if no such engagement should ever be. But whether you will have my grandchild, or whether you will not—and such a chance is rarely offered to a fellow of your standing'—Uncle Ben despised all farmers—'in any case I have at least resolved to let you know my secret; and for two good reasons. The first is that it wears me out to dwell upon it, all alone, and the second is that I can trust you to fulfil a promise. Moreover, you are my next of kin, except among the womankind; and you are just the man I want, to help me in my enterprise.'

'And I will help you, sir,' I answered, fearing some conspiracy, 'in anything that is true, and loyal, and according to the laws of the realm.'

'Ha, ha!' cried the old man, laughing until his eyes ran over, and spreading out his skinny hands upon his shining breeches, 'thou hast gone the same fools' track as the rest; even as spy Stickles went, and all his precious troopers. Landing of arms at Glenthorne, and Lynmouth, wagons escorted across the moor, sounds of metal and booming noises! Ah, but we managed it cleverly, to cheat even those so near to us. Disaffection at Taunton, signs of insurrection at Dulverton, revolutionary tanner at Dunster! We set it all abroad, right well. And not even you to suspect our work; though we thought at one time that you watched us. Now who, do you suppose, is at the bottom of all this Exmoor insurgency, all this western rebellion—not that I say there is none, mind—but who is at the bottom of it?'

'Either Mother Melldrum,' said I, being now a little angry, 'or else old Nick himself.'

'Nay, old Uncle Reuben!' Saying this, Master Huckaback cast back his coat, and stood up, and made the most of himself.

'Well!' cried I, being now quite come to the limits of my intellect, 'then, after all, Captain Stickles was right in calling you a rebel, sir!'

'Of course he was; could so keen a man be wrong about an old fool like me? But come, and see our rebellion, John. I will trust you now with everything. I will take no oath from you; only your word to keep silence; and most of all from your mother.'

'I will give you my word,' I said, although liking not such pledges; which make a man think before he speaks in ordinary company, against his usual practices. However, I was now so curious, that I thought of nothing else; and scarcely could believe at all that Uncle Ben was quite right in his head.

'Take another glass of wine, my son,' he cried with a cheerful countenance, which made him look more than ten years younger; 'you shall come into partnership with me: your strength will save us two horses, and we always fear the horse work. Come and see our rebellion, my boy; you are a made man from to-night.'

'But where am I to come and see it? Where am I to find it, sir?'

'Meet me,' he answered, yet closing his hands, and wrinkling with doubt his forehead, 'come alone, of course; and meet me at the Wizard's Slough, at ten to-morrow morning.'

Chapter LVIII Master Huckaback's Secret

Knowing Master Huckaback to be a man of his word, as well as one who would have others so, I was careful to be in good time the next morning, by the side of the Wizard's Slough. I am free to admit that the name of the place bore a feeling of uneasiness, and a love of distance, in some measure to my heart. But I did my best not to think of this; only I thought it a wise precaution, and due for the sake of my mother and Lorna, to load my gun with a dozen slugs made from the lead of the old church-porch, laid by, long since, against witchcraft.

I am well aware that some people now begin to doubt about witchcraft; or at any rate feign to do so; being desirous to disbelieve whatever they are afraid of. This spirit is growing too common among us, and will end (unless we put a stop to it!) in the destruction of all religion. And as regards witchcraft, a man is bound either to believe in it, or to disbelieve the Bible. For even in the New Testament, discarding many things of the Old, such as sacrifices, and Sabbath, and fasting, and other miseries, witchcraft is clearly spoken of as a thing that must continue; that the Evil One be not utterly robbed of his vested interests. Hence let no one tell me that witchcraft is done away with; for I will meet him with St. Paul, than whom no better man, and few less superstitious, can be found in all the Bible.

Feeling these things more in those days than I feel them now, I fetched a goodish compass round, by the way of the cloven rocks, rather than cross Black Barrow Down, in a reckless and unholy manner. There were several spots, upon that Down, cursed and smitten, and blasted, as if thunderbolts had fallen there, and Satan sat to keep them warm. At any rate it was good (as every one acknowledged) not to wander there too much; even with a doctor of divinity on one arm and of medicine upon the other.

Therefore, I, being all alone, and on foot (as seemed the wisest), preferred a course of roundabout; and starting about eight o'clock, without mentioning my business, arrived at the mouth of the deep descent, such as John Fry described it. Now this (though I have not spoken of it) was not my first time of being there. For, although I could not bring myself to spy upon Uncle Reuben, as John Fry had done, yet I thought it no ill manners, after he had left our house, to have a look at the famous place, where the malefactor came to life, at least in John's opinion. At that time, however, I saw nothing except the great ugly black morass, with the grisly reeds around it; and I did not care to go very near it, much less to pry on the further side.

Now, on the other hand, I was bent to get at the very bottom of this mystery (if there were any), having less fear of witch or wizard, with a man of Uncle Reuben's wealth to take my part, and see me through. So I rattled the ramrod down my gun, just to know if the charge were right, after so much walking; and finding it full six inches deep, as I like to have it, went boldly down the steep gorge of rock, with a firm resolve to shoot any witch unless it were good Mother Melldrum. Nevertheless to my surprise, all was quiet, and fair to look at, in the decline of the narrow way, with great stalked ferns coming forth like trees, yet hanging like cobwebs over one. And along one side, a little spring was getting rid of its waters. Any man might stop and think; or he might go on and think; and in either case, there was none to say that he was making a fool of himself.

When I came to the foot of this ravine, and over against the great black slough, there was no sign of Master Huckaback, nor of any other living man, except myself, in the silence. Therefore, I sat in a niche of rock, gazing at the slough, and pondering the old tradition about it.

They say that, in the ancient times, a mighty necromancer lived in the wilderness of Exmoor. Here, by spell and incantation, he built himself a strong high palace, eight-sided like a spider's web, and standing on a central steep; so that neither man nor beast could cross the moors without his knowledge. If he wished to rob and slay a traveller, or to have wild ox, or stag for food, he had nothing more to do than sit at one of his eight windows, and point his unholy book at him. Any moving creature, at which that book was pointed, must obey the call, and come from whatever distance, if sighted once by the wizard.

This was a bad condition of things, and all the country groaned under it; and Exmoor (although the most honest place that a man could wish to live in) was beginning to get a bad reputation, and all through that vile wizard. No man durst even go to steal a sheep, or a pony, or so much as a deer for dinner, lest he should be brought to book by a far bigger rogue than he was. And this went on for many years; though they prayed to God to abate it. But at last, when the wizard was getting fat and haughty upon his high stomach, a mighty deliverance came to Exmoor, and a warning, and a memory. For one day the sorcerer gazed from his window facing the southeast of the compass, and he yawned, having killed so many men that now he was weary of it.

"Ifackins,' he cried, or some such oath, both profane and uncomely, 'I see a man on the verge of the sky-line, going along laboriously. A pilgrim, I trow, or some such fool, with the nails of his boots inside them.

Too thin to be worth eating; but I will have him for the fun of the thing; and most of those saints have got money.'

With these words he stretched forth his legs on a stool, and pointed the book of heathenish spells back upwards at the pilgrim. Now this good pilgrim was plodding along, soberly and religiously, with a pound of flints in either boot, and not an ounce of meat inside him. He felt the spell of the wicked book, but only as a horse might feel a 'gee-wug!' addressed to him. It was in the power of this good man, either to go on, or turn aside, and see out the wizard's meaning. And for a moment he halted and stood, like one in two minds about a thing. Then the wizard clapped one cover to, in a jocular and insulting manner; and the sound of it came to the pilgrim's ear, about five miles in the distance, like a great gun fired at him.

'By our Lady,' he cried, 'I must see to this; although my poor feet have no skin below them. I will teach this heathen miscreant how to scoff at Glastonbury.'

Thereupon he turned his course, and ploughed along through the moors and bogs, towards the eight-sided palace. The wizard sat on his chair of comfort, and with the rankest contempt observed the holy man ploughing towards him. 'He has something good in his wallet, I trow,' said the black thief to himself; 'these fellows get always the pick of the wine, and the best of a woman's money.' Then he cried, 'Come in, come in, good sir,' as he always did to every one.

'Bad sir, I will not come in,' said the pilgrim; 'neither shall you come out again. Here are the bones of all you have slain; and here shall your own bones be.'

'Hurry me not,' cried the sorcerer; 'that is a thing to think about. How many miles hast thou travelled this day?'

But the pilgrim was too wide awake, for if he had spoken of any number, bearing no cross upon it, the necromancer would have had him, like a ball at bando-play. Therefore he answered, as truly as need be, 'By the grace of our Lady, nine.'

Now nine is the crossest of all cross numbers, and full to the lip of all crochets. So the wizard staggered back, and thought, and inquired again with bravery, 'Where can you find a man and wife, one going up-hill and one going down, and not a word spoken between them?'

'In a cucumber plant,' said the modest saint; blushing even to think of it; and the wizard knew he was done for.

'You have tried me with ungodly questions,' continued the honest pilgrim, with one hand still over his eyes, as he thought of the feminine cucumber; 'and now I will ask you a pure one. To whom of mankind have you ever done good, since God saw fit to make you?'

The wizard thought, but could quote no one; and he looked at the saint, and the saint at him, and both their hearts were trembling. 'Can you mention only one?' asked the saint, pointing a piece of the true cross at him, hoping he might cling to it; 'even a little child will do; try to think of some one.'

The earth was rocking beneath their feet, and the palace windows darkened on them, with a tint of blood, for now the saint was come inside, hoping to save the wizard.

'If I must tell the pure truth,' said the wizard, looking up at the arches of his windows, 'I can tell of only one to whom I ever have done good.'

'One will do; one is quite enough; be quick before the ground opens. The name of one—and this cross will save you. Lay your thumb on the end of it.'

'Nay, that I cannot do, great saint. The devil have mercy upon me.'

All this while the palace was sinking, and blackness coming over them.

'Thou hast all but done for thyself,' said the saint, with a glory burning round his head; 'by that last invocation. Yet give us the name of the one, my friend, if one there be; it will save thee, with the cross upon thy breast. All is crashing round us; dear brother, who is that one?'

'My own self,' cried the wretched wizard.

'Then there is no help for thee.' And with that the honest saint went upward, and the wizard, and all his palace, and even the crag that bore it, sank to the bowels of the earth; and over them was nothing left except a black bog fringed with reed, of the tint of the wizard's whiskers. The saint, however, was all right, after sleeping off the excitement; and he founded a chapel, some three miles westward; and there he lies with his holy relic and thither in after ages came (as we all come home at last) both my Lorna's Aunt Sabina, and her guardian Ensor Doone.

While yet I dwelled upon this strange story, wondering if it all were true, and why such things do not happen now, a man on horseback appeared as suddenly as if he had risen out of the earth, on the other side of the great black slough. At first I was a little scared, my mind being in the tune for wonders; but presently the white hair, whiter from the blackness of the bog between us, showed me that it was Uncle Reuben come to look for me, that way. Then I left my chair of rock, and waved my hat and shouted to him, and the sound of my voice among the crags and lonely corners frightened me.

Old Master Huckaback made no answer, but (so far as I could guess) beckoned me to come to him. There was just room between the fringe of reed and the belt of rock around it, for a man going very carefully to escape that horrible pit-hole. And so I went round to the other side, and there found open space enough, with stunted bushes, and starveling trees, and straggling tufts of rushes.

'You fool, you are frightened,' said Uncle Ben, as he looked at my face after shaking hands: 'I want a young man of steadfast courage, as well as of strength and silence. And after what I heard of the battle at Glen Doone, I thought I might trust you for courage.'

'So you may,' said I, 'wherever I see mine enemy; but not where witch and wizard be.'

'Tush, great fool!' cried Master Huckaback; 'the only witch or wizard here is the one that bewitcheth all men. Now fasten up my horse, John

Ridd, and not too near the slough, lad. Ah, we have chosen our entrance wisely. Two good horsemen, and their horses, coming hither to spy us out, are gone mining on their own account (and their last account it is) down this good wizard's bog-hole.'

With these words, Uncle Reuben clutched the mane of his horse and came down, as a man does when his legs are old; and as I myself begin to do, at this time of writing. I offered a hand, but he was vexed, and would have nought to do with it.

'Now follow me, step for step,' he said, when I had tethered his horse to a tree; 'the ground is not death (like the wizard's hole), but many parts are treacherous, I know it well by this time.'

Without any more ado, he led me in and out the marshy places, to a great round hole or shaft, bratticed up with timber. I never had seen the like before, and wondered how they could want a well, with so much water on every side. Around the mouth were a few little heaps of stuff unused to the daylight; and I thought at once of the tales I had heard concerning mines in Cornwall, and the silver cup at Combe-Martin, sent to the Queen Elizabeth.

'We had a tree across it, John,' said Uncle Reuben, smiling grimly at my sudden shrink from it: 'but some rogue came spying here, just as one of our men went up. He was frightened half out of his life, I believe, and never ventured to come again. But we put the blame of that upon you. And I see that we were wrong, John.' Here he looked at me with keen eyes, though weak.

'You were altogether wrong,' I answered. 'Am I mean enough to spy upon any one dwelling with us? And more than that, Uncle Reuben, it was mean of you to suppose it.'

'All ideas are different,' replied the old man to my heat, like a little worn-out rill running down a smithy; 'you with your strength and youth, and all that, are inclined to be romantic. I take things as I have known them, going on for seventy years. Now will you come and meet the wizard, or does your courage fail you?'

'My courage must be none,' said I, 'if I would not go where you go, sir.'

He said no more, but signed to me to lift a heavy wooden corb with an iron loop across it, and sunk in a little pit of earth, a yard or so from the mouth of the shaft. I raised it, and by his direction dropped it into the throat of the shaft, where it hung and shook from a great cross-beam laid at the level of the earth. A very stout thick rope was fastened to the handle of the corb, and ran across a pulley hanging from the centre of the beam, and thence out of sight in the nether places.

'I will first descend,' he said; 'your weight is too great for safety. When the bucket comes up again, follow me, if your heart is good.'

Then he whistled down, with a quick sharp noise, and a whistle from below replied; and he clomb into the vehicle, and the rope ran through the pulley, and Uncle Ben went merrily down, and was out of sight, before I had time to think of him.

Now being left on the bank like that, and in full sight of the goodly heaven, I wrestled hard with my flesh and blood, about going down into the pit-hole. And but for the pale shame of the thing, that a white-headed man should adventure so, and green youth doubt about it, never could I have made up my mind; for I do love air and heaven. However, at last up came the bucket; and with a short sad prayer I went into whatever might happen.

My teeth would chatter, do all I could; but the strength of my arms was with me; and by them I held on the grimy rope, and so eased the foot of the corb, which threatened to go away fathoms under me. Of course I should still have been safe enough, being like an egg in an egg-cup, too big to care for the bottom; still I wished that all should be done, in good order, without excitement.

The scoopings of the side grew black, and the patch of sky above more blue, as with many thoughts of Lorna, a long way underground I sank. Then I was fetched up at the bottom with a jerk and rattle; and but for holding by the rope so, must have tumbled over. Two great torches of bale-resin showed me all the darkness, one being held by Uncle Ben and the other by a short square man with a face which seemed well-known to me.

'Hail to the world of gold, John Ridd,' said Master Huckaback, smiling in the old dry manner; 'bigger coward never came down the shaft, now did he, Carfax?'

'They be all alike,' said the short square man, 'fust time as they doos it.'

'May I go to heaven,' I cried, 'which is a thing quite out of sight'—for I always have a vein of humour, too small to be followed by any one—'if ever again of my own accord I go so far away from it!' Uncle Ben grinned less at this than at the way I knocked my shin in getting out of the bucket; and as for Master Carfax, he would not even deign to smile. And he seemed to look upon my entrance as an interloping.

For my part, I had nought to do, after rubbing my bruised leg, except to look about me, so far as the dullness of light would help. And herein I seemed, like a mouse in a trap, able no more than to run to and fro, and knock himself, and stare at things. For here was a little channel grooved with posts on either side of it, and ending with a heap of darkness, whence the sight came back again; and there was a scooped place, like a funnel, but pouring only to darkness. So I waited for somebody to speak first, not seeing my way to anything.'

'You seem to be disappointed, John,' said Uncle Reuben, looking blue by the light of the flambeaux; 'did you expect to see the roof of gold, and the sides of gold, and the floor of gold, John Ridd?'

'Ha, ha!' cried Master Carfax; 'I reckon her did; no doubt her did.'

'You are wrong,' I replied; 'but I did expect to see something better than dirt and darkness.'

'Come on then, my lad; and we will show you some-thing better. We want your great arm on here, for a job that has beaten the whole of us.'

With these words, Uncle Ben led the way along a narrow passage, roofed with rock and floored with slate-coloured shale and shingle, and winding in and out, until we stopped at a great stone block or boulder, lying across the floor, and as large as my mother's best oaken wardrobe. Beside it were several sledge-hammers, battered, and some with broken helves.

'Thou great villain!' cried Uncle Ben, giving the boulder a little kick; 'I believe thy time is come at last. Now, John, give us a sample of the things they tell of thee. Take the biggest of them sledge-hammers and crack this rogue in two for us. We have tried at him for a fortnight, and he is a nut worth cracking. But we have no man who can swing that hammer, though all in the mine have handled it.'

'I will do my very best,' said I, pulling off my coat and waistcoat, as if I were going to wrestle; 'but I fear he will prove too tough for me.'

'Ay, that her wull,' grunted Master Carfax; 'lack'th a Carnishman, and a beg one too, not a little charp such as I be. There be no man outside Carnwall, as can crack that boolder.'

'Bless my heart,' I answered; 'but I know something of you, my friend, or at any rate of your family. Well, I have beaten most of your Cornish men, though not my place to talk of it. But mind, if I crack this rock for you, I must have some of the gold inside it.'

'Dost think to see the gold come tumbling out like the kernel of a nut, thou zany?' asked Uncle Reuben pettishly; 'now wilt thou crack it or wilt thou not? For I believe thou canst do it, though only a lad of Somerset.'

Uncle Reuben showed by saying this, and by his glance at Carfax, that he was proud of his county, and would be disappointed for it if I failed to crack the boulder. So I begged him to stoop his torch a little, that I might examine my subject. To me there appeared to be nothing at all remarkable about it, except that it sparkled here and there, when the flash of the flame fell upon it. A great obstinate, oblong, sullen stone; how could it be worth the breaking, except for making roads with?

Nevertheless, I took up the hammer, and swinging it far behind my head, fetched it down, with all my power, upon the middle of the rock. The roof above rang mightily, and the echo went down delven galleries, so that all the miners flocked to know what might be doing. But Master Carfax only smiled, although the blow shook him where he stood, for behold the stone was still unbroken, and as firm as ever. Then I smote it again, with no better fortune, and Uncle Ben looked vexed and angry, but all the miners grinned with triumph.

'This little tool is too light,' I cried; 'one of you give me a piece of strong cord.'

Then I took two more of the weightiest hammers, and lashed them fast to the back of mine, not so as to strike, but to burden the fall. Having made this firm, and with room to grasp the handle of the largest one only—for the helves of the others were shorter—I smiled at Uncle Ben, and whirled the mighty implement round my head, just to try whether I could manage it. Upon that the miners gave a cheer, being honest men, and desirous of seeing fair play between this 'shameless stone' (as Dan Homer calls it) and me with my hammer hammering.

Then I swung me on high to the swing of the sledge, as a thresher bends back to the rise of his flail, and with all my power descending delivered the ponderous onset. Crashing and crushed the great stone fell over, and threads of sparkling gold appeared in the jagged sides of the breakage.

'How now, Simon Carfax?' cried Uncle Ben triumphantly; 'wilt thou find a man in Cornwall can do the like of that?'

'Ay, and more,' he answered; 'however, it be pretty fair for a lad of these outlandish parts. Get your rollers, my lads, and lead it to the crushing engine.'

I was glad to have been of some service to them; for it seems that this great boulder had been too large to be drawn along the gallery and too hard to crack. But now they moved it very easily, taking piece by piece, and carefully picking up the fragments.

'Thou hast done us a good turn, my lad,' said Uncle Reuben, as the others passed out of sight at the corner; 'and now I will show thee the bottom of a very wondrous mystery. But we must not do it more than once, for the time of day is the wrong one.'

The whole affair being a mystery to me, and far beyond my understanding, I followed him softly, without a word, yet thinking very heavily, and longing to be above ground again. He led me through small passages, to a hollow place near the descending shaft, where I saw a most extraordinary monster fitted up. In form it was like a great coffee-mill, such as I had seen in London, only a thousand times larger, and with heavy windlass to work it.

'Put in a barrow-load of the smoulder,' said Uncle Ben to Carfax, 'and let them work the crank, for John to understand a thing or two.'

'At this time of day!' cried Simon Carfax; 'and the watching as has been o' late!'

However, he did it without more remonstrance; pouring into the scuttle at the top of the machine about a baskeful of broken rock; and then a dozen men went to the wheel, and forced it round, as sailors do. Upon that such a hideous noise arose, as I never should have believed any creature capable of making, and I ran to the well of the mine for air, and to ease my ears, if possible.

'Enough, enough!' shouted Uncle Ben by the time I was nearly deafened; 'we will digest our goodly boulder after the devil is come abroad for his evening work. Now, John, not a word about what you have learned; but henceforth you will not be frightened by the noise we make at dusk.'

I could not deny but what this was very clever management. If they could not keep the echoes of the upper air from moving, the wisest plan was to open their valves during the discouragement of the falling evening; when folk would rather be driven away, than drawn into the wilds and quagmires, by a sound so deep and awful, coming through the darkness.

Chapter LIX Lorna Gone Away

Although there are very ancient tales of gold being found upon Exmoor, in lumps and solid hummocks, and of men who slew one another for it, this deep digging and great labour seemed to me a dangerous and unholy enterprise. And Master Huckaback confessed that up to the present time his two partners and himself (for they proved to be three adventurers) had put into the earth more gold than they had taken out of it. Nevertheless he felt quite sure that it must in a very short time succeed, and pay them back an hundredfold; and he pressed me with great earnestness to join them, and work there as much as I could, without moving my mother's suspicions. I asked him how they had managed so long to carry on without discovery; and he said that this was partly through the wildness of the neighbourhood, and the legends that frightened people of a superstitious turn; partly through their own great caution, and the manner of fetching both supplies and implements by night; but most of all, they had to thank the troubles of the period, the suspicions of rebellion, and the terror of the Doones, which (like the wizard I was speaking of) kept folk from being too inquisitive where they had no business. The slough, moreover, had helped them well, both by making their access dark, and yet more by swallowing up and concealing all that was cast from the mouth of the pit. Once, before the attack on Glen Doone, they had a narrow escape from the King's Commissioner; for Captain Stickles having heard no doubt the story of John Fry, went with half a dozen troopers, on purpose to search the neighbourhood. Now if he had ridden alone, most likely he would have discovered everything; but he feared to venture so, having suspicion of a trap. Coming as they did in a company, all mounted and conspicuous, the watchman (who was posted now on the top of the hill, almost every day since John Fry's appearance) could not help espying them, miles distant, over the moorland. He watched them under the shade of his hand, and presently ran down the hill, and raised a great commotion. Then Simon Carfax and all his men came up, and made things natural, removing every sign of work; and finally, sinking underground, drew across the mouth of the pit a hurdle thatched with sedge and heather. Only Simon himself was left behind, ensconced in a hole of the crags, to observe the doings of the enemy.

Captain Stickles rode very bravely, with all his men clattering after him, down the rocky pass, and even to the margin of the slough. And there they stopped, and held council; for it was a perilous thing to risk the passage upon horseback, between the treacherous brink and the cliff, unless one knew it thoroughly. Stickles, however, and one follower, carefully felt the way along, having their horses well in hand, and bearing a rope to draw them out, in case of being foundered. Then they spurred across the rough boggy land, farther away than the shaft was. Here the ground lay jagged and shaggy, wrought up with high tufts of reed, or scragged with stunted brushwood. And between the ups and downs (which met anybody anyhow) green-covered places tempted the foot, and black bog-holes discouraged it. It is not to be marvelled at that amid such place as this, for the first time visited, the horses were a little skeary; and their riders partook of the feeling, as all good riders do. In and out of the tufts they went, with their eyes dilating, wishing to be out of harm, if conscience were but satisfied. And of this tufty flaggy ground, pocked with bogs and boglets, one especial nature is that it will not hold impressions.

Seeing thus no track of men, nor anything but marsh-work, and stormwork, and of the seasons, these two honest men rode back, and were glad to do so. For above them hung the mountains, cowled with fog, and seamed with storm; and around them desolation; and below their feet the grave. Hence they went, with all goodwill; and vowed for ever afterwards that fear of a simple place like that was only too ridiculous. So they all rode home with mutual praises, and their courage well-approved; and the only result of the expedition was to confirm John Fry's repute as a bigger liar than ever.

Now I had enough of that underground work, as before related, to last me for a year to come; neither would I, for sake of gold, have ever stepped into that bucket, of my own goodwill again. But when I told Lorna—whom I could trust in any matter of secrecy, as if she had never been a woman—all about my great descent, and the honeycombing of the earth, and the mournful noise at eventide, when the gold was under the crusher and bewailing the mischief it must do, then Lorna's chief desire was to know more about Simon Carfax.

'It must be our Gwenny's father,' she cried; 'the man who disappeared underground, and whom she has ever been seeking. How grieved the poor little thing will be, if it should turn out, after all, that he left his child on purpose! I can hardly believe it; can you, John?'

'Well,' I replied; 'all men are wicked, more or less, to some extent; and no man may say otherwise.'

For I did not wish to commit myself to an opinion about Simon, lest I might be wrong, and Lorna think less of my judgment.

But being resolved to see this out, and do a good turn, if I could, to Gwenny, who had done me many a good one, I begged my Lorna to say not a word of this matter to the handmaiden, until I had further searched it out. And to carry out this resolve, I went again to the place of business where they were grinding gold as freely as an apothecary at his pills.

Having now true right of entrance, and being known to the watchman, and regarded (since I cracked the boulder) as one who could pay his footing, and perhaps would be the master, when Uncle Ben should he choked with money, I found the corb sent up for me rather sooner than I wished it. For the smell of the places underground, and the way men's eyes came out of them, with links, and brands, and flambeaux, instead of God's light to look at, were to me a point of caution, rather than of pleasure.

No doubt but what some men enjoy it, being born, like worms, to dig, and to live in their own scoopings. Yet even the worms come up sometimes, after a good soft shower of rain, and hold discourse with one another; whereas these men, and the horses let down, come above ground never.

And the changing of the sky is half the change our nature calls for. Earth we have, and all its produce (moving from the first appearance, and the hope with infants' eyes, through the bloom of beauty's promise, to the rich and ripe fulfilment, and the falling back to rest); sea we have (with all its wonder shed on eyes, and ears, and heart; and the thought of something more)—but without the sky to look at, what would earth, and sea, and even our own selves, be to us?

Do we look at earth with hope? Yes, for victuals only. Do we look at sea with hope? Yes, that we may escape it. At the sky alone (though questioned with the doubts of sunshine, or scattered with uncertain stars), at the sky alone we look with pure hope and with memory.

Hence it always hurt my feelings when I got into that bucket, with my small-clothes turned up over, and a kerchief round my hat. But knowing that my purpose was sound, and my motives pure, I let the sky grow to a little blue hole, and then to nothing over me. At the bottom Master Carfax met me, being captain of the mine, and desirous to know my business. He wore a loose sack round his shoulders, and his beard was two feet long.

'My business is to speak with you,' I answered rather sternly; for this man, who was nothing more than Uncle Reuben's servant, had carried things too far with me, showing no respect whatever; and though I did not care for much, I liked to receive a little, even in my early days.

'Coom into the muck-hole, then,' was his gracious answer; and he led me into a filthy cell, where the miners changed their jackets.

'Simon Carfax, I began, with a manner to discourage him; 'I fear you are a shallow fellow, and not worth my trouble.'

'Then don't take it,' he replied; 'I want no man's trouble.'

'For your sake I would not,' I answered; 'but for your daughter's sake I will; the daughter whom you left to starve so pitifully in the wilderness.'

The man stared at me with his pale gray eyes, whose colour was lost from candle light; and his voice as well as his body shook, while he cried,—

'It is a lie, man. No daughter, and no son have I. Nor was ever child of mine left to starve in the wilderness. You are too big for me to tackle, and that makes you a coward for saying it.' His hands were playing with a pick-axe helve, as if he longed to have me under it.

'Perhaps I have wronged you, Simon,' I answered very softly; for the sweat upon his forehead shone in the smoky torchlight; 'if I have, I crave your pardon. But did you not bring up from Cornwall a little maid named "Gwenny," and supposed to be your daughter?'

'Ay, and she was my daughter, my last and only child of five; and for her I would give this mine, and all the gold will ever come from it.'

'You shall have her, without either mine or gold; if you only prove to me that you did not abandon her.'

'Abandon her! I abandon Gwenny!' He cried with such a rage of scorn, that I at once believed him. 'They told me she was dead, and crushed, and buried in the drift here; and half my heart died with her. The Almighty blast their mining-work, if the scoundrels lied to me!'

'The scoundrels must have lied to you,' I answered, with a spirit fired by his heat of fury: 'the maid is living and with us. Come up; and you shall see her.'

'Rig the bucket,' he shouted out along the echoing gallery; and then he fell against the wall, and through the grimy sack I saw the heaving of his breast, as I have seen my opponent's chest, in a long hard bout of wrestling. For my part, I could do no more than hold my tongue and look at him.

Without another word we rose to the level of the moors and mires; neither would Master Carfax speak, as I led him across the barrows. In this he was welcome to his own way, for I do love silence; so little harm can come of it. And though Gwenny was no beauty, her father might be fond of her.

So I put him in the cow-house (not to frighten the little maid), and the folding shutters over him, such as we used at the beestings; and he listened to my voice outside, and held on, and preserved himself. For now he would have scooped the earth, as cattle do at yearning-time, and as meekly and as patiently, to have his child restored to him. Not to make long tale of it—for this thing is beyond me, through want of true experience—I went and fetched his Gwenny forth from the back kitchen, where she was fighting, as usual, with our Betty.

'Come along, you little Vick,' I said, for so we called her; 'I have a message to you, Gwenny, from the Lord in heaven.'

'Don't 'ee talk about He,' she answered; 'Her have long forgatten me.'

'That He has never done, you stupid. Come, and see who is in the cowhouse.'

Gwenny knew; she knew in a moment. Looking into my eyes, she knew; and hanging back from me to sigh, she knew it even better.

She had not much elegance of emotion, being flat and square all over; but none the less for that her heart came quick, and her words came slowly.

'Oh, Jan, you are too good to cheat me. Is it joke you are putting upon me?'

I answered her with a gaze alone; and she tucked up her clothes and followed me because the road was dirty. Then I opened the door just wide enough for the child to to go her father, and left those two to have it out, as might be most natural. And they took a long time about it.

Meanwhile I needs must go and tell my Lorna all the matter; and her joy was almost as great as if she herself had found a father. And the wonder of the whole was this, that I got all the credit; of which not a thousandth part belonged by right and reason to me. Yet so it almost always is. If I work for good desert, and slave, and lie awake at night, and spend my unborn life in dreams, not a blink, nor wink, nor inkling of my labour ever tells. It would have been better to leave unburned, and to keep undevoured, the fuel and the food of life. But if I have laboured not, only acted by some impulse, whim, caprice, or anything; or even acting not at all, only letting things float by; piled upon me commendations, bravoes, and applauses, almost work me up to tempt once again (though sick of it) the ill luck of deserving.

Without intending any harm, and meaning only good indeed, I had now done serious wrong to Uncle Reuben's prospects. For Captain Carfax was full as angry at the trick played on him as he was happy in discovering the falsehood and the fraud of it. Nor could I help agreeing with him, when he told me all of it, as with tears in his eyes he did, and ready to be my slave henceforth; I could not forbear from owning that it was a low and heartless trick, unworthy of men who had families; and the recoil whereof was well deserved, whatever it might end in.

For when this poor man left his daughter, asleep as he supposed, and having his food, and change of clothes, and Sunday hat to see to, he meant to return in an hour or so, and settle about her sustenance in some house of the neighbourhood. But this was the very thing of all things which the leaders of the enterprise, who had brought him up from Cornwall, for his noted skill in metals, were determined, whether by fair means or foul, to stop at the very outset. Secrecy being their main object, what chance could there be of it, if the miners were allowed to keep their children in the neighbourhood? Hence, on the plea of feasting Simon, they kept him drunk for three days and three nights, assuring him (whenever he had gleams enough to ask for her) that his daughter was as well as could be, and enjoying herself with the children. Not wishing the maid to see him tipsy, he pressed the matter no further; but applied himself to the bottle again, and drank her health with pleasure.

However, after three days of this, his constitution rose against it, and he became quite sober; with a certain lowness of heart moreover, and a sense of error. And his first desire to right himself, and easiest way to do it, was by exerting parental authority upon Gwenny. Possessed with this intention (for he was not a sweet tempered man, and his head was aching sadly) he sought for Gwenny high and low; first with threats, and then with fears, and then with tears and wailing. And so he became to the other men a warning and a great annoyance. Therefore they combined to swear what seemed a very likely thing, and might be true for all they knew, to wit, that Gwenny had come to seek for her father down the shaft-hole, and peering too eagerly into the dark, had toppled forward, and gone down, and lain at the bottom as dead as a stone.

'And thou being so happy with drink,' the villains finished up to him, 'and getting drunker every day, we thought it shame to trouble thee; and we buried the wench in the lower drift; and no use to think more of her; but come and have a glass, Sim.'

But Simon Carfax swore that drink had lost him his wife, and now had lost him the last of his five children, and would lose him his own soul, if further he went on with it; and from that day to his death he never touched strong drink again. Nor only this; but being soon appointed captain of the mine, he allowed no man on any pretext to bring cordials thither; and to this and his stern hard rule and stealthy secret management (as much as to good luck and place) might it be attributed that scarcely any but themselves had dreamed about this Exmoor mine.

As for me, I had no ambition to become a miner; and the state to which gold-seeking had brought poor Uncle Ben was not at all encouraging. My business was to till the ground, and tend the growth that came of it, and store the fruit in Heaven's good time, rather than to scoop and burrow like a weasel or a rat for the yellow root of evil. Moreover, I was led from home, between the hay and corn harvests (when we often have a week to spare), by a call there was no resisting; unless I gave up all regard for wrestling, and for my county.

Now here many persons may take me amiss, and there always has been some confusion; which people who ought to have known better have wrought into subject of quarrelling. By birth it is true, and cannot be denied, that I am a man of Somerset, nevertheless by breed I am, as well as by education, a son of Devon also. And just as both of our two counties vowed that Glen Doone was none of theirs, but belonged to the other one; so now, each with hot claim and jangling (leading even to blows sometimes), asserted and would swear to it (as I became more famous) that John Ridd was of its own producing, bred of its own true blood, and basely stolen by the other.

Now I have not judged it in any way needful or even becoming and delicate, to enter into my wrestling adventures, or describe my progress. The whole thing is so different from Lorna, and her gentle manners, and her style of walking; moreover I must seem (even to kind people) to magnify myself so much, or at least attempt to do it, that I have scratched out written pages, through my better taste and sense.

Neither will I, upon this head, make any difference even now; being simply betrayed into mentioning the matter because bare truth requires it, in the tale of Lorna's fortunes.

For a mighty giant had arisen in a part of Cornwall: and his calf was twenty-five inches round, and the breadth of his shoulders two feet and a quarter; and his stature seven feet and three-quarters. Round the chest he was seventy inches, and his hand a foot across, and there were no scales strong enough to judge of his weight in the market-place. Now this man—or I should say, his backers and his boasters, for the giant himself was modest—sent me a brave and haughty challenge, to meet him in the ring at Bodmin-town, on the first day of August, or else to return my champion's belt to them by the messenger.

It is no use to deny but that I was greatly dashed and scared at first. For my part, I was only, when measured without clothes on, sixty inches round the breast, and round the calf scarce twenty-one, only two feet across the shoulders, and in height not six and three-quarters. However, my mother would never believe that this man could beat me; and Lorna being of the same mind, I resolved to go and try him, as they would pay all expenses and a hundred pounds, if I conquered him; so confident were those Cornishmen.

Now this story is too well known for me to go through it again and again. Every child in Devonshire knows, and his grandson will know, the song which some clever man made of it, after I had treated him to water, and to lemon, and a little sugar, and a drop of eau-de-vie. Enough that I had found the giant quite as big as they had described him, and enough to terrify any one. But trusting in my practice and study of the art, I resolved to try a back with him; and when my arms were round him once, the giant was but a farthingale put into the vice of a blacksmith. The man had no bones; his frame sank in, and I was afraid of crushing him. He lay on his back, and smiled at me; and I begged his pardon.

Now this affair made a noise at the time, and redounded so much to my credit, that I was deeply grieved at it, because deserving none. For I do like a good strife and struggle; and the doubt makes the joy of victory; whereas in this case, I might as well have been sent for a match with a haymow. However, I got my hundred pounds, and made up my mind to spend every farthing in presents for mother and Lorna.

For Annie was married by this time, and long before I went away; as need scarcely be said, perhaps; if any one follows the weeks and the months. The wedding was quiet enough, except for everybody's good wishes; and I desire not to dwell upon it, because it grieved me in many ways.

But now that I had tried to hope the very best for dear Annie, a deeper blow than could have come, even through her, awaited me. For after that visit to Cornwall, and with my prize-money about me, I came on foot from Okehampton to Oare, so as to save a little sum towards my time of marrying. For Lorna's fortune I would not have; small or great I would not have it; only if there were no denying we would devote the whole of it to charitable uses, as Master Peter Blundell had done; and perhaps the future ages would endeavour to be grateful. Lorna and I had settled this question at least twice a day, on the average; and each time with more satisfaction.

Now coming into the kitchen with all my cash in my breeches pocket (golden guineas, with an elephant on them, for the stamp of the Guinea Company), I found dear mother most heartily glad to see me safe and sound again—for she had dreaded that giant, and dreamed of him—and she never asked me about the money. Lizzie also was softer, and more gracious than usual; especially when she saw me pour guineas, like peppercorns, into the pudding-basin. But by the way they hung about, I knew that something was gone wrong.

'Where is Lorna?' I asked at length, after trying not to ask it; 'I want her to come, and see my money. She never saw so much before.'

'Alas!' said mother with a heavy sigh; 'she will see a great deal more, I fear; and a deal more than is good for her. Whether you ever see her again will depend upon her nature, John.'

'What do you mean, mother? Have you quarrelled? Why does not Lorna come to me? Am I never to know?'

'Now, John, be not so impatient,' my mother replied, quite calmly, for in truth she was jealous of Lorna, 'you could wait now, very well, John, if it were till this day week, for the coming of your mother, John. And yet your mother is your best friend. Who can ever fill her place?'

Thinking of her future absence, mother turned away and cried; and the box-iron singed the blanket.

'Now,' said I, being wild by this time; 'Lizzie, you have a little sense; will you tell me where is Lorna?'

'The Lady Lorna Dugal,' said Lizzie, screwing up her lips as if the title were too grand, 'is gone to London, brother John; and not likely to come back again. We must try to get on without her.'

'You little—[something]' I cried, which I dare not write down here, as all you are too good for such language; but Lizzie's lip provoked me so—'my Lorna gone, my Lorna gone! And without good-bye to me even! It is your spite has sickened her.'

'You are quite mistaken there,' she replied; 'how can folk of low degree have either spite or liking towards the people so far above them? The Lady Lorna Dugal is gone, because she could not help herself; and she wept enough to break ten hearts—if hearts are ever broken, John.'

'Darling Lizzie, how good you are!' I cried, without noticing her sneer; 'tell me all about it, dear; tell me every word she said.'

'That will not take long,' said Lizzie, quite as unmoved by soft coaxing as by urgent cursing; 'the lady spoke very little to any one, except indeed to mother, and to Gwenny Carfax; and Gwenny is gone with her, so that the benefit of that is lost. But she left a letter for "poor John," as in charity she called him. How grand she looked, to be sure, with the fine clothes on that were come for her!'

'Where is the letter, you utter vixen! Oh, may you have a husband!'

'Who will thresh it out of you, and starve it, and swear it out of you!' was the meaning of my imprecation: but Lizzie, not dreaming as yet of such things, could not understand me, and was rather thankful; therefore she answered quietly,—

'The letter is in the little cupboard, near the head of Lady Lorna's bed, where she used to keep the diamond necklace, which we contrived to get stolen.'

Without another word I rushed (so that every board in the house shook) up to my lost Lorna's room, and tore the little wall-niche open and espied my treasure. It was as simple, and as homely, and loving, as even I could wish. Part of it ran as follows,—the other parts it behoves me not to open out to strangers:—'My own love, and sometime lord,—Take it not amiss of me, that even without farewell, I go; for I cannot persuade the men to wait, your return being doubtful. My great-uncle, some grand lord, is awaiting me at Dunster, having fear of venturing too near this Exmoor country. I, who have been so lawless always, and the child of outlaws, am now to atone for this, it seems, by living in a court of law, and under special surveillance (as they call it, I believe) of His Majesty's Court of Chancery. My uncle is appointed my guardian and master; and I must live beneath his care, until I am twenty-one years old. To me this appears a dreadful thing, and very unjust, and cruel; for why should I lose my freedom, through heritage of land and gold? I offered to abandon all if they would only let me go; I went down on my knees to them, and said I wanted titles not, neither land, nor money; only to stay where I was, where first I had known happiness. But they only laughed and called me "child," and said I must talk of that to the King's High Chancellor. Their orders they had, and must obey them; and Master Stickles was ordered too, to help as the King's Commissioner. And then, although it pierced my heart not to say one "goodbye, John," I was glad upon the whole that you were not here to dispute it. For I am almost certain that you would not, without force to yourself, have let your Lorna go to people who never, never can care for her.'

Here my darling had wept again, by the tokens on the paper; and then there followed some sweet words, too sweet for me to chatter them. But she finished with these noble lines, which (being common to all humanity, in a case of steadfast love) I do no harm, but rather help all true love by repeating. 'Of one thing rest you well assured—and I do hope that it may prove of service to your rest, love, else would my own be broken—no difference of rank, or fortune, or of life itself, shall ever make me swerve from truth to you. We have passed through many troubles, dangers, and dispartments, but never yet was doubt between us; neither ever shall be. Each has trusted well the other; and still each must do so. Though they tell you I am false, though your own mind harbours it, from the sense of things around, and your own undervaluing, yet take counsel of your heart, and cast such thoughts away from you; being unworthy of itself they must he unworthy also of the one who dwells there; and that one is, and ever shall be, your own Lorna Dugal.'

Some people cannot understand that tears should come from pleasure; but whether from pleasure or from sorrow (mixed as they are in the twisted strings of a man's heart, or a woman's), great tears fell from my stupid eyes, even on the blots of Lorna's.

'No doubt it is all over,' my mind said to me bitterly; 'trust me, all shall yet be right,' my heart replied very sweetly.

Chapter LX Annie Luckier Than John

Some people may look down upon us for our slavish ways (as they may choose to call them), but in our part of the country, we do love to mention title, and to roll it on our tongues, with a conscience and a comfort. Even if a man knows not, through fault of education, who the Duke of this is, or the Earl of that, it will never do for him to say so, lest the room look down on him. Therefore he must nod his head, and say, 'Ah, to he sure! I know him as well as ever I know my own good woman's brother. He married Lord Flipflap's second daughter, and a precious life she led him.' Whereupon the room looks up at him. But I, being quite unable to carry all this in my head, as I ought, was speedily put down by people of a noble tendency, apt at Lords, and pat with Dukes, and knowing more about the King than His Majesty would have requested. Therefore, I fell back in thought, not daring in words to do so, upon the titles of our horses. And all these horses deserved their names, not having merely inherited, but by their own doing earned them. Smiler, for instance, had been so called, not so much from a habit of smiling, as from his general geniality, white nose, and white ankle. This worthy horse was now in years, but hale and gay as ever; and when you let him out of the stable, he could neigh and whinny, and make men and horses know it. On the other hand, Kickums was a horse of morose and surly order; harbouring up revenge, and leading a rider to false confidence. Very smoothly he would go, and as gentle as a turtle-dove; until his rider fully believed that a pack-thread was enough for him, and a pat of approval upon his neck the aim and crown of his worthy life. Then suddenly up went his hind feet to heaven, and the rider for the most part flew over his nose; whereupon good Kickums would take advantage of his favourable position to come and bite a piece out of his back. Now in my present state of mind, being understood of nobody, having none to bear me company, neither wishing to have any, an indefinite kind of attraction drew me into Kickum's society. A bond of mutual sympathy was soon established between us; I would ride no other horse, neither Kickums be ridden by any other man. And this good horse became as jealous about me as a dog might be; and would lash out, or run teeth foremost, at any one who came near him when I was on his back.

This season, the reaping of the corn, which had been but a year ago so pleasant and so lightsome, was become a heavy labour, and a thing for grumbling rather than for gladness. However, for the sake of all, it must be attended to, and with as fair a show of spirit and alacrity as might be. For otherwise the rest would drag, and drop their hands and idle, being quicker to take infection of dullness than of diligence. And the harvest was a heavy one, even heavier than the year before, although of poorer quality. Therefore was I forced to work as hard as any horse could during all the daylight hours, and defer till night the brooding upon my misfortune. But the darkness always found me stiff with work, and weary, and less able to think than to dream, may be, of Lorna. And now the house was so dull and lonesome, wanting Annie's pretty presence, and the light of Lorna's eyes, that a man had no temptation after supper-time even to sit and smoke a pipe.

For Lizzie, though so learned, and pleasant when it suited her, never had taken very kindly to my love for Lorna, and being of a proud and slightly upstart nature, could not bear to be eclipsed in bearing, looks, and breeding, and even in clothes, by the stranger. For one thing I will say of the Doones, that whether by purchase or plunder, they had always dressed my darling well, with her own sweet taste to help them. And though Lizzie's natural hate of the maid (as a Doone and burdened with father's death) should have been changed to remorse when she learned of Lorna's real parentage, it was only altered to sullenness, and discontent with herself, for frequent rudeness to an innocent person, and one of such high descent. Moreover, the child had imbibed strange ideas as to our aristocracy, partly perhaps from her own way of thinking, and partly from reading of history. For while, from one point of view she looked up at them very demurely, as commissioned by God for the country's good; from another sight she disliked them, as ready to sacrifice their best and follow their worst members.

Yet why should this wench dare to judge upon a matter so far beyond her, and form opinions which she knew better than declare before mother? But with me she had no such scruple, for I had no authority over her; and my intellect she looked down upon, because I praised her own so. Thus she made herself very unpleasant to me; by little jags and jerks of sneering, sped as though unwittingly; which I (who now considered myself allied to the aristocracy, and perhaps took airs on that account) had not wit enough to parry, yet had wound enough to feel.

Now any one who does not know exactly how mothers feel and think, would have expected my mother (than whom could be no better one) to pet me, and make much of me, under my sad trouble; to hang with anxiety on my looks, and shed her tears with mine (if any), and season every dish of meat put by for her John's return. And if the whole truth must be told, I did expect that sort of thing, and thought what a plague it would be to me; yet not getting it, was vexed, as if by some new injury. For mother was a special creature (as I suppose we all are), being the warmest of the warm, when fired at the proper corner; and yet, if taken at the wrong point, you would say she was incombustible.

Hence it came to pass that I had no one even to speak to, about Lorna and my grievances; for Captain Stickles was now gone southward; and John Fry. of course, was too low for it, although a married man, and well under his wife's management. But finding myself unable at last to bear this any longer, upon the first day when all the wheat was cut, and the stooks set up in every field, yet none quite fit for carrying, I saddled good Kickums at five in the morning, and without a word to mother (for a little anxiety might do her good) off I set for Molland parish, to have the counsel and the comfort of my darling Annie.

The horse took me over the ground so fast (there being few better to go when he liked), that by nine o'clock Annie was in my arms, and blushing to the colour of Winnie's cheeks, with sudden delight and young happiness.

'You precious little soul!' I cried: 'how does Tom behave to you?'

'Hush!' said Annie: 'how dare you ask? He is the kindest, and the best, and the noblest of all men, John; not even setting yourself aside. Now look not jealous, John: so it is. We all have special gifts, you know. You are as good as you can be, John; but my husband's special gift is nobility of character.' Here she looked at me, as one who has discovered something quite unknown.

'I am devilish glad to hear it,' said I, being touched at going down so: 'keep him to that mark, my dear; and cork the whisky bottle.'

'Yes, darling John,' she answered quickly, not desiring to open that subject, and being too sweet to resent it: 'and how is lovely Lorna? What an age it is since I have seen you! I suppose we must thank her for that.'

'You may thank her for seeing me now,' said I; 'or rather,'—seeing how hurt she looked,—'you may thank my knowledge of your kindness, and my desire to speak of her to a soft-hearted dear little soul like you. I think all the women are gone mad. Even mother treats me shamefully. And as for Lizzie—' Here I stopped, knowing no words strong enough, without shocking Annie.

'Do you mean to say that Lorna is gone?' asked Annie, in great amazement; yet leaping at the truth, as women do, with nothing at all to leap from.

'Gone. And I never shall see her again. It serves me right for aspiring so.'

Being grieved at my manner, she led me in where none could interrupt us; and in spite of all my dejection, I could not help noticing how very pretty and even elegant all things were around. For we upon Exmoor have little taste; all we care for is warm comfort, and plenty to eat and to give away, and a hearty smack in everything. But Squire Faggus had seen the world, and kept company with great people; and the taste he had first displayed in the shoeing of farmers' horses (which led almost to his ruin, by bringing him into jealousy, and flattery, and dashing ways) had now been cultivated in London, and by moonlight, so that none could help admiring it.

'Well!' I cried, for the moment dropping care and woe in astonishment: 'we have nothing like this at Plover's Barrows; nor even Uncle Reuben. I do hope it is honest, Annie?'

'Would I sit in a chair that was not my own?' asked Annie, turning crimson, and dropping defiantly, and with a whisk of her dress which I never had seen before, into the very grandest one: 'would I lie on a couch, brother John, do you think, unless good money was paid for it? Because other people are clever, John, you need not grudge them their earnings.'

'A couch!' I replied: 'why what can you want with a couch in the daytime, Annie? A couch is a small bed, set up in a room without space for a good four-poster. What can you want with a couch downstairs? I never heard of such nonsense. And you ought to be in the dairy.'

'I won't cry, brother John, I won't; because you want to make me cry'—and all the time she was crying—'you always were so nasty, John, sometimes. Ah, you have no nobility of character, like my husband. And I have not seen you for two months, John; and now you come to scold me!'

'You little darling,' I said, for Annie's tears always conquered me; 'if all the rest ill-use me, I will not quarrel with you, dear. You have always been true to me; and I can forgive your vanity. Your things are very pretty, dear; and you may couch ten times a day, without my interference. No doubt your husband has paid for all this, with the ponies he stole from Exmoor. Nobility of character is a thing beyond my understanding; but when my sister loves a man, and he does well and flourishes, who am I to find fault with him? Mother ought to see these things: they would turn her head almost: look at the pimples on the chairs!'

'They are nothing,' Annie answered, after kissing me for my kindness: 'they are only put in for the time indeed; and we are to have much better, with gold all round the bindings, and double plush at the corners; so soon as ever the King repays the debt he owes to my poor Tom.'

I thought to myself that our present King had been most unlucky in one thing—debts all over the kingdom. Not a man who had struck a blow for the King, or for his poor father, or even said a good word for him, in the time of his adversity, but expected at least a baronetcy, and a grant of estates to support it. Many have called King Charles ungrateful: and he may have been so. But some indulgence is due to a man, with entries few on the credit side, and a terrible column of debits.

'Have no fear for the chair,' I said, for it creaked under me very fearfully, having legs not so large as my finger; 'if the chair breaks, Annie, your fear should be, lest the tortoise-shell run into me. Why, it is striped like a viper's loins! I saw some hundreds in London; and very cheap they are. They are made to be sold to the country people, such as you and me, dear; and carefully kept they will last for almost half a year. Now will you come back from your furniture, and listen to my story?'

Annie was a hearty dear, and she knew that half my talk was joke, to make light of my worrying. Therefore she took it in good part, as I well knew that she would do; and she led me to a good honest chair; and she sat in my lap and kissed me.

'All this is not like you, John. All this is not one bit like you: and your cheeks are not as they ought to be. I shall have to come home again, if the women worry my brother so. We always held together, John; and we always will, you know.'

'You dear,' I cried, 'there is nobody who understands me as you do. Lorna makes too much of me, and the rest they make too little.'

'Not mother; oh, not mother, John!'

'No, mother makes too much, no doubt; but wants it all for herself alone; and reckons it as a part of her. She makes me more wroth than any one: as if not only my life, but all my head and heart must seek from hers, and have no other thought or care.'

Being sped of my grumbling thus, and eased into better temper, I told Annie all the strange history about Lorna and her departure, and the small chance that now remained to me of ever seeing my love again. To this Annie would not hearken twice, but judging women by her faithful self, was quite vexed with me for speaking so. And then, to my surprise and sorrow, she would deliver no opinion as to what I ought to do until she had consulted darling Tom.

Dear Tom knew much of the world, no doubt, especially the dark side of it. But to me it scarcely seemed becoming that my course of action with regard to the Lady Lorna Dugal should be referred to Tom Faggus, and depend upon his decision. However, I would not grieve Annie again by making light of her husband; and so when he came in to dinner, the matter was laid before him.

Now this man never confessed himself surprised, under any circumstances; his knowledge of life being so profound, and his charity universal. And in the present case he vowed that he had suspected it all along, and could have thrown light upon Lorna's history, if we had seen fit to apply to him. Upon further inquiry I found that this light was a very dim one, flowing only from the fact that he had stopped her mother's coach, at the village of Bolham, on the Bampton Road, the day before I saw them. Finding only women therein, and these in a sad condition, Tom with his usual chivalry (as he had no scent of the necklace) allowed them to pass; with nothing more than a pleasant exchange of courtesies, and a testimonial forced upon him, in the shape of a bottle of Burgundy wine. This the poor countess handed him; and he twisted the cork out with his teeth, and drank her health with his hat off.

'A lady she was, and a true one; and I am a pretty good judge,' said Tom: 'ah, I do like a high lady!'

Our Annie looked rather queer at this, having no pretensions to be one: but she conquered herself, and said, 'Yes, Tom; and many of them liked you.'

With this, Tom went on the brag at once, being but a shallow fellow, and not of settled principles, though steadier than he used to be; until I felt myself almost bound to fetch him back a little; for of all things I do hate brag the most, as any reader of this tale must by this time know. Therefore I said to Squire Faggus, 'Come back from your highway days. You have married the daughter of an honest man; and such talk is not fit for her. If you were right in robbing people, I am right in robbing you. I could bind you to your own mantelpiece, as you know thoroughly well, Tom; and drive away with your own horses, and all your goods behind them, but for the sense of honesty. And should I not do as fine a thing as any you did on the highway? If everything is of public right, how does this chair belong to you? Clever as you are, Tom Faggus, you are nothing but a fool to mix your felony with your farmership. Drop the one, or drop the other; you cannot maintain them both.'

As I finished very sternly a speech which had exhausted me more than ten rounds of wrestling—but I was carried away by the truth, as sometimes happens to all of us—Tom had not a word to say; albeit his mind was so much more nimble and rapid than ever mine was. He leaned against the mantelpiece (a newly-invented affair in his house) as if I had corded him to it, even as I spoke of doing. And he laid one hand on his breast in a way which made Annie creep softly to him, and look at me not like a sister.

'You have done me good, John,' he said at last, and the hand he gave me was trembling: 'there is no other man on God's earth would have dared to speak to me as you have done. From no other would I have taken it. Nevertheless every word is true; and I shall dwell on it when you are gone. If you never did good in your life before, John, my brother, you have done it now.'

He turned away, in bitter pain, that none might see his trouble; and Annie, going along with him, looked as if I had killed our mother. For my part, I was so upset, for fear of having gone too far, that without a word to either of them, but a message on the title-page of King James his Prayer-book, I saddled Kickums, and was off, and glad of the moorland air again.

Chapter LXI Therefore He Seeks Comfort

It was for poor Annie's sake that I had spoken my mind to her husband so freely, and even harshly. For we all knew she would break her heart, if Tom took to evil ways again. And the right mode of preventing this was, not to coax, and flatter, and make a hero of him (which he did for himself, quite sufficiently), but to set before him the folly of the thing, and the ruin to his own interests. They would both be vexed with me, of course, for having left them so hastily, and especially just before dinner-time; but that would soon wear off; and most likely they would come to see mother, and tell her that I was hard to manage, and they could feel for her about it.

Now with a certain yearning, I know not what, for softness, and for one who could understand me—for simple as a child though being, I found few to do that last, at any rate in my love-time—I relied upon Kickum's strength to take me round by Dulverton. It would make the journey some eight miles longer, but what was that to a brisk young horse, even with my weight upon him?

And having left Squire Faggus and Annie much sooner than had been intended, I had plenty of time before me, and too much, ere a prospect of dinner. Therefore I struck to the right, across the hills, for Dulverton.

Pretty Ruth was in the main street of the town, with a basket in her hand, going home from the market.

'Why, Cousin Ruth, you are grown, I exclaimed; 'I do believe you are, Ruth. And you were almost too tall, already.'

At this the little thing was so pleased, that she smiled through her blushes beautifully, and must needs come to shake hands with me; though I signed to her not to do it, because of my horse's temper. But scarcely was her hand in mine, when Kickums turned like an eel upon her, and caught her by the left arm with his teeth, so that she screamed with agony. I saw the white of his vicious eye, and struck him there with all my force, with my left hand over her right arm, and he never used that eye again; none the less he kept his hold on her. Then I smote him again on the jaw, and caught the little maid up by her right hand, and laid her on the saddle in front of me; while the horse being giddy and staggered with blows, and foiled of his spite, ran backward. Ruth's wits were gone; and she lay before me, in such a helpless and senseless way that I could have killed vile Kickums. I struck the spurs into him past the rowels, and away he went at full gallop; while I had enough to do to hold on, with the little girl lying in front of me. But I called to the men who were flocking around, to send up a surgeon, as quick as could be, to Master Reuben Huckaback's.

The moment I brought my right arm to bear, the vicious horse had no chance with me; and if ever a horse was well paid for spite, Kickums had his change that day. The bridle would almost have held a whale and I drew on it so that his lower jaw was well-nigh broken from him; while with both spurs I tore his flanks, and he learned a little lesson. There are times when a man is more vicious than any horse may vie with. Therefore by the time we had reached Uncle Reuben's house at the top of the hill, the bad horse was only too happy to stop; every string of his body was trembling, and his head hanging down with impotence. I leaped from his back at once, and carried the maiden into her own sweet room.

Now Cousin Ruth was recovering softly from her fright and faintness; and the volley of the wind from galloping so had made her little ears quite pink, and shaken her locks all round her. But any one who might wish to see a comely sight and a moving one, need only have looked at Ruth Huckaback, when she learned (and imagined yet more than it was) the manner of her little ride with me. Her hair was of a hazel-brown, and full of waving readiness; and with no concealment of the trick, she spread it over her eyes and face. Being so delighted with her, and so glad to see her safe, I kissed her through the thick of it, as a cousin has a right to do; yea, and ought to do, with gravity.

'Darling,' I said; 'he has bitten you dreadfully: show me your poor arm, dear.'

She pulled up her sleeve in the simplest manner, rather to look at it herself, than to show me where the wound was. Her sleeve was of dark blue Taunton staple; and her white arm shone, coming out of it, as round and plump and velvety, as a stalk of asparagus, newly fetched out of the ground. But above the curved soft elbow, where no room was for one cross word (according to our proverb),* three sad gashes, edged with crimson, spoiled the flow of the pearly flesh. My presence of mind was lost altogether; and I raised the poor sore arm to my lips, both to stop the bleeding and to take the venom out, having heard how wise it was, and thinking of my mother. But Ruth, to my great amazement, drew away from me in bitter haste, as if I had been inserting instead of extracting poison. For the bite of a horse is most venomous; especially when he sheds his teeth; and far more to be feared than the bite of a dog, or even of a cat. And in my haste I had forgotten that Ruth might not know a word about this, and might doubt about my meaning, and the warmth of my osculation. But knowing her danger, I durst not heed her childishness, or her feelings.

'Don't be a fool, Cousin Ruth,' I said, catching her so that she could not move; 'the poison is soaking into you. Do you think that I do it for pleasure?'

*"A maid with an elbow sharp, or knee
Hath cross words two, out of every three."

The spread of shame on her face was such, when she saw her own misunderstanding, that I was ashamed to look at her; and occupied myself with drawing all the risk of glanders forth from the white limb, hanging helpless now, and left entirely to my will. Before I was quite sure of having wholly exhausted suction, and when I had made the holes in her arm look like the gills of a lamprey, in came the doctor, partly drunk, and in haste to get through his business.

'Ha, ha! I see,' he cried; 'bite of a horse, they tell me. Very poisonous; must be burned away. Sally, the iron in the fire. If you have a fire, this weather.'

'Crave your pardon, good sir,' I said; for poor little Ruth was fainting again at his savage orders: 'but my cousin's arm shall not be burned; it is a great deal too pretty, and I have sucked all the poison out. Look, sir, how clean and fresh it is.'

'Bless my heart! And so it is! No need at all for cauterising. The epidermis will close over, and the cutis and the pellis. John Ridd, you ought to have studied medicine, with your healing powers. Half my virtue lies in touch. A clean and wholesome body, sir; I have taught you the Latin grammar. I leave you in excellent hands, my dear, and they wait for me at shovel-board. Bread and water poultice cold, to be renewed, tribus horis. John Ridd, I was at school with you, and you beat me very lamentably, when I tried to fight with you. You remember me not? It is likely enough: I am forced to take strong waters, John, from infirmity of the liver. Attend to my directions; and I will call again in the morning.'

And in that melancholy plight, caring nothing for business, went one of the cleverest fellows ever known at Tiverton. He could write Latin verses a great deal faster than I could ever write English prose, and nothing seemed too great for him. We thought that he would go to Oxford and astonish every one, and write in the style of Buchanan; but he fell all abroad very lamentably; and now, when I met him again, was come down to push-pin and shovel-board, with a wager of spirits pending.

When Master Huckaback came home, he looked at me very sulkily; not only because of my refusal to become a slave to the gold-digging, but also because he regarded me as the cause of a savage broil between Simon Carfax and the men who had cheated him as to his Gwenny. However, when Uncle Ben saw Ruth, and knew what had befallen her, and she with tears in her eyes declared that she owed her life to Cousin Ridd, the old man became very gracious to me; for if he loved any one on earth, it was his little granddaughter.

I could not stay very long, because, my horse being quite unfit to travel from the injuries which his violence and vice had brought upon him, there was nothing for me but to go on foot, as none of Uncle Ben's horses could take me to Plover's Barrows, without downright cruelty: and though there would be a harvest-moon, Ruth agreed with me that I must not keep my mother waiting, with no idea where I might be, until a late hour of the night. I told Ruth all about our Annie, and her noble furniture; and the little maid was very lively (although her wounds were pain-ing her so, that half her laughter came 'on the wrong side of her mouth,' as we rather coarsely express it); especially she laughed about Annie's newfangled closet for clothes, or standing-press, as she called it. This had frightened me so that I would not come without my stick to look at it; for the front was inlaid with two fiery dragons, and a glass which distorted everything, making even Annie look hideous; and when it was opened, a woman's skeleton, all in white, revealed itself, in the midst of three standing women. 'It is only to keep my best frocks in shape,' Annie had explained to me; 'hanging them up does ruin them so. But I own that I was afraid of it, John, until I had got all my best clothes there, and then I became very fond of it. But even now it frightens me sometimes in the moonlight.'

Having made poor Ruth a little cheerful, with a full account of all Annie's frocks, material, pattern, and fashion (of which I had taken a list for my mother, and for Lizzie, lest they should cry out at man's stupidity about anything of real interest), I proceeded to tell her about my own troubles, and the sudden departure of Lorna; concluding with all the show of indifference which my pride could muster, that now I never should see her again, and must do my best to forget her, as being so far above me. I had not intended to speak of this, but Ruth's face was so kind and earnest, that I could not stop myself.

'You must not talk like that, Cousin Ridd,' she said, in a low and gentle tone, and turning away her eyes from me; 'no lady can be above a man, who is pure, and brave, and gentle. And if her heart be worth having, she will never let you give her up, for her grandeur, and her nobility.'

She pronounced those last few words, as I thought, with a little bitterness, unperceived by herself perhaps, for it was not in her appearance. But I, attaching great importance to a maiden's opinion about a maiden (because she might judge from experience), would have led her further into that subject. But she declined to follow, having now no more to say in a matter so removed from her. Then I asked her full and straight, and looking at her in such a manner that she could not look away, without appearing vanquished by feelings of her own—which thing was very vile of me; but all men are so selfish,—

'Dear cousin, tell me, once for all, what is your advice to me?'

'My advice to you,' she answered bravely, with her dark eyes full of pride, and instead of flinching, foiling me,—'is to do what every man must do, if he would win fair maiden. Since she cannot send you token, neither is free to return to you, follow her, pay your court to her; show that you will not be forgotten; and perhaps she will look down—I mean, she will relent to you.'

'She has nothing to relent about. I have never vexed nor injured her. My thoughts have never strayed from her. There is no one to compare with her.'

'Then keep her in that same mind about you. See now, I can advise no more. My arm is swelling painfully, in spite of all your goodness, and bitter task of surgeonship. I shall have another poultice on, and go to bed,

I think, Cousin Ridd, if you will not hold me ungrateful. I am so sorry for your long walk. Surely it might be avoided. Give my love to dear Lizzie: oh, the room is going round so.'

And she fainted into the arms of Sally, who was come just in time to fetch her: no doubt she had been suffering agony all the time she talked to me. Leaving word that I would come again to inquire for her, and fetch Kickums home, so soon as the harvest permitted me, I gave directions about the horse, and striding away from the ancient town, was soon upon the moorlands.

Now, through the whole of that long walk—the latter part of which was led by starlight, till the moon arose—I dwelt, in my young and foolish way, upon the ordering of our steps by a Power beyond us. But as I could not bring my mind to any clearness upon this matter, and the stars shed no light upon it, but rather confused me with wondering how their Lord could attend to them all, and yet to a puny fool like me, it came to pass that my thoughts on the subject were not worth ink, if I knew them.

But it is perhaps worth ink to relate, so far as I can do so, mother's delight at my return, when she had almost abandoned hope, and concluded that I was gone to London, in disgust at her behaviour. And now she was looking up the lane, at the rise of the harvest-moon, in despair, as she said afterwards. But if she had despaired in truth, what use to look at all? Yet according to the epigram made by a good Blundellite,—

Despair was never yet so deep
In sinking as in seeming;
Despair is hope just dropped asleep
For better chance of dreaming.

And mother's dream was a happy one, when she knew my step at a furlong distant; for the night was of those that carry sound thrice as far as day can. She recovered herself, when she was sure, and even made up her mind to scold me, and felt as if she could do it. But when she was in my arms, into which she threw herself, and I by the light of the moon descried the silver gleam on one side of her head (now spreading since Annie's departure), bless my heart and yours therewith, no room was left for scolding. She hugged me, and she clung to me; and I looked at her, with duty made tenfold, and discharged by love. We said nothing to one another; but all was right between us.

Even Lizzie behaved very well, so far as her nature admitted; not even saying a nasty thing all the time she was getting my supper ready, with a weak imitation of Annie. She knew that the gift of cooking was not vouchsafed by God to her; but sometimes she would do her best, by intellect to win it. Whereas it is no more to be won by intellect than is divine poetry. An amount of strong quick heart is needful, and the understanding must second it, in the one art as in the other. Now my fare was very choice for the next three days or more; yet not turned out like Annie's. They could do a thing well enough on the fire; but they could not put it on table so; nor even have plates all piping hot. This was Annie's special gift; born in her, and ready to cool with her; like a plate borne away from the fireplace. I sighed sometimes about Lorna, and they thought it was about the plates. And mother would stand and look at me, as much as to say, 'No pleasing him'; and Lizzie would jerk up one shoulder, and cry, 'He had better have Lorna to cook for him'; while the whole truth was that I wanted not to be plagued about any cookery; but just to have something good and quiet, and then smoke and think about Lorna.

Nevertheless the time went on, with one change and another; and we gathered all our harvest in; and Parson Bowden thanked God for it, both in church and out of it; for his tithes would be very goodly. The unmatched cold of the previous winter, and general fear of scarcity, and our own talk about our ruin, had sent prices up to a grand high pitch; and we did our best to keep them there. For nine Englishmen out of every ten believe that a bitter winter must breed a sour summer, and explain away topmost prices. While according to my experience, more often it would be otherwise, except for the public thinking so. However, I have said too much; and if any farmer reads my book, he will vow that I wrote it for nothing else except to rob his family.

Chapter LXII The King Must Not Be Prayed For

All our neighbourhood was surprised that the Doones had not ere now attacked, and probably made an end of us. For we lay almost at their mercy now, having only Sergeant Bloxham, and three men, to protect us, Captain Stickles having been ordered southwards with all his force; except such as might be needful for collecting toll, and watching the imports at Lynmouth, and thence to Porlock. The Sergeant, having now imbibed a taste for writing reports (though his first great effort had done him no good, and only offended Stickles), reported weekly from Plover's Barrows, whenever he could find a messenger. And though we fed not Sergeant Bloxham at our own table, with the best we had (as in the case of Stickles, who represented His Majesty), yet we treated him so well, that he reported very highly of us, as loyal and true-hearted lieges, and most devoted to our lord the King. And indeed he could scarcely have done less, when Lizzie wrote great part of his reports, and furbished up the rest to such a pitch of lustre, that Lord Clarendon himself need scarce have been ashamed of them. And though this cost a great deal of ale, and even of strong waters (for Lizzie would have it the duty of a critic to stand treat to the author), and though it was otherwise a plague, as giving the maid such airs of patronage, and such pretence to politics; yet there was no stopping it, without the risk of mortal offence to both writer and reviewer. Our mother also, while disapproving Lizzie's long stay in the saddle-room on a Friday night and a Saturday, and insisting that Betty should be there, was nevertheless as proud as need be, that the King should read our Eliza' s writings—at least so the innocent soul believed—and we all looked forward to something great as the fruit of all this history. And something great did come of it, though not as we expected; for these reports, or as many of them as were ever opened, stood us in good stead the next year, when we were accused of harbouring and comforting guilty rebels.

Now the reason why the Doones did not attack us was that they were preparing to meet another and more powerful assault upon their fortress; being assured that their repulse of King's troops could not be looked over when brought before the authorities. And no doubt they were right; for although the conflicts in the Government during that summer and autumn had delayed the matter yet positive orders had been issued that these outlaws and malefactors should at any price be brought to justice; when the sudden death of King Charles the Second threw all things into confusion, and all minds into a panic.

We heard of it first in church, on Sunday, the eighth day of February, 1684-5, from a cousin of John Fry, who had ridden over on purpose from Porlock. He came in just before the anthem, splashed and heated from his ride, so that every one turned and looked at him. He wanted to create a stir (knowing how much would be made of him), and he took the best way to do it. For he let the anthem go by very quietly—or rather I should say very pleasingly, for our choir was exceeding proud of itself, and I sang bass twice as loud as a bull, to beat the clerk with the clarionet—and then just as Parson Bowden, with a look of pride at his minstrels, was kneeling down to begin the prayer for the King's Most Excellent Majesty (for he never read the litany, except upon Easter Sunday), up jumps young Sam Fry, and shouts,—

'I forbid that there prai-er.'

'What!' cried the parson, rising slowly, and looking for some one to shut the door: 'have we a rebel in the congregation?' For the parson was growing short-sighted now, and knew not Sam Fry at that distance.

'No,' replied Sam, not a whit abashed by the staring of all the parish; 'no rebel, parson; but a man who mislaiketh popery and murder. That there prai-er be a prai-er for the dead.'

'Nay,' cried the parson, now recognising and knowing him to be our John's first cousin, 'you do not mean to say, Sam, that His Gracious Majesty is dead!'

'Dead as a sto-un: poisoned by they Papishers.' And Sam rubbed his hands with enjoyment, at the effect he had produced.

'Remember where you are, Sam,' said Parson Bowden solemnly; 'when did this most sad thing happen? The King is the head of the Church, Sam Fry; when did he leave her?'

'Day afore yesterday. Twelve o'clock. Warn't us quick to hear of 'un?'

'Can't be,' said the minister: 'the tidings can never have come so soon. Anyhow, he will want it all the more. Let us pray for His Gracious Majesty.'

And with that he proceeded as usual; but nobody cried 'Amen,' for fear of being entangled with Popery. But after giving forth his text, our parson said a few words out of book, about the many virtues of His Majesty, and self-denial, and devotion, comparing his pious mirth to the dancing of the patriarch David before the ark of the covenant; and he added, with some severity, that if his flock would not join their pastor (who was much more likely to judge aright) in praying for the King, the least they could do on returning home was to pray that the King might not be dead, as his enemies had asserted.

Now when the service was over, we killed the King, and we brought him to life, at least fifty times in the churchyard: and Sam Fry was mounted on a high gravestone, to tell every one all he knew of it. But he knew no more than he had told us in the church, as before repeated: upon which we were much disappointed with him, and inclined to disbelieve him; until he happily remembered that His Majesty had died in great pain, with blue spots on his breast and black spots all across his back, and these in the form of a cross, by reason of Papists having poisoned him. When Sam called this to his remembrance (or to his imagination) he was overwhelmed, at once, with so many invitations to dinner, that he scarce knew which of them to accept; but decided in our favour.

Grieving much for the loss of the King, however greatly it might be (as the parson had declared it was, while telling us to pray against it) for the royal benefit, I resolved to ride to Porlock myself, directly after dinner, and make sure whether he were dead, or not. For it was not by any means hard to suppose that Sam Fry, being John's first cousin, might have inherited either from grandfather or grandmother some of those gifts which had made our John so famous for mendacity. At Porlock I found that it was too true; and the women of the town were in great distress, for the King had always been popular with them: the men, on the other hand, were forecasting what would be likely to ensue.

And I myself was of this number, riding sadly home again; although bound to the King as churchwarden now; which dignity, next to the parson's in rank, is with us (as it ought to be in every good parish) hereditary. For who can stick to the church like the man whose father stuck to it before him; and who knows all the little ins, and great outs, which must in these troublous times come across?

But though appointed at last, by virtue of being best farmer in the parish (as well as by vice of mismanagement on the part of my mother, and Nicholas Snowe, who had thoroughly muxed up everything, being too quick-headed); yet, while I dwelled with pride upon the fact that I stood in the King's shoes, as the manager and promoter of the Church of England, and I knew that we must miss His Majesty (whose arms were above the Commandments), as the leader of our thoughts in church, and handsome upon a guinea; nevertheless I kept on thinking how his death would act on me.

And here I saw it, many ways. In the first place, troubles must break out; and we had eight-and-twenty ricks; counting grain, and straw, and hay. Moreover, mother was growing weak about riots, and shooting, and burning; and she gathered the bed-clothes around her ears every night, when her feet were tucked up; and prayed not to awake until morning. In the next place, much rebellion (though we would not own it; in either sense of the verb, to 'own') was whispering, and plucking skirts, and making signs, among us. And the terror of the Doones helped greatly; as a fruitful tree of lawlessness, and a good excuse for everybody. And after this—or rather before it, and first of all indeed (if I must state the true order)—arose upon me the thought of Lorna, and how these things would affect her fate.

And indeed I must admit that it had occurred to me sometimes, or been suggested by others, that the Lady Lorna had not behaved altogether kindly, since her departure from among us. For although in those days the post (as we call the service of letter-carrying, which now comes within twenty miles of us) did not extend to our part of the world, yet it might have been possible to procure for hire a man who would ride post, if Lorna feared to trust the pack-horses, or the troopers, who went to and fro. Yet no message whatever had reached us; neither any token even of her safety in London. As to this last, however, we had no misgivings, having learned from the orderlies, more than once, that the wealth, and beauty, and adventures of young Lady Lorna Dugal were greatly talked of, both at court and among the common people.

Now riding sadly homewards, in the sunset of the early spring, I was more than ever touched with sorrow, and a sense of being, as it were, abandoned. And the weather growing quite beautiful, and so mild that the trees were budding, and the cattle full of happiness, I could not but think of the difference between the world of to-day and the world of this day twelvemonth. Then all was howling desolation, all the earth blocked up with snow, and all the air with barbs of ice as small as splintered needles, yet glittering, in and out, like stars, and gathering so upon a man (if long he stayed among them) that they began to weigh him down to sleepiness and frozen death. Not a sign of life was moving, nor was any change of view; unless the wild wind struck the crest of some cold drift, and bowed it.

Now, on the other hand, all was good. The open palm of spring was laid upon the yielding of the hills; and each particular valley seemed to be the glove for a finger. And although the sun was low, and dipping in the western clouds, the gray light of the sea came up, and took, and taking, told the special tone of everything. All this lay upon my heart, without a word of thinking, spreading light and shadow there, and the soft delight of sadness. Nevertheless, I would it were the savage snow around me, and the piping of the restless winds, and the death of everything. For in those days I had Lorna.

Then I thought of promise fair; such as glowed around me, where the red rocks held the sun, when he was departed; and the distant crags endeavoured to retain his memory. But as evening spread across them, shading with a silent fold, all the colour stole away; all remembrance waned and died.

'So it has been with love,' I thought, 'and with simple truth and warmth. The maid has chosen the glittering stars, instead of the plain daylight.'

Nevertheless I would not give in, although in deep despondency (especially when I passed the place where my dear father had fought in vain), and I tried to see things right and then judge aright about them. This, however, was more easy to attempt than to achieve; and by the time I came down the hill, I was none the wiser. Only I could tell my mother that the King was dead for sure; and she would have tried to cry, but for thought of her mourning.

There was not a moment for lamenting. All the mourning must be ready (if we cared to beat the Snowes) in eight-and-forty hours: and, although it was Sunday night, mother now feeling sure of the thing, sat up with Lizzie, cutting patterns, and stitching things on brown paper, and snipping, and laying the fashions down, and requesting all opinions, yet when given, scorning them; insomuch that I grew weary even of tobacco (which had comforted me since Lorna), and prayed her to go on until the King should be alive again.

The thought of that so flurried her—for she never yet could see a joke—that she laid her scissors on the table and said, 'The Lord forbid, John! after what I have cut up!'

'It would be just like him,' I answered, with a knowing smile: 'Mother, you had better stop. Patterns may do very well; but don't cut up any more good stuff.'

'Well, good lack, I am a fool! Three tables pegged with needles! The Lord in His mercy keep His Majesty, if ever He hath gotten him!'

By this device we went to bed; and not another stitch was struck until the troopers had office-tidings that the King was truly dead. Hence the Snowes beat us by a day; and both old Betty and Lizzie laid the blame upon me, as usual.

Almost before we had put off the mourning, which as loyal subjects we kept for the King three months and a week; rumours of disturbances, of plottings, and of outbreak began to stir among us. We heard of fighting in Scotland, and buying of ships on the continent, and of arms in Dorset and Somerset; and we kept our beacon in readiness to give signals of a landing; or rather the soldiers did. For we, having trustworthy reports that the King had been to high mass himself in the Abbey of Westminster, making all the bishops go with him, and all the guards in London, and then tortured all the Protestants who dared to wait outside, moreover had received from the Pope a flower grown in the Virgin Mary's garden, and warranted to last for ever, we of the moderate party, hearing all this and ten times as much, and having no love for this sour James, such as we had for the lively Charles, were ready to wait for what might happen, rather than care about stopping it. Therefore we listened to rumours gladly, and shook our heads with gravity, and predicted, every man something, but scarce any two the same. Nevertheless, in our part, things went on as usual, until the middle of June was nigh. We ploughed the ground, and sowed the corn, and tended the cattle, and heeded every one his neighbour's business, as carefully as heretofore; and the only thing that moved us much was that Annie had a baby. This being a very fine child with blue eyes, and christened 'John' in compliment to me, and with me for his godfather, it is natural to suppose that I thought a good deal about him; and when mother or Lizzie would ask me, all of a sudden, and treacherously, when the fire flared up at supper-time (for we always kept a little wood just alight in summer-time, and enough to make the pot boil), then when they would say to me, 'John, what are you thinking of? At a word, speak!' I would always answer, 'Little John Faggus'; and so they made no more of me.

But when I was down, on Saturday the thirteenth of June, at the blacksmith's forge by Brendon town, where the Lynn-stream runs so close that he dips his horseshoes in it, and where the news is apt to come first of all to our neighbourhood (except upon a Sunday), while we were talking of the hay-crop, and of a great sheep-stealer, round the corner came a man upon a piebald horse looking flagged and weary. But seeing half a dozen of us, young, and brisk, and hearty, he made a flourish with his horse, and waved a blue flag vehemently, shouting with great glory,—

'Monmouth and the Protestant faith! Monmouth and no Popery! Monmouth, the good King's eldest son! Down with the poisoning murderer! Down with the black usurper, and to the devil with all papists!'

'Why so, thou little varlet?' I asked very quietly; for the man was too small to quarrel with: yet knowing Lorna to be a 'papist,' as we choose to call them—though they might as well call us 'kingists,' after the head of our Church—I thought that this scurvy scampish knave might show them the way to the place he mentioned, unless his courage failed him.

'Papist yourself, be you?' said the fellow, not daring to answer much: 'then take this, and read it.'

And he handed me a long rigmarole, which he called a 'Declaration': I saw that it was but a heap of lies, and thrust it into the blacksmith's fire, and blew the bellows thrice at it. No one dared attempt to stop me, for my mood had not been sweet of late; and of course they knew my strength.

The man rode on with a muttering noise, having won no recruits from us, by force of my example: and he stopped at the ale-house farther down, where the road goes away from the Lynn-stream. Some of us went thither after a time, when our horses were shodden and rasped, for although we might not like the man, we might be glad of his tidings, which seemed to be something wonderful. He had set up his blue flag in the tap-room, and was teaching every one.

'Here coom'th Maister Jan Ridd,' said the landlady, being well pleased with the call for beer and cider: 'her hath been to Lunnon-town, and live within a maile of me. Arl the news coom from them nowadays, instead of from here, as her ought to do. If Jan Ridd say it be true, I will try almost to belave it. Hath the good Duke landed, sir?' And she looked at me over a foaming cup, and blew the froth off, and put more in.

'I have no doubt it is true enough,' I answered, before drinking; 'and too true, Mistress Pugsley. Many a poor man will die; but none shall die from our parish, nor from Brendon, if I can help it.'

And I knew that I could help it; for every one in those little places would abide by my advice; not only from the fame of my schooling and long sojourn in London, but also because I had earned repute for being very 'slow and sure': and with nine people out of ten this is the very best recommendation. For they think themselves much before you in wit, and under no obligation, but rather conferring a favour, by doing the thing that you do. Hence, if I cared for influence—which means, for the most part, making people do one's will, without knowing it—my first step toward it would be to be called, in common parlance, 'slow but sure.'

For the next fortnight we were daily troubled with conflicting rumours, each man relating what he desired, rather than what he had right, to believe. We were told that the Duke had been proclaimed King of England in every town of Dorset and of Somerset; that he had won a great battle at Axminster, and another at Bridport, and another somewhere else; that all the western counties had risen as one man for him, and all the militia had joined his ranks; that Taunton, and Bridgwater, and Bristowe, were all mad with delight, the two former being in his hands, and the latter craving to be so. And then, on the other hand, we heard that the Duke had been vanquished, and put to flight, and upon being apprehended, had confessed himself an impostor and a papist as bad as the King was.

We longed for Colonel Stickles (as he always became in time of war, though he fell back to Captain, and even Lieutenant, directly the fight was over), for then we should have won trusty news, as well as good consideration. But even Sergeant Bloxham, much against his will, was gone, having left his heart with our Lizzie, and a collection of all his writings. All the soldiers had been ordered away at full speed for Exeter, to join the Duke of Albemarle, or if he were gone, to follow him. As for us, who had fed them so long (although not quite for nothing), we must take our chance of Doones, or any other enemies.

Now all these tidings moved me a little; not enough to spoil appetite, but enough to make things lively, and to teach me that look of wisdom which is bred of practice only, and the hearing of many lies. Therefore I withheld my judgment, fearing to be triumphed over, if it should happen to miss the mark. But mother and Lizzie, ten times in a day, predicted all they could imagine; and their prophecies increased in strength according to contradiction. Yet this was not in the proper style for a house like ours, which knew the news, or at least had known it; and still was famous, all around, for the last advices. Even from Lynmouth, people sent up to Plover's Barrows to ask how things were going on: and it was very grievous to answer that in truth we knew not, neither had heard for days and days; and our reputation was so great, especially since the death of the King had gone abroad from Oare parish, that many inquirers would only wink, and lay a finger on the lip, as if to say, 'you know well enough, but see not fit to tell me.' And before the end arrived, those people believed that they had been right all along, and that we had concealed the truth from them.

For I myself became involved (God knows how much against my will and my proper judgment) in the troubles, and the conflict, and the cruel work coming afterwards. If ever I had made up my mind to anything in all my life, it was at this particular time, and as stern and strong as could be. I had resolved to let things pass,—to hear about them gladly, to encourage all my friends to talk, and myself to express opinion upon each particular point, when in the fullness of time no further doubt could be. But all my policy went for nothing, through a few touches of feeling.

One day at the beginning of July, I came home from mowing about noon, or a little later, to fetch some cider for all of us, and to eat a morsel of bacon. For mowing was no joke that year, the summer being wonderfully wet (even for our wet country), and the swathe falling heavier over the scythe than ever I could remember it. We were drenched with rain almost every day; but the mowing must be done somehow; and we must trust to God for the haymaking.

In the courtyard I saw a little cart, with iron brakes underneath it, such as fastidious people use to deaden the jolting of the road; but few men under a lord or baronet would be so particular. Therefore I wondered who our noble visitor could be. But when I entered the kitchen-place, brushing up my hair for somebody, behold it was no one greater than our Annie, with my godson in her arms, and looking pale and tear-begone. And at first she could not speak to me. But presently having sat down a little, and received much praise for her baby, she smiled and blushed, and found her tongue as if she had never gone from us.

'How natural it all looks again! Oh, I love this old kitchen so! Baby dear, only look at it wid him pitty, pitty eyes, and him tongue out of his mousy! But who put the flour-riddle up there. And look at the pestle and mortar, and rust I declare in the patty pans! And a book, positively a dirty book, where the clean skewers ought to hang! Oh, Lizzie, Lizzie, Lizzie!'

'You may just as well cease lamenting,' I said, 'for you can't alter Lizzie's nature, and you will only make mother uncomfortable, and perhaps have a quarrel with Lizzie, who is proud as Punch of her housekeeping.'

'She,' cried Annie, with all the contempt that could be compressed in a syllable. 'Well, John, no doubt you are right about it. I will try not to notice things. But it is a hard thing, after all my care, to see everything going to ruin. But what can be expected of a girl who knows all the kings of Carthage?'

'There were no kings of Carthage, Annie. They were called, why let me see—they were called—oh, something else.'

'Never mind what they were called,' said Annie; 'will they cook our dinner for us? But now, John, I am in such trouble. All this talk is make-believe.'

'Don't you cry, my dear: don't cry, my darling sister,' I answered, as she dropped into the worn place of the settle, and bent above her infant, rocking as if both their hearts were one: 'don't you know, Annie, I cannot tell, but I know, or at least I mean, I have heard the men of experience say, it is so bad for the baby.'

'Perhaps I know that as well as you do, John,' said Annie, looking up at me with a gleam of her old laughing: 'but how can I help crying; I am in such trouble.'

'Tell me what it is, my dear. Any grief of yours will vex me greatly; but I will try to bear it.'

'Then, John, it is just this. Tom has gone off with the rebels; and you must, oh, you must go after him.'

Chapter LXIII John Is Worsted by the Women

Moved as I was by Annie's tears, and gentle style of coaxing, and most of all by my love for her, I yet declared that I could not go, and leave our house and homestead, far less my dear mother and Lizzie, at the mercy of the merciless Doones.

'Is that all your objection, John?' asked Annie, in her quick panting way: 'would you go but for that, John?'

'Now,' I said, 'be in no such hurry'—for while I was gradually yielding, I liked to pass it through my fingers, as if my fingers shaped it: 'there are many things to be thought about, and many ways of viewing it.'

'Oh, you never can have loved Lorna! No wonder you gave her up so! John, you can love nobody, but your oat-ricks, and your hay-ricks.'

'Sister mine, because I rant not, neither rave of what I feel, can you be so shallow as to dream that I feel nothing? What is your love for Tom Faggus? What is your love for your baby (pretty darling as he is) to compare with such a love as for ever dwells with me? Because I do not prate of it; because it is beyond me, not only to express, but even form to my own heart in thoughts; because I do not shape my face, and would scorn to play to it, as a thing of acting, and lay it out before you, are you fools enough to think—' but here I stopped, having said more than was usual with me.

'I am very sorry, John. Dear John, I am so sorry. What a shallow fool I am!'

'I will go seek your husband,' I said, to change the subject, for even to Annie I would not lay open all my heart about Lorna: 'but only upon condition that you ensure this house and people from the Doones meanwhile. Even for the sake of Tom, I cannot leave all helpless. The oat-ricks and the hay-ricks, which are my only love, they are welcome to make cinders of. But I will not have mother treated so; nor even little Lizzie, although you scorn your sister so.'

'Oh, John, I do think you are the hardest, as well as the softest of all the men I know. Not even a woman's bitter word but what you pay her out for. Will you never understand that we are not like you, John? We say all sorts of spiteful things, without a bit of meaning. John, for God's sake fetch Tom home; and then revile me as you please, and I will kneel and thank you.'

'I will not promise to fetch him home,' I answered, being ashamed of myself for having lost command so: 'but I will promise to do my best, if we can only hit on a plan for leaving mother harmless.'

Annie thought for a little while, trying to gather her smooth clear brow into maternal wrinkles, and then she looked at her child, and said, 'I will risk it, for daddy's sake, darling; you precious soul, for daddy's sake.' I asked her what she was going to risk. She would not tell me; but took upper hand, and saw to my cider-cans and bacon, and went from corner to cupboard, exactly as if she had never been married; only without an apron on. And then she said, 'Now to your mowers, John; and make the most of this fine afternoon; kiss your godson before you go.' And I, being used to obey her, in little things of that sort, kissed the baby, and took my cans, and went back to my scythe again.

By the time I came home it was dark night, and pouring again with a foggy rain, such as we have in July, even more than in January. Being soaked all through, and through, and with water quelching in my boots, like a pump with a bad bucket, I was only too glad to find Annie's bright face, and quick figure, flitting in and out the firelight, instead of Lizzie sitting grandly, with a feast of literature, and not a drop of gravy. Mother was in the corner also, with her cheery-coloured ribbons glistening very nice by candle-light, looking at Annie now and then, with memories of her babyhood; and then at her having a baby: yet half afraid of praising her much, for fear of that young Lizzie. But Lizzie showed no jealousy: she truly loved our Annie (now that she was gone from us), and she wanted to know all sorts of things, and she adored the baby. Therefore Annie was allowed to attend to me, as she used to do.

'Now, John, you must start the first thing in the morning,' she said, when the others had left the room, but somehow she stuck to the baby, 'to fetch me back my rebel, according to your promise.'

'Not so,' I replied, misliking the job, 'all I promised was to go, if this house were assured against any onslaught of the Doones.'

'Just so; and here is that assurance.' With these words she drew forth a paper, and laid it on my knee with triumph, enjoying my amazement. This, as you may suppose was great; not only at the document, but also at her possession of it. For in truth it was no less than a formal undertaking, on the part of the Doones, not to attack Plover's Barrows farm, or molest any of the inmates, or carry off any chattels, during the absence of John Ridd upon a special errand. This document was signed not only by the Counsellor, but by many other Doones: whether Carver's name were there, I could not say for certain; as of course he would not sign it under his name of 'Carver,' and I had never heard Lorna say to what (if any) he had been baptized.

In the face of such a deed as this, I could no longer refuse to go; and having received my promise, Annie told me (as was only fair) how she had procured that paper. It was both a clever and courageous act; and would have seemed to me, at first sight, far beyond Annie's power. But none may gauge a woman's power, when her love and faith are moved.

The first thing Annie had done was this: she made herself look ugly. This was not an easy thing; but she had learned a great deal from her husband, upon the subject of disguises. It hurt her feelings not a little to make so sad a fright of herself; but what could it matter?—if she lost Tom, she must be a far greater fright in earnest, than now she was in seeming. And then she left her child asleep, under Betty Muxworthy's tendance—for Betty took to that child, as if there never had been a child before—and away she went in her own 'spring-cart' (as the name of that engine proved to be), without a word to any one, except the old man who had driven her from Molland parish that morning, and who coolly took one of our best horses, without 'by your leave' to any one.

Annie made the old man drive her within easy reach of the Doone-gate, whose position she knew well enough, from all our talk about it. And there she bade the old man stay, until she should return to him. Then with her comely figure hidden by a dirty old woman's cloak, and her fair young face defaced by patches and by liniments, so that none might covet her, she addressed the young man at the gate in a cracked and trembling voice; and they were scarcely civil to the 'old hag,' as they called her. She said that she bore important tidings for Sir Counsellor himself, and must be conducted to him. To him accordingly she was led, without even any hoodwinking, for she had spectacles over her eyes, and made believe not to see ten yards.

She found Sir Counsellor at home, and when the rest were out of sight, threw off all disguise to him, flashing forth as a lovely young woman, from all her wraps and disfigurements. She flung her patches on the floor, amid the old man's laughter, and let her tucked-up hair come down; and then went up and kissed him.

'Worthy and reverend Counsellor, I have a favour to ask,' she began.

'So I should think from your proceedings,'—the old man interrupted—'ah, if I were half my age'—

'If you were, I would not sue so. But most excellent Counsellor, you owe me some amends, you know, for the way in which you robbed me.'

'Beyond a doubt I do, my dear. You have put it rather strongly; and it might offend some people. Nevertheless I own my debt, having so fair a creditor.'

'And do you remember how you slept, and how much we made of you, and would have seen you home, sir; only you did not wish it?'

'And for excellent reasons, child. My best escort was in my cloak, after we made the cream to rise. Ha, ha! The unholy spell. My pretty child, has it injured you?'

'Yes, I fear it has, said Annie; 'or whence can all my ill luck come?' And here she showed some signs of crying, knowing that Counsellor hated it.

'You shall not have ill luck, my dear. I have heard all about your marriage to a very noble highwayman. Ah, you made a mistake in that; you were worthy of a Doone, my child; your frying was a blessing meant for those who can appreciate.'

'My husband can appreciate,' she answered very proudly; 'but what I wish to know is this, will you try to help me?'

The Counsellor answered that he would do so, if her needs were moderate; whereupon she opened her meaning to him, and told of all her anxieties. Considering that Lorna was gone, and her necklace in his possession, and that I (against whom alone of us the Doones could bear any malice) would be out of the way all the while, the old man readily undertook that our house should not be assaulted, nor our property molested, until my return. And to the promptitude of his pledge, two things perhaps contributed, namely, that he knew not how we were stripped of all defenders, and that some of his own forces were away in the rebel camp. For (as I learned thereafter) the Doones being now in direct feud with the present Government, and sure to be crushed if that prevailed, had resolved to drop all religious questions, and cast in their lot with Monmouth. And the turbulent youths, being long restrained from their wonted outlet for vehemence, by the troopers in the neighbourhood, were only too glad to rush forth upon any promise of blows and excitement.

However, Annie knew little of this, but took the Counsellor's pledge as a mark of especial favour in her behalf (which it may have been to some extent), and thanked him for it most heartily, and felt that he had earned the necklace; while he, like an ancient gentleman, disclaimed all obligation, and sent her under an escort safe to her own cart again. But Annie, repassing the sentinels, with her youth restored and blooming with the flush of triumph, went up to them very gravely, and said, 'The old hag wishes you good-evening, gentlemen'; and so made her best curtsey.

Now, look at it as I would, there was no excuse left for me, after the promise given. Dear Annie had not only cheated the Doones, but also had gotten the best of me, by a pledge to a thing impossible. And I bitterly said, 'I am not like Lorna: a pledge once given, I keep it.'

'I will not have a word against Lorna,' cried Annie; 'I will answer for her truth as surely as I would for my own or yours, John.' And with that she vanquished me.

But when my poor mother heard that I was committed, by word of honour, to a wild-goose chase, among the rebels, after that runagate Tom Faggus, she simply stared, and would not believe it. For lately I had joked with her, in a little style of jerks, as people do when out of sorts; and she, not understanding this, and knowing jokes to be out of my power, would only look, and sigh, and toss, and hope that I meant nothing. At last, however, we convinced her that I was in earnest, and must be off in the early morning, and leave John Fry with the hay crop.

Then mother was ready to fall upon Annie, as not content with disgracing us, by wedding a man of new honesty (if indeed of any), but laying traps to catch her brother, and entangle him perhaps to his death, for the sake of a worthless fellow; and 'felon'—she was going to say, as by the shape of her lips I knew. But I laid my hand upon dear mother's lips; because what must be, must be; and if mother and daughter stayed at home, better in love than in quarrelling.

Right early in the morning, I was off, without word to any one; knowing that mother and sister mine had cried each her good self to sleep; relenting when the light was out, and sorry for hard words and thoughts; and yet too much alike in nature to understand each other.

Therefore I took good Kickums, who (although with one eye spoiled) was worth ten sweet-tempered horses, to a man who knew how to manage him; and being well charged both with bacon and powder, forth I set on my wild-goose chase.

For this I claim no bravery. I cared but little what came of it; save for mother's sake, and Annie's, and the keeping of the farm, and discomfiture of the Snowes, and lamenting of Lorna at my death, if die I must in a lonesome manner, not found out till afterwards, and bleaching bones left to weep over. However, I had a little kettle, and a pound and a half of tobacco, and two dirty pipes and a clean one; also a bit of clothes for change, also a brisket of hung venison, and four loaves of farmhouse bread, and of the upper side of bacon a stone and a half it might be—not to mention divers small things for campaigning, which may come in handily, when no one else has gotten them.

We went away in merry style; my horse being ready for anything, and I only glad of a bit of change, after months of working and brooding; with no content to crown the work; no hope to hatch the brooding; or without hatching to reckon it. Who could tell but what Lorna might be discovered, or at any rate heard of, before the end of this campaign; if campaign it could be called of a man who went to fight nobody, only to redeem a runagate? And vexed as I was about the hay, and the hunch-backed ricks John was sure to make (which spoil the look of a farm-yard), still even this was better than to have the mows and houses fired, as I had nightly expected, and been worn out with the worry of it.

Yet there was one thing rather unfavourable to my present enterprise, namely, that I knew nothing of the country I was bound to, nor even in what part of it my business might be supposed to lie. For beside the uncertainty caused by the conflict of reports, it was likely that King Monmouth's army would be moving from place to place, according to the prospect of supplies and of reinforcements. However, there would arise more chance of getting news as I went on: and my road being towards the east and south, Dulverton would not lie so very far aside of it, but what it might be worth a visit, both to collect the latest tidings, and to consult the maps and plans in Uncle Reuben's parlour. Therefore I drew the off-hand rein, at the cross-road on the hills, and made for the town; expecting perhaps to have breakfast with Master Huckaback, and Ruth, to help and encourage us. This little maiden was now become a very great favourite with me, having long outgrown, no doubt, her childish fancies and follies, such as my mother and Annie had planted under her soft brown hair. It had been my duty, as well as my true interest (for Uncle Ben was more and more testy, as he went on gold-digging), to ride thither, now and again, to inquire what the doctor thought of her. Not that her wounds were long in healing, but that people can scarcely be too careful and too inquisitive, after a great horse-bite. And she always let me look at the arm, as I had been first doctor; and she held it up in a graceful manner, curving at the elbow, and with a sweep of white roundness going to a wrist the size of my thumb or so, and without any thimble-top standing forth, such as even our Annie had. But gradually all I could see, above the elbow, where the bite had been, was very clear, transparent skin, with very firm sweet flesh below, and three little blue marks as far asunder as the prongs of a toasting-fork, and no deeper than where a twig has chafed the peel of a waxen apple. And then I used to say in fun, as the children do, 'Shall I kiss it, to make it well, dear?'

Now Ruth looked very grave indeed, upon hearing of this my enterprise; and crying, said she could almost cry, for the sake of my dear mother. Did I know the risks and chances, not of the battlefield alone, but of the havoc afterwards; the swearing away of innocent lives, and the hurdle, and the hanging? And if I would please not to laugh (which was so unkind of me), had I never heard of imprisonments, and torturing with the cruel boot, and selling into slavery, where the sun and the lash outvied one another in cutting a man to pieces? I replied that of all these things I had heard, and would take especial care to steer me free of all of them. My duty was all that I wished to do; and none could harm me for doing that. And I begged my cousin to give me good-speed, instead of talking dolefully. Upon this she changed her manner wholly, becoming so lively and cheerful that I was convinced of her indifference, and surprised even more than gratified.

'Go and earn your spurs, Cousin Ridd,' she said: 'you are strong enough for anything. Which side is to have the benefit of your doughty arm?'

'Have I not told you, Ruth,' I answered, not being fond of this kind of talk, more suitable for Lizzie, 'that I do not mean to join either side, that is to say, until—'

'Until, as the common proverb goes, you know which way the cat will jump. Oh, John Ridd! Oh, John Ridd!'

'Nothing of the sort,' said I: 'what a hurry you are in! I am for the King of course.'

'But not enough to fight for him. Only enough to vote, I suppose, or drink his health, or shout for him.'

'I can't make you out to-day, Cousin Ruth; you are nearly as bad as Lizzie. You do not say any bitter things, but you seem to mean them.'

'No, cousin, think not so of me. It is far more likely that I say them, without meaning them.'

'Anyhow, it is not like you. And I know not what I can have done in any way, to vex you.'

'Dear me, nothing, Cousin Ridd; you never do anything to vex me.'

'Then I hope I shall do something now, Ruth, when I say good-bye. God knows if we ever shall meet again, Ruth: but I hope we may.'

'To be sure we shall, ' she answered in her brightest manner. 'Try not to look wretched, John: you are as happy as a Maypole.'

'And you as a rose in May,' I said; 'and pretty nearly as pretty. Give my love to Uncle Ben; and I trust him to keep on the winning side.'

'Of that you need have no misgivings. Never yet has he failed of it. Now, Cousin Ridd, why go you not? You hurried me so at breakfast time?'

'My only reason for waiting, Ruth, is that you have not kissed me, as you are almost bound to do, for the last time perhaps of seeing me.'

'Oh, if that is all, just fetch the stool; and I will do my best, cousin.'

'I pray you be not so vexatious; you always used to do it nicely, without any stool, Ruth.'

'Ah, but you are grown since then, and become a famous man, John Ridd, and a member of the nobility. Go your way, and win your spurs. I want no lip-service.'

Being at the end of my wits, I did even as she ordered me. At least I had no spurs to win, because there were big ones on my boots, paid for in the Easter bill, and made by a famous saddler, so as never to clog with marsh-weed, but prick as hard as any horse, in reason, could desire. And Kickums never wanted spurs; but always went tail-foremost, if anybody offered them for his consideration.

Chapter LXIV Slaughter in the Marshes

We rattled away at a merry pace, out of the town of Dulverton; my horse being gaily fed, and myself quite fit again for going. Of course I was puzzled about Cousin Ruth; for her behaviour was not at all such as I had expected; and indeed I had hoped for a far more loving and moving farewell than I got from her. But I said to myself, 'It is useless ever to count upon what a woman will do; and I think that I must have vexed her, almost as much as she vexed me. And now to see what comes of it.' So I put my horse across the moorland; and he threw his chest out bravely.

Now if I tried to set down at length all the things that happened to me, upon this adventure, every in and out, and up and down, and to and fro, that occupied me, together with the things I saw, and the things I heard of, however much the wiser people might applaud my narrative, it is likely enough that idle readers might exclaim, 'What ails this man? Knows he not that men of parts and of real understanding, have told us all we care to hear of that miserable business. Let him keep to his farm, and his bacon, and his wrestling, and constant feeding.'

Fearing to meet with such rebuffs (which after my death would vex me), I will try to set down only what is needful for my story, and the clearing of my character, and the good name of our parish. But the manner in which I was bandied about, by false information, from pillar to post, or at other times driven quite out of my way by the presence of the King's soldiers, may be known by the names of the following towns, to which I was sent in succession, Bath, Frome, Wells, Wincanton, Glastonbury, Shepton, Bradford, Axbridge, Somerton, and Bridgwater.

This last place I reached on a Sunday night, the fourth or fifth of July, I think—or it might be the sixth, for that matter; inasmuch as I had been too much worried to get the day of the month at church. Only I know that my horse and myself were glad to come to a decent place, where meat and corn could be had for money; and being quite weary of wandering about, we hoped to rest there a little.

Of this, however, we found no chance, for the town was full of the good Duke's soldiers; if men may be called so, the half of whom had never been drilled, nor had fired a gun. And it was rumoured among them, that the 'popish army,' as they called it, was to be attacked that very night, and with God's assistance beaten. However, by this time I had been taught to pay little attention to rumours; and having sought vainly for Tom Faggus among these poor rustic warriors, I took to my hostel; and went to bed, being as weary as weary can be.

Falling asleep immediately, I took heed of nothing; although the town was all alive, and lights had come glancing, as I lay down, and shouts making echo all round my room. But all I did was to bolt the door; not an inch would I budge, unless the house, and even my bed, were on fire. And so for several hours I lay, in the depth of the deepest slumber, without even a dream on its surface; until I was roused and awakened at last by a pushing, and pulling, and pinching, and a plucking of hair out by the roots. And at length, being able to open mine eyes, I saw the old landlady, with a candle, heavily wondering at me.

'Can't you let me alone?' I grumbled. 'I have paid for my bed, mistress; and I won't get up for any one.'

'Would to God, young man,' she answered, shaking me as hard as ever, 'that the popish soldiers may sleep this night, only half as strong as thou dost! Fie on thee, fie on thee! Get up, and go fight; we can hear the battle already; and a man of thy size mought stop a cannon.'

'I would rather stop a-bed,' said I; 'what have I to do with fighting? I am for King James, if any.'

'Then thou mayest even stop a-bed,' the old woman muttered sulkily. 'A would never have laboured half an hour to awake a Papisher. But hearken you one thing, young man; Zummerzett thou art, by thy brogue; or at least by thy understanding of it; no Zummerzett maid will look at thee, in spite of thy size and stature, unless thou strikest a blow this night.'

'I lack no Zummerzett maid, mistress: I have a fairer than your brown things; and for her alone would I strike a blow.'

At this the old woman gave me up, as being beyond correction: and it vexed me a little that my great fame had not reached so far as Bridgwater, when I thought that it went to Bristowe. But those people in East Somerset know nothing about wrestling. Devon is the headquarters of the art; and Devon is the county of my chief love. Howbeit, my vanity was moved, by this slur upon it—for I had told her my name was John Ridd, when I had a gallon of ale with her, ere ever I came upstairs; and she had nodded, in such a manner, that I thought she knew both name and fame—and here was I, not only shaken, pinched, and with many hairs pulled out, in the midst of my first good sleep for a week, but also abused, and taken amiss, and (which vexed me most of all) unknown.

Now there is nothing like vanity to keep a man awake at night, however he be weary; and most of all, when he believes that he is doing something great—this time, if never done before—yet other people will not see, except what they may laugh at; and so be far above him, and sleep themselves the happier. Therefore their sleep robs his own; for all things play so, in and out (with the godly and ungodly ever moving in a balance, as they have done in my time, almost every year or two), all things have such nice reply of produce to the call for it, and such a spread across the world, giving here and taking there, yet on the whole pretty even, that haply sleep itself has but a certain stock, and keeps in hand, and sells to flattered (which can pay) that which flattened vanity cannot pay, and will not sue for.

Be that as it may, I was by this time wide awake, though much aggrieved at feeling so, and through the open window heard the distant roll of musketry, and the beating of drums, with a quick rub-a-dub, and the 'come round the corner' of trumpet-call. And perhaps Tom Faggus might be there, and shot at any moment, and my dear Annie left a poor widow, and my godson Jack an orphan, without a tooth to help him.

Therefore I reviled myself for all my heavy laziness; and partly through good honest will, and partly through the stings of pride, and yet a little perhaps by virtue of a young man's love of riot, up I arose, and dressed myself, and woke Kickums (who was snoring), and set out to see the worst of it. The sleepy hostler scratched his poll, and could not tell me which way to take; what odds to him who was King, or Pope, so long as he paid his way, and got a bit of bacon on Sunday? And would I please to remember that I had roused him up at night, and the quality always made a point of paying four times over for a man's loss of his beauty-sleep. I replied that his loss of beauty-sleep was rather improving to a man of so high complexion; and that I, being none of the quality, must pay half-quality prices: and so I gave him double fee, as became a good farmer; and he was glad to be quit of Kickums; as I saw by the turn of his eye, while going out at the archway.

All this was done by lanthorn light, although the moon was high and bold; and in the northern heaven, flags and ribbons of a jostling pattern; such as we often have in autumn, but in July very rarely. Of these Master Dryden has spoken somewhere, in his courtly manner; but of him I think so little—because by fashion preferred to Shakespeare—that I cannot remember the passage; neither is it a credit to him.

Therefore I was guided mainly by the sound of guns and trumpets, in riding out of the narrow ways, and into the open marshes. And thus I might have found my road, in spite of all the spread of water, and the glaze of moonshine; but that, as I followed sound (far from hedge or causeway), fog (like a chestnut-tree in blossom, touched with moonlight) met me. Now fog is a thing that I understand, and can do with well enough, where I know the country; but here I had never been before. It was nothing to our Exmoor fogs; not to be compared with them; and all the time one could see the moon; which we cannot do in our fogs; nor even the sun, for a week together. Yet the gleam of water always makes the fog more difficult: like a curtain on a mirror; none can tell the boundaries.

And here we had broad-water patches, in and out, inlaid on land, like mother-of-pearl in brown Shittim wood. To a wild duck, born and bred there, it would almost be a puzzle to find her own nest amongst us; what chance then had I and Kickums, both unused to marsh and mere? Each time when we thought that we must be right, now at last, by track or passage, and approaching the conflict, with the sounds of it waxing nearer, suddenly a break of water would be laid before us, with the moon looking mildly over it, and the northern lights behind us, dancing down the lines of fog.

It was an awful thing, I say (and to this day I remember it), to hear the sounds of raging fight, and the yells of raving slayers, and the howls of poor men stricken hard, and shattered from wrath to wailing; then suddenly the dead low hush, as of a soul departing, and spirits kneeling over it. Through the vapour of the earth, and white breath of the water, and beneath the pale round moon (bowing as the drift went by), all this rush and pause of fear passed or lingered on my path.

At last, when I almost despaired of escaping from this tangle of spongy banks, and of hazy creeks, and reed-fringe, my horse heard the neigh of a fellow-horse, and was only too glad to answer it; upon which the other, having lost its rider, came up and pricked his ears at us, and gazed through the fog very steadfastly. Therefore I encouraged him with a soft and genial whistle, and Kickums did his best to tempt him with a snort of inquiry. However, nothing would suit that nag, except to enjoy his new freedom; and he capered away with his tail set on high, and the stirrup-irons clashing under him. Therefore, as he might know the way, and appeared to have been in the battle, we followed him very carefully; and he led us to a little hamlet, called (as I found afterwards) West Zuyland, or Zealand, so named perhaps from its situation amid this inland sea.

Here the King's troops had been quite lately, and their fires were still burning; but the men themselves had been summoned away by the night attack of the rebels. Hence I procured for my guide a young man who knew the district thoroughly, and who led me by many intricate ways to the rear of the rebel army. We came upon a broad open moor striped with sullen water courses, shagged with sedge, and yellow iris, and in the drier part with bilberries. For by this time it was four o'clock, and the summer sun, rising wanly, showed us all the ghastly scene.

Would that I had never been there! Often in the lonely hours, even now it haunts me: would, far more, that the piteous thing had never been done in England! Flying men, flung back from dreams of victory and honour, only glad to have the luck of life and limbs to fly with, mud-bedraggled, foul with slime, reeking both with sweat and blood, which they could not stop to wipe, cursing, with their pumped-out lungs, every stick that hindered them, or gory puddle that slipped the step, scarcely able to leap over the corses that had dragged to die. And to see how the corses lay; some, as fair as death in sleep; with the smile of placid valour, and of noble manhood, hovering yet on the silent lips. These had bloodless hands put upwards, white as wax, and firm as death, clasped (as on a monument) in prayer for dear ones left behind, or in high thanksgiving. And of these men there was nothing in their broad blue eyes to fear. But others were of different sort; simple fellows unused to pain, accustomed to the bill-hook, perhaps, or rasp of the knuckles in a quick-set hedge, or making some to-do at breakfast, over a thumb cut in sharpening a scythe, and expecting their wives to make more to-do. Yet here lay these poor chaps, dead; dead, after a deal of pain, with little mind to bear it, and a soul they had never thought of; gone, their God alone knows whither; but to mercy we may trust. Upon these things I cannot dwell; and none I trow would ask me: only if a plain man saw what I saw that morning, he (if God had blessed him with the heart that is in most of us) must have sickened of all desire to be great among mankind.

Seeing me riding to the front (where the work of death went on among the men of true English pluck; which, when moved, no farther moves), the fugitives called out to me, in half a dozen dialects, to make no utter fool of myself; for the great guns were come, and the fight was over; all the rest was slaughter.

'Arl oop wi Moonmo',' shouted one big fellow, a miner of the Mendip hills, whose weapon was a pickaxe: 'na oose to vaight na moor. Wend thee hame, yoong mon agin.'

Upon this I stopped my horse, desiring not to be shot for nothing; and eager to aid some poor sick people, who tried to lift their arms to me. And this I did to the best of my power, though void of skill in the business; and more inclined to weep with them than to check their weeping. While I was giving a drop of cordial from my flask to one poor fellow, who sat up, while his life was ebbing, and with slow insistence urged me, when his broken voice would come, to tell his wife (whose name I knew not) something about an apple-tree, and a golden guinea stored in it, to divide among six children—in the midst of this I felt warm lips laid against my cheek quite softly, and then a little push; and behold it was a horse leaning over me! I arose in haste, and there stood Winnie, looking at me with beseeching eyes, enough to melt a heart of stone. Then seeing my attention fixed she turned her head, and glanced back sadly toward the place of battle, and gave a little wistful neigh: and then looked me full in the face again, as much as to say, 'Do you understand?' while she scraped with one hoof impatiently. If ever a horse tried hard to speak, it was Winnie at that moment. I went to her side and patted her; but that was not what she wanted. Then I offered to leap into the empty saddle; but neither did that seem good to her: for she ran away toward the part of the field at which she had been glancing back, and then turned round, and shook her mane, entreating me to follow her.

Upon this I learned from the dying man where to find his apple-tree, and promised to add another guinea to the one in store for his children; and so, commending him to God, I mounted my own horse again, and to Winnie's great delight, professed myself at her service. With her ringing silvery neigh, such as no other horse of all I ever knew could equal, she at once proclaimed her triumph, and told her master (or meant to tell, if death should not have closed his ears) that she was coming to his aid, and bringing one who might be trusted, of the higher race that kill.

A cannon-bullet (fired low, and ploughing the marsh slowly) met poor Winnie front to front; and she, being as quick as thought, lowered her nose to sniff at it. It might be a message from her master; for it made a mournful noise. But luckily for Winnie's life, a rise of wet ground took the ball, even under her very nose; and there it cut a splashy groove, missing her off hindfoot by an inch, and scattering black mud over her. It frightened me much more than Winnie; of that I am quite certain: because though I am firm enough, when it comes to a real tussle, and the heart of a fellow warms up and tells him that he must go through with it; yet I never did approve of making a cold pie of death.

Therefore, with those reckless cannons, brazen-mouthed, and bellowing, two furlongs off, or it might be more (and the more the merrier), I would have given that year's hay-crop for a bit of a hill, or a thicket of oaks, or almost even a badger's earth. People will call me a coward for this (especially when I had made up my mind, that life was not worth having without any sign of Lorna); nevertheless, I cannot help it: those were my feelings; and I set them down, because they made a mark on me. At Glen Doone I had fought, even against cannon, with some spirit and fury: but now I saw nothing to fight about; but rather in every poor doubled corpse, a good reason for not fighting. So, in cold blood riding on, and yet ashamed that a man should shrink where a horse went bravely, I cast a bitter blame upon the reckless ways of Winnie.

Nearly all were scattered now. Of the noble countrymen (armed with scythe or pickaxe, blacksmith's hammer, or fold-pitcher), who had stood their ground for hours against blazing musketry (from men whom they could not get at, by reason of the water-dyke), and then against the deadly cannon, dragged by the Bishop's horses to slaughter his own sheep; of these sturdy Englishmen, noble in their want of sense, scarce one out of four remained for the cowards to shoot down. 'Cross the rhaine,' they shouted out, 'cross the rhaine, and coom within rache:' but the other mongrel Britons, with a mongrel at their head, found it pleasanter to shoot men who could not shoot in answer, than to meet the chance of mischief from strong arms, and stronger hearts.

The last scene of this piteous play was acting, just as I rode up. Broad daylight, and upstanding sun, winnowing fog from the eastern hills, and spreading the moors with freshness; all along the dykes they shone, glistened on the willow-trunks, and touched the banks with a hoary gray. But alas! those banks were touched more deeply with a gory red, and strewn with fallen trunks, more woeful than the wreck of trees; while howling, cursing, yelling, and the loathsome reek of carnage, drowned the scent of the new-mown hay, and the carol of the lark.

Then the cavalry of the King, with their horses at full speed, dashed from either side upon the helpless mob of countrymen. A few pikes feebly levelled met them; but they shot the pikemen, drew swords, and helter-skelter leaped into the shattered and scattering mass. Right and left they hacked and hewed; I could hear the snapping of scythes beneath them, and see the flash of their sweeping swords. How it must end was plain enough, even to one like myself, who had never beheld such a battle before. But Winnie led me away to the left; and as I could not help the people, neither stop the slaughter, but found the cannon-bullets coming very rudely nigh me, I was only too glad to follow her.

Chapter LXV Falling Among Lambs

That faithful creature, whom I began to admire as if she were my own (which is no little thing for a man to say of another man's horse), stopped in front of a low black shed, such as we call a 'linhay.' And here she uttered a little greeting, in a subdued and softened voice, hoping to obtain an answer, such as her master was wont to give in a cheery manner. Receiving no reply, she entered; and I (who could scarce keep up with her, poor Kickums being weary) leaped from his back, and followed. There I found her sniffing gently, but with great emotion, at the body of Tom Faggus. A corpse poor Tom appeared to be, if ever there was one in this world; and I turned away, and felt unable to keep altogether from weeping. But the mare either could not understand, or else would not believe it. She reached her long neck forth, and felt him with her under lip, passing it over his skin as softly as a mother would do to an infant; and then she looked up at me again; as much as to say, 'he is all right.'

Upon this I took courage, and handled poor Tom, which being young I had feared at first to do. He groaned very feebly, as I raised him up; and there was the wound, a great savage one (whether from pike-thrust or musket-ball), gaping and welling in his right side, from which a piece seemed to be torn away. I bound it up with some of my linen, so far as I knew how; just to stanch the flow of blood, until we could get a doctor. Then I gave him a little weak brandy and water, which he drank with the greatest eagerness, and made sign to me for more of it. But not knowing how far it was right to give cordial under the circumstances, I handed him unmixed water that time; thinking that he was too far gone to perceive the difference. But herein I wrong Tom Faggus; for he shook his head and frowned at me. Even at the door of death, he would not drink what Adam drank, by whom came death into the world. So I gave him a little more eau-de-vie, and he took it most submissively.

After that he seemed better, and a little colour came into his cheeks; and he looked at Winnie and knew her; and would have her nose in his clammy hand, though I thought it not good for either of them. With the stay of my arm he sat upright, and faintly looked about him; as if at the end of a violent dream, too much for his power of mind. Then he managed to whisper, 'Is Winnie hurt?'

'As sound as a roach,' I answered. 'Then so am I,' said he: 'put me upon her back, John; she and I die together.'

Surprised as I was at this fatalism (for so it appeared to me), of which he had often shown symptoms before (but I took them for mere levity), now I knew not what to do; for it seemed to me a murderous thing to set such a man on horseback; where he must surely bleed to death, even if he could keep the saddle. But he told me, with many breaks and pauses, that unless I obeyed his orders, he would tear off all my bandages, and accept no further aid from me.

While I was yet hesitating, a storm of horse at full gallop went by, tearing, swearing, bearing away all the country before them. Only a little pollard hedge kept us from their blood-shot eyes. 'Now is the time,' said my cousin Tom, so far as I could make out his words; on their heels, I am safe, John, if I have only Winnie under me. Winnie and I die together.'

Seeing this strong bent of his mind, stronger than any pains of death, I even did what his feeble eyes sometimes implored, and sometimes commanded. With a strong sash, from his own hot neck, bound and twisted, tight as wax, around his damaged waist, I set him upon Winnie's back, and placed his trembling feet in stirrups, with a band from one to another, under the good mare's body; so that no swerve could throw him out: and then I said, 'Lean forward, Tom; it will stop your hurt from bleeding.' He leaned almost on the neck of the mare, which, as I knew, must close the wound; and the light of his eyes was quite different, and the pain of his forehead unstrung itself, as if he felt the undulous readiness of her volatile paces under him.

'God bless you, John; I am safe,' he whispered, fearing to open his lungs much: 'who can come near my Winnie mare? A mile of her gallop is ten years of life. Look out for yourself, John Ridd.' He sucked his lips, and the mare went off, as easy and swift as a swallow.

'Well,' thought I, as l looked at Kickums, ignobly cropping up a bit of grass, 'I have done a very good thing, no doubt, and ought to be thankful to God for the chance. But as for getting away unharmed, with all these scoundrels about me, and only a foundered horse to trust in—good and spiteful as he is—upon the whole, I begin to think that I have made a fool of myself, according to my habit. No wonder Tom said, "Look out for yourself!" I shall look out from a prison window, or perhaps even out of a halter. And then, what will Lorna think of me?'

Being in this wistful mood, I resolved to abide awhile, even where fate had thrown me; for my horse required good rest no doubt, and was taking it even while he cropped, with his hind legs far away stretched out, and his forelegs gathered under him, and his muzzle on the mole-hills; so that he had five supportings from his mother earth. Moreover, the linhay itself was full of very ancient cow dung; than which there is no balmier and more maiden soporific. Hence I resolved, upon the whole, though grieving about breakfast, to light a pipe, and go to sleep; or at least until the hot sun should arouse the flies.

I may have slept three hours, or four, or it might be even five—for I never counted time, while sleeping—when a shaking more rude than the old landlady's, brought me back to the world again. I looked up, with a mighty yawn; and saw twenty, or so, of foot-soldiers.

'This linhay is not yours,' I said, when they had quite aroused me, with tongue, and hand, and even sword-prick: 'what business have you here, good fellows?'

'Business bad for you,' said one, 'and will lead you to the gallows.'

'Do you wish to know the way out again?' I asked, very quietly, as being no braggadocio.

'We will show thee the way out,' said one, 'and the way out of the world,' said another: 'but not the way to heaven,' said one chap, most unlikely to know it: and thereupon they all fell wagging, like a bed of clover leaves in the morning, at their own choice humour.

'Will you pile your arms outside,' I said, 'and try a bit of fair play with me?'

For I disliked these men sincerely, and was fain to teach them a lesson; they were so unchristian in appearance, having faces of a coffee colour, and dirty beards half over them. Moreover their dress was outrageous, and their address still worse. However, I had wiser let them alone, as will appear afterwards. These savage looking fellows laughed at the idea of my having any chance against some twenty of them: but I knew that the place was in my favour; for my part of it had been fenced off (for weaning a calf most likely), so that only two could come at me at once; and I must be very much out of training, if I could not manage two of them. Therefore I laid aside my carbine, and the two horse-pistols; and they with many coarse jokes at me went a little way outside, and set their weapons against the wall, and turned up their coat sleeves jauntily; and then began to hesitate.

'Go you first, Bob,' I heard them say: 'you are the biggest man of us; and Dick the wrestler along of you. Us will back you up, boy.'

'I'll warrant I'll draw the badger,' said Bob; 'and not a tooth will I leave him. But mind, for the honour of Kirke's lambs, every man stands me a glass of gin.' Then he, and another man, made a rush, and the others came double-quick-march on their heels. But as Bob ran at me most stupidly, not even knowing how to place his hands, I caught him with my knuckles at the back of his neck, and with all the sway of my right arm sent him over the heads of his comrades. Meanwhile Dick the wrestler had grappled me, expecting to show off his art, of which indeed he had some small knowledge; but being quite of the light-weights, in a second he was flying after his companion Bob.

Now these two men were hurt so badly, the light one having knocked his head against the lintel of the outer gate, that the rest had no desire to encounter the like misfortune. So they hung back whispering; and before they had made up their minds, I rushed into the midst of them. The suddenness and the weight of my onset took them wholly by surprise; and for once in their lives, perhaps, Kirke's lambs were worthy of their name. Like a flock of sheep at a dog's attack they fell away, hustling one another, and my only difficulty was not to tumble over them.

I had taken my carbine out with me, having a fondness for it; but the two horse-pistols I left behind; and therefore felt good title to take two from the magazine of the lambs. And with these, and my carbine, I leaped upon Kickums, who was now quite glad of a gallop again; and I bade adieu to that mongrel lot; yet they had the meanness to shoot at me. Thanking God for my deliverance (inasmuch as those men would have strung me up, from a pollard-ash without trial, as I heard them tell one another, and saw the tree they had settled upon), I ventured to go rather fast on my way, with doubt and uneasiness urging me. And now my way was home again. Nobody could say but what I had done my duty, and rescued Tom (if he could be rescued) from the mischief into which his own perverseness and love of change (rather than deep religious convictions, to which our Annie ascribed his outbreak) had led, or seemed likely to lead him. And how proud would my mother be; and—ah well, there was nobody else to be proud of me now.

But while thinking these things, and desiring my breakfast, beyond any power of describing, and even beyond my remembrance, I fell into another fold of lambs, from which there was no exit. These, like true crusaders, met me, swaggering very heartily, and with their barrels of cider set, like so many cannon, across the road, over against a small hostel.

'We have won the victory, my lord King, and we mean to enjoy it. Down from thy horse, and have a stoup of cider, thou big rebel.'

'No rebel am I. My name is John Ridd. I belong to the side of the King: and I want some breakfast.'

These fellows were truly hospitable; that much will I say for them. Being accustomed to Arab ways, they could toss a grill, or fritter, or the inner meaning of an egg, into any form they pleased, comely and very good to eat; and it led me to think of Annie. So I made the rarest breakfast any man might hope for, after all his troubles; and getting on with these brown fellows better than could be expected, I craved permission to light a pipe, if not disagreeable. Hearing this, they roared at me, with a superior laughter, and asked me, whether or not, I knew the tobacco-leaf from the chick-weed; and when I was forced to answer no, not having gone into the subject, but being content with anything brown, they clapped me on the back and swore they had never seen any one like me. Upon the whole this pleased me much; for I do not wish to be taken always as of the common pattern: and so we smoked admirable tobacco—for they would not have any of mine, though very courteous concerning it—and I was beginning to understand a little of what they told me; when up came those confounded lambs, who had shown more tail than head to me, in the linhay, as I mentioned.

Now these men upset everything. Having been among wrestlers so much as my duty compelled me to be, and having learned the necessity of the rest which follows the conflict, and the right of discussion which all people have to pay their sixpence to enter; and how they obtrude this right, and their wisdom, upon the man who has laboured, until he forgets all the work he did, and begins to think that they did it; having some knowledge of this sort of thing, and the flux of minds swimming in liquor, I foresaw a brawl, as plainly as if it were Bear Street in Barnstaple.

And a brawl there was, without any error, except of the men who hit their friends, and those who defended their enemies. My partners in breakfast and beer-can swore that I was no prisoner, but the best and most loyal subject, and the finest-hearted fellow they had ever the luck to meet with. Whereas the men from the linhay swore that I was a rebel miscreant; and have me they would, with a rope's-end ready, in spite of every [violent language] who had got drunk at my expense, and been misled by my [strong word] lies.

While this fight was going on (and its mere occurrence shows, perhaps, that my conversation in those days was not entirely despicable—else why should my new friends fight for me, when I had paid for the ale, and therefore won the wrong tense of gratitude?) it was in my power at any moment to take horse and go. And this would have been my wisest plan, and a very great saving of money; but somehow I felt as if it would be a mean thing to slip off so. Even while I was hesitating, and the men were breaking each other's heads, a superior officer rode up, with his sword drawn, and his face on fire.

'What, my lambs, my lambs!' he cried, smiting with the flat of his sword; 'is this how you waste my time and my purse, when you ought to be catching a hundred prisoners, worth ten pounds apiece to me? Who is this young fellow we have here? Speak up, sirrah; what art thou, and how much will thy good mother pay for thee?'

'My mother will pay naught for me,' I answered; while the lambs fell back, and glowered at one another: 'so please your worship, I am no rebel; but an honest farmer, and well-proved of loyalty.'

'Ha, ha; a farmer art thou? Those fellows always pay the best. Good farmer, come to yon barren tree; thou shalt make it fruitful.'

Colonel Kirke made a sign to his men, and before I could think of resistance, stout new ropes were flung around me; and with three men on either side I was led along very painfully. And now I saw, and repented deeply of my careless folly, in stopping with those boon-companions, instead of being far away. But the newness of their manners to me, and their mode of regarding the world (differing so much from mine own), as well as the flavour of their tobacco, had made me quite forget my duty to the farm and to myself. Yet methought they would be tender to me, after all our speeches: how then was I disappointed, when the men who had drunk my beer, drew on those grievous ropes, twice as hard as the men I had been at strife with! Yet this may have been from no ill will; but simply that having fallen under suspicion of laxity, they were compelled, in self-defence, now to be over-zealous.

Nevertheless, however pure and godly might be their motives, I beheld myself in a grievous case, and likely to get the worst of it. For the face of the Colonel was hard and stern as a block of bogwood oak; and though the men might pity me and think me unjustly executed, yet they must obey their orders, or themselves be put to death. Therefore I addressed myself to the Colonel, in a most ingratiating manner; begging him not to sully the glory of his victory, and dwelling upon my pure innocence, and even good service to our lord the King. But Colonel Kirke only gave command that I should be smitten in the mouth; which office Bob, whom I had flung so hard out of the linhay, performed with great zeal and efficiency. But being aware of the coming smack, I thrust forth a pair of teeth; upon which the knuckles of my good friend made a melancholy shipwreck.

It is not in my power to tell half the thoughts that moved me, when we came to the fatal tree, and saw two men hanging there already, as innocent perhaps as I was, and henceforth entirely harmless. Though ordered by the Colonel to look steadfastly upon them, I could not bear to do so; upon which he called me a paltry coward, and promised my breeches to any man who would spit upon my countenance. This vile thing Bob, being angered perhaps by the smarting wound of his knuckles, bravely stepped forward to do for me, trusting no doubt to the rope I was led with. But, unluckily as it proved for him, my right arm was free for a moment; and therewith I dealt him such a blow, that he never spake again. For this thing I have often grieved; but the provocation was very sore to the pride of a young man; and I trust that God has forgiven me. At the sound and sight of that bitter stroke, the other men drew back; and Colonel Kirke, now black in the face with fury and vexation, gave orders for to shoot me, and cast me into the ditch hard by. The men raised their pieces, and pointed at me, waiting for the word to fire; and I, being quite overcome by the hurry of these events, and quite unprepared to die yet, could only think all upside down about Lorna, and my mother, and wonder what each would say to it. I spread my hands before my eyes, not being so brave as some men; and hoping, in some foolish way, to cover my heart with my elbows. I heard the breath of all around, as if my skull were a sounding-board; and knew even how the different men were fingering their triggers. And a cold sweat broke all over me, as the Colonel, prolonging his enjoyment, began slowly to say, 'Fire.'

But while he was yet dwelling on the 'F,' the hoofs of a horse dashed out on the road, and horse and horseman flung themselves betwixt me and the gun muzzles. So narrowly was I saved that one man could not check his trigger: his musket went off, and the ball struck the horse on the withers, and scared him exceedingly. He began to lash out with his heels all around, and the Colonel was glad to keep clear of him; and the men made excuse to lower their guns, not really wishing to shoot me.

'How now, Captain Stickles?' cried Kirke, the more angry because he had shown his cowardice; 'dare you, sir, to come betwixt me and my lawful prisoner?'

'Nay, hearken one moment, Colonel,' replied my old friend Jeremy; and his damaged voice was the sweetest sound I had heard for many a day; 'for your own sake, hearken.' He looked so full of momentous tidings, that Colonel Kirke made a sign to his men not to shoot me till further orders; and then he went aside with Stickles, so that in spite of all my anxiety I could not catch what passed between them. But I fancied that the name of the Lord Chief-Justice Jeffreys was spoken more than once, and with emphasis and deference.

'Then I leave him in your hands, Captain Stickles,' said Kirke at last, so that all might hear him; and though the news was good for me, the smile of baffled malice made his dark face look most hideous; 'and I shall hold you answerable for the custody of this prisoner.'

'Colonel Kirke, I will answer for him,' Master Stickles replied, with a grave bow, and one hand on his breast: 'John Ridd, you are my prisoner. Follow me, John Ridd.'

Upon that, those precious lambs flocked away, leaving the rope still around me; and some were glad, and some were sorry, not to see me swinging. Being free of my arms again, I touched my hat to Colonel Kirke, as became his rank and experience; but he did not condescend to return my short salutation, having espied in the distance a prisoner, out of whom he might make money.

I wrung the hand of Jeremy Stickles, for his truth and goodness; and he almost wept (for since his wound he had been a weakened man) as he answered, 'Turn for turn, John. You saved my life from the Doones; and by the mercy of God, I have saved you from a far worse company. Let your sister Annie know it.'

Chapter LXVI Suitable Devotion

Now Kickums was not like Winnie, any more than a man is like a woman; and so he had not followed my fortunes, except at his own distance. No doubt but what he felt a certain interest in me; but his interest was not devotion; and man might go his way and be hanged, rather than horse would meet hardship. Therefore, seeing things to be bad, and his master involved in trouble, what did this horse do but start for the ease and comfort of Plover's Barrows, and the plentiful ration of oats abiding in his own manger. For this I do not blame him. It is the manner of mankind.

But I could not help being very uneasy at the thought of my mother's discomfort and worry, when she should spy this good horse coming home, without any master, or rider, and I almost hoped that he might be caught (although he was worth at least twenty pounds) by some of the King's troopers, rather than find his way home, and spread distress among our people. Yet, knowing his nature, I doubted if any could catch, or catching would keep him.

Jeremy Stickles assured me, as we took the road to Bridgwater, that the only chance for my life (if I still refused to fly) was to obtain an order forthwith, for my despatch to London, as a suspected person indeed, but not found in open rebellion, and believed to be under the patronage of the great Lord Jeffreys. 'For,' said he, 'in a few hours time you would fall into the hands of Lord Feversham, who has won this fight, without seeing it, and who has returned to bed again, to have his breakfast more comfortably.

Now he may not be quite so savage perhaps as Colonel Kirke, nor find so much sport in gibbeting; but he is equally pitiless, and his price no doubt would be higher.'

'I will pay no price whatever,' I answered, 'neither will I fly. An hour agone I would have fled for the sake of my mother, and the farm. But now that I have been taken prisoner, and my name is known, if I fly, the farm is forfeited; and my mother and sister must starve. Moreover, I have done no harm; I have borne no weapons against the King, nor desired the success of his enemies. I like not that the son of a bona-roba should be King of England; neither do I count the Papists any worse than we are. If they have aught to try me for, I will stand my trial.'

'Then to London thou must go, my son. There is no such thing as trial here: we hang the good folk without it, which saves them much anxiety. But quicken thy step, good John; I have influence with Lord Churchill, and we must contrive to see him, ere the foreigner falls to work again. Lord Churchill is a man of sense, and imprisons nothing but his money.'

We were lucky enough to find this nobleman, who has since become so famous by his foreign victories. He received us with great civility; and looked at me with much interest, being a tall and fine young man himself, but not to compare with me in size, although far better favoured. I liked his face well enough, but thought there was something false about it. He put me a few keen questions, such as a man not assured of honesty might have found hard to answer; and he stood in a very upright attitude, making the most of his figure.

I saw nothing to be proud of, at the moment, in this interview; but since the great Duke of Marlborough rose to the top of glory, I have tried to remember more about him than my conscience quite backs up. How should I know that this man would be foremost of our kingdom in five-and-twenty years or so; and not knowing, why should I heed him, except for my own pocket? Nevertheless, I have been so cross-questioned—far worse than by young Lord Churchill—about His Grace the Duke of Marlborough, and what he said to me, and what I said then, and how His Grace replied to that, and whether he smiled like another man, or screwed up his lips like a button (as our parish tailor said of him), and whether I knew from the turn of his nose that no Frenchman could stand before him: all these inquiries have worried me so, ever since the Battle of Blenheim, that if tailors would only print upon waistcoats, I would give double price for a vest bearing this inscription, 'No information can be given about the Duke of Marlborough.'

Now this good Lord Churchill—for one might call him good, by comparison with the very bad people around him—granted without any long hesitation the order for my safe deliverance to the Court of King's Bench at Westminster; and Stickles, who had to report in London, was empowered to convey me, and made answerable for producing me. This arrangement would have been entirely to my liking, although the time of year was bad for leaving Plover's Barrows so; but no man may quite choose his times, and on the while I would have been quite content to visit London, if my mother could be warned that nothing was amiss with me, only a mild, and as one might say, nominal captivity. And to prevent her anxiety, I did my best to send a letter through good Sergeant Bloxham, of whom I heard as quartered with Dumbarton's regiment at Chedzuy. But that regiment was away in pursuit; and I was forced to entrust my letter to a man who said that he knew him, and accepted a shilling to see to it.

For fear of any unpleasant change, we set forth at once for London; and truly thankful may I be that God in His mercy spared me the sight of the cruel and bloody work with which the whole country reeked and howled during the next fortnight. I have heard things that set my hair on end, and made me loathe good meat for days; but I make a point of setting down only the things which I saw done; and in this particular case, not many will quarrel with my decision. Enough, therefore, that we rode on (for Stickles had found me a horse at last) as far as Wells, where we slept that night; and being joined in the morning by several troopers and orderlies, we made a slow but safe journey to London, by way of Bath and Reading.

The sight of London warmed my heart with various emotions, such as a cordial man must draw from the heart of all humanity. Here there are quick ways and manners, and the rapid sense of knowledge, and the power of understanding, ere a word be spoken. Whereas at Oare, you must say a thing three times, very slowly, before it gets inside the skull of the good man you are addressing. And yet we are far more clever there than in any parish for fifteen miles.

But what moved me most, when I saw again the noble oil and tallow of the London lights, and the dripping torches at almost every corner, and the handsome signboards, was the thought that here my Lorna lived, and walked, and took the air, and perhaps thought now and then of the old days in the good farm-house. Although I would make no approach to her, any more than she had done to me (upon which grief I have not dwelt, for fear of seeming selfish), yet there must be some large chance, or the little chance might be enlarged, of falling in with the maiden somehow, and learning how her mind was set. If against me, all should be over. I was not the man to sigh and cry for love, like a Romeo: none should even guess my grief, except my sister Annie.

But if Lorna loved me still—as in my heart of hearts I hoped—then would I for no one care, except her own delicious self. Rank and title, wealth and grandeur, all should go to the winds, before they scared me from my own true love.

Thinking thus, I went to bed in the centre of London town, and was bitten so grievously by creatures whose name is 'legion,' mad with the delight of getting a wholesome farmer among them, that verily I was ashamed to walk in the courtly parts of the town next day, having lumps upon my face of the size of a pickling walnut. The landlord said that this was nothing; and that he expected, in two days at the utmost, a very fresh young Irishman, for whom they would all forsake me. Nevertheless, I declined to wait, unless he could find me a hayrick to sleep in; for the insects of grass only tickle. He assured me that no hayrick could now be found in London; upon which I was forced to leave him, and with mutual esteem we parted.

The next night I had better luck, being introduced to a decent widow, of very high Scotch origin. That house was swept and garnished so, that not a bit was left to eat, for either man or insect. The change of air having made me hungry, I wanted something after supper; being quite ready to pay for it, and showing my purse as a symptom. But the face of Widow MacAlister, when I proposed to have some more food, was a thing to be drawn (if it could be drawn further) by our new caricaturist.

Therefore I left her also; for liefer would I be eaten myself than have nothing to eat; and so I came back to my old furrier; the which was a thoroughly hearty man, and welcomed me to my room again, with two shillings added to the rent, in the joy of his heart at seeing me. Being under parole to Master Stickles, I only went out betwixt certain hours; because I was accounted as liable to be called upon; for what purpose I knew not, but hoped it might be a good one. I felt it a loss, and a hindrance to me, that I was so bound to remain at home during the session of the courts of law; for thereby the chance of ever beholding Lorna was very greatly contracted, if not altogether annihilated. For these were the very hours in which the people of fashion, and the high world, were wont to appear to the rest of mankind, so as to encourage them. And of course by this time, the Lady Lorna was high among people of fashion, and was not likely to be seen out of fashionable hours. It is true that there were some places of expensive entertainment, at which the better sort of mankind might be seen and studied, in their hours of relaxation, by those of the lower order, who could pay sufficiently. But alas, my money was getting low; and the privilege of seeing my betters was more and more denied to me, as my cash drew shorter. For a man must have a good coat at least, and the pockets not wholly empty, before he can look at those whom God has created for his ensample.

Hence, and from many other causes—part of which was my own pride—it happened that I abode in London betwixt a month and five weeks' time, ere ever I saw Lorna. It seemed unfit that I should go, and waylay her, and spy on her, and say (or mean to say), 'Lo, here is your poor faithful farmer, a man who is unworthy of you, by means of his common birth; and yet who dares to crawl across your path, that you may pity him. For God's sake show a little pity, though you may not feel it.' Such behaviour might be comely in a love-lorn boy, a page to some grand princess; but I, John Ridd, would never stoop to the lowering of love so.

Nevertheless I heard of Lorna, from my worthy furrier, almost every day, and with a fine exaggeration. This honest man was one of those who in virtue of their trade, and nicety of behaviour, are admitted into noble life, to take measurements, and show patterns. And while so doing, they contrive to acquire what is to the English mind at once the most important and most interesting of all knowledge,—the science of being able to talk about the titled people. So my furrier (whose name was Ramsack), having to make robes for peers, and cloaks for their wives and otherwise, knew the great folk, sham or real, as well as he knew a fox or skunk from a wolverine skin.

And when, with some fencing and foils of inquiry, I hinted about Lady Lorna Dugal, the old man's face became so pleasant that I knew her birth must be wondrous high. At this my own countenance fell, I suppose,—for the better she was born, the harder she would be to marry—and mistaking my object, he took me up:—

'Perhaps you think, Master Ridd, that because her ladyship, Lady Lorna Dugal, is of Scottish origin, therefore her birth is not as high as of our English nobility. If you think so you are wrong, sir. She comes not of the sandy Scotch race, with high cheek-bones, and raw shoulder-blades, who set up pillars in their courtyards. But she comes of the very best Scotch blood, descended from the Norsemen. Her mother was of the very noblest race, the Lords of Lorne; higher even than the great Argyle, who has lately made a sad mistake, and paid for it most sadly. And her father was descended from the King Dugal, who fought against Alexander the Great. No, no, Master Ridd; none of your promiscuous blood, such as runs in the veins of half our modern peerage.'

'Why should you trouble yourself about it, Master Ramsack?' I replied: 'let them all go their own ways: and let us all look up to them, whether they come by hook or crook.'

'Not at all, not at all, my lad. That is not the way to regard it. We look up at the well-born men, and side-ways at the base-born.'

'Then we are all base-born ourselves. I will look up to no man, except for what himself has done.'

'Come, Master Ridd, you might be lashed from New-gate to Tyburn and back again, once a week, for a twelvemonth, if some people heard you. Keep your tongue more close, young man; or here you lodge no longer; albeit I love your company, which smells to me of the hayfield. Ah, I have not seen a hayfield for nine-and-twenty years, John Ridd. The cursed moths keep me at home, every day of the summer.'

'Spread your furs on the haycocks,' I answered very boldly: 'the indoor moth cannot abide the presence of the outdoor ones.'

'Is it so?' he answered: 'I never thought of that before. And yet I have known such strange things happen in the way of fur, that I can well believe it. If you only knew, John, the way in which they lay their eggs, and how they work tail-foremost—'

'Tell me nothing of the kind,' I replied, with equal confidence: 'they cannot work tail-foremost; and they have no tails to work with.' For I knew a little about grubs, and the ignorance concerning them, which we have no right to put up with. However, not to go into that (for the argument lasted a fortnight; and then was only come so far as to begin again), Master Ramsack soon convinced me of the things I knew already; the excellence of Lorna's birth, as well as her lofty place at Court, and beauty, and wealth, and elegance. But all these only made me sigh, and wish that I were born to them.

From Master Ramsack I discovered that the nobleman to whose charge Lady Lorna had been committed, by the Court of Chancery, was Earl Brandir of Lochawe, her poor mother's uncle. For the Countess of Dugal was daughter, and only child, of the last Lord Lorne, whose sister had married Sir Ensor Doone; while he himself had married the sister of Earl Brandir. This nobleman had a country house near the village of Kensington; and here his niece dwelled with him, when she was not in attendance on Her Majesty the Queen, who had taken a liking to her. Now since the King had begun to attend the celebration of mass, in the chapel at Whitehall—and not at Westminster Abbey, as our gossips had averred—he had given order that the doors should be thrown open, so that all who could make interest to get into the antechamber, might see this form of worship. Master Ramsack told me that Lorna was there almost every Sunday; their Majesties being most anxious to have the presence of all the nobility of the Catholic persuasion, so as to make a goodly show. And the worthy furrier, having influence with the door-keepers, kindly obtained admittance for me, one Sunday, into the antechamber.

Here I took care to be in waiting, before the Royal procession entered; but being unknown, and of no high rank, I was not allowed to stand forward among the better people, but ordered back into a corner very dark and dismal; the verger remarking, with a grin, that I could see over all other heads, and must not set my own so high. Being frightened to find myself among so many people of great rank and gorgeous apparel, I blushed at the notice drawn upon me by this uncourteous fellow; and silently fell back into the corner by the hangings.

You may suppose that my heart beat high, when the King and Queen appeared, and entered, followed by the Duke of Norfolk, bearing the sword of state, and by several other noblemen, and people of repute. Then the doors of the chapel were thrown wide open; and though I could only see a little, being in the corner so, I thought that it was beautiful. Bowers of rich silk were there, and plenty of metal shining, and polished wood with lovely carving; flowers too of the noblest kind, and candles made by somebody who had learned how to clarify tallow. This last thing amazed me more than all, for our dips never will come clear, melt the mutton-fat how you will. And methought that this hanging of flowers about was a pretty thing; for if a man can worship God best of all beneath a tree, as the natural instinct is, surely when by fault of climate the tree would be too apt to drip, the very best make-believe is to have enough and to spare of flowers; which to the dwellers in London seem to have grown on the tree denied them.

Be that as it may, when the King and Queen crossed the threshold, a mighty flourish of trumpets arose, and a waving of banners. The Knights of the Garter (whoever they be) were to attend that day in state; and some went in, and some stayed out, and it made me think of the difference betwixt the ewes and the wethers. For the ewes will go wherever you lead them; but the wethers will not, having strong opinions, and meaning to abide by them. And one man I noticed was of the wethers, to wit the Duke of Norfolk; who stopped outside with the sword of state, like a beadle with a rapping-rod. This has taken more to tell than the time it happened in. For after all the men were gone, some to this side, some to that, according to their feelings, a number of ladies, beautifully dressed, being of the Queen's retinue, began to enter, and were stared at three times as much as the men had been. And indeed they were worth looking at (which men never are to my ideas, when they trick themselves with gewgaws), but none was so well worth eye-service as my own beloved Lorna. She entered modestly and shyly, with her eyes upon the ground, knowing the rudeness of the gallants, and the large sum she was priced at. Her dress was of the purest white, very sweet and simple, without a line of ornament, for she herself adorned it. The way she walked. and touched her skirt (rather than seemed to hold it up) with a white hand beaming one red rose, this and her stately supple neck, and the flowing of her hair would show, at a distance of a hundred yards, that she could be none but Lorna Doone. Lorna Doone of my early love; in the days when she blushed for her name before me by reason of dishonesty; but now the Lady Lorna Dugal as far beyond reproach as above my poor affection. All my heart, and all my mind, gathered themselves upon her. Would she see me, or would she pass? Was there instinct in our love?

By some strange chance she saw me. Or was it through our destiny? While with eyes kept sedulously on the marble floor, to shun the weight of admiration thrust too boldly on them, while with shy quick steps she passed, some one (perhaps with purpose) trod on the skirt of her clear white dress,—with the quickness taught her by many a scene of danger, she looked up, and her eyes met mine.

As I gazed upon her, steadfastly, yearningly, yet with some reproach, and more of pride than humility, she made me one of the courtly bows which I do so much detest; yet even that was sweet and graceful, when my Lorna did it. But the colour of her pure clear cheeks was nearly as deep as that of my own, when she went on for the religious work. And the shining of her eyes was owing to an unpaid debt of tears.

Upon the whole I was satisfied. Lorna had seen me, and had not (according to the phrase of the high world then) even tried to 'cut' me. Whether this low phrase is born of their own stupid meanness, or whether it comes of necessity exercised on a man without money, I know not, and I care not. But one thing I know right well; any man who 'cuts' a man (except for vice or meanness) should be quartered without quarter.

All these proud thoughts rose within me as the lovely form of Lorna went inside, and was no more seen. And then I felt how coarse I was; how apt to think strong thoughts, and so on; without brains to bear me out: even as a hen's egg, laid without enough of lime, and looking only a poor jelly.

Nevertheless, I waited on; as my usual manner is. For to be beaten, while running away, is ten times worse than to face it out, and take it, and have done with it. So at least I have always found, because of reproach of conscience: and all the things those clever people carried on inside, at large, made me long for our Parson Bowden that he might know how to act.

While I stored up, in my memory, enough to keep our parson going through six pipes on a Saturday night—to have it as right as could be next day—a lean man with a yellow beard, too thin for a good Catholic (which religion always fattens), came up to me, working sideways, in the manner of a female crab.

'This is not to my liking,' I said: 'if aught thou hast, speak plainly; while they make that horrible noise inside.'

Nothing had this man to say; but with many sighs, because I was not of the proper faith, he took my reprobate hand to save me: and with several religious tears, looked up at me, and winked with one eye. Although the skin of my palms was thick, I felt a little suggestion there, as of a gentle leaf in spring, fearing to seem too forward. I paid the man, and he went happy; for the standard of heretical silver is purer than that of the Catholics.

Then I lifted up my little billet; and in that dark corner read it, with a strong rainbow of colours coming from the angled light. And in mine eyes there was enough to make rainbow of strongest sun, as my anger clouded off.

Not that it began so well; but that in my heart I knew (ere three lines were through me) that I was with all heart loved—and beyond that, who may need? The darling of my life went on, as if I were of her own rank, or even better than she was; and she dotted her 'i's,' and crossed her 't's,' as if I were at least a schoolmaster. All of it was done in pencil; but as plain as plain could be. In my coffin it shall lie, with my ring and something else. Therefore will I not expose it to every man who buys this book, and haply thinks that he has bought me to the bottom of my heart. Enough for men of gentle birth (who never are inquisitive) that my love told me, in her letter, just to come and see her.

I ran away, and could not stop. To behold even her, at the moment, would have dashed my fancy's joy. Yet my brain was so amiss, that I must do something. Therefore to the river Thames, with all speed, I hurried; and keeping all my best clothes on (indued for sake of Lorna), into the quiet stream I leaped, and swam as far as London Bridge, and ate nobler dinner afterwards.

Chapter LXVII Lorna Still Is Lorna

Although a man may be as simple as the flowers of the field; knowing when, but scarcely why, he closes to the bitter wind; and feeling why, but scarcely when, he opens to the genial sun; yet without his questing much into the capsule of himself—to do which is a misery—he may have a general notion how he happens to be getting on.

I felt myself to be getting on better than at any time since the last wheat-harvest, as I took the lane to Kensington upon the Monday evening. For although no time was given in my Lorna's letter, I was not inclined to wait more than decency required. And though I went and watched the house, decency would not allow me to knock on the Sunday evening, especially when I found at the corner that his lordship was at home.

The lanes and fields between Charing Cross and the village of Kensington, are, or were at that time, more than reasonably infested with footpads and with highwaymen. However, my stature and holly club kept these fellows from doing more than casting sheep's eyes at me. For it was still broad daylight, and the view of the distant villages, Chelsea, Battersea, Tyburn, and others, as well as a few large houses, among the hams and towards the river, made it seem less lonely. Therefore I sang a song in the broadest Exmoor dialect, which caused no little amazement in the minds of all who met me.

When I came to Earl Brandir's house, my natural modesty forbade me to appear at the door for guests; therefore I went to the entrance for servants and retainers. Here, to my great surprise, who should come and let me in but little Gwenny Carfax, whose very existence had almost escaped my recollection. Her mistress, no doubt, had seen me coming, and sent her to save trouble. But when I offered to kiss Gwenny, in my joy and comfort to see a farm-house face again, she looked ashamed, and turned away, and would hardly speak to me.

I followed her to a little room, furnished very daintily; and there she ordered me to wait, in a most ungracious manner. 'Well,' thought I, 'if the mistress and the maid are alike in temper, better it had been for me to abide at Master Ramsack's.' But almost ere my thought was done, I heard the light quick step which I knew as well as 'Watch,' my dog, knew mine; and my breast began to tremble, like the trembling of an arch ere the keystone is put in.

Almost ere I hoped—for fear and hope were so entangled that they hindered one another—the velvet hangings of the doorway parted, with a little doubt, and then a good face put on it. Lorna, in her perfect beauty, stood before the crimson folds, and her dress was all pure white, and her cheeks were rosy pink, and her lips were scarlet.

Like a maiden, with skill and sense checking violent impulse, she stayed there for one moment only, just to be admired; and then like a woman, she came to me, seeing how alarmed I was. The hand she offered me I took, and raised it to my lips with fear, as a thing too good for me. 'Is that all?' she whispered; and then her eyes gleamed up at me; and in another instant, she was weeping on my breast.

'Darling Lorna, Lady Lorna,' I cried, in astonishment, yet unable but to keep her closer to me, and closer; 'surely, though I love you so, this is not as it should be.'

'Yes, it is, John. Yes, it is. Nothing else should ever be. Oh, why have you behaved so?'

'I am behaving.' I replied, 'to the very best of my ability. There is no other man in the world could hold you so, without kissing you.'

'Then why don't you do it, John?' asked Lorna, looking up at me, with a flash of her old fun.

Now this matter, proverbially, is not for discussion, and repetition. Enough that we said nothing more than, 'Oh, John, how glad I am!' and 'Lorna, Lorna Lorna!' for about five minutes. Then my darling drew back proudly, with blushing cheeks, and tear-bright eyes, she began to cross-examine me.

'Master John Ridd, you shall tell the truth, the whole truth, and nothing but the truth. I have been in Chancery, sir; and can detect a story. Now why have you never, for more than a twelvemonth, taken the smallest notice of your old friend, Mistress Lorna Doone?' Although she spoke in this lightsome manner, as if it made no difference, I saw that her quick heart was moving, and the flash of her eyes controlled.

'Simply for this cause, I answered, 'that my old friend and true love, took not the smallest heed of me. Nor knew I where to find her.'

'What!' cried Lorna; and nothing more; being overcome with wondering; and much inclined to fall away, but for my assistance. I told her, over and over again, that not a single syllable of any message from her, or tidings of her welfare, had reached me, or any one of us, since the letter she left behind; except by soldier's gossip.

'Oh, you poor dear John!' said Lorna, sighing at thought of my misery: 'how wonderfully good of you, thinking of me as you must have done, not to marry that little plain thing (or perhaps I should say that lovely creature, for I have never seen her), Mistress Ruth—I forget her name; but something like a towel.'

'Ruth Huckaback is a worthy maid,' I answered with some dignity; 'and she alone of all our world, except indeed poor Annie, has kept her confidence in you, and told me not to dread your rank, but trust your heart, Lady Lorna.'

'Then Ruth is my best friend,' she answered, 'and is worthy of you, dear John. And now remember one thing, dear; if God should part us, as may be by nothing short of death, try to marry that little Ruth, when you cease to remember me. And now for the head-traitor. I have often suspected it: but she looks me in the face, and wishes—fearful things, which I cannot repeat.'

With these words, she moved an implement such as I had not seen before, and which made a ringing noise at a serious distance. And before I had ceased wondering—for if such things go on, we might ring the church bells, while sitting in our back-kitchen—little Gwenny Carfax came, with a grave and sullen face.

'Gwenny,' began my Lorna, in a tone of high rank and dignity, 'go and fetch the letters which I gave you at various times for despatch to Mistress Ridd.'

'How can I fetch them, when they are gone? It be no use for him to tell no lies—'

'Now, Gwenny, can you look at me?' I asked, very sternly; for the matter was no joke to me, after a year's unhappiness.

'I don't want to look at 'ee. What should I look at a young man for, although he did offer to kiss me?'

I saw the spite and impudence of this last remark, and so did Lorna, although she could not quite refrain from smiling.

'Now, Gwenny, not to speak of that,' said Lorna, very demurely, 'if you thought it honest to keep the letters, was it honest to keep the money?'

At this the Cornish maiden broke into a rage of honesty: 'A putt the money by for 'ee. 'Ee shall have every farden of it.' And so she flung out of the room.

'And, Gwenny,' said Lorna very softly, following under the door-hangings; 'if it is not honest to keep the money, it is not honest to keep the letters, which would have been worth more than any gold to those who were so kind to you. Your father shall know the whole, Gwenny, unless you tell the truth.'

'Now, a will tell all the truth,' this strange maiden answered, talking to herself at least as much as to her mistress, while she went out of sight and hearing. And then I was so glad at having my own Lorna once again, cleared of all contempt for us, and true to me through all of it, that I would have forgiven Gwenny for treason, or even forgery.

'I trusted her so much,' said Lorna, in her old ill-fortuned way; 'and look how she has deceived me! That is why I love you, John (setting other things aside), because you never told me falsehood; and you never could, you know.'

'Well, I am not so sure of that. I think I could tell any lie, to have you, darling, all my own.'

'Yes. And perhaps it might be right. To other people besides us two. But you could not do it to me, John. You never could do it to me, you know.'

Before I quite perceived my way to the bottom of the distinction—although beyond doubt a valid one—Gwenny came back with a leathern bag, and tossed it upon the table. Not a word did she vouchsafe to us; but stood there, looking injured.

'Go, and get your letters, John,' said Lorna very gravely; 'or at least your mother's letters, made of messages to you. As for Gwenny, she shall go before Lord Justice Jeffreys.' I knew that Lorna meant it not; but thought that the girl deserved a frightening; as indeed she did. But we both mistook the courage of this child of Cornwall. She stepped upon a little round thing, in the nature of a stool, such as I never had seen before, and thus delivered her sentiments.

'And you may take me, if you please, before the great Lord Jeffreys. I have done no more than duty, though I did it crookedly, and told a heap of lies, for your sake. And pretty gratitude I gets.'

'Much gratitude you have shown,' replied Lorna, 'to Master Ridd, for all his kindness and his goodness to you. Who was it that went down, at the peril of his life, and brought your father to you, when you had lost him for months and months? Who was it? Answer me, Gwenny?'

'Girt Jan Ridd,' said the handmaid, very sulkily.

'What made you treat me so, little Gwenny?' I asked, for Lorna would not ask lest the reply should vex me.

'Because 'ee be'est below her so. Her shanna' have a poor farmering chap, not even if her were a Carnishman. All her land, and all her birth—and who be you, I'd like to know?'

'Gwenny, you may go,' said Lorna, reddening with quiet anger; 'and remember that you come not near me for the next three days. It is the only way to punish her,' she continued to me, when the maid was gone, in a storm of sobbing and weeping. 'Now, for the next three days, she will scarcely touch a morsel of food, and scarcely do a thing but cry. Make up your mind to one thing, John; if you mean to take me, for better for worse, you will have to take Gwenny with me.

'I would take you with fifty Gwennies,' said I, 'although every one of them hated me, which I do not believe this little maid does, in the bottom of her heart.'

'No one can possibly hate you, John,' she answered very softly; and I was better pleased with this, than if she had called me the most noble and glorious man in the kingdom.

After this, we spoke of ourselves and the way people would regard us, supposing that when Lorna came to be her own free mistress (as she must do in the course of time) she were to throw her rank aside, and refuse her title, and caring not a fig for folk who cared less than a fig-stalk for her, should shape her mind to its native bent, and to my perfect happiness. It was not my place to say much, lest I should appear to use an improper and selfish influence. And of course to all men of common sense, and to everybody of middle age (who must know best what is good for youth), the thoughts which my Lorna entertained would be enough to prove her madness.

Not that we could not keep her well, comfortably, and with nice clothes, and plenty of flowers, and fruit, and landscape, and the knowledge of our neighbours' affairs, and their kind interest in our own. Still this would not be as if she were the owner of a county, and a haughty title; and able to lead the first men of the age, by her mind, and face, and money.

Therefore was I quite resolved not to have a word to say, while this young queen of wealth and beauty, and of noblemen's desire, made her mind up how to act for her purest happiness. But to do her justice, this was not the first thing she was thinking of: the test of her judgment was only this, 'How will my love be happiest?'

'Now, John,' she cried; for she was so quick that she always had my thoughts beforehand; 'why will you be backward, as if you cared not for me? Do you dream that I am doubting? My mind has been made up, good John, that you must be my husband, for—well, I will not say how long, lest you should laugh at my folly. But I believe it was ever since you came, with your stockings off, and the loaches. Right early for me to make up my mind; but you know that you made up yours, John; and, of course, I knew it; and that had a great effect on me. Now, after all this age of loving, shall a trifle sever us?'

I told her that it was no trifle, but a most important thing, to abandon wealth, and honour, and the brilliance of high life, and be despised by every one for such abundant folly. Moreover, that I should appear a knave for taking advantage of her youth, and boundless generosity, and ruining (as men would say) a noble maid by my selfishness. And I told her outright, having worked myself up by my own conversation, that she was bound to consult her guardian, and that without his knowledge, I would come no more to see her. Her flash of pride at these last words made her look like an empress; and I was about to explain myself better, but she put forth her hand and stopped me.

'I think that condition should rather have proceeded from me. You are mistaken, Master Ridd, in supposing that I would think of receiving you in secret. It was a different thing in Glen Doone, where all except yourself were thieves, and when I was but a simple child, and oppressed with constant fear. You are quite right in threatening to visit me thus no more; but I think you might have waited for an invitation, sir.'

'And you are quite right, Lady Lorna, in pointing out my presumption. It is a fault that must ever be found in any speech of mine to you.'

This I said so humbly, and not with any bitterness—for I knew that I had gone too far—and made her so polite a bow, that she forgave me in a moment, and we begged each other's pardon.

'Now, will you allow me just to explain my own view of this matter, John?' said she, once more my darling. 'It may be a very foolish view, but I shall never change it. Please not to interrupt me, dear, until you have heard me to the end. In the first place, it is quite certain that neither you nor I can be happy without the other. Then what stands between us? Worldly position, and nothing else. I have no more education than you have, John Ridd; nay, and not so much. My birth and ancestry are not one whit more pure than yours, although they may be better known. Your descent from ancient freeholders, for five-and-twenty generations of good, honest men, although you bear no coat of arms, is better than the lineage of nine proud English noblemen out of every ten I meet with. In manners, though your mighty strength, and hatred of any meanness, sometimes break out in violence—of which I must try to cure you, dear—in manners, if kindness, and gentleness, and modesty are the true things wanted, you are immeasurably above any of our Court-gallants; who indeed have very little. As for difference of religion, we allow for one another, neither having been brought up in a bitterly pious manner.'

Here, though the tears were in my eyes, at the loving things love said of me, I could not help a little laugh at the notion of any bitter piety being found among the Doones, or even in mother, for that matter. Lorna smiled, in her slyest manner, and went on again:—

'Now, you see, I have proved my point; there is nothing between us but worldly position—if you can defend me against the Doones, for which, I trow, I may trust you. And worldly position means wealth, and title, and the right to be in great houses, and the pleasure of being envied. I have not been here for a year, John, without learning something. Oh, I hate it; how I hate it! Of all the people I know, there are but two, besides my uncle, who do not either covet, or detest me. And who are those two, think you?'

'Gwenny, for one,' I answered.

'Yes, Gwenny, for one. And the queen, for the other. The one is too far below me (I mean, in her own opinion), and the other too high above. As for the women who dislike me, without having even heard my voice, I simply have nothing to do with them. As for the men who covet me, for my land and money, I merely compare them with you, John Ridd; and all thought of them is over. Oh, John, you must never forsake me, however cross I am to you. I thought you would have gone, just now; and though I would not move to stop you, my heart would have broken.'

'You don't catch me go in a hurry,' I answered very sensibly, 'when the loveliest maiden in all the world, and the best, and the dearest, loves me. All my fear of you is gone, darling Lorna, all my fear—'

'Is it possible you could fear me, John, after all we have been through together? Now you promised not to interrupt me; is this fair behaviour? Well, let me see where I left off—oh, that my heart would have broken. Upon that point, I will say no more, lest you should grow conceited, John; if anything could make you so. But I do assure you that half London—however, upon that point also I will check my power of speech, lest you think me conceited. And now to put aside all nonsense; though I have talked none for a year, John, having been so unhappy; and now it is such a relief to me—'

'Then talk it for an hour,' said I; 'and let me sit and watch you. To me it is the very sweetest of all sweetest wisdom.'

'Nay, there is no time,' she answered, glancing at a jewelled time-piece, scarcely larger than an oyster, which she drew from her waist-band; and then she pushed it away, in confusion, lest its wealth should startle me. 'My uncle will come home in less than half an hour, dear: and you are not the one to take a side-passage, and avoid him. I shall tell him that you have been here; and that I mean you to come again.'

As Lorna said this, with a manner as confident as need be, I saw that she had learned in town the power of her beauty, and knew that she could do with most men aught she set her mind upon. And as she stood there, flushed with pride and faith in her own loveliness, and radiant with the love itself, I felt that she must do exactly as she pleased with every one. For now, in turn, and elegance, and richness, and variety, there was nothing to compare with her face, unless it were her figure. Therefore I gave in, and said,—

'Darling, do just what you please. Only make no rogue of me.'

For that she gave me the simplest, kindest, and sweetest of all kisses; and I went down the great stairs grandly, thinking of nothing else but that.

Chapter LXVIII John Is John No Longer

It would be hard for me to tell the state of mind in which I lived for a long time after this. I put away from me all torment, and the thought of future cares, and the sight of difficulty; and to myself appeared, which means that I became the luckiest of lucky fellows, since the world itself began. I thought not of the harvest even, nor of the men who would get their wages without having earned them, nor of my mother's anxiety and worry about John Fry's great fatness (which was growing upon him), and how she would cry fifty times in a day, 'Ah, if our John would only come home, how different everything would look!'

Although there were no soldiers now quartered at Plover's Barrows, all being busied in harassing the country, and hanging the people where the rebellion had thriven most, my mother, having received from me a message containing my place of abode, contrived to send me, by the pack-horses, as fine a maund as need be of provisions, and money, and other comforts. Therein I found addressed to Colonel Jeremiah Stickles, in Lizzie's best handwriting, half a side of the dried deer's flesh, in which he rejoiced so greatly. Also, for Lorna, a fine green goose, with a little salt towards the tail, and new-laid eggs inside it, as well as a bottle of brandied cherries, and seven, or it may have been eight pounds of fresh homemade butter. Moreover, to myself there was a letter full of good advice, excellently well expressed, and would have been of the greatest value, if I had cared to read it. But I read all about the farm affairs, and the man whe had offered himself to our Betty for the five pounds in her stocking; as well as the antics of Sally Snowe, and how she had almost thrown herself at Parson Bowden's head (old enough to be her grandfather), because on the Sunday after the hanging of a Countisbury man, he had preached a beautiful sermon about Christian love; which Lizzie, with her sharp eyes, found to be the work of good Bishop Ken. Also I read that the Doones were quiet; the parishes round about having united to feed them well through the harvest time, so that after the day's hard work, the farmers might go to bed at night. And this plan had been found to answer well, and to save much trouble on both sides, so that everybody wondered it had not been done before. But Lizzie thought that the Doones could hardly be expected much longer to put up with it, and probably would not have done so now, but for a little adversity; to wit, that the famous Colonel Kirke had, in the most outrageous manner, hanged no less than six of them, who were captured among the rebels; for he said that men of their rank and breeding, and above all of their religion, should have known better than to join plough-boys, and carters, and pickaxemen, against our Lord the King, and his Holiness the Pope. This hanging of so many Doones caused some indignation among people who were used to them; and it seemed for a while to check the rest from any spirit of enterprise.

Moreover, I found from this same letter (which was pinned upon the knuckle of a leg of mutton, for fear of being lost in straw) that good Tom Faggus was at home again, and nearly cured of his dreadful wound; but intended to go to war no more, only to mind his family. And it grieved him more than anything he ever could have imagined, that his duty to his family, and the strong power of his conscience, so totally forbade him to come up and see after me. For now his design was to lead a new life, and be in charity with all men. Many better men than he had been hanged, he saw no cause to doubt; but by the grace of God he hoped himself to cheat the gallows.

There was no further news of moment in this very clever letter, except that the price of horses' shoes was gone up again, though already twopence-farthing each; and that Betty had broken her lover's head with the stocking full of money; and then in the corner it was written that the distinguished man of war, and worshipful scholar, Master Bloxham, was now promoted to take the tolls, and catch all the rebels around our part.

Lorna was greatly pleased with the goose, and the butter, and the brandied cherries; and the Earl Brandir himself declared that he never tasted better than those last, and would beg the young man from the country to procure him instructions for making them. This nobleman, being as deaf as a post, and of a very solid mind, could never be brought to understand the nature of my thoughts towards Lorna. He looked upon me as an excellent youth, who had rescued the maiden from the Doones, whom he cordially detested; and learning that I had thrown two of them out of window (as the story was told him), he patted me on the back, and declared that his doors would ever be open to me, and that I could not come too often.

I thought this very kind of his lordship, especially as it enabled me to see my darling Lorna, not indeed as often as I wished, but at any rate very frequently, and as many times as modesty (ever my leading principle) would in common conscience approve of. And I made up my mind that if ever I could help Earl Brandir, it would be—as we say, when with brandy and water—the 'proudest moment of my life,' when I could fulfil the pledge.

And I soon was able to help Lord Brandir, as I think, in two different ways; first of all as regarded his mind, and then as concerned his body: and the latter perhaps was the greatest service, at his time of life. But not to be too nice about that; let me tell how these things were.

Lorna said to me one day, being in a state of excitement—whereto she was over prone, when reft of my slowness to steady her,—

'I will tell him, John; I must tell him, John. It is mean of me to conceal it.'

I thought that she meant all about our love, which we had endeavoured thrice to drill into his fine old ears; but could not make him comprehend, without risk of bringing the house down: and so I said, 'By all means; darling; have another try at it.'

Lorna, however, looked at me—for her eyes told more than tongue—as much as to say, 'Well, you are a stupid. We agreed to let that subject rest.' And then she saw that I was vexed at my own want of quickness; and so she spoke very kindly,—

'I meant about his poor son, dearest; the son of his old age almost; whose loss threw him into that dreadful cold—for he went, without hat, to look for him—which ended in his losing the use of his dear old ears. I believe if we could only get him to Plover's Barrows for a month, he would be able to hear again. And look at his age! he is not much over seventy, John, you know; and I hope that you will be able to hear me, long after you are seventy, John.'

'Well,' said I, 'God settles that. Or at any rate, He leaves us time to think about those questions, when we are over fifty. Now let me know what you want, Lorna. The idea of my being seventy! But you would still be beautiful.'

'To the one who loves me,' she answered, trying to make wrinkles in her pure bright forehead: 'but if you will have common sense, as you always will, John, whether I wish it or otherwise—I want to know whether I am bound, in honour, and in conscience, to tell my dear and good old uncle what I know about his son?'

'First let me understand quite clearly,' said I, never being in a hurry, except when passion moves me, 'what his lordship thinks at present; and how far his mind is urged with sorrow and anxiety.' This was not the first time we had spoken of the matter.

'Why, you know, John, well enough,' she answered, wondering at my coolness, 'that my poor uncle stlll believes that his one beloved son will come to light and live again. He has made all arrangements accordingly: all his property is settled on that supposition. He knows that young Alan always was what he calls a "feckless ne'er-do-weel;" but he loves him all the more for that. He cannot believe that he will die, without his son coming back to him; and he always has a bedroom ready, and a bottle of Alan's favourite wine cool from out the cellar; he has made me work him a pair of slippers from the size of a mouldy boot; and if he hears of a new tobacco—much as he hates the smell of it—he will go to the other end of London to get some for Alan. Now you know how deaf he is; but if any one say, "Alan," even in the place outside the door, he will make his courteous bow to the very highest visitor, and be out there in a moment, and search the entire passage, and yet let no one know it.'

'It is a piteous thing,' I said; for Lorna's eyes were full of tears.

'And he means me to marry him. It is the pet scheme of his life. I am to grow more beautiful, and more highly taught, and graceful; until it pleases Alan to come back, and demand me. Can you understand this matter, John? Or do you think my uncle mad?'

'Lorna, I should be mad myself, to call any other man mad, for hoping.'

'Then will you tell me what to do? It makes me very sorrowful. For I know that Alan Brandir lies below the sod in Doone-valley.'

'And if you tell his father,' I answered softly, but clearly, 'in a few weeks he will lie below the sod in London; at least if there is any.'

'Perhaps you are right, John,' she replied: 'to lose hope must be a dreadful thing, when one is turned of seventy. Therefore I will never tell him.'

The other way in which I managed to help the good Earl Brandir was of less true moment to him; but as he could not know of the first, this was the one which moved him. And it happened pretty much as follows—though I hardly like to tell, because it advanced me to such a height as I myself was giddy at; and which all my friends resented greatly (save those of my own family), and even now are sometimes bitter, in spite of all my humility. Now this is a matter of history, because the King was concerned in it; and being so strongly misunderstood, (especially in my own neighbourhood, I will overcome so far as I can) my diffidence in telling it.

The good Earl Brandir was a man of the noblest charity. True charity begins at home, and so did his; and was afraid of losing the way, if it went abroad. So this good nobleman kept his money in a handsome pewter box, with his coat of arms upon it, and a double lid and locks. Moreover, there was a heavy chain, fixed to a staple in the wall, so that none might carry off the pewter with the gold inside of it. Lorna told me the box was full, for she had seen him go to it, and she often thought that it would be nice for us to begin the world with. I told her that she must not allow her mind to dwell upon things of this sort; being wholly against the last commandment set up in our church at Oare.

Now one evening towards September, when the days were drawing in, looking back at the house to see whether Lorna were looking after me, I espied (by a little glimpse, as it were) a pair of villainous fellows (about whom there could be no mistake) watching from the thicket-corner, some hundred yards or so behind the good Earl's dwelling. 'There is mischief afoot,' thought I to myself, being thoroughly conversant with theft, from my knowledge of the Doones; 'how will be the moon to-night, and when may we expect the watch?'

I found that neither moon nor watch could be looked for until the morning; the moon, of course, before the watch, and more likely to be punctual. Therefore I resolved to wait, and see what those two villains did, and save (if it were possible) the Earl of Brandir's pewter box. But inasmuch as those bad men were almost sure to have seen me leaving the house and looking back, and striking out on the London road, I marched along at a merry pace, until they could not discern me; and then I fetched a compass round, and refreshed myself at a certain inn, entitled The Cross-bones and Buttons.

Here I remained until it was very nearly as dark as pitch; and the house being full of footpads and cutthroats, I thought it right to leave them. One or two came after me, in the hope of designing a stratagem; but I dropped them in the darkness; and knowing all the neighbourhood well, I took up my position, two hours before midnight, among the shrubs at the eastern end of Lord Brandir's mansion. Hence, although I might not see, I could scarcely fail to hear, if any unlawful entrance either at back or front were made.

From my own observation, I thought it likely that the attack would he in the rear; and so indeed it came to pass. For when all the lights were quenched, and all the house was quiet, I heard a low and wily whistle from a clump of trees close by; and then three figures passed between me and a whitewashed wall, and came to a window which opened into a part of the servants' basement. This window was carefully raised by some one inside the house; and after a little whispering, and something which sounded like a kiss, all the three men entered.

'Oh, you villains!' I said to myself, 'this is worse than any Doone job; because there is treachery in it.' But without waiting to consider the subject from a moral point of view, I crept along the wall, and entered very quietly after them; being rather uneasy about my life, because I bore no fire-arms, and had nothing more than my holly staff, for even a violent combat.

To me this was matter of deep regret, as I followed these vile men inward. Nevertheless I was resolved that my Lorna should not be robbed again. Through us (or at least through our Annie) she had lost that brilliant necklace; which then was her only birthright: therefore it behoved me doubly, to preserve the pewter box; which must belong to her in the end, unless the thieves got hold of it.

I went along very delicately (as a man who has learned to wrestle can do, although he may weigh twenty stone), following carefully the light, brought by the traitorous maid, and shaking in her loose dishonest hand. I saw her lead the men into a little place called a pantry; and there she gave them cordials, and I could hear them boasting.

Not to be too long over it—which they were much inclined to be—I followed them from this drinking-bout, by the aid of the light they bore, as far as Earl Brandir's bedroom, which I knew, because Lorna had shown it to me that I might admire the tapestry. But I had said that no horse could ever be shod as the horses were shod therein, unless he had the foot of a frog, as well as a frog to his foot. And Lorna had been vexed at this (as taste and high art always are, at any small accurate knowledge), and so she had brought me out again, before I had time to admire things.

Now, keeping well away in the dark, yet nearer than was necessary to my own dear Lorna's room, I saw these fellows try the door of the good Earl Brandir, knowing from the maid, of course, that his lordship could hear nothing, except the name of Alan. They tried the lock, and pushed at it, and even set their knees upright; but a Scottish nobleman may be trusted to secure his door at night. So they were forced to break it open; and at this the guilty maid, or woman, ran away. These three rogues—for rogues they were, and no charity may deny it—burst into Earl Brandir's room, with a light, and a crowbar, and fire-arms. I thought to myself that this was hard upon an honest nobleman; and if further mischief could be saved, I would try to save it.

When I came to the door of the room, being myself in shadow, I beheld two bad men trying vainly to break open the pewter box, and the third with a pistol-muzzle laid to the night-cap of his lordship. With foul face and yet fouler words, this man was demanding the key of the box, which the other men could by no means open, neither drag it from the chain.

'I tell you,' said this aged Earl, beginning to understand at last what these rogues were up for; 'I will give no key to you. It all belongs to my boy, Alan. No one else shall have a farthing.'

'Then you may count your moments, lord. The key is in your old cramped hand. One, two, and at three, I shoot you.'

I saw that the old man was abroad; not with fear, but with great wonder, and the regrets of deafness. And I saw that rather would he be shot than let these men go rob his son, buried now, or laid to bleach in the tangles of the wood, three, or it might be four years agone, but still alive to his father. Hereupon my heart was moved; and I resolved to interfere. The thief with the pistol began to count, as I crossed the floor very quietly, while the old Earl fearfully gazed at the muzzle, but clenched still tighter his wrinkled hand. The villain, with hair all over his eyes, and the great horse-pistol levelled, cried 'three,' and pulled the trigger; but luckily, at that very moment, I struck up the barrel with my staff, so that the shot pierced the tester, and then with a spin and a thwack I brought the good holly down upon the rascal's head, in a manner which stretched him upon the floor.

Meanwhile the other two robbers had taken the alarm, and rushed at me, one with a pistol and one with a hanger; which forced me to be very lively. Fearing the pistol most, I flung the heavy velvet curtain of the bed across, that he might not see where to aim at me, and then stooping very quickly I caught up the senseless robber, and set him up for a shield and target; whereupon he was shot immediately, without having the pain of knowing it; and a happy thing it was for him. Now the other two were at my mercy, being men below the average strength; and no hanger, except in most skilful hands, as well as firm and strong ones, has any chance to a powerful man armed with a stout cudgel, and thoroughly practised in single-stick.

So I took these two rogues, and bound them together; and leaving them under charge of the butler (a worthy and shrewd Scotchman), I myself went in search of the constables, whom, after some few hours, I found; neither were they so drunk but what they could take roped men to prison. In the morning, these two men were brought before the Justices of the Peace: and now my wonderful luck appeared; for the merit of having defeated, and caught them, would never have raised me one step in the State, or in public consideration, if they had only been common robbers, or even notorious murderers. But when these fellows were recognised, by some one in the court, as Protestant witnesses out of employment, companions and understrappers to Oates, and Bedloe, and Carstairs, and hand in glove with Dangerfield, Turberville; and Dugdale—in a word, the very men against whom His Majesty the King bore the bitterest rancour, but whom he had hitherto failed to catch—when this was laid before the public (with emphasis and admiration), at least a dozen men came up, whom I had never seen before, and prayed me to accept their congratulations, and to be sure to remember them; for all were of neglected merit, and required no more than a piece of luck.

I answered them very modestly, and each according to his worth, as stated by himself, who of course could judge the best. The magistrate made me many compliments, ten times more than I deserved, and took good care to have them copied, that His Majesty might see them. And ere the case was thoroughly heard, and those poor fellows were committed, more than a score of generous men had offered to lend me a hundred pounds, wherewith to buy a new Court suit, when called before His Majesty.

Now this may seem very strange to us who live in a better and purer age—or say at least that we do so—and yet who are we to condemn our fathers for teaching us better manners, and at their own expense? With these points any virtuous man is bound to deal quite tenderly, making allowance for corruption, and not being too sure of himself. And to tell the truth, although I had seen so little of the world as yet, that which astonished me in the matter, was not so much that they paid me court, as that they found out so soon the expediency of doing it.

In the course of that same afternoon I was sent for by His Majesty. He had summoned first the good Earl Brandir, and received the tale from him, not without exaggeration, although my lord was a Scotchman. But the chief thing His Majesty cared to know was that, beyond all possible doubt, these were the very precious fellows from perjury turned to robbery.

Being fully assured at last of this, His Majesty had rubbed his hands, and ordered the boots of a stricter pattern (which he himself had invented) to be brought at once, that he might have them in the best possible order. And he oiled them himself, and expressed his fear that there was no man in London quite competent to work them. Nevertheless he would try one or two, rather than wait for his pleasure, till the torturer came from Edinburgh.

The next thing be did was to send for me; and in great alarm and flurry I put on my best clothes, and hired a fashionable hairdresser, and drank half a gallon of ale, because both my hands were shaking. Then forth I set, with my holly staff, wishing myself well out of it. I was shown at once, and before I desired it, into His Majesty's presence, and there I stood most humbly, and made the best bow I could think of.

As I could not advance any farther—for I saw that the Queen was present, which frightened me tenfold—His Majesty, in the most gracious manner, came down the room to encourage me. And as I remained with my head bent down, he told me to stand up, and look at him.

'I have seen thee before, young man, he said; 'thy form is not one to be forgotten. Where was it? Thou art most likely to know.'

'May it please Your Most Gracious Majesty the King,' I answered, finding my voice in a manner which surprised myself; 'it was in the Royal Chapel.'

Now I meant no harm whatever by this. I ought to have said the 'Ante-chapel,' but I could not remember the word, and feared to keep the King looking at me.

'I am well-pleased,' said His Majesty, with a smile which almost made his dark and stubborn face look pleasant, 'to find that our greatest subject, greatest I mean in the bodily form, is also a good Catholic. Thou needest not say otherwise. The time shall be, and that right soon, when men shall be proud of the one true faith.' Here he stopped, having gone rather far! but the gleam of his heavy eyes was such that I durst not contradict.

'This is that great Johann Reed,' said Her Majesty, coming forward, because the King was in meditation; 'for whom I have so much heard, from the dear, dear Lorna. Ah, she is not of this black countree, she is of the breet Italie.'

I have tried to write it, as she said it: but it wants a better scholar to express her mode of speech.

'Now, John Ridd,' said the King, recovering from his thoughts about the true Church, and thinking that his wife was not to take the lead upon me; 'thou hast done great service to the realm, and to religion. It was good to save Earl Brandir, a loyal and Catholic nobleman; but it was great service to catch two of the vilest bloodhounds ever laid on by heretics. And to make them shoot one another: it was rare; it was rare, my lad. Now ask us anything in reason; thou canst carry any honours, on thy club, like Hercules. What is thy chief ambition, lad?'

'Well,' said I, after thinking a little, and meaning to make the most of it, for so the Queen's eyes conveyed to me; 'my mother always used to think that having been schooled at Tiverton, with thirty marks a year to pay, I was worthy of a coat of arms. And that is what she longs for.'

'A good lad! A very good lad,' said the King, and he looked at the Queen, as if almost in joke; 'but what is thy condition in life?'

'I am a freeholder,' I answered, in my confusion, 'ever since the time of King Alfred. A Ridd was with him in the isle of Athelney, and we hold our farm by gift from him; or at least people say so. We have had three very good harvests running, and might support a coat of arms; but for myself I want it not.'

'Thou shalt have a coat, my lad,' said the King, smiling at his own humour; 'but it must be a large one to fit thee. And more than that shalt thou have, John Ridd, being of such loyal breed, and having done such service.'

And while I wondered what he meant, he called to some of the people in waiting at the farther end of the room, and they brought him a little sword, such as Annie would skewer a turkey with. Then he signified to me to kneel, which I did (after dusting the board, for the sake of my best breeches), and then he gave me a little tap very nicely upon my shoulder, before I knew what he was up to; and said, 'Arise, Sir John Ridd!'

This astonished and amazed me to such extent of loss of mind, that when I got up I looked about, and thought what the Snowes would think of it. And I said to the King, without forms of speech,—

'Sir, I am very much obliged. But what be I to do with it?'

Chapter LXIX Not to Be Put-Up With

The coat of arms, devised for me by the Royal heralds, was of great size, and rich colours, and full of bright imaginings. They did me the honour to consult me first, and to take no notice of my advice. For I begged that there might be a good-sized cow on it, so as to stamp our pats of butter before they went to market: also a horse on the other side, and a flock snowed up at the bottom. But the gentlemen would not hear of this; and to find something more appropriate, they inquired strictly into the annals of our family. I told them, of course, all about King Alfred; upon which they settled that one quarter should be, three cakes on a bar, with a lion regardant, done upon a field of gold. Also I told them that very likely there had been a Ridd in the battle fought, not very far from Plover's Barrows, by the Earl of Devon against the Danes, when Hubba their chief was killed, and the sacred standard taken. As some of the Danes are said to be buried, even upon land of ours, and we call their graves (if such they be) even to this day 'barrows,' the heralds quite agreed with me that a Ridd might have been there, or thereabouts; and if he was there, he was almost certain to have done his best, being in sight of hearth and home; and it was plain that he must have had good legs to be at the same time both there and in Athelney; and good legs are an argument for good arms; and supposing a man of this sort to have done his utmost (as the manner of the Ridds is), it was next to certain that he himself must have captured the standard. Moreover, the name of our farm was pure proof; a plover being a wild bird, just the same as a raven is. Upon this chain of reasoning, and without any weak misgivings, they charged my growing escutcheon with a black raven on a ground of red. And the next thing which I mentioned possessing absolute certainty, to wit, that a pig with two heads had been born upon our farm, not more than two hundred years agone (although he died within a week), my third quarter was made at once, by a two-headed boar with noble tusks, sable upon silver. All this was very fierce and fine; and so I pressed for a peaceful corner in the lower dexter, and obtained a wheat-sheaf set upright, gold upon a field of green.

Here I was inclined to pause, and admire the effect; for even De Whichehalse could not show a bearing so magnificent. But the heralds said that it looked a mere sign-board, without a good motto under it; and the motto must have my name in it. They offered me first, 'Ridd non ridendus'; but I said, 'for God's sake, gentlemen, let me forget my Latin.' Then they proposed, 'Ridd readeth riddles': but I begged them not to set down such a lie; for no Ridd ever had made, or made out, such a thing as a riddle, since Exmoor itself began. Thirdly, they gave me, 'Ridd never be ridden,' and fearing to make any further objections, I let them inscribe it in bronze upon blue. The heralds thought that the King would pay for this noble achievement; but His Majesty, although graciously pleased with their ingenuity, declined in the most decided manner to pay a farthing towards it; and as I had now no money left, the heralds became as blue as azure, and as red as gules; until Her Majesty the Queen came forward very kindly, and said that if His Majesty gave me a coat of arms, I was not to pay for it; therefore she herself did so quite handsomely, and felt goodwill towards me in consequence.

Now being in a hurry—so far at least as it is in my nature to hurry—to get to the end of this narrative, is it likely that I would have dwelled so long upon my coat of arms, but for some good reason? And this good reason is that Lorna took the greatest pride in it, and thought (or at any rate said) that it quite threw into the shade, and eclipsed, all her own ancient glories. And half in fun, and half in earnest, she called me 'Sir John' so continually, that at last I was almost angry with her; until her eyes were bedewed with tears; and then I was angry with myself.

Beginning to be short of money, and growing anxious about the farm, longing also to show myself and my noble escutcheon to mother, I took advantage of Lady Lorna's interest with the Queen, to obtain my acquittance and full discharge from even nominal custody. It had been intended to keep me in waiting, until the return of Lord Jeffreys, from that awful circuit of shambles, through which his name is still used by mothers to frighten their children into bed. And right glad was I—for even London shrank with horror at the news—to escape a man so bloodthirsty, savage, and even to his friends (among whom I was reckoned) malignant.

Earl Brandir was greatly pleased with me, not only for having saved his life, but for saving that which he valued more, the wealth laid by for Lord Alan. And he introduced me to many great people, who quite kindly encouraged me, and promised to help me in every way when they heard how the King had spoken. As for the furrier, he could never have enough of my society; and this worthy man, praying my commendation, demanded of me one thing only—to speak of him as I found him. As I had found him many a Sunday, furbishing up old furs for new, with a glaze to conceal the moths' ravages, I begged him to reconsider the point, and not to demand such accuracy. He said, 'Well, well; all trades had tricks, especially the trick of business; and I must take him—if I were his true friend—according to his own description.' This I was glad enough to do; because it saved so much trouble, and I had no money to spend with him. But still he requested the use of my name; and I begged him to do the best with it, as I never had kept a banker. And the 'John Ridd cuffs,' and the 'Sir John mantles,' and the 'Holly-staff capes,' he put into his window, as the winter was coming on, ay and sold (for everybody was burning with gossip about me), must have made this good man's fortune; since the excess of price over value is the true test of success in life.

To come away from all this stuff, which grieves a man in London—when the brisk air of the autumn cleared its way to Ludgate Hill, and clever 'prentices ran out, and sniffed at it, and fed upon it (having little else to eat); and when the horses from the country were a goodly sight to see, with the rasp of winter bristles rising through and among the soft summer-coat; and when the new straw began to come in, golden with the harvest gloss, and smelling most divinely at those strange livery-stables, where the nags are put quite tail to tail; and when all the London folk themselves are asking about white frost (from recollections of childhood); then, I say, such a yearning seized me for moory crag, and for dewy blade, and even the grunting of our sheep (when the sun goes down), that nothing but the new wisps of Samson could have held me in London town.

Lorna was moved with equal longing towards the country and country ways; and she spoke quite as much of the glistening dew as she did of the smell of our oven. And here let me mention—although the two are quite distinct and different—that both the dew and the bread of Exmoor may be sought, whether high or low, but never found elsewhere. The dew is so crisp, and pure, and pearly, and in such abundance; and the bread is so sweet, so kind, and homely, you can eat a loaf, and then another.

Now while I was walking daily in and out great crowds of men (few of whom had any freedom from the cares of money, and many of whom were even morbid with a worse pest called 'politics'), I could not be quit of thinking how we jostle one another. God has made the earth quite large, with a spread of land large enough for all to live on, without fighting. Also a mighty spread of water, laying hands on sand and cliff with a solemn voice in storm-time; and in the gentle weather moving men to thoughts of equity. This, as well, is full of food; being two-thirds of the world, and reserved for devouring knowledge; by the time the sons of men have fed away the dry land. Yet before the land itself has acknowledged touch of man, upon one in a hundred acres; and before one mile in ten thousand of the exhaustless ocean has ever felt the plunge of hook, or combing of the haul-nets; lo, we crawl, in flocks together upon the hot ground that stings us, even as the black grubs crowd upon the harried nettle! Surely we are too much given to follow the tracks of each other.

However, for a moralist, I never set up, and never shall, while common sense abides with me. Such a man must be very wretched in this pure dearth of morality; like a fisherman where no fish be; and most of us have enough to do to attend to our own morals. Enough that I resolved to go; and as Lorna could not come with me, it was even worse than stopping. Nearly everybody vowed that I was a great fool indeed, to neglect so rudely—which was the proper word, they said—the pushing of my fortunes. But I answered that to push was rude, and I left it to people who had no room; and thought that my fortune must be heavy, if it would not move without pushing.

Lorna cried when I came away (which gave me great satisfaction), and she sent a whole trunkful of things for mother and Annie, and even Lizzie. And she seemed to think, though she said it not, that I made my own occasion for going, and might have stayed on till the winter. Whereas I knew well that my mother would think (and every one on the farm the same) that here I had been in London, lagging, and taking my pleasure, and looking at shops, upon pretence of King's business, and leaving the harvest to reap itself, not to mention the spending of money; while all the time there was nothing whatever, except my own love of adventure and sport, to keep me from coming home again. But I knew that my coat of arms, and title, would turn every bit of this grumbling into fine admiration.

And so it fell out, to a greater extent than even I desired; for all the parishes round about united in a sumptuous dinner, at the Mother Melldrum inn—for now that good lady was dead, and her name and face set on a sign-post—to which I was invited, so that it was as good as a summons. And if my health was no better next day, it was not from want of good wishes, any more than from stint of the liquor.

It is needless to say that the real gentry for a long time treated my new honours with contempt and ridicule; but gradually as they found that I was not such a fool as to claim any equality with them, but went about my farm-work, and threw another man at wrestling, and touched my hat to the magistrates, just the same as ever; some gentlemen of the highest blood—of which we think a great deal more than of gold, around our neighbourhood—actually expressed a desire to make my acquaintance. And when, in a manner quite straightforward, and wholly free from bitterness, I thanked them for this (which appeared to me the highest honour yet offered me), but declined to go into their company because it would make me uncomfortable, and themselves as well, in a different way, they did what nearly all Englishmen do, when a thing is right and sensible. They shook hands with me; and said that they could not deny but that there was reason in my view of the matter. And although they themselves must be the losers—which was a handsome thing to say—they would wait until I was a little older and more aware of my own value.

Now this reminds me how it is that an English gentleman is so far in front of foreign noblemen and princes. I have seen at times, a little, both of one and of the other, and making more than due allowance for the difficulties of language, and the difference of training, upon the whole, the balance is in favour of our people. And this, because we have two weights, solid and (even in scale of manners) outweighing all light complaisance; to wit, the inborn love of justice, and the power of abiding.

Yet some people may be surprised that men with any love of justice, whether inborn or otherwise, could continue to abide the arrogance, and rapacity, and tyranny of the Doones.

For now as the winter passed, the Doones were not keeping themselves at home, as in honour they were bound to do. Twenty sheep a week, and one fat ox, and two stout red deer (for wholesome change of diet), as well as threescore bushels of flour, and two hogsheads and a half of cider, and a hundredweight of candles, not to mention other things of almost every variety which they got by insisting upon it—surely these might have sufficed to keep the people in their place, with no outburst of wantonness. Nevertheless, it was not so; they had made complaint about something—too much ewe-mutton, I think it was—and in spite of all the pledges given, they had ridden forth, and carried away two maidens of our neighbourhood.

Now these two maidens were known, because they had served the beer at an ale-house; and many men who had looked at them, over a pint or quart vessel (especially as they were comely girls), thought that it was very hard for them to go in that way, and perhaps themselves unwilling. And their mother (although she had taken some money, which the Doones were always full of) declared that it was a robbery; and though it increased for a while the custom, that must soon fall off again. And who would have her two girls now, clever as they were and good?

Before we had finished meditating upon this loose outrage—for so I at least would call it, though people accustomed to the law may take a different view of it—we had news of a thing far worse, which turned the hearts of our women sick. This I will tell in most careful language, so as to give offence to none, if skill of words may help it.*

Mistress Margery Badcock, a healthy and upright young woman, with a good rich colour, and one of the finest hen-roosts anywhere round our neighbourhood, was nursing her child about six of the clock, and looking out for her husband. Now this child was too old to be nursed, as everybody told her; for he could run, say two yards alone, and perhaps four or five, by holding to handles. And he had a way of looking round, and spreading his legs, and laughing, with his brave little body well fetched up, after a desperate journey to the end of the table, which his mother said nothing could equal. Nevertheless, he would come to be nursed, as regular as a clock, almost; and, inasmuch as he was the first, both father and mother made much of him; for God only knew whether they could ever compass such another one.

Christopher Badcock was a tenant farmer, in the parish of Martinhoe, renting some fifty acres of land, with a right of common attached to them; and at this particular time, being now the month of February, and fine open weather, he was hard at work ploughing and preparing for spring corn. Therefore his wife was not surprised although the dusk was falling, that farmer Christopher should be at work in 'blind man's holiday,' as we call it.

But she was surprised, nay astonished, when by the light of the kitchen fire (brightened up for her husband), she saw six or seven great armed men burst into the room upon her; and she screamed so that the maid in the back kitchen heard her, but was afraid to come to help. Two of the strongest and fiercest men at once seized poor young Margery; and though she fought for her child and home, she was but an infant herself in their hands. In spite of tears, and shrieks, and struggles, they tore the babe from the mother's arms, and cast it on the lime ash floor; then they bore her away to their horses (for by this time she was senseless), and telling the others to sack the house, rode off with their prize to the valley. And from the description of one of those two, who carried off the poor woman, I knew beyond all doubt that it was Carver Doone himself.

The other Doones being left behind, and grieved perhaps in some respects, set to with a will to scour the house, and to bring away all that

*The following story is strictly true; and true it is that the country-people rose, to a man, at this dastard cruelty, and did what the Government failed to do.—Ed.

was good to eat. And being a little vexed herein (for the Badcocks were not a rich couple) and finding no more than bacon, and eggs, and cheese, and little items, and nothing to drink but water; in a word, their taste being offended, they came back, to the kitchen, and stamped; and there was the baby lying.

By evil luck, this child began to squeal about his mother, having been petted hitherto, and wont to get all he wanted, by raising his voice but a little. Now the mark of the floor was upon his head, as the maid (who had stolen to look at him, when the rough men were swearing upstairs) gave evidence. And she put a dish-cloth under his head, and kissed him, and ran away again. Her name was Honour Jose, and she meant what was right by her master and mistress; but could not help being frightened. And many women have blamed her, as I think unduly, for her mode of forsaking baby so. If it had been her own baby, instinct rather than reason might have had the day with her; but the child being born of her mistress, she wished him good luck, and left him, as the fierce men came down-stairs. And being alarmed by their power of language (because they had found no silver), she crept away in a breathless hurry, and afraid how her breath might come back to her. For oftentime she had hiccoughs.

While this good maid was in the oven, by side of back-kitchen fire-place, with a faggot of wood drawn over her, and lying so that her own heart beat worse than if she were baking; the men (as I said before) came downstairs, and stamped around the baby.

'Rowland, is the bacon good?' one of them asked with an oath or two; 'it is too bad of Carver to go off with the only prize, and leave us in a starving cottage; and not enough to eat for two of us. Fetch down the staves of the rack, my boy. What was farmer to have for supper?'

'Naught but an onion or two, and a loaf and a rasher of rusty bacon. These poor devils live so badly, they are not worth robbing.'

'No game! Then let us have a game of loriot with the baby! It will be the best thing that could befall a lusty infant heretic. Ride a cock-horse to Banbury Cross. Bye, bye, baby Bunting; toss him up, and let me see if my wrist be steady.'

The cruelty of this man is a thing it makes me sick to speak of; enough that when the poor baby fell (without attempt at cry or scream, thinking it part of his usual play, when they tossed him up, to come down again), the maid in the oven of the back-kitchen, not being any door between, heard them say as follows,—

'If any man asketh who killed thee,
Say 'twas the Doones of Bagworthy.'*

Now I think that when we heard this story, and poor Kit Badcock came all around, in a sort of half-crazy manner, not looking up at any one, but dropping his eyes, and asking whether we thought he had been well-treated, and seeming void of regard for life, if this were all the style of

*Always pronounced 'Badgery.'

it; then having known him a lusty man, and a fine singer in an ale-house, and much inclined to lay down the law, as show a high hand about women, I really think that it moved us more than if he had gone about ranting, and raving, and vowing revenge upon every one.

Chapter LXX Compelled to Volunteer

There had been some trouble in our own home during the previous autumn, while yet I was in London. For certain noted fugitives from the army of King Monmouth (which he himself had deserted, in a low and currish manner), having failed to obtain free shipment from the coast near Watersmouth, had returned into the wilds of Exmoor, trusting to lurk, and be comforted among the common people. Neither were they disappointed, for a certain length of time; nor in the end was their disappointment caused by fault on our part. Major Wade was one of them; an active and well-meaning man; but prone to fail in courage, upon lasting trial; although in a moment ready. Squire John Whichehalse (not the baron) and Parson Powell* caught him (two or three months before my return) in Farley farmhouse, near Brendon. He had been up at our house several times; and Lizzie thought a great deal of him. And well I know that if at that time I had been in the neighbourhood, he should not have been taken so easily.

John Birch, the farmer who had sheltered him, was so fearful of punishment, that he hanged himself, in a few days' time, and even before he was apprehended. But nothing was done to Grace Howe, of Bridgeball, who had been Wade's greatest comforter; neither was anything done to us; although Eliza had added greatly to mother's alarm and danger by falling upon Rector Powell, and most soundly rating him for his meanness, and his cruelty, and cowardice, as she called it, in setting men with firearms upon a poor helpless fugitive, and robbing all our neighbourhood of its fame for hospitality. However, by means of Sergeant Bloxham, and his good report of us, as well as by virtue of Wade's confession (which proved of use to the Government) my mother escaped all penalties.

It is likely enough that good folk will think it hard upon our neighbourhood to be threatened, and sometimes heavily punished, for kindness and humanity; and yet to be left to help ourselves against tyranny, and base rapine. And now at last our gorge was risen, and our hearts in tumult. We had borne our troubles long, as a wise and wholesome chastisement; quite content to have some few things of our own unmeddled with. But what could a man dare to call his own, or what right could he have to wish for it, while he left his wife and children at the pleasure of any stranger?

The people came flocking all around me, at the blacksmith's forge, and the Brendon alehouse; and I could scarce come out of church, but

*Not our parson Bowden, nor any more a friend of his. Our Parson Bowden never had naught whatever to do with it; and never smoked a pipe with Parson Powell after it.—J.R.

they got me among the tombstones. They all agreed that I was bound to take command and management. I bade them go to the magistrates, but they said they had been too often. Then I told them that I had no wits for ordering of an armament, although I could find fault enough with the one which had not succeeded. But they would hearken to none of this.

All they said was 'Try to lead us; and we will try not to run away.'

This seemed to me to be common sense, and good stuff, instead of mere bragging; moreover, I myself was moved by the bitter wrongs of Margery, having known her at the Sunday-school, ere ever I went to Tiverton; and having in those days, serious thoughts of making her my sweetheart; although she was three years my elder. But now I felt this difficulty—the Doones had behaved very well to our farm, and to mother, and all of us, while I was away in London. Therefore, would it not be shabby, and mean, for me to attack them now?

Yet being pressed still harder and harder, as day by day the excitement grew (with more and more talking over it, and no one else coming forward to undertake the business, I agreed at last to this; that if the Doones, upon fair challenge, would not endeavour to make amends by giving up Mistress Margery, as well as the man who had slain the babe, then I would lead the expedition, and do my best to subdue them. All our men were content with this, being thoroughly well assured from experience, that the haughty robbers would only shoot any man who durst approach them with such proposal.

And then arose a difficult question—who was to take the risk of making overtures so unpleasant? I waited for the rest to offer; and as none was ready, the burden fell on me, and seemed to be of my own inviting. Hence I undertook the task, sooner than reason about it; for to give the cause of everything is worse than to go through with it.

It may have been three of the afternoon, when leaving my witnesses behind (for they preferred the background) I appeared with our Lizzie's white handkerchief upon a kidney-bean stick, at the entrance to the robbers' dwelling. Scarce knowing what might come of it, I had taken the wise precaution of fastening a Bible over my heart, and another across my spinal column, in case of having to run away, with rude men shooting after me. For my mother said that the Word of God would stop a two-inch bullet, with three ounces of powder behind it. Now I took no weapons, save those of the Spirit, for fear of being misunderstood. But I could not bring myself to think that any of honourable birth would take advantage of an unarmed man coming in guise of peace to them.

And this conclusion of mine held good, at least for a certain length of time; inasmuch as two decent Doones appeared, and hearing of my purpose, offered, without violence, to go and fetch the Captain; if I would stop where I was, and not begin to spy about anything. To this, of course, I agreed at once; for I wanted no more spying, because I had thorough knowledge of all ins and outs already. Therefore, I stood waiting steadily, with one hand in my pocket feeling a sample of corn for market; and the other against the rock, while I wondered to see it so brown already.

Those men came back in a little while, with a sharp short message that Captain Carver would come out and speak to me by-and-by, when his pipe was finished. Accordingly, I waited long, and we talked about the signs of bloom for the coming apple season, and the rain that had fallen last Wednesday night, and the principal dearth of Devonshire, that it will not grow many cowslips—which we quite agreed to be the prettiest of spring flowers; and all the time I was wondering how many black and deadly deeds these two innocent youths had committed, even since last Christmas.

At length, a heavy and haughty step sounded along the stone roof of the way; and then the great Carver Doone drew up, and looked at me rather scornfully. Not with any spoken scorn, nor flash of strong contumely; but with that air of thinking little, and praying not to be troubled, which always vexes a man who feels that he ought not to be despised so, and yet knows not how to help it.

'What is it you want, young man?' he asked, as if he had never seen me before.

In spite of that strong loathing which I always felt at sight of him, I commanded my temper moderately, and told him that I was come for his good, and that of his worshipful company, far more than for my own. That a general feeling of indignation had arisen among us at the recent behaviour of certain young men, for which he might not be answerable, and for which we would not condemn him, without knowing the rights of the question. But I begged him clearly to understand that a vile and inhuman wrong had been done, and such as we could not put up with; but that if he would make what amends he could by restoring the poor woman, and giving up that odious brute who had slain the harmless infant, we would take no further motion; and things should go on as usual. As I put this in the fewest words that would meet my purpose, I was grieved to see a disdainful smile spread on his sallow countenance. Then he made me a bow of mock courtesy, and replied as follows,—

'Sir John, your new honours have turned your poor head, as might have been expected. We are not in the habit of deserting anything that belongs to us; far less our sacred relatives. The insolence of your demand well-nigh outdoes the ingratitude. If there be a man upon Exmoor who has grossly ill-used us, kidnapped our young women, and slain half a dozen of our young men, you are that outrageous rogue, Sir John. And after all this, how have we behaved? We have laid no hand upon your farm, we have not carried off your women, we have even allowed you to take our Queen, by creeping and crawling treachery; and we have given you leave of absence to help your cousin the highwayman, and to come home with a title. And now, how do you requite us? By inflaming the boorish indignation at a little frolic of our young men; and by coming with insolent demands, to yield to which would ruin us. Ah, you ungrateful viper!'

As he turned away in sorrow from me, shaking his head at my badness, I became so overcome (never having been quite assured, even by people's praises, about my own goodness); moreover, the light which he threw upon things differed so greatly from my own, that, in a word—not to be too long—I feared that I was a villain. And with many bitter pangs—for I have bad things to repent of—I began at my leisure to ask myself whether or not this bill of indictment against John Ridd was true. Some of it I knew to be (however much I condemned myself) altogether out of reason; for instance, about my going away with Lorna very quietly, over the snow, and to save my love from being starved away from me. In this there was no creeping neither crawling treachery; for all was done with sliding; and yet I was so out of training for being charged by other people beyond mine own conscience, that Carver Doone's harsh words came on me, like prickly spinach sown with raking. Therefore I replied, and said,—

'It is true that I owe you gratitude, sir, for a certain time of forbearance; and it is to prove my gratitude that I am come here now. I do not think that my evil deeds can be set against your own; although I cannot speak flowingly upon my good deeds as you can. I took your Queen because you starved her, having stolen her long before, and killed her mother and brother. This is not for me to dwell upon now; any more than I would say much about your murdering of my father. But how the balance hangs between us, God knows better than thou or I, thou low miscreant, Carver Doone.'

I had worked myself up, as I always do, in the manner of heavy men; growing hot like an ill-washered wheel revolving, though I start with a cool axle; and I felt ashamed of myself for heat, and ready to ask pardon. But Carver Doone regarded me with a noble and fearless grandeur.

'I have given thee thy choice, John Ridd,' he said in a lofty manner, which made me drop away under him; 'I always wish to do my best with the worst people who come near me. And of all I have ever met with thou art the very worst, Sir John, and the most dishonest.'

Now after all my labouring to pay every man to a penny, and to allow the women over, when among the couch-grass (which is a sad thing for their gowns), to be charged like this, I say, so amazed me that I stood, with my legs quite open, and ready for an earthquake. And the scornful way in which he said 'Sir John,' went to my very heart, reminding me of my littleness. But seeing no use in bandying words, nay, rather the chance of mischief, I did my best to look calmly at him, and to say with a quiet voice, 'Farewell, Carver Doone, this time, our day of reckoning is nigh.'

'Thou fool, it is come,' he cried, leaping aside into the niche of rock by the doorway; 'Fire!'

Save for the quickness of spring, and readiness, learned in many a wrestling bout, that knavish trick must have ended me; but scarce was the word 'fire!' out of his mouth ere I was out of fire, by a single bound behind the rocky pillar of the opening. In this jump I was so brisk, at impulse of the love of life (for I saw the muzzles set upon me from the darkness of the cavern), that the men who had trained their guns upon me with goodwill and daintiness, could not check their fingers crooked upon the heavy triggers; and the volley sang with a roar behind it, down the avenue of crags.

With one thing and another, and most of all the treachery of this dastard scheme, I was so amazed that I turned and ran, at the very top of my speed, away from these vile fellows; and luckily for me, they had not another charge to send after me. And thus by good fortune, I escaped; but with a bitter heart, and mind at their treacherous usage.

Without any further hesitation; I agreed to take command of the honest men who were burning to punish, ay and destroy, those outlaws, as now beyond all bearing. One condition, however, I made, namely, that the Counsellor should be spared if possible; not because he was less a villain than any of the others, but that he seemed less violent; and above all, had been good to Annie. And I found hard work to make them listen to my wish upon this point; for of all the Doones, Sir Counsellor had made himself most hated, by his love of law and reason.

We arranged that all our men should come and fall into order with pike and musket, over against our dung-hill, and we settled early in the day, that their wives might come and look at them. For most of these men had good wives; quite different from sweethearts, such as the militia had; women indeed who could hold to a man, and see to him, and bury him—if his luck were evil—and perhaps have no one afterwards. And all these women pressed their rights upon their precious husbands, and brought so many children with them, and made such a fuss, and hugging, and racing after little legs, that our farm-yard might be taken for an out-door school for babies rather than a review ground.

I myself was to and fro among the children continually; for if I love anything in the world, foremost I love children. They warm, and yet they cool our hearts, as we think of what we were, and what in young clothes we hoped to be; and how many things have come across. And to see our motives moving in the little things that know not what their aim or object is, must almost or ought at least, to lead us home, and soften us. For either end of life is home; both source and issue being God.

Nevertheless, I must confess that the children were a plague sometimes. They never could have enough of me—being a hundred to one, you might say—but I had more than enough of them; and yet was not contented. For they had so many ways of talking, and of tugging at my hair, and of sitting upon my neck (not even two with their legs alike), and they forced me to jump so vehemently, seeming to court the peril of my coming down neck and crop with them, and urging me still to go faster, however fast I might go with them; I assure you that they were sometimes so hard and tyrannical over me, that I might almost as well have been among the very Doones themselves.

Nevertheless, the way in which the children made me useful proved also of some use to me; for their mothers were so pleased by the exertions of the 'great Gee-gee'—as all the small ones entitled me—that they gave me unlimited power and authority over their husbands; moreover, they did their utmost among their relatives round about, to fetch recruits for our little band. And by such means, several of the yeomanry from Barnstaple, and from Tiverton, were added to our number; and inasmuch as these were armed with heavy swords, and short carabines, their appearance was truly formidable.

Tom Faggus also joined us heartily, being now quite healed of his wound, except at times when the wind was easterly. He was made second in command to me; and I would gladly have had him first, as more fertile in expedients; but he declined such rank on the plea that I knew most of the seat of war; besides that I might be held in some measure to draw authority from the King. Also Uncle Ben came over to help us with his advice and presence, as well as with a band of stout warehousemen, whom he brought from Dulverton. For he had never forgiven the old outrage put upon him; and though it had been to his interest to keep quiet during the last attack, under Commander Stickles—for the sake of his secret gold mine—yet now he was in a position to give full vent to his feelings. For he and his partners when fully-assured of the value of their diggings, had obtained from the Crown a licence to adventure in search of minerals, by payment of a heavy fine and a yearly royalty. Therefore they had now no longer any cause for secrecy, neither for dread of the outlaws; having so added to their force as to be a match for them. And although Uncle Ben was not the man to keep his miners idle an hour more than might be helped, he promised that when we had fixed the moment for an assault on the valley, a score of them should come to aid us, headed by Simon Carfax, and armed with the guns which they always kept for the protection of their gold.

Now whether it were Uncle Ben, or whether it were Tom Faggus or even my own self—for all three of us claimed the sole honour—is more than I think fair to settle without allowing them a voice. But at any rate, a clever thing was devised among us; and perhaps it would be the fairest thing to say that this bright stratagem (worthy of the great Duke himself) was contributed, little by little, among the entire three of us, all having pipes, and schnapps-and-water, in the chimney-corner. However, the world, which always judges according to reputation, vowed that so fine a stroke of war could only come from a highwayman; and so Tom Faggus got all the honour, at less perhaps than a third of the cost.

Not to attempt to rob him of it—for robbers, more than any other, contend for rights of property—let me try to describe this grand artifice. It was known that the Doones were fond of money, as well as strong drink, and other things; and more especially fond of gold, when they could get it pure and fine. Therefore it was agreed that in this way we should tempt them; for we knew that they looked with ridicule upon our rustic preparations; after repulsing King's troopers, and the militia of two counties, was it likely that they should yield their fortress to a set of ploughboys? We, for our part, felt of course, the power of this reasoning, and that where regular troops had failed, half-armed countrymen must fail, except by superior judgment and harmony of action. Though perhaps the militia would have sufficed, if they had only fought against the foe, instead of against each other. From these things we took warning; having failed through over-confidence, was it not possible now to make the enemy fail through the selfsame cause?

Hence, what we devised was this; to delude from home a part of the robbers, and fall by surprise on the other part. We caused it to be spread abroad that a large heap of gold was now collected at the mine of the Wizard's Slough. And when this rumour must have reached them, through women who came to and fro, as some entirely faithful to them were allowed to do, we sent Captain Simon Carfax, the father of little Gwenny, to demand an interview with the Counsellor, by night, and as it were secretly. Then he was to set forth a list of imaginary grievances against the owners of the mine; and to offer partly through resentment, partly through the hope of gain, to betray into their hands, upon the Friday night, by far the greatest weight of gold as yet sent up for refining. He was to have one quarter part, and they to take the residue. But inasmuch as the convoy across the moors, under his command, would be strong, and strongly armed, the Doones must be sure to send not less than a score of men, if possible. He himself, at a place agreed upon, and fit for an ambuscade, would call a halt, and contrive in the darkness to pour a little water into the priming of his company's guns.

It cost us some trouble and a great deal of money to bring the sturdy Cornishman into this deceitful part; and perhaps he never would have consented but for his obligation to me, and the wrongs (as he said) of his daughter. However, as he was the man for the task, both from his coolness and courage, and being known to have charge of the mine, I pressed him, until he undertook to tell all the lies we required. And right well he did it too, having once made up his mind to it; and perceiving that his own interests called for the total destruction of the robbers.

Chapter LXXI A Long Account Settled

Having resolved on a night-assault (as our undisciplined men, three-fourths of whom had never been shot at, could not fairly be expected to march up to visible musket-mouths), we cared not much about drilling our forces, only to teach them to hold a musket, so far as we could supply that weapon to those with the cleverest eyes; and to give them familiarity with the noise it made in exploding. And we fixed upon Friday night for our venture, because the moon would be at the full; and our powder was coming from Dulverton on the Friday afternoon.

Uncle Reuben did not mean to expose himself to shooting, his time of life for risk of life being now well over and the residue too valuable. But his counsels, and his influence, and above all his warehousemen, well practised in beating carpets, were of true service to us. His miners also did great wonders, having a grudge against the Doones; as indeed who had not for thirty miles round their valley?

It was settled that the yeomen, having good horses under them, should give account (with the miners' help) of as many Doones as might be despatched to plunder the pretended gold. And as soon as we knew that this party of robbers, be it more or less, was out of hearing from the valley, we were to fall to, ostensibly at the Doone-gate (which was impregnable now), but in reality upon their rear, by means of my old water-slide. For I had chosen twenty young fellows, partly miners, and partly warehousemen, and sheep farmers, and some of other vocations, but all to be relied upon for spirit and power of climbing. And with proper tools to aid us, and myself to lead the way, I felt no doubt whatever but that we could all attain the crest where first I had met with Lorna.

Upon the whole, I rejoiced that Lorna was not present now. It must have been irksome to her feelings to have all her kindred and old associates (much as she kept aloof from them) put to death without ceremony, or else putting all of us to death. For all of us were resolved this time to have no more shilly-shallying; but to go through with a nasty business, in the style of honest Englishmen, when the question comes to 'Your life or mine.'

There was hardly a man among us who had not suffered bitterly from the miscreants now before us. One had lost his wife perhaps, another had lost a daughter—according to their ages, another had lost his favourite cow; in a word, there was scarcely any one who had not to complain of a hayrick; and what surprised me then, not now, was that the men least injured made the greatest push concerning it. But be the wrong too great to speak of, or too small to swear about, from poor Kit Badcock to rich Master Huckaback, there was not one but went heart and soul for stamping out these firebrands.

The moon was lifting well above the shoulder of the uplands, when we, the chosen band, set forth, having the short cut along the valleys to foot of the Bagworthy water; and therefore having allowed the rest an hour, to fetch round the moors and hills; we were not to begin our climb until we heard a musket fired from the heights on the left-hand side, where John Fry himself was stationed, upon his own and his wife's request; so as to keep out of action. And that was the place where I had been used to sit, and to watch for Lorna. And John Fry was to fire his gun, with a ball of wool inside it, so soon as he heard the hurly-burly at the Doone-gate beginning; which we, by reason of waterfall, could not hear, down in the meadows there.

We waited a very long time, with the moon marching up heaven steadfastly, and the white fog trembling in chords and columns, like a silver harp of the meadows. And then the moon drew up the fogs, and scarfed herself in white with them; and so being proud, gleamed upon the water, like a bride at her looking-glass; and yet there was no sound of either John Fry, or his blunderbuss.

I began to think that the worthy John, being out of all danger, and having brought a counterpane (according to his wife's directions, because one of the children had a cold), must veritably have gone to sleep; leaving other people to kill, or be killed, as might be the will of God; so that he were comfortable. But herein I did wrong to John, and am ready to acknowledge it; for suddenly the most awful noise that anything short of thunder could make, came down among the rocks, and went and hung upon the corners.

'The signal, my lads,' I cried, leaping up and rubbing my eyes; for even now, while condemning John unjustly, I was giving him right to be hard upon me. 'Now hold on by the rope, and lay your quarter-staffs across, my lads; and keep your guns pointing to heaven, lest haply we shoot one another.'

'Us shan't never shutt one anoother, wi' our goons at that mark, I reckon,' said an oldish chap, but as tough as leather, and esteemed a wit for his dryness.

'You come next to me, old Ike; you be enough to dry up the waters; now, remember, all lean well forward. If any man throws his weight back, down he goes; and perhaps he may never get up again; and most likely he will shoot himself.'

I was still more afraid of their shooting me; for my chief alarm in this steep ascent was neither of the water nor of the rocks, but of the loaded guns we bore. If any man slipped, off might go his gun, and however good his meaning, I being first was most likely to take far more than I fain would apprehend.

For this cause, I had debated with Uncle Ben and with Cousin Tom as to the expediency of our climbing with guns unloaded. But they, not being in the way themselves, assured me that there was nothing to fear, except through uncommon clumsiness; and that as for charging our guns at the top, even veteran troops could scarcely be trusted to perform it properly in the hurry, and the darkness, and the noise of fighting before them.

However, thank God, though a gun went off, no one was any the worse for it, neither did the Doones notice it, in the thick of the firing in front of them. For the orders to those of the sham attack, conducted by Tom Faggus, were to make the greatest possible noise, without exposure of themselves; until we, in the rear, had fallen to; which John Fry was again to give the signal of.

Therefore we, of the chosen band, stole up the meadow quietly, keeping in the blots of shade, and hollow of the watercourse. And the earliest notice the Counsellor had, or any one else, of our presence, was the blazing of the log-wood house, where lived that villain Carver. It was my especial privilege to set this house on fire; upon which I had insisted, exclusively and conclusively. No other hand but mine should lay a brand, or strike steel on flint for it; I had made all preparations carefully for a goodly blaze. And I must confess that I rubbed my hands, with a strong delight and comfort, when I saw the home of that man, who had fired so many houses, having its turn of smoke, and blaze, and of crackling fury.

We took good care, however, to burn no innocent women or children in that most righteous destruction. For we brought them all out beforehand; some were glad, and some were sorry; according to their dispositions. For Carver had ten or a dozen wives; and perhaps that had something to do with his taking the loss of Lorna so easily. One child I noticed, as I saved him; a fair and handsome little fellow, whom (if Carver Doone could love anything on earth beside his wretched self) he did love. The boy climbed on my back and rode; and much as I hated his father, it was not in my heart to say or do a thing to vex him.

Leaving these poor injured people to behold their burning home, we drew aside, by my directions, into the covert beneath the cliff. But not before we had laid our brands to three other houses, after calling the women forth, and bidding them go for their husbands, and to come and fight a hundred of us. In the smoke and rush, and fire, they believed that we were a hundred; and away they ran, in consternation, to the battle at the Doone-gate.

'All Doone-town is on fire, on fire!' we heard them shrieking as they went; 'a hundred soldiers are burning it, with a dreadful great man at the head of them!'

Presently, just as I expected, back came the warriors of the Doones; leaving but two or three at the gate, and burning with wrath to crush under foot the presumptuous clowns in their valley. Just then the waxing fire leaped above the red crest of the cliffs, and danced on the pillars of the forest, and lapped like a tide on the stones of the slope. All the valley flowed with light, and the limpid waters reddened, and the fair young women shone, and the naked children glistened.

But the finest sight of all was to see those haughty men striding down the causeway darkly, reckless of their end, but resolute to have two lives for every one. A finer dozen of young men could not have been found in the world perhaps, nor a braver, nor a viler one.

Seeing how few there were of them, I was very loath to fire, although I covered the leader, who appeared to be dashing Charley; for they were at easy distance now, brightly shone by the fire-light, yet ignorant where to look for us. I thought that we might take them prisoners—though what good that could be God knows, as they must have been hanged thereafter—anyhow I was loath to shoot, or to give the word to my followers.

But my followers waited for no word; they saw a fair shot at the men they abhorred, the men who had robbed them of home or of love, and the chance was too much for their charity. At a signal from old Ikey, who levelled his own gun first, a dozen muskets were discharged, and half of the Doones dropped lifeless, like so many logs of firewood, or chopping-blocks rolled over.

Although I had seen a great battle before, and a hundred times the carnage, this appeared to me to be horrible; and I was at first inclined to fall upon our men for behaving so. But one instant showed me that they were right; for while the valley was filled with howling, and with shrieks of women, and the beams of the blazing houses fell, and hissed in the bubbling river; all the rest of the Doones leaped at us, like so many demons.

They fired wildly, not seeing us well among the hazel bushes; and then they clubbed their muskets, or drew their swords, as might be; and furiously drove at us.

For a moment, although we were twice their number, we fell back before their valorous fame, and the power of their onset. For my part, admiring their courage greatly, and counting it slur upon manliness that two should be down upon one so, I withheld my hand awhile; for I cared to meet none but Carver; and he was not among them. The whirl and hurry of this fight, and the hard blows raining down—for now all guns were empty—took away my power of seeing, or reasoning upon anything. Yet one thing I saw, which dwelled long with me; and that was Christopher Badcock spending his life to get Charley's.

How he had found out, none may tell; both being dead so long ago; but, at any rate, he had found out that Charley was the man who had robbed him of his wife and honour. It was Carver Doone who took her away, but Charleworth Doone was beside him; and, according to cast of dice, she fell to Charley's share. All this Kit Badcock (who was mad, according to our measures) had discovered, and treasured up; and now was his revenge-time.

He had come into the conflict without a weapon of any kind; only begging me to let him be in the very thick of it. For him, he said, life was no matter, after the loss of his wife and child; but death was matter to him, and he meant to make the most of it. Such a face I never saw, and never hope to see again, as when poor Kit Badcock spied Charley coming towards us.

We had thought this man a patient fool, a philosopher of a little sort, or one who could feel nothing. And his quiet manner of going about, and the gentleness of his answers (when some brutes asked him where his wife was, and whether his baby had been well-trussed), these had misled us to think that the man would turn the mild cheek to everything. But I, in the loneliness of our barn, had listened, and had wept with him.

Therefore was I not surprised, so much as all the rest of us, when, in the foremost of red light, Kit went up to Charleworth Doone, as if to some inheritance; and took his seisin of right upon him, being himself a powerful man; and begged a word aside with him. What they said aside, I know not; all I know is that without weapon, each man killed the other. And Margery Badcock came, and wept, and hung upon her poor husband; and died, that summer, of heart-disease.

Now for these and other things (whereof I could tell a thousand) was the reckoning come that night; and not a line we missed of it; soon as our bad blood was up. I like not to tell of slaughter, though it might be of wolves and tigers; and that was a night of fire and slaughter, and of very long-harboured revenge. Enough that ere the daylight broke upon that wan March morning, the only Doones still left alive were the Counsellor and Carver. And of all the dwellings of the Doones (inhabited with luxury, and luscious taste, and licentiousness) not even one was left, but all made potash in the river.

This may seem a violent and unholy revenge upon them. And I (who led the heart of it) have in these my latter years doubted how I shall be judged, not of men—for God only knows the errors of man's judgments—but by that great God Himself, the front of whose forehead is mercy.

Chapter LXXII The Counsellor and the Carver

From that great confusion—for nothing can be broken up, whether lawful or unlawful, without a vast amount of dust, and many people grumbling, and mourning for the good old times, when all the world was happiness, and every man a gentleman, and the sun himself far brighter than since the brassy idol upon which he shone was broken—from all this loss of ancient landmarks (as unrobbed men began to call our clearance of those murderers) we returned on the following day, almost as full of anxiety as we were of triumph. In the first place, what could we possibly do with all these women and children, thrown on our hands as one might say, with none to protect and care for them? Again how should we answer to the justices of the peace, or perhaps even to Lord Jeffreys, for having, without even a warrant, taken the law into our own hands, and abated our nuisance so forcibly? And then, what was to be done with the spoil, which was of great value; though the diamond necklace came not to public light? For we saw a mighty host of claimants already leaping up for booty. Every man who had ever been robbed, expected usury on his loss; the lords of the manors demanded the whole; and so did the King's Commissioner of revenue at Porlock; and so did the men who had fought our battle; while even the parsons, both Bowden and Powell, and another who had no parish in it, threatened us with the just wrath of the Church, unless each had tithes of the whole of it.

Now this was not as it ought to be; and it seemed as if by burning the nest of robbers, we had but hatched their eggs; until being made sole guardian of the captured treasure (by reason of my known honesty) I hit upon a plan, which gave very little satisfaction; yet carried this advantage, that the grumblers argued against one another and for the most part came to blows; which renewed their goodwill to me, as being abused by the adversary.

And my plan was no more than this—not to pay a farthing to lord of manor, parson, or even King's Commissioner, but after making good some of the recent and proven losses—where the men could not afford to lose—to pay the residue (which might be worth some fifty thousand pounds) into the Exchequer at Westminster; and then let all the claimants file what wills they pleased in Chancery.

Now this was a very noble device, for the mere name of Chancery, and the high repute of the fees therein, and low repute of the lawyers, and the comfortable knowledge that the woolsack itself is the golden fleece, absorbing gold for ever, if the standard be but pure; consideration of these things staved off at once the lords of the manors, and all the little farmers, and even those whom most I feared; videlicet, the parsons. And the King's Commissioner was compelled to profess himself contented, although of all he was most aggrieved; for his pickings would have been goodly.

Moreover, by this plan I made—although I never thought of that—a mighty friend worth all the enemies, whom the loss of money moved. The first man now in the kingdom (by virtue perhaps of energy, rather than of excellence) was the great Lord Jeffreys, appointed the head of the Equity, as well as the law of the realm, for his kindness in hanging five hundred people, without the mere brief of trial. Nine out of ten of these people were innocent, it was true; but that proved the merit of the Lord Chief Justice so much the greater for hanging them, as showing what might be expected of him, when he truly got hold of a guilty man. Now the King had seen the force of this argument; and not being without gratitude for a high-seasoned dish of cruelty, had promoted the only man in England, combining the gifts of both butcher and cook.

Nevertheless, I do beg you all to believe of me—and I think that, after following me so long, you must believe it—that I did not even know at the time of Lord Jeffreys's high promotion. Not that my knowledge of this would have led me to act otherwise in the matter; for my object was to pay into an office, and not to any official; neither if I had known the fact, could I have seen its bearing upon the receipt of my money. For the King's Exchequer is, meseemeth, of the Common Law; while Chancery is of Equity, and well named for its many chances. But the true result of the thing was this—Lord Jeffreys being now head of the law, and almost head of the kingdom, got possession of that money, and was kindly pleased with it.

And this met our second difficulty; for the law having won and laughed over the spoil, must have injured its own title by impugning our legality.

Next, with regard to the women and children, we were long in a state of perplexity. We did our very best at the farm, and so did many others to provide for them, until they should manage about their own subsistence. And after a while this trouble went, as nearly all troubles go with time. Some of the women were taken back by their parents, or their husbands, or it may be their sweethearts; and those who failed of this, went forth, some upon their own account to the New World plantations, where the fairer sex is valuable; and some to English cities; and the plainer ones to field work. And most of the children went with their mothers, or were bound apprentices; only Carver Doone's handsome child had lost his mother and stayed with me.

This boy went about with me everywhere. He had taken as much of liking to me—first shown in his eyes by the firelight—as his father had of hatred; and I, perceiving his noble courage, scorn of lies, and high spirit, became almost as fond of Ensie as he was of me. He told us that his name was 'Ensie,' meant for 'Ensor,' I suppose, from his father's grandfather, the old Sir Ensor Doone. And this boy appeared to be Carver's heir, having been born in wedlock, contrary to the general manner and custom of the Doones.

However, although I loved the poor child, I could not help feeling very uneasy about the escape of his father, the savage and brutal Carver. This man was left to roam the country, homeless, foodless, and desperate, with his giant strength, and great skill in arms, and the whole world to be revenged upon. For his escape the miners, as I shall show, were answerable; but of the Counsellor's safe departure the burden lay on myself alone. And inasmuch as there are people who consider themselves ill-used, unless one tells them everything, straitened though I am for space, I will glance at this transaction.

After the desperate charge of young Doones had been met by us, and broken, and just as Poor Kit Badcock died in the arms of the dead Charley, I happened to descry a patch of white on the grass of the meadow, like the head of a sheep after washing-day. Observing with some curiosity how carefully this white thing moved along the bars of darkness betwixt the panels of firelight, I ran up to intercept it, before it reached the little postern which we used to call Gwenny's door. Perceiving me, the white thing stopped, and was for making back again; but I ran up at full speed; and lo, it was the flowing silvery hair of that sage the Counsellor, who was scuttling away upon all fours; but now rose and confronted me.

'John,' he said, 'Sir John, you will not play falsely with your ancient friend, among these violent fellows, I look to you to protect me, John.'

'Honoured sir, you are right,' I replied; 'but surely that posture was unworthy of yourself, and your many resources. It is my intention to let you go free.'

'I knew it. I could have sworn to it. You are a noble fellow, John. I said so, from the very first; you are a noble fellow, and an ornament to any rank.'

'But upon two conditions,' I added, gently taking him by the arm; for instead of displaying any desire to commune with my nobility, he was edging away toward the postern; 'the first is that you tell me truly (for now it can matter to none of you) who it was that slew my father.'

'I will tell you truly and frankly, John; however painful to me to confess it. It was my son, Carver.'

'I thought as much, or I felt as much all along,' I answered; 'but the fault was none of yours, sir; for you were not even present.'

'If I had been there, it would not have happened. I am always opposed to violence. Therefore, let me haste away; this scene is against my nature.'

'You shall go directly, Sir Counsellor, after meeting my other condition; which is, that you place in my hands Lady Lorna's diamond necklace.'

'Ah, how often I have wished,' said the old man with a heavy sigh, 'that it might yet be in my power to ease my mind in that respect, and to do a thoroughly good deed by lawful restitution.'

'Then try to have it in your power, sir. Surely, with my encouragement, you might summon resolution.'

'Alas, John, the resolution has been ready long ago. But the thing is not in my possession. Carver, my son, who slew your father, upon him you will find the necklace. What are jewels to me, young man, at my time of life? Baubles and trash,—I detest them, from the sins they have led me to answer for. When you come to my age, good Sir John, you will scorn all jewels, and care only for a pure and bright conscience. Ah! ah! Let me go. I have made my peace with God.'

He looked so hoary, and so silvery, and serene in the moonlight, that verily I must have believed him, if he had not drawn in his breast. But I happened to have noticed that when an honest man gives vent to noble and great sentiments, he spreads his breast, and throws it out, as if his heart were swelling; whereas I had seen this old gentleman draw in his breast more than once, as if it happened to contain better goods than sentiment.

'Will you applaud me, kind sir,' I said, keeping him very tight, all the while, 'if I place it in your power to ratify your peace with God? The pledge is upon your heart, no doubt, for there it lies at this moment.'

With these words, and some apology for having recourse to strong measures, I thrust my hand inside his waistcoat, and drew forth Lorna's necklace, purely sparkling in the moonlight, like the dancing of new stars. The old man made a stab at me, with a knife which I had not espied; but the vicious onset failed; and then he knelt, and clasped his hands.

'Oh, for God's sake, John, my son, rob me not in that manner. They belong to me; and I love them so; I would give almost my life for them. There is one jewel I can look at for hours, and see all the lights of heaven in it; which I never shall see elsewhere. All my wretched, wicked life—oh, John, I am a sad hypocrite—but give me back my jewels. Or else kill me here; I am a babe in your hands; but I must have back my jewels.'

As his beautiful white hair fell away from his noble forehead, like a silver wreath of glory, and his powerful face, for once, was moved with real emotion, I was so amazed and overcome by the grand contradictions of nature, that verily I was on the point of giving him back the necklace. But honesty, which is said to be the first instinct of all the Ridds (though I myself never found it so), happened here to occur to me, and so I said, without more haste than might be expected,—

'Sir Counsellor, I cannot give you what does not belong to me. But if you will show me that particular diamond which is heaven to you, I will take upon myself the risk and the folly of cutting it out for you. And with that you must go contented; and I beseech you not to starve with that jewel upon your lips.'

Seeing no hope of better terms, he showed me his pet love of a jewel; and I thought of what Lorna was to me, as I cut it out (with the hinge of my knife severing the snakes of gold) and placed it in his careful hand. Another moment, and he was gone, and away through Gwenny's postern; and God knows what became of him.

Now as to Carver, the thing was this—so far as I could ascertain from the valiant miners, no two of whom told the same story, any more than one of them told it twice. The band of Doones which sallied forth for the robbery of the pretended convoy was met by Simon Carfax, according to arrangement, at the ruined house called The Warren, in that part of Bagworthy Forest where the river Exe (as yet a very small stream) runs through it. The Warren, as all our people know, had belonged to a fine old gentleman, whom every one called 'The Squire,' who had retreated from active life to pass the rest of his days in fishing, and shooting, and helping his neighbours. For he was a man of some substance; and no poor man ever left The Warren without a bag of good victuals, and a few shillings put in his pocket. However, this poor Squire never made a greater mistake, than in hoping to end his life peacefully upon the banks of a trout-stream, and in the green forest of Bagworthy. For as he came home from the brook at dusk, with his fly-rod over his shoulder, the Doones fell upon him, and murdered him, and then sacked his house, and burned it.

Now this had made honest people timid about going past The Warren at night; for, of course, it was said that the old Squire 'walked,' upon certain nights of the moon, in and out of the trunks of trees, on the green path from the river. On his shoulder he bore a fishing-rod, and his book of trout-flies, in one hand, and on his back a wicker-creel; and now and then he would burst out laughing to think of his coming so near the Doones.

And now that one turns to consider it, this seems a strangely righteous thing, that the scene of one of the greatest crimes even by Doones committed should, after twenty years, become the scene of vengeance falling (like hail from heaven) upon them. For although The Warren lies well away to the westward of the mine; and the gold, under escort to Bristowe, or London, would have gone in the other direction; Captain Carfax, finding this place best suited for working of his design, had persuaded the Doones, that for reasons of Government, the ore must go first to Barnstaple for inspection, or something of that sort. And as every one knows that our Government sends all things westward when eastward bound, this had won the more faith for Simon, as being according to nature.

Now Simon, having met these flowers of the flock of villainy, where the rising moonlight flowed through the weir-work of the wood, begged them to dismount; and led them with an air of mystery into the Squire's ruined hall, black with fire, and green with weeds.

'Captain, I have found a thing,' he said to Carver Doone, himself, 'which may help to pass the hour, ere the lump of gold comes by. The smugglers are a noble race; but a miner's eyes are a match for them. There lies a puncheon of rare spirit, with the Dutchman's brand upon it, hidden behind the broken hearth. Set a man to watch outside; and let us see what this be like.'

With one accord they agreed to this, and Carver pledged Master Carfax, and all the Doones grew merry. But Simon being bound, as he said, to see to their strict sobriety, drew a bucket of water from the well into which they had thrown the dead owner, and begged them to mingle it with their drink; which some of them did, and some refused.

But the water from that well was poured, while they were carousing, into the priming-pan of every gun of theirs; even as Simon had promised to do with the guns of the men they were come to kill. Then just as the giant Carver arose, with a glass of pure hollands in his hand, and by the light of the torch they had struck, proposed the good health of the Squire's ghost—in the broken doorway stood a press of men, with pointed muskets, covering every drunken Doone. How it fared upon that I know not, having none to tell me; for each man wrought, neither thought of telling, nor whether he might be alive to tell. The Doones rushed to their guns at once, and pointed them, and pulled at them; but the Squire's well had drowned their fire; and then they knew that they were betrayed, but resolved to fight like men for it. Upon fighting I can never dwell; it breeds such savage delight in me; of which I would fain have less. Enough that all the Doones fought bravely; and like men (though bad ones) died in the hall of the man they had murdered. And with them died poor young De Whichehalse, who, in spite of his good father's prayers, had cast in his lot with the robbers. Carver Doone alone escaped. Partly through his fearful strength, and his yet more fearful face; but mainly perhaps through his perfect coolness, and his mode of taking things.

I am happy to say that no more than eight of the gallant miners were killed in that combat, or died of their wounds afterwards; and adding to these the eight we had lost in our assault on the valley (and two of them excellent warehousemen), it cost no more than sixteen lives to be rid of nearly forty Doones, each of whom would most likely have killed three men in the course of a year or two. Therefore, as I said at the time, a great work was done very reasonably; here were nigh upon forty Doones destroyed (in the valley, and up at The Warrens) despite their extraordinary strength and high skill in gunnery; whereas of us ignorant rustics there were only sixteen to be counted dead—though others might be lamed, or so,—and of those sixteen only two had left wives, and their wives did not happen to care for them.

Yet, for Lorna' s sake, I was vexed at the bold escape of Carver. Not that I sought for Carver's life, any more than I did for the Counsellor's; but that for us it was no light thing, to have a man of such power, and resource, and desperation, left at large and furious, like a famished wolf round the sheepfold. Yet greatly as I blamed the yeomen, who were posted on their horses, just out of shot from the Doone-gate, for the very purpose of intercepting those who escaped the miners, I could not get them to admit that any blame attached to them.

But lo, he had dashed through the whole of them, with his horse at full gallop; and was nearly out of shot before they began to think of shooting him. Then it appears from what a boy said—for boys manage to be everywhere—that Captain Carver rode through the Doone-gate, and so to the head of the valley. There, of course, he beheld all the houses, and his own among the number, flaming with a handsome blaze, and throwing a fine light around such as he often had revelled in, when of other people's property. But he swore the deadliest of all oaths, and seeing himself to be vanquished (so far as the luck of the moment went), spurred his great black horse away, and passed into the darkness.

Chapter LXXIII How to Get Out of Chancery

Things at this time so befell me, that I cannot tell one half; but am like a boy who has left his lesson (to the master's very footfall) unready, except with false excuses. And as this makes no good work, so I lament upon my lingering, in the times when I might have got through a good page, but went astray after trifles. However, every man must do according to his intellect; and looking at the easy manner of my constitution, I think that most men will regard me with pity and goodwill for trying, more than with contempt and wrath for having tried unworthily. Even as in the wrestling ring, whatever man did his best, and made an honest conflict, I always laid him down with softness, easing off his dusty fall.

But the thing which next betided me was not a fall of any sort; but rather a most glorious rise to the summit of all fortune. For in good truth it was no less than the return of Lorna—my Lorna, my own darling; in wonderful health and spirits, and as glad as a bird to get back again. It would have done any one good for a twelve-month to behold her face and doings, and her beaming eyes and smile (not to mention blushes also at my salutation), when this Queen of every heart ran about our rooms again. She did love this, and she must see that, and where was our old friend the cat? All the house was full of brightness, as if the sun had come over the hill, and Lorna were his mirror.

My mother sat in an ancient chair, and wiped her cheeks, and looked at her; and even Lizzie's eyes must dance to the freshness and joy of her beauty. As for me, you might call me mad; for I ran out and flung my best hat on the barn, and kissed mother Fry, till she made at me with the sugar-nippers.

What a quantity of things Lorna had to tell us! And yet how often we stopped her mouth—at least mother, I mean, and Lizzie—and she quite as often would stop her own, running up in her joy to some one of us! And then there arose the eating business—which people now call 'refreshment,' in these dandyfied days of our language—for how was it possible that our Lorna could have come all that way, and to her own Exmoor, without being terribly hungry?

'Oh, I do love it all so much,' said Lorna, now for the fiftieth time, and not meaning only the victuals: 'the scent of the gorse on the moors drove me wild, and the primroses under the hedges. I am sure I was meant for a farmer's—I mean for a farm-house life, dear Lizzie'—for Lizzie was looking saucily—'just as you were meant for a soldier's bride, and for writing despatches of victory. And now, since you will not ask me, dear mother, in the excellence of your manners, and even John has not the impudence, in spite of all his coat of arms—I must tell you a thing, which I vowed to keep until tomorrow morning; but my resolution fails me. I am my own mistress—what think you of that, mother? I am my own mistress!'

'Then you shall not be so long,' cried I; for mother seemed not to understand her, and sought about for her glasses: 'darling, you shall be mistress of me; and I will be your master.'

'A frank announcement of your intent, and beyond doubt a true one; but surely unusual at this stage, and a little premature, John. However, what must be, must be.' And with tears springing out of smiles, she fell on my breast, and cried a bit.

When I came to smoke a pipe over it (after the rest were gone to bed), I could hardly believe in my good luck. For here was I, without any merit, except of bodily power, and the absence of any falsehood (which surely is no commendation), so placed that the noblest man in England might envy me, and be vexed with me. For the noblest lady in all the land, and the purest, and the sweetest—hung upon my heart, as if there was none to equal it.

I dwelled upon this matter, long and very severely, while I smoked a new tobacco, brought by my own Lorna for me, and next to herself most delicious; and as the smoke curled away, I thought, 'Surely this is too fine to last, for a man who never deserved it.'

Seeing no way out of this, I resolved to place my faith in God; and so went to bed and dreamed of it. And having no presence of mind to pray for anything, under the circumstances, I thought it best to fall asleep, and trust myself to the future. Yet ere I fell asleep the roof above me swarmed with angels, having Lorna under it.

In the morning Lorna was ready to tell her story, and we to hearken; and she wore a dress of most simple stuff; and yet perfectly wonderful, by means of the shape and her figure. Lizzie was wild with jealousy, as might be expected (though never would Annie have been so, but have praised it, and craved for the pattern), and mother not understanding it, looked forth, to be taught about it. For it was strange to note that lately my dear mother had lost her quickness, and was never quite brisk, unless the question were about myself. She had seen a great deal of trouble; and grief begins to close on people, as their power of life declines. We said that she was hard of hearing; but my opinion was, that seeing me inclined for marriage made her think of my father, and so perhaps a little too much, to dwell on the courting of thirty years agone. Anyhow, she was the very best of mothers; and would smile and command herself; and be (or try to believe herself) as happy as could be, in the doings of the younger folk, and her own skill in detecting them. Yet, with the wisdom of age, renouncing any opinion upon the matter; since none could see the end of it.

But Lorna in her bright young beauty, and her knowledge of my heart, was not to be checked by any thoughts of haply coming evil. In the morning she was up, even sooner than I was, and through all the corners of the hens, remembering every one of them. I caught her and saluted her with such warmth (being now none to look at us), that she vowed she would never come out again; and yet she came the next morning.

These things ought not to be chronicled. Yet I am of such nature, that finding many parts of life adverse to our wishes, I must now and then draw pleasure from the blessed portions. And what portion can be more blessed than with youth, and health, and strength, to be loved by a virtuous maid, and to love her with all one's heart? Neither was my pride diminished, when I found what she had done, only from her love of me.

Earl Brandir's ancient steward, in whose charge she had travelled, with a proper escort, looked upon her as a lovely maniac; and the mixture of pity and admiration wherewith he regarded her, was a strange thing to observe; especially after he had seen our simple house and manners. On the other hand, Lorna considered him a worthy but foolish old gentleman; to whom true happiness meant no more than money and high position.

These two last she had been ready to abandon wholly, and had in part escaped from them, as the enemies of her happiness. And she took advantage of the times, in a truly clever manner. For that happened to be a time—as indeed all times hitherto (so far as my knowledge extends), have, somehow, or other, happened to be—when everybody was only too glad to take money for doing anything. And the greatest money-taker in the kingdom (next to the King and Queen, of course, who had due preeminence, and had taught the maids of honour) was generally acknowledged to be the Lord Chief Justice Jeffreys.

Upon his return from the bloody assizes, with triumph and great glory, after hanging every man who was too poor to help it, he pleased his Gracious Majesty so purely with the description of their delightful agonies, that the King exclaimed, 'This man alone is worthy to be at the head of the law.' Accordingly in his hand was placed the Great Seal of England.

So it came to pass that Lorna's destiny hung upon Lord Jeffreys; for at this time Earl Brandir died, being taken with gout in the heart, soon after I left London. Lorna was very sorry for him; but as he had never been able to hear one tone of her sweet silvery voice, it is not to be supposed that she wept without consolation. She grieved for him as we ought to grieve for any good man going; and yet with a comforting sense of the benefit which the blessed exchange must bring to him.

Now the Lady Lorna Dugal appeared to Lord Chancellor Jeffreys so exceeding wealthy a ward that the lock would pay for turning. Therefore he came, of his own accord, to visit her, and to treat with her; having heard (for the man was as big a gossip as never cared for anybody, yet loved to know all about everybody) that this wealthy and beautiful maiden would not listen to any young lord, having pledged her faith to the plain John Ridd.

Thereupon, our Lorna managed so to hold out golden hopes to the Lord High Chancellor, that he, being not more than three parts drunk, saw his way to a heap of money. And there and then (for he was not the man to daily long about anything) upon surety of a certain round sum—the amount of which I will not mention, because of his kindness towards me—he gave to his fair ward permission, under sign and seal, to marry that loyal knight, John Ridd; upon condition only that the King's consent should be obtained.

His Majesty, well-disposed towards me for my previous service, and regarding me as a good Catholic, being moved moreover by the Queen, who desired to please Lorna, consented, without much hesitation, upon the understanding that Lorna, when she became of full age, and the mistress of her property (which was still under guardianship), should pay a heavy fine to the Crown, and devote a fixed portion of her estate to the promotion of the holy Catholic faith, in a manner to be dictated by the King himself. Inasmuch, however, as King James was driven out of his kingdom before this arrangement could take effect, and another king succeeded, who desired not the promotion of the Catholic religion, neither hankered after subsidies, whether French or English), that agreement was pronounced invalid, improper, and contemptible. However, there was no getting back the money once paid to Lord Chancellor Jeffreys.

But what thought we of money at this present moment; or of position, or anything else, except indeed one another? Lorna told me, with the sweetest smile, that if I were minded to take her at all, I must take her without anything; inasmuch as she meant, upon coming of age, to make over the residue of her estates to the next-of-kin, as being unfit for a farmer's wife. And I replied with the greatest warmth and a readiness to worship her, that this was exactly what I longed for, but had never dared to propose it. But dear mother looked most exceeding grave; and said that to be sure her opinion could not be expected to count for much, but she really hoped that in three years' time we should both he a little wiser, and have more regard for our interests, and perhaps those of others by that time; and Master Snowe having daughters only, and nobody coming to marry them, if anything happened to the good old man—and who could tell in three years' time what might happen to all or any of us?—why perhaps his farm would be for sale, and perhaps Lady Lorna's estates in Scotland would fetch enough money to buy it, and so throw the two farms into one, and save all the trouble about the brook, as my poor father had longed to do many and many a time, but not having a title could not do all quite as he wanted. And then if we young people grew tired of the old mother, as seemed only too likely, and was according to nature, why we could send her over there, and Lizzie to keep her company.

When mother had finished, and wiped her eyes, Lorna, who had been blushing rosily at some portions of this great speech, flung her fair arms around mother's neck, and kissed her very heartily, and scolded her (as she well deserved) for her want of confidence in us. My mother replied that if anybody could deserve her John, it was Lorna; but that she could not hold with the rashness of giving up money so easily; while her next-of-kin would be John himself, and who could tell what others, by the time she was one-and-twenty?

Hereupon, I felt that after all my mother had common sense on her side; for if Master Snowe's farm should be for sale, it would be far more to the purpose than my coat of arms, to get it; for there was a different pasture there, just suited for change of diet to our sheep as well as large cattle. And beside this, even with all Annie's skill (and of course yet more now she was gone), their butter would always command in the market from one to three farthings a pound more than we could get for ours. And few things vexed us more than this. Whereas, if we got possession of the farm, we might, without breach of the market-laws, or any harm done to any one (the price being but a prejudice), sell all our butter as Snowe butter, and do good to all our customers.

Thinking thus, yet remembering that Farmer Nicholas might hold out for another score of years—as I heartily hoped he might—or that one, if not all, of his comely daughters might marry a good young farmer (or farmers, if the case were so)—or that, even without that, the farm might never be put up for sale; I begged my Lorna to do as she liked; or rather to wait and think of it; for as yet she could do nothing.

Chapter LXXIV Driven Beyond Endurance

[Also known as BLOOD UPON THE ALTAR in other editions]

Everything was settled smoothly, and without any fear or fuss, that Lorna might find end of troubles, and myself of eager waiting, with the help of Parson Bowden, and the good wishes of two counties. I could scarce believe my fortune, when I looked upon her beauty, gentleness, and sweetness, mingled with enough of humour and warm woman's feeling, never to be dull or tiring; never themselves to be weary.

For she might be called a woman now; although a very young one, and as full of playful ways, or perhaps I may say ten times as full, as if she had known no trouble. To wit, the spirit of bright childhood, having been so curbed and straitened, ere its time was over, now broke forth, enriched and varied with the garb of conscious maidenhood. And the sense of steadfast love, and eager love enfolding her, coloured with so many tinges all her looks, and words, and thoughts, that to me it was the noblest vision even to think about her.

But this was far too bright to last, without bitter break, and the plunging of happiness in horror, and of passionate joy in agony. My darling in her softest moments, when she was alone with me, when the spark of defiant eyes was veiled beneath dark lashes, and the challenge of gay beauty passed into sweetest invitation; at such times of her purest love and warmest faith in me, a deep abiding fear would flutter in her bounding heart, as of deadly fate's approach. She would cling to me, and nestle to me, being scared of coyishness, and lay one arm around my neck, and ask if I could do without her.

Hence, as all emotions haply, of those who are more to us than ourselves, find within us stronger echo, and more perfect answer, so I could not be regardless of some hidden evil; and my dark misgivings deepened as the time drew nearer. I kept a steadfast watch on Lorna, neglecting a field of beans entirely, as well as a litter of young pigs, and a cow somewhat given to jaundice. And I let Jem Slocombe go to sleep in the tallat, all one afternoon, and Bill Dadds draw off a bucket of cider, without so much as a 'by your leave.' For these men knew that my knighthood, and my coat of arms, and (most of all) my love, were greatly against good farming; the sense of our country being—and perhaps it may be sensible—that a man who sticks up to be anything, must allow himself to be cheated.

But I never did stick up, nor would, though all the parish bade me; and I whistled the same tunes to my horses, and held my plough-tree, just the same as if no King, nor Queen, had ever come to spoil my tune or hand. For this thing, nearly all the men around our parts upbraided me; but the women praised me: and for the most part these are right, when themselves are not concerned.

However humble I might be, no one knowing anything of our part of the country, would for a moment doubt that now here was a great to do and talk of John Ridd and his wedding. The fierce fight with the Doones so lately, and my leading of the combat (though I fought not more than need be), and the vanishing of Sir Counsellor, and the galloping madness of Carver, and the religious fear of the women that this last was gone to hell—for he himself had declared that his aim, while he cut through the yeomanry—also their remorse, that he should have been made to go thither with all his children left behind—these things, I say (if ever I can again contrive to say anything), had led to the broadest excitement about my wedding of Lorna. We heard that people meant to come from more than thirty miles around, upon excuse of seeing my stature and Lorna's beauty; but in good truth out of sheer curiosity, and the love of meddling.

Our clerk had given notice, that not a man should come inside the door of his church without shilling-fee; and women (as sure to see twice as much) must every one pay two shillings. I thought this wrong; and as church-warden, begged that the money might be paid into mine own hands, when taken. But the clerk said that was against all law; and he had orders from the parson to pay it to him without any delay. So as I always obey the parson, when I care not much about a thing, I let them have it their own way; though feeling inclined to believe, sometimes, that I ought to have some of the money.

Dear mother arranged all the ins and outs of the way in which it was to be done; and Annie and Lizzie, and all the Snowes, and even Ruth Huckaback (who was there, after great persuasion), made such a sweeping of dresses that I scarcely knew where to place my feet, and longed for a staff, to put by their gowns. Then Lorna came out of a pew half-way, in a manner which quite astonished me, and took my left hand in her right, and I prayed God that it were done with.

My darling looked so glorious, that I was afraid of glancing at her, yet took in all her beauty. She was in a fright, no doubt; but nobody should see it; whereas I said (to myself at least), 'I will go through it like a grave-digger.'

Lorna's dress was of pure white, clouded with faint lavender (for the sake of the old Earl Brandir), and as simple as need be, except for perfect loveliness. I was afraid to look at her, as I said before, except when each of us said, 'I will,' and then each dwelled upon the other.

It is impossible for any who have not loved as I have to conceive my joy and pride, when after ring and all was done, and the parson had blessed us, Lorna turned to look at me with her glances of subtle fun subdued by this great act.

Her eyes, which none on earth may ever equal, or compare with, told me such a depth of comfort, yet awaiting further commune, that I was almost amazed, thoroughly as I knew them. Darling eyes, the sweetest eyes, the loveliest, the most loving eyes—the sound of a shot rang through the church, and those eyes were filled with death.

Lorna fell across my knees when I was going to kiss her, as the bridegroom is allowed to do, and encouraged, if he needs it; a flood of blood came out upon the yellow wood of the altar steps, and at my feet lay Lorna, trying to tell me some last message out of her faithful eyes. I lifted her up, and petted her, and coaxed her, but it was no good; the only sign of life remaining was a spirt of bright red blood.

Some men know what things befall them in the supreme time of their life—far above the time of death—but to me comes back as a hazy dream, without any knowledge in it, what I did, or felt, or thought, with my wife's arms flagging, flagging, around my neck, as I raised her up, and softly put them there. She sighed a long sigh on my breast, for her last farewell to life, and then she grew so cold, and cold, that I asked the time of year.

It was Whit-Tuesday, and the lilacs all in blossom; and why I thought of the time of year, with the young death in my arms, God or His angels, may decide, having so strangely given us. Enough that so I did, and looked; and our white lilacs were beautiful. Then I laid my wife in my mother's arms, and begging that no one would make a noise, went forth for my revenge.

Of course, I knew who had done it. There was but one man in the world, or at any rate, in our part of it, who could have done such a thing—such a thing. I use no harsher word about it, while I leaped upon our best horse, with bridle but no saddle, and set the head of Kickums towards the course now pointed out to me. Who showed me the course, I cannot tell. I only know that I took it. And the men fell back before me.

Weapon of no sort had I. Unarmed, and wondering at my strange attire (with a bridal vest, wrought by our Annie, and red with the blood of the bride), I went forth just to find out this; whether in this world there be or be not God of justice.

With my vicious horse at a furious speed, I came upon Black Barrow Down, directed by some shout of men, which seemed to me but a whisper. And there, about a furlong before me, rode a man on a great black horse, and I knew that the man was Carver Doone.

'Your life or mine,' I said to myself; 'as the will of God may be. But we two live not upon this earth, one more hour together.'

I knew the strength of this great man; and I knew that he was armed with a gun—if he had time to load again, after shooting my Lorna—or at any rate with pistols, and a horseman's sword as well. Nevertheless, I had no more doubt of killing the man before me than a cook has of spitting a headless fowl.

Sometimes seeing no ground beneath me, and sometimes heeding every leaf, and the crossing of the grass-blades, I followed over the long moor, reckless whether seen or not. But only once the other man turned round and looked back again, and then I was beside a rock, with a reedy swamp behind me.

Although he was so far before me, and riding as hard as ride he might, I saw that he had something on the horse in front of him; something which needed care, and stopped him from looking backward. In the whirling of my wits, I fancied first that this was Lorna; until the scene I had been through fell across hot brain and heart, like the drop at the close of a tragedy. Rushing there through crag and quag, at utmost speed of a maddened horse, I saw, as of another's fate, calmly (as on canvas laid), the brutal deed, the piteous anguish, and the cold despair.

The man turned up the gully leading from the moor to Cloven Rocks, through which John Fry had tracked Uncle Ben, as of old related. But as Carver entered it, he turned round, and beheld me not a hundred yards behind; and I saw that he was bearing his child, little Ensie, before him. Ensie also descried me, and stretched his hands and cried to me; for the face of his father frightened him.

Carver Doone, with a vile oath, thrust spurs into his flagging horse, and laid one hand on a pistol-stock; whence I knew that his slung carbine had received no bullet since the one that had pierced Lorna. And a cry of triumph rose from the black depths of my heart. What cared I for pistols? I had no spurs, neither was my horse one to need the rowel; I rather held him in than urged him, for he was fresh as ever; and I knew that the black steed in front, if he breasted the steep ascent, where the track divided, must be in our reach at once.

His rider knew this; and, having no room in the rocky channel to turn and fire, drew rein at the crossways sharply, and plunged into the black ravine leading to the Wizard's Slough. 'Is it so?' I said to myself with a brain and head cold as iron; 'though the foul fiend come from the slough, to save thee; thou shalt carve it, Carver.'

I followed my enemy carefully, steadily, even leisurely; for I had him, as in a pitfall, whence no escape might be. He thought that I feared to approach him, for he knew not where he was: and his low disdainful laugh came back. 'Laugh he who wins,' thought I.

A gnarled and half-starved oak, as stubborn as my own resolve, and smitten by some storm of old, hung from the crag above me. Rising from my horse's back, although I had no stirrups, I caught a limb, and tore it (like a mere wheat-awn) from the socket. Men show the rent even now, with wonder; none with more wonder than myself.

Carver Doone turned the corner suddenly on the black and bottomless bog; with a start of fear he reined back his horse, and I thought he would have turned upon me. But instead of that, he again rode on; hoping to find a way round the side.

Now there is a way between cliff and slough for those who know the ground thoroughly, or have time enough to search it; but for him there was no road, and he lost some time in seeking it. Upon this he made up his mind; and wheeling, fired, and then rode at me.

His bullet struck me somewhere, but I took no heed of that. Fearing only his escape, I laid my horse across the way, and with the limb of the oak struck full on the forehead his charging steed. Ere the slash of the sword came nigh me, man and horse rolled over, and wellnigh bore my own horse down, with the power of their onset.

Carver Doone was somewhat stunned, and could not arise for a moment. Meanwhile I leaped on the ground and awaited, smoothing my hair back, and baring my arms, as though in the ring for wrestling. Then the little boy ran to me, clasped my leg, and looked up at me, and the terror in his eyes made me almost fear myself.

'Ensie, dear,' I said quite gently, grieving that he should see his wicked father killed, 'run up yonder round the corner and try to find a pretty bunch of bluebells for the lady.' The child obeyed me, hanging back, and looking back, and then laughing, while I prepared for business. There and then I might have killed mine enemy, with a single blow, while he lay unconscious; but it would have been foul play.

With a sullen and black scowl, the Carver gathered his mighty limbs, and arose, and looked round for his weapons; but I had put them well away. Then he came to me and gazed; being wont to frighten thus young men.

'I would not harm you, lad,' he said, with a lofty style of sneering: 'I have punished you enough, for most of your impertinence. For the rest I forgive you; because you have been good and gracious to my little son. Go, and be contented.'

For answer, I smote him on the cheek, lightly, and not to hurt him: but to make his blood leap up. I would not sully my tongue by speaking to a man like this.

There was a level space of sward between us and the slough. With the courtesy derived from London, and the processions I had seen, to this place I led him. And that he might breathe himself, and have every fibre cool, and every muscle ready, my hold upon his coat I loosed, and left him to begin with me, whenever he thought proper.

I think that he felt that his time was come. I think he knew from my knitted muscles, and the firm arch of my breast, and the way in which I stood; but most of all from my stern blue eyes; that he had found his master. At any rate a paleness came, an ashy paleness on his cheeks, and the vast calves of his legs bowed in, as if he were out of training.

Seeing this, villain as he was, I offered him first chance. I stretched forth my left hand, as I do to a weaker antagonist, and I let him have the hug of me. But in this I was too generous; having forgotten my pistol-wound, and the cracking of one of my short lower ribs. Carver Doone caught me round the waist, with such a grip as never yet had been laid upon me.

I heard my rib go; I grasped his arm, and tore the muscle out of it* (as the string comes out of an orange); then I took him by the throat, which is not allowed in wrestling; but he had snatched at mine; and now was no time of dalliance. In vain he tugged, and strained, and writhed, dashed his bleeding fist into my face, and flung himself on me with gnashing jaws. Beneath the iron of my strength—for God that day was with me—I had him helpless in two minutes, and his fiery eyes lolled out.

'I will not harm thee any more,' I cried, so far as I could for panting, the work being very furious: 'Carver Doone, thou art beaten: own it, and thank God for it; and go thy way, and repent thyself.'

It was all too late. Even if he had yielded in his ravening frenzy—for his beard was like a mad dog's jowl—even if he would have owned that, for the first time in his life, he had found his master, it was all too late.

The black bog had him by the feet; the sucking of the ground drew on him, like the thirsty lips of death. In our fury, we had heeded neither wet nor dry; nor thought of earth beneath us. I myself might scarcely leap, with the last spring of o'er-laboured legs, from the engulfing grave of slime. He fell back, with his swarthy breast (from which my gripe had rent all clothing), like a hummock of bog-oak, standing out the quagmire; and then he tossed his arms to heaven, and they were black to the elbow, and the glare of his eyes was ghastly. I could only gaze and pant; for my strength was no more than an infant's, from the fury and the horror. Scarcely could I turn away, while, joint by joint, he sank from sight.

Chapter LXXV Life and Lorna Come Again

When the little boy came back with the bluebells, which he had managed to find—as children always do find flowers, when older eyes see none—the only sign of his father left was a dark brown bubble, upon a newly formed patch of blackness. But to the center of its pulpy gorge the greedy slough was heaving, and sullenly grinding its weltering jaws among the flags and the sedges.

With pain, and ache, both of mind and body, and shame at my own fury, I heavily mounted my horse again, and, looked down at the innocent Ensie. Would this playful, loving child grow up like his cruel father, and end a godless life of hatred with a death of violence? He lifted his noble

*A far more terrible clutch than this is handed down, to weaker ages, of the great John Ridd.—Ed.

forehead towards me, as if to answer, "Nay, I will not": but the words he spoke were these:—

'Don,'—for he could never say 'John'—'oh, Don, I am so glad that nasty naughty man is gone away. Take me home, Don. Take me home.'

It has been said of the wicked, 'not even their own children love them.' And I could easily believe that Carver Doone's cold-hearted ways had scared from him even his favorite child. No man would I call truly wicked, unless his heart be cold.

It hurt me, more than I can tell, even through all other grief, to take into my arms the child of the man just slain by me. The feeling was a foolish one, and a wrong one, as the thing has been—for I would fain have saved that man, after he was conquered—nevertheless my arms went coldly round that little fellow; neither would they have gone at all, if there had been any help for it. But I could not leave him there, till some one else might fetch him; on account of the cruel slough, and the ravens which had come hovering over the dead horse; neither could I, with my wound, tie him on my horse and walk.

For now I had spent a great deal of blood, and was rather faint and weary. And it was lucky for me that Kickums had lost spirit, like his master, and went home as mildly as a lamb. For, when we came towards the farm, I seemed to be riding in a dream almost; and the voices both of man and women (who had hurried forth upon my track), as they met me, seemed to wander from a distant muffling cloud. Only the thought of Lorna's death, like a heavy knell, was tolling in the belfry of my brain.

When we came to the stable door, I rather fell from my horse than got off; and John Fry, with a look of wonder took Kickum's head, and led him in. Into the old farmhouse I tottered, like a weanling child, with mother in her common clothes, helping me along, yet fearing, except by stealth, to look at me.

'I have killed him,' was all I said; 'even as he killed Lorna. Now let me see my wife, mother. She belongs to me none the less, though dead.'

'You cannot see her now, dear John,' said Ruth Huckaback, coming forward; since no one else had the courage. 'Annie is with her now, John.'

'What has that to do with it? Let me see my dead one; and pray myself to die.'

All the women fell away, and whispered, and looked at me, with side glances, and some sobbing; for my face was hard as flint. Ruth alone stood by me, and dropped her eyes, and trembled. Then one little hand of hers stole into my great shaking palm, and the other was laid on my tattered coat: yet with her clothes she shunned my blood, while she whispered gently,—

'John, she is not your dead one. She may even be your living one yet, your wife, your home, and your happiness. But you must not see her now.'

'Is there any chance for her? For me, I mean; for me, I mean?'

'God in heaven knows, dear John. But the sight of you, and in this sad plight, would be certain death to her. Now come first, and be healed yourself.'

I obeyed her, like a child, whispering only as I went, for none but myself knew her goodness—'Almighty God will bless you, darling, for the good you are doing now.'

Tenfold, ay and a thousandfold, I prayed and I believed it, when I came to know the truth. If it had not been for this little maid, Lorna must have died at once, as in my arms she lay for dead, from the dastard and murderous cruelty. But the moment I left her Ruth came forward and took the command of every one, in right of her firmness and readiness.

She made them bear her home at once upon the door of the pulpit, with the cushion under the drooping head. With her own little hands she cut off, as tenderly as a pear is peeled, the bridal-dress, so steeped and stained, and then with her dainty transparent fingers (no larger than a pencil) she probed the vile wound in the side, and fetched the reeking bullet forth; and then with the coldest water stanched the flowing of the life-blood. All this while my darling lay insensible, and white as death; and needed nothing but her maiden shroud.

But Ruth still sponged the poor side and forehead, and watched the long eyelashes flat upon the marble cheek; and laid her pure face on the faint heart, and bade them fetch her Spanish wine. Then she parted the pearly teeth (feebly clenched on the hovering breath), and poured in wine from a christening spoon, and raised the graceful neck and breast, and stroked the delicate throat, and waited; and then poured in a little more.

Annie all the while looked on with horror and amazement, counting herself no second-rate nurse, and this as against all theory. But the quiet lifting of Ruth's hand, and one glance from her dark bright eyes, told Annie just to stand away, and not intercept the air so. And at the very moment when all the rest had settled that Ruth was a simple idiot, but could not harm the dead much, a little flutter in the throat, followed by a short low sigh, made them pause, and look and hope.

For hours, however, and days, she lay at the very verge of death, kept alive by nothing but the care, the skill, the tenderness, and the perpetual watchfulness of Ruth. Luckily Annie was not there very often, so as to meddle; for kind and clever nurse as she was, she must have done more harm than good. But my broken rib, which was set by a doctor, who chanced to be at the wedding, was allotted to Annie's care; and great inflammation ensuing, it was quite enough to content her. This doctor had pronounced poor Lorna dead; wherefore Ruth refused most firmly to have aught to do with him. She took the whole case on herself; and with God's help she bore it through.

Now whether it were the light and brightness of my Lorna's nature; or the freedom from anxiety—for she knew not of my hurt;—or, as some people said, her birthright among wounds and violence, or her manner of not drinking beer—I leave that doctor to determine who pronounced her dead. But anyhow, one thing is certain; sure as stars of hope above us; Lorna recovered, long ere I did.

For the grief was on me still of having lost my love and lover at the moment she was mine. With the power of fate upon me, and the black cauldron of the wizard's death boiling in my heated brain, I had no faith in the tales they told. I believed that Lorna was in the churchyard, while these rogues were lying to me. For with strength of blood like mine, and power of heart behind it, a broken bone must burn itself.

Mine went hard with fires of pain, being of such size and thickness; and I was ashamed of him for breaking by reason of a pistol-ball, and the mere hug of a man. And it fetched me down in conceit of strength; so that I was careful afterwards.

All this was a lesson to me. All this made me very humble; illness being a thing, as yet, altogether unknown to me. Not that I cried small, or skulked, or feared the death which some foretold; shaking their heads about mortification, and a green appearance. Only that I seemed quite fit to go to heaven, and Lorna. For in my sick distracted mind (stirred with many tossings), like the bead in the spread of frog-spawn carried by the current, hung the black and central essence of my future life. A life without Lorna; a tadpole life. All stupid head; and no body.

Many men may like such life; anchorites, fakirs, high-priests, and so on; but to my mind, it is not the native thing God meant for us. My dearest mother was a show, with crying and with fretting. The Doones, as she thought, were born to destroy us. Scarce had she come to some liveliness (though sprinkled with tears, every now and then) after her great bereavement, and ten years' time to dwell on it—when lo, here was her husband's son, the pet child of her own good John, murdered like his father! Well, the ways of God were wonderful!

So they were, and so they are; and so they ever will be. Let us debate them as we will, are ways are His, and much the same; only second-hand from Him. And I expected something from Him, even in my worst of times, knowing that I had done my best.

This is not edifying talk—as our Nonconformist parson says, when he can get no more to drink—therefore let me only tell what became of Lorna. One day, I was sitting in my bedroom, for I could not get downstairs, and there was no one strong enough to carry me, even if I would have allowed it.

Though it cost me sore trouble and weariness, I had put on all my Sunday clothes, out of respect for the doctor, who was coming to bleed me again (as he always did twice a week); and it struck me that he had seemed hurt in his mind, because I wore my worst clothes to be bled in—for lie in bed I would not, after six o'clock; and even that was great laziness.

I looked at my right hand, whose grasp had been like that of a blacksmith's vice; and it seemed to myself impossible that this could be John Ridd's. The great frame of the hand was there, as well as the muscles, standing forth like the guttering of a candle, and the broad blue veins, going up the back, and crossing every finger. But as for colour, even Lorna's could scarcely have been whiter; and as for strength, little Ensie Doone might have come and held it fast. I laughed as I tried in vain to lift the basin set for bleeding me.

Then I thought of all the lovely things going on out-of-doors just now, concerning which the drowsy song of the bees came to me. These must be among the thyme, by the sound of their great content. Therefore the roses must be in blossom, and the woodbine, and clove-gilly-flower; the cherries on the wall must be turning red, the yellow Sally must be on the brook, wheat must be callow with quavering bloom, and the early meadows swathed with hay.

Yet here was I, a helpless creature quite unfit to stir among them, gifted with no sight, no scent of all the changes that move our love, and lead our hearts, from month to month, along the quiet path of life. And what was worse, I had no hope of caring ever for them more.

Presently a little knock sounded through my gloomy room, and supposing it to be the doctor, I tried to rise and make my bow. But to my surprise it was little Ruth, who had never once come to visit me, since I was placed under the doctor's hands. Ruth was dressed so gaily, with rosettes, and flowers, and what not, that I was sorry for her bad manners; and thought she was come to conquer me, now that Lorna was done with.

Ruth ran towards me with sparkling eyes, being rather short of sight; then suddenly she stopped, and I saw entire amazement in her face.

'Can you receive visitors, Cousin Ridd?—why, they never told me of this!' she cried: 'I knew that you were weak, dear John; but not that you were dying. Whatever is that basin for?'

'I have no intention of dying, Ruth; and I like not to talk about it. But that basin, if you must know, is for the doctor's purpose.'

'What, do you mean bleeding you? You poor weak cousin! Is it possible that he does that still?'

'Twice a week for the last six weeks, dear. Nothing else has kept me alive.'

'Nothing else has killed you, nearly. There!' and she set her little boot across the basin, and crushed it. 'Not another drop shall they have from you. Is Annie such a fool as that? And Lizzie, like a zany, at her books! And killing her brother, between them!'

I was surprised to see Ruth excited; her character being so calm and quiet. And I tried to soothe her with my feeble hand, as now she knelt before me.

'Dear cousin, the doctor must know best. Annie says so, every day. What has he been brought up for?'

'Brought up for slaying and murdering. Twenty doctors killed King Charles, in spite of all the women. Will you leave it to me, John? I have a little will of my own; and I am not afraid of doctors. Will you leave it to me, dear John? I have saved your Lorna's life. And now I will save yours; which is a far, far easier business.'

'You have saved my Lorna's life! What do you mean by talking so?'

'Only what I say, Cousin John. Though perhaps I overprize my work. But at any rate she says so.'

'I do not understand,' I said, falling back with bewilderment; 'all women are such liars.'

'Have you ever known me tell a lie?' Ruth in great indignation—more feigned, I doubt, than real—'your mother may tell a story, now and then when she feels it right; and so may both your sisters. But so you cannot do, John Ridd; and no more than you can I do it.'

If ever there was virtuous truth in the eyes of any woman, it was now in Ruth Huckaback's: and my brain began very slowly to move, the heart being almost torpid from perpetual loss of blood.

'I do not understand,' was all I could say for a very long time.

'Will you understand, if I show you Lorna? I have feared to do it, for the sake of you both. But now Lorna is well enough, if you think that you are, Cousin John. Surely you will understand, when you see your wife.'

Following her, to the very utmost of my mind and heart, I felt that all she said was truth; and yet I could not make it out. And in her last few words there was such a power of sadness rising through the cover of gaiety, that I said to myself, half in a dream, 'Ruth is very beautiful.'

Before I had time to listen much for the approach of footsteps, Ruth came back, and behind her Lorna; coy as if of her bridegroom; and hanging back with her beauty. Ruth banged the door, and ran away; and Lorna stood before me.

But she did not stand for an instant, when she saw what I was like. At the risk of all thick bandages, and upsetting a dozen medicine bottles, and scattering leeches right and left, she managed to get into my arms, although they could not hold her. She laid her panting warm young breast on the place where they meant to bleed me, and she set my pale face up; and she would not look at me, having greater faith in kissing.

I felt my life come back, and warm; I felt my trust in women flow; I felt the joys of living now, and the power of doing it. It is not a moment to describe; who feels can never tell of it. But the rush of Lorna's tears, and the challenge of my bride's lips, and the throbbing of my wife's heart (now at last at home on mine), made me feel that the world was good, and not a thing to be weary of.

Little more have I to tell. The doctor was turned out at once; and slowly came back my former strength, with a darling wife, and good victuals. As for Lorna, she never tired of sitting and watching me eat and eat. And such is her heart that she never tires of being with me here and there, among the beautiful places, and talking with her arm around me—so far at least as it can go, though half of mine may go round her—of the many fears and troubles, dangers and discouragements, and worst of all the bitter partings, which we used to have, somehow.

There is no need for my farming harder than becomes a man of weight. Lorna has great stores of money, though we never draw it out, except for some poor neighbor; unless I find her a sumptuous dress, out of her own perquisites. And this she always looks upon as a wondrous gift from me; and kisses me much when she puts it on, and walks like the noble woman she is. And yet I may never behold it again; for she gets back to her simple clothes, and I love her the better in them. I believe that she gives half the grandeur away, and keeps the other half for the children.

As for poor Tom Faggus, every one knows his bitter adventures, when his pardon was recalled, because of his journey to Sedgemoor. Not a child in the country, I doubt, but knows far more than I do of Tom's most desperate doings. The law had ruined him once, he said; and then he had been too much for the law: and now that a quiet life was his object, here the base thing came after him. And such was his dread of this evil spirit, that being caught upon Barnstaple Bridge, with soldiers at either end of it (yet doubtful about approaching him), he set his strawberry mare, sweet Winnie, at the left-hand parapet, with a whisper into her dove-coloured ear. Without a moment's doubt she leaped it, into the foaming tide, and swam, and landed according to orders. Also his flight from a public-house (where a trap was set for him, but Winnie came and broke down the door, and put two men under, and trod on them,) is as well known as any ballad. It was reported for awhile that poor Tom had been caught at last, by means of his fondness for liquor, and was hanged before Taunton Jail; but luckily we knew better. With a good wife, and a wonderful horse, and all the country attached to him, he kept the law at a wholesome distance, until it became too much for its master; and a new king arose. Upon this, Tom sued his pardon afresh; and Jeremy Stickles, who suited the times, was glad to help him in getting it, as well as a compensation. Thereafter the good and respectable Tom lived a godly (though not always sober) life; and brought up his children to honesty, as the first of all qualifications.

My dear mother was as happy as possibly need be with us; having no cause for jealousy, as others arose around her. And everybody was well pleased, when Lizzy came in one day and tossed her bookshelf over, and declared that she would have Captain Bloxham, and nobody should prevent her. For that he alone, of all the men she had ever met with, knew good writing when he saw it, and could spell a word when told. As he had now succeeded to Captain Stickle's position (Stickles going up the tree), and had the power of collecting, and of keeping, what he liked, there was nothing to be said against it; and we hoped that he would pay her out.

I sent little Ensie to Blundell's school, at my own cost and charges, having changed his name, for fear of what anyone might do to him. I called him Ensie Jones; and we got him a commission, and after many scrapes of spirit, he did great things in the Low Countries. He looks upon me as his father; and without my leave will not lay claim to the heritage and title of the Doones, which clearly belong to him.

Ruth Huckaback is not married yet; although upon Uncle Reuben's death she came into all his property; except, indeed, 2000 pounds, which Uncle Ben, in his driest manner, bequeathed 'to Sir John Ridd, the worshipful knight, for greasing of the testator's boots.' And he left almost a mint of money, not from the mine, but from the shop, and the good use of usury. For the mine had brought in just what it cost, when the vein of gold ended suddenly; leaving all concerned much older, and some, I fear, much poorer; but no one utterly ruined, as is the case with most of them. Ruth herself was his true mine, as upon death-bed he found. I know a man even worthy of her: and though she is not very young, he loves her, as I love Lorna. It is my firm conviction, that in the end he will win her; and I do not mean to dance again, except at dear Ruth's wedding; if the floor be strong enough.

Of Lorna, of my lifelong darling, of my more and more loved wife, I will not talk; for it is not seemly that a man should exalt his pride. Year by year her beauty grows, with the growth of goodness, kindness, and true happiness—above all with loving. For change, she makes a joke of this, and plays with it, and laughs at it; and then, when my slow nature marvels, back she comes to the earnest thing. And if I wish to pay her out for something very dreadful—as may happen once or twice, when we become too gladsome—I bring her to forgotten sadness, and to me for cure of it, by the two words 'Lorna Doone.'